THE DARK VOLUME

By the same author

The Glass Books of the Dream Eaters

THE DARK VOLUME

G. W. Dahlquist

VIKING BOOKS

VIKING

Published by the Penguin Group
Penguin Books Ltd, 80 Strand, London WC2R 0RL, England
Penguin Group (USA) Inc., 375 Hudson Street, New York, New York 10014, USA
Penguin Group (Canada), 90 Eglinton Avenue East, Suite 700, Toronto, Ontario, Canada M4P 2Y3
(a division of Pearson Penguin Canada Inc.)
Penguin Ireland, 25 St Stephen's Green, Dublin 2, Ireland (a division of Penguin Books Ltd)
Penguin Group (Australia), 250 Camberwell Road, Camberwell, Victoria 3124, Australia
(a division of Pearson Australia Group Pty Ltd)
Penguin Books India Pvt Ltd, 11 Community Centre, Panchsheel Park, New Delhi – 110 017, India
Penguin Group (NZ), 67 Apollo Drive, Rosedale, North Shore 0632, New Zealand
(a division of Pearson New Zealand Ltd)
Penguin Books (South Africa) (Pty) Ltd, 24 Sturdee Avenue, Rosebank, Johannesburg 2196, South Africa

Penguin Books Ltd, Registered Offices: 80 Strand, London WC2R 0RL, England

www.penguin.com

First published 2008
1

Set in 11/15.5pt Bodoni Book
Typeset by Rowland Phototypesetting Ltd, Bury St Edmunds, Suffolk
Printed in Great Britain by Clays Ltd, St Ives plc

A CIP catalogue record for this book is available from the British Library

HARDBACK
ISBN: 978–0–670–91653–5

TRADE PAPERBACK
ISBN: 978–0–670–91756–3

www.greenpenguin.co.uk

Penguin Books is committed to a sustainable future
for our business, our readers and our planet.
The book in your hands is made from paper
certified by the Forest Stewardship Council.

For Morgan and Ali, and for Anne

Transitional periods, especially between worlds not strictly real, can be trying at the best of times. This book is indebted to the following, and I am grateful for the chance to thank them all.

Liz Duffy Adams, Danny Baror, Vincent Barrett, Maxim Blowen-Ledoux, Karen Bornarth, Venetia Butterfield, CiNE, Cupcake Café, Shannon Dailey, Joseph Goodrich, David Levine, Todd London, John McAdams, E. J. McCarthy, Patricia McLaughlin, Bill Massey, Kate Miciak, Honor Molloy, Rachel Neuburger, New Dramatists, Octocorp@530, Suki O'Kane, Tim Paulson, Molly Powell, Anne Washburn, Mark Worthington, Margaret Young.

The events contained within *The Glass Books of the Dream Eaters* are many and ornate. However much this present volume stands apart as a discrete narrative, where former assurances have fallen to dust, the introduction of these few personages may prove useful.

Celeste Temple, a plantation heiress from the West Indies of twenty-five sharp years, her engagement to Roger Bascombe (a rising figure in the Foreign Ministry) summarily terminated by Mr Bascombe without explanation, found herself in the position, some three days later, of shooting him dead in a sinking dirigible.

Cardinal Chang, a criminal with disfiguring scars across both of his eyes (thus his habit to wear dark glasses at all times), who first made the acquaintance of Miss Temple on a train at 4 a.m.

Doctor Abelard Svenson, a naval surgeon in service to a pleasure-seeking young prince. Despite the Doctor's efforts, both the Prince and his fiancée, Lydia Vandaariff, were viciously slain en route to the Duchy of Macklenburg by the Contessa di Lacquer-Sforza.

Robert Vandaariff, recently ennobled financier, perhaps the richest man of the age. In funding the Cabal's efforts, Lord Vandaariff believed himself its master, right to the very moment his mind was wiped as clean as a dish plate licked by a dog.

Henry Xonck, munitions magnate, business rival to Vandaariff, also believed himself to be master of the Cabal. The contents of his mind were harvested into a blue glass book and his body left an idiot husk.

Francis Xonck, youngest sibling of the arms magnate, a well-travelled dandy whose disreputable ways concealed a formidable appetite for violence; shot in the chest by Doctor Svenson.

Deputy Foreign Minister Harald Crabbé, a diplomatic *éminence grise* whose manipulations gave a legal veneer to the Cabal's actions and put a regiment of dragoons at its command; killed on the dirigible by Contessa di Lacquer-Sforza and dropped into the sea.

Comte d'Orkancz, mysterious aesthete, alchemical genius, the discoverer of indigo clay and the fabricator of the blue glass books, whose unnatural science informed every inch of the Cabal's ambitions; run through with a sabre on the dirigible by Cardinal Chang.

Mrs Marchmoor, three weeks previously a courtesan known as Margaret Hooke, now the only survivor of the Comte's most audacious experiment, to transform a woman into living glass.

Colonel Arthur Trapping, a middling drone of the Cabal, married to Charlotte Trapping – née Xonck – an unhappy woman whose two brothers allowed her no role in the family empire.

Elöise Dujong, tutor to the children of Arthur and Charlotte Trapping, fell foul of the Cabal in her efforts to find the murdered Colonel; in the process a portion of her memory was drained from her mind into a glass book.

Caroline Stearne, a protégée of the Contessa; she killed Colonel Trapping as part of her own secret alliance with Roger Bascombe. Caroline was also slain quite savagely by the Contessa di Lacquer-Sforza.

Contessa di Lacquer-Sforza, a noblewoman of Italian extraction, who – it must be admitted – possesses a temper.

PROLOGUE

She did not know what time it was, because of the new rule. It had been the girl's habit to creep up the stairs and then, depending on the day and who might be home or what servants watching, slip into her mother's rooms, at the end of the hallway, or into her father's, to the right of the landing. Her mother's bedchamber was filled with the deliberate clicking of a clock made of Chinese porcelain, all creamy white with a flickering of red flowers. If she was careful and again unseen, she could lift it off its stand and put her ear against the brass-ringed face. Her father's rooms were altogether different: seldom occupied, and smelling of tobacco and dust. Here stood the tall, dark pendulum clock, with a glass front through which she could dimly see the swinging metal disc, lurking in its permanent shadow. It was this clock that most satisfyingly rang the hour, and the smaller Chinese clock that more reliably gave out the minutes in between. But it had been three days since the girl had seen her mother, and another three before that since her father had kissed her cheek at breakfast, the stiff collar of his uniform tunic scraping against her chin, then marched out to the street, already lighting his first cheroot of the morning. Mr Flempton had shut both rooms – telling all the other servants that the three children were forbidden the entire floor. The girl knew there were other timepieces in the house, indeed that her merest question to Cook, or their maid Amelia, or even the forbidding Mr Flempton, would give her the time in a trice, yet she refused to ask. If she could not go upstairs to find it for herself, she did not care to know.

Her brothers asked all sorts of things, persistent questions – especially Charles – but received no answers at all. This upset her, because she knew there *were* answers – her parents were *some* place – and she did

not understand why people she had trusted would avoid the truth so
cruelly. She had retreated instead, for hours every day to their schoolroom, also empty, since their lessons had been suspended as well (she
could not remember when she had last seen their tutor, Elöise – it was
almost as if the woman had vanished along with her parents). As Charles
hated lessons and Ronald was too young, the room became a place no other
occupant of the house had any cause to visit. And so the girl passed her
time with books, with picture paints, and with looking out the window to
the square, where the coaches came and went as if the world was not
profoundly amiss.

What vexed her the most, as she strove ever more diligently to read or
draw or arrange the paint pots into a wall and jump the collection of her
brother's carved wooden horses over it, like the soldiers in her father's
regiment – the black horse always being her father's and always making
the highest jump of all – was that those moments, her father at breakfast,
her mother kissing her goodbye after supper, would be the last for so long
a time. The girl had not fixed her parents into her mind – their smiles,
their moods, their final very important words. If she could only get into
her mother's clothes closet, she could shut her eyes and lean her face into
the line of hanging dresses, breathing in the perfume. Instead she had the
smells of servants and well-scrubbed common rooms, and worried whispers
from the kitchens that stopped whenever she was seen.

It was after Cecile had collected her for afternoon tea, after so many
hours of silence the maid's voice echoing up the stairway harsh as a crow's,
that the girl found herself, hands washed and dress changed, waiting for
Ronald – her younger brother was always troubled by shoes – and staring
down the main hall, through the foyer to the closed front door.

The door chime was pulled, then after the briefest interval pulled again.
Mr Flempton rushed past her, tugging at the cuffs of his jacket. Cecile
touched the girl's shoulder to guide her away, but she ignored it. Mr
Flempton opened the door wide to reveal three men in long black coats
and high black hats. The men to either side held leather portfolios. The
coat of the man in the centre was draped limply over one shoulder, the arm
beneath it wrapped with white plaster.

'May I help you?' asked Mr Flempton.

'Ministry orders,' said the man with the plaster cast. 'We'll require your complete cooperation.'

ONE

WOLVES

One of his hands tugged cruelly at her hair as the other squeezed her throat. Miss Temple could not breathe – he was too strong, too angry – and even as part of her mind screamed that she must not, that there must be another way, she ground the revolver into the man's body and pulled the trigger. It kicked against her wrist with a deafening crack, and Roger Bascombe was thrown into the cabin wall. The red imprint of his fingers marked her windpipe, but his shocked blue eyes – the fiancé who had cruelly thrown her over – showed only dismay at *her* betrayal. His gaze punctured her heart like a blade. What had she done? She stumbled, aware for the first time that her feet were freezing, that she stood in six inches of icy sea water. The airship had spiralled into the ocean. They were sinking. She would drown.

Dimly, Miss Temple heard her name – *Celeste! Celeste!* – the calls of Doctor Svenson and of Chang. Her memory seemed two steps behind . . . They had climbed to the roof, with Elöise. She must follow, it was her only chance to survive . . . but she looked again at Roger, crumpled and wan, and could not move – would they die together after all? But then something nudged Miss Temple's leg. She cried out, thinking of rats on a ship, and saw it was a body, floating with the rising water . . . the Comte d'Orkancz, the alchemist-savant who had discovered the blue glass, run through with a sabre by Cardinal Chang. Miss Temple forced herself past the dead man's bulk, barely able to feel her legs. Other bodies loomed as she crossed the cabin, each more gruesome than the last: Francis Xonck, with his flaming red hair and elegant silk waistcoat, shot by Doctor Svenson . . . Lydia Vandaariff, decapitated with a blue glass book . . . the Prince of Macklenburg, legs broken clean away. Miss Temple crawled up the stairs, the foaming water keeping pace as her fingers clawed the cold metal. The cries above were fainter. With a piercing shock she remembered the one body she had not seen, that of the Contessa di Lacquer-Sforza . . . Had she jumped to her death? Had she somehow hidden and killed the others? Was she even then waiting for Miss Temple?

The cold salt water reached her throat, splashing at her mouth. Her arms became too heavy to lift. Behind lay Roger . . . her terrible guilt. Above floated the open hatch. She could not move for the ice forming around her legs, locking her joints stiff. She would perish after all . . . just as she deserved –

Miss Temple woke – weak, starving, and riddled with aches – to a sour-smelling room, with dark, raw-cut beams. A single smeared window framed the feeble light of a heavy, cloud-covered sky, the very image of boiled wool. She sat up in the frankly noisome bed, doing her best to shake away the vision of the sinking airship.

'At least it does not reek of fish,' she muttered, and looked about her for any sign of where she was or – for that matter – her clothing. But the room was bare.

She crept gingerly off the bed, feeling the unsoundness of her limbs and the lightness of her head, and peered under the frame to find a chipped porcelain chamber pot. As Miss Temple squatted down, she rubbed her eyes and looked at her hands, which were flecked with half-healed abrasions and cuts. She stood, slid the pot back from view beneath the bed with her foot, and noticed a small rectangle of glass, no bigger than a page of poetry, hanging from a nail – a mirror. She was forced to stand on her toes, but, despite the effort, stayed staring into the glass for some minutes, curious and dismayed at the young woman she there met.

Her chestnut curls hung flat and lank, which had the effect of making her face – from a certain vantage somewhat round – even rounder. This was set off by her sunken cheeks, the dark circles of distress beneath each eye, and once more a scattering of livid marks – the searing trace of a bullet above one ear, welts across both cheekbones, and greenish bruises on her throat that perfectly matched a vicious, squeezing palm. All this Miss

Temple took in with a sigh, grateful she had not, for instance, lost a tooth – that all could be mended by time, food, and the touch of a skilful maid. What struck her more forcefully, however – what she found *mysterious* – was what had happened to her eyes. They were still grey, still insistent, impatient, and sharp, but possessed a new quality she could not at first name. A moment later the truth appeared. She was a killer.

Miss Temple sat back on the bed and stared up at the darkening clouds. She had shot Roger Bascombe and left his body to the sea. Certainly the man had betrayed her, betrayed everything, and yet . . . what had she become in defeating him, in thwarting the powerful figures Roger had chosen to serve, chosen over her love, their marriage . . . what had she herself cast away?

Such thoughts were impossible on an empty stomach. She would eat, bathe, dress, locate her friends – still an oddly foreign notion to Miss Temple – and take assurance from their survival that it had all been necessary.

But when she called to the door, her voice an alarmingly ragged croak, there came no answer. Instead of calling again, Miss Temple lay down and pulled the blankets up over her face.

As she lay sniffing the dusty wool, she recalled what she could of her coming ashore. They had been on the roof of the dirigible's cabin, waiting to drown as it dropped into the sea, but instead of sinking they came aground on fortunate rocks, saved. She reached the sand on her hands and knees, half drowned and cold to the bone, frozen anew by the pitiless wind whose lashing impact curled her to a shivering ball. Chang carried her beyond the narrow ribbon of beach and over a hedge of sharp black rocks, but already she felt her body failing, unable to form words for her chattering teeth. There were black trees, the Doctor banging on a wooden door, racks of drying and salted fish, and then she was bundled in front of a burning hearth. Outside it was morning, but inside the hut the air was close and foul, as if it had been nailed tight against the cold all winter. The dirigible's original destination had been the Duchy of Macklenburg, on the Baltic Sea – but how far north had the airship flown? Someone held hot tea for her to drink, then they — Elöise? — took off her clothes and wrapped her in blankets. Miss Temple felt her chills swiftly escalate into fever . . . and then dreams had swallowed her whole.

Miss Temple sighed heavily, the sound quite muffled beneath the bedding, and slept.

When she next awoke the window had gone dark and there were sounds outside the door. Miss Temple crawled from the bed and stood more steadily than before. She plucked at her simple shift, wondering where it had come from, and pushed the hair from her face. How much must have happened while she slept? Yet, instead of forming the many questions she ought to have had — about her companions, their location, the very date — Miss Temple found her attention drawn to a lurid flickering — *already* — beneath the surface of her mind, like tiny bubbles in a pot growing to boil. This was the Contessa's blue glass book of memories that Miss Temple had absorbed — and she shuddered to realize that each tiny bubble of memory found an echo in her flesh, each one threatening to expand to prominence in her mind, until the memory blotted out the present altogether. She had peered into the shimmering depths of the blue glass and been changed. How many of its memories had she consumed — experienced in her *own* body — and thus made her own? How many acts that she had never performed did she now *remember*? The Contessa's book was a catalogue of insidious and unmentionable delight, the sensual experience of a thousand souls crammed together. The more Miss Temple thought about it, the more insistent the memories became. Her face flushed. Her breath quickened. Her nostrils flared with anger. She would not have it.

She jerked open the door. Before her two women huddled over a large woven basket near an iron stove. At the sound of the door both looked up, faces blank with surprise. They wore plain dresses, soiled aprons, and heavy shoes, with their hair stuffed tightly under woollen caps — a mother and a daughter, sharing a thick nose and a certain flatness about the eyes. Miss Temple smiled primly and noticed that the basket was bundled full of linens quite broadly stained with blood. The younger of the two abruptly upended the pile to obscure the stains and shoved the entire basket from view behind the stove. The elder turned to Miss Temple with a doting smile – which Miss Temple would have been less disposed to despise had it not appeared as so open a distraction from the basket – and rubbed her chapped hands together.

'Good-day,' said Miss Temple.

'You are awake!' The woman's voice bore an accent Miss Temple had heard before, from the mouths of sailors.

'Exactly so,' replied Miss Temple. 'And, though I do not intend any inconvenience, it is true that I require rather many things in a short time. I should like breakfast – I have no sense of the time, so perhaps it is more supper I should ask for – and if possible a bath, and then some clothing, and more than anything information: where precisely might I be, and where are my companions? And of course, who are you?' she added, smiling again. 'I am sure you have been instrumental to my recovery. I trust I was not a burden. One never enjoys being ill – often one calls out, sometimes brusquely. I have no memory of calling out at all – I have no memory of coming here – so I trust you will accept my open regrets for any – well, for anything *untoward*. I do indeed feel much better. Some tea would be lovely. And toast – toast of any kind. And, yes, something to wear. And news. Indeed, most of all, *news*.'

She smiled at them, expectant and, she hoped, the picture of kind gratitude. The women stared at her for perhaps four seconds, when the elder suddenly clapped her hands, startling a squeak from the girl, as if she had been pinched. At once the poor thing darted from the room, pausing only to snatch up the basket as she went.

'Bette will come back with food,' the woman announced, lips pursed, her hands again rubbing together. 'Perhaps you will sit by the stove.'

She indicated a rough wooden stool, but before Miss Temple could respond the woman took her arm and guided her to it. Wood chips and cinders beneath her feet, Miss Temple sat – for it *was* cold outside of her blanket, and much warmer by the stove.

'What is your name?' asked Miss Temple. 'And where are we? I expect you know my name – undoubtedly my companions have spoken of how we came to be here. I should actually be quite curious as to what they said –'

'I am Lina,' the woman said. 'I will make tea.'

The woman brusquely turned away, stepping closer to the stove and placing an iron kettle onto its flat, oily top. Keeping her back to Miss Temple, Lina crossed to a low, humble cupboard for a teapot and metal mug, and a small stoppered jar that held a dusty inch of black tea – each action making clear there was scarce hope of a lemon.

'And where are we exactly?' asked Miss Temple, even in her weakened state not entirely pleased with having to repeat herself.

Lina did not respond, pretending – poorly – not to have heard. Rolling her eyes, Miss Temple stood and without another word walked past the woman to the door through which Bette had disappeared. There was a sharp exhalation from Lina as she pulled it open, but a moment later she was through, shutting it behind her and slipping a conveniently placed wooden latch. Lina yanked on the door from the other side. Miss Temple ignored her.

Bette – who, Miss Temple now saw, as the girl looked up at her with shock – was, if not exactly fat, what one might in charity term *healthy*, with a wide, pale, pink neck and heavy arms that shook the entirety of her torso when they worked. At the moment Miss Temple entered, Bette had been fully occupied – not with any meal at all but in scrubbing the blood-soaked bedding in a steaming bucket of water, crimson-tinged soap suds lathering nearly to each elbow.

'Hello again,' said Miss Temple. 'Lina is making my tea. I have been alone so long that I am quite keen for company. And whatever are you doing?'

Bette shifted on her feet, torn between the urge to hide the blood and to curtsy to a social superior, and succeeded only in losing her balance and sitting down on the floor. The impact caused one black-booted foot to kick the tub, launching a jet of bloody foam into the air.

The latched door rattled again. Miss Temple studied the room, of a piece with where she had slept – dark, wooden beams with a wall of inset shelves, all covered with boxes and pots and jars, one half taken up with soaps and oils and the other equally occupied with fishing tackle. There were two more wooden tubs the size of the one Bette presently used, and the width of the room was spread with hanging cords upon which to dry things. Miss Temple saw these were strung with more bedding, and nothing she might wear.

'That seems a lot of blood,' said Miss Temple. 'I am hopeful that it represents a happy outcome – the birth of a child?'

Bette shook her head.

Miss Temple nodded seriously. 'I see. Someone has been injured?'

Bette nodded.

'*Killed?*'

Bette nodded again.

'And poor you, with the horrid task of washing it out.' Miss Temple continued to ignore the rattling door behind her. She stepped to one of the other tubs, perching herself on its edge. 'Do you know what happened?'

Bette glanced past Miss Temple to the door. Miss Temple leant closer to the girl.

'Between *ourselves*.'

Bette's hesitant answer was so hushed as to be nearly inaudible. 'It was the *storm . . .*'

She wriggled back onto her toes and sank her hands once more into the tub, as if resuming her work would balance the impulse to gossip.

'What storm?'

'After you came ashore.'

'I remember no *storm*,' said Miss Temple. 'But perhaps I was in no state to mark it – go on.'

'It rained for two days,' whispered the girl. 'And when it was over, the beaches were different, and trees had come down, and the river had flooded the forest. That was why they said – because of the forest –'

'The *blood*, Bette.' Miss Temple attempted to be patient. '*Blood*, not forests.'

'But they said that was why. No one had called on Jorgens since the storm, because he lived near the river, and the path was washed away. When someone did think to call, they found . . . they found them *dead*.

Jorgens *and* his wife. The door opened, dogs gone, their . . . their *throats* . . . and *then* –'

Lina banged on the door, frightening the girl to silence. Miss Temple spun round and barked with annoyance: 'I will have my tea when I am *ready* for it!'

'Celeste!' cried Elöise Dujong. 'You must come out at once – there is no time!'

Miss Temple dashed to the door and shoved the latch aside, just as Elöise yanked it open and took her hand. She felt a rush of pleasure at the sight of her friend and wanted nothing more than to wrap her arms around her and crush Elöise to her body, realizing in the moment how alone she had felt, and how delicate had become her fears. Instead, Elöise called to Lina that Miss Temple would need a bath at once, and then some food to take with them, for they must travel. These orders shouted – and they *were* shouted, Miss Temple heard with surprise, and they *were* orders (she had never seen Elöise so in command – but was she not a tutor or governess, and were they not prime whiphands all?) – Elöise yanked Miss Temple into her bedroom and swung the door shut with her other arm, which, Miss Temple noticed for the first time, was draped with clothing. She led Miss Temple to the bed and they sat together, Miss Temple's bare feet dangling above the floor, Elöise flushed and out of breath, her boots quite caked with mud.

'As I say, my dear, there is no time – it is nearly dawn. I did not know you were awake. I am so sorry not to have been here; I can only wonder what you thought. The fever was prodigious. Abelard – the Doctor' – here Elöise blushed and dropped her eyes – 'left only when he was certain the danger had passed – I have remained until you revived –'

'The Doctor is *gone*?' asked Miss Temple.

'And Cardinal Chang – there is too much to explain – you must see if any of this fits while they heat water. We really haven't time, but you must be craving a bath after so long – and there is no telling when we may find another –'

She thrust the mass of clothing onto Miss Temple's lap and began to sort it into piles – undergarments, shifts, petticoats, a corset or two, stockings, and several actual dresses. Miss Temple watched Elöise's fingers darting about, and she struggled to make sense of her news. Chang was gone? And the Doctor?

'But where –'

'Back to the city. My dear, so much has happened. It has been over a week – there was, my goodness, *such* a storm –'

'I have been told.'

'We are far north, in a fishing village on what is called the Iron Coast – no harbours to speak of, no trains, the only roads washed out by this tempest.'

Miss Temple shivered to recall the terrible last minutes on the damaged airship, as it settled onto the freezing waves and began to fill – the dark rush of sea water lifting the bodies of the Prince, of Lydia, of Xonck, and of the Comte, transforming each from a person to an object. She shook the thought away.

'But what is so pressing? Our enemies were destroyed!'

'Try these,' said Elöise, pointing to a sorted stack of worn white underthings.

'I'm sure they will fit well,' replied Miss Temple, already regretting the absence of her silks and suspiciously curious what had become of them, 'but I do not understand the *urgency*.'

'At least try the dresses,' insisted Elöise.

'Where did you get them?' asked Miss Temple, holding up a cotton dress of a faded royal blue – simple but pretty enough in its way, and an admittedly fetching colour with her hair.

'A local woman, Mrs Jorgens – the match in size was fortuitous.'

'And she parted with them willingly?'

'Please put it *on*, Celeste. I must see about the water. We must hurry.'

Through the door she could hear Elöise speaking to Lina, and then a general buzz of preparation that she knew had nothing to do with baths and everything to do with imminent departure. She stood naked with a dead woman's dress pulled up to her waist, looking at her face and body in the tiny square of mirror. Her skin was pale as milk, a fact that seemed less a part of her than the bruises and shadows traced across it, evidence of another life, just as the ruddy thumb smears of her lips and at the tip of each breast were signs of an interior hunger that struck her now – as she slipped her arms into each sleeve and shrugged the dress in place across her chest – as fully at odds with the colder creature she had perforce become. She pulled it from her shoulders and then brought it up to her nose. There was no scent of its previous owner, only salt air, dust, and camphor. It must have been her finest dress, worn but three times a year and scrupulously cleaned.

Miss Temple glanced behind her and saw, laid to the side of the pile of clothing, a tiny white shift and a cotton dress to match it, to fit a girl of five years at the very most. Elöise must have gathered them up along with the rest of Mrs Jorgens' things. Bette had not mentioned a child . . . had one been killed as well?

Elöise knocked on the door and opened it enough to say the bath was ready. From beyond the far room, Miss Temple heard the stamping of horses.

As she crouched in the wooden tub, the water none too warm but nevertheless welcome, Miss Temple saw Elöise pass Lina several silver coins, dug from one of Miss Temple's sea-battered green boots. How much money had been left in them – and how much had now been spent without her knowledge? Bette poured another bowlful of water over Miss Temple's head, interrupting her calculations, and worked the soap through her hair with thick fingers, as Lina packed food into a wrapped bundle. Glancing over to Miss Temple, Elöise saw that she was being watched.

'We will speak as we travel, Celeste,' she said. 'But we must travel at once.'

'Will not the Doctor or Chang expect to collect us? Will they not be confused when we are gone?'

'They will not.'

'Why? What are they doing? Where will we go?'

'Excellent questions – you are yourself once more –'

'What has happened to our enemies?'

If Elöise replied, Miss Temple did not hear it. Bette emptied another bowl over her head, and another after that, pouring slowly to wash out the suds. Miss Temple carefully stepped free of the tub as Bette dabbed at her dripping hair.

'I suppose it is impossible that my hair be curled,' she said to Elöise.

'The curls are quite natural to you, are they not?' Elöise carefully replied.

'Of course they are,' snapped Miss Temple; 'but that does not mean they are not better when *managed*.'

She raised her arms, the better for Bette to dry her, and nodded at Elöise's hands rather pointedly. 'Where is my other boot?'

Green-shod once more, Miss Temple stepped from the wooden house into a pallid light. The trees above were leafless, and the path to their wagon – a simple affair drawn by one weathered nag – was still moist from the rains. She smelt the sea and even heard the distant waves somewhere behind the house, tracing the air like a restless rope of wind. Lina and Bette stood in the door, watching them go with, Miss Temple recognized with annoyance, expressions of relief. She turned to Elöise to remark on the fact but saw for the first time the line of men that waited on the far side of the wagon – raw, hard-faced fellows with knives at their belts and staves in their hands.

'Are they coming with us?' she whispered to Elöise.

'Ah, no,' Elöise replied with a tight smile. 'They have come to make sure we *go*.'

Miss Temple looked with more attention – perceiving women and children now peering out behind the line of men – and felt their gazes could not have been more cold had she and Elöise been diseased interlopers with the plague. She opened her mouth to speak, but stopped at the sight of a small girl with a haunted, pale face, hands gripped by two grey matrons – no mother or father near her. Her view of the girl was blocked by one of the men with staves, who met Miss Temple's curiosity with a frown. The man sported a new pair of knee-high black leather riding boots, incongruous with his rough wool garments and fisherman's beard.

Before she could point this out to Elöise, their driver – an aged man whose wrinkled face seemed crushed between an untamed beard and a close-pulled woollen cap – reached down with hard knobbed hands to lift Miss Temple aboard. A moment later Elöise stood beside her, and a moment after that they groped for awkward seats on a pallet of straw, as the driver snapped the reins without a word. The bitter nameless village and its silent people receded from view.

Miss Temple frowned and hissed sharply to her companion, 'I do not know what they think we have done – were they not paid?'

Elöise glanced at the driver's back. Miss Temple huffed, quite out of patience. 'What has *happened*, Elöise? I quite insist you say!'

'I plan to – but you must know, these people –'

'Yes yes, the rising river in the forest, I have been told –'

'Indeed –'

'People were *killed*.'

Elöise nodded, and spoke carefully. 'The implication is a wolf. Or wolves, actually –'

'Which is no reason to glower at *me*.' Miss Temple looked up at their driver. 'How *many* wolves?' she asked waspishly.

'It depends on how one reads the attacks.'

'Well, how many attacks were there? Bette mentioned the Jorgens. I saw her washing the bloody linen.'

'Mr and Mrs Jorgen died two nights ago – or that is when they were *found*. Without the Doctor no one could specify when in fact they died. But before that a fisherman was found in his boat. And before *that* two grooms at the nearest stable.'

Miss Temple snorted. 'What sort of wolf goes in a *boat*?'

Elöise did not reply, as if, the question having no answer, nothing further might be said. Miss Temple felt no such hesitation. 'Where is the Doctor? Where is Chang?'

'I have told you –'

'You have told me nothing at all!'

'They have each gone ahead of us.'

'*Why?*'

'The roads, for one – they have been ruined by the weather, and, as you were so very ill, we did not know if you could travel – the last thing one wanted was to be two days out and then stranded without shelter, if *another* storm –'

'That might perhaps convince me for the Doctor, but never Chang.'

'No, indeed, Chang departed earlier.'

'*Why?*'

'Did you see that Lina has put together a parcel of food? How kind of her.'

Elöise smiled at Miss Temple, mildly but determined. Miss Temple pursed her lips, grudgingly working for a topic that might be safely overheard.

'This *storm*,' she offered with patently false interest. 'One gathers it was *prodigious*.'

'You did well to sleep through the thing,' replied Elöise at once. 'In truth we felt – for it was the very night after we'd come ashore – that all the anger of our enemies was being vented through the heavens – as if the waves were the late Comte's attempts to dash us to pieces, and the lightning bolts sent down from the dead Contessa's furious eyes.'

Miss Temple said nothing, aware that the other woman could not have mentioned the Contessa lightly. When she finally replied, her own voice had become distressingly small. 'The Contessa is dead, then?'

'Of course she is,' said Elöise.

'I did not know you'd found the body.'

'We did not need to, Celeste. She fell from the airship into the frozen sea. You and I could barely swim in our merest underthings – that woman's dress would have taken in enough water within one minute to sink her down to hell itself.'

'It is just that . . . I spoke to her on the roof of the airship – it must have been just before she leapt to the sea . . . her face . . . even then so proud, so uncaring. She haunts me still.'

'She is dead, Celeste. I promise you.'

Elöise put her arm around Miss Temple's shoulders and squeezed. Never one to anticipate affection of any kind, Miss Temple did not know what to do, and so did nothing, looking instead at her salt-cracked boots and the dirty planking. Elöise squeezed again and took her arm away, a trim smile on her lips, as if she were not entirely sure of the gesture either, but then she reconsidered and reached up to smooth the hair from Miss Temple's face.

'I know you feel better,' she said, 'but we are travelling while you would still be best in bed. Lean against my shoulder and I will tell you what I know' – her voice dropped to a whisper – 'and what has taken the Cardinal and the Doctor from our sides.'

'The first night was spent in a fisherman's hut. I do not exaggerate to say the Doctor was hard pressed to keep you alive, while tending to Chang – for the icy sea had done nothing kindly to his lungs – and to myself, for I admit to very nearly drowning. That night the heavens erupted in a storm the likes of which I have never seen – a raging sea, the land awash, trees torn from the earth by the winds. In the morning Chang and the Doctor went for help, and that afternoon, during the briefest break in the tempest, you were moved to Lina's house. You lay there for six days, quite incoherent. It was only on the fourth day that your fever finally broke and the Doctor saw fit to leave.'

'But where was Chang?' Miss Temple burrowed more tightly into the crook of Elöise's arm and allowed her eyes to slip closed.

'The Doctor felt it vital that, once the storm was over, we get a boat and return to the fallen airship: to collect what remained of the glass books, to find any papers that might tell of our enemies' agents in Macklenburg, and to bring ashore what bodies we could for decent burial.'

Miss Temple's thoughts went to Roger, imagining with dismay what her fiancé must have looked like after two days in the sea. She had seen a drowned sailor once on a beach and remembered – indeed, could never forget – his swollen and shapeless cast, as if submersion had half transformed him to a fish, with only his unseeing eyes and hanging, open mouth showing protest at the horrid injustice done to his body. She imagined Roger's thin, nimble fingers, bobbing bloated and pale in the dark water, already subject to the gnawing of scavenger fish or industrious crabs. She pictured his softening face –

'But the airship was gone,' Elöise went on. 'Dragged out to sea no doubt by the water-logged balloon. Scraps of canvas washed ashore . . . but that was all.'

'What', Miss Temple forced herself to ask, 'of the . . . bodies?'

'We saw no sign. But they were inside the craft. They would be carried with it, down below.'

'And all the glass books?'

'All of them. And all the Comte's machines – everything they had brought to conquer Macklenburg.'

Miss Temple exhaled. 'Then it is truly finished.'

Elöise shifted slightly. 'And *then* the dead grooms were discovered – horses driven from the stable – and then the poor fisherman in his boat. The local folk have little doubt of the killer – the victims' throats were all torn out most savagely, and this *is* a land where wolves are *known*. But, after this – after Chang and Doctor Svenson had both taken their leave – the Jorgens were discovered –'

'But why *did* Chang go?'

Elöise shifted her position to look into Miss Temple's face. 'You and I have lived in the city. The villagers who took us in became frightened, in the sober light of day, by our strange appearance – you and I dressed as if we'd escaped a *seraglio*, and the Doctor a foreign *soldier* – but most of all by the Cardinal – his figure, the scars, the long red coat, the obvious capacity for violence – all of this brought suspicion upon *us* as these deaths began to appear so suddenly, one after another. And of course Chang *is* a killer. Once the villagers began to whisper amongst themselves – once there were *deaths* – well, Doctor Svenson –'

'And where is *he*? If he went to make sure of the road, why did he not *return*?'

'I do not know.' Elöise's voice sounded hollow. 'The Doctor left the day before yesterday. We . . . I am ashamed to say we quarrelled. I am a fool. In any event I knew that I must stay with you, and that the two of us must leave as soon as you were fit. That we were to meet them –'

'Where?'

'My family has a cottage, outside the city. It will be safe, and a peaceful place for you to get your strength.'

Miss Temple was silent. None of this made a bit of sense, from the wolves to the feeble excuses given for her own abandonment. Did Elöise think her so credulous, or was Elöise still speaking for the driver to hear? Surely *she* did not believe such nonsense . . .

Miss Temple cleared her throat. 'Will you and Doctor Svenson be married?' she asked.

Elöise stiffened beside her. 'I beg your pardon?'

'I merely wondered.'

'I – I'm sure I have not given it a thought – we have been too busy seeing to you, haven't we? And, my goodness, it feels we have not exchanged ten words of friendly conversation.'

'You seemed quite disposed to one another.'

'I barely know him, truly.'

'When you were captured by the Comte, and taken away by Francis Xonck – at Harschmort House – the Doctor was especially keen that we save you.'

'He is a kindly man.'

'Why did you quarrel?'

'I'm sure I do not remember.'

'Perhaps you prefer Cardinal Chang,' wondered Miss Temple, her voice airy and musing. 'He is more . . . dangerous . . .'

'I have had enough of danger,' replied Elöise, with a touch of tartness. 'Though I owe the Cardinal my life –'

'What do you think of his *eyes*?' asked Miss Temple.

'It is a terrible thing,' Elöise said, after a careful moment. 'Impossibly cruel.'

Miss Temple recalled seeing Chang's scars for the first time at the Hotel Boniface, when he removed his glasses to look into the blue glass card Doctor Svenson had found. After several strange glimpses of one another, on trains, across the ballroom of Harschmort, in secret tunnels, the three had met unexpectedly at Miss Temple's own hotel and, in an even more unlikely turn of events, joined forces. Chang had looked into her eyes upon taking off his glasses, a deliberate mocking challenge to what he assumed was her tender, ladylike sensibility. But Miss Temple had seen such scarring before, in fact quite regularly, on the faces of her own plantation. Yet even so, she had never considered disfigurement as a regular part of her life, for it had never afflicted anyone for whom she cared. She wondered if she could have loved Roger if he had been lacking one hand, and knew in all truth she never would have opened her heart to begin with. But that was the queer thing – for she had not purposely opened her heart to Cardinal Chang – or to the Doctor or to Elöise – yet somehow he had entered its confines. It was nothing like what Miss Temple had felt upon choosing Roger Bascombe – that *was* a choice, and for a type of life as much as for the man himself, though she had not fully understood it at the time. Of course it was impossible to relate men like Chang or Svenson to any reasonable type of life whatsoever.

She looked up again at the trees, aware that a nagging itch had grown between her legs as her thoughts had wandered. If she had been alone in her room, she might have allowed her hands beneath her petticoats, but with Elöise so near Miss Temple merely pressed her thighs together with a frown. It was the glass book again, the one she had looked into – been swallowed by – in the Contessa's rooms at the St Royale. The book had contained thousands of memories – the lives of courtesans, adventurers, villains of every kind, decadent sensualists, the indulgent and the cruel – together creating a sort of opium den that had trespassed over every border of her own identity, and from which she had wrenched herself free only with the most desperate effort. The problem for Miss Temple was the way the glass books captured memories – insidious, delicious, and terrifying. Looking into a book caused the viewer to physically experience the memory from the point of view – the *experiential* point of view – of the original source, whether this was a man or woman. It was not as if Miss Temple had merely *read* a lurid account of the goings on at the Venetian *Carnevale*; she now remembered performing the same deeds with her own body. Her mind teemed with false memories so vivid they left her breathless.

She had not spoken of the glass book to anyone. Yet a part of her craved a moment of conversation with the only people who could comprehend the true extent of what she'd undergone – her darkest enemies, the Comte and the Contessa. She felt the warmth of Elöise's arm around her – for Miss Temple was a woman unused to being touched by any person save a maid doing up her corset – and at even this meagre contact unbidden visions began to rise, like smoke from a slow-catching fire, abetted by the jostling cart wheels, until every tingling nerve had grown to glowing. She could help it no more and shut her eyes . . .

Suddenly she was inhabiting a man's body, with such wonderful strength in her arms and in her deliciously thrusting hips . . . then it was the rushing thrill of another girl's greedy tongue between her legs . . . her hands caught the girl's head and raised her up, a smiling kiss and she tasted herself . . . one after another the visions flowed together – Miss Temple's face flushed as red as if her fever had returned – until another kiss, another liquid tongue, became – she realized quite abruptly with horror – the Contessa di Lacquer-Sforza dragging her tongue across Miss Temple's eye with a knowing, angry, sensuous sneer. Miss Temple gasped aloud. That incident had really taken place, in Harschmort House. What did it mean that Miss Temple's true memories could be entwined so seamlessly with what she remembered from the book, as if such a distinction was a boundary for the weak, or no real boundary at all? If she could not keep her own life apart from what she had consumed from the lives of others, how could she retain who she was? She sat up at once.

'Celeste?' asked Elöise. 'Are you all right? Are you too cold?'

'I am fine,' said Miss Temple. She dabbed a pearling of sweat from her upper lip. 'Perhaps there is something to eat?'

Lina had packed cold mutton, hard cheese, and some loaves of country bread. Miss Temple unhappily chewed a mouthful of meat while gazing about her. The woods had continued to deepen.

'Where exactly are we?' she asked Elöise.

'Heading south. Beyond that I cannot say – apparently past the forest there are hills. On the other side of *them* we may have hope of a train.'

'The road seems perfectly fine,' Miss Temple observed.

'It does.'

Miss Temple watched Elöise closely until the woman met her gaze. Miss Temple made a point of speaking loudly.

'This forest . . . is this where the people were killed?'

'I've no idea,' said Elöise.

'I would think it must be.'

'It is entirely possible –'

'Did you not go there?'

'Of course not, Celeste. The clothing was brought to me – Lina knew what we needed –'

'So no one has seen the Jorgens' cabin?'

'Of course people have *seen* it – the villagers who *found* them –'

'But that is not the same at all,' cried Miss Temple. She called to the driver in her firmest voice, 'Sir, we will require you to take us to the cabin of Mr and Mrs Jorgens. It is most urgent.'

The man pulled his horse to a stop and turned. He glanced once at Miss Temple but then settled on Elöise as the person in charge.

Miss Temple sighed and spoke in the most patient tone she could muster. 'It is necessary we visit the cabin of Mr and Mrs Jorgens. As you can see, I am wearing the poor woman's dress. It is incumbent upon me – for *religious* reasons, you understand – to pay my respects to her memory. If I do not, it is impossible that I shall sleep soundly *ever again*.'

The man looked again at Elöise. Then he turned and snapped the reins.

Miss Temple took another bite of mutton, for she was extremely hungry still.

It was perhaps twenty more minutes until he stopped the cart and pointed to their left. Through the trees Miss Temple saw a winding path washed away in more than one spot, like a pencilled line incompletely marred by the jagged pass of a gum eraser. She scrambled from the cart without assistance and then gave a hand to Elöise, whose expression was far from her own excitement.

'We will not be long,' Elöise called to their driver. 'It is just – just along that path?'

He nodded – Miss Temple wondered if the man possessed a tongue – and pointed. Miss Temple took her companion's hand and pulled her away.

The washed-out sections were moist and required careful steps to avoid thick mud, but in minutes they were out of sight of the cart, even though Elöise kept glancing back.

'He will not leave us,' Miss Temple finally said.

'I'm glad you think so,' answered Elöise.

'Of course he won't. He has not been fully paid.'

'But he has.'

'*You* think he has – but *he* surely plans to charge us that much more again once we are stranded with him in the hills.'

'How do you know that?'

'Because I am used to people wanting money – it is the dullest of things. But now we can speak – and *look*, Elöise . . . there it is!'

The cabin was small, and nestled comfortably between the trees on one side and a lush meadow. All around them Miss Temple could see the flotsam left from the flooding rain and its recession. The air was tinged with a certain whiff of corruption, of river mud churned and spread like a stinking condiment amidst the grasses and the trees.

'I'm sure I don't know what you hope to find,' said Elöise.

'I do not either,' replied Miss Temple, 'but I do know I have never seen a wolf in a boat. And now we can speak freely – I mean, honestly – *wolves*!'

'I do not know what you would like me to say.'

Miss Temple snorted. 'Elöise, are our enemies dead or not?'

'I have told you. I believe they are dead.'

'Then who has done *this* killing?'

'I do not know. The Doctor and Chang –'

'Where are they? Truthfully now – why did they leave?'

'I have *been* truthful, Celeste.'

Miss Temple stared at her. Elöise said nothing. Miss Temple wavered between dismay, mistrust, and condescension. As this last came most easily to her nature, she allowed herself an inner sneer. 'Still, as we are *here*, it seems perfectly irresponsible not to investigate.'

Elöise pursed her lips together, and then gestured about them at the ground. 'You see the many bootprints – the village people collecting the bodies. There is no hope of finding the sign of an animal's paw; nor of disproving such signs were here.'

'I agree completely,' said Miss Temple, but then she stopped, cocking her head. To the side of the cabin steps, pressed into the soft earth, was the print of a horse's shoe – as if the horse had been tethered near the door. Miss Temple leant closer but found no more. What she did find, on the steps themselves, was one muddy bootprint, followed by a thin, trailing line.

'What is that?' she asked Elöise.

Elöise frowned. 'It is a horseman's *spur*.'

For all her bravado, Miss Temple found herself taking a deep breath when she opened the cabin door – slowly and with as little sound as possible – and wishing she'd some kind of weapon. The interior was as simple as the outside promised: one room with a cold stove, a table and workbench, and a bed – plain and small, yet large enough to hold a marriage. Beyond the bed was an achingly little cot, and beyond this Miss Temple saw the trunk where her dress had undoubtedly been kept. She felt Elöise behind her, and the two stepped fully into the room, amidst the trappings of dead lives.

'I'm sure the others have ... have cleaned,' said Elöise, her voice dropping to a whisper.

Miss Temple turned back to the door, to the hinges and the handle. 'Do you see scratch marks? Or anything that would suggest a forceful entry?'

Elöise shook her head. 'Perhaps Mr Jorgens opened the door himself upon hearing a noise – they apparently had dogs, if there was barking –'

'They were killed in bed – I saw the bedding, quite covered in blood.'

'But that could be only one of them – when the other had opened the door, allowing the animal inside.'

Miss Temple nodded. 'Then perhaps there are signs of violence in the door's *vicinity* ...'

'Celeste,' began Elöise, but then stopped, sighed, and started to look as well.

But there was nothing – no scratches, no blood, no sign at all. Miss Temple crossed to the bed – at least someone had been killed *there*.

'Can you search the stove, in case anything untoward has been burnt?'

'Such as what?'

'I'm sure I do not *know*, Elöise, but I speak from experience. When the Doctor, Cardinal Chang, and I searched the workroom of the Comte d'Orkancz – we knew the Comte had been keeping a woman there who had been injured by contact with the blue glass – I located a remnant of the woman's dress, which proved a helpful clue.'

Elöise took all this with a tolerant sigh and set to clanging about with a poker. Miss Temple pulled back the bed's patchwork quilt. The mattress below was marked with rust-brown stains, soaked through the absent sheets. The marks were heaviest near one end of the bed – the head, she assumed – but spread across its width in a series of lines and whorls.

'There is nothing here but ash,' muttered Elöise, setting down the poker and wiping her hands with a grimace.

'I believe both husband and wife were in the bed,' said Miss Temple. 'If the Doctor were here, he might confirm it – but the stains suggest two occupants. Of course, we have no idea where the bodies were found –'

'With their throats torn out,' said Elöise, 'the blood would be prodigious.'

'Where was the child?'

'What child?'

'There is her cot,' said Miss Temple. 'Surely you would have been told –'

Elöise sighed. 'After a certain point it was simpler not to mix with the villagers at all. Perhaps there is an orphan. Lina never said.'

'But was she *here*?' asked Miss Temple. 'Did she see it?'

'Of course she wasn't,' said Elöise. 'Any wolf would have killed a child as well.'

Miss Temple did not reply. She stepped past the bed to the small cabin's only window. It was latched, but she could see, fine as the tip of a needle drawn across the worn wood, a tiny scratch. Something sharp had been driven between the frame and the pane. Miss Temple slipped the latch and pulled the window open, only to have it stick half-way.

'The wood has warped,' said Elöise, pointing to an imperfection in the upper frame.

Miss Temple leant forward and looked out the window to the ground, some five feet below. Who could say what climbing or jumping might be possible? She was about to shove it closed when her eye caught something flicked by the wind. At first it seemed a shred of cobweb, but when she reached out to take it she saw it was a hair. She plucked it from the splinter where it had snagged. A very black hair, and some two feet long.

If there was anything else to find in the cabin, it escaped them. Retracing their steps across the moist forest floor, Miss Temple glanced up at Elöise, who walked ahead. The one black hair was wound in a loop and stuffed into the pocket of her dress – Miss Temple's dress had no pockets (not that she normally sought pockets; it was why one carried a bag or walked with servants). Elöise's hand persisted in absently plucking at it as they went, as if her mind wrestled with the truth behind their discovery.

Miss Temple took the moment to study Elöise – for she had not before in all their time together taken any particular time to examine the woman, involved as they had been with fires and killings and airships. The tutor's brown hair was piled sensibly behind her head and held in place with small black pins. To her sudden surprise Miss Temple noticed within Elöise's hair one thin strand of grey, and then upon searching two or three more. Exactly how old was she? To Miss Temple the very idea of a grey hair was outlandish, but she accepted that time did grind all before it (if not in equal measure) and became curious about how such a thing felt. Such projection of interest, if not sympathy, drew Miss Temple's eyes down Elöise's body, where she found herself satisfied by the woman's practical carriage, her slim but sturdy shoulders, and her ability to walk without whingeing over muddy and rough terrain. Of course, she knew Elöise had been married, and that married life expanded a woman's experience in a way that left Miss Temple morally ambivalent. On the one hand, experience tended to improve a person by removing illusions – and at the least giving them more to speak of at the table – but, on the other, there was so often in married women a certain vein of mitigation, of knowledge that served to reduce rather than expand their thoughts. She suddenly wondered if Elöise had children. Had she *ever* had children? Had they possibly *died*?

With a sudden urge, for she had no vocabulary to express the deep unsettled thoughts behind such questions, Miss Temple stepped up her pace and took Elöise's restless hand in hers. 'We must be careful,' she said, looking down at her boots and away from the surprise on her companion's face. 'Never having been acquainted with the late Mrs Jorgens, it is strictly possible the hair is hers . . .'

Elöise nodded. Miss Temple took a breath and went on. 'But I have a memory, from the airship, that the Contessa carried – well, a vicious sort of spike upon one hand – and you see, it is how they have described the wolves – the woman's throat *torn out*' – Miss Temple's voice went hoarse, to her great frustration – 'with such *slashes*. I simply cannot forget poor Caroline Stearne's forlorn face above the wound . . . any more than I could forget the Contessa's *smile*.'

Elöise squeezed Miss Temple's hand. 'There is our cart, Celeste. You were correct, our man has waited.'

Miss Temple looked back to the cabin. 'We are fools,' she said. 'I am sure we might have availed ourselves of some weapons from the house –'

'Not to worry,' whispered Elöise. For the first time Miss Temple noticed the tight bundle in the woman's other hand. 'I have borrowed a pair of Mr Jorgens' knives.'

It was another hour before the trees began to thin and one more after that before the land changed to brown and tangled meadows, full of stones and rising gently to a line of hills whose rocky tops looked as if they had been blackened by a flame.

Through some of this Miss Temple had managed to sleep, and she woke, blinking, surprised by the flat open light around her, now that the trees had gone. The cart had stopped, and she saw their driver walking into the grass to relieve himself.

'Do you know where we will rest tonight?' she asked Elöise, who had used the man's absence to unroll the cloth she'd taken from the cabin.

'I was told it is an inn,' she replied. 'A mining town within the hills.'

She looked up to see Miss Temple's attention on the knives. One was three inches long and perhaps one fat inch across, razor sharp on one side and dull on the other, with the blade curving quite as much as a Turk's scimitar.

'Might it be for *skinning*?' offered Miss Temple.

The other knife was slightly longer, stabbing to a needle-sharp point, with a heavier blade than its length would seem to warrant.

'I would hazard it serves to strip meat from a bone,' answered Elöise. 'Mr Jorgens may have been a hunter.'

'I have no pockets,' Miss Temple announced crisply, and reached for the longer, straighter blade, 'but this will slip easily in my boot.' She glanced once at their returning driver, then settled the weapon neatly alongside her right instep.

Elöise palmed the other and balled up the cloth as the cart shifted, their driver swinging himself into his seat. He peered at them with the sour expression of a man unjustly burdened, spat a brackish jet of tobacco juice, and snapped the reins.

Feeling after another rest nearly her peremptory, impatient self, Miss Temple nevertheless did not speak of the matters most pressing to her mind. Instead, she plied her companion with the polite questions there had never been time to ask before – where her people were from, her preferred blend of tea, favourite fruit, and colour of sealing wax. This lead naturally enough to Elöise describing her life as tutor to the Trapping children. She spoke not at all of the Trappings themselves, or of the two Xonck brothers (Mrs Trapping's powerful siblings – the elder, Henry, as mighty and distant as the younger, Francis, was cunning and wicked), as if Elöise's position in life had no relation whatsoever to the adventures that had swept her up like a rising tide in the past weeks, or of any urgent questions that might still face them.

As a lady of property, Miss Temple had been well trained for conversation about family and social ritual (for amongst her social peers, such talk was a currency vital as gold coin), and so she nodded and smiled in turn as Elöise described in suffocating detail the parkland cottage of her uncle, with its stone wall lined with yellow rose bushes that had been tended by her mother as a girl. Yet it was ultimately of no use, for Miss Temple's tender mind, like a mill trembling with the motion of turbines and wheels, simply contended with too many forces to permit distraction.

Elöise had just confessed her love for the opera, despite the difficulty of securing tickets, and was offering an account of a particular favourite from some seasons ago, *Les Jardins Glacés*, an apparently wandering adventure from the mountains of deepest China. Upon reaching a point of pause – where Miss Temple might enquire politely about the music or the scenery

– she instead found the young woman's grey eyes fixed on the scrub-filled meadows around them.

'Celeste?' Elöise ventured, after the silence had taken full root.

Miss Temple looked at her and flicked the corners of her mouth in a smile. 'I am sorry,' she said. 'I had a thought.'

Elöise put away her neglected story of the opera and smiled gamely. 'What thought?'

'Actually several thoughts, or several that make one large thought clustered together – like chairs around a table, don't you know –'

'I see.'

'One of those cunning tables one can *extend*.'

'What thoughts, Celeste?'

'I was thinking about killing.'

'*Killing?*'

Miss Temple nodded.

'I'm sure it is a subject to weigh upon us both,' began Elöise, with a careful air. 'We have seen so much of it in so short a time – the killings at Tarr Manor, people hunted through the hallways of Harschmort, the truly savage battle on the rooftop before the airship could fly, and then death after death once we were aloft – and for you an even more difficult and sensitive question, in your unfortunate and foolish and corrupted former fiancé –'

The cautious deliberacy of her words was mortifying. Miss Temple waved her hands. 'No no – it is not that at all! I am occupied with our *present* business. We are miles away, and it is all my mind can hold – certainly there is no room there for a wolf! If we are to help the Doctor and Chang, who must have become caught up in these same events –'

'But these recent deaths,' protested Elöise, 'we know very little –'

'We can extrapolate!' cried Miss Temple. 'We are not fools. If one has studied dogs, one then knows how to lead a pack of hounds. If we assume the three incidents are part of one tale –'

'What three incidents?'

Miss Temple huffed with exasperation. 'In the fishing village! The grooms killed in the stable, the fisherman dead in his boat, the Jorgens in their cabin. By stitching them together we will see whether the resulting narrative reveals the raw hunger of a beast or the calculated actions of a villain. We can *then* determine where *next* –'

'How can we? Not having witnessed the incidents – not having seen the stable or the boat, not knowing how the bodies were disposed –'

'But you must know! Doctor Svenson must have told you –'

'But he did *not*.'

'We at least know in what order the killings occurred, and at what times –'

'But we *don't*. We know only when the bodies were *found*, Celeste.'

Miss Temple did not enjoy others referring to her Christian name at whim, and enjoyed it even less as punctuation to a thought she was supposed to find self-evident.

'Then perhaps you will tell me when *that* was, Elöise.'

After a wary glance at their silent driver and another sigh of resignation, Elöise shifted closer to Miss Temple and spoke in a voice barely above a whisper. 'The two grooms were discovered first, after the storm. The wind was still quite high, but the rains had eased enough for people to leave their homes. Several horses were found roaming free. When they were led back to the stable, the doors were found open, and the grooms dead. The Doctor and Chang were both there. I was tending to you, not that I regret being deprived of the sight.'

'And some horses are still missing.'

'Apparently, yes –'

'And there was a hoofprint at the Jorgens' cabin – along with the mark of spurs. Did you see the man in the village wearing new boots?'

'I did not.'

'*Riding* boots. In a *fishing* village!'

'With spurs?'

'No,' snapped Miss Temple. 'But that barely matters – such boots are as unlikely in that village as a tiara.'

'I disagree – they are fishermen, there was a storm – they all increase their living through salvage.'

'What of the *boat*?' asked Miss Temple.

'The fisherman's boat was found after the grooms. Since a savage animal was already settled on as the killer, there was only curiosity at how such a beast had managed to come aboard.'

'Did the Doctor venture an opinion, having seen the bodies?'

'Doctor Svenson did not share his opinions with me.'

'Why *not*?'

'You will have to ask *him*, Celeste!'

Miss Temple tossed her hair. 'It is all quite obvious! The Contessa was rescued by the fisherman. Upon landing, he was of no further use to her and she killed him. Then she came across the unfortunate Jorgens. Killing them provided her with new clothing, food, and a place to warm herself. Thus restored, she finally proceeded to the stable, where she killed the grooms and took a horse, driving the others away to make the attack look like a wolf.'

'That does not explain the hoofprints at the cabin. Or your spurs.'

'I cannot be expected to answer *everything*.'

Elöise was silent, running her tongue against the inside of her teeth, which Miss Temple realized was a sign of the woman's irritation.

'*What?*' snapped Miss Temple.

'It is geography,' answered Elöise. 'You have seen the forest, and where the river runs – and the width of its flood during the storm. Believe me when I say it was impassable for at least two days – exactly why the Jorgens were not found sooner. Further, both the fisherman's boat and the livery stable were divided from each other by still *more* flooding. There truly is *no* way, in the given span of days, that a single person, however viciously inclined, might have accomplished all five of these killings.'

'But we found the hair,' Miss Temple said, frowning.

'It could have been Mrs Jorgens'.'

'You know it wasn't,' Miss Temple replied coolly. 'Why did you and Doctor Svenson quarrel?'

'I should prefer not to speak of it,' replied Elöise.

'Is it related to our peril?'

'It is not.'

Miss Temple flounced her dress across her legs. 'I expect it weighs upon you cruelly,' she observed.

Elöise said nothing.

Miss Temple pulled another hank of dark bread from their second loaf. She was not especially hungry, but gave herself over to an earnest series of bites and swallows, studying the rocky hills. She'd no experience with such landscapes, stones driving up through the earth like some primeval carcass whose flesh had been melted away by a thousand years of rain, the bones blackened with rot but remaining, stiff and unfathomably hard. The soil was gritty and coarse, sustaining only tough, greasy grasses and squat, knotted trees, like sclerotic pensioners bent under the weight of impending death.

Staring into this barren landscape, Miss Temple cast her mind back to the airship. She attempted to recall the fate of each member of the villainous Cabal – it *had* been frenetic. The Contessa had leapt – unseen by anyone – from the dirigible's roof into the freezing sea. Francis Xonck and Roger Bascombe had been shot, the Comte d'Orkancz shot *and* stabbed, the Prince of Macklenburg horribly killed, and of course poor Lydia Vandaariff . . . Miss Temple closed her eyes and shook her head to dispel the image of the blonde girl's head splitting off from her body even as the crack of stiffening blood echoed out from her mouth. The airship had become a tomb of icy water as the cabin filled – she herself had seen the sodden corpse of Caroline Stearne, murdered by the Contessa, bobbing against the rooftop hatch – but if no one had survived, or no one aside from the Contessa, then how could she explain identical murders on the shore?

Miss Temple sighed again. Was this not a good thing? Was it not better the hair had belonged to Mrs Jorgens, and the plague of wolves exactly that? Was it simply that she could not trust such luck, or was it that the absence of further intrigue forced her to face her recent actions in a more sober light? It was all well and good to have killed in the heat of battle, but what of life afterwards? And could she truly convince herself that Roger Bascombe had been shot in battle? Certainly her fiancé had been angry, even perhaps dangerous – but she had been *armed*. Why had she not simply left him there alone, locked into a wardrobe? Miss Temple took another bite of bread, swallowing it with difficulty, her throat gone dry. The airship had been sinking – would she have allowed Roger to drown? Would drowning have been any less a murder? She saw no way past what she had done, apart from wishing – and then taking it back at once – that Chang or Svenson had taken Roger's life instead. The task had been hers – to kill him or set him free.

And could she not have done that? Did not her entire adventure prove how little Roger Bascombe had come to matter? Could he not have lived? Why had she pulled the trigger?

Miss Temple had no answer it did not hurt to think on.

The sun had set by the time their cart entered the tiny town of Karthe, a stretch of low stone huts, and here and there a larger storehouse or barn. The driver had stopped in front of a two-storey wooden structure – wood seeming to Miss Temple to be an expensive commodity, given the total lack of trees – with a hanging painted sign, its image a flaming star passing across a black sky.

'The inn,' he muttered. In an uncharacteristic gesture of politeness, the driver climbed from his bench and helped first Elöise and then Miss Temple down from the cart. 'I will settle the horse. I will stay at the livery, but return to take you to the morning train.'

He paused and turned his slightly damp eyes towards Elöise. 'As to the price we had discussed –'

Though she had anticipated (and looked forward to smashing) this strat-agem for extracting more money from two ostensibly helpless women, Miss Temple barely marked what the man was attempting to say. 'We must discuss your suggestions between ourselves,' she announced firmly, stopping the driver's narrative of desert in its tracks. Immediately she hooked her arm in Elöise's and pulled the woman a half-turn, so Miss Temple's mouth was pressed against her ear. 'It is the perfect opportunity to answer all of our questions! I will ascertain if any village horses have arrived – whether there have been any riders from the north – while *you* locate signs of any unexpected persons here at the inn. Also the Doctor and Chang – we will know they have travelled safely!'

'But – wait – Celeste, if they have left us – and they *have* – perhaps they have no wish to be found.'

'Don't be ridiculous,' said Miss Temple. 'I will find you in our room.'

She pressed two coins into Elöise's hands – having taken a moment during the day to pull off her boot and ascertain their financial state – and then indicated with an extended arm that their driver ought to remount and proceed directly to the stable with her as a passenger. Neither Elöise nor the driver seemed particularly pleased, but neither could they find any persuasive reasons to protest. The driver helped her back into the cart and climbed into his seat. Miss Temple went so far as to wave as her companion receded into the dark.

The stable was as modest as the rest of Karthe, making plain by a meagre number of stalls exactly how few horses were owned in the environs. Miss Temple watched the driver arrange for his nag – an earnest, ageing creature who would certainly prick her heart if allowed to do so, thus her choice to ignore it utterly – before stepping herself into a sharp haggle with the groom, agreeing to cover the costs for both man and beast as a fair extension of their original bargain. Hoping for more but sensing the steel in her tone, the driver agreed – yet was more than a bit surprised when she followed along as the groom installed the horse and acquainted the man with his place of rest. Miss Temple did so solely intent upon her investigation. It did not occur to her that she was seeing where the man would lay, perhaps in advance of some later assignation – the idea was too absurd – until the curious glance of the groom to the driver and the driver, somewhat abashed, back to the groom stopped her cold. She reddened with anger and waved brusquely at the stalls.

'As a livery this seems rather *meagre*,' she huffed. 'I suppose you must depend on strangers for your pay – are we your only tenants?'

The groom grinned at what now seemed to be an enquiry about *privacy*.

And it was then, in the midst of her sneering exasperation at the foul minds of men in general, that Miss Temple's thought was seized from within, overborne for a desperately clotted instant with a swirl of memory from the blue glass book. As ever, these experiences – and her own unnatural participation in them – were in that first moment irresistible. Set off by the smirking men, the details of the stable dredged into her memories like hooks, catching echoes of straw, horse stalls, leather, sweat, and musk. Miss Temple became in her flashing mind both man and woman – and indeed man and man – as each detail of an assignation caught hold: her ripened lady's body, shoulders braced against a wall, pushing her hips back like a stretching cat . . . or feeling, as a boy, the rough imprint of straw on her knees, quivering at the difficult entry of the older boy behind . . . or her own hard, masculine fingers mauling the soft flesh of a farm girl, legs wrapped round his waist, pulling tight inside her, the fervid quickening . . . She bit her lip to draw blood and blinked.

The driver and the groom were staring at her. How much time had passed?

'I ask, of course, because I will be staying at the inn,' explained Miss Temple. 'A lady is often well prepared to know who else may be in residence at such an establishment – whether to expect gentlemen, or figures of trade, or unsavoury adventurers, all of whom must in turn billet their mounts with you.'

The groom opened his mouth, then shut it, his hand floating up to indicate the stalls. For the first time Miss Temple noticed the pallor of the young fellow's complexion. Was he ill? She cleared her throat importantly, rising up to her toes and peeking into a stall. 'I see we are not your only tenants after all – excellent. Are these animals locally owned?' The horse inside ignored her, snuffling at its feed. 'Who in a mining town such as this would own a horse?'

'P-people need to ride,' stammered the groom.

'Yes, but who could *afford* one?' asked Miss Temple.

'Foremen,' offered her driver. 'Or to let out to travellers.'

Miss Temple could not imagine anyone travelling to Karthe for any reason at all. She peeked into the next stall. It was empty but strewn with straw and droppings.

'This horse is gone,' she called. 'Is it let out, as he says, or did it belong to a traveller?' She turned to face the groom.

'T-traveller.'

'And this traveller has *gone*?'

The groom's stretched throat bobbed nervously as he swallowed. Miss Temple could not prevent her mind, for it was now a trait she associated with grooms in general, from drifting to an image of that bobbling throat slashed wide.

'One horse or two?'

'T-two.' The single word emerged in parts, as if traversing an ill-swallowed bone. What was possibly making the fool so unsettled?

'And when? When did these *two* travellers leave? And who *were* they? Were they together?'

'I never saw them.'

'Why not? Who did?'

'Willem. The morning boy – but – but he – he –'

'He *what*?'

'You should ask the others.'

'What others?'

'If anyone's there.'

'*Where*?'

'At the inn.'

The driver laughed lewdly, as if even mentioning the inn was to conjure rooms and assignations. Miss Temple brusquely pushed past both men to the tack room, where the driver was to sleep. The humble room was wholly unremarkable, as was the tattered straw pallet the man would use.

'A whole silver penny for this?' Miss Temple scoffed loudly. 'It is not worth the half!'

'Beg pardon –'

'No doubt he is used to no better,' she sneered. 'Yet on principle – this pallet, for example –'

With a heave she lifted up one corner, wincing at the dust that rose to her face. Feeling ridiculous – why had she gone further into the stable instead of just walking away? – she flung the pallet from her, flipping it over. Miss Temple looked down, turned back at the now silent groom, and then down again. Seeped into the pallet's canvas cover was a brilliant blue stain the size of a china saucer.

A further search before the gaping faces of her social inferiors revealed no more than the Jorgens' cabin had disclosed after the single hair. Miss Temple strode back up the darkened lane to the inn, dismissing any suggestion that she be accompanied by either man. What did it mean that the blue stain was positioned on the pallet precisely near a sleeper's head? Or that there were two horses from the north? Could *this* be what the Doctor had discovered – why he had so swiftly followed the Cardinal? But how could the two men have left her – both of them! – with such danger in the village, and only Elöise to protect her – or, as Miss Temple was already refiguring their likely dealings in her busy mind – for *her* to *protect*?

Miss Temple turned at a rustling noise. There was nothing. She looked at the tiny cottages, each showing a chink of light beneath a bolted door or between closely drawn shutters . . . but one, just ahead to her left, showed no light at all, nor did a plumed shadow of smoke rise from its chimney. Miss Temple stared. The door was ajar. Something was wrong in Karthe . . . something had been wrong with the groom . . . she had found the blue stain . . . Miss Temple stepped quickly off the road. The door opened silently at a push and she went in.

She allowed her eyes to penetrate the dark until she located a standing bureau where one might expect to find, and then did, a tallow candle and a match. Shutting the door to hide her house-breaking from any prying eyes in the street, she examined the room with a light in one hand and, after a deft reach to her boot, Mr Jorgens' sharp knife in the other.

The hut differed from the Jorgens' cabin in that it contained at least three rooms, receding one after another in a line, but the size and low ceiling of the first main room was nearly the same, a fact that only accentuated Miss Temple's disquiet upon seeing a bed stripped of its linens, a cold stove, and a large trunk whose lock had been prised open with force. The floor was such a jumble of footprints that no inferences – apart from a lamentable lack of house care – could be made. The trunk was empty. She turned to the various shelves and cupboards. These were also bare. The only exceptions were the candles to one side of the door, and to the other, on the floor, a wadded ball of cloth. Miss Temple was not at all surprised to find it stained with blood.

The next room was windowless. It was clotted with furniture, chairs and tables and bureaus, stacked all against each other and pressed to each wall, the piles topped with a spinning wheel, wrapped burlap bundles, and heaps of bedding. Either the occupants were leaving Karthe or someone had died.

On the threshold of the final room Miss Temple paused. At her feet lay the crushed stub of a cigarette. She crouched down but could not determine if the unlit edge had been crimped in the Contessa's lacquered holder, or if it had been consumed by Doctor Svenson, again availing himself of that filthy habit.

The last room – and then she really must rejoin Elöise – was as empty of furnishings as the second was full, but its smell – a smell Miss Temple never would forget – remained pungent. It was a stomach-turning mix of burning tar and sulphurous, smoking ore – the smell of indigo clay, the noxious raw mineral the Comte d'Orkancz used to make the blue glass. She'd had a whiff of it off the stable pallet, but that was nothing compared to the saturation in the hut – almost as if someone had been smelting clay, or some hapless citizen of Karthe had fallen victim to the Process – the Cabal's cruel procedure to imprint their authority onto a victim's mind, making the man or woman a willing slave to the dreams of indifferent masters. But this required machinery, and there could be none – it was all back at Harschmort, or under the sea in the sunken airship. She held the candle high and turned slowly – nothing but an empty room with cheap, patterned paper pasted to each wall. Miss Temple crossed to the one window, leaning close to the sill. At first she saw nothing, then suddenly squeaked with shock and dropped the candle to the floor, where it went out, plunging the room into darkness.

She'd seen a face, and stumbled back blind before crouching and scuttling until she reached the wall, the knife held before her. She heard nothing save her own breath, and held her breath only to hear her pounding heart. She waited. The face had been pale, disfigured – no face she felt she

knew by sight, yet exuding in the scarcely remembered instant the baleful
malevolence of a ghoul.

She must leave at once.

But she could not do so without one last look at the window. Miss Temple
crept to the wall beneath, peered into the darkened doorway, then seized
her courage and popped to her feet, staring into the glass. A clouded fluid
had been sprayed, dark and clinging, on the glass. It had not been there
before. Miss Temple turned and ran.

With a surge of fear she pulled the door open and dashed outside. She
looked back at the house, the wide night sky and the open street underscor-
ing how alone she was. The cabin door hung slack and empty, a mocking
mouth in the dark.

Her breathless arrival at the inn minutes later did not in any way forestall
Miss Temple's fears, nor, stepping into the common room, with its low
glowing fire and wooden benches, did she find the hoped for comfort of
numbers inside. The room was empty. Miss Temple closed the door behind
her and dropped into place a wrought-iron latch.

'Excuse me?' she called, her voice not yet as controlled as she might
prefer. There was no answer. The only sound was the popping of embers.

'Elöise?' she called, her tone encouragingly firmer. 'Elöise Dujong?'

But Elöise answered no more than any innkeeper.

Miss Temple stepped towards the kitchen. There she found, again, no
person, but the complete trappings of a half-prepared meal: fresh loaves,
salted meat, pickled vegetables floating in an earthenware dish.

'Hello?' called Miss Temple.

Past the high wooden table was a door to the sort of yard where one
might house chickens or tend a garden or dry laundry on poles – or perhaps
store barrels of ale (it being the *only* inn in the village, she guessed that
the Flaming Star's ale being good or indifferent did not so much matter).
But Miss Temple did not explore further. Instead, she closed the door,
slipped its latch into place and returned through the common room to
stand at the base of a stairway.

'Elöise?' she called.

There was a glowing lantern somewhere above, but not in view, as the stairway turned back at a tiny landing. She climbed up, boots echoing despite her care. At the top of the stairs were three doors. The two to either side were closed. The lantern light came from the middle one, open wide.

On its narrow bed lay the wrapped bundle Lina had prepared that morning, but there was no other sign of Elöise. Miss Temple took up the lantern and returned to the landing. She looked at the two closed doors and weighed – given that the inn seemed empty, and that no light came from beneath either door – what to her mind was a very minor moral choice.

The first room was certainly let out, for there were several leather travel bags – one on the bed and three on the floor, and an odd, long, leather case, as if for a parasol, set into the corner. The bags were lashed tightly, however, and, aside from a chipped white dish smeared with ash, she saw no sign of a particular occupant.

The third room had no occupant at all, for the bed was stripped of blankets. Miss Temple sniffed for the slightest whiff of indigo clay, but she perceived only a problem with mice under the floorboards. She dropped to a crouch to look under the bed. Directly before her lay a slender book. She picked it up. The book's cover of pale white pasteboard – *Persephone: Poetic Fragments* (translated by a Mr Lynch) – was finger-smeared with long-dried blood.

She recalled their first meeting, on the train – a man reading such a volume, a straight razor open on the seat beside. The book was Chang's.

Below her someone rattled the inn's front door. Miss Temple leapt out of the empty room, hurriedly set the lantern and the book back next to Lina's bundle, and ran down the stairs. As she dashed into the common room, wondering who could be at the door and whether running to them so openly was a very stupid thing, a woman emerged from the kitchen, wiping her hands on an apron.

'You must be the other young lady.' The woman smiled tolerantly as she crossed to unlatch the door. 'I was told you'd arrive.'

Before Miss Temple could say a word – or even fully form the question as to where the woman had been hidden – Elöise Dujong burst in from the street, followed by two men. She rushed to Miss Temple and clasped hold of her hands. 'O Celeste – there you are!' Elöise turned back to the men with a relieved smile. 'You see – she is no figure of my imagination!'

'I had begun to think it, I confess,' chuckled the elder of the two, a tall, broad fellow with black hair that curled about his ears. He wore a thick travelling cloak that covered his body, down to a pair of black leather riding boots.

'This is Mr Olsteen,' said Elöise, extending her hand, 'a fellow guest at the Flaming Star who quite nobly agreed to walk with me!'

'Can't have a lady alone in the street.' Olsteen chuckled again. 'Not with everything I hear about these mountains.'

'And this is Franck.' The second man was shorter than Olsteen and young, with rough, sullen eyes. His hands – which the fellow persisted in squeezing into fists – were unpleasantly callused. 'Franck is Mrs Daube's hired man here at the inn – our hostess, whose acquaintance I see you have already made –'

'I haven't, actually,' managed Miss Temple, ignoring the gaze of both men upon her person.

'We have been searching for you, Celeste,' continued Elöise, as though this was not perfectly obvious. 'Apparently some of the regrettable events from further north have anticipated our arrival. When you did not return at once, I became worried.'

'We walked all the way to the stables,' said Olsteen. 'But they said you had already gone.'

'And yet we did not pass in the street,' observed Miss Temple innocently. 'How very queer.'

'Mr Olsteen is one of a party of hunters just back from the mountains. And both Mrs Daube and Franck informed me –'

'Of the deaths, I expect,' said Miss Temple, turning to their hostess. 'The wretched occupants of that particular squat cottage – across the road and some twenty yards along? Quite recent, I should think – and one can only guess how horrid.'

To this no one replied.

'Because it had no *lights*,' Miss Temple went on, 'nor smoke from the chimney – alone of the entirety of Karthe. Thus one draws *conclusions*. But, tell me, how many were killed – and, if I might be so pressing, *who* were they? And killed by *whom*?'

'A boy, Willem,' said Franck, 'and his poor father –'

'Not young Willem,' Miss Temple asked with sympathy, 'the morning boy at the stables?'

'How did you know that?' asked Franck.

'She's just come from the stables,' said Olsteen with a shrewd smile. 'No doubt this Willem's death was all the other lad could speak of.'

'You are correct, sir.' Miss Temple nodded severely. 'People will peck at another person's tragedy like daws at a mislaid seed cake.'

Elöise reached out for Miss Temple's hand. 'But the groom did not say who had *done* the murders,' added Miss Temple, a touch too hopefully.

'I shouldn't expect he did,' said Mrs Daube.

'Shall we retire for a moment to our room?' Elöise asked Miss Temple.

'Of course.' Miss Temple smiled at Olsteen and Franck. 'I am obliged to both of you for your kindness, however unnecessary.'

Elöise dipped her knee to Mr Olsteen, gently turned Miss Temple towards the stairs, and then respectfully addressed their hostess. 'Mrs Daube, if it would be no trouble for us to dine in some twenty minutes?'

'Of course not, my dear,' answered the innkeeper evenly. 'I shall just be carving the joint.'

The women sat side by side on their bed, door latched, whispering closely.

'It is *Chang's*,' exclaimed Miss Temple, holding out the blood-stained book. 'I found it in the other room.'

'I'm sure it must be. And *here* . . .' Elöise dug in the pocket of her dress and came out with a small smooth purple stone and a cigarette butt. She snatched the stone away with her other hand and held out the cigarette butt to Miss Temple. '. . . is evidence of Doctor Svenson.'

Miss Temple studied the butt end without success for any sign of crimping.

'Are you sure it must be his?'

'It was crushed to the floor just *here*.'

'But perhaps Mr Olsteen or one of his fellows – may they not have been in this very room?'

'As I'm certain many men read poetry.'

Miss Temple did not see the comparison at all. 'I have seen Chang with this very book,' she explained. 'The consumption of tobacco is as common as cholera in Venice.'

'Doctor Svenson purchased a quantity of Danish cigarettes from a fisherman,' answered Elöise. 'You will see the maker's mark.'

She turned the foul thing in her hand until Miss Temple could indeed discern a small gold-inked bird.

'Well, then,' Miss Temple said, 'perhaps it tells us more. I found another such *remnant* – though I do not know if it bore this mark – in the abandoned house I examined on my way back from the livery. If the Doctor had *also* been inside it –'

'You went into an abandoned house? Alone? In the midst of these *murders*?'

'I did not know I was in the midst of *anything*,' began Miss Temple.

'And you just brazenly lied to us all downstairs!'

'What *ought* I to have said? I do not know those people, I do not know what involvement they might have had –'

'Involvement?' cried Elöise. 'Why should they have any *involvement* – they were trying to help you!'

'But why?'

'Kindness, Celeste! Plain decency –'

'O Elöise! The hair, the bootprints – and now there have been murders *here*! That empty house belonged to these most recent victims –'

Elöise threw the cigarette butt to the floor. 'We went looking for you, Celeste – as soon as I learnt what had happened, we went the length of the road to the stables! We should have seen you on our way! But you had vanished! I was quite disturbed and frightened!'

'O, you had your burly fellows,' said Miss Temple.

'I was frightened for *you*!'

'But I have discovered –'

'We have discovered we are in great danger! We have discovered the
Doctor and Cardinal were both here – but we do not know if they *survived*
to leave!'

It was not a thought that had occurred to Miss Temple. So happy had she
been to find Chang's book that the notion of its somehow being a token of
his *peril* seemed too cruel a contradiction. It was then, looking up at Elöise
– whose gaze had fallen to the cigarette stub – that Miss Temple noticed
the tears brimming about the woman's eyes. She saw in an instant that
Elöise was right, that anything could have happened, that Chang and
Svenson could have been killed.

'No no,' she began with a dutiful cheer. 'I'm sure our friends are
quite safe –'

But Elöise cried out sharply, even as twin lines of tears broke forth down
her cheeks. 'Who are you to know anything, Celeste Temple? You are a
wilful thing who has been happily asleep these past cruel days – who
has money and confident ease, who has been rescued from your brazen
presumption time and again by these very men who may now be dead – or
who knows where? Who I have watched over, night after night, watched
alone, only to have you abandon me at every adventuresome whim that
pops into your spoilt-brat's brain!'

Miss Temple's first impulse was to slap the other woman's face quite
hard, but she was so taken aback by this outburst that her only response
was a certain cold loathing. It settled behind her grey eyes and imbued
their formerly eager expression with the watchful, heartless gaze of an
ambivalent cat.

Just as immediately Elöise placed a hand over her mouth, her eyes wide.
'O Celeste, I am sorry – I did not mean it – forgive me –'

But Miss Temple had heard such words before, throughout the whole of
her life, from her imperious father to the lowest kitchen maid, so often that
she divided the persons she knew into those who had voiced – or, she
suspected, harboured – such criticisms and those, like Chang, Svenson,
and up to this very instant Elöise, who had not. She was routinely obliged

to retain regular contact with those in the former category, but future dealings were irrevocably changed – and, as she stared coolly at Mrs Dujong, Miss Temple ignored what a less forceful person might have recognized on the woman's face as evident regret. Instead, taking care and interest as things once more to bury fully within her own heart, Miss Temple shifted her attention, as if it were a heavy case on a train platform, to the very real and pressing tasks at hand, next to which any *intimate* misunderstandings must be insignificant.

'We shall not speak of it,' she said quietly.

'No no, it was horrid, I am so sorry' – here Elöise stifled an actual, presumptuous sob – 'I am merely frightened! And after my quarrel with the Doctor, our foolish, foolish quarrel –'

'It is surely no matter to me either way.' Miss Temple took the opportunity to rise and straighten her dress, stepping deftly beyond the reach of any guilt-driven comforting hand. 'My only concern is to confound and defeat this party of murdering villains – and learn who is responsible for these crimes – and whether anyone else survived the airship! Lives are at stake – it is imperative we find *answers*, Elöise.'

'Of course – Celeste –'

'Which brings me to ask, as it was impossible to do so downstairs, whether in your search you glimpsed any other *figure* in the village streets?'

'Was there someone we *ought* to have seen?'

Miss Temple shrugged. Elöise was watching her closely, obviously on the point of apologizing once more. Miss Temple smiled as graciously as she could. 'It is only this morning that I have been from my bed. Suddenly I should like nothing more than to shut my eyes.'

'Of course. I will tell Mrs Daube that we shall be some minutes more – you must take all the time you like.'

'That is most kind,' said Miss Temple. 'If you would take the lantern with you and close the door.'

As she lay in the dark, facing the pine plank wall, holding Chang's volume of poetry between her hands, Miss Temple told herself that in all truth it was simpler this way – and who knew, perhaps Elöise's quarrel with Doctor

Svenson had been similarly impulsive and short-sighted, the outburst of an unreliable, skittish woman who had, quite frankly, always been something of a bother. She took in a deep breath and let it out slowly, feeling a catch in her throat. Nothing was changed – apart from it being that much more important to get back to the city. If she slept on the train, there would be no need for her to speak to Elöise at all, apart from the sorting of tickets – and no reason to visit her family's cottage either. Miss Temple could find a new hotel. Chang and Svenson could seek her out there. If they were alive.

She sighed again, then sat up in an abrupt rustle of petticoats, fumbling for a candle and a match. She did not want to think about Elöise, or the disfigured, corpse-white face in the window, or her visions from the glass book, or the Contessa, or Roger. She didn't want to *think* about anything. Miss Temple looked down at the book in her hand and leant closer to the light.

She was never one for poetry or, if it must be said, reading in particular. It was an activity most often undertaken at the behest of someone else – a governess, a tutor, some relative – and so a source of resentment and disdain. Yet Miss Temple imagined Chang must feel about poetry the same way she felt about maps, maps being the one sort of reading she could happily essay. She opened the book and began to flip the pages, gauging the amount of text per page (not very much) and the number of pages in all (not very many) – an easy sort of read that would have appealed to her impatience save that this sparsity gave off at the same time an unwelcome whiff of pride.

She closed the book, and then, on an impulse, opened both covers at the same time, allowing the pages to open on a random poem. The one that fell to view did so because the binding had been repeatedly doubled back, and the page's corner deliberately folded down to mark its place.

It was composed of but one simple stanza, titled 'Pomegranate':

> Six blood-swept seeds, consumed in grief
> A dismal realm of fetid torp'rous air
> No sky above her for relief
> Compacted with damnation, beyond care.

Miss Temple closed the book. She was not against poetry as a rule – the *idea* of its density even appealed to her. Yet to Miss Temple this meant nothing *written* but knotted, sensual experiences she could not imagine bound into mere words – moments too unwieldy, too crammed with what shivered her bare spine: the rage of a September surf, the snarl of her sweet cat upon catching a bird, the smoke of burning cane fields drifting across her morning veranda . . . distilled instants in which she perceived some larger inkling of the hidden world . . . moments that left her feeling both wiser and bereft.

If she concentrated she could of course recall the legend of Persephone, or enough of it to make her sigh with impatience, but she did not know what kidnapping, pomegranates, and so forth meant to Chang. That the binding had been bent and the page folded spoke to the poem's significance in his mind. She did take a certain pleasure at 'blood-swept' and appreciated the hopelessness of a realm lacking a sky, as one supposed an underworld must. But as to the poem's *subject*, a princess taken into the underworld . . . Miss Temple sniffed, supposing it must refer to Chang's courtesan love, Angelique. She pursed her lips to recall the regrettable whore who, like a foolish girl in a fairy tale, had rejected Chang in favour of vain promises from the Comte d'Orkancz – a choice that had led to Angelique's enslavement, disfigurement, and death. Such things of course happened – a great many unwelcome men had cared for Miss Temple any number of times – and yet it seemed that the Cardinal, who was so *able*, ought to have been immune to so common an affliction. And yet, far from spurring a dislike of Chang for this failing, Miss Temple found herself sighing in unexpected sympathy for his pain.

She sighed again, looking into the candle flame. A sensible course would have been to go downstairs, eat a good meal, and then sleep through to the morning. But her thoughts were still too restless (nor was she especially looking forward to sharing a bed with Elöise). It occurred to her that the other guest, the hunter, Mr Olsteen, must have used a local horse for his hunting. Perhaps he could answer some of the questions she would have put to the murdered groom . . .

Miss Temple tucked the book under the pillow and blew out the candle. She stepped onto the landing and again straightened her dress, wondering if Mrs Daube might be prevailed upon in the morning to curl her hair, a thought that quite unbidden brought a smile to her face. She descended the stairs breathing in the smells of food and a crackling fire, the hardening of her heart so normal a sensation as to be but scarcely noticed.

Miss Temple found Mrs Daube in the kitchen pouring a very dark gravy from a pan on her stove into a small pewter cruet. The innkeeper had set a modest table with two places. But Elöise was not there.

Mrs Daube looked up at Miss Temple, her eyes kind and bright. 'There you are! The other lady said you were resting, but I am sure a hot supper will do you nicely.'

'Where is Mrs Dujong?'

'Is she not by the fire?'

'No.'

'Then I'm sure I do not know. Perhaps she is speaking to Mr Olsteen.'

'Why would she be doing that?' asked Miss Temple.

'Perhaps to apologize for his needless searching for you?' said Mrs Daube with a smile, as she placed a bowl of steaming vegetables onto the table, next to a brown loaf dusted with flour.

'Where would she be?' asked Miss Temple. 'They are not upstairs.'

'Will you sit?' asked Mrs Daube. 'It is much better eaten when ready.'

Miss Temple hesitated, both annoyed and relieved at Elöise's absence, but then she considered that time with Mrs Daube was an opportunity of its own. She slipped past with a trim smile to a chair on the table's far side, where she could speak to the innkeeper without turning.

'Here you go.' Mrs Daube set a meagre chop on a heavy Dutch blue plate before her. 'The end of last week's mutton. I make no apologies, for you'll get no better in Karthe. There have been no stores come north these last five days – as if we have not the needs of finer folk. One vexation after *another*. I am not sure I ever got your name.'

'I am Miss Temple.'

'I am poor with names,' said Mrs Daube tartly. 'It is good I am an excellent cook.'

Miss Temple occupied herself with the pewter cruet, the bread, and a wooden bowl of what looked like mashed turnips with some scrapings of nutmeg – a grace note that indeed bettered her opinion of her hostess.

'I believe you have recently seen a friend of Mrs Dujong and myself,' Miss Temple observed, pasting a smear of butter across her slice of bread. 'A rather daunting person, in a red coat and dark glasses?'

Mrs Daube shifted two pots to different places on the stove, making room for an iron kettle. When she looked back to the table, her lips were thinly pressed together. 'The gentleman, if I may call him such, is not one to slip the mind. Yet he paid for one meal only and went on his way. We barely spoke ten words, and most of those with regard to passing the salt.'

'Would Mr Olsteen have spoken to him?'

'Mr Olsteen had not yet returned from the mountains.'

'What about Franck?'

'Franck does not speak to guests.'

As if the young man had just been brought back to mind, Mrs Daube turned to a small door to the side of the stove that Miss Temple had not before noticed, draped as it was with a hanging piece of cloth, and shouted like a sailor: '*Franck! Supper!*'

No answer came from the hidden room.

'This bread is delicious,' said Miss Temple.

'I'm glad to hear it,' said Mrs Daube.

'I am quite fond of bread.'

'It is hard to go wrong with bread.'

'Especially bread with jam.'

Mrs Daube felt no need to comment, jam not presently available on the table.

'And what of our other friend?' Miss Temple continued.

'You have a great many friends for someone so far from home.'

'Doctor Svenson. He must have passed through Karthe at most two days after the Cardinal –'

'Cardinal? That fellow – all in red, and with those *eyes*? He was no churchman!'

'No no,' said Miss Temple, chuckling, 'but that – in the city – is what everyone *else* calls him. In truth I have no knowledge of his Christian name.'

'Do Chinamen have Christian names?'

Miss Temple laughed outright. 'O Mrs Daube, he is no more from China than you or I are black Africans! It is merely a name he has acquired – from the scars across his eyes, you see.'

Miss Temple happily pulled her own eyelids to either side, doing her best to approximate Chang's disfigurement.

'It is unnatural,' declared Mrs Daube.

'Horrid, to be sure – the result of a riding crop, I believe – and it would indeed be difficult to call the Cardinal *handsome*, and yet – for his world is a harsh one – their ferocity speaks to his *capacity*.'

'What world is that?' asked Mrs Daube, her voice a bit more hushed. She had stepped closer, one hand worrying the scuffed edge of the table.

'A world where there are murders,' replied Miss Temple, realizing how much pleasure she took in disturbing her hostess, and that it was all a sort of boasting. 'And people like Cardinal Chang – and Doctor Svenson, and – though I know you will not credit such a thing – myself, have done our best to discover who has been doing the killing. You did meet Doctor Svenson, I know it. Mrs Dujong found one of his crushed cigarettes upstairs – it is *proved* he was here.'

Miss Temple gazed up at the woman – older, taller, stronger, in her own home – with the clear confidence of an inquisitor not to be trifled with. She set down her knife and fork, and indicated the empty chair opposite her. Mrs Daube sank into it with a grudging sniff.

'Karthe does not take to strangers, much less those that walk about looking like the devil himself.'

'How long after Chang arrived did the Doctor –'

'And then came the murders – of course men from the town went looking, even your other friend, the foreign Doctor –'

'He is a surgeon, to be precise, in the Macklenburg Navy. Where is the Doctor *now*?'

'I told you – he joined the party of men to search. I'm sure I don't know what's taken them so long to return.'

'But where did they go – to the train?'

Mrs Daube snorted at this ridiculous suggestion. 'The mountains, of course. Dangerous any time of year, and even more so after winter, when what beasts that have survived are ravenous.'

'Beasts?'

'Wolves, my dear – our hills are full of them.'

Miss Temple was appalled at two such violently complementary thoughts – the missing men and a propensity for wolves – existing so placidly next to one another in the woman's mind.

'I beg your pardon, Mrs Daube, but you seem to be saying that Doctor Svenson left Karthe with a party of men, travelling into the wolf-ridden mountains, and has failed to return. Is no one worried? Surely the missing townsmen have families –'

'No one tells *me*,' snapped Mrs Daube sullenly. 'Merely a poor widow, no one cares for an old woman –'

'But who *would* know where they went?'

'Anyone else in Karthe! Even Franck,' the woman huffed. 'Not that he's breathed a word to me, though one would only think – after my generosity –'

'Did either of you mention this to Mrs Dujong?'

'How am I expected to know that?' she snapped, but then grinned with poorly hidden relish. 'But I can guess how the likes of *him* would enjoy frightening her with stories.'

Miss Temple shut her eyes, imagining how news of the Doctor's vanishing must have been taken by Elöise.

'My goodness, yes,' Mrs Daube went on, 'ever since the first strangers – and then your man Chang –'

'Wait – what *first* strangers? Do you mean Mr Olsteen and his fellows – or someone else?'

'The Flaming Star is extremely popular with travellers of all sorts –'

'What travellers? From the north, like us?'

'I'm sure I do not know,' the woman whispered; 'that is the very *mystery* of it.' She leant over the table with a conspiratorial leer that revealed the absence of an upper bicuspid. 'A boy – the same that died – came running from the livery to say a room would be wanted, the finest we had. But then the fool ran on before we knew for who or how many! Every effort was made, rooms cleaned and food prepared – such expense! – only to have not a single soul appear! And then your man Chang arrived – *not* from the stables, for he had no horse – and the *next* day, before I could switch that lying horse groom raw, I was told both he and his shiftless father had been *killed*!'

'But . . . you don't actually believe that wolves, driven down from the hills, could have stalked into the streets of this village?'

Mrs Daube, apparently revived for having voiced her pent-up discontent, took it upon herself to dunk a piece of bread into the turnips and spoke through her chewing. 'It has not happened since my grandmother's time, but such a dreadful thing is *possible*. Indeed, my dear, what ever else but *wolves* could explain it?'

Two minutes later, the sharp knife in her hand, Miss Temple again strode down the main road of Karthe. The air was cold – she could see her breath – and she regretted not having a wrap, impulsively refusing the musty brown cloak offered by Mrs Daube (ingrained as she was to reject any brown garment out of hand). The moon had dropped closer to the shadowed hills, but still shone bright. She felt sure Elöise would have sought the murdered stable boy's hut, and all too soon Miss Temple found herself, unsettled, at its door – no longer hanging open, a sliver of yellow light winking out where it met the ground.

The door was latched from within and would not open. Miss Temple knocked – the noise absurdly loud in the night. There was no answer. She knocked again, and then whispered sharply. 'Elöise! It is Miss Temple.' She sighed. 'It is *Celeste*!'

There was still no answer. She pulled on the handle with no more success than before.

'Mr Olsteen! Franck! I insist that you open this door!'

She was getting chilled. She rapped on the window shutters but could not pry them apart. Miss Temple stalked to a narrow passage that ran between the cottage and the stone wall of its neighbour, straight through to the rear of the house. She swallowed. Was it likely that Elöise had gone instead to the stables? Where were the two men? Had *they* done something to Elöise, luring her to such an isolated place? Or was it someone else in the house entirely? Someone with a corpse-like, ravaged face?

She took another breath and entered the passage, slipping from the moonlight like a ghost, her feet rustling through grass thick with dew, wetting her dress and swatting at her ankles. This wall held no windows, and she heard nothing from inside the house as she went. Miss Temple made sure of her grip on the knife and slowly, like a drop of grudging honey into a cup of tea, leant around the rear corner.

A waft of evening wind nearly smothered her with the fumes of indigo clay.

She swallowed, throat burning and eyes blinking tears, but forced herself to look once more. Behind the cottage was a patch of grass strewn with an odd assortment of wooden hutches – abandoned now but once housing chickens or rabbits – all brightly illuminated by a square of yellow light thrown from the house, from the very window she had peered through in the rearmost room, its frame and glass now fully shattered, as if by a brutal series of kicks. Miss Temple studied the snapped remnants of the panes that dotted the window's edge like a sailor's meagre teeth, and realized they were bent back into the room. The force to smash the window had come from outside.

She crept closer. The window was too high to see through – but there had to be a rear door if there was a yard. She padded past the window and found it behind the hutches, made of hammered-together planking and hanging feebly from a pair of rusted hinges. Her first pull on the handle told her it was held by a chain from within, which made sense – if the door was open, why would anyone kick in the window?

Reasoning that between rattling the chain and calling out for Elöise at the front door she had already alerted anyone inside as to her presence, Miss Temple noisily dragged one of the hutches over to the window, tested its strength gingerly with one foot, and then carefully climbed up. From this height she could just see over the battered sill. On the floor lay Franck, curled away from her on his side. Set down in the centre of the room was a lantern, its bright beams revealing the glittering shards that covered the floor.

More glass still stuck out in brittle needles across the length of the sill – she could not possibly climb through without injuring herself. She exhaled, happy for a good excuse not to ruin her dress, and then, remembering her first visit, looked down at the centre of the frame. A dark, sticky stain had soaked into the wood. She sniffed at it and was rewarded with the loathsome, mechanical odour of indigo clay. But Miss Temple frowned and sniffed again, shutting her eyes to concentrate . . . salt . . . and iron. She opened her eyes and grimaced. Mixed into the noxious blue fluid was blood.

Miss Temple leapt off the hutch and strode back to the rickety door. With a satisfying thrust she shoved the knife blade between the planking and the frame and tugged upward, catching the chain. She jerked it upwards again, exclaiming with irritation as a sliver of wood caught on her hand, and dislodged the chain from its post. In an instant she stood at the room's threshold, holding her nose with one hand and licking a bead of blood from the other. The man on the floor was quite dead. Glass crunching beneath her boots, Miss Temple moved cautiously into the middle room, stacked with furniture, aware that it afforded ample nooks for concealment and ambush. She did her best to peer underneath, but found her attention taken by details she'd not noticed before – heaped clothing, a box of battered toys, a folded Sunday jacket and shoes. With an uncomfortable swallow she went on to the final room – darkest, being furthest from the lantern – which remained as empty as ever. Though it gave her no pleasure, she returned to the body.

Miss Temple set her knife on the floor, needing both hands to turn Franck, but as his face rolled into view she covered her mouth and wheeled away, fighting nausea. The hired man's features were pale as paste and his eyes stuck despairingly wide, but his plaintive expression was not the source of Miss Temple's horror. Steeling herself, she carefully peeked back, then spun away again, waving the indigo fumes away from her face, a prickling tang of bile in her mouth. Miss Temple had never seen anything like it – Franck's throat was *gone*. She could see the gleaming ridges of his spine.

She forced her eyes away from the wound to the rest of his body, doing her best to imagine how Doctor Svenson would proceed. Were there other scratches or cuts – as there surely must be to credit an animal with the killing? Miss Temple found nothing . . . and then, more than this, she realized that she was not – as she surely ought to have been – standing in a spreading pool of the poor man's blood.

In point of fact, there was no blood anywhere. How could that be? Could he have been killed out of doors and then thrown *through* the window? It was possible, but still such a massive wound must flow even then, and there was not a drop that she could see, not even on the fellow's *shirt*. With trepidation, Miss Temple knelt and extended the knife, using the tip to peel back the dead man's collar.

In a crease of skin between his battered neck and shoulder was a tiny crust of blue flakes . . . of dark blue glass.

The murder had been done by an insertion of blue glass, freezing the flesh around it without the slightest spray of blood. Then, the killer must have taken the time to prise out – with a knife? with their fingers? – every morsel of flesh that had been alchemically transformed, leaving an appalling wound no one would think to question.

Miss Temple lurched towards the dim front room. But how had Franck come to be here by himself? And what had he seen to make his death necessary? And where were Elöise and Mr Olsteen? Miss Temple had assumed the three to be together – had the others simply fled? Or had Franck come alone? But then where *was* Elöise – in the company of the broad-shouldered huntsman, with whom she seemed far too taken . . .

And how was it that the front door was still latched? Even if Franck *had* been killed outside and then thrown through the window, the window showed no evidence of anyone returning through it *back* to the yard – the glass splinters were proof enough of that. Yet both doors were latched from the inside, indicating that whoever latched them to begin with . . . must still be inside . . .

The noise of a wooden chair scraping against a floorboard pierced her thoughts. She wheeled towards the middle room. The scrape was redoubled as a bureau was pushed – and then the end table that must have been atop it clattered – was thrown! – to the floor, bouncing into view with the shocking force, in the tiny still cottage, of a cavalry charge. Miss Temple screamed. Behind her the table was kicked aside. She heard *footsteps* –

heavy, stomping – tore the latch free and wrenched on the handle as a sickening wave of indigo fumes reached around her shoulders like a pair of clutching hands. The door was open. Miss Temple leapt through it.

The door of the Flaming Star yawned open when she reached it. Something was wrong. Miss Temple burst into the common room, shouting for Mrs Daube, for Elöise, only to receive no answer. She clawed the latch in place on the door and then launched herself up the stairs – snatching Chang's book from beneath her pillow – no sign of Elöise, but Olsteen's door was open, and his bags ransacked and scattered across his room. She careered to the kitchen, calling again, her breath coming raw and her head palpably beginning to swim. She was not well. She ought to be in bed with tea, with someone kind in a chair reading ridiculous items from a newspaper as she slipped into sleep. But instead Miss Temple rounded the corner into the kitchen and skidded off balance into the wall as her boot slid through an overturned bowl of turnips. The table lay on its side, the food was strewn everywhere amidst sharp blue-white chips of broken plates and upended dripping pans. The door to the yard hung wide, and Miss Temple rushed to it. Behind her the front door rattled against the vicious kick of what sounded like a plough horse.

Mrs Daube was on her knees in the grass, gasping for air. Strewn all around her, tangled and wet, lay linens and clothing, as if a wilful child had sorted through a week's worth of laundry, only to toss whatever he did not fancy to the ground.

Miss Temple dug her hand under the innkeeper's arm, trying to haul her up. 'Mrs Daube – you are in peril . . .'

The woman did not seem to hear, or even note being moved. She muttered and shook her head, a bead of clear saliva suspended from her lips.

'Mrs Daube – *this way* – have you seen Mrs Dujong?'

Dragging the innkeeper, Miss Temple kicked through the balled-up sheets towards a gate at the far end of the yard. Another kick roared from inside the inn, and then a third – a savage battering the door could never bear.

'Mrs Daube! *Please!* Have you seen Elöise? Have you seen Mr Olsteen?'

At last the innkeeper looked up, eyes wide and black, blood at the corner of her mouth. 'Mr Olsteen?'

'Do you know where he is?'

'She – she came back –'

'Elöise? Where did they go?'

'She . . .' Mrs Daube choked with fright, still overtaken by what she must have seen. 'She – she made me help her – but then Mr Olsteen – *no!*'

This last came at the realization that Miss Temple was dragging her towards the gate – swinging open, another sign of Elöise's flight. Mrs Daube moaned like a beast, dug in her heels, and fought away from Miss Temple's grip, only to topple back to her knees, dissolving into tears. Elöise had made Mrs Daube help her how – search through Olsteen's bags? But why tip the table and scatter the laundry? Had Olsteen caught up with them – had Elöise escaped, with him in pursuit?

Miss Temple spun to the kitchen door with a sudden chill. The kitchen lamp had blown out – the only glow the creeping firelight from the common room. Then this was blotted out by a shadow in the door, thick and impenetrable. With a cry of her own, Miss Temple abandoned the sobbing innkeeper and clawed her way through the gate.

She had not gone fifteen steps before the night was split with a scream from Mrs Daube. Miss Temple sobbed aloud and drove herself on, desperate as a hawk-sought hare. If she could only find Elöise – dear, stupid Elöise – perhaps the two together might defend themselves. Yes, Miss Temple scoffed, with their little *knives*. The bark of her breath fogged in the cold.

The rough dirt path ran to the rear of the other houses of Karthe village, but each was bordered by a stone fence with a heavy gate. By the time she might reach any one and raise the house with shouting, she would be captured. Her gasps were ragged and her body slick with sweat – she would get another fever, she would die, she would trip and snap her ankle like a twig. She looked to the rising hills – could she leave the path and hide in the rocks? No. Such a choice was to abandon Elöise, which Miss Temple could not – perhaps as much in pride as care – allow herself to do.

The path abruptly dropped into a ravine split by a trickling watercourse tumbled with smooth stones. On its other side, flat on the path in the moonlight, lay the broad figure of Mr Olsteen. Miss Temple hurdled the dribbling stream and crept near. Olsteen's throat was whole, but the pulsing stain on his once-white shirt betrayed a wicked puncture near his heart. His eyes caught hers, and his hand slapped towards her, ineffectual and weak. It held the curved skinning knife carried by Elöise Dujong.

'Should have killed you both on sight,' he gasped. A welling of gore spat past his lips, and Olsteen's further words were wetly smothered by blood.

She heard a noise on the opposite bank. To turn was to face whoever hunted her. Fear gripped Miss Temple as fiercely as a hand around her neck. She ran on.

The way abruptly forked – to the right curving back towards the town, to the left winding away through a squat tumble of boulders. She paused, chest heaving, willing herself with a brutal severity to look behind her: she saw nothing. Was she a fool – imagining ghosts? No – no, she swallowed, Mrs Daube's horrid scream still rang in her ears. She forced her tired mind to study the two paths for the slightest sign as to which way Elöise might have gone, knowing she could spare but seconds. The fork to the town led over an open flat meadow; the one to the rocks disappeared almost at once. If Elöise were frightened, she would want to hide. Miss Temple flung herself towards the blackened stones.

Not twenty steps on a flashing stripe across a moonlit boulder caught her eye – a smear of blood, a hand hurriedly wiped clean. She had chosen correctly. Elöise must be running as fast and as fearfully as she herself was now. Perhaps she thought Olsteen was still in pursuit – or had she seen the Contessa? Had Elöise been a witness to Franck's death? What had happened for Olsteen to attack them, Elöise and Mrs Daube? Could Olsteen be in league with the Contessa? Could he have travelled not to the mountains but to the north, leaving his bootprints outside the Jorgens' cabin? But why was he warm and sound at the Flaming Star while his mistress skulked in the shadows? Yet if the man was not the Contessa's ally, why had Elöise taken his life?

The path dropped downhill across a moonlit meadow towards a copse of gnarled trees. Miss Temple's heart leapt at the sight of a woman running across the knee-high grass and into the shadowed wood. She brushed the hair from her eyes, skin damp, shambling on in an exhausted trot. Elöise was running to the train! Appalled at the evident ease with which Elöise had seen fit to abandon her (granting peril, granting fear, but *still*), Miss Temple imagined with disdain the feeble excuses the woman might offer Chang and Svenson to explain her own consignment to death. In the time it took to reach the copse of woods, Miss Temple had fully restored her earlier feelings of outrage, chasing Mrs Dujong as much as anything to fiercely box her ears.

The trees were dark and dense, and she made her way quickly to the other side. Below her yawned another, deeper ravine, split not by a watercourse but by the rail tracks themselves. Miss Temple stumbled to the edge, looking down, and then saw smoke rising into the air around a turn, some hundred yards away. There would be engineers, firemen, a guard – surely enough to forestall the actions of one woman! She craned her head down the tracks and saw Elöise just vanish around the bend, too far to hear any call. Miss Temple began a hesitant shuffle down the slope. Half-way down, she was compelled by gravity to sit, scooting the rest of the way like a crab. She swatted the dirt from her dress as she jogged alongside the tar-soaked wooden sleepers.

Miss Temple found herself suddenly taken with another question that had slipped her mind: the smell of the blue fluid on the windowsill. It had without doubt been infused with blood . . . yet that made no sense. From what she had seen in the dirigible and from what she could guess from Franck's body, the blue glass acted in an instant to solidify human blood, and thus the flesh seethed with it, into glass. So how was the blood-tinged liquid on the sill, spat from the mouth of the ghostly face, *still* a liquid? How could the blue fluid, which utterly, utterly stank of indigo clay, be taken inside a body without hardening whatever flesh it touched? If only the Doctor were there! Perhaps this was one more reason he'd gone ahead to warn Chang. Miss Temple fought away a tentative impulse of pity for the Contessa, for the ghastly, pale face spoke to an unthinkable price paid for survival. Yet the disfigurement of so cruel a seductress could be no cause for sorrow – such ironies of justice were more aptly met with outright glee.

Miss Temple saw the train. Most of the carriages were open and piled high with what must be ore to be taken south for smelting. Miss Temple needed to lie down, to sleep, to bathe, and she kicked at a nearby stone with irritation. She reached the rearmost carriages, hissing aloud.

'Elöise! Elöise Dujong!'

The woman must have gone on towards the engine, where she would find more protection. Miss Temple sighed – she was not in any state to meet anyone, much less unfamiliar men smothered in coal dust – and followed on.

Near the front of the train was a squat building topped with skeletal scaffolding and a metal chute – whence the ore was poured into the carriages – and next to it a more modest cabin whose windows gleamed with yellow light. Miss Temple padded on, cautious at an eruption of voices, trainmen shouting to each other with sudden urgency. A gang of nine or ten burly fellows in helmets and long coats had gathered around a figure on the ground, directly beneath the loading chute. The figure writhed and moaned as some of his fellows held him down and the others ran about for bandages or water or whisky to ease his pain. She crept forward in the shadow of the train.

'Elöise?' she whispered.

The carriage seemed empty, and, with a sudden surge of effort, Miss Temple tossed the book and the knife in before her and jumped up, catching the carriage's floor just above her waist. She hung for an awkward second before heaving herself inside and crawling inelegantly from view. The trainmen still ringed their fallen fellow – someone knelt over him, tending a wound on his face. Miss Temple ducked from sight, doing her best to still her heaving breath.

She looked down at the book in her hands and on a whim let it fall open, expecting to take comfort at its opening to the same poem. But the book

did not. Instead, to Miss Temple's great dismay, it fell to the *next* page –
the reverse side of 'Pomegranate'. How had she not seen! The folded-over
page was bent in the opposite direction – it was to mark not *that* poem but
the *next*! This poem, 'Lord of Sighs', was even shorter (*two* meagre lines!),
leaving more room for Cardinal Chang to write his own words in the
open space:

> Our enemies live. Leave this inn.
> Trust no one. Travel by night. Stay together.
> I will wait at noon the Lord's Time.

Outside the carriage a footstep turned the gravel. Miss Temple slipped
further from the door into shadow. Was it one of the trainmen? What if
the fellow locked the door? Was she prepared to remain on the train for its
journey south to the city? What had happened to Elöise? What would *she*
say to Svenson and Chang – what feeble excuses? The steps crunched
closer, and, curling like an unseen cobra into the chilled air of the carriage,
she smelt the first creeping, reeking tendrils of scorched indigo clay.

An unnaturally long shadow stretched across the open doorway, the smell
becoming harsh. Miss Temple sank into a crouch behind a barrel, no longer
able to see. She realized with a spark of hope that she was in a goods van
and that the barrels were full of fish oil, giving out a stench that would
hopefully hide her own scent from her pursuer. But would they? The
indigo fumes made her head swim, and the sniffing came on, insistent as a
bloodhound but broken by hideous swallows and spitting. The reek made
Miss Temple's eyes water and her throat clench. The shadow came closer.
She felt as if she must faint or cry out.

From the darkness behind her a firm hand fell hard across her mouth
and soft lips pressed full against Miss Temple's ear, the words that slipped
between them scarcely louder than a sigh. 'Be *still*, Celeste,' breathed the
Contessa di Lacquer-Sforza, 'or it will mean the death of us *both*.'

TWO

EXILE

Cardinal Chang took another sip from the metal mug, less from any desire for tea than a restless need to measure, again, exactly how tender his throat still was and if, upon clearing it, he found any residual taste of blood. He did not, though the rawness persisted. It had been a week since they'd come ashore. The Doctor had done what he could to leach the ground blue glass from Chang's lungs. Indeed, he had saved his life with the foul-tasting orange liquid. Chang abruptly drank off the rest of the mug and with a tight grimace walked back down the corridor to return it to the three trainmen crouched around their stove. Looking again as he went, Chang's quarry was not to be found in any of the compartments he passed.

Chang sank back into his seat and looked out the window at the utterly uninteresting countryside. He'd spent each moment in that godforsaken village in those godforsaken woods ridiculously unable to see beyond regret and reproach. He had never realized the degree to which his heart had held Angelique at its core – it had taken her death to spell it out. The courtesan had rejected him utterly, but the only sin he could charge her with was honesty. Chang swallowed and winced. Honesty was the cruellest thing of all.

He remembered carrying Celeste to the fisherman's hut, but the rest of that first night blurred in his memory as any catalogue of endless work – building a fire, rummaging for food, and coping with the storm, the likes of which he'd never seen. The hut was all but flooded, its roof torn open, tree branches crashing around them, the downpour endless – and through it all, with each worsening moment, Chang had been driven further from

his companions and deeper within his own brooding soul. He did whatever
was required. He carried Celeste to the cart the next morning, and from
the cart on to Sorge and Lina's cabin, one small bare foot slipping free of
the blanket as they climbed the steps. He helped Elöise gather clothing, he
went with Svenson to arrange matters with the fishermen and their hard-
bitten wives – until it became plain that his presence only complicated
things, and so he spent even more time alone.

At one point he realized he had not spoken a word for five hours. He
had carried an armload of wood to stock the stove and found himself in
Celeste's sparse room, looking down at her body on the bed. He could hear
the whisper of her breath, its rasp as delicate as any lacework. Her skin was
wet, her hair darkly coiled, the bruises marking her neck and face like a
language Chang alone could read. At another time it would have aroused
him, but instead Cardinal Chang found himself wondering who this young
woman was to have changed his life so much. He watched her chest rise
and fall – the size of her ribcage, the sweet proportionality of her breasts,
abstractly curious as to their softness – while at the same time keenly aware
of the pain in his chest, his tattered appearance, his poverty, his profession,
and, perhaps more than anything, the steady grasp with which sorrow was
taking hold of his heart. That two so unsuitable people might be alone in
a room together under any circumstances – much less in a tiny fishing
village on the Iron Coast – was not to be imagined.

Chang would finish this business as quickly as he could and disappear
into the opium den. He would remain beyond every well-intentioned effort
of Doctor Svenson to find him, until those efforts ceased. He would remember them all, two more kindly anchors to weigh him down, until the end of
his days – the arrival of which, in his present mood, Cardinal Chang would
not have resisted at all.

He had been interrupted standing over the bed by Elöise, come to place
a fresh cool cloth over Celeste's forehead. As soon as she leant over to
smooth the hair from Celeste's face, Chang left the room.

He had walked to the water, stalking through the sodden woods to stand
at the band of sharp black rocks that bordered the shore. A creature of the
city, Chang stared at the line of breaking waves as if he were looking at

some strange undiscovered continent. The biting wind brought a grim pleasure, the roaring of the water echoed his spinning thoughts, and the expanse of sky conveyed the futility of his struggles. He wondered how he had been able to leave Angelique's shattered body, how he had gone on, fought on the airship – how, in truth, he had not died with her. The answer, of course, was because she had never wanted him to.

He sat on the rocks and took a volume of poetry from his coat pocket, Lynch's *Persephone*. Yet the very first poem, 'Arcadia' – an ironic account of the Princess's innocent life in the Edenic gardens of her mother – caused him to close the book. Chang stuffed it back into his coat and winced at the coldness of the wind.

He looked down at his boots and scuffed the sand. He frowned. There was something buried . . . something blue. Making sure he was unobserved, Chang used a small, flat black stone to dig and quickly uncovered the broken remains of a blue glass book. The pieces were of various size and jagged – if he hadn't known better, the fragments might have come from a large, brightly coloured bottle. With a great deal of care he excavated a deep hole in the sand, then pushed all the glass he could find into it with his boot. He refilled the hole and covered it with stones, then continued down the sand, watching closely for any further flash of blue, but there was nothing.

Inside the cabin, Elöise was speaking to Lina. Chang did not enter, turning back to the barren yard and the stark trees beyond it. The cabin felt like an overlarge coffin. He thought wistfully of his city routines, longing to be standing in the cool, dusty darkness of the Library stacks. But then he sighed. It did not matter where he was – his world would still seem lost.

Behind him the door abruptly opened. 'Cardinal Chang!' called Elöise. Chang turned to her. She waited for him to speak, realized he did not intend to, then nodded with a smile. 'Good-morning. I was wondering if you had seen the Doctor.'

'I believe he was dragooned by Sorge – something about an ailing goat.'

'Ah.'

'Is Miss Temple in danger?'

'She is unchanged, which, as the Doctor says, is good news. She has even been able to drink a little of the Doctor's herbal tea.'

'She is awake?'

'For instants only, and never herself within them, but able to take a swallow and slip back to sleep, or into dreams. She dreams constantly, I think . . . like clouds passing before the moon, they cross her face . . . and her hands clutch so . . .'

'The Doctor will return as soon as possible,' said Chang flatly, wondering when and for who else Elöise had evoked the moon and clouds. 'He cannot love goat tending.'

Elöise nodded at the sand still clinging to Chang's boots. 'You walked to the sea?'

'I did.'

'I so love the sea,' said Elöise. 'It lightens my heart.'

'On the Doctor's suggestion I searched again for any refuse from the airship, or any corpse washed ashore.'

'I'm sure that's very wise. And what did you find?'

'That the sea does not lighten my heart at all,' said Chang.

Svenson called to them from the muddy lane behind the house that ran to the village. Limping a step behind came Lina's husband, Sorge, whose conversational skills were such that Chang was certain the Doctor had shouted to them as soon as he could, to escape the torpor.

'The fellow himself,' Chang observed to Elöise, smiling at Svenson's awkward waving.

'He is a very good man,' replied Elöise quietly, and they said no more until the Doctor reached them. Svenson shook hands with Sorge, refusing his thanks, then waited until the fisherman stumped up the steps and into the house.

'How fares the goat?' asked Chang.

Svenson waved the question away and turned to Elöise. 'Our patient?'

'Very well, I think – of course, you must see for yourself.'

'At this point your observations are fully the equal of mine, but I will be in momentarily.' He paused, and Chang was on the verge of excusing himself, so obviously did Svenson long to say more to Elöise. Instead, before he could, the Doctor turned to him, glanced down at his boots, then back up at his face. 'Did you find anything?'

'Nothing at all,' said Chang.

He was not sure why he did not mention the broken glass to Elöise – hadn't she as much right to know as Svenson? Wasn't her life as much at risk? Could it be that he did not fully trust her, even now?

'Yet I am unsure if I have walked the same ground you searched before. Sorge has mentioned the power of the tides – something might have come ashore some distance away . . .'

A complete fabrication – the Doctor and Chang had never spoken of this at all.

'Why don't I show you?' offered Svenson. He turned to Elöise. 'We shall just be two minutes.'

'I will see if Lina will make tea,' Elöise replied, smiling, with the exact same careful tone.

As they walked to the sand, Chang quickly described finding the blue glass shards. They stopped at the ring of black rocks, where Svenson lit a cigarette, hands cupped round a match. The tobacco caught, and, after a deep breath and an exhaled plume of pale smoke, the Doctor waved a pale spidery hand back towards the house.

'I did not want to say in front of Mrs Dujong, for I do not know what it means – and after your own discovery I am even less sure. Something has happened in the village.'

'Something aside from sick goats?'

Svenson did not smile. 'The men will not speak of it openly . . . I am convinced we must go with Sorge and see it for ourselves.'

The bodies were laid out on flat squares of canvas that would, once the families were satisfied, be sewn around them for burial. Several men from the village were still there – to Chang all alike, with their drab woollen coats, bearded faces, and wrinkled hard stares – and they made way silently for the two outsiders. The Doctor knelt by each corpse. From Chang's perspective, the damage was clear enough – the throat of each groom gaped wide, the wounds nearly black with clotted blood – and so he turned his attention instead to the stable. The double wooden doors were open, the muddy yard marked by too many foot and hoof prints to untangle. Chang could see from his clothing and plastered hair that one of the dead men had lain in the rain. Any traces of blood would have been quickly obliterated by such a storm.

He looked to the village men. 'Where was the other?'

Chang followed them inside. A stall door had been cracked at the hinges, as if the groom had been driven – or thrown – against it with great force. The floor was covered with damp straw, and, while there were grooves and hillocks indicating a struggle, there was no way to know who or what had made them. Several stalls were now closed off with rope, their wooden slats snapped or broken. Something had stirred the horses to violence.

He turned at the approach of Svenson. The Doctor studied the straw, the stall door, and then, completing the circuit, the rest of the main stable room. He glanced once to Chang with a deliberately blank expression, then turned to the villagers.

'It seems plain enough, I am sorry to say. Sorge has suggested a wolf, or even wolves, driven out by the storm. You see the wounds required great strength.'

'And teeth?' asked Chang mildly.

'Indeed.' Svenson frowned. 'The narrative is unfortunately clear. The first groom hears a disturbance and opens the doors to see what it might be – from the distress demonstrated by the horses, we know the disturbance was significant. Once outside he was attacked. The door still open, the beasts gained entry and slew the second groom, again' – Svenson gestured to the battered stall – 'with notable ferocity.'

The men nodded at each point the Doctor made. The horse snorted.

'Would it be possible', Svenson asked, smiling encouragingly, 'to see where these fellows slept?'

Their quarters were undisturbed: two bunks, an iron stove, moth-eaten blankets, and a rack of woollen stockings set to dry. Only a metal box of biscuits had been knocked from its shelf, the pale contents, more than likely rife with weevils, spilt out on the straw. Chang cleared his throat and met the ever suspicious faces of the villagers.

'Where is their privy?'

He had merely wanted to be away from these piggish stabbing eyes, but once he strode down the path to the tiny wooden shed Chang felt the effect of too much tea – drinking being the simplest way to avoid conversation with their hosts – at that morning's breakfast. The privy's door was ajar. As he pulled it open, Chang saw its upper hinge had become dislodged. He wrinkled his nose. The hole cut into the seat of sawn planking was spattered darkly around its edge. Even he could smell – burning through the standard reek of the pit beneath – the foul acrid traces of indigo clay. He leant forward, squinting at the stained wood . . . a viscous smear . . . stinking dark blue mucus. To either side of the hole were smaller marks . . . fingerprints. He pictured the position of the hands – the *forward* position, from the placement of each thumb. Someone had vomited their twisted blue guts out.

They said nothing more on their return, accompanied as they were by the villagers. Chang had managed to subtly direct the Doctor to the privy – forcing himself to discuss wolves with their hosts in the interval. Though he did learn that of five horses driven into the woods, two remained unaccounted for – and in the fishermen's opinion most likely eaten.

Once back at Sorge and Lina's cabin the two men paused at the base of the steps. Chang knew why *he* did not want to enter, but was curious about Svenson's obvious hesitation.

'They will wonder where we have been,' said Chang. 'Or at least Elöise will.'

Svenson looked back through the wood to the shore. 'Perhaps we should walk a bit,' he said.

They retraced their steps to where they had spoken before, the wind having grown bitter in the intervening time. Svenson lit another cigarette with difficulty, Chang tolerantly holding his leather coat open to block the wind. Svenson straightened, exhaled, and looked over the sea, grey fatigue lining his pale face. 'The blue stains. We must assume our enemies from the airship survive . . . in some fashion.'

Chang said nothing – this much seemed obvious.

'Miss Temple is not free from fever,' Svenson went on. 'She cannot be moved. Our hosts here – their goodwill, their suspicions. I do not like to say it, but you have seen the way they stare at you.'

'What has that to do with anything?' snapped Chang.

'You did not hear the villagers gabbling as soon as they got the news. They are all wondering if you had been at the stables, if you had come ashore to kill them all – if you were in fact a living devil.'

'A *devil?*'

'One assumes they are inspired by your coat.'

'And if I am a devil, it reflects upon yourself and Mrs Dujong –'

'Miss Temple cannot survive a disruption of place or care – she is our only concern.'

'I disagree,' snarled Chang. 'You hazard that our enemies live. It seems obvious that, with the horses missing, they are on their way back to the city.'

Svenson sighed heavily. 'I do not see how it can be helped –'

'*Helped?*' Chang cried out. 'Do you not know what this means? Missing on that dirigible is the Prince of Macklenburg – and a government minister! As soon as word reaches the city of our survival, we will be hunted by the law! Our descriptions will be published – bailiffs, soldiers, men like *me* – out in droves for the reward. What sort of disruption will *that* be?'

'We do not know this for certain – the stains in the privy suggest grave illness –'

'The two grooms were *slaughtered!*'

'I am aware of it. What do you suggest we do?'

'Find their killer. It is the only way to protect ourselves.'

'*You* cannot,' insisted Svenson. 'If these people see you rampaging back and forth, their every suspicion will seem to be confirmed. They'll burn us all for witches!'

'So I should stay indoors while *you* hunt the killer? Or should we give the task to Mrs Dujong?'

'Do not be ridiculous —'

The rest of Svenson's words were torn away by the wind. Chang had turned on his heel, striding away, his white face even paler with rage.

Miss Temple lay on her side, turned away from the door, hair dark in the dim room and sticking to her throat where it was damp with sweat. One bare arm lay outside the woollen blanket, fingers — shorter and slimmer than he had recalled   clenched feebly. Chang tugged the glove from his right hand and reached out, hooking the curls from her face and tucking them behind her ear, the back of his fingers brushing across her cheek. He looked down at the thin scored plum line above her ear that tucking the hair back had revealed . . . if the bullet had flown but half an inch to the side . . . he could easily imagine the bone-shattering damage, her crumpled body, the gasps as she expired — how different everything might have been . . .

He heard footsteps outside, Elöise and Svenson talking. With a sudden darting movement Cardinal Chang leant down, brushed his lips across Miss Temple's cheek, and stalked out of the room.

'Cardinal Chang —' began Elöise, startled by his sudden appearance. Chang strode past her to the door.

'Cardinal Chang,' said Elöise again, 'please —'

'I require some air.'

In seconds he was down the steps and marching away into the trees, the calls behind him like the cries of crows.

For the first minutes he did not mark where he walked at all — generally south through the trees, away from the village. But the further he went, the closer he came to the flooded part of the forest. He cursed aloud at the effort required to pull his boot free of the sucking mud, and shifted his course towards the shore.

Chang had not been to this part of the woods before. He leapt a rushing watercourse and climbed a small rise, beyond which he expected to see the ocean. With a bitter smile, he realized that once on the other side he would be happily hidden from any prying villager's eye.

But just before his head cleared the crest, Chang stopped. His hand twitched with an instinctive urge to draw a weapon, but he had none. He dropped to a crouch. He was certain he'd heard the snuffle of a horse.

It would have been difficult to steal a horse from the stables and remain unseen, especially with the flooding. Apparently someone had done it . . . but who? Chang raised his head over the bracken and was surprised to see, their long necks rising up from the foliage, not one horse but two, and saddled as if their masters were ready to ride. Chang waited, and was rewarded by a sharp hiss and then, his eyes turning towards where it had come, a faint curl of ash in the air. Someone had just thrown water on a skilfully made fire whose smoke he had not noticed, even ten yards away.

A man with a shaven head stood struggling into a dark greatcoat. Near his stocking feet were travel bags, a grey blanket tied into a tight roll, and a pair of leather boots. Chang appreciated the variety of people's personal habits, yet knew from experience how incalculably stupid it was to leave one's footwear for last when dressing, especially in a dangerous forest. He launched himself into a dead run as the man lifted his left foot to its boot-top.

The bald man heard the rustling leaves but only turned in time for Chang's right forearm to catch him square on the jaw and send him sprawling by the fire. Chang wheeled around for a second man – why else would the other horse be saddled? – but saw nothing. The bald man swept a snubbed pepperbox pistol from his coat, but Chang kicked the weapon into the underbrush. Another kick landed just below the man's ribcage, doubling him onto his side, and a third, lower still, had him gasping. Chang placed a foot hard on the man's face, pinning it to the earth, scanning around him again, unable to hear any sound over the stamping, startled horses.

'Who are you?' he asked, not bothering to wait for a reply before grinding down with his boot. He relaxed the pressure and asked again.

The man spat the dirt from his lips and coughed. 'My name is Josephs – I'm a hunter –'

Chang noticed for the first time the long leather holsters slung near each saddle. 'Those are carbines.'

'No,' the man said hastily. 'You can't hit deer with a carbine.'

'I agree,' said Chang. 'Only men. Where's your friend?'

'What friend?'

Chang pressed again with his boot. The other man must be near – he had to assume it. He had to assume he carried a pistol as well.

He stepped away from Josephs and towards the horses, untying their leads.

'What are you doing?' gasped Josephs.

'Where is your friend?' repeated Chang.

'In the village! Buying coffee.'

'You'll find the Pope before you'll find coffee there,' muttered Chang, stepping between the beasts and drawing out the carbine from its sheath. He opened the chamber to confirm it held a shell and slammed it home.

'If you want the horses, take them,' wheezed Josephs.

'I will. And you with them, back to the stables.'

'What stables?'

Chang raised the carbine to his shoulder, taking aim. 'It is the last time I will ask. *Where is your friend?*'

Chang's thought in standing between the horses was to protect himself from being shot, but now he wheeled awkwardly at a rustle of leaves, lifting the carbine barrel to clear the horse's neck, and realized too late that the sound had come from a stone being thrown. At once Chang dropped between the horses – he hated horses – and threw himself towards the rustling, reasoning it to be his one safe refuge. He rolled downhill, came up to his knees and raised the carbine, but no one was there. Josephs had taken the horses, pulling them so the animals blocked his body from Chang's aim.

Where was the second man? Chang charged in a circle to the left, boots digging in the soft earth, crouching low. It was a risk – either he was running into safety or straight into a bullet – but the second man must have been on the opposite side. Josephs hauled at the horses, but the animals were confused, and Chang rushed forward, bursting out of the leaves and outflanking Josephs completely.

Josephs dropped the reins and stumbled back, a wide bladed hunting knife in his hand.

'It is *him*!' he cried over his shoulder. 'The criminal!'

Chang reversed the carbine in his hands – shots would alert the villagers. Josephs's lips twisted into a satisfied grimace, as if he were perfectly happy to weigh his knife against the carbine butt. The man was near as tall as Chang and quite a bit more solid. Josephs came at him with a snarl.

Why did the second man hold back?

The knife required Josephs to close quickly, to reach Chang with the blade and render the swinging carbine useless, and so Chang fell back against the charge, swiping once at Josephs's knife hand to slow him down. Josephs paused, feinted at Chang's abdomen, and then slashed at his face. Like most deadly grapples, this would be over in an instant – Josephs would land his blow or die.

Chang whipped the carbine against Josephs's forearm, cracking it hard and driving the knife stroke wide – by perhaps an inch – which threw Josephs off balance. Chang spun and drove a knee hard into his back, near the kidney, staggering the man enough for Chang to spin again, this time with room to swing the carbine. The blow caught Josephs flat across the jaw and dropped him flat. At once Chang flipped the carbine again and jammed the barrel into the gagging man's soft throat. Chang looked around him in the trees.

'If you do not come out, he dies.'

Josephs swallowed, his eyes askew from the blow. Chang waited. Silence. *Where were the horses?*

Chang wheeled around. The second man had crept up to collect them while they grappled. Chang snatched up the hunting knife and dropped the carbine. A quick stroke across Josephs's neck and Chang was running again.

Criminal. These hunters were hunting *them.*

He'd not gone thirty yards before he saw them, for the fool still led both horses – too greedy to drive one off. The man looked back and Chang saw his face – pointed and fair-haired with a girlish moustache and side whiskers. The fair man reached to the nearest saddle and drew out, like a music hall magician revealing a silver scarf, a gleaming and wickedly curved cavalry sabre. He stepped to the side of the horses, dropping the reins and allowing them to walk past, and fell into an easy *en garde*, his boots taking their position with a soft jingle of spurs. No wonder he had thrown the stone – any movement and the spurs would have betrayed him.

Chang stopped, aware that the hunting knife was no match for the heavy blade. He considered throwing it, but the knife's hilt was an awkward curve of brass and badly weighted. Instead, Chang spat into the leaves and nodded at the sabre. 'Strange weapon for hunting.'

'Not true.' The man smirked. 'Given the prey.'

'You must have ridden hard to get here.'

The man shrugged.

'That you are only two says you are part of a larger effort – searching the entire Iron Coast. I suppose there's less need to search a populated area – one would have heard of a fallen airship crammed full of dignitaries –'

'And criminals.'

Chang nodded at the sabre. 'Is that yours, or have you robbed some soldier?'

'You want to know if I can use it?'

'I want to know how much of a criminal you are too.'

'Why not come at me and see?'

By the man's obvious comfort with a military blade, Chang knew he was a soldier. Who had sent the search parties so quickly? Who could have known so soon of the crash, or guessed its location? Every fear of exposure and retribution he had expressed to Svenson was staring him in the face.

Why had he dropped the carbine? Because the noise would rouse the villagers to something he wouldn't want to explain. And because he would miss his shot and die in the bargain.

Assuming his opponent knew his business, the attack would be a snapping overhead slash, the whole happening so fast that Chang must choose blindly where to parry – and, with the short-bladed knife, there was not the slightest margin for error. He would have to make one parry – he could not hope for more – and then dive forward, slashing and stabbing before the soldier could land a second blow.

Chang stepped forward until he was just at the far reach of the sabre, the hunting knife held before him. 'You will have much to answer for with these villagers.'

In response, the man feinted once at Chang's legs and then hacked upwards at Chang's face. Chang stopped the blow but was caught flat-footed by its strength and could not charge. The man swung again, this time the overhead slash that Chang had dreaded. Chang moved his knife and felt the ringing of steel at his correct guess. On sudden impulse, he twisted his wrist. The brass hilt of the hunting knife pinned the sabre blade and for just an instant held it fast. The soldier grunted in anger and ripped the sabre free, but Chang followed the sabre as it pulled back and sent the tip of the hunting knife lancing straight for the soldier's eye. At the last moment the man's left hand seized Chang's wrist and the knife went wide. Chang lowered his shoulder and tackled his opponent to the ground.

The soldier landed hard but flailed his sword's brass pommel into Chang's back. Chang swore aloud and clubbed his forearm across his opponent's throat, but then let pass the chance to bring the hunting knife down into the man's heart. He knew he should take him alive – as proof to the village and to learn their true peril – so instead snapped his fist into the soldier's face. The brass guard left a cruel red mark, but to Chang's surprise the soldier arched his back and flipped Chang over. The man clawed to get away. Chang seized his boot and dropped him back face down in the leaves. He stabbed the knife at the back of the man's knee, but the soldier rolled again, and the edge cut across his leather boot. Chang snarled with frustration, aching to simply kill the man, and chopped the hunting knife at the soldier's ribs, hoping for a bloody wound that would break his spirit without piercing any organs. But the soldier stopped it with a desperate parry, the metal ringing through the trees. Both pulled free – Chang on his knees, the soldier on his back – gauging their next blow. But Chang knew he had his opponent. As soon as the soldier swung, Chang would deflect the blade and leap forward, the knife against the man's neck. As if he too was perfectly aware of his peril, the soldier cried out with effort, sweeping the sabre with all his strength at Chang in a wild slash. Chang threw himself just clear of the blow, ready to attack – but his rear foot slipped straight over the edge of a five-foot drop. The rest of him followed, landing only to roll through fallen branches and leaves for another ten yards, where the woods began to give way to the sea.

Chang shook his head and looked up. There was no sign of the soldier.

Chang stopped, bent over and gasping. The leaves had given way to a muddy clearing spattered with prints. He saw one line of hoofs, and then – wide apart and deep, as if made at a run – the prints of a man. Was the soldier trailing his own horse? They would worry for him back at the village, no doubt, but the man's knowledge was too great a danger. Chang paused long enough to drink muddy water from the pooling bootprints.

He had followed as quickly as possible, hoping the man had lost his horses, or lost enough time in recovering them to allow Chang to catch up. By the time Chang was sure the soldier had regained his mount, the village was far behind him. He recalled from Svenson's torporous talks with Sorge after supper that the next town to the south, Karthe, was a mining settlement, with a distant spur of the train line. If the soldier was part of a larger force, their search would be headquartered there. It was also possible, given the town's isolation, that the trains ran on an irregular basis. If so, Chang might catch up with the soldier in town – no matter if he'd arrived a day earlier by horse – and take him, along with whatever fellows were there, before the news could spread south to their masters.

The forest gave way to tall grasses and hard, gnarled shrubs. The land began to rise, and Chang reached the tall blackened rocks as darkness fell, deciding it would be as good a place as any to stay the night – continuing on was idiotic, given his eyesight and ignorance of the area. He'd no means to make a fire, nor food to cook. Chang curled himself to the most wind-protected nook of rock. He stared up at the sky, starless, shrouded in black cloud, waiting far too long for sleep.

When he woke the ground was wet with dew. Ten minutes after opening his eyes Chang was on his way.

*

It took him another day to reach Karthe. There had been no further signs of the soldier, though, as he had spent so much time cutting across open country and then still more lost amongst identical piles of rock, this was no surprise. Chang trudged up the last turn of the road into the town, assuming the worst: that his enemies would be fully prepared and waiting for revenge.

Chang's battered red coat blended in with the brown dirt road and the grey rock houses, rendering him all but invisible in the twilight. The doors of Karthe were closed and its shutters drawn. As he stalked its length, Chang heard snatches of talk, the ringing of pans, the high voices of children, but everything remained hidden behind layers of wood and stone.

He passed the village's only inn – a ramshackle wooden building that filled Chang with a palpable longing for a bed, warm food, and several pints of ale – in favour of going directly to the train. Knowing whether the soldier had already escaped would dictate everything.

He looked up at the sound of footsteps and saw a young boy in a pale canvas coat racing towards him without heed.

'You! Boy!'

The boy stopped short, eyes widening at Chang's appearance, and began to edge backwards.

Chang calmed him with an open hand. 'I am a traveller in need of the train. Where is the train yard?'

The boy backed up another two steps and pointed over his shoulder, to where the road wound from sight beyond the last few buildings.

'When did the last train leave – to the south?'

'Not for these two days.'

'Two days? You're sure?'

The boy nodded, his eyes darting between Chang's red coat and his black glasses.

'And when is the next?'

'This night, sir. As soon as they finish loading the ore – it'll be some hours.'

Chang looked behind him, back towards the inn. It could not be more than five o'clock now, by the light. Would the soldier be there?

'Where were you running –'

But the boy had dashed back to where he'd come from – a tall wooden structure that, from its wide, high, double doorway, must be the village stables. One door was open, yellow lantern light pooling through it across the muddy yard. Chang strode after him. If he did not need to reach the train at once, the stable was an excellent way to discover if the soldier had arrived by horseback, and if he might have any companions with him at the inn.

The boy was nowhere to be seen as Chang walked in, one hand loosely on the hilt of the hunting knife in his belt, though he could hear scuffling from a tack room in the rear. The last stall held a white horse he knew he'd never seen. The horse snorted, sensing his gaze, and pawed the straw. It was obviously spent, still wet with perspiration, nostrils pink and flaring, and shifting its feet with an unsettled, stumbling fearfulness. Was the animal ill, or had it been driven mad from mistreatment? Chang stepped away, uncomfortable as ever in the presence of infirmity, and crossed to the tack room.

The boy he'd seen in the street stood in the doorway. He looked up to Chang as he entered, his face already turned to a grimace of nausea. Curled at his feet lay another groom – breath ragged and face pale – the planking before him pooled with vomit. Near the stricken groom's hands – shaking and compulsively clutching together – lay a dagger-sized spike of blue glass.

Chang took the young boy's shoulder and turned his face to his. 'What is your name?'

'Willem, sir.'

'Willem, your fellow is sick from that piece of glass. Bring me water.'

Chang scuffed a wad of straw into the vomit with his foot and stepped carefully around it, scooping up the groom and dragging him to a rolled straw pallet, which lay beneath a row of pegs dangling bridles and stirrups. Chang very carefully picked up the wedge of glass and laid it on the seat of a wooden stool. Willem reappeared with a wooden bucket and a cup. Chang dipped the cup and without ceremony splashed the water in the older groom's face. He refilled the cup as the older groom coughed and snorted.

'Drink,' he said, and then called over his shoulder to Willem, as the boy was even then peering at the dagger of glass. 'Get *away* from that – can you not see what it's done to him?'

The groom gagged on the water, but Chang was able to turn his head before what he'd drunk shot back out on top of the pallet, staining the dirty canvas bright blue. Chang refilled the cup and forced it into the groom's hands.

'Keep drinking,' he said, and once more took Willem's shoulder, pulling the boy after him back to the stalls.

Chang nodded to the bay gelding. 'Whose horse is this?'

'Mr Bolte's, sir – one of the mine directors.'

'He's the only man with a horse in Karthe?'

'No, sir – the others are let out – to other folk coming to Karthe – traders, hunters – Mr Bolte's too. To the Captain – just came back today!'

'Who is this Captain?'

'A hunter! The Captain has a whole party, sir – hunting wolves!'

'But he came back alone?'

'I expect he'll be riding out again –'

Chang leant closer to the boy. 'Did your friend over there perhaps help himself to the Captain's saddlebags?'

'No, sir!' The boy was touchingly vehement, and Chang shook his head tolerantly.

'*I* do not care, Willem –'

'But he did not! He found that in the yard – outside!' Willem wheeled and pointed to the crazed white horse. 'Christian – that's him there – found the mare and the glass too, and didn't tell me about it either. Half mad she is – you can see for yourself.'

'Found *when?*'

'Not two hours,' said the boy, and he pointed to the fresh oats and hay in the trough. 'She won't eat anything!'

Chang stared at the horse, and its too-large rolling eyes. 'Where is the saddle? What do you call them – the traces, the bridle –'

'She didn't have any.' Willem bobbed his head fearfully at Chang. 'She wouldn't be *your* horse . . . would she, sir?'

'You mean you don't know whose it is?'

Willem shook his head.

'Can you tell me if this horse has come from a particular stable – from the north?'

'Are you from the north too, sir?' asked Willem.

'Can you *tell* me?' repeated Chang more sharply.

'If she has their mark.'

'I will give you this to know,' said Chang, and he took a silver penny from his pocket – Chang had, without the slightest scruple, filched his own small supply from Miss Temple's boot while the Doctor and Elöise were elsewhere. The boy slithered over the stall door and carefully approached the skittish animal, his calming whispers at odds with his eagerness to earn the penny. Chang took two steps closer to the animal – just enough to detect the odour of indigo clay clinging to its flesh.

'I have found the mark, sir!' Willem cried. 'It belongs to a merchant in fish oil. He lives here in Karthe, but his team and driver have been trading between villages in the north.'

Chang flipped the silver penny into the air and the boy snatched it from the air with a smile.

'You are quite sure the train will not leave for two hours at the soonest?'

'At the very soonest, sir.'

'Then let us see what else your comrade can say.'

Christian still gripped the wooden cup between his hands, but his senses had cleared enough for him to look up as Chang re-entered the tack room.

'Willem says you found that glass next to the white mare.'

'Is it your glass, sir?' His words were thick and slurred. 'I'm ever so sorry –'

'Did you touch it?' asked Chang, but then he saw the groom wore leather gloves. 'Did you look *into* it?'

The groom nodded haltingly.

'Tell me what you saw.'

'It was a rainstorm . . . a *trampled* rainstorm . . . every drop was . . . *broken* . . .'

Chang picked up the glass shard with his gloved hands and squinted, holding it at an angle. The entire shard was riven with cracks, finer than a spider's thread, a ruined lacework just beneath its surface. What effect would this have on the memories inside – would they remain legible? Would looking into broken glass offer only broken memories, or something worse? If the boy had looked longer, would it have burnt a hole in his mind, like the tip of a cigar punching through a sheet of parchment?

Chang kicked open the stove with his boot. He shot the shard of glass into the bed of white-orange coals and closed it again. Then he turned back to the groom with a smile as false as any quack physician's.

'You will be fine. I know you both for honest lads . . . perhaps you will tell me more about this *Captain* . . .'

Chang looked around him for the younger boy, but he was gone.

'Where is Willem?' he asked.

The older groom smiled weakly. 'Gone to announce you at the inn, sir, so they can prepare a room and a proper dinner. As you have been good to us, Willem was happy to go.'

Chang cursed under his breath as he loped back through Karthe, just imagining the way he would be eagerly described. Alone or with a gang of allies, the Captain would now have ample time to lay an ambush. Above Chang lurked the same dim carpet of cloud, seemingly fed by the pale twists of smoke from each smug little stone house in the town. The illusion of safety provided by stone walls so easily climbed and wooden shutters so simply prised apart – the naivety made him suddenly sick.

The white horse had carried the reek of indigo clay – and the privy had been stained with blue. He had allowed himself to assign all those killings to Josephs and this Captain, yet neither man had shown signs of any sickness, nor were their mounts deranged, as the white horse so obviously was. Did this mean someone else had survived the airship? Or had another of the Captain's party run as afoul of the blue glass as the naive groom? Had there perhaps been another broken book in the sand – had the man looked into it or tried to transport the pieces and exposed the horse? Perhaps this man was even now with the Captain at the inn, fouling an upstairs room . . .

Chang stood below the inn's hanging sign, deciding how best to enter. The windows above were shuttered. No doubt there was an exit to the rear, but if the Captain intended to bolt out the back, it only postponed their meeting until the train yard. Chang reached into his coat and took firm hold of the hunting knife. Then he rapped on the door.

It was opened by an older woman in an apron, her hair wrapped tight with a cloth. Chang's gaze went past her to the room beyond – lined with benches, a fire freshly laid – and then back to the woman. Her face bore a practised smile, and her eyes balanced with a professional skill the likelihood of his having money against his causing trouble. It did not seem any man with a weapon lurked behind her door. Chang brushed past, turning when the hearth was at his back and he could see the entire room in a glance.

'I will need a meal,' he said. 'Have you any other guests?'

'A meal, you say?' answered the woman. 'Let me see –'

'Yes. I will be taking this evening's train.'

'My name is Mrs Daube –'

'I have not asked your name, madam. Have you any other guests?'

Chang craned his gaze towards a staircase leading to rooms upstairs. The woman looked back to the still open door behind her, as if he should consider leaving.

'I cannot discuss my tenants – present or future – with every fellow – unsavoury fellow – coming in off the street –'

'There is no street! In a town like this one is known by all or is a stranger.' He stepped closer to her. 'Like the Captain.'

'Captain?'

Instead of answering, Chang advanced past her to the front door and quietly closed it.

The innkeeper pursed her lips. 'I do not think there will be room at table –'

A movement in the kitchen caused Chang to turn. A burly young man with his sleeves rolled up and his hands black with coal dust stood in the doorway.

He stared darkly at Chang. 'Mrs Daube?'

Chang held out an open palm, his words deliberate and simple. 'I require this Captain. Is he alone?'

'What Captain?' called the one with dirty hands.

'We do get so few travellers in Karthe –' began the woman.

Chang ignored her. He stepped to the staircase, drawing the hunting knife and reaching the first landing in two long strides. The rooms above him were dark and silent. Normally he would not trust his sense of smell, but even he could detect the reek of indigo clay . . . yet there was no trace. Chang darted up to the upper landing, bracing for an attack. When none came, he stepped quickly into each room, looking behind the doors and under the beds. When he reappeared from the third, he found Mrs Daube on the lower landing, holding a lantern, her eyes fixed to the wide-bladed weapon in his hand.

'When did he go?' Chang asked.

'I'm sure I haven't –'

'There has been murder, madam – more than one innocent life taken, in the north.' He returned the knife to his belt. 'This Captain came to Karthe and then rode north, did he not?'

Mrs Daube frowned but did not deny it. Chang gently took the lantern from her hand.

Under lantern light the three rooms revealed nothing. With a sudden thought Chang sat on the bed of the centre room and pulled a book of poetry from his coat. He folded the spine back and scrawled a terse warning on the open page to whoever followed. He bent the corner of the page and stuffed the book beneath the pillow. A futile gesture, but what wasn't?

When he reached the kitchen, the young man had installed himself behind the table, gripping a mug of beer, his blackened hands reminding Chang of an animal's paws. Mrs Daube muttered bitterly, moving efficiently between her stove and table, tending a large number of steaming and bubbling pots while slicing a loaf of bread, pouring a mug of beer, and placing salt and butter in front of an empty chair. She looked up and saw him in the door.

'It will be two silver pennies,' she announced.

'I thought there was no room,' said Chang with a smile.

'Two pennies,' she replied, 'or you are welcome to go elsewhere.'

'I would not dream of it.' Chang reached into his pocket and came out with two bright coins. 'What an excellent seeming meal. You must be the finest cook in Karthe village.'

Mrs Daube said nothing, looking at his hand.

'We have not understood each other,' continued Chang. 'I am strange to you – it is only natural for a woman to have suspicions. Will you sit with me, that I may explain, as I ought to have done when first I reached your door?'

He smiled, impatient, tired, and wanting nothing more than to shove the woman so hard into a seat that she squawked. She sniffed girlishly. 'As long as Franck is here, I am sure you will be civil.'

She sat at the table, helping herself to a slice of thick black bread. She chewed it closely like a rabbit, peering over the slice at her guest. Franck eyed the knife in Chang's belt and took another pull of beer. Chang remained standing, the various mashed piles suddenly nauseating.

'My name is Chang.' He sighed heavily for their benefit, as if deciding against his better instincts to trust them. 'As you have guessed, I too am from the city, to which I must return as soon as possible, by train. I am in Karthe to find this Captain and his men.'

'Why?' asked Mrs Daube. 'The Captain was a proper gentleman, you are a – a – just *look* at – at – at –'

Her twitching fingers stabbed at his ruined leather coat, his unshaven face, and then up at his shuttered eyes.

'I am indeed,' nodded Chang gravely.

'And admitting it!' sneered the woman. 'Proud as a peacock!'

Chang shook his head. 'And I'm sure neither the Captain nor the men with him could hide what they are any better – soldiers for the Queen, on a secret errand. At times such work requires the efforts of men like myself, who ply the darker ways of life, if you will understand me.'

'What secret errand?' whispered the young man, his upper lip wet with beer froth.

'And why were you waving that wicked knife about?' asked the innkeeper, still suspicious.

'Because terrible things have happened up north,' said Chang. 'You will remember Mr Josephs.'

'Mr Josephs and the Captain rode together,' said Franck.

'Then the Captain will know what attacked his fellow. I myself was to meet them by way of a fishing vessel – you will see I have no horse – but Mr Josephs was killed –'

'Killed!' gasped Mrs Daube.

'Dead as a stone,' Chang said. 'And the Captain driven away . . . by *something*.' He paused, giving them both significant looks.

'What is the secret errand?' the young man whispered.

Chang sighed and glanced quickly back into the common room, then leant forward, speaking low, wondering how much time he still had to reach the train. 'There is a sunken craft, of an enemy nation, driven to the rocks, a craft containing certain stolen *documents* . . . detailing hidden ways . . . by which an unprincipled foreigner might enter the Queen's unguarded treasury.'

Mrs Daube and her man were silent, and Chang could sense the breathless reverberations of his last word within their minds.

'You still have not said why the likes of *you* would be part of it,' she said.

Chang smiled, the better to resist his natural impulses in the face of such disdain. 'Because the documents are in code, a complicated cipher that only a man like myself – or a certain elderly savant of the Royal Institute – is able to make clear. With the old gentleman too feeble to make the trip, only I can tell the Captain if the documents are genuine. If I do not, my own debts to the Crown – for you are right, I have been a criminal – will not be paid. Thus, I must ask you again, for your own souls, if you know where I may find the Captain.'

'What will you do with those, then?' Mrs Daube nodded at the hand that held the silver pennies.

Had she listened to a single word? He slapped the coins onto the table top. 'There is no time –'

'I have not seen him,' said Mrs Daube with a smirk. 'And, as you have seen, neither he nor his fellows are in Karthe –'

The innkeeper's hands darted out to collect the coins. Chang caught her wrist. Her expression hovered between fear and greed.

'What I've said is true, Mrs Daube,' he whispered. '*Pitiless* murder. If I find you have lied to me, you are doomed.'

Chang swept back to the street and had not walked five steps before the sudden sound of a galloping horse rose out of the darkness behind him, from the north. He had just time to see the looming shape of the animal before flinging himself clear of its hoofs. He winced – one knee had landed on a stone – and looked up, but the rider was already beyond sight, tearing through the whole of Karthe in a matter of seconds. Could this have been another one of the Captain's men, racing to meet him at the train? But how would they have coordinated their rendezvous? Chang was sure that without his own intervention, the Captain and Josephs would still be doing their vicious work in the fishing village.

And what was that work? They'd known of him – 'the criminal' – which meant they must have known of Svenson and Miss Temple as well. But the soldiers' primary errand must have been to recover the airship and any survivors. Perhaps they'd seen enough of the Iron Coast to assure themselves there were none, and that the craft lay stricken beyond salvage. But none of that explained the origin of this new rider, or the terrified horse that stank of indigo clay.

As he came in sight of the stables, he saw young Willem pushing the door closed. Chang waved, but he was too far away in the dark. He kept on until he reached the muddy yard and paused, looking above him at the sky. Six o'clock at the latest – he still had an hour. Chang straightened his coat on his shoulders, rapped his fist on the door, and called out for the boy. There was no reply. He pulled on the door. It had been barred. He pounded again, then pressed his ear against the gap . . . the muffled sound of horse's hoofs

. . . voices . . . they *must* have heard him . . . was someone else preventing Willem or Christian from opening the door?

Directly above was a wooden half-door for loading hay into the loft. Chang set his foot on the door handle and launched himself up.

He balanced for one precarious moment with one knee on the rotten lip above the doorway before stabbing a hand beyond it to the loft door. At his touch it swung open just enough to slip a hand through the gap. It was held with a loop of rope, and he wormed his arm in. The rope was knotted. The wooden lip sagged beneath his weight. If it gave way, he would most likely break his arm, jammed as it was into the loft. Chang swore under his breath, pulled his hand free, and fished out the knife. He sliced through the rope with one stroke.

The loft door swung open. Chang tossed the knife onto the straw and hauled his body up and in. He reclaimed the knife and picked his way silently to a hole sawn in the floor, through which rose the end of a wooden ladder. Below, he heard more clearly . . . Willem stowing the new horse into a stall . . . and the voices – just the boy . . . no, two boys . . . or was there a woman?

His blood suddenly ran cold. Chang slipped down the ladder, dropping the last five rungs to land on his feet in the straw.

The Contessa di Lacquer-Sforza stood near the doorway of the tack room.

When had he last seen her? On the airship . . . she had just slaughtered the Prince and Lydia . . . her eyes had been wild, like a blood-soaked *bacchante*, like a sense-drugged Minoan priestess with an axe, driven to violence merely by holding two blue glass books in her bare hands. Then she had fled to the rooftop, black hair whipped by the wind . . .

Chang carefully stepped away from the ladder.

Behind her sat Christian, insensible in a chair. At her feet was an oddly shaped trunk, like a leather-bound, octagonal hat box.

'Contessa . . .'

'Cardinal Chang.'

She was tired, and her head tilted to the side as she spoke as if to tell him so – that she was only a woman, and one who, however resourceful, stood near the end of her rope. In truth, Chang had never see the Contessa look so . . . *human*, so subject to fate. Her hair was pinned back without care and her pale face uncharacteristically drawn with fatigue. The dress was, for her, extremely plain, a cheap sort of silk that had been dyed violet – someone's wedding dress refit for fancy usage, and he wondered whose home she had ransacked to find it. He saw no weapon in her hands, but that meant nothing – the woman was a weapon in herself.

He turned at the sound of Willem emerging from the stall – the horse behind him was spent but not visibly deranged. The boy cradled a canvas-wrapped bundle in his arms.

'I have your parcel from the saddlebag –' he began, but his words stopped when his eyes met Cardinal Chang's.

'It is all right, Willem,' the Contessa said, quite calmly. 'The Cardinal and I are old friends.'

Chang snorted.

'I understood your wounds to be quite *mortal*,' she said.

'I understood *you* to be drowned.'

'One's life is indeed a *parade* of disappointment.'

She stretched the fingers of each hand, like a cat rising up from sleep. Chang did not shift his gaze from hers, but pitched his voice to the boy.

'Willem, you must leave. Set her parcel down and go home.'

The boy's eyes darted to the Contessa, and then to Chang. He did not move.

'He will not harm me, dear,' said the Contessa softly. 'You may do what you like. I am grateful for your kindness.'

'I won't leave you,' whispered the boy.

'She is not your mother!' shouted Chang, and then muttered, 'You do not have eight legs . . .'

The Contessa laughed, a throaty chuckle, like dark wine poured in a rush. 'Cardinal Chang and I have much to . . . *discuss*. You may be sure I am not in danger, dear Willem.'

The boy looked at Chang with a new distrust but slowly set down the canvas bag. Chang backed away to give him room, waiting as the boy shifted the bar and slipped out the door. Chang snorted again and spat into the straw.

'Not everyone around you will perish, then – even if he has no sense of his escape.'

'Is your own company any less perilous, Cardinal? I do not see Miss Temple or Doctor Svenson.'

Chang pointed with the knife to the remaining groom, still inert in his chair. 'And what have you done to him?'

The Contessa shrugged, utterly indifferent. 'Not a thing. I am quite recently arrived.'

'He reeks of the glass, of indigo clay. He was bewitched by it – sickened by a shard of shattered glass.'

The Contessa raised her eyebrows. 'My *goodness*. Blue glass? Surely it was all destroyed in the airship.'

'The glass was fissured with cracks. The groom has looked into it. Whatever memories were stored inside have been altered –'

'Well, yes, I expect they might be.' She sighed like a heartsick schoolgirl. 'How little I know about such practical matters. If only the Comte were here to *explain* to us –'

'It has damaged the boy's mind – perhaps permanently.'

'How terrible. He is so *young* –'

'Contessa!'

Chang's voice was harsh, impatient. The Contessa waved one delicate hand dismissively at the dazed groom and beamed at Chang with something bordering on affection. 'Poor Cardinal – it seems you are unable to protect *anyone*. Of course, since nearly everyone hates or fears you – that Asiatic trollop, for example –'

He stepped forward and brought the back of his hand sharply across the Contessa's jaw. She stumbled but did not fall, raising one hand to her cheek, her eyes wild with something close to pleasure, meeting his gaze as the tip of her tongue dabbed at the blood beading on her lower lip.

'We must understand one another,' he whispered.

'O but we do.'

'No,' hissed Chang. 'Whatever you hope to achieve, you will not.'

'And *you* will prevent me?'

'Yes.'

'You will *kill* me?'

'Why not – as you killed the two grooms in the north?'

The Contessa rolled her eyes. 'What grooms?'

'Do not pretend –'

'When have I *ever* pretended?'

'You hacked out their throats. You took a horse –'

'I *found* a horse.'

'Do not –'

'Will you strike me again?' She laughed unpleasantly. 'Do you know what fate befell the last man to lay a hand on my body in anger?'

'I can imagine.'

'No, I do not think you *can* . . .'

He gestured to the strange hide-covered trunk. 'What is that? You could not have taken it from the airship. You leapt from the roof.'

'Did I?'

'*Where did it come from!*'

'Such emotion. I found it, obviously . . . with the horse.'

'What is inside?'

'I haven't the first idea.' She smiled. 'Shall we find out together?'

'Do not think to remove a weapon,' he hissed. 'Do not think of anything but the ease with which I can end your life.'

'How could I, now you have reminded me?'

She knelt in the straw and reached for the trunk, turning it this way and that in search of a catch.

'There is no evident hinge,' observed Chang.

'No,' she agreed, pressing each corner carefully. 'Though I know it *does* open . . .'

'How do you know?'

'Because I have seen it, of course. Before I took it.'

'You said "found" before.'

'Found – took – the point being –'

'Did you see inside?'

'*Perhaps . . .*'

She looked up at him with a triumphant smile, then pushed firmly. From within the case Chang heard a muffled metallic click.

The Contessa grinned, set the trunk down, and stood. 'There you are,' she said, stepping away and indicating the trunk with an open hand.

Chang motioned her back towards it. 'Open it fully.'

'Are you afraid of something?'

'Do it slowly. Then step away.'

'So many *commands* . . .'

The Contessa kept her eyes fixed on Chang's as she sank down to the straw. Both hands reached out for the lid, gripping it delicately. She glanced down into it, then back to Chang, biting her lip.

'If you do insist . . .'

The iron pole landed hard against the side of Cardinal Chang's head and he dropped to his knees. The boy swung again. Chang deflected the blow, barking his forearm and knocking the knife away. He cried out, his head swimming, shouting at Willem – misguided idiot! – swaying on his feet, blinking with the pain. The Contessa rushed at him, the trunk snatched up and held high. She brought it down hard on Chang's head and he collapsed into the straw.

For a moment he could not move – neither his body nor, it seemed, his thoughts, the whole of his sensibility stalled like an insect in a ball of thickening sap. Then the pain lanced across Chang's skull like a fire. His fingers twitched. He felt the straw sticking into his face. He heard the Contessa rustling near by but could not move.

'Where is the knife?' she hissed.

'Did I – did I –' The boy's voice was fearful and wavering.

'You did what was right and brave,' the Contessa assured him. 'Without you, my dear boy, I should have been – well, it is too frightful to imagine. Cardinal Chang is exactly the brute he appears. Ah!'

She had found the knife, and Chang felt her footsteps coming near. Her fingers pulled at his coat collar as she called back to Willem, 'If you would collect my parcel from where you set it down – there's an angel – and close the door.'

Chang pushed at the straw, trying to roll away, the strength in his arms no more than an infant's. The Contessa chuckled and ground a boot onto his nearest hand, as if she were crushing a spider. Chang braced for the tug of the knife against his jugular, the gush of his own hot blood against his skin –

The Contessa's gaze must have fallen across Christian in his chair, and she paused just long enough to call again to Willem.

'And perhaps you will tell me just *when* your fellow found this bit of glass –'

Her words stopped. The white horse began to neigh, horrible and high-pitched, like a screaming child. It kicked furiously in its stall, and Chang could hear the breaking wood. The boy called to the animal, but the Contessa's voice cut across his, suddenly sharp as iron. '*Willem!* Run with the parcel – now! Out the door – to the train! I will find you – fast as you can – let no one see you – *no one –*'

The cries of the animal escalated to outright panic, spreading to the other horses, drowning out her further words. The Contessa was shouting – someone was shouting – Chang could not concentrate with the roaring pain.

He realized after the fact that his mind had drifted, and that the stables had gone silent. He rolled onto one side. The stable door hung open. The air reeked of indigo clay. He was alone.

He pushed himself first to his hands and knees, and then, with an audible grunt, onto his knees alone. Across the room lay the trunk, open and empty, the top broken. The insides were lined with orange felt and moulded to contain an instrument of a shape he did not recognize – but it had held a tool of the Comte d'Orkancz, the orange felt alone told him that. The Comte – bear of a man, an aesthete whose proclivities were as jaded as an octogenarian sultan's – had been brilliant enough to discover the secret of indigo clay, laying the insidious foundation for the Cabal's every dream. However much the man's 'science' struck Chang as an addled mixture of refined engineering and alchemical nonsense, he could not dispute its effects, nor shake a fear that its true dark power remained untapped – exactly why he took particular satisfaction in having run the Comte through with a cavalry sabre.

The felt depression was not large, and Chang wondered if the tool it had held might have been damaged in the scuffle. Was the Contessa lying about finding it with the horse? But how else *had* she acquired the trunk? It had not been with her on the roof of the airship.

Chang closed his eyes at the excruciating ache in his skull. He walked stiffly towards the tack room, but there was no drink at all. The knife was gone, so as he left the stables Chang snatched up the iron pole the boy had used to strike him, and swung it back and forth like a sword, testing the weight. He was frankly eager to thrash the next person he met.

He found the way to the train, a well-worn cart track beyond the edge of town. He stopped at a sound beyond the immediate hills . . . the howling of a wolf. Chang looked back a last time at Karthe, spat into the darkness, and pressed on through a thicket of scrub, the twisted branches like the supplicating fingers of the bitter, wicked poor. He emerged to see, above an intervening rise of ground, a glow shot with rising smoke: the train. He swung the pole to loosen his arm, wondering whether he would find the Contessa or the Captain first. He did not especially care, as long as he got a chance at both before the end.

On curved spurs of track to either side stood empty open-topped carriages to carry ore. Ahead were two squat wooden buildings, one fitted with scaffolding to load ore, the windows of the other glowing with yellowed lamplight. Beyond these, a short line of passenger carriages – he could hear the engineers shouting to men on the trackside – was being connected to a steaming engine. His enemies could have gone inside the square building to wait, but, given their mutual desire for secrecy, it seemed unlikely.

Behind the passenger carriages and the engine, but not yet connected to them, ran a longer line of ore cars, piled with rock, at the end of which was a brake van whose windows were dark. Chang crouched next to a rusted pair of iron wheels and studied the yard: no sign of the Captain, of the Contessa, or even of Willem. If the Captain had indeed gone to the train some hours before, he might be in a passenger carriage, if only because the presence of other passengers and a guard might provide, with witnesses, more security. At the same time, he might well be hiding in an ore car . . . but such logic made sense only if he was frightened, and the man with the sabre had not seemed frightened at all.

Chang loped to the rear passenger carriage, its platform bracketed by two lamps, and vaulted silently over the rail. He heard nothing from inside. The door was not locked – was there such confidence and trust still in the world? – and Chang eased it open to find the rear compartment had been converted into a comfortable little room for the guard, with a stove, wooden chairs, lanterns, maps, and any number of small metal tools set on hooks in the wall. On a side table sat a welcome pot of tea, and he poured half a cup into a nearby metal mug – the brew still steaming as it met the air – and drank it off in one set of swallows. He set the cup down, moved to an inner door and carefully, silently, turned the knob.

Chang stepped into the hallway of a standard passenger carriage, with glass-doored compartments to his right-hand side, bathed in the dim half-light of lanterns hung at either end. The carriages formed one long inter-locked corridor straight to the engine, where he assumed the guard presently was. But before the train left, the guard would make his way down the length of the train, accounting for every passenger. It would be better if Chang could locate the Captain before that happened. He strode quickly down the length of the carriage, glancing into each compartment, and then through the next, with the same result – every compartment was empty. The train shuddered: the line of ore cars had been attached. They would leave momentarily.

He entered the third carriage. The Contessa di Lacquer-Sforza burst through the far door, out of breath, her expression hard as hell itself. She saw Chang just an instant after he saw her. Neither moved. Then the Contessa launched herself straight at him with all speed, dress held up with both hands, black boots pounding against the polished planking.

Chang's lips curled back with pleasure. 'Contessa! How completely *superb* . . .'

He raised the iron pole and strode deliberately forward – free hand raised, fingers open, to catch or turn aside whatever she might fling – awaiting their collision with an animal eagerness.

The Contessa suddenly dodged from the corridor into a compartment. Chang swore under his breath and leapt forward, tearing at the compartment door. She had shot the bolt, and he could see her through the glass clawing at the window latches. Chang stabbed the pole through the glass and cleared a ragged hole. The Contessa turned once as he thrust his gloved through to grope for the bolt, and then, with all her strength, the latches not yet free, hurled herself full against the window. Its glass cracked, starring raggedly like the web of an opium-sick spider. She cried out, stumbled back, and Chang saw the bleeding slash across her shoulder. He wrenched the door open. The Contessa threw herself at the cracked window again, sailing through in a shower of dagger-sharp shards to land in a glittering heap on the rocky trackside below. Chang leapt to the window, looking down. The Contessa groped to her hands and knees, blood gleaming on her dress.

'Don't be a fool, woman! You cannot escape!'

The Contessa groaned with a savage, desperate effort and reached a stumbling, drunken run. Chang looked at the shattered window with distaste and cleared as much of the remaining glass as he could with the iron pole, sweeping it along the lower frame.

He turned in time to see a dark shadow filling the entire doorway, the compartment air suddenly thick with indigo clay. He turned a thrust with the pole, raising it swiftly before him, and heard more shattering of glass.

The second blow, fast upon the first, was the man's stone-hard fist, catching Chang square on the jaw and sprawling him into the compartment seats. At once Chang rolled to his side, just evading a shard of glass slicing down to shred the upholstery where his head had been. Chang rolled again, whipping the iron pole at his assailant's face. The man blocked it on his forearm without the slightest cry – a blow meant to shatter bone – but as he did Chang landed a kick square in the fellow's stomach. The man grunted and staggered back. Chang scrambled to his feet, jaw numb, trying to see who – for it was *not* the Captain – had determined to kill him.

His attacker was tall, wrapped in a black woollen cloak, its hood pulled forward. Chang could see only his pale jaw, a mouth with broken teeth, lips nearly black, and shining with what might have been blood but for the smell. It was the same blue discharge Chang had seen on the lips of Lydia Vandaariff, after the doomed heiress's body had been corrupted by the Comte's alchemical injections. The man snarled – a mean, rasping exhalation like the grinding of flesh between two stones – and Chang's eyes darted to his hands. The left was wound thick with cloth and held a squat spear of blue glass, the shattered edge bristling like a box of needles, while the right – no wonder Chang's jaw felt as if it had been broken – was wrapped in *plaster*. Then the instant was over. As the man surged forward, Chang cracked the pole against the left hand, knocking the blue glass to the floor, and received another blow from the plaster-covered right that drove the air from his lungs. He was thrown back through the open compartment door and slammed into the corridor wall. The man was right after him, groping for Chang's throat with one hand and clubbing at his head with the other. Chang dropped the pole and tore at the ice-cold, squeezing grip with both hands, his boots slipping on broken glass. The man pressed close. The indigo stench was near to nauseating, pricking the back of Chang's throat – part of his mind vaguely curious as to whether it was possible to vomit while being strangled to death. Chang found his footing at last and snapped forward, sharply striking the man's face with his forehead, then driving his knee between them, sending his assailant back into the doorway.

But the man was incredibly fast and lashed out with his plaster-cast fist,

catching Chang's shoulder like a hammer. Chang gasped at the impact as
if he had been nailed to the wall behind him. The man dug under the black
cloak and came out with another dagger-length spike of blue glass.

The man spat a rope of fluid from the side of his mouth and extended
the dagger mockingly towards Cardinal Chang's right eye. Chang could not
run – he'd only be gashed in the back. His mind ran through each feint
and counter-feint he might attempt, and every possible attack – just as he
knew his enemy was doing the very same, the entirety of a chess match in
one instant.

'She's escaped you,' Chang whispered. 'Just like at the stables.'

'No matter.' The man's voice was a slithering, limestone grind.

'She will survive us all.'

'*You*, certainly.'

'You are no portrait of good health.'

'*You have no idea.*'

Like a bullet from a gun, the man's stone fist swept forward, smashing
past into the wall as Chang dodged away and then dropped to his knees,
just below the dagger hacking at his face. Chang dived forward, catching
his opponent around the waist, and bullrushed him backwards into the
compartment. The man roared, but in three quick steps was pinned against
the shattered window frame, then toppled through with a cry. His flailing
boot caught Chang across the face as he fell, knocking the Cardinal to the
glass-littered floor. By the time Chang could lurch to his knees and peer
out of the window his mysterious enemy had vanished.

Chang stood wincing at the pain scored across the whole of his body,
catching his rasping breath and taking in the ruined compartment – window
and door destroyed, upholstery slashed, the floor scratched and pitted by
the glass ground beneath their boots. He took in the fact that the Contessa
had never especially feared Chang at all, that her only concern – at the
stable and on the train – had been this hooded, implacable killer. This man
had chased her from the front of the train towards Chang – what did that
mean with regard to the Captain? Chang had assumed the disfigured man
was another of the Captain's soldiers who'd run afoul of the blue glass . . .

but Chang realized that the man – and, by extension, the Captain? – had been trying to *kill* the Contessa. One of the most subtle achievements of the Cabal had been their insinuation into the highest levels of government – suborning powerful figures throughout the Ministries and the Palace to the extent that state policy would be now executed to serve their particular interests. What was more, an entire regiment of dragoons had been reassigned to 'unspecified duties' at the Palace, an unprecedented gesture that had allowed the key figures in the Cabal – Minister Crabbé, the Comte, Francis Xonck, the Contessa – to protect their every endeavour with seasoned troops. Chang frowned, for, given all of this, what he'd seen made little sense. If the search party had been sent by the Palace, were they not the Contessa's *allies*?

Was the Captain in one of the carriages or had he talked his way into the engine itself? Chang wanted to leap out the window and run after the Contessa, but knew that stopping the Captain, stopping any discovery of their survival – *especially* if he did not truly understand who the Captain served – was more important than revenge. Yet if he remained on the train, Chang was now leaving two deadly enemies behind him, when all of his companions would be passing through Karthe village.

But who knew when Svenson and the women might arrive? It could be another week, even more. By driving the Captain and Josephs away from the fishing village, Chang had ensured his companions would be safe there. The Contessa wanted only to escape Karthe, and the disfigured man had shown he would pursue her above anything.

The Contessa was one woman. If no one stopped the Captain delivering his news, Chang and the others would be hunted everywhere, by hundreds of men . . . and he *had* left his warning note at the Flaming Star . . .

The splitting ache in his head prevented further thought. There was no clean choice – either way he risked damning both the others and himself. He needed to sleep, to eat – to eat opium, he thought with no small longing.

Chang staggered against the row of seats. The train was moving. He looked at the dark trackside moving past, weighing the possibility of leaping out, but did not move. The decision had been made.

*

It had taken the whole of that night's travel to descend from the dark
mountains into a land of treeless hills marked, as by the scrawls of a child's
pencil, with arbitrary seams of lichen-speckled slate. He had bartered
with the trainmen for some meat and bread and tea. To his great frustration,
the Captain was *not* in any of the carriages, or in the coal wagon, or with
the engine. Nothing was said of the ruined compartment – the glass was
swept up and the broken doorway stretched with canvas by the time he had
finished his search in the forward carriages – even if the men seated around
the stove cast more than one wary glance at Chang's unsettling eyes and his
battered, nonsensical garments. He paced the length of the train, fruitlessly
hoping he had overlooked some nook or cupboard, but only frightened the
other passengers – three men with business at the mines, an old woman,
and two young labourers on their way to shackle their lives to a mill, or
one of the new *factories* setting up outside of the city.

Given that Chang had no way to search the ore cars himself while they
were in motion, and barring an open attack on his person, there was nothing
he could do for the remaining journey.

He did not know who the disfigured man was – either one of the Captain's
men . . . or not. Had the Contessa contaminated some woodsman? Chang
shivered to recall the agony of the ground blue glass inside his own lungs.
If this fellow had the same torment . . . was he even in his own mind? And
what had been in the strange trunk? The orange felt marked it as salvage
from the dirigible . . . if a priceless glass book had been brought to shore
only to smash into weaponry, what else could be still *more* valuable?

The question made Chang think of the airship. Just when the members
of the Cabal had stood at the very brink of success – unimaginable wealth
and power all but in their grasp – the suspicions and rivalries between them
had been inflamed to open, violent antagonism. Chang had seen it before,
thieves turning on each other in the midst of a crime, but these were no
common thieves. What they had schemed to steal was nothing less than the
free thought of a nation – of *many* nations – to fashion an empire of oxen.
That extreme ambition had fed their fears and distrust of one another, of
which the violence on the dirigible was only the final, sudden flowering.
Chang knew that Xonck, the Contessa, the Comte, and Crabbé had all

hatched their own secret plans against the others – either for insurance or outright betrayal. As he wondered what was in the trunk, he also wondered what private schemes remained in place, like loaded weapons in an unlocked cupboard, just waiting to be found.

Chang spent the next day paralysed with waiting, watching the landscape descend from the brown hills to cultivated fields and villages and then small towns, each indicated from afar by its brittle spire. By the time night had fallen again, he sat slumped in the seat, his glasses folded in his lap and a hand pressed over his eyes, hating the confinement, hating the docile passengers around him, hating every prim little town he passed. It was ridiculous, patently ridiculous. The woman was dead. He pulled away his hand and looked up, squinting at the yellow lantern light that came from the corridor.

Then for no particular reason he thought of the Contessa on her knees at the trackside. The image was impossibly vivid – her face flushed, hair wild, the scarlet gash on her shoulder. He recalled striking her in the stable, and the exquisite movement of her body as she had stumbled back but kept her feet . . . the elegance of her pale hand touching her new-bruised jaw . . . Cardinal Chang covered his eyes with a groan. He was insane.

The sky was dark when the train pulled into Stropping Station. Chang dropped down on the gravel trackside a good distance from the main station floor and its crowd. He looked down the line of ore cars, knowing the Captain could be anywhere. The scattered pages of a newspaper blew towards him with a blast of steam from the engine, and Chang reached down to catch one. Although his eyesight made reading anything but the largest type difficult, he'd been gone from the city for days and knew he ought to see where things stood. It was the *Courier*, an inflammatory, vulgar rag, of two days previous. The headline read MARKET CRISIS! Chang sneered – the markets were *always* in crisis – and allowed his eyes to drift down the page. The other stories seemed no less dire – BLOOD-FEVER FEAR, INDUSTRY AT STANDSTILL, PRIVY COUNCIL DELAY – but that was the *Courier*. Chang balled up the paper and threw it aside.

A flicker of movement caught his eye. Behind the ore cars, between the wheels – for an instant only – had been a shadow. It was a crouching man, and that man was watching him. Chang broke into a jog across the tracks, ducking beneath the carriages until he reached a side exit he'd found on a Royal Engineers' architectural survey plan some years before and employed on numerous occasions since. A quick kick to the half-rusted door, up two storeys of metal staircase in pitch-blackness – just slow enough for the Captain to follow – and Chang was groping for the bolt of a small iron door. He paused . . . smiled at the sound of footfalls in the darkness below . . . and emerged onto Helliott Street, narrow and high-walled, and dangerous at any time to the careless or unarmed. Chang left the door ajar behind him and smiled again, pleased to be back where he knew his way.

Helliott Street fed into the Regent's Star, a square formed by the meeting of five roads and once dominated by the apartments of the old Queen's utterly unregretted father. The district was steeped in the louche sort of traffic those apartments housed – at the Prince's death the royal apartments had been vacated, but the place only became more deeply the province of the lawless and depraved.

The hideous Stropping clock had marked the time as nine o'clock. Even without being followed, Chang could not go back to his rooms until he knew his status with the law, nor could he show his face at the Raton Marine tavern. Chang knew he must choose a path. But he waited – detecting the slightest squeak of the rusted door – then loudly cleared his throat and spat towards the gutter.

Two men, one of them abnormally large, had stepped forth from the shadows of St Piers Lane and walked towards him . . . the exact last thing he needed.

The large man, whose throat bulged like a toad's above a soiled, tightly knotted cravat, wore a shapeless wool cap pulled close around his ears. Chang knew him to be bald, with a mouth full of worn-to-stump brown teeth, and that his hands, presently in the pockets of a too-small greatcoat, were caged in chain-mail gloves. The second man wore a battered top hat and a green military jacket, all of its gold braid removed. His face was thin, unshaven, and his yellow hair flattened back on his skull with grease. This man's left hand, scratching a groove along his scalp as they advanced, was empty. His right, tucked neatly behind his back, would hold a belled brass cutlass hilt set with a fat, squat, double-edged blade. Chang drifted along the square so his back was no longer to Helliott Street. He did not care for the Captain to strike from behind.

'Cardinal Chang,' the big fellow called. 'It was said you'd run away.'

'That you'd come to your senses.' The other man shook his head ruefully. 'Yet here you are, mad as ever.'

'Horace,' Chang called to the large man, and then with a wry nod to his companion, 'Lieutenant Sapp. I suppose I ought to have expected such a meeting.'

'Why is that?' asked Sapp.

'Because I am sought by parties with little knowledge of the town,' said Chang. 'Being ignorant, they were certain to employ the likes of you to find me.'

Horace exhaled with a snort and took his chain-sheathed fists from his coat. Chang carefully measured the distance between them – perhaps four feet of cobbled walkway – and exhibited his own empty hands for them to see. 'Unfortunately, I am quite helpless.'

Horace snorted again.

'Will you convey me to your employer?' asked Chang.

'We will *convey* you to the dog-heap,' Sapp told him. 'A pleasure I have been anticipating these long years.'

Chang smiled back coolly. 'And whose feet are you licking tonight, Sapp? Do you even know? Or are you licking something other than a foot and enjoying yourselves too much to care?'

Chang snapped his head back as Sapp's arm swept forward, attempting – with some skill – to cut a small canal across the width of Chang's throat. The stroke went wide. Sapp slashed again, then feinted at Chang's stomach as Chang hopped back another step, keeping Sapp between him and Horace's meaty fists.

'Slow as ever, Sapp,' observed Chang.

'Choke on your own blood,' snarled the former officer. Sapp had been cashiered for selling his regiment's ammunition to the local population to pay his gambling debts, but persisted in wearing his rank-stripped coat in defiance of his shame.

Sapp stabbed across Chang's face – too close. This time, Chang did not give ground but shifted so the blade shot past, then seized hold of Sapp's wrist. Sapp tried to pull away, which gave Chang room to kick him viciously in the groin. As the wheezing Sapp crumpled to the cobbles, Chang tore his blade free and called sharply to the big man, who stood murderously flexing his ring-wrapped fingers.

'Stay and think, Horace,' hissed Chang. 'As you say yourself, I am mad. It also means I will have no qualms about killing you. I *will* kill you, Horace. I will bury this blade in your throat if you take one more step in my direction.'

Horace did not move. Sapp whimpered, his breath huffing clouds against the night-wet stone.

'No,' Horace announced. 'I'm killing *you*.' He came at Chang like a bull.

It was all Chang could do not to laugh. For the stinging impact of one blocked fist on his forearm, Chang slashed Sapp's very sharp blade once across Horace's bulging stomach, opening a seething, surging line of red. Horace grunted and swung again. This time Chang merely stepped aside and chopped at the man's extended arm, severing the cords at his elbow. When Horace clutched at the spurting wound with his other hand – his upper body now utterly open – Chang drove the blade hilt-deep into the bulging flesh below his chin. He released the weapon and Horace toppled backwards to the street.

The Captain was nowhere to be seen. With the commotion, Chang's pursuer had gone his way. Chang swore aloud, the words echoing across the filthy bricks of the Regent's Star. Everything was ruined – his entire purpose in taking the train, the risk in leaving the Contessa and the disfigured man behind . . .

He spun to Sapp – gaping at his companion's demise – and sent a swinging kick across the man's jaw, dropping him flat. Still snarling with anger, Chang took firm hold of Sapp's uniform collar and dragged the moaning man away from his comrade's corpse back into the shadows.

A quick search of Sapp's pockets produced a razor, and Chang held the open edge before the former lieutenant's blinking right eye. Chang's other hand grasped Sapp's neck, pressing the man against a brick wall. 'Who has asked you to kill me?'

'I would kill you in any case –'

Chang squeezed Sapp's throat until the words rattled to a stop. 'Who has asked you to kill me?'

'You killed Horace –'

'He had his chance, Sapp. This – right *now* – is yours.'

Chang squeezed again. Sapp gasped, and whined with discomfort – had the kick broken a tooth? – but then nodded vigorously. 'I'll tell you. Don't kill me. I'll tell you.'

Chang waited, not easing his grip.

Sapp swallowed. 'Word came down, to the Raton Marine – money to be made. Everyone had seen the soldiers, outside your room – and the dead German in the alley behind – more Germans watching the Library –'

Soldiers of the Prince of Macklenburg. With his disappearance and the death of their commander, Major Blach – at Chang's hand in the depths of Harschmort – Chang assumed they had been recalled to the Macklenburg diplomatic compound.

'Word from where?'

'Nicholas –'

Nicholas was the barman at the Raton Marine. Chang's dealings with him had always been respectful, but he knew – for this was the heart of the tavern's unique marketplace – that the barman held himself scrupulously neutral with regard to fugitives, feuds, even outright assassinations.

'What *about* Nicholas?'

'Said a man had come. In a black coat – from the Palace – *official*.'

'No one in the Palace knows the Raton Marine exists!'

'Then someone told them, didn't they?' spat Sapp.

'And he told you to watch the trains?'

'Of course he didn't! I *know* you, Chang! I know how you think!'

Chang lowered the blade from Sapp's eyes and released his throat, taking a moment to pat the street grime from each ragged epaulette. 'Now why should the Palace care about the likes of me?'

'Because of the *crisis*.'

'What crisis?'

'The Ministry men. I'm not so stupid I can't follow them just as well – and I heard them whispering . . .'

'I've seen the *Courier*. Nothing new.'

'Men of power, Chang. Men used to half a dozen fools leaping around at a flick of their little finger. I heard them myself. And they were *terrified*.'

'I'm supposed to believe I'm wanted by the Palace – because they're *frightened* of me?'

'Believe what you want.' Sapp's contempt returned with his confidence. 'Or maybe you don't want to admit that you don't know already – from your *Library* –'

Chang dipped the razor just beneath Sapp's jaw, slicing just deeply enough towards the man's gnarled right ear, and with his other hand spun Sapp's shoulder so the spray shot onto the wall behind them. He folded the razor into his coat and returned to the light of the Regent's Star. His footfalls scattered two curious dogs already sniffing at Horace. The sputtering gasps of Lieutenant Sapp were inaudible beneath the clipped echo of Chang's boots against the city stone.

He had no money for a proper hotel, and the sorts of rooms he could afford would put him in view of a bothersome host of fools, less clever than Sapp if just as bloody, all chasing the same reward. Chang shrugged his coat closer around his shoulders. Of course he could find *some* place . . . yet if he had no safe haven of his own, did it make sense to bring the battle to his enemies?

The Contessa surely retained her rooms at the St Royale – but there would be no information there, and secret entry would be difficult. There was Harschmort House, the home of Lord Robert Vandaariff . . . With the mighty financier reduced to the status of a mindless slave and his daughter

Lydia brutally murdered on the airship, might not their sprawling mansion be the perfect place to do mischief? Chang shook his head – mischief was not the point. He was being hunted by men from the Palace, but the Palace – the many, many Ministry buildings, the Queen's residence, the Assembly chambers, Stäelmaere House – was a labyrinth. It made even Harschmort look like a country-garden maze. Each option brought danger without any clear sense of advantage – he did not know enough, nor who to truly fear.

In the morning he would buy every newspaper and confirm Sapp's information, just as he would find out the fates of those Cabal underlings left behind – whether the Duke of Stäelmaere and Colonel Aspiche were still alive . . . and, perhaps most important of all, what had befallen Mrs Marchmoor, the last of the Comte's most powerful creations, three women he had transfigured into living glass. Was she still alive – if her present state of existence could be termed *life* at all? Or had she too been destroyed? They were all questions for tomorrow. Tonight Chang needed another refuge, unexpected, yet not without *some* purpose.

After so long in the train, Chang was happy enough to walk, and made for the empty lanes behind the White Cathedral. Named for the pale stone used to rebuild it after a fire, the Cathedral had remained unfinished for years, its broken toothed dome, crusted with scaffolding, a mighty testament to corruption. The streets were narrow and had been meticulously lined with a spiked iron fence, but for Chang they made a convenient path between the evening crowds at the Circus Garden and the less savoury gatherings closer to the river. He swung his arms with satisfaction, passing through the motions of parry and attack and slash. It had pleased him immensely to despatch Horace and Sapp. He had despised them for years, of course, but, after so much that had been inconclusive, simply *doing* something was a profound relief. And he had even *warned* them!

In another thirty minutes he had entered a world of well-kept street lamps and shade trees, of courtyards and small private parks. Chang made a slow ambling circuit of an especially neat and proud little square, first along the main walk and then, with the silent hop of a locked gate, through the servants' alley behind, to crouch in the shadows of an impressive townhouse. It was well after ten o'clock. The rooms on the ground floor were still lit, as were the gabled attic rooms that housed the servants. Executing a plan whose origin seemed to lie in another lifetime, Cardinal Chang followed a line of sculpted juniper bushes to a drain pipe bolted to the wall. He took hold with both gloved hands and pulled himself rapidly to a narrow eave, his legs hanging free, and then swept first one and then the other over the ledge, until he knelt outside a dark second-storey window. The window had not been locked during his previous reconnoitre. It was not locked now. Chang silently slid up the sash and stepped through, starting with one long leg – his boot soft against a runner of rose-coloured carpet – then his torso and finally the remaining leg, which he carefully folded through like an insect tucking in its wing. Chang eased Sapp's razor from his pocket, orienting himself from his research as to the exact location of Mrs Trapping's bedroom.

How long ago had Chang been hired by Adjutant-Colonel Noland Aspiche – the very beginning of his involvement in this wretched affair – to murder his commanding officer, Arthur Trapping, Colonel of the Prince's Own 4th Dragoons? Trapping was an ambitious rake, rising by virtue of his wife's powerful brother, the arms magnate Henry Xonck. It was Xonck who had purchased Trapping's commission and then manoeuvred the 4th Dragoons' assignment to Ministry service, thus inserting his brother-in-law at the centre of the Cabal's activity. For Trapping, it was a chance to climb to the Cabal's upper ranks, playing them off against one another – his intentions unfortunately far outstripping his ability. Both Trapping and Henry Xonck had been outmanoeuvred by the youngest of the three Xonck siblings – Francis, as capable an adversary as Chang had ever seen. Decadent and disregarded, Francis Xonck had manipulated his brother's use of Trapping, Trapping himself, and his sister's hope that her worthless husband's rise might provide the social status her dour eldest brother denied her. Francis Xonck's plans to usurp the family empire even went so far as to involve the Trapping children's tutor, Elöise Dujong. Only a bullet from the Doctor on the sinking dirigible had finally forestalled the man's ambition.

But before any of this, hired by Aspiche, Chang had crafted a detailed plan to penetrate the Trapping home in secret, to eliminate Colonel Trapping in his bed, if necessary. He had never employed it – Chang had instead followed the Colonel to Harschmort, the mansion of Robert Vandaariff, where his quarry had been murdered by someone else before he could act. But now . . . now, even though she was a marginal figure in the whole intrigue, Chang was certain Trapping's widow might possess *some* insight on what had transpired during the week he had been marooned in the north. With any luck a few good words about her children's missing tutor would gain him a clean bed and breakfast . . . once the woman got over the shock of his arrival, of course.

His study of Arthur or Charlotte Trapping had not shown either to be an especially doting parent: at this time of night the children should be asleep in their rooms – directly behind him – and their mother in her own chamber on the third floor. The lights down below would be servants, some cleaning up that night's dinner and others preparing the meals and linens for tomorrow. Chang strode quietly to the staircase. Keeping close to the wall, he climbed three steps at a time to the next landing, pausing to crane his head around the corner. He heard nothing. To the right lay Colonel Trapping's bedchamber. To the left was that of the Colonel's new widow. A bar of yellow gaslight peeked out beneath the door. Chang took gentle hold of its ivory knob. From within he heard a muffled squeak . . . the opening of a drawer. Was Mrs Trapping awake? Would her back be to the door? If he could just enter without her screaming . . .

Chang turned the knob with the deliberate patience of a man stroking a woman's leg during church service, but then the bolt released with a *snap* that echoed down the hall. He thrust the door wide. A trim man in a long black coat wheeled in alarm from a writing table strewn with papers, his mouth open and his eyes wide – a man perhaps of Chang's same age, hair combed flat, each cheek bristling with side whiskers. Chang backhanded the man savagely across the face, knocking him past the table and onto a tasselled square of Turkish carpet, where he lay still. Chang returned to the open door, listening for any alarm, heard nothing, and eased it closed.

Charlotte Trapping was not in the room.

The drawers of each cupboard and trunk had been pulled open, their contents put in piles, the bedding heaped on the floor, and her papers spread wide for meticulous scrutiny. The man – one of Sapp's Palace functionaries? – remained insensible. Chang picked up a letter from the table – by its signature, from Colonel Trapping – and turned it over to see if there was a date.

He frowned, set it down, sorted through three more letters in turn, and then set them down as well, gazing around him at the room.

It was quite large, and a mirror in size of the Master's suite at the opposite end of the hallway. Chang entered its expansive closet. The locked door inside led without question to an identical closet in Colonel Trapping's own rooms – just what one might expect between a modern husband and his wife. He looked at the clothing hanging about him, none of it overly fine, but there – no doubt freshly cleaned because it had been more recently worn – was a pale, demure dress he knew. He had seen it at Harschmort House, watching from afar on the night of Lydia Vandaariff's engagement celebration . . . the night it had all begun, not thirty minutes before the Colonel had been poisoned.

Chang walked back to the bed and stood over the unmoving man. Everything in this room belonged to Elöise Dujong.

THREE

APPARITION

U pon waking from his first sleep after the frozen, all-night struggle to save Miss Temple from fever, Doctor Svenson felt an unaccountable lightness of heart, so unfamiliar that he wondered if he'd succumbed to fever too. He had slept in the workroom to the side of Sorge's kitchen, on a pile of linens waiting to be washed, until the fellow's wife had dragged him from sleep with her rattling pans. Svenson rubbed his face, felt his stubbled jaw, and then shook his head like a dog. He stood, plucked at his steel-grey uniform shirt – still smelling of its immersion in the sea – and rolled each sleeve to the elbow as he worked first one foot and then the other into his boots. The Doctor smeared his pale hair back and smiled. They might all die within the day, but what did it matter? They had survived so far.

His sleep had been a few snatched hours, but, after collecting a mug of milky sweet tea from Sorge's daughter Bette, hot water to shave, and a buttered slice of black bread folded over a slab of salted cod, the Doctor threw himself back into his work, resmearing Miss Temple's many cuts and bruises with a salve he had concocted from local herbs. The fever remained high and his options in this place were impossibly few – perhaps another mixture of herbs could be brewed into a tea. The door to Miss Temple's room opened – Bette with a new pile of towels. He had not seen Elöise. No doubt she was sleeping herself.

They had not spoken at any length since the sinking of the airship – nor had they ever, save for those few impulsive words at Tarr Manor. And yet Elöise had kissed him – or had he kissed her? Did that matter? Did it retain any *momentum* in the present?

He applied a fresh layer of damp, cool cloths to Miss Temple's body.

She had worsened while he slept. He should have insisted she stay on the airship until a boat could be fetched from the village. It might not have made any difference – the airship might have gone under before any boat could arrive – but Svenson berated himself for not even considering it, for not even realizing the danger.

He returned to the kitchen, hoping to find Elöise, but met only the concerned faces of Lina and Bette, wondering about the poor young lady. Svenson served them a practised lie – all was improving – and excused himself to the porch, where Cardinal Chang stood at the rail with his own cup of tea. The Doctor suggested that Chang might avail himself of the salve for his own welter of cuts, but he knew even before he had finished describing where it was kept that the man would not. They dropped into silence, gazing at the muddied yard and the three very squat huts: one for chickens, one for drying fish, and one for nets and traps. Beyond these were the woods, mainly birch, pale bark gashed with black, branches hanging slack and dripping from the fog.

'Have you seen Mrs Dujong?' Svenson asked.

'She went walking.' Chang nodded towards the trees. 'Not that there is any notable destination.'

Svenson did not reply. He found the isolated woods and the heavy sky splendid.

'Celeste?' asked Chang.

'Grave.' Svenson patted his pocket by instinct for the cigarettes he knew were not there. 'The fever has worsened. But she is a fierce young woman, and strength of character may turn the tide.'

'But as far as what you can do?'

'I will continue to do it,' said Svenson.

Chang spat over the rail. 'Then it is quite impossible to say how long we are marooned here.'

Chang glanced behind him to the door, then out again at the muddy forest, for all the world trapped on the porch like a tiger in a cage.

'Perhaps I will have a walk myself,' Svenson observed mildly.

*

He had no particular memory of Elöise's shoes – and wondered on the fact that he'd paid them no mind – but the muddy path to the shore showed small fresh prints with a pointed rear heel he doubted came from any fisherman. The surf was a brilliant churning line dragged between the nearly black sea water and the grey sky hanging heavily above it. Perhaps fifty yards away, her feet just above the reaching waves, stood Elöise.

She turned, saw him coming, and waved. He waved back with a smile, stepping clear of a sudden swipe of surf at his boot. Her cheeks were red with the cold, and her hands – in gloves but thin wool – tucked under her arms. She wore a plain bonnet borrowed from Sorge's wife, but the wind had pulled strands of her hair loose and whipped them eagerly behind her head. Svenson was tempted to put his arm around her – indeed upon seeing her his feelings were quite suddenly carnal – but instead he merely nodded, calling above the surf.

'Very fresh, is it not?'

She smiled and hugged her arms. 'It is very *cold*. But a change from the sickroom.'

He saw she held something in her hand. 'What have you found?'

She showed it to him – a small wet stone, the water darkening its colour to plum.

'How lovely,' he said.

She smiled, and tucked it into the pocket of her dress.

'Thank you for tending Miss Temple while I slept,' he said.

'Thank Lina – you see I am here, having left well before you were awake. You did not sleep long – you must still be quite tired.'

'Naval surgeons are made of iron, I assure you – it is *required*.'

She smiled again and turned to continue walking. He fell in step beside her, closer to the rocks where the wind was less, and they could speak without shouting.

'Will she die?' Elöise asked.

'I do not know.'

'Have you told Chang?'

Svenson nodded.

'What did he say?'

'Not a thing.'

'That is ridiculous,' muttered Elöise. She shivered.

'Are you too cold?' Svenson asked.

She gestured vaguely with her hand at the waves. 'I have been walking . . .'

She stopped and took another breath to start again. 'When we spoke on the stairs at Tarr Manor, when you had saved me – so long ago, a lifetime ago – well, since we have properly survived, we have not properly spoken *again* –'

Svenson smiled despite his desire to keep his feelings discreet. 'There *has* been little time –'

'But we must,' she insisted. 'I told you that I came to Tarr Manor on the advice of Francis Xonck, the brother of Mrs Trapping, my mistress –'

'To find Colonel Trapping. But you did not know Xonck was part of the Cabal, and had that very morning put the Colonel's body in the river –'

'Please. I have been attempting to order these words for some hours –'

'But Elöise –'

'A train full of people came to Tarr Manor, to sell secrets about their betters to the Cabal – and I went with them. I was told they might know where the Colonel –'

'You cannot hold yourself to blame, if Mrs Trapping authorized your journey –'

'The point is that they collected these secrets – *my* secrets – into a glass book –'

'And the experience almost killed you,' said Svenson. 'You are uniquely sensitive to the blue glass –'

'Please,' she said. 'You must listen to me.'

Svenson heard the tension in her voice and waited for her to go on.

'What I told them,' she said, 'whatever I had to offer . . . you must understand . . . I cannot *remember* it –'

'Of course not. Memories taken into a book are erased from a person's brain. We saw the same with those seduced to Harschmort: their minds were drained into a book, and they left idiot husks. Yet perhaps for you this is even fortunate – if these were secrets you yourself were ashamed of sharing –'

'No – you must *understand*. Confusing, *intimate* details of my life are missing – not about my employers but about *me*. I have tried to make sense of what I *do* remember, but the more I try, the more my fears have left me wretched! Every *erasure* is surrounded by scraps and clues that describe a woman I don't recognize. I truly do not know who I am!'

She was weeping – so suddenly, the Doctor did not know what to do or say – hands over her eyes. His own hands hovered before him, wanting to take her shoulders, to draw her in, but when he ought to have moved he did not, and she turned away.

'I must apologize –'

'Not at all, you must allow me –'

'It is unfair to you, terribly unfair – please forgive me.'

Before he could reply, Elöise was walking back where they had come as fast as she could, her head shaking as if she were chiding herself bitterly – whether for what she felt or for attempting to speak at all he could not tell.

When he returned to the house, Chang seemed not to have moved, but as the Doctor climbed the wooden steps the Cardinal cleared his throat with a certain pointed speculation. Svenson looked into Chang's black lenses and felt again the extremity of the man's appearance and how narrow – like a South American bird that eats only a weevil found in the bark of a particular mangrove – his range of habitation actually was. Then Svenson considered his own condition and scoffed at the presumption of comparing Chang to a parrot. He himself might well be some sort of newt.

He could hear Elöise inside, speaking to Lina. The Doctor paused, and then tormented himself for pausing, only to be interrupted by a call from behind him: Sorge, limping across from the shed, accosting Svenson with yet another request for medical expertise – this time for a family in the village whose livestock were ailing after the storm. The Doctor dredged a hearty smile from the depths of his service at the Macklenburg Palace. He glanced at Chang. Chang was staring at Sorge. Sorge pretended the scowling figure in red did not exist. The Doctor stumped down the stairs towards their host.

After the livestock it had been the suppurated tooth of an elderly woman, and then setting the broken forearm of a fisherman injured during the storm. Svenson knew these errands established goodwill to compensate for the strangeness of their arrival, and also for the haunting figure of Cardinal Chang, whose company – the villagers made quite clear – was unanimously loathed. But the Doctor was left with little time for Elöise, and when he was free – brief moments in the kitchen or on the porch, perfectly willing for another walk to the shore – she became unaccountably busy herself.

At their evening meal, however, they must finally be together. Lina preferred the three of them to eat apart from the family, the better to isolate the cost of their board. Svenson was more than happy to oblige. He stood over the stove, watching the kettle, having offered to make tea. Chang pushed open the door, his arms full of split wood, which he carefully stacked next to the stove. The kettle began spitting steam and Svenson, his hand wrapped in a rag, lifted it up, poured into the open pot, and placed it back on a cooler part of the stove. Elöise entered from Miss Temple's room. She caught his eye and smiled quickly, then gathered an armful of dishes to lay the table. Svenson replaced the top on the teapot and stepped away, rubbing his temples with a sudden grimace. Chang smirked and sat, allowing Elöise to weave around him.

'You have my sympathies, Doctor,' Chang said.

'Sympathies for what?' asked Elöise, setting out three metal mugs for tea.

'His headache, of course,' smiled Chang. 'The cruelties of tobacco deprivation . . .'

'O *that*,' replied Elöise. 'Hardly the best of habits.'

'Tobacco quite sharpens the mind,' observed the Doctor mildly.

'And yellows the teeth,' replied Elöise, equally genial.

Lina came between them with a steaming pot of soup – her usual steep of potatoes, fish, cream, and pickled onion. Chang had announced he could not taste it at all, by way of explaining his regular second helpings. At least the bread was fresh. Svenson wondered if Elöise ever baked bread. His cousin Corinna had. Not that she had needed to, there had always been servants – but Corinna had enjoyed the work, laughing that a country woman ought to do things with her hands. Corinna . . . killed by blood fever while Svenson had been at sea. He tried to remember what sorts of bread she had made – all he recalled was the flour on her hands and forearms, and her satisfied smile.

'Sorge can get tobacco,' said Lina, speaking to no one in particular.

'Sweet Jesus,' said Svenson, far too eagerly.

'Fishermen chew it. But smoke also. Talk to Sorge.'

She ran her eyes across the table to see if her obligations for their meal were met. A sharp nod to Elöise – they were – and Lina excused herself into the inner room. As soon as the door closed, Svenson held a chair for Elöise and pushed it in after she had settled herself. He took his own seat, then snapped up again to pour the tea.

'It seems you are saved,' said Elöise tartly.

'By the saint of foul habits, I am sure.'

They did not speak while the soup was served and the bread passed, each tearing off a piece with their hands.

'How is Miss Temple?' asked Chang.

'Unchanged.'

Svenson dunked his bread in the broth, biting off the whole of the dampened portion.

'She dreams,' said Elöise.

Chang looked up.

'She is delirious,' said Svenson, chewing.

Elöise shook her head. 'I am not so sure. We spoke very little together, at Harschmort – I do not presume to *know* her – yet she holds her life quite tightly, with such *purpose*, for someone so young . . .'

She looked up to find both men watching her closely.

'I do not *criticize*,' said Elöise. 'Did either of you know she looked into a book? A glass book?'

'Not at all,' answered Svenson. 'Are you sure?'

'She said nothing,' muttered Chang.

'But when would she have?' admitted Svenson. 'What did she say about it?'

'Nothing at all, apart that she had done it – if I remember correctly she mentioned the fact to comfort *me*. But the book I looked into was empty – the book looked into *me*, if that does not sound mad –'

'I saw the same at Harschmort,' said Chang. 'You are fortunate to retain your mind, Mrs Dujong.'

'It quite nearly killed her,' said Svenson, a touch importantly.

'The point is that my glass book was *empty*,' said Elöise, 'its intent being to *take* my memories. But Miss Temple looked into a book that was *full*.'

Doctor Svenson set down his spoon. 'My Lord. A full *book* . . . instead of the few incidents captured in a single glass card, one could experience entire *lifetimes* – and dear heaven, you would remember those experiences from other lives as things you *yourself* had done. An entire book . . . and depending on the memories it contained . . . and given the decadent tastes of the Comte . . .' The Doctor paused.

'So I suppose I merely wonder what she dreams,' said Elöise quietly.

Svenson looked across the table at Chang, who was silent. He glanced at Elöise. Her hand shook as she held her mug. She saw his gaze and set it down with another brisk smile.

'I find I cannot sleep,' she said. 'Perhaps it is the excess of light this far north.'

A single candle burnt in a dish near the bed in Miss Temple's room. Svenson sat down on the bed next to her, holding the light close to see her clearly. He took her pulse at the throat, feeling the heat of her glistening skin. Her heart was restless and fast. Was there so little else to do? He rose, opened the door and nearly collided with Elöise, her hands occupied with a basin of water, new towels draped over each arm.

'I thought you'd gone with Sorge,' she said.

'Not at all. I set more herbs to steep, which should be ready. A moment.'

When he returned with the recharged teapot, he found Elöise on the opposite side of the bed, bathing Miss Temple's body, one limb at a time. The Doctor swirled the tea before pouring it into Miss Temple's small china cup to cool, his eyes caught by the sensual competency of Elöise's fingers. Elöise carefully bent one leg at the knee and sponged along underneath, the beads of water running down the girl's pale thigh into the shadows at her hips. Elöise resoaked the cloth and reached carefully under the shift to wash – Svenson made a point of looking away – between Miss Temple's legs, the movements of her hand a gentle burrowing beneath the fabric. Elöise removed the cloth, dipped it back in the basin, and squeezed it out.

'That will ease her sleep a bit, surely,' she said softly. She handed the cloth to Svenson and nodded to the limb nearest to him. 'Will you do that arm?'

He ran the cloth along Miss Temple's pale, thin arm, the cool water trickling to the stubbled pale pit and under the shift to her ribs.

'We were speaking of memory,' he said.

'We were.'

'A curious . . . *phenomenon*.'

Elöise did not answer, but instead reached out to glide a strand of hair from Miss Temple's face with an extended finger.

'My own circumstance, for example,' the Doctor continued. 'In the course of these past weeks I have squandered all hope of returning as anything but a traitor to my home, my own duty invisible next to a murdered prince, a slaughtered envoy, a diplomatic mission in ruins –'

'Doctor – Abelard –'

'Your turn.' He handed the cloth to her and nodded at the other arm. 'I am not finished. The point being that while I am presently banished – my mind *spinning* to imagine a life in exile – what work, what hope, what love' – he did not meet her eyes – 'I am made aware by this crisis that the only force binding me to Macklenburg, indeed that has bound me to the world these past six years, is *memory*. A woman I loved. She died. All has been futility – and yet, that loss – which is also her – seems to be all I know. How can I go forwards and not betray what I have been? A fool's dilemma – life being life, corpses being many – and yet, such is my mind.'

'She was . . . your wife?'

Svenson shrugged. 'Never so much – or still more ridiculous. She was my cousin. Corinna. Fever, years ago. Useless regret. And I only say this, any of this, my dear, as a way of explaining my sympathy for your own difficulty – your life, to wonder what that life *is*, with so much disrupted . . . memory and time, all you have lost . . . and within that missing time, all that you feel you may have done . . .'

Elöise said nothing, absently stroking Miss Temple's arm.

He took a deep breath. 'I say all of this so you will understand, when I speak of remaining here, when I see your own tears . . . so you will know . . . I am determined –'

Elöise looked up, and he stopped speaking. The silence widened and became unbearable.

'It is not that I do not possess feelings for you,' she said softly. 'Of course I do, and most tenderly. It is the most awkward thing, and you must think me a terrible person. It would give me no greater pleasure than to offer myself to you, to kiss you right this moment. If I were free. But I am not. And my *mind* – it cannot be wholly present –'

'Of course not, we are in a wilderness –'

'No – no, please – it is what I *recall*, and what I *feel* within those recollections . . . even if I do not know fully why . . . or know . . . who.'

Svenson's throat was at once horribly dry. '*Who?*'

'There is a locked room in my mind. But there are paths to the room, and from it – there are words I remember being spoken – there are clues about what I cannot recall. As I brood upon them . . . they imply everything – inescapably, even if –'

'But . . . you do not *know*? You mean – there is *someone* – but –'

'You must think very poorly of me. I think poorly of myself. Not to remember *such* a thing – though I know the thing to be true. I cannot describe it. I have no faith in who I am.'

She was silent, looking into his eyes. Her own were rimmed with tears, and impossibly sad. He struggled to catch up with her words. She was a *widow* – with a *suitor*. Of course she had a suitor, she was beautiful, intelligent, well placed . . .

But that was not the thing at all.

Svenson recalled her words on the beach. It was all to do with the book, with the memories having been *taken* – which meant for a *reason*. No memories of a simple suitor – no *lover* – would have been added to the glass book and thus expunged from her mind. For the memories to be worth taking, Elöise's lover could only have been someone of value to the Cabal. The number of men this could describe was unpleasantly small.

'Elöise –'

'The tea has cooled. I have been enough of a burden.'

Elöise stood, wiping her eyes. In an instant she was out the door.

The Doctor sat alone, his head pounding, the room a roar of silence. Without a hope in the world he picked up the teacup and eased his other hand behind Miss Temple's head, tilting it so she might drink.

The next morning, having passed most of the night on Miss Temple's floor, the Doctor rose early, shaved, and threw on his coat, finding Sorge with the chickens. A brief conversation pointed Svenson to the most likely fisherman to accommodate his errand. He left word for Chang to join him at the village piers.

The walk did nothing for his mood – the woods were thick with fog, the ground soft beneath his boots, the entire landscape only reminded him of home, and thus of misery. What else had he expected? And why – just because they had survived when they ought to have died ten times? Had luck in one instance ever trumped his unhappiness in another? He had only to remember first entering the halls of Macklenburg Palace – uniform crisp, boots gleaming, a far cry from the ice-rimed cabin of a ship – while the palace of his mind housed only despair. If being the protégé of Baron von Hoern had not assuaged Corinna's death, why should the heroic pleasure of shooting Francis Xonck on the airship grant him happiness with Elöise?

It was an easy enough matter, once money was offered, to arrange for the journey. A few minutes' poring over a map of the local sandbars with the fisherman quickly isolated the likely spots where the dirigible must lay. This settled, Svenson inspected the boat's supply of canvas. If they were to bring out the bodies – assuming the storm had not cracked the ship open and scattered the corpses with the tides – he would need enough to hold them.

Chang was not yet there – Svenson was not frankly sure where Chang slept, much less when he woke – and so the Doctor tracked down another fisherman, the one Sorge suggested might have cigarettes. After a minute or two of evasive haggling, the man showed Svenson a brick of waxed paper sealed with a dab of red wax marked with a two-headed bird.

'Danish,' the man explained.

'My habitual brand is Russian,' countered Svenson, doing his best to sound sceptical when he was so hungry. 'One can only acquire them through an agent in Riga – Latvia – as St Petersburg is barred to Macklenburg merchants.'

The man nodded, as if this was of no interest but he was willing to assume some point lay beyond it.

'The tobacco is quite strong,' said Svenson. 'Have you smoked a Russian cigarette?'

'I prefer to chew.' In proof of his claim the fisherman spat into a pewter cup Svenson had assumed to contain an especially bitter-looking coffee.

'Eminently understandable – a sailing man can never depend on a flame. No matter. I will be happy to take them off your hands.'

He gathered up the parcel and placed the price they had agreed to on the table – outrageous by the village's standards, but nothing compared to what he might pay in town – or what the vile sticks were worth to his clear mind.

Puffing away with the intensity of a fox tearing into a slaughtered hare, Svenson returned to the fishing boat – waiting any longer for Chang's sullen appearance would cost the tide. It took half an hour to pass through the surf into the sea. The Doctor, while no real practical sailor, knew enough to pull on the proper ropes when the fisherman called them out. As they approached the most likely sandbar, Svenson lit up another smoke and did his best to relax in the fresh cold air. But even with the familiar nicotine spur in his lungs, he wondered that he could have surrendered to optimism – from such an unlikely and unlooked-for corner – so very easily.

The airship was not at that sandbar, nor any other, nor any place they could spy as they ran the length of the coastline. The fisherman explained the depth of the sea away from the bars, the action of the tide, the force of the storm. The craft must have been pulled from its fortunate perch and then rolled down – keeping together or tearing apart, depending on the strength of its construction and whether it smashed into any outcroppings of rock on its way – to the very deep bottom of the sea.

Miss Temple's condition did not change. Doctor Svenson had again been dragooned by Sorge, to give his precious medical opinion on a neighbour's afflicted swine, and once back had pounded willow bark at the table for a plaster. It was a task he had hoped to share with Elöise, but instead young (and well intentioned, and fat) Bette had expressed an interest, committing the Doctor to an hour of the girl's belaboured enthusiasm. By the time Svenson finally left the table, he could hear Elöise helping Lina with the laundry. One could no more speak around Lina than exchange pleasantries with a Jesuit. When he returned from administering the plaster to Miss Temple, none of the women were in the house. He stepped onto the porch and fumbled a cigarette from his restocked silver case. At the other end of the rail, like a statue in its customary spot, stood Chang.

'Have you seen Mrs Dujong?' Svenson asked, rather casually. They had not spoken of the missed appointment with the fishing boat.

'I have not,' answered Chang.

The Doctor smoked the rest of his cigarette in silence, shivering at the evening chill, and ground the butt beneath his heel.

He woke in near darkness, on the floor next to Miss Temple's bed, covered with his pea jacket. The tallow candle was close to guttering, and he'd no idea of the time. Had Miss Temple made a sound? He had been dreaming, and already the fragments were fading – a tree, bright leaves, his own hands caked with ice. He inhaled deeply to push away his thickened thoughts and shifted closer to the bed.

Miss Temple opened her eyes.

'Celeste?' he whispered.

'*Mmmn*,' she sighed, though it seemed no sort of reply.

'Can you hear me? How do you feel?'

She turned her head away with a whispered exhalation and said no more.

Doctor Svenson tucked the blanket over her exposed shoulder, allowing –
and quite viciously disapproving of the gesture the instant he performed it
– the tips of his fingers to trace along her skin. He returned to his place on
the floor and stared up at the single window, the candle reflected in its dark
pool like a distant, dying sun.

He tried again at breakfast, lingering at the table while Elöise piled the
plates on a tray for Bette to scrub. The girl clomped outside with the tray,
and Svenson, fingering a cigarette, spoke in as general a tone as possible
before Elöise could leave the room.

'We must talk about our return. Sorge tells me a train may be caught
in Karthe, a mining settlement in the hills, some days' ride away on good
roads – though of course the roads are poor after the storm. The forest
between has been flooded –'

She turned from the window to face him, and he began to stammer.

'In – *ah* – any event – there is a score of questions about our enemies,
about the law, we must also – each of us – because I am not . . . unmindful
– and yet –'

The door opened and Chang stepped into the room.

'That child is an *animal*,' he snarled.

Svenson turned to him, his face a mask of frustration.

'Doctor Svenson has raised the very important question of our return,
of what waits for us,' said Elöise.

Chang nodded but said nothing.

'The state of our remaining enemies,' Elöise continued. 'The law. What
is known –'

Chang nodded again but did not speak.

Svenson sighed – it was not what he wanted to talk about at *all* – nor
did he want to be talking to Chang – but he carried on, thoughts tumbling
out of order, hoping to catch Elöise's eye. But even when he did, she
showed nothing beyond attention to his words.

Then, with a sudden chill, Doctor Svenson saw himself, standing in the
kitchen. He saw these last days with a startling clarity, with *foreboding* –
tending Miss Temple, desiring Elöise, their isolation – it was all vanity,

distraction, a witch's illusion from a tale, a false offer of a life Svenson knew he could not have.

He had delayed. He had tried to turn away. He had dropped his guard.

He stopped talking. He left them standing there and walked into the dirty yard, looking up at the oppressive, heavy sky. Sorge called to him from the boat shed, waving both arms to penetrate the Doctor's thoughts.

This newest errand had involved goats, but their owner occupied one of a small cluster of houses and so the appearance of the Doctor had become a social occasion for all of the neighbours. Into this knot of villagers came the news about dead men at the stable . . . and a rumour of wolves. At once children were bundled inside, livestock penned, and a party of men gathered to investigate. The nerves on the back of his neck tingling with dread, Svenson volunteered to go along and provide a medical opinion. Sorge looked at him strangely.

'But it is a wolf.'

'Perhaps there is more than one,' said Svenson quickly. 'A proper examination of wounds, you see, can make such details clear.'

The men around them murmured approval – and approval of Doctor Svenson in general – but Sorge became noticeably less talkative. Before he could broach the news to Chang – whom he found, to his annoyance, standing with Elöise on the porch – Chang suggested they walk to the shore, so they might search more effectively for any flotsam. Svenson agreed to the obvious lie, and was soon presented with Chang's discovery of blue glass. While it did not prove anything either way, it increased his dread as the two men travelled with Sorge to the stable.

The dead grooms' wounds were vicious and savage enough for a wolf, but lacked teeth marks. Indeed, the edges of the wounds were ragged, like a hank of bread torn from a loaf. He looked up for Chang, who was not there, and found himself forced to explain the sequence of death to his observers, all the time growing more convinced no animal was to blame at all. When Chang did return, subtly directing him to the privy and its indigo blue stench and finger stains, the Doctor knew they were all in danger.

The journey back passed in silence because of the proximity of the villagers, more than one of whom eyed Chang with ill-concealed suspicion. Without any relish for the task, Svenson sought a quiet moment to speak frankly about how the villagers' distrust of Chang must be dealt with in the light of the murdered grooms. Before he even knew what had happened, Chang had angrily stalked off.

Svenson was more than happy to see the man's back for the afternoon. Even if Chang's warning about their enemies – whether any had survived, what havoc might erupt were they to reach the city first – was perfectly sound, his *own* worries – that the villagers' reaction to Chang jeopardized their safety while Miss Temple's life still hung in the balance – were equally sensible, and serious. In the sober, dank air of the sickroom, it was obvious that both opinions could be managed together, though given Chang's pride it would be up to Svenson to smooth things over. Truly, sharing the cabin with the man was like living with a high-strung horse.

But Chang did not return that night for their meal. They had waited in awkward silence – Sorge, Lina, and Bette waiting with them, until the food had gone quite cold – and Svenson was forced to concoct a story that Chang had taken it upon himself to search the coastline to the south, travelling so far that perhaps it seemed simpler to make camp where he was, especially if he had found any sign of wreckage. He'd no idea if Sorge believed him – he knew full well Elöise did not – but hoped it would be enough until Chang finally reappeared. As soon as he could reasonably escape to the porch for a cigarette, Svenson snatched up a lantern and walked through the woods to where he and Chang had argued and well beyond, to the water, into the trees, knowing the search was haphazard and fruitless. Two hours later, his face numb and his breath frosting before him as he scraped his boots on the porch steps, Svenson was no more the wiser. All the lights were doused. He crept inside in silence, boots in one hand.

'Where were you?' asked Elöise softly, from the shadows near the stove.

'Walking,' he whispered, and sat awkwardly at the table.

'Did you find him?'

'No.'

'Where did he go? If you know anything, please –'

'Elöise, I have no idea. We argued. He stalked off in a rage and has not returned.'

'Argued? About what?'

'About the villagers – you must have seen it yourself, *heard* their whispers – I merely suggested he make himself less *visible* . . .'

Elöise was silent. He knew he ought to mention the grooms. Why did he hesitate?

'Did Sorge say anything, while I was gone? Or Lina?'

'I do not know that they trust me enough to speak. Bette, however, once her parents had retired, was less reticent.'

'What did she say?'

'One of the village boats has been missing since the storm. They fear the man is dead.'

'They say this *now*? Has he no family?'

'No. And apparently this fellow sailed alone.'

Svenson said nothing – again, knowing he should mention the grooms, the blue stains. Instead, as the silence grew – his eyes now adjusted to the dark – he realized she was quite lost in thought.

'I am appalled at myself,' he said. 'I have never asked – of course I know you were married. Do you have children, Elöise?'

She shook her head, smiling away both the question and his concern. 'I do not. My husband died soon after our marriage.'

'What was his profession?'

'He was a soldier. I thought you knew.'

Svenson shook his head.

'It was a very long time ago,' said Elöise. 'I scarcely remember the girl I must have been – in truth I recall him even less. A dear boy. He did not seem a boy at the time. We knew so very little.' Elöise paused, and then spoke rather carefully. 'This woman you mentioned . . . your cousin –'

'Corinna,' said Svenson.

'Your silver case. The engraving on it – "*vom* CS" – Corinna Svenson?'

'You remember that?'

'Of course I do,' said Elöise. 'Miss Temple had wondered who it was from.'

'A gift upon my last promotion.'

She smiled. He sighed, then knowing it was wrong, plunged ahead.

'I have wanted to say – perhaps I can help you – to discover what you remember, what you do not –'

She shook her head quickly. 'I'm sure it is impossible.'

'But – this other man –'

'I cannot speak of it.'

'But – Elöise – you are a grown woman – a respectable widow –'

She looked away from him. His words faltered. 'But you and I – At Tarr Manor – did we not –'

He stopped.

'I am a fool.' Her face was hard but her eyes stricken. 'You saved my life. But at times – so many times – I think I should have died.'

She stood and walked without another word into the room she shared with Bette.

The next morning, the fisherman's boat was found. It lay on its side, flung onto the line of sharp black rocks as if by a disdainful child, the mast snapped and the tattered, dragging sails half buried in the sand. Three men were there to meet them – the same men who had been at the stable, their expressions visibly colder and more grim. As he nodded in greeting – no man offered his hand – Svenson frowned to see that one of the fishermen now wore a well-kept pair of leather riding boots.

The man saw his gaze and redirected the Doctor's attention with a jab of his unshaven chin. The body had been placed, as if sitting upright, on one of the angled benches that spanned the width of the boat.

'A moment first,' said Svenson, and he climbed past the corpse, over the skewed gunwale to the cabin, poking his head into the dim little chamber.

The cabin's contents had been thrown to the floor and sent into a pile by the vessel's tilt. The floorboards were still damp, but the upper walls had not been submerged. The one small window bore a spattered line of reddish brown, and a patient search revealed another half-dozen drips and flecks. He rooted through the littered debris without any particular expectation, and found nothing.

He stepped back to the tilting deck. Sorge stood with the other men, some several yards further away, as if they had sought to speak without Svenson overhearing. As he knelt to examine the corpse, their scrutiny was palpable on the back of the Doctor's neck.

The fisherman's throat had been gashed, ear to ear and more than once, but the repeated strokes had not carved the same *cavity* seen on the bodies at the stable.

'Are those . . . from *claws*?' Sorge leant forward, pointing.

'Or *teeth*?' called one of the others.

'Or is it a *knife*?' called the man with boots.

Svenson calmly indicated the empty sheath at the fisherman's belt. 'Did anyone *find* his knife?'

They had not. Svenson returned to the corpse, delicately holding the head and moving it in his hands to better see the overlapping incisions. He stood and faced the fishermen, picking his words carefully.

'No doubt you can read these signs for yourselves. The weapon was likely a short, squat blade.'

'Do you know how long he's been dead?' asked Sorge.

'My guess would be two days. During the storm. Is it strange he should be found only now?'

'It was the flooding,' said the booted man, gesturing back towards the town. 'The land was flooded four feet this last half-mile.'

The men all stared at Svenson, as if this comment required his answer.

'The stables,' said Sorge awkwardly. 'The stables are on the other side of the village, to the south. These waters have only just receded . . .'

'Quite impassable,' the booted man spat. 'Since the storm.'

Svenson felt his heart sink like a stone. Whoever slew *this* man could not possibly be to blame for the two dead grooms and the scattered horses.

'So . . . more than one wolf?' muttered Sorge.

He found Elöise alone in Miss Temple's room. He spoke quickly – the grooms, the fisherman, the flooding, the unrest in the village.

'What can we do?' she asked.

He had not yet mentioned the blue stains, or the villager's new boots.

'Something has happened. Something they will not tell me –'

'Have they killed Chang?'

'I do not know – I cannot think so –'

A knock came on the door, and Svenson quickly sat next to Miss Temple, taking her wrist just as Sorge entered, nodding an apology for intruding but asking if he might have a word with the Doctor alone.

Svenson stepped into the kitchen but Sorge had already walked out onto the porch. Svenson took out his silver case, selected a cigarette, and tapped it on the case before lighting it. Sorge exhaled sharply – miserably, for Svenson had so recently been such a stroke of good fortune – and his words came tumbling out.

'What about the flooding? Where is your Chang? The others say you must deliver him up! Or they will blame you! I have told them – but – but –'

Svenson blew a stream of smoke over the yard. The other men were gone. Miss Temple could not yet leave. He tapped his ash over the rail.

'It cannot be easy for you, my friend – you who have been so kind to us all – who have saved our lives. I will of course – of *course* – do all I can to make things right with your village.' Svenson took another puff of his cigarette. 'Sorge . . . you are quite sure that none of your fellows has seen Chang themselves? They *would* tell you, yes?'

'Of course they would!'

'Indeed – now, these deaths. We must sort them out – we must sort them to everyone's satisfaction. Will you trust me this much? Will you let me speak to the other men?'

Sorge did not reply and Svenson put his hand on the man's shoulder. 'It would be better for everyone – for the *women* – that no one be left afraid.'

Svenson wondered if the man had already sent his wife and daughter to hide in one of the sheds.

'I will call them together,' said Sorge. 'An hour, at the boats.'

'I'm sure that will do perfectly.'

He slipped into Miss Temple's room. Elöise sat on the opposite side of the bed, looking down.

'Sorge claims they have not found Chang.'

She nodded but did not reply.

Svenson rubbed his eyes. 'Before anything else – I am sorry for not telling you about the dead grooms. I had hoped they did not portend anything. I am sorry.'

'And do they? Portend anything?' Her voice was hoarse with worry. 'Did Chang believe so – is that why he has gone?'

'I don't know where Chang is.'

'Perhaps he simply left us,' she said. 'The man was miserable –'

Svenson's words came out in a cold rush. 'The dead grooms and the dead fisherman had different killers. At the stable we found traces of indigo clay. Something is known by the villagers – about Chang or the deaths – that they hide from me.'

She stared at him. 'Indigo clay? You say this *now*? Are we *safe*?'

'I will make sure we are.'

To this bald promise Elöise said nothing, smoothing her dress over her legs. The dress was spare and black – gathered from someone's period of mourning and lucky to fit, he knew. In the dim room Elöise's hair looked black as well, and her face half wrought from shadow. He wondered – with a strange, despairing detachment he did not fully understand – what his feelings for her truly were. A piece of her mind was missing. There was another man, a man she loved. Was this such a disappointment? Could she dislodge the stone of grief he had carried so long?

It seemed to Doctor Svenson that he had the power to choose – she was right before him, a woman in life, and he saw the flaws in her face or body as he saw her fundamental beauty. He felt the tipping balance of his own heart and mind. Prudence, sanity even, demanded he fold his hopes back where they had lain and do his very best to return her to that life, to whatever mystery shook her soul, and then, that done, to step away. To choose differently led nowhere – or to the exact same place, after agonizing cost.

Yet the proximity . . . the terrible possibility, however illusory, however doomed, that here was a woman he might love – after so much time, after all the world. How could a man turn away from that?

'It seems her breath is not so shallow tonight,' she said.

'No.'

'Hopefully we may leave soon.'

Elöise paused, as if there might be some other thing to say, but then smiled tightly.

'I must meet Sorge and the village men at the boats,' he said. 'I will convince them of Chang's innocence, and our own – I must find out what they know, do my best to find Chang. If our enemies do live, then the more I do – the more visible these efforts are –'

'Why do you meet them at the boats?'

'It is Sorge's idea. My hope is to draw all this away from you –'

'Where are you going?' asked Elöise. 'Where are you *going*?'

'I am *not* – I merely – whatever *needs* to be done –'

'What of me? What of Celeste?'

'You will be *safe*. Believe me. Only promise not to go out alone – to the shore or the woods. Until all this has been settled.'

They stood in silence, the bed between them, and the girl upon it. He so wanted to speak to her, yet sensed with an unassailable sharpness how little he must count for in her thoughts.

'They are all dead,' Elöise whispered. 'They simply must be.'

He strode through the woods, late for Sorge, his thoughts running wild. What did his own unhappiness matter? Elöise would disappear into her former life . . . or what might be left of it – a widow now caring for another widow's children. Elöise would tell Charlotte Trapping everything – perhaps sparing a few details about the louche habits of the late Colonel . . . but were they not confidantes? He had seen the two women together at Harschmort, Elöise whispering in Charlotte Trapping's ear . . . as he had seen Elöise whispering to Arthur Trapping . . . attempting to persuade him to remain in the ballroom, as opposed to going off with Harald Crabbé, the Deputy Foreign Minister. But Trapping had ignored the women and gone off with Crabbé . . .

The hole in Elöise's memory. Francis Xonck convincing her to visit Tarr Manor, to share whatever shameful secrets she might keep . . . shameful secrets Xonck must have known . . . all in order to save Arthur Trapping's life.

Svenson stopped walking. He stood, acutely aware of the high cocoon of the night, miles wide and cold, holding his thoughts fast.

Arthur Trapping . . . a man of no account . . . his Colonel's commission purchased by his wife's money . . . an unprincipled and ambitious rake . . . Svenson had seen the man's behaviour for himself . . .

Elöise's lover was Arthur Trapping.

Svenson felt numb.

Or was it Francis Xonck?

Or *both* of them?

Svenson's thinking snagged on the image, like a fish hooked sharply through its jaw.

Perhaps he was wrong. Perhaps Elöise was engaged to the greengrocer, or an officer in the local militia . . . but why should any such unimportant attachment have been selected for inclusion in the glass book?

It would not have been. He was not wrong.

Svenson laughed bitterly. He was an idiot. Of course she had kissed him. Her brown hair, curling onto her startling white neck. They had been ready to die.

He looked up. He had reached the docks without realizing it, and at least ten men stood watching him, waiting in a knot outside a row of huts. Sorge raised a hand to wave him on, but the others remained silent as Svenson forced himself forward, following Sorge under a hanging sheet of oilcloth and out of the wind. The hut smelt of fish, but had a burning stove and room for them all. Svenson waited until the last man had come in – the fellow with the boots – and lit up another cigarette. Everyone stared at him. Svenson cleared his throat, stuck the cigarette in his mouth to free his hands, and peeled off his pea jacket.

'You know me as a man of medicine . . .' Svenson swatted his battered tunic with both hands. 'But you will see that what I wear is the uniform of a soldier – the uniform of Macklenburg. I am a foreigner – yet you all know the meaning of duty, of honour, of loyalty – and such is the code of my own service. I speak of Sorge's family, and your entire village, whose kindness saved our lives.'

No one had interrupted him yet, which he chose to take as an encouraging sign.

'The man who gave his name as Chang is a stranger to me. I do not *know* him, any more than I know where he is now. But the lives of two women are my responsibility – and so I am here to help as best I can.'

Svenson met the gaze of the man in the riding boots.

'This Chang is without question a criminal. And yet, such men easily become phantoms – scapegoats –'

At this several men began to mutter. Svenson held out his hands. 'If more people are not to die, we need to understand *exactly* what has happened!'

'That's clear enough,' called the man with the boots.

'Is it?' asked Svenson. 'What did you yourself say this afternoon? That the grooms and the dead boatman must have been killed by different hands?'

'What of it?' snarled the man. 'The grooms were killed by a wolf – the boatman by your *criminal*.'

'The fisherman –' began Svenson.

'His name was *Sarn*!' called one of the others angrily.

'I'm sorry – *Sarn* – my apologies, but *Sarn* was murdered two days ago. *Before* the grooms. Chang was at Sorge's – you all saw him. He could no more have reached the fishing boat than any of you, because of the flooding!'

'But he could have gone to the stables –'

'Like any of us, indeed. But you saw those wounds. The grooms were not killed by any blade I know – not unless it was a cutlass, or a boarding axe. Think, all of you! If the grooms were murdered – not by a wolf – they were murdered for horses, which means whoever killed them then *left*! On a horse! Chang did not so leave – nor, as he was here in your sight that entire day, did he have any horse tucked under his coat. I do not *excuse* Chang, but my reasoning tells me that someone else has done this killing. Perhaps they have now killed Chang. Perhaps there is something else we do not know . . .'

He looked out hopefully, but no one replied. Svenson turned to Sorge. 'Is there paper, something to write on?'

There was no paper, but Sorge passed him a mostly white patch of sailcloth, which Svenson spread on the table, plucking a stub of charcoal from near the stove. With quick strokes he drew out the coastline as he knew it, the pathways of the village, the line of the river, and the expanded width – as he guessed – of its storm-fuelled flood. Then, explaining as he went, he drew an X to mark the stables, another to mark the fishing boat.

'I am trying to *reason* why these people have been killed. Killing the grooms would have given their killer a mount – but also blankets, food, clothing. If you look, you will see from the map that, having killed them, the killer's path south would have been unimpeded by the flood.'

'What if they did not want to go south?' asked an older man. Svenson had tended his pigs.

'Where else would they go?' the Doctor replied. 'They could not have gone north – since they could not have passed the flood. We should have heard the horses in the village.'

Svenson lit another cigarette, snapping it out from his silver case. 'My point is that the grooms' killer is gone. As for Sarn – well, first, there would have been no horse, little food, no clothing – why was he killed at all?

Secondly, because of the flooded river, there would have been no path south until last night at the earliest. His killer was marooned.'

Even the booted man nodded. Svenson began drawing small X's.

'Those are houses,' said Sorge, unnecessarily narrating for the others.

Svenson was touched by this spot of loyalty and nodded. 'They are. Anyone coming from the fishing boat must have passed by *someone's* house. I suggest that men go to each one, asking questions about what was heard, what was seen . . .'

Svenson looked up and saw the booted man studying the crude map. He reached across the table, took the charcoal from Svenson, and marked an area to the *west*, in the thick of the woods. This house lay on the exact route, from the vantage of the wreck, of a person attempting to skirt the village entirely.

'Whose home is that?' Svenson asked.

'Jorgens,' Sorge answered. 'More a hunter than a fisherman. He prefers the woods.'

'Has anyone seen Mr Jorgens since the storm?'

Sorge looked up at Svenson with a blank expression.

At once the men were shouting to each other – calling for lights, for weapons – but the man with the riding boots hissed sharply and brought them all to silence.

'What if your man Chang is at Jorgens'? What if that's where he's been hid?'

'Then you must seize him,' said Svenson.

'And what if he's already *gone*?' The man stabbed his finger back onto the map, tracing a line south. 'We need to search both ways – some to Jorgens', and some by sea, around the forest.'

'But that's full of wolves,' hissed Sorge, and other men muttered in agreement. 'No matter what else is true – that way is asking for death.'

The Doctor felt a sudden peaceful symmetry. 'Not at all,' he said. 'I'll go. It is the simplest way to prove myself and guarantee the safety of Mrs Dujong and Miss Temple. If I do find Chang, I can get closer to him than any of you – and if I find wolves, well – I shall do my best to make a wolfskin hat.'

'That is madness,' whispered Sorge.

'Do I have a choice?' asked Svenson. 'If I am to convince you of my intentions?'

No one answered. The man with the boots nodded sharply, signalling the end of discussion.

'We will go to Jorgens' and walk south – you, Doctor, will skirt around the forest and come back north to the village.'

'Excellent,' said Svenson.

It was decided.

The tide had changed, and Svenson clambered aboard the fishing boat, directed to a seat in the bow. He had not said goodbye to Elöise. He was leaving Miss Temple, but Miss Temple had passed the crisis – it was merely a question of when she might regain her strength. Elöise would be safer without him, safer with the village mollified. The craft's sail filled easily, and they pulled away, bobbing over small breaking waves. The water darkened beneath the bow, and he looked back to find the land had curved – so quickly – and the village was already out of sight. Doctor Svenson held a hand over his eyes, for they were tearing in the bitter wind.

The sky was black by the time the boat reached the swollen estuary lined with reeds. Svenson thanked the fishermen, and followed their directions up the banks and through the trees. But instead of following the path deeper into the forest, the Doctor cut across a wide, wet meadow to a line of hills he could sense only as shadows. He dismissed the idea of wolves – there was no danger at all – as he now dismissed the notion of following the forest road back to the fishing village. Their enemies had already fled – the *danger* would be returning to the city. He would go on to this mining town and seek Chang, not that he expected to find Chang either. He would continue to travel ahead of the women, clearing the way of danger without the painful necessity of actual contact. The villagers might assume his death – but he could leave word in the town; any sorrow on his behalf would be brief, if it existed at all. The more he thought of it, the less he believed

Elöise would want to see him anyway – would this not be the cleanest break?

Once he reached drier ground he made camp, not wanting to blunder about in the dark. He built a small fire, ate his meagre supper, and spread his coat over his body. He woke with the sun and walked steadily past noon, winding to the dark hills, grateful for the physical effort to distract his mind and wear his limbs. He knew next to nothing about Karthe and was mildly worried about his arrival – a foreigner in a military uniform, in a town that saw few travellers at any time and scarcely one in a half a century from abroad. So much would depend on who else had reached the town before him, and what story they had told. Yet there must be an inn, and he had money. Once the place was sure, he would take the train back to the city. He wondered which of his countrymen might be left at the mission compound, and what word had been sent to Macklenburg. Could it possibly be safe for him to appear there? Perhaps he ought to go straight on to Cap Rouge . . . on to the sea, and some other ship.

If she loved another man – Trapping or Xonck – what did it change? And why was it so surprising – such terrible men? When did love ever care for facts? Did Corinna mouldering in a grave shift Svenson's feeling for her?

The twilight was just creeping from the hills when he came to a wider road, rutted by the passage of mining carts. He hoped with the appearance of the road that the town was near, but after another half an hour the Doctor stopped for a drink from his water bottle, sweat damp under his collar. He looked around him. His gaze was taken by a stand of high black stones, each the size of a house but sharply upthrust through the earth, one on top of the other, like a spectacularly unfortunate tangle of teeth. If he did not think the town so close, he would have investigated it at once for a campsite. He corked the bottle and returned it to the rucksack.

He heard a noise . . . perhaps a bird, perhaps an animal, but not the wind . . . faint, but clearly coming from the stones. The Doctor stepped off the road, his pace quickening to a run, boots clumping over the knotted grass.

'Is someone here?' he called aloud, his own voice sounding foolish after being so long alone. The clearing was abandoned, but there was a ring of blackened rocks for a fire, flat slabs to sit or sleep upon, and even a collection of coal, most likely stolen from the mines, or from an unguarded scuttle in the town.

In answer came the same huffling wail that had reached him on the road. It was above him. He dug a candle from his coat and dragged a match on the rock to light it. Some ten feet above he saw a cracked seam between two larger stones, not a cave as such but large enough to shelter something small. The smooth surface of the rock face below it gleamed wet. He knew it at once for blood, and called to whoever had crammed themselves into the tiny crease.

'What has hurt you? Is it an animal? Can you come down? I am a doctor – if you are injured, I can help.'

He received no reply. The rivulets of blood were smeared and spattered and dragged. The injured person had done their best to climb away, even as his attacker had persisted in trying to reach him.

'I am here to help you,' called Svenson. 'I cannot get up – you must come down! Who are you? What is your name?'

In an abrupt answer the figure toppled off the rock, nearly knocking Svenson flat. He raised his arms without thinking and managed to half catch the bloody, wind-milling tangle of limbs . . . but as he held the weight he saw it was only a boy. Svenson eased him to the ground, recovered the candle, and lit another match, moving the light to identify what wounds he could.

'What is your name?' he repeated, dropping his voice to a soothing whisper. The boy did not reply. He had been gashed at the throat and chest, and then repeatedly along his legs. Svenson could only too vividly imagine how these last had been received – the boy's assailant relentlessly scrabbling up the rock, slashing again and again at whatever could be reached, the cave so shallow that the child had not room enough to pull his legs clear. Svenson winced at a brutal gash below the child's knee, a shining, near-black drag of blood . . . but then reached out to touch it. The dark shining line was not blood at all. He held the candle close. The line was blue . . . a shooting vine of glass beneath the boy's opened flesh. The Doctor hoisted the child in his arms and stumbled back to the road.

His shouting brought a rush of people from the doorways of Karthe. Svenson handed the boy into the arms of others, and gasped out that he was a doctor and required a table and some light. The townsmen did not question him – neither his voice nor appearance – as he removed his bloody coat and rolled up his sleeves, stepping into someone's kitchen, vaguely aware of the pale faces of a woman and her children as they cleared the table and attempted to lay down a sheet.

  ˙Svenson waved it away. 'It will merely be ruined,' he said, and then turned to the nearest man – older than he and with luck someone in authority. 'I found him in a stand of black rocks outside the town. He has been attacked – perhaps by an animal. Do you know him? Do you know his name?'

  'It is Willem,' the man replied, unable to shift his gaze from the blood crusting the boy's mouth and nose. 'A groom at the stable. His father –'

  'Someone should find his father,' said Svenson.

  'The father has been killed this night.'

The boy did not regain his senses before death. Given the absence of opiates or ether, Svenson counted it as a blessing. The Doctor had staunched the deeper cuts at the throat and across the ribs, but neither of these had been mortal. Instead, he blamed the many gashes across each leg, all with some trace of blue glass in the wound. He recalled the freezing, snapping deaths of Lydia Vandaariff and Karl-Horst von Maasmärck on the airship, the chemical reaction of indigo blue glass and human blood, and was astonished the boy had remained alive as long as he had. He took the once-proffered sheet and pulled it over the body, shutting the child's eyes with a sad sweep of his hand.

  Svenson looked up and saw the ring of faces. How long had he worked to save the boy? Thirty minutes? He hoped the effort had at least gone some way towards establishing his own good intentions. He nodded to the same woman, her wide-eyed children around her (had no one thought to shoo them from the room?), and indicated the pea jacket bundled over a chair. She handed it to him, and the Doctor dug out his case, selected a cigarette and leant towards a tallow light in a wooden dish next to the dead boy's arm. Svenson straightened, exhaled, and cleared his throat.

'My name is Svenson, Captain-Surgeon Abelard Svenson from the Macklenburg Navy. Macklenburg is a German duchy – perhaps you do not know it. Through a complicated set of events I have found myself ashore in your country, some days' travel north, in the company of several companions. Upon nearing Karthe I heard this boy cry out. He had climbed into a nook in the rocks, where something or someone attempted to drag him down with a savage determination. I find it hard to conceive of a reason any sane person should so fiercely desire the death of a child. Is that stand of rocks someone's property? Was the boy trespassing?'

He had no interest in the answer to either question, but as long as he diverted conversation away from the blue glass he would have that much more time to make sense of the situation himself. One of the men was answering him – the rocks were common land, no one would have harmed the boy for his presence there. Svenson nodded, reminding himself to search the boy's pockets as soon as he had a private moment.

'But you say his father is newly dead as well?'

The man nodded.

'Where? How?' He paused at the silence in the room. 'Murdered?'

The man nodded again. Svenson waited for him to go on. The man hesitated.

'Could it have been the same killer?' the Doctor asked. 'Perhaps the boy ran to a hiding place he thought would be safe.'

The man looked at the other faces around him, as if asking each a question he did not care to voice. Then he turned back to Svenson. 'You should come with us,' he said.

It was exactly like the murdered grooms – the gaping throat that on first glance seemed simply an especially vicious laceration but that, upon further inspection, betrayed a substantial removal of flesh. Svenson held a candle close to the wound, aware that his examination caused the townsfolk around him to blanch and turn away. He was certain, especially after seeing the murdered boy's legs, that the father had been killed by a weapon of blue glass.

He tilted the man's head to the side, frowning at the discoloured band of skin that stretched on either side of the wound. He looked up, and saw the head townsman – who had on their walk to this house introduced himself as Mr Bolte – notice his discovery.

'He was hanged once,' said Mr Bolte. 'Neck didn't break, and he was cut down – proved innocent, he said.'

'Or freed by his friends,' muttered one of the women.

'What did he do?' asked Svenson. 'What work in the town?'

'In the mines,' said Bolte. 'But he'd been ill. The boy supported them both.'

'How could those wages be enough?' asked Svenson. 'Was the man also perhaps . . . a thief?'

He received no reply – but no denial. Svenson spoke carefully. 'I am wondering if any person might have reason to kill him.'

'But why kill his son?' asked Bolte.

'What if the boy saw the murder?' said Svenson.

Bolte looked to the faces around him and then back to Svenson. 'We will take you to Mrs Daube.'

Mr Bolte and one of his fellows – Mr Carper, a very short man whose torso was the exact size of a barrel – accompanied Svenson to the inn. The Flaming Star's landlady met them in the perfectly hospitable common room. The Doctor smelt food from the kitchen and gazed jealously past her shoulder to the crackling fire. He nodded kindly at Mrs Daube as she was named to him, but her eyes darkened as Bolte narrated the circumstances of the Doctor's arrival in Karthe.

'It is that villain,' she announced.

Mr Bolte paused at the vicious look on the woman's face. 'What villain, Mrs Daube?'

'He threatened me. He threatened Franck. He had a knife – waved it right in my face – in this very room!'

'A knife!' Mr Carper spoke across Svenson to Bolte. 'You saw how the boy was cut!'

Mr Bolte cleared his throat and called gravely to the young man now visible near the kitchen door.

'What man, Franck?'

'In red, with his eyes cut up, dark glasses. Like a *devil*.'

'He *is* a devil!' growled Mrs Daube.

Svenson's heart sank. Who knew what Chang might have done?

Another voice broke into his thoughts, from the foot of the stairs. 'Who are you *exactly*, sir? I confess I did not hear your introduction.'

The speaker was younger than Svenson – perhaps an age with Chang – with combed, well-oiled, black hair and wearing, of all things, black business attire for the city.

'Abelard Svenson. I am a doctor.'

'From Germany?' The man's smile floated just short of a sneer.

'Macklenburg.'

'Long way from Macklenburg.'

'And yet not so far away to introduce one's self politely,' observed Svenson.

'Mr Potts is a guest of the Flaming Star,' said Mrs Daube importantly. 'One of a hunting party –'

Svenson looked at the man's pale hands and walking shoes, his well-pressed trouser crease.

He caught Svenson's gaze and cut the woman off with a crisp smile. 'So sorry, to be sure. Potts. Martin Potts. And is it true you know this – this *devil*?'

'I know *of* him. He had been to the same village, up north –'

'Was there trouble?' asked Mr Carper.

'Of course there was trouble,' hissed Mrs Daube.

'But who is he?' demanded Mr Bolte. 'Where is he now?'

'I do not know,' said Svenson, looking straight at Potts. 'He is called Chang. My *understanding* is that he returned to the city.'

'And yet now there has been murder,' observed Mr Potts mildly, and cocked his head to Bolte. 'I heard you mention a boy?'

'Young Willem,' explained Bolte. 'A stable groom. This gentleman found him at the black rocks, savagely attacked – we were unable to save him. You know his father –'

'Murdered this night!' whispered Franck.

'Just like that devil promised!' cried Mrs Daube. 'He told me plain as day that any person crossing him would die. No doubt he went from here to the stables! Now that I remember, I am *sure* he said it quite clear – "If that boy *crosses* me –"'

The two townsmen erupted in astonished and outraged shouts, demanding that Mrs Daube explain more, demanding of Svenson where his *friend* was hiding, insisting (this was Mr Carper) that the fellow be hanged. Svenson put up his hands and called out, his eyes darting between the strangely satisfied innkeeper and her watchful guest.

'Gentlemen – please! I am sure this woman is wrong!'

'How am I wrong?' she sneered. 'I know what I saw – and what he said! And now you say the boy's been slaughtered!'

'The many cuts –' began Mr Bolte.

'The knife!' cried Mr Carper.

'I understand!' shouted Svenson, raising his hands again to quiet them.

'Who are you anyway?' muttered Mrs Daube.

'I am a surgeon,' said Svenson. 'I have spent the last hour attempting to save that poor boy's life – I am not *unmindful* of the savage way in which he was killed. Mrs Daube – you have told us what Chang –'

'He is a Chinaman?' asked Mr Bolte, with open distaste.

'No. It – it does not *matter* – Mrs Daube claims that Chang told her –'

'He *did* tell me!'

'I do not doubt you, madam.' Indeed, Svenson was surprised not to find the imprint of Chang's hand still raw on the woman's face. 'But *when* . . . when did this conversation occur?'

Mrs Daube licked her lips, as if she did not trust this line of questioning at all.

'Yesterday evening,' she replied.

'Are you *sure*?' asked Svenson.

'I am.'

'And after this conversation Cardinal Chang departed –'

'He is a *churchman*?' asked Mr Bolte.

'He is a *demon*,' muttered Mrs Daube.

'A demon you last saw yesterday evening?' asked the Doctor.

Mrs Daube nodded with a sniff.

'Why are you *defending* this man?' Mr Potts asked Svenson.

'I am trying to learn the *truth*. The boy was only attacked some hours ago, and, by his wounds, the father at most only hours before that –'

'That proves nothing,' offered Mr Potts. 'This fellow might have spent the whole next day tracking them, only to make his attack tonight.'

'Certainly true,' nodded Svenson. 'The question is whether Chang had left the town in the intervening hours or not. You did not see him yourself, Mr Potts?'

'Regrettably, no.'

'Mr Potts and his fellows have each travelled in different directions from Karthe,' explained Mrs Daube, 'the better to find the best hunting.'

'And none of your fellows were back either?' asked Svenson.

'I fear I am the first to return – being less of an outdoorsman –'

'Not like the Captain,' said Mrs Daube with a smile, 'who has come and gone again. As handsome a man as this Chang is a terror –'

'No one was here,' Potts insisted over her words. 'Suspicion naturally falls on this man Chang.'

'Who *else* could have done these things?' asked Mr Bolte.

'Why else would anyone do them?' asked Mr Carper.

'Why would Chang?' countered Svenson. 'He is a stranger here – like myself and Mr Potts – and come to Karthe only in order to leave it, and leave *before* these killings occurred.'

'And yet,' began Carper, 'if he *is* a natural villain –'

'How would we learn whether he had gone?' asked Mr Bolte.

'Quite simply,' said Svenson. 'Did a train depart last night or this morning?'

Mr Bolte looked at Mr Carper.

'Last night,' answered Carper. 'But we do not know this Chang was on it.'

'Is there anyone who *might* know?' asked Svenson. 'Usually this sort of thing is quite easily proved, you see.'

'Perhaps we could ask at the train yard,' Mr Bolte said.

An hour later Doctor Svenson walked back with Mr Bolte – Mr Carper, connected to the mines, was still speaking with the trainmen. There had indeed been an *incident* – the talk of the train yard – on the previous night's train: a passenger compartment with its window and glass door shattered, and a mysterious figure, wearing a blind man's glasses and a long red coat, stalking through the corridor like a wraith. The damaged compartment had been splashed with blood, as had the glass on the trackside, but no victim – dead or alive – had been found. But the trainmen were sure: the strange figure in red *had* been aboard when the train had finally left

With Chang regrettably eliminated as a suspect, the two townsmen had speculated about who, or what, might have killed the boy and his father, seizing on the possibility of a wolf with enthusiasm. Svenson nodded where politeness required it.

All of Chang's suspicions had stood before him in the form of Mr Potts – obviously no simple *hunter*. If Potts was on any official Ministry errand, there would be no fiction of a hunting party – there would be soldiers in uniform. Since there were not, Svenson had to conclude that the remnants of the Cabal in the city – all those masked guests at Harschmort who had received their instructions in specially coded leather-bound volumes – had not yet claimed power openly. Because of the disaster with the airship? Perhaps there was still time to stop them – the question was what Potts *knew*. Did he have their names? Was he informed about the glass? Would he denounce Svenson to the town? What were his exact instructions . . . and from whom?

And, of course, to the side of this, there was the unfortunate boy himself. Both he and his father – and, by the similarity of wounds, the two grooms in the fishing village – had been slain by shards from a broken blue glass book. Could this have been one of Potts's soldiers, penetrating that far north, coming across the glass? But why the grooms and not Svenson himself? Surely anyone in the fishing village would have directed the soldiers to Sorge's cabin.

Was it possible someone else had survived the airship? Svenson recalled the crude map drawn on Sorge's table, the killings ascribed to two sources. He groaned aloud. Did that mean *two* survivors?

'Are you quite well, Doctor?'

'Perhaps I ought to eat,' he replied, smiling weakly.

'I will show you back to the inn,' said Bolte, 'and have one of the men on watch collect you later.'

'Watch?'

'Indeed, yes!' Bolte patted Svenson heartily on the shoulder. 'While you are having your dinner, Mr Carper and I must rouse the town. We have a wolf to hunt!'

Mr Potts was not at the inn when Svenson returned. After Mr Bolte had explained Chang's innocence, and how it was certain their culprit was a wolf, Mrs Daube had grudgingly shown the Doctor upstairs to a small room with a bare mattress on a wooden frame. The woman sniffed, not at all ready to ease her disapproval, and asked again what place Svenson was from (this being a clear implication Macklenburg did not truly exist). Svenson took the opportunity to draw a map with his finger on the dusty top of the room's one little table, but he had not finished placing Macklenburg to the far side of Schleswig-Holstein before she broke in to ask what he desired for his meal. The Doctor swept his hand across the dust with a thin smile and replied that anything ready and warm would do – along with, if she had it, a pot of beer. Mrs Daube briskly announced what this would cost and told him he was free to sit in the common room or to come down to the table in half an hour.

He listened to her footsteps on the stairs, sitting on the bed in his coat, and then stretched out on his back. The discovery of the boy had launched him into hours of unexpected activity, the obligations of medicine that provided – as they had so often in his life – an illusion of purpose and place. But now, staring up at the slanted split pine roof of an overpriced, underkempt room in a town he had no desire to know, the Doctor felt the weight of his isolation. Chang, by catching that train, could even at that moment have reached Stropping Station – back in a city where he lived as easily as a crow amongst carrion. But Svenson's escape from Karthe meant merely another destination for exile.

Should he offer himself to a workhouse hospital? Or to the brothels as an abortionist? He lit the cigarette and blew smoke above his head. How recently – how very recently – had his heart been as light a fool's? What ridiculous visions had inflected the corners of his mind? During one evening meal at Sorge's, Elöise had described her uncle's cottage, near some park, her summers there as a child . . . a glimpse of another sort of life. It was all veneer, the very idea of taking *walks*, for goodness' sake, or possessing genuine concern for a garden, or tending the feelings of another. The more the Doctor imagined it, the more it seemed beyond his abilities – as well as quite beyond hope.

Svenson sat up, listening to Mrs Daube's distant puttering, and used both hands to quickly remove his boots. Walking softly in his stockinged feet, the Doctor crept with the candle to the other guest rooms. The first was empty, the pallet rolled up against the bed frame. The next held Mr Potts's things – travel valise, trousers, and two shirts hanging from hooks on the wall, and a small pile of books on the bedside table – the Navy's official book of tide tables, an engineering pamphlet on salvaging shipwrecks, and a distressingly thick serial novel, *Handmaids to Messalina*, which, from randomly opened pages, proved to be quite vigorously obscene.

Svenson peered beneath the bed. A second pair of shoes, a ragged newspaper – the *Herald*, folded to dire proclamations on PRIVY COUNCIL DEFIANCE and EPIDEMIC SILENCES INDUSTRY – and beyond them both, poking out from the far side of the bed frame, what looked like another book. Svenson stood, leant carefully over the bed, and extracted a thin volume of poetry – without question the same he had seen belonging to Chang. Svenson craned his head towards the stairway, heard no one, and flipped through the book with both hands. What could have made Chang forget it – especially if his time with Mrs Daube was so fraught with suspicion?

Chang would *not* have forgotten it – the man was, in his habits if not in his person, as fastidious as a cat. He had left it for a reason, but it had been discovered by Mr Potts. Svenson found a folded-down page and a terse note from Chang: 'Our enemies live. Leave this inn . . .'

He crept back to his own room and hid the book beneath his bed.

The Doctor sat near the hearth with a mug of beer. It was not especially good, but to the first beer to pass his lips in nearly a fortnight he was forgiving. Mrs Daube clattered away in the kitchen. He wondered what Elöise was doing even then − most likely dismal conversation with Lina and Sorge. He wondered if Miss Temple was awake.

The front door opened to admit Mr Bolte.

'I am afraid I must borrow your guest for a little time, Mrs Daube,' he called, smiling in such a way as to let the woman know she had no say in the matter.

Mrs Daube snorted at the Doctor. 'What's it to me if you eat it cold?'

'We have found something,' Mr Bolte explained once they were outside. 'A *clue*.'

In the road waited Mr Potts, and − his work at the train yard evidently finished − Mr Carper, both with lanterns, and more men Svenson did not recognize, each standing with either a new-sharpened stave or a bright lantern.

'It was Mr Potts's idea.' Bolte nodded to the crisply dressed city man. 'Perhaps you will show the Doctor, Martin.'

Doctor Svenson disliked this new-found familiarity, but forced himself to smile with curiosity at Potts, aware that the man's own earnest expression was an untrustable veil. Svenson had been attached to the Macklenburg diplomatic party as Personal Physician to the late Prince, but everyone with a brain knew his true task: to control the young man's penchant for excess and scandal. If Potts was from the Ministry, he *must* know of Svenson . . . which meant he must also know that Macklenburg had declared Svenson a criminal. Yet here was Potts, saying nothing, leading them all to a patch of scrub grass near the road, half-way between the dead boy's house and the Flaming Star.

Mr Potts stroked his chin like a preening bird. 'Indeed – well, it was this notion of the killer – the wolf – chasing the boy from the deathbed of his father to the rocks. I simply took a lantern and searched for any signs connecting the two – for example, a trail of blood.'

'And was there?' asked Svenson.

'My word, yes,' said Potts with a smile. 'But not of blood! It's most strange, you see – nothing other than marbles! Beads of what to me looks like *glass*!' He crouched low, holding the lantern.

There in the dirt lay a scatter of flattened, bright stones that in the flickering light seemed to contain the blue shimmer of a tropical sea. Svenson instantly saw that this had been some fluid ejected in a stream – a jet of coagulating blood or clotted saliva – that had then hardened in the cold air. Could the boy have been wounded in the house? Had he fled to the rocks, leaving this unnatural trail?

He realized Potts was watching him closely. Svenson cleared his throat. 'Do you gentlemen know their . . . source?'

'We rather hoped *you* did,' replied Bolte.

'I am afraid this is beyond my knowledge. But perhaps Mr Potts . . .'

'Not I.' Potts fixed his gaze on Svenson.

'Then let us hurry on,' Mr Bolte urged. 'Back to the rocks.'

As they walked, Mr Bolte speculated on whether the blue marbles might have come from some hitherto unknown mineral deposit or whether the boy's father had cadged them from unsavoury dealings – here Bolte's voice dropped low – with a *gypsy*.

'I should not think Karthe has traffic with gypsies,' offered Svenson.

'We do *not*,' insisted Bolte.

'Because of the isolation, I mean.'

'*Precisely*.'

'Then perhaps' – Potts risked a glance to the Doctor – 'we have not found a *gypsy's* marble. Perhaps it comes from a wolf . . . eating something unnatural.'

Mr Carper called over their shoulders, for he had fallen behind, his voice thick with effort.

'A hungry wolf will eat anything!'

Svenson felt Potts watching him and groped for some reply, but then they reached the rocks. With so many lanterns lighting up the inner clearing like an unnatural dark-skied summer day, the horrifying nature of the boy's last hour was inescapable. The rock face below his cleft of refuge was thickly striped in both blood and gleaming blue. The child had been clawed to pieces like a cornered rat – his assailant striking again and again from below, hacking at the legs but never able to catch a grip to pull the boy to the ground. Svenson turned away, dismayed to his heart. His gaze fell upon a ring of blackened stones, a fire pit.

Potts called to him. 'It seems to have been recently used, does it not?'

'It might have been the boy,' Svenson speculated aloud. 'Or a miner in transit with no money for the inn.'

'But if it wasn't?' asked Potts.

'Who do you mean?' asked Bolte.

'I do not know. But if someone else might have been here –'

'I saw no one,' said Svenson, 'when I found the boy.'

'Perhaps they too fell victim,' wheezed Mr Carper – who did not seem the better for the walk. 'Or perhaps they ran away.'

'Perhaps they left a trail themselves,' observed Svenson, and he looked meaningfully at Mr Potts. Immediately Potts was snapping orders at the other men – without a qualm for Mr Bolte's ostensible authority – spreading them out to search the ground.

Svenson looked up at the mournful crevice where the boy had lain. He turned to Mr Carper. 'If I might trouble you for a push, sir?'

Carper was entirely obliging – it gave him an excuse not to search – and allowed the Doctor to press one foot off his cradled hands, and then another off his shoulder. Svenson clawed his way up the rock, gritting his teeth and refusing to look beneath him – even this minor height made his palms sweat. Why must he always find himself in these situations?

'What do you see?' called Carper, holding up his lantern.

Svenson reached the crevice and pulled himself to the side of the sticky blood, exhaling with effort. The crevice was tiny but extended further than he'd thought, the depths too narrow for the boy to use. Svenson squinted

. . . a pale object in the very distant dark . . . he flattened his body and extended one arm . . . his fingers touched cloth . . . he pulled on it, gently, and it came free – a grain sack . . . with something particularly heavy inside it.

He slid to the ground. Before Mr Carper could ask what Svenson had found, the Doctor leant close. 'We must find Mr Bolte, alone.'

The rest of the men were assisting Mr Potts, nosing about like dogs in the shadows. Svenson crossed quickly, took Bolte's arm, and walked him out of the rocks altogether, Carper trailing behind with the lantern.

'The Doctor has something to show you,' whispered Carper, a bit too dramatically.

'Found in the crevice,' said Svenson, 'where the boy was attacked. I believe it was what he was protecting – why he was killed.'

'I do not understand. Is it food?'

'It is not.'

'Why would a wolf care about anything it could not eat?'

'Mr Bolte . . . and Mr Carper, you too must know.'

The two men exchanged a glance and drew closer.

'There is no wolf,' said Svenson. 'At least no wolf in Karthe. Before you say a word – believe me, my proof for all I say is longer than we have time to tell – you saw the "marbles" Mr Potts found on the road, and you saw the dead boy's legs – the gashes of blue?'

'But you said that you did not know –'

'I had hoped it was not necessary. It has become so.'

He opened the sack and carefully held it open, rolling down the sides so they could see, but keeping his fingers in contact only with the canvas. All three flinched as Carper's lantern was reflected back into their eyes, a bewitching, luminous indigo.

'It . . . appears to be . . . a sort of book . . .'

'Made of . . . glass,' whispered Carper. 'The *same* glass!'

'But of what use is a glass book?' asked Bolte. 'It cannot hold *printing* –'

Svenson stood, gathering the top of the sack into a knot. Mr Potts was approaching from the stand of black stones.

'You must trust me and say nothing,' the Doctor whispered quickly. 'What this holds is unnatural – to even touch it is to put your very life at risk.'

Mr Potts informed them with a satisfied smile that someone *had* been using the rocks as a campsite, and that this person possessed a horse. The searchers had also discovered another spray of blue pebbles leading away from the rocks into the hills. He looked at the sack in Svenson's hand but did not ask about it.

'Is the person with the horse related to the blue stones?' asked Svenson.

'I cannot say,' replied Potts, his eyes carefully moving across their faces.

Mr Bolte nodded sharply and announced that the search must continue, pursuing the trail of stones. Potts shouted over his shoulder to the other men, but paused, staring narrowly at the Doctor, before stalking off to lead them.

Svenson turned to Mr Carper. 'How many fellows exactly are with us?'

Carper frowned. 'I believe it is six, and Mr Bolte and myself. And yourself.'

'Six counting Mr Potts?'

'Yes, six with Potts. Nine with everyone – including you. Why do you ask?'

'Mere idleness. And apart from those staves – do any possess . . . weapons?'

'The staves are quite stout,' answered Carper. 'Do you mean firearms?'

'I suppose I do.'

'I would doubt there are five guns in all of Karthe. I believe Mr Potts possesses a pistol.'

'He does?'

'Well, he *is* a hunter.'

'I did not know hunters often *used* pistols.'

'No,' said Carper, smiling, 'that is what is so convenient for *us*! I should much prefer to shoot a wolf than kill it with our staves.'

'Indeed.'

'And yet . . . as you say . . . it may be no wolf at all.'

Svenson did not reply at once, then dropped his voice even lower. 'It may – I hesitate to say – but our quarry may in fact be . . . a woman.'

'A *woman?*'

'It is possible – perhaps I am wrong –'

'You must be, sir! For a woman to do such violence – and to a child!'

Svenson exhaled, not entirely sure where to begin, but Carper had reached his own conclusion, the fat man's breath rasping in clouds before his face.

'If you are correct – with so many of us, she *must* surrender. We will not be called on to shoot a *woman.*'

There were calls from the darkness ahead of them.

'I believe Mr Potts has found something,' said the Doctor.

At the turning were signs of another struggle: flattened grass, a dark woollen wrap, and more glass – but this in smooth, broken wedges, not the rounded drips they had followed. Mr Potts knelt over the glass, Mr Bolte standing above him. It was clear by Potts's dark glare as the Doctor approached that the Ministry man had been told about the book.

Svenson called out sharply as he saw Potts extend his hand. 'Do not touch it!'

Potts jerked his hand away and stood with a triumphant sneer, making room for Svenson.

'It is just like what you discovered in the rocks,' whispered Mr Bolte.

'Exactly,' said Svenson, to cut him off.

The pieces of glass were impossibly thin, snapped from an inner page of a book, and starred along their length, as if they had been shattered.

'I should be grateful to know your thoughts,' said Potts.

'You would be even more grateful not to, I assure you,' the Doctor told him.

'I do insist. I will have no more *secrets.*'

'Then tell us where your fellow hunters are now? Your *party.*'

'What is that to do with our search?' asked Mr Bolte. 'Surely we are enough –'

'It is to do with *what* they hunt, as Mr Potts well knows.'

'My companions are reputable men –'

'Soldiers of the Queen?'

'They are not well-known criminals,' spat Potts, 'like your Cardinal Chang –'

'Cardinal Chang has been accounted for,' interrupted Svenson. 'Your party has not. Your own arrogance shows exactly how little you do understand your prey – dangerous prey, as that poor child has proved with his life –'

'What *prey*, Doctor?' snarled Potts. 'Tell us all!'

'The Doctor mentioned a woman,' said Mr Carper.

Svenson wheeled to find Carper directly behind him, holding up the woollen wrap.

'Do you know it?' Mr Bolte asked Svenson.

'Not at all,' replied the Doctor.

Mr Bolte turned to Potts. 'Do you? Do you know any women here?'

Mr Potts shook his head. He glanced down at the glass shards and then back to Svenson with a cold, knowing gaze. As if in silent answer to all of their questions, Doctor Svenson stepped forward and with deliberate strikes of his boot heel smashed the glass fragments into glittering powder, then scuffed as much dirt as would come loose on top of the pile.

Potts pointed above them, further into the hills. 'The trail continues. Perhaps we've argued enough.'

It was another hour of steady climbing before they stopped again, by which time the air had grown cold. Without the slightest regard for propriety Mr Carper had thrown the woollen wrap across his shoulders. Ahead, at the front of the line – a line that had become distended as their journey increased and the urgency of their errand diminished with the deepening chill – Svenson saw Mr Potts conferring earnestly with Mr Bolte, and knew he ought to take part, if only to defend himself. But Doctor Svenson was tired and still too generally touched with despair not to instead take a cigarette from his case and light a match. He looked above him at the dense carpet of low cloud, so near it seemed he might exhale directly into its smoky mass. He offered the case to Mr Carper, who shook his head, and then looked up to approaching footsteps – Bolte and Potts bringing the conversation to him.

'It has grown late,' began Mr Bolte. 'Mr Potts suggests we stop.'

'And go back?' asked Mr Carper hopefully.

'That would take half-way to morning,' announced Potts. 'Apparently there is an old mine just ahead. Shelter enough, and we may make a fire.'

'Have we any food?' asked Carper.

'We did not think to bring it,' snapped Potts, glaring at Svenson, as if the lack of a dinner was his doing.

The fire was made in a long, roofless hut; the far end – where a deep shaft had been sealed with a hammered-together wall of boards – sloped into shadows. Across a small clearing were two more huts, one also roofless and the other – because of the roof – a haven for nesting birds, its floor crusted and foul.

'I have told you exactly the truth,' said Potts, his sharp features etched deeper in the firelight. 'I joined a hunting party –'

'Hunting what?' asked Svenson.

'*Deer*,' replied Potts. 'And wild boar.'

'Boar?' asked Mr Bolte. 'At this time of year?'

'I am no expert,' said Potts. He sighed with a sudden peevishness. 'I am no particular hunter at all.'

'No,' said Svenson. 'That would be your Captain . . . what was his name?'

'Captain Tackham,' yawned Carper. 'I came up with them on the train. Elegant fellow for a soldier, I must say.'

'Mrs Daube told me the party went separate ways to hunt,' said Svenson to Potts. 'I wonder who went north . . . and if they have returned.'

'The Captain,' said Potts. 'According to Mrs Daube he returned and then went out again, searching elsewhere – there can be nothing – no good *game* – in the north.'

'And what about this woman?' asked Mr Bolte, poking the fire and looking seriously at Svenson across the rising sparks. 'A woman is responsible for all this death? I confess *that* makes no sense to me.'

Svenson met the gaze of Mr Potts, who seemed just as concerned about the question as he himself. Perhaps, as far as the men of Karthe were concerned, they shared a desire to keep their business as hidden as possible . . .

'I will tell you all I know,' Svenson replied, and reached into his coat for another cigarette. 'Though I cannot pretend to possess an answer to her particular *mystery*. Even her name may be a fiction – Rosamonde, Contessa di Lacquer-Sforza.' He glanced at Potts, but the man's face betrayed nothing.

'She is Italian?' asked Bolte.

'Venetian, I was told,' said Svenson, deliberately deepening his own accent. 'Though that too is most likely a lie . . . I myself first made her acquaintance in a private room of the St Royale Hotel, in search of my charge – the Crown Prince of Macklenburg, Karl-Horst von Maasmärck. Do you know the St Royale? It is an extraordinary place – the lobby is like an Ottoman palace, with carved columns and walls of mirror and marble – you can just imagine the sort of woman who keeps a whole suite of rooms there to herself! But – yes – the Prince – I was the Prince's Personal Physician – the Contessa was an intimate of the Prince's fiancée, Miss Lydia Vandaariff, though she was more truly an intimate of the girl's father, Lord Robert Vandaariff, whose name you must know, even in Karthe, for he is reckoned one of the wealthiest men of the age – the Contessa being in fact a member of Lord Vandaariff's inner circle of advisers with regard to a particular business strategy involving my country of Macklenburg – thus his daughter's alliance in marriage with the Prince – mining rights, to be precise, which must interest you gentlemen *very* much, and then in turn manufacturing, shipping – markets in general – in any case, in this particular private room, the Contessa was, if I recall correctly – and I'm sure I do, for if ever there was a striking woman, it is she – wearing a dress of red silk, a *Chinese* red – which as you will know is a colour that possesses more yellow in it than, for example, what one would call *crimson* – a very striking choice when set against the woman's very black hair . . .'

He was gratified to see Mr Bolte yawn, and pressed ahead with this pattern of detail and digression, giving at all times the impression of complete cooperation without ever revealing anything of substance regarding the Cabal, not even the airship and why such a woman would be in Karthe to begin with. Instead, by the time his narrative had paused to describe the labyrinthine interiors of Harschmort House his only remaining listener was Mr Potts, across the fire. The Doctor allowed his sentence to drift into silence, and he reached for another cigarette. Mr Potts smirked at the slumbering men around them.

'An amusing stratagem.'

'They have no need to know,' said Svenson. 'I do not claim to know who precisely has sent you –'

'You will accompany me back to the city,' snarled Potts.

Svenson looked up at him. 'Quite possibly.'

'Without *question*.'

'Mr Potts, I appeal to you – you have seen for yourself this violence, the unnatural effects of the blue glass – the wickedness –'

'I know that, alone amongst my fellows, I have discovered my enemy.'

Svenson snapped with exasperation. 'Alone amongst your fellows? Mr Potts, what does that *tell* you? What do you think has *happened* to them?'

Potts chuckled greedily. 'They are unluckily blundering about the woods, while *I* capture – from your own description – the prime quarry of them all!'

'*Quarry?* Not ally? Not *mistress*?'

'It can be none of your concern.'

'You tempt fate to speak before you have her in hand.'

'Not in the slightest,' said Potts, smiling. 'If I read these signs correctly, she is gravely ill. Your proud villainess has been reduced to killing *children*. Speaking of which . . .' From his pocket the man extracted a large naval revolver, the black metal gleaming with oil. 'You will give me what you found.'

The large revolver was an unlikely weapon for the dapper Ministry man, one that required strength to be accurate, given the recoil, or simply a knowledge that anyone he was likely to shoot would be at point-blank range. It meant that either Potts was a cold killer or that he was ignorant of firearms altogether.

'I will not,' said Svenson, nodding to the sleeping men around them. 'You will do nothing.'

Potts hesitated and then stuffed the weapon away. Svenson breathed a sigh of relief for the lack of bloodshed, but in the same moment knew he was dealing with a dangerous fool.

'It is not the time,' sniffed Potts officiously. 'And, as you say, the business is not finished. But do not doubt me, Doctor. If you try to escape I will shoot you dead – no matter who sees it.'

Potts shoved more wood onto the fire, and Svenson took the opportunity to excuse himself, aware that the other man would have the pistol trained on his back the entire time. He stumbled to the bird-stinking hut and relieved himself in its shadow. When he returned Potts too had lain down next to the fire, his eyes closed. Svenson smoked a last cigarette, tossed the butt into the embers, pulled the pea jacket more tightly around him, and shut his eyes, the glass book in its sack at his side.

When he opened his eyes, the hut was dark. The stone pit still smoked, but the fire was dead. Mr Potts was gone. Svenson's hand went instantly to the sack, felt the weight of the book – but it wasn't right, it wasn't smooth. He opened it up, could not see inside, and with an instant's hesitation thrust his hand in and touched not glass but a rough block of stone. With a snarl, he scrambled to his feet, winding the sack around his hand so he could swing the rock like a mace.

He did not have far to walk. Mr Potts stood in the centre of the clearing, under the cloud-shrouded moon. He was not holding the book. Had the fool dropped it?

'Mr Potts,' Svenson whispered. '*Mr Potts!*'

Potts turned, eyes unfocused, as if unable to place Svenson yet knowing he ought to. The man's chin was streaked with a dark film, and Svenson wrinkled his nose at the smell of bile.

'Where is the book, Mr Potts?'

'Who?'

'Not who, *what*! The book! Where is it?'

In response, Mr Potts whimpered and rubbed his eyes. His hand was smeared with black liquid.

'Potts – yes, of course – I remember.'

'Where is the book?' Svenson reached out to shake the man's shoulder. Mr Potts smiled weakly, but his eyes were wild.

'Most important is the quality of paint – the chemicals ground into the paint to make colours – every chemical in life possesses *properties* –'

'Mr Potts –'

'Chemical properties – fundamental energies!' whispered Potts, abruptly terrified, as if this were a secret he did not care to know. 'One might even ask if there is anything else to life at all!'

Svenson slapped Mr Potts across the face. Potts staggered, blinked, opened his mouth, but found no voice. He looked into Svenson's eyes, blinked again, and the words came out in a fearful croak. 'What . . . has . . . happened?'

'Mr Potts –'

'Who *am* I?'

'Where is the *book*, Mr Potts? Where did you leave it?'

But Mr Potts was biting his trembling lip, attempting not to cry.

Svenson dragged Potts to the roofless shed. He shoved Potts in and snapped a match to a candle stub – another ring of blackened stones, travellers' rubbish, with the far end of this shed also blocked off with planking – another shaft . . . and there, the canvas sack. It was empty.

'An important problem is viscosity,' whispered Potts.

'Tell me!' hissed Svenson. 'Where is it?'

Now the man was sobbing. 'She was only a *girl*. I have a daughter myself . . .'

Svenson wrinkled his nose with distaste. A new draught in the open shed had filled it with a tell-tale reek . . . was it from Potts or the shaft? The planking had been pulled away and then hastily pressed back into place, but at the simplest touch – as Svenson himself proved with a tug – the boards came off. The reek of indigo clay rose even stronger. He thought of the blue vomit in the privy . . .

'Mr Potts . . . you are confused and frightened but in no danger. You must help me find the book if I am going to help you –'

But Potts shook free, stumbling into the yard. He pointed to the larger shed, where the other men still slept.

'They are doomed,' he whispered.

A sudden spike of fear shot the length of Doctor Svenson's spine. He strode past Potts – the candle going out – and then wheeled around, digging without apology in the man's pockets and pulling out the revolver. He entered the larger shed, cocking the hammer with his other hand . . . each man seemed to be where he had left them, undisturbed by Mr Potts's babbling. Svenson sighed with relief, then looked back. Potts had dropped into a crouch, hugging his knees and muttering. The Doctor's attention was taken by a shadow in the far corner, near the blocked-off shaft. Was someone else awake? Keeping his eye fixed on a darkness he could not penetrate, Svenson dug with his free hand for another match. He struck it and looked down at Bolte. A glittering line of blue, like the drag of a paint-clogged brush across the man's throat.

Svenson dropped the match with a start. He raised the pistol towards the shadow in the corner, only to see it swell in size before him. He fired, the sound impossibly loud, but the shadowed figure – a man in a cloak? – darted to the side and was on Svenson before he could shoot again. A shocking blow knocked the Doctor down, the pistol flying from his hand. He groped to his knees, shouting to wake the others – the shadow was between him and the outside yard – and took another hideous blow to his shoulder, toppling him back again. Utterly dazed, Svenson felt himself picked up by the lapels of his coat. He looked into a reeking, dark-lipped, dripping mouth, a pale face whose eyes were wild. The Doctor was thrown with savage force through the wall of planking, a rag-doll tumbling down into the shaft.

He awoke with his head pointing downwards and his legs above in an uncomfortable tangle. Something pulled at his hair and he very carefully reached down to it, probing the area with half-numbed fingers. A gash had opened on the side of his skull, not too bad, but it had bled and the blood had dried. How long would that have taken? He was terribly cold. His head throbbed cruelly, as did his shoulder and the left side of his ribcage. He feebly groped around him – damp rock and earth, a steeply angled slope. He felt for a match, wondering how many he had left, but could not find the box – had it flown from his pocket? Svenson looked above him . . . a fretful penumbra of light, yards above. He listened, heard absolutely nothing save his own ragged breath, and began, with the grace of an upended turtle, to turn his body and climb.

He reached the first of the broken boards that had accompanied his fall and carefully brushed them aside, mindful of the noise but still convinced that his attacker was long gone. When he emerged into the roofless hut, he saw the men of Karthe just as he had left them. In the stark day, each huddled shape held a poignance he could not endure: they had been slain in sleep.

The bear-like form of Mr Carper lay curled like a snuggling child, a glittering orchid of blue glass blooming from his jugular. Svenson staggered to the yard and saw the sprawled body of Mr Potts, the man's chalk-white face smeared with greasy, stinking, black film. Svenson sat down with his head in his hands and tried to think of simply one thing he could do.

He washed the blood from his hair with one man's water bottle, and took another's to drink. He located the pistol amongst the bodies. The glass book was gone.

He had no real idea of the time – he had not thought to purloin Mr Bolte's pocket watch – and the heavy clouds did not aid his attempt to guess it. As he descended, the fog stayed with him, lurking over each new valley and preventing any long-range view that might point his way with more confidence. He simply followed what seemed to be the trail, and trusted it would deposit him back at the stand of black rocks. Even when the Doctor attempted to pay attention to the path, his attention wandered within minutes – back to the ravings of Mr Potts, and to the face he had seen in shadow.

It was Francis Xonck – he was sure, though terribly, terribly altered by exposure to the blue glass. Xonck had slain the village grooms, the boy and his father . . . and all these men. Could a single book be so precious? Svenson scoffed – measured against human life, a hot breakfast would have been more precious to Francis Xonck.

But now . . . what had happened to him? Xonck had been shot in the chest on the airship . . . days ago now. Could he have saved himself with a spike of blue glass, desperately inserted to cauterize the wound? The airship had been flooding – the only option was death. Yet if the glass had saved him then, it was killing him now, by agonizing, disfiguring increments.

And what *was* the book – merely the nearest Xonck could snatch up in the final moments on the airship? Or had he chosen it deliberately? Mr Potts had looked inside it and been deranged. From what Svenson had witnessed at Harschmort, most of the books were populated with the memories of the rich and powerful . . . what dignitary's memories could have so terrified Potts? Could his rambling about chemicals and viscosity relate to ordnance – powder and explosives? Could the missing book contain the memories of Henry Xonck, the arms magnate?

He stood once more in Karthe, doors shut tight, smoke pluming from its chimneys and stove-pipes, its people unaware of all those they had so recently lost. His conscience gnawed at him, but Svenson was exhausted, hungry, cold, and full of his own aches. That very night was the next train – had he missed it? Xonck would surely be on it now too. Svenson told himself this was more important than speaking to widows – it was a way to make the deaths matter.

He passed by the inn with a curious frown . . . its door hung open. He hesitated . . . then forced himself to walk on – Mrs Daube's grievances were not his concern. But then on his right came another open door . . . a darkened hut . . . he had been inside – the body of the boy's father. Was that so strange? The family were dead, and the place had not been tidy . . . but Svenson walked even faster, into a loping half-jog to the end of the village road, suddenly sure that he was already too late. Ahead of him in the hills, a wolf howled. Doctor Svenson reached the narrow road to the train and began to run.

*

The way curved through a small collection of unused ore cars, and their cold emptiness struck the Doctor as another omen, like the yawning doorways, of something gone wrong. The muddy road gave out onto the gravelled yard, and Svenson finally saw the tracks themselves and the waiting train, its engine building up steam: two passenger carriages, and all the rest either open-topped cars filled with ore or boxed carriages to carry goods.

Before him were men with lanterns, clustered about a figure on the ground. At Svenson's call they turned, suspicion and anger on their faces.

Svenson raised both hands. 'I am Doctor Svenson – I was here yesterday with Mr Carper and Mr Bolte. What has happened here? Who is hurt?'

Without waiting for a reply he sank to his knees, frowning professionally at the bright quantities of blood pouring from a deep gash across the fallen man's face. He snatched a rag from the hand of a trainman and pressed it hard down on the wound.

'Who did this?' the Doctor demanded.

A half-dozen ragged voices began to answer. Svenson cut them off, realizing that the attack had already accomplished its purpose: to distract every pair of eyes around the train.

'Listen to me. There is a man – dangerous and determined to be aboard this train when it leaves. He must be found.' Svenson looked down at the injured man. 'Did *you* see who attacked you?'

The cut across the fellow's cheek was deep and still bleeding . . . still bleeding – the man had not been cut with blue glass. The man tried to speak between gasps. 'Came from behind me – no idea –'

The Doctor pushed the cloth back against the wound and then seized one of the other men's hands to replace his own. He stood, wiping his hands on his coat, then drew the revolver.

'Maintain this pressure for as long as you can – until the bleeding slows. It will have to be sewn – find a seamstress with a strong stomach. But we must search – a man – and also quite possibly a woman –'

The trainmen were staring at him, almost quizzically. 'But we already found a woman,' one said.

'Where?' Svenson sputtered. 'Why didn't you say so? I must speak to her!'

The man pointed to the first carriage. But another reached out and opened his palm to Svenson. In it he held a small purple stone.

'She had this in her hand, sir. The woman's dead.'

FOUR

CORRUPTION

Miss Temple did not make a sound. She could not tell if the shadow in the doorway – hissing in ragged gasps – was climbing in or not. The Contessa's hand tightened hard across her mouth.

There was a shout from outside, from the trainmen. With the barest scrape of gravel the shadowed figure was gone. Miss Temple struggled to peek, but the Contessa sharply pulled her down. A moment later came the sound of more bootsteps, jostling bodies in the doorway, mutters about the god-awful smell – and then, like the sudden crash of a cannon, the door to the carriage slammed shut. Another agonizing minute, for the woman was nothing if not careful, and the Contessa at last released Miss Temple's mouth.

Miss Temple spun so her back was against the barrels and raised her knife. Her heart was pounding. The carriage was as dark as a starless night.

'Wait now . . .' whispered the Contessa. 'Just a few moments more . . .'

Then the entire carriage shook, jolting Miss Temple and the barrels behind her, then settled to a regular motion as it gathered speed.

The Contessa laughed out loud. Then she sighed – a pretty, sliding sound.

'You may put away your knife, Celeste.'

'I will not,' replied Miss Temple.

'I have no immediate interest in harming you – I am not hungry, nor am I especially disposed to make a pillow of your lovely hair.'

The Contessa laughed again and Miss Temple heard her rummaging in the darkness. Then the Contessa lit a match and set it to a white wax candle she had wedged into a knothole in the carriage's plank floor.

'I do not like to waste them,' the Contessa said, 'but a little light will aid our *negotiation*. The journey will best be served by a short-term mutually beneficial agreement.'

'What sort of agreement?' hissed Miss Temple. 'I cannot imagine it.'

'Simple things. An agreement whereby – for *example* – we trust each other enough to sleep without fear of never waking.'

'But you are a liar,' said Miss Temple.

'Am I indeed? When have I *ever* lied to you?'

Miss Temple thought for a moment, and then sniffed. 'You are vicious and cruel.'

'But not a *liar*, Celeste –'

'You lied to the others – to the Comte and Francis Xonck! You lied to Roger!'

'I did not *need* to lie to Roger, my dear – no one ever did. As for Francis and Oskar, I will admit it. But one always lies to friends – if you *had* friends, you would know friendship relies on that very tradition. But lying to enemies . . . well, it lessens one's spark.'

'I do not believe you.'

'You would be a fool to believe me. And yet, I am offering a bargain. While we share this carriage, I will not harm you.'

'Why not?'

'Because I do not *need* anything from you, Celeste. What I need is sleep. And sleep in a cold carriage will be more restful if we are not barricaded behind barrels of fish oil ready to kill one another. Truly, it is a *civilized* gesture – a logic beyond morals, if that speaks to you.'

Miss Temple shifted slightly – one of her legs was getting a cramp, and the sweat on her back had cooled. She could feel the weight of her exertions waiting to fall. If she did not sleep well, she would slip back into her fever.

'Do you have any food?' she asked.

'I do. Would you like some?'

'I had a perfectly fine supper,' said Miss Temple. 'But I expect I will be hungry again in the morning.'

The Contessa smirked, and for the first time Miss Temple saw the woman's sharp spike had been ready if their conversation had gone another way.

*

The Contessa removed a small cork-stoppered bottle and a handkerchief from her bag. She tugged the cork free and tamped the cloth over the bottle, tipping it once to soak a small circle. Without a glance to Miss Temple she wiped her face and neck as deliberately and thoroughly as a cat giving itself a bath. Miss Temple watched with some fascination as the woman's face slipped through so many guileless formations: shutting her eyes as the cloth dabbed around them, stretching her lips as she swabbed around her nose and mouth, lifting her jaw as she swept the cloth – resoaked – up and down her throat and under the collar of her dress.

'What is that?' Miss Temple finally asked.

'An alcoholic tincture of rosewater. The scent is horrid, of course, but the alcohol a welcome enough astringent.'

'Where did you get it?'

'Would you like to clean your face, Celeste? In truth, you do not appear at all well.'

'I have had fever,' said Miss Temple.

'Goodness, did you nearly die?'

'As I did not, it does not especially matter.'

'Come here, then.'

The Contessa soaked a new spot on the handkerchief. She held it out and, not wanting to seem either docile or ill-bred, Miss Temple scooted closer. The Contessa took gentle hold of Miss Temple's jaw and started at her forehead, working down. Miss Temple flinched as the cloth came near the bullet weal above her ear, but the woman took account of the rawness and her touch did not hurt at all.

'Did you ever *think* you would die?' asked the Contessa musingly.

'When?' replied Miss Temple.

The Contessa smiled. 'At any time at all.'

'I'm sure I did. Did you?'

Finished with the face, the Contessa redrenched the cloth and swabbed brusquely at Miss Temple's neck. 'Your hair.'

Miss Temple obligingly lifted both arms and held the curls to either side. A few more swipes with the cloth and the Contessa was finished, but then she blew a cool breath across the newly clean and dampened skin.

Miss Temple shivered. The Contessa set down the bottle and cloth, and looked up.

'Perhaps you will help *me*,' she said.

Miss Temple watched the Contessa's fingers undo one line of ebony buttons and then ease her right arm, pale as a swan's wing, from the dark silk dress with wincing difficulty. Miss Temple gasped at the bloody gash on the woman's shoulder blade.

'I can reach it myself,' the Contessa said, 'but if you could assist me we would waste less of the tincture.'

The cut was deep but had closed with a near-black clotting seam. Miss Temple frowned, not knowing quite how to begin, a little transfixed by the sweep of the Contessa's shoulder and the smooth line of the Contessa's vertebrae – these were her *bones* – disappearing down her back like something whispered but not understood. She returned her gaze to the wound.

'It must be soaked,' said the Contessa. 'It does not matter – this far north I cannot prevent a scar.'

Miss Temple took up the bottle and poured carefully along the wound, catching the drips with the cloth. The Contessa winced again but said nothing. The cut seeped blood as Miss Temple pressed against it, refolding the stained cloth several times until the bleeding stopped. At last the Contessa's hand came over hers, holding the cloth in position herself.

'I am obliged to you, my dear.'

'What happened?' asked Miss Temple.

'I was forced to pass through a window.'

'By whom?'

'Cardinal Chang.'

'I see.' Miss Temple's heart leapt. Chang was alive.

'But I was not *fleeing* Cardinal Chang. I was fleeing Francis Xonck.'

'Francis Xonck is alive?'

'If you can call it life. You smelt him yourself, didn't you?'

'*He* was chasing me? Just now? The monster?'

'I say this with kindness, my dear, but you really must keep the pace . . .'

'But Xonck stinks of the blue glass!'

'He does.'

'But the Doctor shot him!'

'One did not think the Doctor had it in him – yet it does seem Francis has taken *drastic* steps to survive . . .'

The Contessa carefully returned her arm to her dress and did up the buttons. The close working of her fingers drew Miss Temple's eyes as if their repeated movement was a conjuring sign.

'How did you escape the airship?' Miss Temple asked.

'How do you think?'

'You must have jumped.'

The Contessa tilted her head, encouraging her to go on.

'But your dress – the Doctor said it would have soaked in the water and pulled you down.'

'The Doctor is astute.'

'You took it off!'

The Contessa tilted her head once more.

'I should never have done that,' whispered Miss Temple.

'Then you should have died,' the Contessa told her. 'But I think you would have done it. And anything else you needed to. That is how we recognize one another, Celeste.'

Miss Temple's words came suddenly, hot and loud. 'But you did *not* recognize me, madam. You consigned me to death. On more than one occasion!'

The Contessa's eyes glittered, but her voice remained even. 'Why should wanting you dead change a thing?'

Miss Temple opened her mouth, then shut it with a snap.

She listened to the rattling wheels, wondering what stops there might be between Karthe and the city, and if the contents of their carriage were even destined for the city. The doors might well open in an hour at another mountain town, or two hours after that in some village that stank of pigs. And would Francis Xonck be waiting for them?

'Where is Elöise Dujong?' she asked.

'I'm sure I've no idea.'

'I thought I was chasing her,' said Miss Temple. 'But I was chasing *you*. The man on the path – Mr Olsteen, the hunter –'

'The *soldier*, Celeste.'

Miss Temple ignored her. 'He had her knife in his hand.'

'What a *conundrum*. A shame he cannot explain it.'

'You killed him.'

'*Someone* had to.'

'How do you know he was a soldier?'

'Because I went to great trouble to avoid him – and his fellows – for some days, while they went to not quite enough trouble to find *me*.'

'Did they find Chang?' Miss Temple asked, suddenly afraid. 'Did they find the Doctor? Who *are* they?'

'I thought you wanted to know about Mrs Dujong.'

'I want you to answer my *questions*.' Miss Temple fixed her gaze on the Contessa quite firmly.

The Contessa studied Miss Temple's face, then yawned, covering her mouth with her hand, and then lowered the hand to reveal another knowing smile.

'I am tired. As you look like without sleep you will *die*, I would suggest that you do so next to me. It is still the mountains, and we have no blankets. Think of it as a pact for warmth between animals.'

Before Miss Temple could reply, the Contessa blew out the candle.

Miss Temple did not move from her barrel, listening with consternation to the rustling of the Contessa's petticoats as the woman sorted herself out on the floor. The Contessa was a wicked, wicked creature – it would be the act of an idiot to trust her. Miss Temple was exhausted and shivering. What had happened to Chang? He'd left his note – and then done what, simply vanished to the city, knowing the Contessa was alive and free? And was Doctor Svenson any better? Miss Temple hugged her knees to her chest. She did not wish to find either man a source of disappointment, and yet they had clearly done less than they might have in her service.

The Contessa sighed, rather contentedly. Miss Temple yawned, not even bothering to cover her mouth, and blinked. She was trembling with cold, and felt utterly ridiculous. Staying awake would only waste whatever strength she still possessed – she knew this for a fact and bitterly resented that in being sensible she was doing the Contessa's bidding.

Miss Temple crawled to the Contessa's side and then, rather hesitantly, pressed her body close, curling her knees behind the other woman's and nestling her face against the nape of the Contessa's neck, which smelt of the alcohol and rosewater. At her touch the Contessa pushed her body gently back into Miss Temple's. Miss Temple held her breath at the suddenly intimate press of the woman's silk-wrapped buttocks into her own pelvis. The Contessa shifted again, nuzzling her body still closer. Miss Temple's impulse was to draw away, though already she was shivering less and it *was* pleasant to have something as soft as the Contessa's hair upon which to rest her head. From the smell of alcohol and roses she realized that the shoulder inches from her face bore the bloody gash. She found herself tempted to touch it, to even – her eyes were heavy and her thoughts slipping adrift – dab at it with her tongue. But before this thought could even spark her own disapproval, the Contessa reached back, groped between them, and took firm hold of Miss Temple's hand. The hand was pulled across the Contessa's body and tucked tightly between the woman's breasts. The Contessa wriggled a last time – now the hand was no longer in the way – tight against Miss Temple, and sighed deeply. Miss Temple had no idea what to do at all. She gently squeezed the Contessa's hand. The Contessa squeezed hers in return, slipping two of her fingers into Miss Temple's half-formed fist. Within worries that she very much should get back to her barrel, Miss Temple fell asleep.

She opened her eyes in a dim light that peeped cautiously through the very few gaps and knotholes in the wall of the goods van. The train had stopped. Outside, she heard footsteps on the gravel; they passed by, followed by an exchange of shouts. Then with a slow, grinding rhythm the train pulled back into life.

Miss Temple realized with a shock that her hand was cupping the Contessa's breast, and that the woman's own hand held hers in place. Miss Temple did not move. Had she shifted her hand to its present location or had the Contessa done it for her? Miss Temple had, with an interest at times abstract and at other times less so, of course held her own breasts, wondering at their shape and sensitivity, convinced they were both bother-some and perfectly splendid. But the Contessa's breast felt very different – being somewhat larger and connected to an altogether different body – and it was all she could do not to gently squeeze her fingers. Miss Temple bit her lip. At the margins of her mind she felt the seeping presence of the blue glass book, insistent and intoxicating, sparking an undeniable itch between her legs (. . . wrapped naked in furs in the back of a sledge . . . a smearing of musk and blood across her lips . . . her own inner thighs stroked with a feather . . .), and she squeezed her hand, ever so softly, breath held tight, then squeezed again, her whole body warming with desire.

The Contessa's hips pushed luxuriously back into her own. Miss Temple yanked her arm free with a gasp, sitting up. In a moment she was across and against her barrel, knees drawn up, smoothing back her hair. When she could no longer prevent her eyes from glancing towards the Contessa, she saw that the woman was leaning on her elbow, still drowsy from sleep, smiling back at her with a mild sort of hunger.

'We stopped,' said Miss Temple. 'I've no idea where. Did it wake you?'

'It must have,' said the Contessa, a little dreamily for Miss Temple's taste. The Contessa plucked idly at her hair. 'I must look a fright.'

'You do not,' said Miss Temple, 'as I am sure you know. I am the one who is frightful – my hair has not been curled, my hands are scabbed, my complexion is quite ruined with sundry disfigurements and bruising and what-have-yous – not that I care a jot for any of it.'

'Why should you?'

'Exactly,' snorted Miss Temple, not exactly sure why she was suddenly so cross.

'How did you sleep?'

'Quite poorly. It was very cold.'

The woman was smiling at her again, and Miss Temple nodded peremp-torily in the direction of the Contessa's bag.

'Would you have anything to eat?'

'I might.'

'I would even more enjoy a cup of tea.'

'I cannot help you there.'

'I am aware of it,' said Miss Temple, and then observed, 'Some people prefer coffee.'

'I am one of those people,' said the Contessa.

'Coffee is too bitter.'

The Contessa let this stand and opened her bag, then looked back at Miss Temple before removing any article from it. 'And what do I get in return for sharing my food?'

'What would you expect?'

'Not a thing. That is, I would not *rely* upon it.'

'Then we understand each other quite well.'

The Contessa chuckled and produced two dried apples and a gold-crusted pie wrapped in a grease-stained cloth. She handed one of the apples to Miss Temple and took the pie between her hands. Miss Temple thought to offer her knife to cut it in two and reached down to her boot. The knife was no longer there. She looked up at the Contessa, who had broken the pie between her fingers and was handing across one half.

'It is too much to hope for anything but mutton,' she said. 'Is something wrong?'

'Not at all,' replied Miss Temple, taking the pie. The crust flaked onto her wrist and she brought it to her mouth, catching the flake on her tongue like a toad. 'I am much obliged to you.'

'You needn't be,' said the Contessa, chewing, and rather more frank in her manners than Miss Temple had expected. 'I have no further interest in any memory of Karthe, much less its food. As I have no desire to eat more than half this pie – in fact, hardly enough to eat any at all – giving that much to you costs me nothing.'

Miss Temple had no response to this, so she simply ate. Despite every-thing she felt well rested, and stronger than she had the day before. She bit into the apple, finding it too chewy but still tart.

'You took my knife, didn't you?'

'Do you always insist on asking questions to which you know the answer?'

'It was a way of letting you know I was aware of it.'

'Only a fool would not be, Celeste.'

'I must have slept deeply, then.'

'Like a mewling kitten.' The Contessa swallowed another bite of pie. 'You mentioned our stopping. But that was the third time we had stopped – you slept through the others.'

'Will you give it back?'

'I shouldn't think so.'

The Contessa saw her cross expression and leant forward. 'Understand, Celeste, slitting your throat would have been as easy as patting your head. I did not, because we had an agreement.'

'But *after* the agreement – *after* we arrive –'

'I will not give it back then either. Who knows when you will want to cut mine?'

Miss Temple frowned. It was far too easy to imagine some future meeting – in the city, in a train carriage, on a marble staircase – where the Contessa would without pause slash her glittering spike at Miss Temple's unprotected face. Could she do the same, after pressing herself against the Contessa's warm and splendid body in the dark? How could mere familiarity change anything between them? But how could it not?

Miss Temple cleared her throat. 'If we are so agreeable, perhaps you will now tell me of Elöise. You did promise to do so.'

'It is a very boring thing to ask.'

'Did you hurt her?'

'I did not. Mrs Dujong and a young man entered a house in Karthe – a house I myself was *observing*.'

'Why?'

'Because I *lost* something, Celeste.'

'But the boy who lived there was murdered!'

'Yes, I *know*. Once they went in, I saw the soldier lurking in the street – he'd followed *them*. I took this as my own opportunity to slip past him to the inn, but before I was finished with the innkeeper the soldier returned and insisted on being unpleasant to everyone.'

'And Elöise?'

'Since she did not come back to the inn with the soldier – either he killed her, or Francis killed her . . . or something else.'

'What else do you mean?'

'Once again, Celeste, if you simply made a habit of *thinking* before speech –'

'Xonck *knows* her?'

'Of course Francis *knows* her. She is his sister's loyal confidante.'

'She never said any such thing to me!' Miss Temple sniffed doubtfully. 'Francis *Xonck* –'

'But that is what is so delicious!' cried the Contessa. 'She does not even know herself!'

'Know what?'

'That she is already *his*!'

Miss Temple recalled Elöise's determination not to explain why Chang and the Doctor had vanished, indeed her determination to explain as little as possible . . . but Francis Xonck? Miss Temple was appalled.

'But what has *happened* to her?'

'I've no idea,' said the Contessa. 'When I got to the train yard, I did what I could to create a disturbance – to make it that much harder for Francis to move about freely – and found my place to hide. Perhaps there was a scream or two outside – I was securing my place with the fish oil.'

'I should not think he would scare you,' observed Miss Temple mildly.

'Francis does not *scare* me,' the Contessa replied pointedly. 'But he is very dangerous, and in Karthe I had no way to combat him. In the city I shall. Most *definitely*.'

The Contessa idly patted her bag, then realized she had done so and that Miss Temple had noticed the gesture. Miss Temple smirked with great satisfaction, and nodded to the closed carriage door. 'If we stopped three times, do you know where we are, or what time it is?' she asked.

'I do,' replied the Contessa, 'and see no profit whatsoever in telling you. But you did sleep so beautifully.'

The Contessa set the rest of her pie on the floor, pulled up her dress to wipe her hands on her petticoats, then flounced the dress back into position and crawled deliberately towards Miss Temple on her hands and knees, until their faces were very near. Miss Temple swallowed, suddenly afraid, but her fear was of a different order than that of the night before. The Contessa had become more *known* . . . a woman who ate and slept and yawned and flexed her hips with restless hunger . . . somehow it made her even more monstrous. Despite everything the Contessa had said, Miss Temple did not know why she was still alive – there must be a reason – some role the woman hoped she would perform. What other explanation was there?

'The thing is . . . I have slept as well. I am no longer tired, nor does my shoulder so vex my movement – I am indebted to you for your . . . ministrations.'

The Contessa's tongue caught a last crumb of pie crust from the corner of her dark mouth.

'Not to worry,' croaked Miss Temple.

'I am not in the slightest worried. Though I do *wonder* . . . I wonder what you *intend*.'

'Me?' whispered Miss Temple. 'Nothing at all.'

'O *tush*. Our journey together is a parenthesis, and upon disembarkation we must once more become active enemies. In truth, you are lucky that you have been isolated with me, for, alone among my companions, I am . . . whimsical. I helped the Doctor to rescue his Prince once, just to confound the Comte. I lied to Francis – O goodness, how he was angry – and of course all of us betrayed Lord Vandaariff quite utterly. So it is not for squeamishness regarding a promise that I have not killed you in your sleep. But . . . that, as I say . . . I am curious.'

'About what?'

'About you, of course.'

The Contessa nudged her face closer, dipping her nose towards Miss Temple's curls, and inhaled. Miss Temple could not meet the woman's eye, but found her own caught by the other's pale throat, the two jet buttons still undone at the top of her bodice. She could feel the strange memories within her mind, pushing forward, shining their insidious light through each crack in her resolve.

'You must be full of flames,' whispered the Contessa. 'The book . . . in which you nearly drowned . . . I *know* it haunts you, Celeste. It was *my* book – I know everything that was in it . . . everything that must be preying on your heart – it was my own calculated entrapment. I expect you struggle against it even now. Look at you *trembling* . . . do you fear I will *bite* you?'

At this the Contessa did just that, snapping her teeth gently onto Miss Temple's cheek. Miss Temple cried out and the Contessa let go, laughing, and then swept her tongue across the blushing, bitten spot.

'All of this can be over for you, Celeste. Roger is dead – you've had your revenge. As you said yourself on the roof of the airship, my plots are finished. Macklenburg is unreachable – with the Prince and Lydia dead, there is no marriage, and all the money and land remain in Lord Vandaariff's name, beyond my control . . . no doubt *he* has been placed in a madhouse . . .'

She nipped again at Miss Temple's face and then pushed her mouth onto Miss Temple's. The Contessa's lips were even softer than Miss Temple had feared, and the woman's tongue darted past her teeth so very deliciously. Miss Temple groaned. The Contessa pulled back, breathing just a touch deeper herself, and went on as if there had been no interruption.

'You can go back to your hotel, back to your husband-hunting, back to your little island . . . there is no need for the two of us . . . to come . . . to *blows* . . .'

The Contessa feinted another kiss and smiled at Miss Temple's indecision, whether to turn her head or open her mouth.

'You must stop,' Miss Temple whispered.

'Stop what?' asked the Contessa, stabbing her mouth forward again. This time Miss Temple's tongue responded, pushing into the Contessa's mouth. Miss Temple's hands were balled into fists against the desire to seize the Contessa's body. Her mind was spinning, so many flickering memories leaping to feed her senses. She did not know how much of what she felt came from the book and how much from the Contessa – did it matter? Was she any less subject either way? The Contessa broke contact and kissed her a third time, pushing forward. Miss Temple's left hand groped to keep her balance, while her right shot out to push the woman away, but felt the stiff corset beneath the cheap silken dress and then slid further along, smoothing past the corset's edge to the sweet soft rounded sweep of her hip, where she could not help but squeeze. The Contessa broke away to bite Miss Temple's little chin.

'You must stop . . .'

'I do not believe you,' breathed the Contessa against Miss Temple's throat.

'Your plots,' gasped Miss Temple, despite herself turning her head away so the Contessa's tongue might trace itself more freely. 'Your intrigues – you must be content with survival . . .'

'What did you say?'

'You have corrupted my heart –'

'O . . . nothing of the kind . . . you were always so . . .'

'They will kill you if you do not disappear.'

'Who will kill me?'

'Cardinal Chang – the Doctor –'

'Those *heroes* . . . but what, Celeste, of *you*?'

'I would kill you myself –'

'And how very brave – and how *principled*.'

This did not seem like a compliment. Miss Temple's breath was still rapid – when had the Contessa's knee lodged itself between her legs?

'Such principles just show how much you understand . . .' The Contessa planted small speculative kisses along Miss Temple's jaw. 'And how little . . . a gratifying thing to have displayed by an enemy.'

'I *am* your enemy.' Miss Temple writhed against the Contessa's grinding knee.

'You always have been, dear.'

'Then why have you kept me alive?'

'Because even I cannot be everywhere at once.'

To Miss Temple's surprise, even as once more her tongue was darting within the warm and slipping confines of the Contessa's mouth, the Contessa's hand pinched her nose tightly closed. Merging oddly with the tingle of her loins and the flush she was sure had spread all down her front . . . was the realization that she could not breathe. She tried to gently shift the Contessa's arm but found her own sharply pinned by the woman's elbow. She tried to turn away, but the Contessa did not loosen her grip. Miss

Temple arched her back. She tried to bite the Contessa's tongue, but the woman merely brought up her other hand to clamp shut Miss Temple's jaw. Miss Temple thrashed her legs. She slapped at the Contessa's face, groped for her hair. The Contessa did not budge, the seal of her soft lips as fast as an oyster to a stone. Miss Temple became dizzy and afraid. She could not think. She heaved with all her strength but could not dislodge her succubus. With a last, desperate thought that such an end was exactly what she had come to deserve, Miss Temple's mind went black.

She opened her eyes to an unmoving carriage and the Contessa gone. Attempting to sit up, she found herself pinned to the wooden floor, the tip of her own knife driven through her dress at the very juncture of her legs. Miss Temple wrenched it free with both hands, snorting that to the Contessa such a gesture would pass for wit, and returned the blade to her boot. She crawled to the doorway of the carriage and, heaving with both arms, pulled it three inches wide, enough to peer through.

The land before her was a blend of fen and forest, perfectly suited for the construction of canals. She remembered Elöise's description of her uncle's cottage, annoyed that she had listened with such disinterest, for she was certain his home lay in this very part of the country. It had been in a park of some sort – what had it been called? *Parchfeldt!* Yet the idea of leaping off the train in the deluded hope that anyone – if there *was* anyone – might direct her to Parchfeldt Park was ridiculous. Miss Temple slumped back against the wall. Her actions in the goods van – from the first decision to sleep next to the Contessa to this last humiliating struggle – flayed her conscience like a whip.

If she ever found Chang and Svenson, what would she say to them – about her own failures of character, or about her loss of Elöise? Where would she possibly find the two men? She did not know where Parchfeldt was. She did not know what Chang's message possibly meant – 'the Lord's *Time*' – no doubt it was the secret name for some gambling club or brothel.

The Contessa's words echoed in her heart. She could choose to leave her adventure as something finished, be satisfied with her revenge and her survival. She could return to her life with lessons learnt and precious few scars to prove it. But then she clenched her legs tightly together, shivering at the memory of the Contessa's touch, pulling her knees to her chest in fervid misery.

The train at last pulled forward. Miss Temple curled onto her side, though the rest she found was thin and brought no comfort.

She woke to whistles and the rushing racket of other trains passing near. Miss Temple straightened her dress and wiped her face, making sure of the knife in her boot. They had entered the tunnels surrounding Stropping

Station. The train slowed and crawled agonizingly to a stop. She opened
the door with a determined, prolonged shove, wriggled through, legs dangling, and pushed herself off to land with a grunt on the soot-blackened
gravel. Miss Temple ducked her head down and scuttled like a crab beneath
the next train over. Emerging unseen on the far side, she advanced briskly
towards the main station hall.

She was still in a quandary as to her path. She was tempted by so many
sensible tasks: to find a hotel, arrange a draft of money from her bank, refit
herself – a new bag from Nesbit's, undergarments from Clauchon, a dress
from Monsieur Massée (who would have her sizes, and could be counted on
to be discreet), and before everything a hot bath with rosemary oil.

Miss Temple ducked into the space between two carriages. Ahead of her
a figure in a long hooded black cloak crept from under a railway carriage,
escaping her own train just as she had done. The figure paused there, for
the path to the thronging open plaza of Stropping Station had been blocked
by two men in long black coats and top hats and, behind them, four
red-coated soldiers. The men in black looked very much like Roger – like
government officials – and gazed grimly down the trackside, but they saw
neither the cloaked man nor Miss Temple. With a shrug of agreement they
marched from view, the soldiers in stomping unison behind them. The
hooded man flowed soundlessly forward like a shadow against the side of
the train.

Miss Temple scampered after him. She reached the spot where he had
hidden and wrinkled her nose at the reek of indigo clay. She was following
Francis Xonck. But why was Xonck hiding from the government officials
and soldiers who had been his allies? Her heart rose with sudden hope. Did
it mean that the Cabal had been overthrown?

Then she sighed bitterly. If only she knew where to meet Chang or
Svenson, she could satisfy herself with having seen Xonck, and make her
way directly to a hotel, perhaps the Beacon, or – her heart leapt just a little
– Anburne House, which boasted an especially excellent tea. But she did
not know.

Xonck rushed into the bright lights of the main station floor and disappeared. Miss Temple reached down for her knife and, holding the thing as discreetly as she could in her fist, dashed after him.

The massive angel-flanked clock, hanging over Stropping terminal like an oppressive omen of guilt, set the time at just before noon. As she turned away from its unwelcome image, Miss Temple realized that something in the station had changed. The teeming crowds coursed between the high staircases and the ticket counters and the different platforms, with eddies and pools around the various shops and kiosks scattered across the floor . . . but their formerly free movement was now directed by an army of brown-coated railway constables. What had happened? She saw travellers driven in harried groups, resentful sheep under the rule of nipping hounds. She saw uncooperative individuals pulled aside and escorted brusquely away – respectably dressed people – given over to the custody of soldiers! Had there been some rail crash or catastrophe? Had there been another riot at a mill? At the kiosks and shops, each purchase was observed by constables – even small groups standing in conversation were ordered to move along. Across the station Miss Temple saw bright knots of scarlet – dragoons in uniform, each group accompanied by figures in crisp city black. They peered down the track lines as different trains pulled in and out of Stropping, obviously engaged in a massive search . . . and a preponderance were gathered near her own quadrant of the station's platforms . . . where trains arrived from the north.

Francis Xonck thrust himself past two quarrelling constables into the crush of waiting travellers, crouching low. Miss Temple threw herself into his wake, into the bags and elbows, the jabbing umbrellas and ankle-catching canes, finally stumbling to a halt against an elderly gentleman's back. She looked up to apologize and saw his face was wrinkled with nausea. With a hop she glimpsed Xonck's black hood. He had changed direction.

Thinking quickly, Miss Temple joined a group of schoolchildren led by hectoring tutors, for whom the constables made way – and when one of the children turned curiously back to her she hissed '*Face front!*' with such authority that the young thing instantly complied. Suddenly Xonck was

almost directly before her . . . waiting for an opening between the patrols
of soldiers. From behind she could see how tall Xonck truly was, and she
could too easily recall his deadly movements . . . the man was actually quite
a bit like Chang. Of course Xonck was a preening dandy, a wicked vampire
of a man, while Chang . . . well, one had to admit the red coat was ostenta-
tious . . . and Chang's character *was* wicked. He had abandoned them all,
hadn't he?

Xonck dashed forward. At either side of the platform's edge stood
black-coated men and dragoons, but Xonck slipped skilfully past them all,
down a gravelled alleyway beside a waiting, steaming train. She leapt after
him, but Xonck did not look back, racing straight to the furthest carriage.
He craned his head ahead to the coal wagon, first looking for any trainmen
– warning Miss Temple, who threw herself down – then glanced behind
him. When she peeked again, he had climbed to an odd-shaped window at
the carriage's front, perhaps to a lavatory. Miss Temple crept closer. The
window would not open, and Xonck shoved again, striking the sash with
the heel of his fist. He shifted his grip to push with both hands, but lost
his balance and dropped to the ground with a snort of disgust. Xonck
flipped his cloak over his shoulder to reveal a heavy canvas bag looped
around his right hand – which Miss Temple now saw was wrapped with
plaster. Setting the sack on the rocks, he rescaled the carriage, now clubbing
at the window latch with the cast and pushing at the sash with his more
nimble left hand.

Miss Temple advanced across the gravel, quiet as a trotting cat. He did
not see her. Without hesitation she snatched up the sack and ran.

The sack was heavy and bounced against her thigh. She'd not gone five
yards before she heard Xonck roar. A rush of delirious fear rose to the
very roots of her hair. Xonck's bootsteps pounded behind her. At the
platform stood a man in a black coat with three soldiers at his side, not a
single one of them looking her way. Miss Temple screamed, high-pitched
and helpless. She darted to the side and heard Xonck – so very close behind
her – stumble to change direction. She screamed again, and the idiots on
the platform at last turned their faces. The man gaped at her, then *finally*

called to his men. The dragoons drew their sabres and followed. Miss Temple screamed a third time and cannoned into the official's arms, knocking him back a full two steps as the soldiers charged by. She turned, chest heaving, to see the path behind her utterly empty. Francis Xonck was gone.

A soldier stalked along each flanking train, peering beneath every carriage. The third remained on guard, his sabre drawn. The man in the black coat studied her with concern, a thin-faced fellow with a waxed black moustache and side whiskers a touch more full than his jaw could attractively bear.

'He was chasing me,' she gasped.

'*Who* was chasing you, child? Who was it?'

'I do not know!' cried Miss Temple. 'He was quite wicked looking and smelt foul!'

'She says there's a smell!' he called out to the dragoons. As if this were not at all strange, both searching soldiers bent forward to sniff.

'Yes, sir!' one called back. 'Cordite and *corruption* – just like we were told!'

The man in the black coat raised Miss Temple's chin in a way she did not appreciate. 'What is your name?'

'I am Miss Isobel Hastings.'

'And what are you doing running about between trains at Stropping Station, Miss Hastings?'

'I did not intend to be between trains at all, I promise you. I was chased. Of course I am so grateful for my rescue.'

'What is in your parcel?'

'Only my supper. I was to travel on to Cap Rouge, you see, to meet my aunt.'

'All the way to Cap Rouge?'

'Indeed,' she said, hefting the sack, 'and so I have packed enough for two meals. A pork pie and a wedge of yellow cheese and a jar of pickled beetroot –'

'Cap Rouge is to the south,' said the man condescendingly. 'These trains ride to the east'

'Do they?' asked Miss Temple, curious as to why Francis Xonck had not simply fled into the city.

The man spoke to the soldier near him. 'Call them back. I must make my report.' He took hold of Miss Temple's shoulder. 'Miss Hastings, I shall require a bit more of your time.'

She was escorted to a larger group of soldiers, with two Ministry officials instead of her one, whom she overheard addressed as Mr Soames. When Soames returned, his face was more grave, and he again took firm hold of her arm, pulling her towards the large staircase. Miss Temple was about to inform Mr Soames that she was perfectly able to accompany him without physical contact – in fact to wrench her arm away – but in that moment they passed a shop stall selling hats and scarves to forgetful travellers, which was to say she passed a stall that housed a *mirror*. With a shock, she first realized the standing rectangle *was* a mirror, and to her full mortification Miss Temple realized that she had seen herself without any recognition whatsoever. Every part of her body belonged to a different person: her splendid hair was tangled and lank, her dress was out of date, dirty, and plain, her boots cracked and scuffed, her skin streaked with grime where it was not marked with a cut or bruise – even the sack in her hand spoke to poverty and weakness. For the first time in her life Miss Temple was without control of her own *character*. In the eyes of the world she had been transformed to a completely and commonly *known* type of woman – unvalued, poor, untrustworthy – which left her at the unquestioned mercy of a man like Mr Soames.

They reached the stairway, the soldiers falling in line behind, and began to climb. Had she eluded her enemies only to face the disinterested cruelty of the law? In vain she looked below her, the milling snakes of the ticket queues, the crowds at each platform, the tangle of bodies below the clock . . . the clock . . . Miss Temple's heart fell in an instant to her feet. *The Lord's Time!* Below the angel-flanked clock stood a tall, lean figure in red, motionless amidst the swirling crowd. It was Cardinal Chang. She had missed him completely. Soames pulled her arm and she stumbled. They had reached the top of the stairway. She looked back again, but the soldiers blocked any sight of the terminal floor. Chang was gone.

Only Soames joined her in the coach, rapping his knuckle imperiously on the roof to start it forward.

'Where are we going?' asked Miss Temple, the canvas sack held tightly on her lap. At least Mr Soames was crisp in his appearance, his hat set on the seat beside him, his dark hair parted in the middle, not over-oiled, and his coat well cut and clean.

'Do you know the man who chased you?'

'Not at all – he quite surprised me, and as I told you, smelt terrible –'

'Between the tracks.'

'I beg your pardon.'

'Between the tracks,' repeated Soames. 'It is not an especially safe place, nor where one might expect to find a lady.'

'I have told you. He *chased* me there.'

Soames raised one warning eyebrow at her tone. 'The man in question is sought by the highest levels of government,' he announced. 'He is a dangerous *traitor*.'

'What Ministry do you work for?'

'Excuse me?'

'I am acquainted with many men at the Foreign Ministry –'

'A word of advice, Miss Hastings. It is the wise trollop who holds her *tongue* – and survives.'

Miss Temple was stunned. Soames studied her closely, as if weighing a decision, and then leant back and glanced too casually at the window, as if none of what he had said was of the slightest importance.

'I have been recently promoted,' sniffed Soames. 'I have been seconded to the Privy Council.'

Would he proposition her then and there in the coach? Soames took off his gloves one finger at a time as if the task was serious business, and then slapped them together on his knee. 'It is a very different matter than what you are used to,' he said with a tolerant smile. 'Very easy for a girl to get in over her head – to quite lose herself, without an ally –'

He was interrupted by a cry from outside. The coach lurched and came to a sudden stop. Before Soames could call to the driver, they heard the driver calling himself, a torrent of abuse immediately echoed by a swell of shouting from the street.

'What is going on?' asked Miss Temple.

'It is nothing – agitators – malcontents –'

'Where are we?'

Soames did not answer, for the harsh voice of the dragoon sitting next to the driver now threatened whoever blocked the coach. Soames waited – the voices in the street remained defiant – but then the coach moved again. Soames sank back in his seat with a frustrated sigh, snapping the curtain closed on the small window as they passed the still-shouting crowd apparently lining both sides of the street.

'Do not be concerned,' he muttered. 'All this rabble will soon be settled.'

'As all rabble ought to be,' said Miss Temple, and then she smiled. 'Privy Council! My goodness – then perhaps you can tell me if the Duke of Stäelmaere is still alive?'

Soames sputtered, then shot an arm out to the door to steady himself as the coach went round a turn too fast 'Of course he is alive!'

'Are you *sure*?'

'He rules the Privy Council!'

'And Colonel Aspiche?' asked Miss Temple.

'Colonel Aspiche?' cried Soames. 'By God, someone has schooled you in any number of topics you have no business knowing!'

He leant forward, and Miss Temple feared he might strike her, or worse. She looked up at Mr Soames and batted her eyes hopefully. 'I should be more than happy to answer your questions, Mr Soames, but you can see for yourself that I am tired and – well, indeed – *dishevelled*. I have an excellent proposal that will help us both. If you would let me off near the Circus Garden, I should be most grateful, and we can speak tomorrow when I will be rested and not so unpleasantly insolent. The fright of my escape, you understand, has rattled my nerves –'

'I cannot oblige you.' There was a distinct note of pleasure in his voice.

'Any person having contact with traitors must be transported directly for questioning.'

'Traitors?' asked Miss Temple. 'You only mentioned the one.'

'It is hardly your concern.'

'It becomes mine when you detain me.'

'What do you expect?' replied Soames. 'You obviously know more than you will say!'

'Say? You have barely asked a thing!'

'I will ask however it pleases me!'

'What apparently pleases you most is to waste my time,' muttered Miss Temple.

The coach pulled up, forestalling Soames's defiant reply. Miss Temple saw nothing through the little window save a waist-high wall of white brick. Beyond it rose a very musty old hedge, blocking the sky. Soames reached for the door handle.

'You had your chance. Now we shall see how you answer your betters –'

But instead of opening the door, Soames exhaled with a strange rattle. Both eyelids fluttered, the eyes themselves rolled back in his head. Then the fluttering stopped, and he very slowly turned towards her, his jaw slack. Miss Temple retreated to the far corner of her seat.

'Mr Soames?' she whispered.

He did not seem to hear. The coach rocked as the soldier climbed down. Miss Temple heard bootsteps on the cobbles. Then, like the prick of a needle puncturing her skin, Soames's eyes snapped into focus – he *saw* her . . .

Then Soames was shaking his head and swallowing awkwardly, smacking his lips like a dog that has snapped at a bee. He pulled open the door and stepped through, turning behind to take her hand.

'This way, Miss Hastings.' He cleared his throat and then smiled heartily. 'It will be for the best. Better manners always are . . .'

He did not release her hand as they made their way to a small open gate in the wall. Before they reached it, two more men emerged. They wore coats identical to Soames's.

'Mr Phelps,' called Soames in greeting.

Phelps, whose coat hung slack over his right shoulder, ignored Soames. Instead he met Miss Temple's gaze with an expression of dismay, as if her existence were simply more evidence of a disappointing world. His hair was brushed forward in an old-fashioned manner, and, strangely, his right arm, like Francis Xonck's, was wrapped in plaster, from the hand up to the elbow.

'What is that bag?' His voice was crisp and high-pitched, as if belonging to a smaller animal.

'Her supper,' answered Soames.

'Give it to me.'

Soames reached for the canvas sack. Miss Temple knew she could not maintain her grip in the face of so many and let it go. Phelps did not look into the bag – nor did he even seem tempted – merely looped it over his plaster-wrapped hand. Without another word he led them through an ill-trimmed archway in the hedge to a little courtyard with a weed-choked pool, from which rose a non-working fountain: a stone statue of a naked youth with broken arms, a corroded metal spout protruding from his mouth.

Across the plaza was another archway in another hedge, this time leading to a heavy wooden door set with an iron-barred window. The third man fished out an iron key and unlocked it. Miss Temple followed them into a dark, dank, stone corridor with a low ceiling. The door was locked, the dragoons remaining on the other side.

They passed through narrow pools of light let in by a series of oval, barred windows, footsteps echoing off the stone. Another wooden door was opened with another key. Mr Phelps indicated that Miss Temple should enter – a room of pale plaster walls, the floor bare, two simple wooden chairs and a battered table of planking.

'Would you care for anything while you wait?' he asked. 'Tea?'

'I should appreciate that very much.'

She saw Soames bite back a comment as the third man marched away at once, a small satisfaction that allowed Miss Temple to enter the room with poise. To her surprise, the door was not locked behind her.

'Go ahead and sit down.' Phelps gestured with his protruding pink fingers towards the nearest chair. Miss Temple did not move. He stepped into the room.

'I appreciate the oddness of the occasion. You have no need to be afraid.'

'I am *not* afraid,' replied Miss Temple.

He looked as if he expected her to say more, but, being rather afraid indeed, she did not. Phelps turned to Soames. 'What is your name again?'

'Soames. Joseph Soames. One of Lord Acton's special *liaisons*.'

'Soames.' Phelps intoned it, committing the name to memory. 'Perhaps you could discover what delays this woman's tea.'

Soames's footsteps echoed down the corridor. Phelps reached into the pocket of his topcoat, pulling out one black leather glove. Still watching her expression – which remained wilfully bland – he tugged the glove onto his non-plastered hand and then carefully opened the canvas sack. As if he were unpacking a cobra, Phelps removed a shining blue glass book. He set it down on the table and took two steps away, removing the glove.

'What was your name again?' he asked, a bit too idly. 'Because I feel I have seen you before.'

'Isobel Hastings. May I ask what happened to your arm?'

'It was broken,' said Phelps.

'Did it hurt?'

'It did indeed.'

'Does it hurt still?'

'Only when I am attempting to sleep.'

'You know, I myself am fascinated by that exact sort of thing – how in the middle of a sleepless night a sore tooth can seem to have become the size of one's entire fist – so much *room* does it take up in one's thoughts, you see. What did you actually do to break it?'

'A German doctor broke it for me – at a place called Tarr Manor. Do you know it?'

'Do you insinuate I ought to?'

'Heavens no, I merely pass the time.'

Miss Temple settled herself on one of the chairs, both because she was bored by standing like a servant and to bring the knife in the boot nearer to her hand.

'I'm sure it is a lesson to steer clear of Germans to begin with,' she observed. 'Am I your prisoner?'

'I will tell you as soon as I know myself,' said Mr Phelps.

Mr Soames returned alone, holding a metal tray with a pot, a stack of cups without saucers, a small jug of milk, and, Miss Temple noted bitterly, not one biscuit on a plate. He stopped abruptly in the doorway, his eyes fixed on the book on the table, then caught himself and turned to Phelps, raising the tray as if to ask where – the table taken – he should put it. Phelps gestured with disdain to the floor. Soames set the tray on the tiles and knelt, pouring tea, looking to Miss Temple to see if she wanted milk, then pouring milk at her indication that she did. He took the cup to her, returned to the tray and looked to Phelps, who shook his head with impatience. Soames looked down briefly at the tray, measuring whether, with Phelps's demurral, he might avail himself of a cup, but then clasped his hands behind his back, looking sharply at Miss Temple. She held the warm cup cradled on her lap and smiled back at him brightly. 'We were just discussing the manner in which pain can preoccupy the mind –'

Her words were cut off by the loud clatter of Mr Soames's foot kicking the teapot, scattering the tray and its contents across the floor. He staggered where he stood, his face blank as it had been in the coach, arms dangling at his side. Miss Temple looked to Phelps, but Phelps had already crossed to the doorway. He slammed it shut and turned a metal key in its lock. Miss Temple's hand reached towards her boot. Soames blinked and cocked his head, watching her with intent, flickering eyes.

'Celeste Temple.' His voice was an unpleasant, uninflected hiss.

'Mr Soames?'

'It is not Mr Soames,' whispered Phelps. 'If you value your life, you must answer every question put to you.'

Mr Soames drew back his lips in the unnatural leer of an ape in a cage. 'Where is she, Celeste? Where are the others?'

It was a small number of people who might presume to call her Celeste and a smaller number still to whom she might grant the privilege – not half a dozen in life, and nowhere in this number stood Mr Soames. The troubling, hideous spectacle was not – at least terms of *mind* – Mr Soames at all.

Mr Phelps cleared his throat, and Miss Temple looked to him. 'You must answer.'

Mr Soames watched her closely, a bit of foam having appeared at each corner of his mouth.

'What others do you mean precisely?' she said to him.

'You *know* what I want,' hissed Mr Soames.

She glanced fearfully at Mr Phelps, but the man's attention seemed split between discomfort and curiosity.

Miss Temple forced herself to shrug and began to rattle away in as blithe a tone as possible. 'Well, it all depends on where one starts – I don't know if the events at Harschmort House are known to you – but on the airship nearly everyone was killed, and the airship itself, with all the books and machinery and most of the bodies, has been sunk beneath the sea. The Prince, Mrs Stearne, Doctor Lorenz, Miss Vandaariff, Roger Bascombe, Harald Crabbé, the Comte d'Orkancz I saw dead with my own eyes –'

'Francis Xonck is still alive,' spat Mr Soames. 'You were with him. You were seen.'

Miss Temple felt an icy blue pressure against her skull, the pressure escalating to pain.

'He was in Karthe,' squeaked Miss Temple. 'I saw him get off the train and followed him.'

'Where did he go?'

'I don't know – he disappeared! I took his book and ran!'

'Where is the Contessa?' asked Soames. 'What will she do?'

'I cannot say – her body was not found –'

'Do not *lie*. I can feel her.'

'Well, you know more than I do –'

Mr Soames twitched his fingers. 'I can see her near you,' he whispered. 'I can sense her . . . on your mouth.'

'I beg your pardon,' said Miss Temple.

'Tell me I am wrong,' rasped Mr Soames.

Mr Phelps crossed to Soames. He placed a hand on Soames's forehead, and then – with some distaste – peeled back the lid from the man's left eye. Its white had acquired a milky blue cast that, as Miss Temple watched, crossed into the brown iris.

'There is not much time,' whispered Mr Phelps.

'Where is the Contessa?' cried Soames.

'I do not know!' insisted Miss Temple. 'She was on the train. She left in the night.'

'*Where?*'

'I do not know!'

'Scour the length of the train tracks!' Soames barked to Phelps. 'Every man you have – near the canals! She must be near the canals!'

'But,' began Phelps, 'if it was Francis Xonck –'

'Of *course* it was Xonck!' screeched Soames.

'Then surely we must keep searching –'

'Of course!' Soames coughed thickly, spattering saliva on his moustache and chin. He turned his attention back to Miss Temple. 'Xonck's book!' he cried hoarsely. 'Why did you take it?'

'Why would I *not* take it?' replied Miss Temple.

Soames coughed again. His eyes were almost entirely blue.

'Bring her upstairs,' he croaked. 'This one is spent.'

In an instant, like the snuffing of a candle, the presence that had inhabited Mr Soames was gone. He toppled to the floor and lay still, gasping like a fish in the bottom of a boat, a ghastly rasp that filled the room. She looked up to Phelps.

'I will escort you to His Grace's chambers,' he said.

Waiting outside the door were two servants with an assortment of mops and bottles.

'You will manage the gentleman,' Phelps said to them. 'Be sure to scrub well with vinegar.'

He took Miss Temple's arm and guided her down to the corridor. Her eyes darted at each new door and alcove they passed.

Phelps cleared his throat discreetly. 'Any attempt to flee is useless. As is any hope to employ that weapon in your boot. At the slightest provocation

– and I do mean slightest – you will be *occupied*. You have seen the consequences.'

His tone was stern, but Miss Temple had the distinct feeling that Mr Phelps also found himself a prisoner, for ever wondering when he in his turn would become as expendable as a non-entity like Soames.

'Will you tell me where we are?' she asked.

'Stäelmaere House, of course.'

Miss Temple saw no 'of course' about it. Stäelmaere House was an older mansion that lay between the Ministries and the Palace, connecting each to each through its ancient drawing rooms – a stucco-encrusted architectural pipe-joint. It was also home, she assumed, to the very horrid Duke.

In the ballroom of Harschmort House, Miss Temple had seen the Duke of Stäelmaere addressing the whole of the Cabal's gathered minions – making clear, for he was the new head of the Privy Council, how powerful the Cabal had finally become. But Miss Temple knew that the Duke had been shot through the heart not two hours before that speech. Using the blue glass and the mental powers of the glass women, the Comte d'Orkancz had extended the Duke's existence by transmuting him into a marionette, without anyone seeing through the trick. This fact had left Miss Temple, Svenson, and Chang with a dilemma: whether to prevent the Duke from seizing power or to stop the airship sailing to Macklenburg.

But Miss Temple had discovered that every 'adherent' undergoing the alchemical Process (a fearsome alchemical procedure that instilled loyalty to the Cabal) had their minds inscribed with a specific *control phrase*. This was a sort of verbal cipher that, when invoked, allowed the speaker to command the adherent at will. Miss Temple had learnt the control phrase of Colonel Aspiche, and when the Duke of Stäelmaere returned to the city with Mrs Marchmoor, the sole surviving glass woman, Miss Temple had sent Aspiche in pursuit, with orders to assassinate the Duke at all costs.

She had hoped that the unrest at Stropping and in the streets might be because of the Duke's assassination by the Colonel. But Mr Soames had insisted it was not the case. Her cunning plan had failed.

*

They reached a wooden door. Phelps rapped the wrought-iron knocker, and the door was opened by a crisply dressed servant. Miss Temple noticed with some alarm – did the fellow have mange? – that a patch of hair was missing from behind the man's ear. His complexion was even paler than Mr Phelps's and his lips unpleasantly chapped. As the servant closed the door behind them, she saw a smudge of bloody grime beneath his stiff white shirt cuff, as if the fellow's wrist had been cut and poorly bandaged.

Phelps led her past high, dark paintings and massive ebony glass-fronted cabinets stuffed with every conceivable dining article one might fashion out of silver. Apparently ancient servants darted silently around them, but then Miss Temple saw with some alarm that they were not old at all, merely *exhausted* – faces horribly drawn, eyes red, and their swan-white collars and cuffs chafed with rust-coloured smears. She looked fearfully to Phelps, wondering if he had delivered her to some hideous epidemic. What she had first taken to be a well-kept corridor was in fact littered with smatterings of – she could find no other words – interior decay: dust thick on the paintings, a tangle of cleaning rags pushed into a shadowy corner, candle wax pooled onto a Turkish carpet, another carpet blackened by coal dust. And yet there were servants everywhere. She stepped around a man crouched with a dustpan and a brush, and looked back to see him sag against the wall, eyes shut, succumbing to thin, sickly sleep.

'This way,' muttered Phelps. They climbed to another high-ceilinged hallway, the landing littered with loose pages of parchment. Three men in black coats stood with their arms full of similar documents, while a fourth crouched on his hands and knees, attempting to peel a sheet of paper from the floor without removing his white gloves. Near them sat an elderly man with a close-trimmed beard and a steel-rimmed monocle. Phelps bowed and addressed him with grave respect.

'Lord Acton.'

Lord Acton ignored Phelps, barking impatiently at the secretary on his knees. 'Pick it up, man!'

With a protesting whine the secretary raised a hand to his mouth, caught the tip of one gloved finger in his teeth – his gums unpleasantly vivid – and pulled it off, leaving the thing to dangle as his bare hand scrabbled to gather the parchment. Miss Temple winced to see the fellow's nails were ragged, split, and yellow as a crumbling honeycomb.

Phelps made to edge past them when Lord Acton turned and, as if echoing his servant, called to Phelps in a bleating complaint. 'If we are to do the Council's business, we must see him, sir! His Grace cannot take hold of the Council if he will not lead!'

'Of course, My Lord.'

'We cannot even gather enough of our number for the simplest work – Lord Axewith, Henry Xonck, Lord Vandaariff – none will answer my entreaties! Nor have we any news from Macklenburg – none at all! We are prepared – all the instructions have been observed – the regiments, the banks, the canals, the sea ports – but they must hear from the Duke!'

'I will inform His Grace at once,' said Phelps, nodding.

'I have no desire to *trouble* him –'

'Of course, My Lord.'

'It is simply – he now *rules* – yet remains absent – and I have been waiting outside his door for so very long . . .'

'Of course, My Lord.'

Lord Acton said nothing, out of breath, waiting for Phelps to respond more fully. When Phelps did not, he then abruptly nudged a foot at the man on the floor, still collecting pages.

'At this rate we will be here all *day*,' he complained to no one in particular. 'While my head, you know . . . it aches most cruelly –'

While Phelps muttered his condolences for Lord Acton's head, and the Lord's aide continued to grapple with his armload of papers, Miss Temple's attention turned to the far end of the corridor, where a man in a red dragoon's uniform had just stumbled into view. The man was tall and slim, with fair hair and side whiskers, and held his brass helmet under one arm. With his other arm against the far wall he bent over, as if gasping for breath or vomiting. Without looking in her direction, the officer recovered himself, squared his shoulders, and strode out, disappearing down a much smaller staircase. She looked back to Phelps.

'You will *tell* him, won't you?' whined Lord Acton. 'I am not without enthusiasm!'

'Of course, My Lord – if you will excuse me . . .'

Lord Acton sneezed, which gave Phelps exactly enough time to reclaim Miss Temple's arm and sweep her directly towards the set of high, carved doors from which the dizzied officer had emerged.

'The Duke's chambers. You will be presented by his manservant.' Phelps passed a hand over his brow, and sighed. 'In your interview . . . downstairs . . . you mentioned Deputy Minister Crabbé. That he is dead. We . . . we at the Ministry did not know.'

Miss Temple indicated Mr Phelps's broken arm. 'I think you knew enough, sir.'

Phelps looked back down the corridor, his expression once more pained, and absently scratched at his shirt front. Miss Temple's eyes widened as she noticed a tiny bead of red soaking up into the fabric from where Phelps's nail had touched.

'Perhaps,' he said. 'Perhaps we are beyond them all . . .'

He rapped the iron door knocker, cast in the shape of a snarling hound's head.

The door opened, and Miss Temple suppressed a gasp. If the other occupants of Stäelmaere House had seemed unwell, the man before her looked as if he'd spent a fortnight in the grave. While his body may have once stood tall and thin, now it was skeletal. His stiff topcoat tented like a bed sheet hanging from a tree. His pale hair hung lank and unkempt, and there were clumps of it on his lapel. Miss Temple flinched against the foulness of his breath.

'Mr Fordyce,' said Phelps, his gaze still to the wall.

'Mr Phelps.' The voice was moist and indistinct – Miss Temple heard it as *Fauwlpth* – as if the man's tongue had lost the ability to shift within his mouth. 'The lady will follow me . . .'

Fordyce stepped aside and extended a brittle arm, his gloved hand and white cuff divided by a wrist wrapped with a rust-soaked twist of cloth. Miss Temple entered a dimly lit ante-room. A single silver candelabrum flickered on a small writing desk. The room's massive windows were curtained tightly, and when the door was closed behind her the darkness deepened that much more.

'Etiquette,' slurred Mr Fordyce, 'demands you not speak . . . unless the Duke requests that you do so.'

He crossed to the candelabrum and raised it to the level of his face, the orange glow dancing unpleasantly across the man's mere scattering of teeth. In his other hand he held the canvas sack.

'In the Duke's presence, you are no longer required to keep to your knees. You are *free* to do so, but such deference is no longer *enforced*.'

He led her across a carpet littered with tumbled books and cups and plates that clinked or snapped beneath Fordyce's feet; never once did he look down, or show any sign of minding the wax that dripped freely from the candelabrum. She walked with a hand over both her mouth and nose. The reek of the man extended to every corner of the apartments. What had happened? What sort of disease might be so *eroding* everyone within the confines of Stäelmaere House? Would she too succumb to its effects?

Fordyce knocked discreetly at a heavy door, meticulously carved from ebony wood. She was just realizing that the carving was actually a picture – an enormous man, flames coming off from his body like the sun, in the act of swallowing a writhing child whole – when Fordyce opened the door and coughed hideously, as if gargling a piece of his own disintegrating throat.

'Your Grace . . . the young woman . . .'

There was no reply. Miss Temple darted forward, before the rancid man could take hold of her arm, into an even dimmer chamber hung with high tapestries and even larger paintings – dark oil portraits whose faces loomed like drowning souls staring up through the sea. The door closed behind her, and the room was silent, save for her own breath and the thudding of her heart. A faintly glowing gas-lit sconce, shaped like a tulip, floated in the gloom near a large straight-backed chair. In it sat a very tall man, staring into the darkness, his spine as rigid as the wood he leant against. She recognized the collar-length iron-grey hair and sharply forbidding features that would not have seemed amiss on an especially intolerant falcon.

'Your Grace?' Miss Temple ventured.

The Duke did not stir. Miss Temple crept carefully closer. The smell

here was different, the noisome, waxy reek smothered in jasmine perfume.
Still he did not move, not even to blink his glassy eyes. She took another
hesitant step, slowly extending one arm and, at the tip of that arm, a finger
towards his nearest hand, large-knuckled, and knotted with rings. When
her finger touched the clammy skin, the Duke's face snapped towards her,
a movement as sharp as a cleaver cutting meat. Miss Temple yelped in
surprise and leapt back.

Before she could gather words to speak, her ears – though not her ears
at all, for she felt the noise erupt within her head – rebounded with brittle,
sliding laughter. The glass woman emerged through a gap in the tapestries,
wrapped in a heavy cloak, her hands and face reflecting the gaslight's glow.

'You are alive!' whispered Miss Temple.

In answer, the unpleasant laughter came again – like a needle dragged
across her teeth – and with a sudden flick of intention Mrs Marchmoor –
the glass woman – caused the Duke to turn his head just as sharply away.

Miss Temple ran for the door. It had been locked. She turned to face the
woman – the glass *creature* – the slick blue surface of her flesh, the impassive
fixity of her expression belied by the wicked amusement in her laugh, and
the subtle curl of her full, gleaming lips.

She had seen three glass women paraded by the Comte before the
gathered crowds at Harschmort, each naked but for a collar and leash –
like strange beasts from deepest Africa captured and sent to Rome to
astonish a dissolute Emperor. The last of the three, Mrs Marchmoor – a
courtesan, born Margaret Hooke, the daughter of a bankrupt mill owner –
was quite obviously no longer *human*. But was she *sane*?

'At your feet,' hissed the voice inside Miss Temple's skull. 'Bring it
to me.'

The canvas sack lay on the carpet, where Fordyce must have set it.

'Do it. No one will come. No one will hear you.'

Miss Temple walked forward with the sack and set it onto the desk with
care. Then, glancing once into the unsettling and predatory blue pearl eyes,
she peeled the canvas away without touching the surface of the blue glass,
exposing it to the air.

'Explain.'

'I took it from Francis Xonck,' said Miss Temple, with a sort of shrug
that hoped to convey that this had been no particular challenge for her.
'I can only assume he took it from the trunk of books on the airship.'

Mrs Marchmoor floated closer to the book, gazing intently into its depths.

'It is not from the trunk . . .'

'But it must be,' said Miss Temple. 'Where else?'

'The book itself perhaps, but not what lies within . . . the *mind* . . .
is *new* . . .'

Mrs Marchmoor extended one slender arm towards the book, the cloak
falling away to either side, the fingers of her hand uncurling like the stalks
of some unclassified tropical plant. Miss Temple gasped. At the point where
the woman's finger tip ought to have clicked against the cover like a tumbler
striking a tabletop, it instead passed directly through, as if into water.

'Glass . . . is a liquid . . .' whispered Mrs Marchmoor.

At the first intrusion of her finger the book began to glow. She slowly
inserted the whole of her hand, and then, like the curling smoke from a
cigarette, twisting, glowing azure lines began to swirl inside the book. Mrs
Marchmoor cocked her head and extended her fingers, as if she were
tightening the fit of a leather glove. The lines wrapped more tightly around
her and glowed more brightly . . . yet Miss Temple was sure that something
was wrong. Then the gleam went out, and Mrs Marchmoor retracted her
hand, the surface of the book top never once betraying a single ripple at
her passage.

'Can you . . . can you *read* it?' asked Miss Temple.

Mrs Marchmoor did not respond. Miss Temple felt a harsh pressing at
her mind, cold and uncaring, and stumbled backward in fear.

'Simply ask me!' she squealed.

'You will *lie*.'

'Not when I know you can enter my mind as easily as one sticks a spoon
in a bowl!' Miss Temple held out her hand. 'Please – I have seen what you
have done to the people in this place – I have no desire to lose my hair or
see my skin split by sores!'

'Is that what I have done?' asked Mrs Marchmoor.

'Of course it is – you must know very well!'

The glass woman did not respond. Miss Temple heard her own quick breath and was ashamed. She forced herself to swallow her fear, to pay attention – to *think*. Why was her enemy silent?

'I do not *see* anyone, Celeste,' whispered Mrs Marchmoor carefully. 'I remain in this room and only rummage what minds are near. I *cannot* go out. I am not unaware of your reaction to my . . . *form* – yours and everyone else's. I am alone. I am alone in the *world*. I have been waiting for word, but no word has come.'

'You sent soldiers, didn't you?' asked Miss Temple. 'Did they tell you nothing?'

'What happened on the airship?'

'Quite a lot happened,' replied Miss Temple nervously. She pointed to the Duke. 'What happened to Colonel Aspiche?'

A trilling series of clicks in Miss Temple's head told her Mrs Marchmoor was chuckling. 'That was very clever of you. But I stopped the Colonel in time. I cleansed his mind. I can do that. I have discovered that I can do all kinds of things.'

'But you can't do anything with *him*.' Miss Temple gestured again towards the sepulchral Duke. 'If anyone but Fordyce gets a glimpse – or a *whiff* – of him, they'll know something's wrong. Everyone outside is most agitated, you know –'

Mrs Marchmoor's rage struck Miss Temple's mind like a hammer. 'I could kill you,' the glass woman snarled. 'I could skin your mind like a cat and keep it dancing in an agony you cannot conceive.'

'The city is in turmoil,' spat Miss Temple, on her hands and knees, a strand of saliva hanging from her lip. 'Someone will force their way in, or the Duke will decay beyond what perfume can hide. His palace will be burnt to the ground like a plague house –'

Another hammer blow and Miss Temple felt the carpet fibres prickling against her cheek. She was lying flat, unable to think. How much time had passed? Had the glass woman already ransacked her memories? Her eyes stung and her teeth ached. The unnatural face loomed above her, its eyes shining as if they'd been slickened with oil. The fingers of Mrs Marchmoor's hands moved slowly as her mind worked, like sea grasses in a gentle current.

'In the airship,' Miss Temple gasped, 'every one of your masters plotted against the others. You say you have discovered new talents, yet I am certain the Comte set controls on your independence. Why else would you hide in this tomb?'

'I am not hiding. I am *waiting*.'

Despite her aching mind, Miss Temple smiled. 'I wonder – are you more frightened that *none* of the others possesses his knowledge . . . or that one of them *does*?'

'I have nothing to fear from the Contessa or from Francis Xonck.'

'Is that why you sent men to kill them?'

'I sent men to *find* them, Celeste. And to find you. I can take whatever I need from your mind. I can leave you dead.'

'Of course you can,' admitted Miss Temple, with a nervous breath. 'You kept me alive to talk to me . . . but if I live still, it has to do with that book . . . and everything you fear.'

Mrs Marchmoor was silent, but Miss Temple could see flecks of brightness flitting inside her like sparks from an open fire at night. There was no telling what secrets the woman had plucked from the minds of those around her. Like a hidden spider at the heart of the Palace, with every day Mrs Marchmoor extended her knowledge beyond the Cabal, and became less and less vulnerable without them.

The door opened for Fordyce, shuffling his feet and breathing wetly. He tottered directly to the seated Duke and executed as deferential a bow as his precarious balance might allow. From the Duke's rot-riddled chest came a rotting meat wheeze that drove Miss Temple to put a hand across her mouth.

'Fordyce . . . the large brougham . . . private steps . . . at once.'

'At once, Your Grace.'

'And those fellows . . .'

'Fellows, Your Grace?' Fordyce tipped towards the desk and reached out a subtle hand to steady himself.

'*Phelps* . . .' rasped the Duke, stretching the name on the rack of his breath to three ugly syllables. 'Crabbé's man . . . and the other . . . newly posted . . . *Soames* . . . I *require* them.'

'Excellent, Your Grace.'

'And the corridors . . . as always . . . *cleared*.'

'As always, Your Grace. At once.'

Fordyce tottered from the room without the slightest glance in their direction. Miss Temple flinched as the abrasive hiss filled her mind.

'You will take the Duke's arm.'

The corridors were indeed empty of all human traffic. With everyone in Stäelmaere House waiting anxiously for the Duke's appearance, the decaying chamberlain's announcement of his departure must have been a blow. Were there top-coated diplomats and ministers kneeling behind every keyhole as they walked? The Duke's steps were deliberate and slow, but he was stable enough – or Mrs Marchmoor's control so powerful – that she could brace him with one hand and keep the other over her mouth, for the Duke's perfumed stench was extremely disagreeable. The glass woman herself followed behind, swathed in her thick, dark cloak, its hood pulled forward. Only the muffled click of her footfalls betrayed her to Miss Temple's ears, though to anyone else the sound would have merely suggested fashionably Spanish, metal-capped boots.

Fordyce led the way, his left leg dragging more than before, to a portrait of the young Duke dressed in a dashing hussar's uniform, his vicious face and long black hair at odds with the merry profusion of tassels and plumes. To the side of the portrait – the background of which, Miss Temple noticed with a shock, showed a line of severed brown heads on fence spikes – was another over-carved wooden door. Fordyce clawed it open with shaking hands and stepped aside for them to enter a narrow vestibule, waiting for Mrs Marchmoor without ever seeming to acknowledge her presence. He nodded gravely and shut them in. Miss Temple grimaced – the air was impossibly close. Were they hiding here while the rest of the Privy Council crept past? She gagged into her hand. Suddenly the entire chamber shuddered. Miss Temple looked over at the glass woman, whose lip curled with a stiff amusement. The entire vestibule was a dumbwaiter – and they were descending.

The vestibule came to a stop. The door was unlocked from the outside by Mr Phelps. Behind him waited Mr Soames – face drawn, eyes ringed with red – earnestly staring down at the floor. Neither man acknowledged Mrs Marchmoor as she glided past them into a corridor flagged with slate tiling. The air was cooler, as if they had descended far beneath the house.

'The large brougham . . .' rasped the Duke. 'It is *prepared*?'

'It is, Your Grace,' answered Phelps. 'May I ask our destination?'

The Duke's voice was a baleful scrape. 'The driver knows.'

Before them waited a large black coach, strangely constructed with two distinct compartments, the whole pulled by six enormous black horses. The rear compartment was windowless – almost as if it were part of a hearse – while the forward was every bit a normal sort of carriage. Liveried footmen stood waiting, utterly attentive though avoiding any eye contact, as Mrs Marchmoor very slowly scaled the small steps into the rear compartment, whose interior was as lushly upholstered as a Turkish sofa. The footmen relieved Miss Temple of the Duke's arm and eased their master up. Once he was settled, they shut the door and opened the front compartment. Miss Temple raced to the far corner without anyone's help. Phelps sat across from her. Soames perched nervously next to Phelps, plucking at the frayed skin of his lower lip with his teeth. The footmen shut the door and called out to the driver, and the coach eased forward so gently it might have been carrying a cargo of eggs.

At first the way around them was dark, but then they safely emerged into a cobbled avenue dotted with well-dressed scowling men striding about importantly.

'The rear of the Kingsway,' observed Phelps, and then, as Miss Temple had no comment, 'We are behind the Ministries.'

'A shame you've no more idea than I where we are off to,' replied Miss Temple.

Phelps said nothing.

'What of you, Mr Soames?' she called, doing her best to smile brightly.

'I'm sure I couldn't say!' he managed, in an earnest sort of yelp.

The coach left the white stone warren of the Ministries and flanked the river itself, for she recognized its stone walls and iron railings and saw beyond them open sky.

For a moment it seemed as if Soames might speak, but he glanced first to his superior and thought better of it. Miss Temple exhaled with a sharp little huff. That she found herself – so quickly upon her return – in the exact sort of situation she had been determined to avoid galled her extremely. So much was happening – the glass woman had forsaken her lair! – and yet here she was cocooned with two utterly bloodless drones. She thought again of Chang standing by the clock, and her anger rose, as if her predicament was entirely his doing.

'If you think I care that she hears us, you are mistaken,' Miss Temple said. 'And if you think fawning will save your disease-ridden skins, then you are outright fools.'

'She?' asked Mr Soames.

Miss Temple ignored Soames altogether and leant to Phelps. 'Deputy Minister Crabbé is *dead*,' she hissed. 'Roger Bascombe is dead. That part of your plot died with them. She is looking for something in that book! Once she finds it, she will rule every soul in Stäelmaere House as easily as you can butter hot toast.'

Phelps looked to Soames, but Soames bore the troubled expression of an ailing man whose physicians have begun to speak across his head in Latin.

'The deprivations of poverty and despair,' Soames offered to Phelps. 'Once a girl sheds her virtue, her thoughts become every bit as corrupted as her body –'

'Be *quiet*!' spat Phelps to his shocked colleague. Phelps turned back to Miss Temple. 'It is pointless to speculate, pointless to discuss. I am bound by an oath to my Queen.'

'Your *Queen*?' Miss Temple sneered. 'And who do you think that will be in a fortnight? A blue glass *monstrosity* who but one week ago was an upper-echelon *whore*!'

The pain took hold of her mind like an iron hand, its fingers bunching tight to a fist through the very fabric of her thoughts, an excruciating crush that shot a thread of blood from each nostril. The two men before her faded to the palest glimmers, as if the coach had been flooded with the brightest summer sun, as if each of her eyes had been somehow smeared with fire. She squeezed shut her eyes, but the brightness blazed through her lids. Into her very soul she felt the malevolent burn of Mrs Marchmoor's violent disapproval. Miss Temple arched her back, gagging against what felt like an impossibly sustained whipcrack along her spine.

She sat up on one elbow and dabbed at her nose with one hand, pulling it away and looking at her red-tipped fingers. Phelps passed her a folded handkerchief, and she struggled to a sitting position, wiping her face and where the blood had dripped onto her dress. In the centre of her thoughts was a buzzing, as if she had not slept for three days.

Was this how it had begun, for Soames and Fordyce and the other servants of Stäelmaere House? Would she have sores and splitting nails and her hair dropping out in clumps? Did she already? Miss Temple sniffed deeply, refolded the handkerchief, and pressed it quickly to each corner of her eyes. She looked out the window. They had left the city altogether and were riding along a country road bordered to either side by wide, flat, brown fields of marsh grass. Fen country – and as she formed the thought she smelt a tang of salt in the cooler air. She looked up to meet the gaze of Mr Phelps.

'We are going to Harschmort House,' she said.

The journey lasted another hour, during which time there was little talk. Phelps had shut his eyes, with only his left hand's restless plucking at a spot of loose plaster on his cast to betray his wakefulness. Soames slept without any disguise, his mouth open and his posture slack, like a switched-off machine. Despite her own weariness, Miss Temple did not follow their example. There was no reason not to, she knew – even if she were to open the coach door and fling herself to freedom, Mrs Marchmoor could still reach out and stop her. Miss Temple examined the front of her dress with annoyance, and lifted the stained portions to her mouth and sucked on them one after another, tasting the blood and working the fabric back and forth between her tongue and teeth. Her thoughts sank into a brood.

If she had followed Francis Xonck and stolen his book out of a determined antagonism to evil, she would have happily curled herself up for a proper nap. But Miss Temple knew, for hers was a habitually lacerating scrutiny, that the daring theft had been spurred by the confusion she felt in the wake of the Contessa's seduction and rebuff – that her stabbing action was in fact a running away. With a growing conviction she began to wonder if the entirety of her adventures – from first following Roger's coach to ending his life inside the airship – had not been a flight from a deeper and unflattering truth about her character and its essential paucity.

She had no answer to such thoughts save assertion, and her powers of insistence were low. The Contessa had advised her to abandon her adventure utterly. Even Elöise had attempted to dissuade her from any further investigation – was she so certain these warnings were wrong? Her adventures *had* altered her character – into that of a woman who had done murder, a woman whose body inflamed to depravity at the merest spark. It was a feral life like Chang's, and rootless like the Doctor's – marked by isolation and anonymity, by danger and – without any question – eventual doom. It was also – and Miss Temple bit her lip to admit it – a life like the Contessa di Lacquer-Sforza's.

Her thoughts were jarred by a sudden shift in the surface of the road. They had reached the cobbled drive leading to the Vandaariff estate. She cleared her throat rather deliberately and was gratified to see Mr Phelps open one eye in response.

'Have you ever *been* to Harschmort House?' she asked.

He exhaled wearily and shrugged himself to a more respectable posture. 'I have.'

'With Deputy Minister Crabbé?'

'Indeed.'

'And Roger Bascombe?'

Phelps glanced at the still sleeping Soames, and then out the window at the dispiriting landscape. 'Before the disappearance of the Deputy Minister, there were regular communications between his office, Lord Vandaariff's people, and officials of the Privy Council. It was in no small part owing to Lord Vandaariff that the Duke was able to achieve the control over the Privy Council that he presently enjoys.'

'I would say the Duke enjoys very little,' said Miss Temple, '*these* days.'

'My *point*', continued Phelps, 'is that since the disappearance of the Deputy Minister, no word has arrived from Lord Vandaariff whatsoever.'

'Of course there hasn't,' said Miss Temple.

'It is easily explained by the epidemic at Harschmort House of blood fever . . .'

'Blood *fever*!' She tossed her head at the compartment behind them. 'Have you asked *her*?'

Phelps licked his lips. 'Who?'

'*Who?*' she said, mocking him openly. '*Her!* Mrs Marchmoor! Margaret Hooke! Not saying her name will not change the fact of her existence, nor lessen her power.'

'I cannot say I am . . . personally . . . acquainted with the lady.'

Miss Temple delicately blew her nose into the wadded handkerchief. 'A pity, for she is perfectly acquainted with *you*.'

The coach crossed the flagstone plaza to the wide steps. Mr Phelps jogged Soames awake, and the man was still blinking and unpleasantly smacking his lips as he stepped from the coach. Miss Temple realized she had never seen Robert Vandaariff's mansion during the day. Without the enfolding night, the structure's harsh simplicity was even more oppressive. The building had first been constructed as a coastal fortress, then turned into a

prison. Lord Vandaariff had refitted the interiors to his own lavish specifications, but to Miss Temple, Harschmort – isolated between a featureless
landscape and the vast, and therefore somehow inherently disapproving,
sky – seemed a prison once again.

Phelps followed her from the coach and shut the door. The Duke's
footmen carefully extricated the Duke – Soames taking His Grace's elbow
– and then, with all the relish they might have shown towards a similarly
sized spider, Mrs Marchmoor. The footmen remained with the coach, heads
lowered, as the party made its deliberate way to the stairs: Phelps in the
lead, then Soames and the Duke, and last Miss Temple next to the glass
woman. Miss Temple sniffed sharply and wiped her nose. 'You hurt me
very much,' she said.

'You insulted me,' echoed the voice of Mrs Marchmoor in her head.

'Resenting a fact does not make it untrue,' replied Miss Temple. 'Besides,
I thought the Process made that sort of *shyness* unimportant.'

'It is not too late for you to discover first-hand,' answered the glass
woman. 'All the necessary machinery is here. How very smart of you to
suggest it.'

Miss Temple swallowed, her fears augmented by the ruthless grip of the
glass woman's hand on her arm. They had reached the stairs, and she was
compelled to assist her captor's awkward climb.

'There are no servants to meet us, Your Grace,' Phelps called.

'Of course there are servants,' croaked the Duke in reply.

As if he had been pushed, Phelps stumbled to the still-shut double doors.
He lifted the enormous metal knocker and brought it down with a crash,
the sound echoing across the empty plaza like the bark of an enormous,
lonely dog. The echoes faded to silence, and Phelps rapped the knocker
twice more. He was rewarded by a metal snapping from inside as the lock
was turned. One door swung open enough to reveal a man in Harschmort's
black livery.

'The Duke of Stäelmaere,' announced Mr Phelps. 'To see Lord Robert
Vandaariff.'

The man looked up at Phelps, hesitating, 'I am sorry to inform you that
Lord Vandaariff – '

He got no further. The servant staggered backwards, and Miss Temple heard the awkward clatter of his fall. Phelps pushed the door wide and motioned them in.

Vandaariff's footman lay inert on the tile, breathing in shallow puffs like an agitated spaniel, but his eyes were vacant and dull. The main foyer of the mansion was empty of any other person. Miss Temple wrinkled her nose, and saw Phelps and Soames doing the same.

'There has been a fire,' Phelps said.

Miss Temple turned to Mrs Marchmoor, but the glass woman was already moving. Miss Temple followed with the others, hoping Mrs Marchmoor's probing mind might become distracted such that a resourceful person might avail themselves of something like a heavy brass candlestick or a flingable Chinese urn. A sudden snap of pain between Miss Temple's eyes made her stumble. Phelps glanced back at her, his mouth a clenched, disapproving line.

The stench of smoke was most intolerable at the centre of the house, though any actual sign of what had been burnt remained hidden. An elderly man in black livery toppled onto the marble floor as his mind fell subject to Mrs Marchmoor's need. He lay on his back, blood flowing from his ears, and they swept to a winding staircase Miss Temple had taken before — down to an old library where the Comte d'Orkancz had set up a smaller, experimental laboratory. The smell of smoke worsened as they traversed the curving corridor to the blackened door. The Comte's laboratory was littered with the charred wreckage of fallen balconies and the bookcases that had propped them up, the walls peeled and streaked with soot, the domed ceiling pitted by flame. The stone worktops were cracked and seared with brilliant colours where his stores of chemical compounds had succumbed to the blaze. Miss Temple stepped gingerly into the room, her feet crunching on cinders, gazing with a grim fascination at the charred feather bed where Lydia Vandaariff had undergone the loathsome ministrations of the Comte d'Orkancz.

Miss Temple turned to Mrs Marchmoor. Clearly she had hoped to find the Comte's tools and his supply of refined blue glass, his copious notes and specially designed machines. Had Mrs Marchmoor left the protection of Stäelmaere House, risked exposure, risked everything only to find herself outwitted by an adversary she did not know existed?

But Mrs Marchmoor was not looking at the wall, or the ruined chemical machinery, or even the bed. As Miss Temple watched, the glass woman carefully advanced into the ruined chamber, stopping only when she stood within a wide circle of smoke-blackened blue glass fragments. Miss Temple covered her mouth with one hand, recalling the first glass woman she had encountered . . . the Comte's prize . . . Cardinal Chang's love . . . the glass woman she had herself destroyed in this very room with Doctor Svenson's pistol. Mrs Marchmoor turned to Miss Temple, impassive, her unseen feet grinding against the broken remains of Angelique.

No one spoke as they retraced their steps to the main floor. Directed by two more unfortunate servants, the glass woman stalked slowly across the empty ballroom. The smell of fire grew strong again, and then openly oppressive as they stepped through the French doors into the ornamental garden. As if a massive explosion had taken place (a level of destruction one associated only with newspaper accounts of full-scale battle), the centre of the garden had fallen in on itself, collapsing utterly into the massive cathedral chamber beneath it, which now lay open to the air, and in ruins. Here the fire had been far more massive and savage, melting the bright pipes that lined the walls, consuming the roof timbers, toppling the tiers of prison cells into a mangle of misshapen steel. In the centre of it all still rose the iron staircase tower, broken and jagged as a black rotting tooth. The platform at its base, where all the Comte's machinery had been installed, where Mrs Marchmoor had been strapped to a table – for the last time flesh and blood – lay smothered in debris.

Mrs Marchmoor's head whipped to the right, towards the interior of the house, the action so sharp as to dislodge her hood and reveal her shining face. In the doorway to the ballroom stood another figure in a cloak, as dark but much more ragged, tall but bent with fatigue. His red hair was shocked with lifeless white, as if it had been wiped with paste. His skin, deathly pale, was at every margin – the rims of each eye, the discoloured flare within each nostril, both livid dripping lips – cast in varying shades of blue, as if he were a monochrome portrait of a frozen corpse. In Francis Xonck's left hand glittered a narrow lancet of blue glass.

'You've travelled quite a way, Margaret. How very *brave* of you.'

'So you are alive, Francis.'

The woman's response insinuated itself into Miss Temple's mind, like the sound of a knife being sharpened in another room.

Xonck snorted and spat a knot of blue matter on the grass. 'When did it become Francis? Whatever happened to "Mr Xonck"? Even when I was rogering you sideways at the Old Palace you still kept your sense of *respect*. I suppose that also explains the pack of *spaniels* out searching for me.' He nodded contemptuously at Phelps and Soames, then passed his gaze more deliberately over the Duke, stiff as statuary, and then Miss Temple. Xonck's voice dropped into a low snarl. 'If you have *her*, then you have my book. Will you give it back, Margaret?'

'I cannot, Francis. I know what it holds.'

'If I understand things correctly, the contents would be useless to you.'

'Useless in that I cannot *penetrate* them directly. But I am determined to influence whoever does.'

'*Influence?* I think you mean *control*.'

'A great deal has changed.'

'You are no longer bound by the Process?'

'The Process opens one's eyes to the truth – you've only yourself to blame.'

Miss Temple remembered Xonck as dandyish – a rake, as well as a wit – but within that pose he'd been as vicious and deadly as any viper. If Mrs Marchmoor were not there, the whole of their party would have without question been at his mercy. Xonck took another step, and his cloak gaped open to reveal a white shirt horribly stained with dried brown blood . . . and a spot within that stain boasting a bright blue crust.

Xonck cocked his head and studied the Duke. 'Is he beginning to rot yet? I'm sure the Comte concocted all sorts of preparations to sustain longevity . . . such a shame he is not here to apply them.'

'You are as bereft without the Comte as I am,' hissed Mrs Marchmoor. 'Why else are you at Harschmort, if not to find his secrets?'

'I admit it freely,' replied Xonck, stepping just a bit closer. 'A shame what's happened to the place, isn't it?'

'You claim *not* to have caused this destruction?'

'Don't be a fool,' laughed Xonck. 'Look into the mind of any servant here and you will see the fire predates my return. What they will *not* tell you – for none of them know what to look for – is that the Comte's machinery had all been removed beforehand.'

'Who would have known to do that? Rosamonde –'

'She could not have returned any earlier than I. Truly, Margaret, who else could it be but *you*? Everyone else the Comte enlisted to help him is dead –'

'Where is Robert Vandaariff?' Miss Temple called out. 'We did not see him *anywhere*.'

Xonck turned to her with a nasty look, and in the same moment she felt a prick inside her skull from Mrs Marchmoor's irritation. She winced but spoke again. 'I am well aware Lord Vandaariff's mind was *emptied*, but are the effects of an emptied mind permanent? Could some portion of the man remain? Before you betrayed him, Robert Vandaariff knew as much about your plots as anyone – indeed he thought he was in *command*. One is curious, in these intervening days, who was given the task of *minding* him?'

Mr Phelps stepped forward, sparking an immediate response from Xonck, the glass stiletto poised. Phelps raised his own empty hands before him and spoke clearly, despite his obvious fear. 'It is a simple enough matter for the servants to tell us where their master is, or at least when he left them. If his departure is coincidental with these fires, then the situation is all the clearer. Yes?'

Xonck nodded and stepped aside. Phelps walked quickly past him and into the house. Miss Temple wondered if he might not take the opportunity to run for his life.

'Elspeth Poole was to have tended Vandaariff,' said Xonck. 'In her absence . . .'

He paused, his concentration broken by a spasm of discomfort. Miss

Temple clucked her tongue. Xonck met her eyes with an intense distaste.

'May I ask why this woman is alive?' he snarled.

'Because I can force her to action where the two of you cannot. And I don't care if she dies.'

'Do you care if anyone dies, Margaret?'

'Do you?'

'Do not be frightful,' said Xonck with a smile, his broken teeth dark and slick; 'my *own* life I hold extremely dear.' He gestured with the dagger towards the massive reeking pit. 'And I think there has been enough wanton destruction for the time being. Who has done this, if not you and if not me? Has your fellow found someone to talk to, Margaret? Eavesdrop in his brain – save us the misery of waiting!'

Mrs Marchmoor did not reply, but Miss Temple could see the twitch in her posture. Xonck took another step. Miss Temple glanced over at Mr Soames, but he remained holding the Duke's arm, as if that simple duty might protect him.

'He has . . .' replied Mrs Marchmoor, and Miss Temple winced to imagine Phelps tottering on his feet as she possessed him, foam on his lips, eyelids batting like the wings of a moth in the dark. Mrs Marchmoor held up one hand, sorting through the conversation they could not hear.

'The fires occurred in the night . . . two days ago. Lord Vandaariff was discovered missing the next morning. At first it was thought he might have set the blazes himself and perished in them –'

Xonck interrupted her: 'Ask about the machinery – there must have been carts to haul it – or a freight launch on the canal –'

'Yes . . . the previous day – there were men –'

'Mrs Marchmoor!' Miss Temple cried. Francis Xonck had advanced within range of a sudden lunge. The glass woman cocked her head and took a careful step back.

'What do you play at, Francis? Do you think I won't scruple to seize your mind? Do you think I would not *enjoy* it all the more? You rogering *me*? What of my rogering the stuffing from your very *soul*?'

'By all means, Margaret – your cause is perfectly just.' Francis Xonck leered at her, wide and hideous, and opened his arms in invitation. 'But I do not think you can. I too have been touched by the glass – and my *alchemy* changed . . .'

He took another deliberate, challenging step forward. Mrs Marchmoor raised her arm. Xonck staggered, as if he had been struck by a hammer, and wavered on his feet. But then he rolled his head to the side, easily, as if he were resisting an unwelcome caress, and came on.

With a flick of the glass woman's arm, Mr Soames flew forward at Xonck, grappling for the dagger. Mrs Marchmoor retreated as fast as possible with her slow, careful pace. Miss Temple hesitated – should she fight or run? The unattended Duke sank to the grass like a balloon losing its air. Soames had Xonck's forearm with both hands, but Xonck shifted his weight and slammed the plaster-wrapped fist into Soames's head, knocking him to his knees. Still – perhaps this was the force of Mrs Marchmoor's control – Soames did not let go. Xonck hammered him again, the impact spattering the cast with blood. Xonck shoved Soames clear.

'Give me the book, Margaret! Set it down this instant!'

Mrs Marchmoor retreated two more steps, and the edge of her cloak rippled to reveal the canvas sack, which she set down on the grass. She continued backwards and Xonck followed, pausing to snatch up his prize, until they stood face to face.

'Very wise, Margaret. Stay where you are. You will be mine. You know it – there is no other way. I will keep you here in this garden – what can the rain or fog matter to *you*? – and if you set foot in the house or attempt to leave, I will smash you piece by piece and keep you alive through all of it!' He waved the book. 'Because I will know *how*, Margaret, and I will know how to remake you, just to destroy you all over again –'

The pistol shot caught him above the right knee, the spray of blood blowing out onto the grass. Xonck crumpled with a cry of pain, but with a heave of effort he surged up and turned to face Mr Phelps, who stood with a smoking pistol, a handful of black-coated Harschmort servants behind him.

'You fool!' cried Xonck. 'Any shot that misses me *shatters* her!'

With an ungainly leap he took hold of Mrs Marchmoor and pulled her roughly to him, with a force that Miss Temple was sure must crack the glass woman's arm. But it did not crack, and she stumbled, an unnatural embrace – Xonck's free hand swiftly circling her waist and his heavy cast braced against her neck, as if prepared to snap it clean.

It seemed as if Mr Phelps would not stop – that he did not care – and his gaze passed over both the Duke, face down on the lawn, and the unmoving Mr Soames. But then Phelps's eyes went dull and he paused. The pistol point drifted to the side. A stream of blood opened from Phelps's nose and dripped down to stain his starched collar. Mrs Marchmoor had taken his decision into her own hands.

Xonck laughed again, harsh as a crow, and then swore as he shifted the weight from his bleeding leg. This caused Mrs Marchmoor to turn, and their faces came as close as two lovers'.

Suddenly Xonck's spine stiffened. The canvas sack slipped from his hand.

In the open space between them Miss Temple saw that Mrs Marchmoor had plunged her finger into the blue-crusted wound in Xonck's chest, well up to the third knuckle, just as she had inserted it into the book. Xonck arched his back and roared, a bull beneath the axe, but he could not tear free.

Miss Temple dashed forward and snatched up the canvas sack, running away into the ruins of the Harschmort gardens, dodging behind hedges and between lines of gnarled rose bushes, her boots stumbling over sudden bands of cobblestone or crunching gravel . . . Xonck was screaming behind her . . . a pistol shot crashed into the air.

Miss Temple cried out at a sudden burst of pain. Something had happened to Mrs Marchmoor. The glass woman's distress chopped viciously into the minds of everyone around her. Miss Temple shook her head. She lay on the grass – unaware of the fall – and awkwardly crawled forward, heedless of the distant cries and shouting. Before her was a low stone wall – the edge of the garden? – and she scrambled over the thing with a desperate grunt of fear. The fear told her to keep running, but Miss Temple crouched low against the cover of the wall, breathing hard, listening for pursuit.

She did not feel the glass woman in her mind. Could Francis Xonck and Mrs Marchmoor both have been destroyed?

Miss Temple looked down at the canvas sack in her hand and, just to make sure nothing had been damaged in the fracas, peeked inside. The book lay whole and gleaming. She knew how dangerous it must be. The first book she had looked into had changed her so profoundly . . . it was already impossible to recall what she had been like before. That this book too contained something powerful was obvious — Mrs Marchmoor had been determined it should not fall into the hands of an enemy. Miss Temple bit her lip. Was *she* not an enemy? What if the book contained the knowledge that would allow her to smash the remaining members of the Cabal once and for all? What if it taught her the one true way to crush the Contessa for ever?

Miss Temple looked over her shoulder . . . the garden was silent. If she merely touched the outside cover with one extended finger, she might but glimpse its contents . . . the merest graze and she would pull away . . .

Miss Temple looked behind her once more. Then, taking a breath, she touched her finger to the cover of the book. Nothing happened, though her fingertip began to feel cold. She pulled it away, took another breath, and then put forward *two* fingers. Still nothing. Then she took a deep breath and laid the entirety of her open palm upon the book.

A blast of sensation, like the sharp choking rush of black smoke from a stove-pipe, shot through the flesh of her arm and without warning enveloped her mind before she could even blink. Miss Temple flew back with a strangled cry, struck the wall, and rolled into the grass, her eyes blind, vomiting without heed, moaning through each spasm like a terrified animal. For she knew now that what Xonck's book contained was death, and its obliterating taste had taken root inside her soul.

FIVE

CARAPACE

As the nearest place certain to be void of any occupant, Chang had dragged the insensible man into the closet and through the connecting door into Colonel Trapping's private rooms, locking the door and lighting a single candle after making sure every window shade had been tightly drawn. His captive's topcoat, black suit, and shoes were well made and crisp – Chang was reminded of the odious Roger Bascombe. He held the candle close to the man's face, pulling back the lid of each eye. The whites were bloodshot and yellowed, but the pupils reacted to the candlelight. Chang turned the man's jaw – already a bruise was darkening where his blow had landed – and frowned to see his lips were also bleeding. Had he broken a tooth? With some distaste he peeled back the lower lip, surprised by the raw colour of the gums and a newly missing canine. The gap was on the opposite side of the man's mouth from where Chang had struck him.

Chang rolled back on his heels and slapped his captive on the face. The man coughed, and Chang slapped him again, noticing a patch of scalp above his left ear, pink and raw, like the mistake of a razor, or – he was not sure why the thought came to mind – as if his prisoner had sacrificed a lock of hair to some witch's ceremony. Chang glanced at the room, well kept and undisturbed. Any secrets it held would require a thorough search . . . and yet – the Ministry man was now blinking and wheezing – Chang felt there was more to it, that the room was not well kept so much as *embalmed*. The Colonel's desk was completely clean: not a blotter, not pens or an inkpot; even the square sorting compartments empty of envelopes, as if the desk were new. Every trace of Arthur Trapping had been discreetly removed.

The man coughed again and made to sit up. Chang's free hand easily gathered up the lapels of the fellow's coat, and twisted the fistful of fabric into a knot beneath his jaw.

'You will answer my questions,' he whispered, 'quietly and with speed. Or I will cut your throat. Do you understand?'

The man looked into Chang's covered eyes with dismay. Chang was aware – what with the candlelight – that his appearance must be even more mysterious than normal, and he permitted himself a satisfied smile.

'Whom do you serve? What Ministry?'

'Privy Council,' the man whispered.

'The Duke is alive?'

The man nodded.

'Then what about the woman?'

'I'm sorry?'

'Margaret Hooke. Mrs *Marchmoor*. The *glass* woman.'

The man swallowed. 'I'm afraid I am not acquainted –'

Chang casually tipped the candle and dropped a spatter of wax onto the functionary's forehead. The man hissed with pain and clenched shut his eyes.

'She would be with the Duke,' Chang explained patiently. 'If you have seen the Duke, you must have seen her.'

'No one has seen the Duke!' the man protested. 'Everyone is waiting – all the Ministers – the generals and admirals – the men of business. There are rumours – blood fever at Harschmort House, quarantine –'

'Where is he now?'

'In his rooms! The Duke does not appear – merely sends his servants on – on – on – errands – as he requires information –'

'What information?'

'Whatever we can find –'

Chang dripped another stream of wax and used the man's subsequent writhing as a pause, allowing a shift in his questions.

'What is your name?'

'Rawsbarthe!' the man whined. 'Andrew Rawsbarthe – assistant to the Deputy Under-Secretary of the Foreign Ministry –'

'Who is the Deputy Under-Secretary?'

'Roger Bascombe.'

Chang laughed out loud. 'You are *Bascombe's* assistant? You are older than he by five years!'

Rawsbarthe sputtered. 'Mr Bascombe's ascent at the Foreign Ministry is due to his great talents – and once Mr Bascombe discovers how I have been so roundly mistreated –'

'Roger Bascombe is *dead*.'

'*What?*' Rawsbarthe licked his swollen lips. 'May I ask how you know this?'

'My name is Chang.'

For a moment Rawsbarthe looked up without understanding, and then suddenly his entire body burst into a thrashing attempt to get away. As the fellow was on his back and in no way strong, it was simple for Chang to pin him with one knee and shift his grip to the fellow's throat, squeezing tight.

'You are a criminal!' Rawsbarthe gasped.

'And you were searching Mrs Trapping's private room. I do not believe a woman's bedchamber is the lawful province of any Ministry.'

'Mrs Trapping has been summoned to the Duke's presence! She has not complied. My investigation is fully within the scope of the Privy Council's powers –'

'Then why are you alone in the dead of night? Where are your soldiers? Where is your writ?'

'I . . .' Rawsbarthe gulped and twitched his cheek where a fleck of wax had hardened, a milky teardrop. 'I . . . I do not answer to the likes of . . . ah . . .'

'Why does the Duke want to see Mrs Trapping?'

'Her brother –'

'Which brother?'

Rawsbarthe frowned as if this were the question of an idiot. 'Henry Xonck has withdrawn to his home in the country – an attack of fever. With his munitions works, such incapacity becomes a matter of national interest –'

Before the man could finish, Chang hauled Rawsbarthe to a sitting position against the side of a bedpost. Chang stood, ready to send a kick wherever it might prove necessary.

'So what *did* you find *here*? In the national interest?'

'Well, firstly – *goodness* – it seems the room is not *Mrs Trapping's* room at all –'

'Goodness indeed,' sneered Chang. 'Empty your pockets.'

Rawsbarthe shrugged his coat back into place and patted it vaguely, as if trying to remember where the pockets actually were. He plucked out an envelope and peered at the writing. 'Yes – here – and the woman whose belongings *do* in fact fill it – one – ah – one – *Elöise Dujong* –'

'Tutor to the Trapping children.'

Rawsbarthe's eyes went wide. 'You know her?'

Chang snatched the envelope from Rawsbarthe's grasp. 'Keep talking.'

'The room is hers! *Her* clothes fill the closet connecting to the Colonel's chamber. Yet the children have no rooms on this floor of the house! It may well be that Elöise Dujong is the Colonel's mistress! Yet, with such a settled inhabitation of the nearby room, Mrs Trapping must herself be fully aware of the arrangement!'

Chang dealt enough with the back staircases and alleyways of society to know this sort of arrangement was far more common than was believed. What he did not know – and must discern, for his own safety – was where Elöise's involvement stopped. Was she merely Trapping's mistress . . . or more? Trapping had been on the periphery of the Cabal, a go-between serving the Xoncks and Vandaariff . . . but Elöise was hardly unobservant . . . or a fool . . .

Chang looked down at the envelope, sorting his earliest memories of Elöise at Harschmort – she had been whispering advice into Charlotte Trapping's ear. But on their last night . . . when she had been captured in the Comte's laboratory . . . it had been Francis Xonck who had taken personal charge of her. Could it be that Elöise was dear to Xonck – that he had manipulated events to spare her?

'Why take this?' Chang asked Rawsbarthe. 'There were many others.'

'N-no reason at all, merely to satisfy my superiors that I had successfully entered –'

Chang sent the toe of his boot sharply into Rawsbarthe's ribs, turning the man's words into a wheeze. The letter was a single page, folded over, covered in script, addressed to *Mrs Elöise Dujong, 7 Hadrian Square . . .* the postal marks were smudged, with no clear date, nor was there any other writing to indicate who the envelope was from. He glanced to Rawsbarthe, who was looking up at him with some trepidation.

Mrs Dujong,

I trust you will forgive my presumption, yet the matters at hand are too vital for etiquette to prevent sharing what I have learnt. Your loyal attachment to Colonel and Mrs Trapping is well known, and so I fear you may be the only person in a position to give warning about the imminent danger that now threatens them both. I say both, yet it is for the Lady I am most urgently concerned. You must perceive the depth of interests arrayed against Mrs Trapping's recent and misguided efforts of enquiry. I have included such tokens that may convince you of my good intentions, and implore you to reveal this letter to no one, most particularly the Lady herself.

Word may be left in my name at the St Royale Hotel and I shall respond directly. In this I am your humble and obedient servant,

Caroline Stearne

There was nothing else in the envelope. Chang crouched down, leaning his face closer to Rawsbarthe's. 'Where is the rest of it?' he asked.

'I've no idea!' the man squeaked.

'Who is your immediate superior after Bascombe?'

'M-Mr Phelps!'

This was going nowhere.

'Why give him this? Of all her things? The *truth* – or I shall cut off your nose.'

'Because it mentions Mrs Trapping! And she has vanished!'

'Vanished as of *when*?'

'Three days ago.'

'Then who is in charge of the Xonck family interests?'

Rawsbarthe shook his head. 'Stewards, directors, factory managers – but *no one* can step forward. They all wait for Henry Xonck to recover, though the doctors give no hope – but the nation's defence, our capacity for military action –'

'I am not aware of any need for war.'

Rawsbarthe sputtered. 'Simply because *you* are not aware does not mean that genuine threats –'

Chang snapped the envelope at Rawsbarthe's nose. 'What "misguided efforts" was Charlotte Trapping engaged in? Is she being blackmailed? By someone who wants her newly expanded share of the Xonck empire?'

'I've n-no idea!'

'Do you know this Caroline Stearne?'

'Unfortunately not – however, as soon as you allow me to leave, I assure you that one of my very first points of business will be to enquire for her at that very hotel –'

'Do not bother. The woman's throat has been cut ear to ear this last week.'

Chang stood. If only the letter had a date! How had Caroline Stearne known to write Elöise? *When* had she known? Such a warning may have steered Charlotte Trapping away from discovering the Cabal's plot, but might it not also have protected the woman when her husband and elder brother were both marked for ruin? Serious and stable like Bascombe, Caroline Stearne had been in the first rank of the Cabal's minions, but Chang had no illusion that she would do such a thing on her own impulse . . . so who amongst the Cabal had directed her?

Chang turned to Rawsbarthe, who had grown rather accustomed to looking up at the ceiling. 'Where is Colonel Aspiche?' asked Chang.

'Who?'

'Colonel of Dragoons – the 4th Dragoons.'

'How on earth should I know?'

'Is he *alive*?'

'Is there a reason he *wouldn't* be?'

Chang dropped to his knees and drove his fist hard across Rawsbarthe's jaw, knocking the man senseless once more. He stood, flexed the fingers in his glove, and tucked the envelope into the inner pocket of his coat. He'd been in the Trapping house far too long.

Five minutes later Chang was on the street, unseen and unremarked, threading his way towards the White Cathedral, itself no particular destination but on the way to others he had not yet chosen amongst. One possibility would be the Palace — Stäelmaere House itself — to find out first-hand about the Duke and the glass woman. Charlotte Trapping had been missing for three days . . . yet for the Captain and his soldiers to reach Karthe, they must have been sent well before that, soon after the airship had set forth. He was sure the true sequence of events would tell him who lay behind it, and their true intentions . . . but it was very late, and the pleasure Chang had felt from his encounter with Sapp and Horace had faded before the unremarkable complexity of what he had learnt of Elöise. She was an intelligent woman, but the idea that an intelligent woman would make the choices her room had spelt out, as he knew perfectly intelligent people did every day of the week, was nevertheless dismaying.

He reached the Cathedral and kept on, up St Margaret's to the Circus Garden, but turned well before he reached its lights — even at this hour burning brightly — wending by habit back towards the Library. In another five minutes he reached the squat hut housing the sewer entrance, and ten minutes after that heaved open the hatch in the Library basement. He climbed the inner staircases in silence, located the pallet in the dark — quietly displacing the bottles around it (the spot was used in the afternoons by an especially gin-steeped catalogue clerk), and gratefully stretched the whole of his frame onto its welcome softness. He laid his coat over his body like a stiffened blanket and folded his glasses into the outside pocket. He exhaled in the dark, feeling the bones in his shoulders settle into the pallet, the edges of his mind already beginning to fray into dream . . . he recalled a stanza from the Cœurome retelling of *Don Juan*, extending the story into the new world — 'that eternal optimism of desire/Persistent as plague' — but then the words blurred, flowing from line to line like a bubbling stream of broken ink . . . then the lines became smoke against a white sky, Doctor Svenson's cigarettes, curling up . . . smoke rising from Angelique's shattered torso . . . from the Contessa's lacquered cigarette holder. Chang's last thought was of that same smoke, exhaled from the Contessa's mouth into the ear of Celeste Temple, still feverish on her bed. Then Celeste opened her eyes, the whites swirling with the filth that had been blown into each blinking globe.

Chang woke to shafts of dimmest morning falling five floors through a lattice of metal catwalks and staircases, all the way from skylights of thick streaked glass on the roof. The effect was very much like that of a prison — or how Chang imagined a prison to be — but he enjoyed it nevertheless, taking pleasure in wilful limitation. He padded his way to the archivist's cupboard, where he found water, a mirror, and a chamber pot. The water was not hot, so he did not shave, but rinsed his neckcloth, wrung it out, and then draped it across his shoulders to dry. He grimaced at the state of his once-fine leather coat, ruined first by passage through the furnace pipes of Harschmort and second by immersion in the sea. But Chang had no money to replace it. As the lining was whole and the coat still kept him warm, he resigned himself to being mistaken, with his glasses, for a blind beggar.

Morning ablutions as complete as they were ever going to be, Chang climbed to the ninth floor of stacks, emerging on the third floor of high-vaulted public rooms. He crossed to the Document Annexe, where the government publications were housed. Like every public room in the Library, the Annexe was graced with a pink-streaked marble floor and a large cartouche above the door bearing the arms of the aristocratic family funding that particular room's construction (in this case the extinct and unregretted Grimps). In direct opposition to its opulent trappings, the Annexe, owing to its ever-expanding contents, had been crammed with shelving, covering the walls and in free-standing rows, some fifteen feet tall; ladders, as well as the help of Library staff, were required to find anything whatsoever.

For Chang, the collection was a ready source of information about land

holdings, changes in law, marriages, estates, legacies, census surveys –
anything (which meant everything) the dogged grind of the government
decided ought to be set down for posterity. He started at the beginning.
The Duke was alive, which meant his puppet mistress, Mrs Marchmoor,
must be as well. Charlotte Trapping was not in her house, and the Palace
bureaucracy sought her. By all accounts she was no idiot (unless one took
into account her marriage), only a woman who had been routinely shunted
aside from her family's power . . .

Chang rolled a wooden ladder into position and climbed to its highest
rung. On the top shelf was a wooden tray holding the newest reports not
yet of a quantity to be bound. Chang scooped up the contents and stepped
easily down the ladder with his arms full, sure as a cat, crossing to a wide
table. He dropped the pile onto it without ceremony.

When the 4th Dragoons had been reposted to serve at the Palace, Chang
had used Ministry announcements to trace where the order had come from.
Thus he had uncovered a bargain made between Henry Xonck and Deputy
Minister Crabbé. While Chang was not a man to imagine purity in the
intentions of others, even he had been surprised by the nakedness with
which a man of business like Xonck had insinuated his agenda into that of
the government. By placing Colonel Trapping – his own brother-in-law –
at the centre of the Palace, Xonck ensured that he would receive advance
notice of all military actions, diplomatic agreements, tariff decisions – an
almost infinite number of events that he could then skilfully exploit to his
financial advantage. In turn, Crabbé had been given – quite without lawful
precedent – the equivalent of a private army at his own command, which
also – being now executed by the Queen's soldiers – put an official government stamp on all of the Cabal's actions. The arrangement had been
audacious and arrogant. But now Chang was curious about the finer details
that – because of the grind of bureaucracy – might not have been published
initially. What had Henry Xonck been promised for his part in the bargain?
And, by extension, what might Charlotte Trapping have discovered since
that final night at Harschmort House?

The reports were an uncollected jumble, from every Ministry and each
department, but Chang sorted rapidly, discarding documents on agriculture,

legal reform, medical patents, cheese, livestock, and stamps. He paused at a mention of royal game preserves, his squinting eyes caught by a reference to Parchfeldt Park. Chang held the paper up to his face and read more closely: a portion of land running directly through the park's southern quarter had been given over to the public interest, to allow an arm of the Orange Canal to be extended across the width of the preserve. Chang frowned. What was on the far side of Parchfeldt Park that required access to the canals, and through them the sea? He set this aside and sorted through the rest of the unbound papers, but nothing else caught his interest. He shrugged. That a Parchfeldt canal had anything to do with the Xoncks was mere speculation. On a whim he crossed to the Interior Ministry documents, looking for any previous attempts to open this portion of Parchfeldt to private usage. With some satisfaction he found a cluster of petitions brought forward by a certain Mr De Groot, the apparently ill-favoured owner of a local mill. All had been denied. The requests had persisted for ten years and then abruptly ceased, leaving a gap of some three years with no requests whatsoever . . . until this last winter, when one was put forward by a Mr Alfred Leveret.

This request had been granted.

He left the Annexe and crossed the marble landing to the reference room, vaulting behind the archivist's counter without a qualm. Moving like a deliberate half-blind bee amongst dusty blossoms, Chang dipped in and out of heavy, flaking volumes – registries of business, of death, catalogues of land transfer. Thirty minutes later he slipped off his glasses and spat into his handkerchief, rubbing the moistened cloth over each tender eye. He had learnt what he needed to know: August De Groot had died bankrupt in a debtor's cell. After three years unclaimed and empty, his mill works had been purchased – just this last October – by Alfred Leveret, a senior employee of Xonck Armaments. And now, in the wake of all the recent transactions between Henry Xonck and the Privy Council, the precious canal access had been granted.

He snorted at the way wealth so effortlessly got its own, De Groot's misery bringing to mind the story of Margaret Hooke, the daughter of a

northern mill owner gone bankrupt, no doubt hounded to ruin, just as De
Groot had been, by others waiting to snap up the leavings for cheap. And
what had happened to De Groot's children, or his displaced workers – were
any of them driven to a life in the brothels? Were such costs ever considered
in the transactions of high finance? Certainly they lay outside the care of
any official counting – and thus beyond what the nation could ever admit
had occurred. Chang swatted the book dust from his hands.

It was near eight o'clock. The staff would be arriving. De Groot's factory and
its proximity to Parchfeldt struck Chang as the exact sort of circumstance he
had been looking for, though his rational mind told him it was far more
likely that the widowed Charlotte Trapping had decamped to the cottage
of some cousin by the sea, or even to a welcoming foreign capital. But was
Charlotte Trapping really who he wanted to follow? He'd gone into her
home only to have his search dislocated by the mysteries of Elöise Dujong
. . . ought he to be investigating *her*? He climbed quietly up to the map
room, hoping to investigate all three quarries at the same stroke.

Perhaps his distrust finally had the better of him, and he was overestimat-
ing the reach of his enemies, and their capacity . . . or perhaps he was
finally learning that their plans for profit and control spread beyond any
boundary he had formerly understood. Chang opened the surveyor's *Codex*
and found the map number for Parchfeldt Park, then turned to the large
cases of the maps themselves, located the proper drawer, and finally hauled
the item in question onto the table.

Like many royal preserves Parchfeldt was enormous. The park was
shaped like a tall Norman shield, and with the Ministry report in mind
Chang turned his attention to the southernmost spike, now crossed by the
band of a newly laid canal. The park was nearer to the sea than Chang had
realized, close to the northern spur of the Orange Canal. Just to the edge
of his map he picked out the abandoned – or soon to be so, depending on
when the map had actually been made – mill works of the late Mr De Groot.
Chang shook his head. From the mill to the nearest canal had been an
awkward circular path, adding days to any delivery, notwithstanding the
tolls and duties levied along the way – a minor concern to someone like

Henry Xonck, but the exact margin of cost to drive a man like De Groot into collapse. With the canal extended the factory would be but a day from the open sea itself – a shocking advantage, with few or no duties at all. It would be a perfect manufacturing point for goods going abroad . . . to such a place as Macklenburg.

He dug Caroline Stearne's letter from his pocket. Two things struck him, the first of which was that Elöise had been contacted at all. Xonck had persuaded Elöise to visit Tarr Manor to find Colonel Trapping only *after* Trapping had been killed. But this letter meant some other member of the Cabal had targeted Elöise and Mrs Trapping well *before* . . . which was also to say that they had their eyes on outflanking Xonck with regard to his family's fortune. Chang snorted at the brazen strategy . . . and the letter *did* mention the St Royale Hotel. It had to have come from the Contessa.

Chang turned his attention to the second point – the 'efforts' of Charlotte Trapping. The very fact that she was a woman meant that his usual tactic – sorting through the footpaths of paper that nearly every respectable man left in his wake – was useless. It would be nearly impossible for Charlotte Trapping to exercise her desires apart from the consent of her husband or brothers in any way that would be so recorded. That she possessed all manner of personal resources he did not doubt, but discovering their workings would be very difficult.

Yet if he could not guess what *she* had done, perhaps he could deduce what might have provoked the Contessa.

Any objective look at the Xonck family would have found Henry by far the most important, with Charlotte and her socially promoted husband a distant second, and Francis – the rakish dilettante – an ill-considered third. To all appearances, the Cabal was dominated by Robert Vandaariff and Henry Xonck, its true architects posing as mere hangers-on to these great men. If Mrs Trapping had been curious about her husband's activities, her enquiries would have naturally centred on his relations with those two most powerful men . . .

Chang began to pace between the tables, hands clasped behind his back. He was near to something, he knew. Through Caroline Stearne and Elöise Dujong, the Contessa had warned Charlotte Trapping – the distance kept between she and her object making clear the need for subterfuge and care. Chang strode back to the Annexe. On the stairs he saw one of the cataloguers from the second floor climbing slowly ahead of him, holding a bulging satchel. Chang ignored the fellow's nod, stalking back to the report about canal-building, flipping the pages . . . and found an address cited for Mr Alfred Leveret. This done, he crossed to the volumes of property holdings. Another two minutes told him that Alfred Leveret had recently become the owner of a Houlton Square townhouse. In no way fashionable, Houlton Square offered its residents an unquestionable, drab respectability – the perfect address for an ambitious underling of industry.

The property record cited another entry, in an appendix . . . which in turn documented bank drafts . . . which in turn . . . Chang flipped page after page, tracking a deliberate trail of obfuscation that spawned a litter of paper across the Annexe. But then he slipped his fingers beneath his glasses, rubbing his tender eyes with a smile. He had found it after all. The Contessa had frightened Charlotte Trapping away from prying into Henry Xonck's affairs – like the purchase of De Groot's mill – precisely because they were *not* Henry Xonck's affairs at all. The money for Leveret's house had come from a bank in Vienna representing *Francis* Xonck. The factory was *his*, and the Contessa knew it – which meant she was determined no one else, much less a disenfranchised prying sister, ought to.

By the time Chang slipped from the rear entrance, it was almost ten o'clock. He'd spent far longer than he'd intended in the Library. Through a roundabout route, winding as far north as Worthing Circle – stopping there for a pie and a hot mug of tea from a stall – Chang returned to the shuttered building at the next corner from his own lodging house and forced the door. No one followed. He climbed rapidly to the empty attic and located the floorboard under which he'd stashed the sabre of the Macklenburg lieutenant, killed in his own rooms so long ago. He stuffed the weapon under his coat and returned to the street, ready to draw it in defence if need be, but there was no one.

Another brisk walk took him to Fabrizi's, to exchange the sabre for his repaired stick, apologizing for the loss of his loan. The old man eyed the sabre with professional detachment and accepted it with a clicking sound as adequate payment. The gold on the hilt and scabbard alone would have bought the stick twice over, but Chang never knew when he would need to presume on Fabrizi for special treatment, and this was a simple enough way to build up a balance. It was nearly eleven. There was just time for a visit to Houlton Square.

The servant answering the door was stout and white whiskered, a man who some years ago might have been of a height with Chang but had since lost an inch to age. His expression upon seeing Chang was admirably impassive, for it was broad daylight, with any number of people in the road to notice an unsavoury character calling on so respectable a man as Alfred Leveret.

'Mr Leveret,' he said. 'My name is Chang.'

'Mr Leveret is not at home.'

'Might one enquire when he will return?'

'I am unable to say.'

Chang curled his lip in a very mild sneer. 'Perhaps because you do not know yourself?'

The servant ought to have slammed the door – and Chang was poised to interpose a boot and then drive his shoulder forward to force himself through – but the man did not. Instead, he merely sketched a careful peek at whoever might be watching from the street or nearby windows.

'Are you *acquainted* with Mr Leveret?' he asked.

'Not at all,' Chang answered. 'Yet it appears we have interests in common.'

The servant did not reply.

'Charlotte Trapping, for example. And Mr Francis Xonck.'

The man's crisp professional veneer – the collar, the coat, the clean-scrubbed nails, the impeccable polish of his shoes – was suddenly belied by his eyes, twitching with the encapsulated worry of two nervous mice.

'May I ask you a question . . . Mr?'

'Mr Happerty.'

'Mr Happerty. That you entertain a character like myself in the middle of the morning on your own doorstep tells me you have certain . . . *cares*

. . . about your master. That I *am* here, never having met the man, is signal enough of his grave situation. I would suggest we speak more frankly – for speak we must, Mr Happerty – indoors.'

Happerty sucked on his teeth but then stepped aside.

'I am *obliged*,' whispered Cardinal Chang. Things were far worse than he had assumed.

The foyer of Leveret's townhouse was all one would have imagined, which was to say it expressed an imagination utterly contained: a black and white chequered marble floor, a high domed ceiling with an ugly chandelier dangling from a chain like a crystallized urchin, a staircase marked at regular intervals with paintings nakedly selected to match the upholstery of the reception chairs – optimistic river scenes showing the city's waters in a hue Chang doubted they would possess if Christ Himself walked across them on the brightest day in June.

Mr Happerty shut the door but did not invite Chang further into the house, so Chang took it upon himself to stalk a few steps towards the open archway.

'The house is new to Mr Leveret,' Chang stated. 'Were you in his service at his previous residence?'

'I have allowed your entry only so as to not be further seen from the street,' said Happerty firmly. 'You must tell me what you know.'

'Tell me how long your master has been missing.'

It was a guess but a reasonable one. The real question was whether Leveret had fallen victim to the Cabal, or whether something else had occurred in the confusion of the past week – that is, whether the man was simply in hiding, or whether he was dead.

'I have let you in this house,' said Happerty again. 'But I must know more who you are.'

'I am exactly what I seem,' Chang replied. 'I do not care two pins for your master – I am not interested in *harming* him, if that is what you ask. Or harming *you* – or I would already have done so.'

There were no other servants – no crowd of footmen at call to throw him out of doors. Had they all gone? Or been sent away?

'It has been four days,' said Happerty at last, with a sigh.

'And to your mind, when you last saw him, did he *expect* to be gone?'

'I do not believe so.'

'No valise? No pocket of ready cash? No changes to his social calendar?'

'None of those things.'

'And where is his place of business?'

'Mr Leveret travels to the different gun-works throughout the week. But that day . . .' Happerty hesitated.

'Can he *defend* himself?' asked Chang.

Happerty said nothing.

'Your employer is in danger,' said Chang. 'Henry Xonck is an imbecile and Francis Xonck is dead. Forces more powerful than they, thus very powerful indeed, have made your master their target.'

Chang found his eye caught by the grain of the close-shaven skin on the underside of Happerty's jaw, reminding him unpleasantly of sliced salmon. The way it rubbed against the white starched collar, Chang expected to see a greasy pink stain. Then the old servant cleared his throat, as if he had made a decision. 'Mr Leveret had an appointment at the Palace.'

'Is that normal?'

'Such appointments are a regular consequence of government contracts, though Mr Leveret never appeared himself – they were the province of Mr Xonck –'

'Henry Xonck?'

Happerty frowned. 'Of course Henry Xonck. Yet in Mr Xonck's absence – the *quarantine* – Mr Leveret was summoned, to present delivery time-tables related to shore defences.'

'Deliveries by way of the western canals?'

'I only keep Mr Leveret's *house*.'

'Do you know who he met at the Palace?'

'Apparently he never arrived. They were most insistent he appear. An officer came. Quite beyond all decorum and without any further explanation, his men searched the premises for Mr Leveret, despite everything I might do to persuade them otherwise!'

Happerty had become more animated, describing the disruption of his own domain. Chang nodded in sympathy. 'But who was he meeting? At the Palace?'

'Mr Leveret's calendar names a "Mr Phelps", of the Foreign Ministry — itself a thing that makes no sense for coastal defences. I do not believe Mr Leveret had ever met with him before.'

Happerty gestured, affronted, beyond the archway. In the far room a window had been cracked, the fine lace curtains lay on the floor in a heap, the expensive Italian floor tiles had been scratched . . .

'Do you recall the officer in command?' Chang asked.

'It is my duty to recall everyone. Colonel Noland Aspiche, 4th Dragoons.'

Chang recalled the looping scars from the Process around Aspiche's eyes, the temporary disfigurement an apt sign of the man's internal distemper. Though he had hated Trapping's corruption, Colonel Aspiche had been seduced by the Cabal with ease. Chang was sure any remorse lay curled like a worm within the Colonel's conscience, making him that much more severe in executing his new masters' agenda.

'Two more questions, and I must go,' he said, 'though I am in your debt, and will do my best to find Mr Leveret. First, did your master ever visit Harschmort House?'

Mr Happerty shook his head no.

'Second — in the last fortnight — did you ever see his face discoloured, a scarring around the eyes? Or was he ever absent for some days at a time when such a condition might have healed without your knowing it?'

Happerty shook his head again. 'Mr Leveret is a prompt man with regular habits, dining at home each night at half-past six.'

'In that case I will ask a third question,' said Chang, his hand on the crystal knob of the door. 'You are a man who pays attention. Are you acquainted with Mrs Elöise Dujong?'

'She is the widow,' said Happerty. 'Mrs Trapping's woman.'

'Would Mr Leveret know her?'

'Mr Leveret is most attentive to social nuance.'

He was forced to cut through the Circus Garden, a district he preferred at all times to avoid and found especially onerous with his presently battered appearance. His path was momentarily blocked by a coach of young ladies, and Chang was stung by the trust cocooning them, even to the colour of their merry hats, the blitheness – in a city of filth and smoke and blood and tobacco juice and layered grease – that allowed *anyone* to wear *anything* the colour of a lemon meringue.

In his hurry, he'd not gone the extra streets to enter hidden through Helliott Street, and he was jostled down Stropping's main staircase into what appeared to be an especially restive and hostile crowd of travellers . . . but then he saw a line of constables at the foot of the wide stone steps, barking at people to form lines and group themselves by destination. What in the world was this? Chang paused, as angry bodies pushed past him – people muttering at the constables, constables answering the travellers with sharp shoves. What was more, beyond the constables he picked out pockets of red – dragoons scattered across the whole of the terminal, with each little crimson band led by men in Ministry topcoats – in the midst of a search the scale of which Chang had never seen in a lifetime of crime and its consequences. He was shoved forward, swept down by the crowd's momentum, waiting with rising dread for a constable to pick him out. Just before the foot of the stairs Chang muttered a sudden apology, as if he had dropped his stick, and crouched below the shoulders of the travellers around him, scuttling quickly ahead and past the harassed constables. He kept low until he reached the cover of an advertising kiosk, and then carefully took stock of his predicament.

Rawsbarthe, while knowing clearly who Chang was, had not been searching *for* him – perhaps it was the same with the men here. Even if the constables knew Chang from the Captain's description, he could not merit *this*. Could things actually be so desperate that the Palace would so openly search for Charlotte Trapping or even Leveret – as if *they* were criminals? But the constables did not even seem to be searching. Rather, they were positioned to quell unrest amongst the people themselves. What else had happened in the city? He remembered the newspapers – but one *always* ignored the newspapers, they were written for fools. Was it possible their shrill warnings had been real?

He looked up at the clock – it was just before noon – and then beneath it. There was no sign of the Doctor or Miss Temple – or, for that matter, Elöise Dujong.

The meeting place was extremely exposed, and he had no desire to linger. He inched up on his toes, trying to determine if the search was directed at trains coming or going from a particular place. Along the southern platforms, to Cap Rouge and other coastal resorts he had never seen (Chang took some satisfaction at how freezing the wind would be at this time of year), roamed a pair of dragoons, with one portly man in black standing in place while the soldiers marched back and forth. For the entire bank of western platforms, which would have included Tarr Manor, the detachment of dragoons had been expanded to six.

It was noon. Since his allies would arrive from the north, he made his way to the clock by a looping path that brought him close enough to the northern platforms to see that each of these trains had its own black-clad functionary, with at least an entire squadron of dragoons arranged between them. Neither the Doctor or Miss Temple would have the knowledge – or the sense, honestly – to slip out the side door to Helliott Street. They would be taken. And yet . . . a train from the north *had* apparently arrived; he could see a small line of disembarked passengers under scrutiny, but he did not see Svenson or Miss Temple – nor did he see anyone being dragged away. Chang took up his position at the clock, wondering how long he could realistically expect to stand unnoticed, and in which direction, when he *was* noticed, he would flee.

He gave them three minutes – any more would be idiotic – and berated himself for setting up a rendezvous that had become a trap for anyone credible enough to trust him. The seconds ticked by. The constables came near with their charges. He could hear soldiers calling above the train whistles. Enough. Chang stalked abruptly into the thickest part of the crowd. As long as he was there, his time could be far better spent with the last quadrant of trains, those going back and forth from the east – towards the coastal canals, and Harschmort. He rose to his full height. The red and black coats of his enemies were laced through the swirling crowd, as sure and as hard as whalebone in a woman's corset.

A heavy hand gripped his right shoulder. Chang spun and raised his stick. Before him stood Colonel Aspiche, bawling out to the red-coated troopers behind him: 'Dragoons! Arrest this man!'

Chang knocked away the Colonel's arm, but the moment when Chang might have landed a kick or chopped the handle of his stick into Aspiche's throat was lost in his shock at the man's appearance. Where before the Colonel had been hale and fierce, now his eyes were shot through with blood, his skin was lividly blistered around both nostrils, and his closely cropped grey hair had gone entirely white.

The dragoons surged forward, and Chang dived away into the crowd. But the simmering anger he had witnessed on the staircase had been inflamed, as if the Colonel's cry had tarred Chang as a scapegoat for every humiliation and inconvenience that had been inflicted on them. He heard shouts and insults, and knew – he had his own experience of hostile mobs – that any moment some angry idiot would try to bring him down, and then a dozen others would follow suit. He seized an elderly man by the arm and yanked him squawking into the path of whoever might be behind. He heard the ring of sabres being drawn, Aspiche shouting at the crowd to make way, the screams of women – he had no idea where to go, he could not *see* – another scream – but then he bulled through to an open area of the terminal floor, the people shrinking away and pointing. To hesitate was death – Chang flung himself forward in a dead run towards a gap between two waiting east-bound trains.

Blocking the way stood a man in black and another four dragoons, their backs to the commotion, intent on something down the track. Aspiche roared out for Chang to stop. The Ministry man turned, paled, and flapped his arms at his men – but Chang measured the distance in an instant, they were too far away, he was moving too fast. He slammed into the Ministry man, screaming upon impact to further terrify his quarry, seized his black lapels, and spun him, limbs flailing, into the dragoons at his heels. Chang sprinted for the nearest train carriage, diving beneath and crawling furiously out the far side, tearing his trousers on the gravel, up on his feet as the soldiers fell to their knees in pursuit. Emerging in another corridor between two trains, he found he had gained perhaps five seconds of distance. More soldiers appeared at the head of this corridor's platform, shouting, pointing – Chang broke into a run away from them all.

The train he'd crawled beneath had just arrived – that is, its engine faced the platform – but the other train, on his right, was preparing to leave Stropping, and Chang dashed alongside, towards its steaming engine. Without looking back, he dived beneath it, scrambling out the other side.

The row of track before him was empty. Chang ran at an angle towards the next train over, painted yellow. He considered doubling around – back to the terminal – or climbing into the train through a window, just to get out of view. But what he needed more was distance. Another twenty yards and he dived under again. On the other side of the yellow train, Chang began to sprint: the train beyond it was in motion, leaving Stropping, its distant front end disappearing into the black tunnels at the station's edge. He glanced over his shoulder – no dragoons.

He reached the train just as its final carriage swept by. He leapt between the tracks proper, running hard to catch up. The train was gaining speed but so was Chang. His gloved fingers just brushed the rear rail. He looked up to see a figure in the doorway of the guard's van, wrapped in a hooded black cloak. It was his assailant from the train compartment in Karthe. The man's arm lashed down, a blue spike in his hand. Chang let go before the blow could land and nearly stumbled onto his face. The man stared malevolently at Chang as the train disappeared into the tunnel, his hood opened by the wind. Or maybe that was wrong – maybe he had *wanted* Cardinal Chang to see his face after all. Chang bent over, gasping for breath, hands on his knees, as any number of nagging questions began to fall into place.

Francis Xonck was still alive.

Some distance behind him, but still closer than he would have liked, a determined pair of dragoons emerged from under the yellow train. Chang broke into a ragged run, following Xonck's train into the dark tunnel. At the very least it would serve as a place to turn and set his own ambush. With any luck, the dragoons would simply give up once they saw him go in — as well they ought to, for the tunnels were insanely dangerous, with tracks crossing each other without any warning and trains screaming out of nowhere from every direction. He'd no desire to enter it himself, and only hoped the passage of Xonck's train would keep these particular tracks clear for at least the time it took to lose the dragoons.

But the tunnel was further away than it seemed. By the time he reached it, Chang was winded and the darkness echoed with the sounds of other trains. What was worse, the dragoons had not stopped. Instead, the ones in front had paused, allowing the rest to catch up — some ten men in all, sabres out, forming a line between the tracks. Chang spat out another curse and pulled off his glasses, stuffing them into the inner pocket of his coat. He could barely see a thing. He held his stick out before him to find the tunnel's wall, hoping for an alcove to hide in. Instead he tripped over a half-buried stretch of unused track and fell to his knees. He groped for his stick and looked back, blinking. The line of dragoons raced directly towards him, moving faster than Chang had anticipated. He found the stick and plunged into the darkness, landing hard on the tar-soaked stones. The train roared past — inches away, it seemed, though he knew this was but the speed and violence of its passage. In the doorway of its final car stood a guard with a lantern, illuminating for a teasingly brief instant the vaulted tunnel where Chang crouched.

One line of tracks veered into a deeper side tunnel. It was the sort of place that might be a trap — even the best ambush would not catch Aspiche and all of his men — but Chang was drawn to it anyway on the chance of another side exit, and an easy escape. Once he'd stumbled in, however, the side tunnel's isolation became its own difficulty, for the blackness was total. Chang felt his way, knocking with his stick, wasting time. He could hear the dragoons calling to one another and then, shadows playing about the cavern, saw with a sick realization that they had fetched lanterns. They would pick him out like a rat cornered in the pantry.

But the flickers of light at least showed him where to go. He broke into a reckless run as the neglected side cavern echoed with the approach of another train. Yet, instead of roaring past, this train broke speed to actually enter the cavern. Knowing there were only seconds before he must be found, Chang sprinted towards the curving cavern wall, the bricks black with soot. The wall was a series of arches, each one penetrated by a set of rail tracks, all fanning out from a central spur. Chang ducked inside the nearest arch and flattened himself against the wall. The cavern had become much brighter, both for the train – now easing its way slowly and backwards into the vast hall – and the dragoons waving their lanterns. Chang retreated further, and was suddenly surprised to see the lantern light reflecting back. His alcove archway was not empty, but exactly designed to house – as it did now – a detached train carriage.

He edged between the carriage and the filthy wall. The dragoons came nearer. Chang flung himself down and rolled beneath the carriage. He felt for the cross-braces above and hauled himself up off the sleepers, wedging his boots to each side and wrapping his arms around the braces. In a matter of seconds his tunnel was bright with lantern light. Chang held his breath. The gravel crunched as two soldiers marched the length of each side of the carriage. Their light passed by and left him in a momentary shadow. He released the air in his lungs and carefully inhaled. The men came back. They thrust their lanterns beneath the carriage, but Chang remained suspended just out of view. The light was withdrawn. He heard the soldiers walk on to the next tunnel.

Chang slowly lowered himself onto the bed of railway sleepers, listening to the sounds in the cavern, feeling the pressure of the wood and gravel against his back, and the cool, foul air of the cavern on his face. What if he merely died where he was? How long until his bones would be discovered? Or would they be taken apart by rats and scattered across the whole of the tunnel?

He peered past his boots. The light in the cavern was moving again. Divested of its carriages, the engine had reversed direction back towards the station proper. In its wake came the smaller bobbing glows of the individual dragoons. Chang relaxed on the wooden sleepers – he would wait another few minutes before moving – and turned his mind to more useful matters. Francis Xonck was alive. Colonel Aspiche was diseased. There was growing unrest in the city.

In hindsight, it seemed stupid not to have recognized Xonck during their struggle in the train compartment at Karthe, and his reappearance was a reminder that Chang could take nothing for granted when dealing with the Cabal. For all he knew, not a single person had perished aboard the dirigible. But then Chang recalled the severing of Lydia Vandaariff's head and the Prince of Macklenburg's legs, and then Caroline Stearne floating face down in the rising flood. The servantry always died.

Chang rolled out from under the carriage, brushing at his coat from habit. Barely able to see a thing but suddenly curious . . . he walked, one hand against the wall, to carriage's far end. Chang patted his hands across the platform and found a metal ladder welded to its side. He climbed up and felt for a waist-high railing of chain around the platform's edge. He threw a leg over it and ran his hands across the door. It was metal, cold, and lacking any handle.

Chang retraced his way to the carriage's other end, finding an identical platform, ladder, and flat metal door. He pulled the glove from his right hand and ran it over the cold surface. His fingers found the depression of a key hole.

He fished out a ring of skeleton keys, sifting through them by feel for three particularly heavy and squat specimens he had acquired in trade from a Dutch thief named Rüud, after Chang had secured him a hiding space on a smuggler's ship to Rotterdam. Chang had more than once contemplated discarding them, annoyed by the weight they added to the ring and having only a thief's word as to their value. He brought the first key to bear with the keyhole, but it would not go in. The second key slipped inside, but did not turn. He jiggled it free with some effort and no little irritation. The third key went in – again the fit was tight – and turned to the right. It did not move. With another burst of impatience, Chang turned the key sharply to the left. The lock caught and the key spun a complete circle, rolling the bar free with a muffled clank.

The interior of the carriage glowed blue from a hundred bright points, as if he had wandered into a grotto of fairies. He stood inside the Comte's specially fabricated carriage. Chang leant to the closest glowing array – bulbs of blue glass set into a hanging rack, drilled with holes the size of the

Doctor's monocle. Similar racks were hung along each wall of the open
room. Chang wondered why, with such a supply of glass, the carriage had
been sent to storage, and in such a relatively public space. Perhaps because
the order had come from the Comte, and no one yet dared to countermand
him? Were the tunnels under Stropping parcelled out to the wealthy to
store their private carriages? Was the old Queen's own silver anniversary
carriage, made at such public expense (for a figure so dyspeptically viewed),
gathering soot but another stone arch away?

Chang left the door ajar – the last thing he wanted was to be locked in
by yet another mechanism he didn't understand – and stepped to a glowing
rack of glass. It held perhaps thirty bright bulbs and reminded Chang of
an array of ammunition for an imaginary weapon. If this was just-refined
blue glass, there would be no memory imprinted on it, merely the substance's own raw, untreated properties . . . of which Chang had no real idea.
Each hole was covered by a disc of clear glass, held in place by a thin metal
ring. Chang frowned. Was the metal copper . . . or brighter than that, more
distinctively . . . *orange*? Chang dug a fingernail under the metal ring – the
instant of pressure conjuring the image of his entire nail peeling hideously
back – and popped both the metal ring and the clear disc out of place.
With his gloved hand, he extracted the bolt of blue glass, the size of a
very large bullet – for elephants, perhaps – but completely smooth and
symmetrical.

Against all of his better judgements, Cardinal Chang slipped it into the
pocket of his coat. In an afterthought he put the orange metal ring in with
it. The clear glass cover he fitted back over the empty hole.

The carriage's interior had been designed to resemble an elegant parlour:
windows with tasteful sashes and drapery, carpets and stucco mouldings,
with the appropriate furnishings – all nailed down – an assortment of
fauteuils and chaise longues and spindle-legged sideboards. Chang sneered
at the desire to at all times be accompanied by the familiar. Did not the
pleasure of having one's own *railway carriage* lay in its being exclusive
and unique? The décor ought to be proudly unsuited to any place *else*,
expressing the soul of this new environment of privilege. Instead, he saw
the trappings of staid comfort, a train carriage styled on the ante-room of

a gentleman's club – or, he sneered, a dirigible fitted with sofas. New places ought to be platforms of discovery, not merely venues for drinking port in a chair.

Not that Cardinal Chang drank port, but poverty of means did not contradict his conviction regarding his enemies' poverty of mind. And yet . . . the carriage was the work of the Comte d'Orkancz, hardly a slave to conventional taste. He looked around him more closely, and the interior began to take on a certain irony, precisely *because* of its banality. Now he saw that the staid interior fittings were all an arrogant black – the carpet, the walls, the loops of stucco, even the upholstery – as if the comfort and security they projected was itself a source of wicked, contemptuous pleasure. The Comte was an artist, and he saw the world in terms of metaphor – however dark his sensibilities, the worlds he created remained expressions of beauty and wit. One elegant chaise longue was fitted with leather restraints. The wide, soft fauteuils bore lacquered trays that folded out like square wasp wings, where one might lay out food, drink . . . or medical implements . . .

Chang's amusement stuck in his throat. A ventilation grille had been set into the ceiling, and at his feet, in a pristine square of slate, lay a metal drain. The square of slate was edged with a thin band of orange metal, the same orange metal that ringed every bulb of glass. He looked up. The ventilation grille as well. And the stucco moulding, running the entire circuit of the carriage, bore a line of orange the width of an infant's finger along its upper edge.

He took a breath and then sharply exhaled. The air in the carriage nearly vibrated with dread. On the far end of the room was a low wooden cabinet, its top wide enough to serve as a desk for examining the documents sequestered within its many thin drawers. To his right stood a more unusual fixture, braced at either end by mechanical standing cabinets – the same species, but not full-grown, as the brass-bound kiosks the Comte had used in the cathedral tower to transform his three women to glass. These versions bore fewer black hoses and brass switches, but the sight of them made Cardinal Chang's throat go dry. The black hoses ran into the side of the large object that lay between them: a high metal box the shape of a large coffin, with a curved lid of thick glass. This was where they had kept Angelique.

The glass cover was smoked, and he could not see in. With a grimace Chang set his stick against the box, replaced his glove, and lifted the cover carefully with both hands, looking down with revulsion. The interior of the coffin, for he could call it no other thing, was lined with black rubber. Its centre depression was dusted with a small ring of sediment, like the sigil of a parched, departed sea, the salts of her body – of whatever had been *done* to her – the waters all having dried away. His eyes flicked quickly about the box's interior – more tubes, and holes where liquid or gas had been pumped inside. Chang dropped the cover loudly back into place, his own breath coming raw with anger. He stalked to the cabinet, pulling open the drawers one after another, pawing the papers inside, until he realized he was not seeing them at all. He ought to feel none of this – it was nothing he had not seen before, nothing he had not resigned himself to bear. Chang pulled out his glasses. The blue glow made him squint.

He sorted the cabinet's contents with a grim concentration. One drawer was given over to the plans for the carriage itself, others held purely alchemical formulae – all of it in the same hand, assumedly the Comte's. Next came designs for various small machines. Here the Comte's notations were augmented by another hand, with some pages attached with pins to others that were more technically detailed. These bore a different notation in the corner. Chang held it up to his eyes: a stamp of several horizontal lines, each of which was initialled. It was a way to track production, Chang realized – these were all designs for machines that had been *made*. The top lines were all initialled 'C d'O' . . . the second line – perhaps referring to the mechanical details – was initialled 'GL' or 'JC' – Lorenz or Crooner, engineers from the Royal Institute recruited by the Comte to construct his fever dreams in iron and brass. A fourth line bore simply a stylized mark, identifying the Xonck Armament Works – indicating where the fabrication had been done – but the third line, in every instance, was initialled 'AL' . . .

Every machine had been made for the Comte d'Orkancz by the Xoncks. The construction itself had been completely overseen by Alfred Leveret.

Chang went back to the case. Three drawers had been emptied. He assumed he would find specifications for the great cathedral tower, and for the creation of the glass books, but they did not appear. The rest held more alchemical scribblings, half legible and meaningless to anyone save d'Orkancz. He shoved the last drawer home and heard the rustle of something caught in it. Curious, Chang reached to the back of the drawer and found a balled-up piece of vellum, which looked as if it had slipped out of the drawer above . . . one of the drawers that had been emptied. Chang carefully smoothed it out on the cabinet top.

It was smaller than the rest and depicted a device the size of a black-powder pistol. The design was executed entirely in the hand of the Comte d'Orkancz and labelled 'marrow sparge' – an insidious term that meant nothing to Chang. There was no Xonck stamp in the corner. Had this implement been fabricated? Or did it exist solely in the Comte's ecstatic brain?

With a sudden curiosity Chang studied the tool's dimensions and wondered – trying to recall the impression set into the velvet – if this, or something very like it, might have fitted in the Contessa's mysterious trunk. He could not say. He stuffed it into the inner pocket of his coat.

No doubt there remained more crucial information about the workings of the glass, but Chang knew it was beyond his own understanding. He wished Svenson were there – at least *he* understood the medical issues. It seemed inarguable that, in the Comte's absence, whoever *did* best understand the glass must destroy their rivals. Chang strode to the door, but then paused at a sudden impulse of responsibility. Working deliberately, he began to dig the orange metal rings from one rack of glass, stuffing one after another into his pockets. He'd no idea of their value, but Svenson might, and if they gave any protection whatsoever, it was worth his hauling them around.

He abruptly looked up. A noise outside the carriage. Chang stepped to the door, listening carefully. There were voices, bootsteps. Without hesitation he eased the door closed, sealing himself in, and looked around the room, hating every inch of it, hating the fools outside who had trapped him.

The entire carriage lurched, and Chang was nearly thrown to his knees, grabbing a rack of glass to stay upright. He cursed the black-painted windows and the thick steel doors. He could not hear a thing. The carriage shook again and then settled into a regular rhythm. Chang wanted to spit with frustration. The black carriage was being collected. He was a prisoner.

He could drag the chaise longue in front of one door and use the squat cabinet to block the other, but this would turn the situation into a siege, which must end in his death. He wondered where the carriage was being taken, and by whom. Could it be merely trainmen executing an order in which they had no personal interest? Such men would hardly care if Chang were to slip out and vanish into the shadows of Stropping . . . but if there were dragoons . . . if the carriage was being added onto a train chartered and occupied by his enemies, any appearance would be the end of him. There was simply no way to know.

The movement stopped. Then the black carriage shook at an impact from the other side. It was now bracketed between carriages. The carriage resumed its movement, rising to a regular jogging motion as the train took up speed. Was it possible that the front of the carriage was attached to the coal wagon? Could he slip out that way and hide, while they were still in the tunnels? Before he could sort his thoughts further, he heard a key being thrust into the lock. Thanking fate for the difficulty of the lock itself, Chang strode to the coffin and flipped up the lid. Bile rose in his throat. The lock was turning. If he fought them he would probably die. Did it matter? Chang tossed his stick into the box. He swung himself in flat on his back, shuddering at the vile feel of the soiled black rubber, and pulled the smoked glass cover into place. He could see nothing through it. Then the door to the black carriage opened and Chang poured all his will into silence.

The first thing he heard was a whistle, low and under someone's breath.

'Indeed,' observed a hard voice somewhat thickened with phlegm. 'The construction is . . . *unique.*'

'We are to retrieve what we came for and that is all.' This was a thinner voice, also male.

'Don't be such a woman,' the hard-voiced man snarled. 'Mr Fochtmann must make an estimation – it is the entire purpose of our errand.'

'It is not our *entire* purpose,' replied the man by the door. 'There are materials to gather, documents to find –'

'Don't be a fool,' growled the hard voice, 'and step *inside*!'

Chang could hear footsteps as someone came further into the carriage, and then knuckles rapping against the glass lid of the coffin. He gripped his stick, ready to draw the dagger and slash upwards. With a good first cut he could scramble out before these two were on him –

At once Chang started – the thin voice – it was Rawsbarthe, the Ministry man he'd found at the Trappings' house – he was sure of it! And the hard voice . . . could that be Aspiche? The tone was clotted . . . and Colonel Aspiche *had* looked very ill . . .

'I have no wish to come between you gentlemen,' said a third voice, smooth and diplomatic. This was the third man, who had whistled; Aspiche had said his name – Fochtmann. 'Indeed, though I have been summoned by the Privy Council –'

'By the Duke of Stäelmaere,' corrected Rawsbarthe.

'Of course – by His Grace himself. Yet whether I may be of *service* to the Duke remains to be seen. Though I know *of* him, I am unfamiliar with the precise, ah, practical . . . *achievements* of the Comte d'Orkancz . . . though their scope is evident just from where we stand.'

'You are a colleague of Doctor Lorenz,' observed Aspiche, as if this were evidence enough.

'Certainly,' replied Fochtmann. He rapped again on the curved glass, directly above Chang's face, as if gauging the thickness. 'Though in truth more his *rival*. I am curious . . . is Doctor Lorenz *aware* you have contacted me?'

Neither of the other two men answered until, the moment having become awkward, Rawsbarthe muttered, 'It is, ah, possible that Doctor Lorenz is dead.'

'*Indeed?*'

'It is, more precisely . . . probable.'

'Does that change anything?' Aspiche's hard tone was obliquely threatening.

'No change at all,' replied Fochtmann smoothly, adding with a smile Chang could not see but knew was there, 'save perhaps the size of my fee.'

At this Fochtmann stepped away from the coffin-chest and began taking formal stock of the room, calling notes or instructions to Rawsbarthe, who was writing them down. Between these calls and the sound of Fochtmann's rummaging, Chang was unable to make out the private conversation between Aspiche and Rawsbarthe, low and under their breaths . . . 'Bascombe assured me' . . . 'depletion of the quarry' . . . 'despatched vessels' . . . 'no word from Macklenburg' . . .

Fochtmann fell silent, a slick clicking indicating that he was occupied with a rack of the glass bullets. Chang heard Aspiche remark quietly, 'You say he asked about *me*? About my *health*?'

'He did, Colonel,' replied Rawsbarthe, 'and rather implied that your being alive was a surprise.'

'What the devil does he know?' snarled Aspiche, and then sneezed loudly and moistly, twice. 'My apologies – this damned . . . condition –'

'It is seasonal, I think,' sniffed Rawsbarthe. 'The shifting weather – as the days become warmer, one's body is never prepared –'

'I am sure you are right. And these wretched *chills* . . .'

Fochtmann resumed calling out figures – perhaps the number of glass bullets, or their estimated weight, or – who knew? – the purity of refinement. The man's tone remained cheerful with each detail: Chang became certain that Fochtmann and Lorenz were the bitterest of enemies, and that Fochtmann's presence signified a desperation to understand the science of the slain Comte. Chang smiled at being that odious man's executioner, and causing so much trouble for so many who deserved it.

Fochtmann's investigations moved to the large cabinet, sorting through the same papers Chang had so recently ransacked.

'And all this time I thought Lorenz was a fool,' he whispered. 'Even if the ideas belonged to d'Orkancz, the construction is magnificent, delightful!'

'Delightful?' asked Colonel Aspiche.

'What other word for such cleanly made machines?' cried Fochtmann. 'They can be *improved* – my own revisions already suggest themselves – but the *flow*, the clarity of . . .' The man chuckled merrily. 'Of *power*! And you are certain Lorenz is dead?'

'It is likely,' said Rawsbarthe.

Fochtmann cackled. 'And you *promise* me, it is *only* Lorenz – of men at the Institute, in industry – who *knows* of this, this *vein* of – of –'

'Alchemy,' said Aspiche.

Fochtmann rolled his eyes.

'According to the Comte,' continued Aspiche.

Fochtmann exhaled in pointed exasperation. 'While the basic properties of the glass alone are beyond question –'

'They are a matter of fact,' Aspiche snapped.

'The Comte's writings are the ravings of a madman,' replied Fochtmann. 'A madman with some small sense of insight. One sees the approving notations of others – engineers, architects of science – and so one studies that insight more scrupulously than the mania would suggest. These machines, this very carriage – one cannot gainsay concrete *results* . . .' Fochtmann paused. 'Or . . . for another example . . . these books . . .'

'Books?' asked Rawsbarthe innocently.

'Prominently described in the notes. Apparently a most singular exploitation of the . . . *acquisitive* . . . properties of indigo glass.'

'I would not know,' said Rawsbarthe.

Aspiche remained silent.

'Not that I have seen such a thing,' Fochtmann went on easily. 'Indeed "book" may merely be a term for compiling knowledge. Every visionary has his own vocabulary, and such terms are always strange to those outside its understanding. What is significant about the mention of "book", of course, is how as a device it embodies the capacity of indigo clay – in an explicit indication of *function*. Indeed, many of the major machines seem to employ these "glass books" in their actual workings. But then again – as a man of science, one looks for clues! You gentlemen will see yourselves, in this very carriage, the prevalent inlay of *orange* metals – an alloy made to very exact specifications – around the ceiling, between the floor tiles, around each piece of glass . . .'

'What is it?' asked Rawsbarthe, with concern.

'Rather, *why* is it?' chuckled Fochtmann. 'The effect is deliberate – could it have been solely in the service of *beauty*? Where is the serious intent? *I* cannot say – you must give me time to read before we arrive – I will take these papers to a compartment where I may commune with my own thoughts.'

'Does this mean you have accepted the Duke's commission?' asked Rawsbarthe.

'It does indeed, sir. How could I refuse His Grace's personal invitation?'

'Excellent,' said Rawsbarthe. 'Welcome news. Our situation –'

Aspiche cleared his throat.

'Colonel?' asked Fochtmann.

'I am sure His Grace will cherish your dedication,' said Aspiche. 'But *I* wonder . . . if . . . for the time being . . . the three of us might keep word of your . . . *discoveries* . . . amongst ourselves.'

No one spoke.

Rawsbarthe sniffed. 'Ah . . . well . . . yes, that seems to me a rather . . . interesting . . . and *prudent* suggestion. Especially as Mr Fochtmann has made clear the *value* of this – what is the word? – *lode* of unknown science.'

'Unknown and *provocative*,' said Aspiche.

'Provocative and *powerful*,' said Rawsbarthe.

'Mr Fochtmann?' asked Aspiche.

'Why should I object to that?' replied Fochtmann. 'I should hardly expect the Queen's own brother to attend to every small detail.'

'Then we have an understanding?'

'I believe we do. I will share my immediate findings only with you two gentlemen, and the three of us together will determine . . . further steps.'

'It is *sensible*,' said Rawsbarthe.

'It is.' Chang could imagine the greedy smile on Fochtmann's lips. 'Yet this material is copious, and we have a very little time. If you gentlemen would excuse me . . .'

A hand rapped sharply on the glass cover above Chang's face.

'And what is this large thing?' asked Rawsbarthe, his voice only inches away.

Chang looked up to see the hand now rubbing on the glass, as if to clear away the darkness and peer more clearly inside.

'Do you know its purpose?'

'Not until I've done more study,' answered Fochtmann.

'Should we not open it and look?'

'If you are keen to do so,' replied Fochtmann, 'by all means.'

Rawsbarthe's hand moved to the edge of the glass and gave it an exploratory nudge, realized how heavy it was, and then put both hands upon it, ready to push harder.

'It was where the Comte had the woman,' said Aspiche.

'What woman?' asked Fochtmann.

'His oriental harlot. *Angelique*. Something had been done to her, she became ill. He kept her alive there, to reach Harschmort – you see the brass boxes, and the tubes that feed inside. Blue water was pumped through them, thick as glue –'

'She was ill?' asked Rawsbarthe.

'The Comte called it an "imbalance of heat" or some such.'

'What happened to her?'

'She *died*.'

No one spoke. Fochtmann cleared his throat.

'On the chance – seeing there is much we do not yet understand – that her illness might be . . . *catchable* . . .'

Rawsbarthe plucked his hands away as if the coffin had become a hot stove.

'Indeed, yes. Besides, we have more than enough to occupy our time.'

Chang waited to make sure that they'd closed the steel door behind them before he raised the glass top with both hands. He knew by the carriage's rocking gait that they had left the tunnels under Stropping and were crossing open country. He extricated himself, one long leg at a time, from Angelique's coffin, replaced the lid, and crossed to each window in turn, all equally shuttered in black-painted steel. Not that he needed to see a thing – Chang knew he was being taken back to Harschmort.

There were immediate questions he needed to answer – where the black carriage had been placed in the whole of the train, how many dragoons were aboard and where – and there were decisions to make, most importantly whether he ought to accept his fate and take his enquiries to Harschmort directly or do his best to escape the train while it was still close to the city. Chang stretched his shoulders – tight after his time in the coffin

– and turned his neck, the bones answering with an audible click. Fochtmann might not have wanted to deal with the coffin when his arms were
full of papers that piqued his curiosity, but he would certainly do so upon
arrival. The black carriage would be studied, perhaps even dismantled, as
a means of explaining the Comte's science. This might begin even sooner –
it was at least another hour to Harschmort. He needed to leave immediately.

The door the three men had used to enter and exit led to a carriage of
passenger compartments – Fochtmann had said as much – so Chang crossed
to the opposite door and took out his keys. Unless a dragoon had been
posted on the outer platform, it was highly unlikely, with the noise of the
train, anyone would hear the turning of his key. Still, it was with a deliberate
slowness that Chang twisted his hand until the inner lockings caught. He
snatched up his stick before opening the door, ready to strike at anyone
there. No one. Chang stepped into the roar of the train track, the wind
flapping his coat around him.

Ahead was another passenger carriage, the flaring sunlight preventing
him from seeing anything inside. Chang crossed the jouncing platform and
pressed his face against the window. Coming straight towards him was a
red-coated dragoon, wearing his brass helmet, in that very instant glancing
down to take something from an inside pocket. He would look up and see
Chang. Chang spun and launched himself onto the narrow metal ladder
bolted to the passenger carriage. As the door opened, he flattened himself
against the vibrating ladder, the tracks racing past below his feet.

The dragoon stepped out onto the platform, a half-smoked cheroot in
his mouth, sabre knocking against the door, the horse-hair crest of his
helmet whipping wildly in the wind. In his gloved hand was a pewter flask.
The marks on his collar and epaulettes showed a captain's rank . . . then
Chang saw the fair whiskers slipping out from beneath the brass helmet,
pale as corn silk . . . It had to be his adversary from the north – the very
Captain who had evaded him in the forest and in Karthe and in the darkness
of Helliott Street. What was he doing with the black carriage – alone, and
apart from his commanding officer? Or was he just nipping whisky?

It was not the whisky. The officer peered back where he'd come –
pressing his face to the glass (helmet clicking at impact), just as Chang had

done against the glare – before crossing to the metal door. Chang wondered
at the fact he had not been seen, but knew that where one did not expect
something one often neglected to look. The dragoon stuffed the flask back
in his tunic and came out with something else . . . a large metal key. He
inserted it quickly into the black carriage's lock, standing casually so
anyone who happened to see him might think he was merely smoking.
Chang heard the snap of the bolts in the door . . . but instead of pushing it
open, the officer merely sealed it shut again and then tucked the key back
in his tunic.

The dragoon turned and saw him.

The soldier's hand shot to his sabre hilt. Holding tightly to the ladder,
Chang kicked both legs at the Captain, one sharply to his chest and the
other across his jaw, knocking him back into the metal door and then, with
a dangerous stumble, into the rail of chain. Abandoning his attempt to
draw his weapon, the man desperately caught hold with both hands to
prevent toppling over. The kick left Chang hanging for a sickening moment
by his hands, boots just above the implacably deadly wheels. He caught a
leg on the lowest rung and tried another kick – but the Captain, his face
red where Chang's boot had landed, snatched hold of Chang's ankle and
yanked hard to pull him from the ladder to his death.

Chang held fast. The Captain pulled again, grunting aloud, boots slipping
on the metal platform. Chang held, less certainly, and then, because he
could not withstand a third pull, let go with one hand and stabbed his stick
like a blunt court sword into the Captain's face. The officer flinched and
swore aloud – blood welling under his eye. Dangling by one hand, Chang
swung his other boot in a sweeping kick that caught the officer square on
the ear, bouncing his brass helmet onto the trackside and the man again
into the rail of loose chain, where he overbalanced and began to jackknife
off the platform.

Before he could fall, Chang shot both legs forward and wrapped them
tightly around the fellow's neck. The Captain leant perilously forward,
suspended over an abyss of rushing rail track, the chain caught uselessly
below his waist, his open hands pawing the air. It seemed as if he must fall,
but Chang held strong, looping both arms tight around the iron rungs,

grimacing with the effort. Neither man moved, the train roaring around them. Then the officer carefully twisted his head to meet Chang's gaze. He said nothing, but his eyes burnt with hatred and with fear.

'Whose key?' called Chang, loud enough for the man to hear above the wheels.

'Yours, if you want it,' sneered the Captain. 'Of course, if you drop me –'

'I *have* one.' Chang dug his heel hard into the man's jugular. 'Where did you get *yours*? Aspiche?'

'Leveret.'

'You searched Leveret's home. Does Aspiche know you have that key?'

The man spat. 'If he knew, why would I be out here on my own?'

'What about the woman?'

'What about her? No one knows where she went!'

Chang's question had been about Mrs Marchmoor, not Charlotte Trapping. But he nodded, playing along. 'Where do *you* think she went?'

'We can have this chat perfectly well on the damned platform,' the officer grunted. 'I can feel your bloody legs slipping. We may well be of use to one another –'

'You're a liar.'

'My point exactly,' the Captain wheezed. 'You have caught me out on forbidden business . . . the advantage is all yours . . .'

The man's point was echoed by a growing ache in Cardinal Chang's arms. With a grunt he heaved the Captain back towards the platform. The man wavered, his fair hair blowing around his face, then caught the chain and dropped safely to his knees. By the time he looked up, Chang had vaulted onto the shaking platform and pulled apart his stick, the dagger held ready at the level of the Captain's eyes. The officer looked past Chang at the carriage door.

'Not the best place for a private conversation,' he called.

Chang ignored this. 'Why were you in that carriage at all? Why not in the back – with your betters?'

'Would *you* trust them – my *betters*?'

'If I were you, or your betters' . . . master?'

The man shrugged, as if the question answered itself.

'What is your *duty* here?' asked Chang impatiently.

'What was my duty in the north?' the Captain replied. 'As one says in the Latin, *ad hoc*.'

The man's features were boyish, but his eyes were hard, as if too early disillusioned by the temptations available to his station.

'A great deal has changed in the city since we both left it,' said Chang.

The man shrugged again. Chang nodded at the key in the man's tunic. 'But I suppose change begets opportunity.'

'Have you *seen* their faces?' replied the Captain, with a wicked smile. 'My God, by the *smell* alone – very soon there will be gaps in the upper echelons. And every gap needs filling –'

'You were telling me about the woman.'

The officer smiled, rubbing his throat. As he did, Chang noticed the man's face seemed more pale than it had in the woods, only days earlier. Fatigue? Or was he sick too, without knowing it?

'Mrs Trapping has disappeared.'

'So has Leveret.'

'Leveret's a dull clot. He will be as obvious in his hiding place as a schoolboy crouching under a table.'

'Is Charlotte Trapping a clot?'

'Even more than Leveret. She is a society widow. She is marooned – she has no *skills*. The powerful brother has lost his mind, and the other brother . . . has vanished.'

'Along with the Contessa . . . and everyone else on the airship.'

'Quite a tragic journey, that,' said the Captain. 'A comprehensive loss for the nation.'

Chang studied the man's face, as he knew the man studied his. The Captain had been in the train yard along with Chang; it was entirely possible he too had seen the Contessa and Xonck. In fact, he *must* have seen them – why else would the Ministries be searching Stropping with such vigour?

'As you say . . . there may be opportunities . . . Mrs Trapping –' The Captain spoke carefully.

'What can a woman matter?' Chang interrupted. 'Especially her?'

'The Privy Council believes Mrs Trapping matters a great deal. Makes a fellow think . . .'

'Think *what*?' asked Chang, stepping closer.

The dragoon glanced at the knife blade and then up to Chang, girlish curls framing a mirthless smile. 'That the Privy Council has lost its *head*.'

'Get out your key.'

Chang tossed the dragoon's sabre behind him on the chaise longue. He looked into the open coffin, where the Captain lay, arms tucked tightly to his side, face set with displeasure.

'What is your name?' asked Chang.

'Tackham. David Tackham.'

'They will find you when we arrive, if not before.'

'I assure you, it is not necessary –'

'It is this or cutting your throat,' said Chang.

'My point being such a choice does not *have* to be –'

'What do you know of this Fochtmann?'

Tackham sighed. 'Nothing at all. Engineer – invented some useful . . . thingummy –'

'And Rawsbarthe?'

'Another Foreign Ministry stick insect. Why the Duke entrusts such weak tea to do his bidding –'

'Where is Margaret Hooke?'

'Who?'

'Mrs *Marchmoor*.'

'*Who?*'

'Where is Charlotte Trapping?'

'As I have *told* you –'

'Who is Elöise Dujong?'

'I've not the slightest idea –'

'Then where is Captain Smythe?'

Tackham was taken aback and smiled, unsure of the question's intent.

'I beg your pardon?'

'Captain *Smythe*,' snarled Chang. 'Your brother officer.'

'Yes, of course – I just don't know why *you* would be asking, of all people!'

'*Answer* me.'

'Captain Smythe is dead. Shot in the back and strangled where he lay – on the roof of Harschmort House, before the airship went aloft. Shot and strangled by *you*, according to every account I have heard. Assuming you *are* the infamous Cardinal Chang –'

Chang was no longer listening. He dropped the glass lid into place and shot the bolts, trapping Tackham inside. Perhaps the man would be able to kick his way free. Chang did not especially care.

The light of the next car was all wrong – brighter than it should have been. Chang craned his head around the wall of what he assumed was the first compartment, only to see that the compartment was not only empty of people but of seats and luggage racks as well. Moreover, the walls between this compartment and the next two had been knocked down. Chang silently crossed this opened space, and craned round again to find another three compartments enlarged into one. This new room was cluttered with boxes and occupied by a man in a black coat, sitting with his back to Chang at a table of stacked crates piled high with notebooks. Chang did not move . . . and neither did the man. Chang stalked closer, slipping the dagger from his stick. The man's face was pale, red around the nose and eyes. A crust of blood lined his nearest ear. He rocked gently with the motion of the train, upright but quite asleep.

If the train was going to Harschmort with so much empty space, its aim must be to collect whatever of the Comte's scientific paraphernalia still remained. What would prompt such an expedition, and on such a scale? It could not have been the return of Francis Xonck – Aspiche and his men had received orders to collect the black carriage before Xonck arrived at Stropping, probably even before Tackham could have confirmed Xonck was alive. Chang imagined all the titled and moneyed adherents the Cabal had suborned for various schemes, all waiting greedily, desperate for the orders that would make them exceedingly rich and powerful . . . and yet it was clear, from the soldiers controlling Stropping Station and the reclamation of the black carriage, that something *was* happening. Was the plotting of Aspiche and Rawsbarthe part of it? Or were they already the first sign of rebellion?

There was one more compartment. Going to it would put Chang in the line of sight of the sleeping man, but even if the fellow woke, who could he call on for help?

Chang peered around the wall. Curled on the far seat lay a girl in a lilac dress, perhaps eight years old, and next to her, his head having sagged into the girl's lap, a boy of five in a black velvet suit. The near row of seats held a still younger boy, in a matching suit, save he had kicked off his shoes. He sat next to another sleeping man in a black coat with a sheaf of papers on his lap. Chang tilted his head to see the man's face: fair, with a pale, waxed moustache, just enough like the diplomat Bascombe to spark contempt. The face bore no signs of the degenerative pallor. The man's fingernails, however, were splitting and red. Another look at the man's face – the eyelids were noticeably gummed – and Chang stepped back from view.

These were Charlotte Trapping's three children.

He looked again, only to find the girl, eyes now open, staring directly back at him. Chang froze. The girl did not make a sound. She glanced quickly to her sleeping Ministry guardian, then to Chang's black lenses. Her face betrayed no fear – though he knew her world had been uprooted like a tree: both parents gone, in the custody of men she did not know. His own appearance must seem to her like something from a carnival. Yet the girl merely watched him.

> The chilling air above a winter stream
> A stab of doubt enrobing every day

Why did this come into his head now? More of DuVine's 'Christina', a poem Chang did not so much enjoy as feel subject to. With his painstaking reading habits he had lived in the work's incandescent world for *days*: an archaic story of a woman bewitched by a wizard who had died, taking to his grave the secret of her enchantment, and of her doomed lover, unable to penetrate the magic – 'a sheet of lead enwrapping a corse' – yet unwilling to abandon his love . . . or was it merely impossible to remember a life before his efforts?

None of this was helping.

He could do nothing for the Trapping girl. In two steps Chang was through the far door, hoping the sudden rush of noise from the platform did not wake the other children or the man. Before him was the coal wagon. As he climbed to it, the train rattled past Raaxfall Station without slowing. At this pace they would reach the Orange Locks in under an hour.

Chang leapt off the train – hanging from the coal wagon ladder – half-way between St Porte and Orange Locks. He landed without breaking his ankle and rolled into the cover of a copse of low trees. He stayed down until the train was well past, collected his stick from where he had thrown it before jumping, and began his hike to Robert Vandaariff's mansion.

Why had he not cut Tackham's throat? Was it because the man had revealed himself as the greedy minion of fools? Or was Chang still hesitant to spill the blood of any 4th Dragoon? Captain Smythe had saved his life more than once, *and* the lives of Miss Temple and Svenson. Chang felt his jaw tighten at the utter waste of the man's death – shot from behind on the roof of Harschmort, and no doubt finished off by Francis Xonck. Was that a surprise? What other reward did decency receive in this world? Chang shook his head. Tackham must be newly promoted in Smythe's stead – Aspiche's hand-picked favourite. And yet, for all that he despised Aspiche as a hypocritical ass, Chang had to allow the man knew his soldiering – and knew his men. Tackham's character was no mystery to Aspiche – and the choice simply confirmed where Aspiche's intentions truly lay, as fully evidenced by the conversation he'd just overheard in the black carriage. It was the ambition of such trusted underlings as Roger Bascombe and Caroline Stearne that had brought the Cabal to ruin in the airship. Why should Colonel Aspiche be any more loyal?

Chang's mind went back to Tackham. That he had been an instant away from killing him in the woods meant nothing – such careening circumstances could happen to anyone. The man was unquestionably dangerous. Chang spat into a ditch as he jumped across, his heels sinking into the muddy earth. No, it did mean *one* thing – that Tackham would be particularly keen to cut him down.

The idea was a whetstone for Chang's bitterness. He vaulted another ditch, wider than the last, the water's surface swirling with what looked like ash. Harschmort was visible now, like the ridged scar of a bullet in an expanse of unblemished skin. He wondered about its master, shut indoors under false quarantine. Was there *anything* remaining of the man who had once bent a continent to his will?

Bearing in mind that the party from the train might arrive before him in their coaches, Chang angled his approach well to the far side of the gardens, between the estate and the sea. Several hollows within the dunes had been flecked with ash, probably just the normal burning of leaves or scrub that came with any garden the ridiculous size of Harschmort's. By the time he approached a scatter of outlying sheds, his attention was focused on anyone watching from the French doors or an upstairs window. Chang waited, saw no one, and dashed across to the nearest fragile glass door. A quick jab of his dagger into the lock, and one sharp turn to pop the bolt. He was in.

Robert Vandaariff's office and private apartments lay on the opposite side of the massive house, but Chang was near to at least one of his targets. He poked his head into a white-tiled corridor that ran the length of the entire wing, off of which lay the stairway to the lower levels. He readied his stick, for the corridor was not empty.

An elderly man in black livery lay on his back, his face dark and wet. Chang advanced quietly, close to the wall. The servant's eyelids fluttered. Blood had poured from his nose and smeared itself over the near half of his face, but the nose itself was not bruised or red – it did not seem he had been *struck*. Chang looked up. Further down the hallway, towards the centre of the house . . . a strangled cry . . . a man's voice? He waited. Silence, but in it as he listened, even to his limited senses, penetrated the odour of smoke. Could the garden fires have drifted indoors? Chang abruptly stepped to the staircase door and hurried down.

*

The Comte's laboratory was a blackened shambles. Chang stood in the doorway, attempting to remember the room as it had been, the better to discern the intentions of whoever had set the fire. That it was deliberate he had no question, and from the density of the reek he knew it had occurred within the last few days. He stepped over a fallen beam and the half-charred remnants of a wooden chair. To the left had been the Comte's laboratory proper. This had been the centre of the fire (not surprising, given the density of volatile chemicals), and the balcony above it was completely consumed, the stone walls behind scorched to the cracked and blackened ceiling. Books had been pulled from the walls and hurled into the flames, along with the Comte's implements, now reduced to twisted lumps of metal sticking up from the ashes. Indeed, it seemed like every sign of the Comte d'Orkancz's work had been purposefully destroyed . . . except . . .

Chang's eyes went to the walls, where the *Annunciation* had been hung. This was an enormous canvas cut into thirteen parts, portraying the Comte's blasphemous interpretation of Mary's visitation from the angel (whose skin was a tell-tale blue). When the painting was seen in isolated fragments, its lurid, sexual intent might not have been immediately apparent, but with the slightest study the nasty amusement infusing the artist's composition was both obvious and appalling. But, most importantly, the rear of each canvas had been covered with alchemical formulae – explaining, if one knew how to read the Comte's symbolic codes, vital secrets about the properties of indigo clay. That these too had been destroyed . . .

Chang frowned, comparing the scorch marks on that part of the wall with the rest of the room . . . there was no difference at all. If the thirteen paintings had burnt, the chemicals embedded in the paint should have marked the walls with the same livid whorls of burnt colour scored across the marble worktop. He took another few steps, wondering if the paintings had simply been taken from the walls and thrown into the fire directly . . . it was possible, to be sure . . . but was it also possible they had been saved? It all depended on who had set the blaze and why. Chang took another step and a curl of glass popped to pieces beneath his boot.

The skin at the back of his neck suddenly went cold. The floor was littered with glass – broken, blackened, but still glinting blue . . . Angelique.

Chang knelt despite himself, setting his stick on the floor, and reached out a gloved hand, touching the pieces – faceted pebbles, with one or two long, curving fragments – with just the tips of his fingers, gently, as if he were tracing them across her skin.

In the corridor were footsteps, and he spun on his heels, one hand snapping up the stick and the other – the most natural and yet the stupidest impulse in the world – stabbing down at the floor to maintain his balance. Chang felt the sharp pain in his palm, just as the black cloak of Francis Xonck flitted past the doorway. But then Xonck was forgotten, for when the blue glass shard penetrated his flesh, Chang's mind was suddenly swallowed up . . . with *hers*.

Angelique stood in her small room at the Old Palace brothel, wearing a pale silk robe, her hair hanging wet and fragrant with sandalwood – Chang knew the smell only because she herself had taken such pleasure in it, but he experienced it now, the sensation of scent, in his *mind*, with a deranging vividness well beyond him in life – facing an open cabinet set with five empty shelves. On a chair next to her and on the small pallet bed were piles of clothing, dresses and robes and underthings and shoes and then a small carved wooden box, cheaply bought from the markets near St Isobel's. From her memory he knew the box contained every bit of meagre jewellery that she owned. As she looked at the empty shelves, Chang felt from Angelique such a *surge* of pleasure – of arrival, of security, of an answer so gratefully received to a question Chang himself had never wanted to ask – and realized that this was her first ever room of her own, where her things would not be stolen, where she might put a printed postcard or a picture cut from a coloured newspaper on the wall without it disappearing the next day – and her *happiness*, to begin to place her clothing in the cabinet, rejoicing in the extent of her possessions, shifting each piece with delight from shelf to shelf just to stretch out the task, beaming with pleasure at her escape from the degradations of the brothels that had so far been her life, chuckling with anticipation at the advantages she was sure to find – at the mere prospect of –

*

Chang wrenched out the shard from his palm and threw it away into the wreckage, tearing the glove from his stricken hand, his concentration desperately held in the face of the continuing – a pulsing echo even after the glass was gone – repetition of Angelique's captured happiness pressing inescapably at his brain. The glove came off at last, and he saw his palm starred with blue glass – newly made from contact with his own blood – a fat, flattened, still-biting spider, his fingers clutching at its impossibly cold burn. Thankful it had gone into his left hand, Chang pulled the razor from his pocket and flicked it open. With an excruciating burst of pain he sliced under the glass and then, blood pooling brightly beneath the blade, did his best to prise it up. For a moment it would not come, pulling cruelly. Chang bit his lip, digging deeper with the razor. The spiked lozenge of glass flipped free, leaving his palm a raw seething mess. Chang swore aloud. He wrapped a handkerchief tight around the wound, pulling the knot with his teeth. He snatched up his stick and stumbled after Xonck – how much time had he lost? Chang reeled like a drunkard but kept going, the smell of her hair in his mind like a poison.

He burst back onto the main floor, past the unmoving elderly servant, striding too recklessly towards the centre of the house. Ahead of him were jostling footsteps, voices – a crowd of people – Aspiche and his dragoons? No, it was a gang of servants from Harschmort, all in Vandaariff's black livery, rushing ahead of him into the ballroom. Chang felt a spur of curiosity – it was easier than thinking – and followed. Someone shouted over the tumble of voices – a man just come in from the French doors. Chang could not see him, but his voice was loud and very angry.

'Let me have it!' the man cried. 'There is no time!'

'But it is *mine*!' protested the servant.

'There is no *time*!' the man cried again, and lunged – Chang could tell from the sudden swirl of bodies – wrestling desperately for whatever it was he sought.

Without warning, the memory of Angelique in her room rose to swallow him once more. Again he was in her body, but this time more deeply, feeling so intimately the strength of her limbs, the weight of them, the particular distribution of female flesh, the pins in her hair, and all of it infused with her *happiness*.

He shook his head like a dog, keeping his glasses in place with his bandaged hand, wondering what had set off the spell – a perfume, the sight of an open cabinet? He had prised the glass out of his hand – the memory ought to be gone! And yet he could sense it still, gliding beneath the surface of his thought like a pikefish in a pond, waiting to sink its sweet teeth into his scarcely coherent will. He snapped his eyes to the open French door and the suddenly motionless crowd of servants.

From the garden came a pistol shot, and then a hideous scream.

He shouldered his way into the garden. A second, more terrible fire had caused the ornamental garden to collapse in on the cathedral chamber below, leaving a massive ruined pit from which fumes and foul vapours continued to rise. Near to the edge, grappling like unnatural statues amidst the scorched greenery, were Francis Xonck and Mrs Marchmoor. Xonck writhed against the glass woman's hand, two fingers of which were buried in his chest like a dagger. On the grass lay two men – one, by his iron-grey hair and blue sash, Chang knew as the Duke of Stäelmaere. The other, his head bloodied, looked like a Ministry peon. Directly in front of Chang but facing the garden stood a second Ministry official, a smoking pistol extended in his hand. But the man hesitated to shoot again, for Mrs Marchmoor and Francis Xonck were still entwined.

Chang had no such scruples. He stabbed the tip of his stick hard into the Ministry man's right kidney, deftly snatched the pistol as the man arched his back in pain, and then kicked the back of the fellow's knee, dropping him to the grass. Chang strode towards the conjoined pair of his enemies and fired, the pistol kicking at his grip. The bullet flew between them – it was not his weapon, or perhaps he could not choose which of the two he wanted to kill more – and cut across Margaret Hooke's wrist, chipping the glass and sending a single pale fissure forward into her hand. Xonck grunted with pain and twisted, exerting pressure on the damaged hand. As Chang aimed again, her wrist began to give, puffs of blue smoke rising out from the cracks. Xonck hurled himself away, screaming with agony, and the hand sheared off, its jagged stump sparking glass chips like the spout of a spitting kettle.

Chang staggered, as if he had borne the great blast of a silent explosion. He looked behind him. The servants of Harschmort had as one collapsed to their hands and knees, holding their heads in pain. He could not hear. He looked back to Mrs Marchmoor, waving her broken limb like a smoking branch, staggering. Xonck was on his back, pulling at the shattered fingers still penetrating his chest. How had the silent explosion of Margaret Hooke's anguish left him standing while flattening everyone else?

Chang raised the pistol for another shot. Angelique . . . he felt the rising sensation of her flesh once more, in every limb – he shook his head, it was no time – it was *never* time, was not right, could not be borne – how could she be *in* him when he knew she had not cared? He blinked his eyes – he could not free his mind – he could not *see* – he fired blindly at the woman, then just as recklessly at Xonck. Angelique would not leave him. Chang thrashed like a bull beset with stinging bees, except the bees were all beneath his skin. He moaned at the complete idiocy of his predicament, even as he sank, helpless, to his knees, and his mind surrendered to the feel of silk pyjamas.

SIX

CANAL

Doctor Svenson stared at the purple stone in the trainman's open palm for three seconds, just long enough for the men encircling him to take in his silence and the stricken pallor of his face, before reaching to take it with his left hand, his right occupied with Mr Potts's revolver. The man who had spoken still indicated with an extended arm the first carriage of the train. Without a word Svenson walked towards it, his pace quickening. He was up the five iron stairs in two steps, and then, far too soon it seemed, standing at the compartment's open door.

Elöise lay in her black dress, with one arm pinned beneath her and the other awkwardly splayed above her head. Svenson set the revolver on the nearest seat and sank to his knees, whispering her name. Behind in the corridor came shuffling bootsteps. Svenson turned, aware that his face was flushed and that his voice held firm by the scarcest margin.

'Send men to search! The killers! They could still be anywhere!'

Svenson shifted forward, stuffing the purple stone into the pocket of his trousers, again whispering her name as if it were a spell. He placed two fingers against the pulse in her throat. Her flesh was still warm . . . but cooling . . . he felt nothing . . . but then – some birdlike tremor, was it possible? No, his own hands were shaking – he was unable to perform a simple examination, nerves of an untempered student. If he had only been here sooner, even a few minutes! His boots ground unpleasantly against the floor. He looked down and saw glittering dust – a scattering of shattered blue glass across the polished wood.

Francis Xonck. If Svenson had not been such a helpless wretch at the mining camp – if it had been Chang instead of him – Elöise might still be living.

He delicately rolled her onto her back, wincing at the lifeless loll of her head . . . at the base of her sternum, a dark circle, smaller than his monocle, soaking the black fabric and catching the lantern light . . . blood. The relatively small amount spoke to a deep, suddenly mortal wound. He touched the stain with a finger to judge how long ago it had occurred.

The stain was solid and clicked against his nail, like a shining black coin set into the cloth. It was glass.

'A knife – sharp as you have – at once!'

He snapped his fingers as the men hurriedly patted their pockets, aware he was again burying heartbreak under a shovelful of useless effort. He looked down at Elöise's impossibly pale face . . .

Doctor Svenson's breath stopped. Was it only the light? At once he feverishly dug into his coat. A man stepped forward with a knife.

'Not now – not now!' he cried, and pulled free his silver cigarette case.

He rubbed the shining surface violently across his trouser-leg and leant forward, cradling her head and holding the polished metal directly before her parted lips. He waited . . . waited . . . bit his lip to draw blood . . . and then felt a surge of desperate joy as the surface fogged ever so delicately, an infinitesimal pearling.

'This woman is alive!' he cried. 'Hot water! Clean linen – whatever you have! At once!'

Svenson thrashed out of the horrible stiff coat. He snapped his fingers again at the man with the knife and snatched it away – an old pen-knife, its thin blade nothing like sharp enough. He put a hand again to Elöise's throat and then her forehead, which was cold and moist, and unbuttoned the black dress to either side of the tight glass disc, which seemed fixed through to her skin. Svenson carefully plucked up the dress and sawed a quick circle around the glass. The wound was just at the lowest joint of her ribcage. Had the cartilage shattered Xonck's glass stiletto, or had the blade thrust past, penetrating her vital organs? That would be an injury he could scarcely address with a fully equipped surgical theatre.

He gently palpated the paper-white skin around the dark lozenge, seeking the submerged hardness of a deeper plume of glass. The skin was colder around the wound. Her lips had darkened in the seconds she'd been on her back.

Svenson turned savagely to the men clustered at the door. 'Where is the water? She will die without it!'

A man in blue uniform edged towards Svenson and cleared his throat. 'The train, sir – the schedule –'

'I do not give a damn for your schedule!' cried Svenson.

A ring of blued flesh was spreading before his eyes across Elöise's abdomen. He could not wait for the water. He pulled the skin taut with the fingers of his left hand and edged the knife beneath the disc of glass. A sharp chop and the glass came free with only a few splintered chips. Elöise gasped, but when he glanced to her face she was no closer to her senses. What was more, part of the wound had coagulated at once back into glass. The remaining hole was small, perhaps a half-inch wide – but how deep did it go? How could he dig without any way to control the bleeding? Would more bleeding simply transform into more blue glass and make things worse? Svenson was sure it was the toxic quality of the glass itself, more than the puncture, that was killing her. He thought back to Chang's damaged lungs. The orange liquid – if only he had some now! – had dissolved the glass Chang had inhaled, allowing him to spit it up like the gelatinous detritus of any chest cold, removing it in a way surgery never could have. And once it was done the man had regained his strength with striking rapidity.

But Svenson had no orange liquid. There was nothing else for it. He inserted the knife blade into the wound – and then cursed out loud in German as the entire compartment lurched around him. The train was moving.

'God damn!' he cried to the men in the doorway. 'What is this idiocy?'

'It is the schedule,' protested the uniformed guard. 'I have tried to explain –'

'She will die!' barked Svenson.

None of the clustered men spoke, stepping away as the guard appeared in the doorway.

'I hope the lady will not. And I am happy to postpone any questions of payment – of your fares – until – ah – we know if there will be – that is – one or two of you.'

Svenson glared at the man, thought better of anything he could possibly say, and spun back to Elöise, painfully aware of the tiny shakes now racking her body. He parted the wound again, his own fingers unsteady, the edge of the glass flecking new chips into the shimmering, tight cavity as it nicked her flesh. The knife would not work. He set it down and dug in his pocket for a handkerchief, and then wrapped it around his fingers. With a sharp push that sparked another gasp from Elöise, Svenson took hold of the spike and wrenched it out. He folded the handkerchief and held it over the wound – clean flowing blood staining the cloth – and eased it away. The wound was not deep. The glass was gone.

When the hot water and linen finally arrived, Svenson cleaned and dressed the wound, and settled Elöise onto a row of seats. He brooded with a cigarette, watching her face for some sign he could not quite name. Perhaps he simply wanted to know she would survive, so he could leave with a clear conscience, as he had left Miss Temple . . .

Svenson sat bolt upright in his seat. What had he been thinking? He was an idiot, a negligent fool – they were miles beyond Karthe with no way to return. Miss Temple must have travelled to Karthe with Elöise . . . was she marooned at the inn awaiting Elöise's return? Was she dead in the shadows of the train yard, another glass spike in *her* heart? Was Xonck even then stalking her through the streets, as he had hunted the men of the village?

Svenson stuffed the pistol into his belt, pulling his uniform tunic down to cover the butt. He strode to the front of the train and found the guard chatting with two men of business, perhaps from the mines. Svenson cleared his throat. The guard did not respond, but when Svenson cleared his throat more pointedly the man looked up, wary at what the troubling foreigner might want *now*, as if delay, disruption, and women mysteriously reclaimed from death were not enough for an evening. With a nod to the two businessmen he joined Svenson in the corridor.

'Something else?' he asked crisply.

'Is there is another woman on the train?'

'Who requires a rescue?'

'I beg your pardon –'

'No other *women* at all that I am aware of,' said the guard with a smile. 'And I am quite correct in my counting.'

'I'm sure you are,' said Svenson. 'Yet this woman is very small, and may be *hidden*.'

'To avoid paying her fare?'

Svenson shook his head. 'She may have been subject to the same *assailant* –'

'Assailant?'

'The woman who was attacked – Mrs Dujong – by the same man who attacked the fellow in the train yard!'

'Impossible. He was attacked by a woman.'

'What?' said Svenson. 'Who says so?'

'*Everyone*, of course. The man himself.' The guard glanced at the businessmen, raising his eyebrows.

'Why did no one tell me?'

'You were tending to the lady.'

Had the Contessa truly been at the train yard? Could Xonck have mistaken Elöise for *her*?

'There are no other female passengers?' Svenson asked. 'You are certain?'

'There are not,' replied the guard.

'But the carriages for freight, from the mines –' Svenson pointed to the rear of the train.

'These hold no *passengers*.'

'Not *normally* –'

'They are full of *freight*.'

'Have you inspected them?' pressed Svenson. 'Some must be empty, to pick up goods further down your line –'

'Empty carriages would be locked.'

'But locks can be picked – is there no way one might examine –'

'There are no connecting *doors*, you see.' The two businessmen were now openly eavesdropping, and the guard appealed to them for the obviousness of his logic.

'But it might be possible when we stop?' Svenson asked.

'We are not stopping for some time.'

'Yes, of course – but when we *do* –'

'I will be sure to advise you of that fact,' said the guard. 'You will *excuse* me . . .'

The Doctor stalked the length of the train's two passenger carriages. The guard had told the truth. Besides the two mining men, only one other compartment in the first carriage was occupied – a quartet of labourers heading south to work in the mills. Might Miss Temple have found refuge in the brake van? He would have to wait until the train stopped to reach the van.

Elöise's forehead was warmer to the touch. Svenson lit another cigarette. He pulled the pistol from his waistband, dropped it on the coat, and stretched his legs out on the seats. After another minute of restless thought he fished out the purple stone. Elöise had been clutching it in her hand . . . he could not allow the fact any significance . . . yet it was with a disgusting ease that his mind slipped to the two of them standing on the sand, the sound of the sea, and the wind against her glowing face . . .

He put the stone away. He had abandoned the woman without fully apprising her of the dangers he knew to exist. If he was now in a position to help, it was a matter of expiating guilt, not of reclaiming affection. Svenson forced his mind to the facts at hand – it was the only way he was going to help anyone.

What had Elöise been doing in Karthe so soon? Obviously Miss Temple had recovered . . . or, he realized helplessly, had died . . . but no, if that had been the case, Elöise would have been occupied for at least an additional day with a burial. Yet if Miss Temple had simply come to her senses, fever passed, the Doctor would have expected the women to delay another day to build up her strength. What could have driven them from the fishing village with such precipitous haste? Clearly the villagers had not loved their presence . . . could there have been *more* murders? What *had* they found at the Jorgens' cabin?

It seemed obvious that Xonck had killed the grooms in the fishing village. If the Contessa truly lived, then she must be responsible for the fisherman

– and the man in the train yard, whose face had been slashed. This placed the Contessa in the train yard at the same time as Elöise – so perhaps Xonck *had* mistaken her identity.

Svenson shut his eyes. What *was* the connection between Francis Xonck and Elöise?

He wondered again what he might say to her. Once in the city they would pursue their separate paths, and for ever. But before that, he would search the train when it stopped. If he found no sign of Miss Temple, he would return to Karthe, to track the poor girl down . . . but perhaps once Elöise was able to speak, she might know perfectly well where Miss Temple was . . . perhaps the women had hatched some plan together . . . perhaps . . . the Doctor's eyes closed . . . perhaps he would never wake at all . . .

It took him a moment to remember where he was, but the instant he did the Doctor sat up straight. The train was stopped. He looked to Elöise, still asleep – and groped for the pistol, couldn't find it, then stood and snatched up the coat he had sometime in the night bundled up for a pillow. The weapon had maliciously worked its way beneath. He seized it with one hand and smeared his hair back with the other. He rushed into the corridor, only to be thrown into the far wall as the train pulled forward.

'God damn!' Doctor Svenson cried aloud, and he stumbled down the corridor in search of the hateful guard. He'd no sense of the time – the sky remained dark and he had no watch. He had completely missed a stop! How long had he slept? The four labourers sat slumped against one another, and each of the two businessmen was stretched across three seats in their compartment. A third compartment had been occupied by an elderly woman and two heavy-lidded children. The woman looked up at Svenson as he paused by her open door.

'Have you seen the guard?' he asked.

She nodded towards the front of the train. Taking this for an answer, Svenson continued forward, but when he reached the head of the carriage the guard was not there. Svenson slid open the door and stood in the cold rushing air. Before him lay a narrow railed platform, the greasy coupling, beyond it the blank wall of the coal wagon, and beyond that the engine.

The plume from the smokestack blew over him, suffusing the air with an acrid, moist, and smoky odour. Could the guard have been behind him, in the second carriage? He made his way to the rear door and wrenched it open. Barring a leap from the railed platform to the ladder on the goods van, there was no exit here.

If the train had stopped . . . the guard might have walked back to the brake van, or forward to the engine. But why – especially when new passengers had been taken on? Svenson re-entered their compartment and set the pistol (had he been waving it at the old woman?) onto a seat cushion. Where *was* the man?

Elöise abruptly gasped, as if waking from an especially fearful dream, her eyes snapping open.

'Francis?'

The name was a spike of ice in Svenson's heart.

'No, my dear,' he said. 'It is Doctor Svenson.'

She did not hear him, her eyes still wide. She attempted to sit up and cried out. Svenson darted across to her, sank to his knees and eased one hand behind her head and with the other caught the hand that sought to explore her bandages.

'You must not move,' he whispered to her. 'Elöise –'

'Francis –'

'You have been stabbed. You very nearly died.'

He eased her back until her head lay fully on the seat once more, and squeezed her hand.

'You were very brave, and very fortunate the blade of glass penetrated only as far as it did. The blow was meant to kill.'

For the first time her eyes found his with recognition – his face, his hands, their physical proximity. Svenson stepped away at once. He waited for her to speak.

'We are on a train?'

'We are, from Karthe to the city.'

'You were in Karthe?'

'I was – quite luckily. My own story is too long to tell, and yet –' He took a breath. 'Elöise. I must apologize. The peremptory, indeed, even *cowardly* manner –'

'Where is Celeste?' asked Elöise, interrupting him.

'I have been waiting for you to tell *me*.'

'But she will be killed!'

'How? By whom?'

In answer Elöise only groaned, for she had tried again to rise. Svenson caught her with both hands and eased her down.

'You have been *stabbed*. I have done what I can and the wound has closed, but it will tear if you –'

'She was in town – with *them*.' Elöise stifled a bitter cry. 'It was my own fault – *again* – I went to a house . . . he was killed –'

'I know, my dear,' whispered Svenson, going so far as to brush the sweat-curled hair from her brow. 'The poor boy had not even ten years –'

'No no.' She shook her head. '*Franck* was dead. But we smelt *him* – and I thought I could lead him away from Celeste, that he might follow . . . I went to the train, to find help. But he did *not* follow. I was alone. I knew I should go back, to help her, to face him –'

Svenson nodded, finally catching up to her pronouns. 'Francis Xonck.'

'But instead . . . instead . . . I hid under the train. I was afraid. And then I saw *her* – running past, and then men were shouting – and I stepped out – right into him. He chased me –' The words choked in her throat.

'There is no shame. Francis Xonck has this last day killed far too many to add you to that number – he near as did for me as well.'

'But – but –'

'You have survived. The wound is minor, but the properties of the glass are especially disagreeable to you. The men on the train thought you were dead.' On a sudden whim he opened his palm and showed it to her. 'They gave me this.'

Elöise was silent. Doctor Svenson pressed the purple stone back into her hand, and once more stepped away.

'But Celeste had recovered?' he asked. 'She came with you to the town, but then you separated?'

Elöise nodded. Despite his own guilt, Svenson could scarcely credit the decision to leave someone so recently ill alone. Yet he also knew Miss Temple enough to wonder if it had not been entirely Elöise's doing.

'She is . . . at times . . . *wilful* –'

'She is a girl. It was entirely my fault. I was upset, about everything – you speak of cowardice. I could no more say the truth to Celeste than you could say it to me. And now –'

'If Miss Temple is left behind in Karthe, the best we can do for her is to find our enemies. Both the Contessa and Francis Xonck were at the train. In his attack he may have mistaken you for her.'

Svenson paused and met her eyes, discomfort hardening his voice. 'Did he speak to you?'

'No – it was too sudden – he caught me from behind –'

'But did he see you? What I mean – of *course* he saw you – but did he *know* you?'

'Why does that matter?'

'You are acquainted with the man – from before all of this, in the Trapping household.' The name stuck in Svenson's mouth like a too-large bite of unboned fish. 'I promise you I do not care – it is no matter of *feeling*. The matter is Miss Temple's life – and ours.'

'I do not remember,' whispered Elöise.

'You do. You remember *enough*.'

'I cannot –'

'No, Elöise. You *must*.' His tone had grown sharp. 'You took a lover – very well, we are adults, it is the world. But that man was Arthur Trapping. Or – yes, I am not a fool – that man was Francis Xonck. It is all done. What *matters* is your loyalty *now*, what we know *now*!'

'Loyalty? But – but they have tried to kill me –'

Svenson waved his hand angrily. 'Who have they *not* tried to kill? How many of their *own* have they not sacrificed pell-mell – as if they were laying tricks at whist!'

'Abelard –'

Doctor Svenson stood. 'You must hear me. I do not care for your past, save how it can help us *now*. As for the hole in your mind – to *my* mind it gives you a choice. If you were with them before –'

'I – I was not – I *cannot* have been –'

He overrode her words. 'You have the opportunity for a clean slate. I will do all I can to help and protect you. If you will excuse me, I must locate our guard.'

He wheeled from the compartment, blindly snatching up the pistol, his own idiotic words echoing in his head. He had only exposed himself as a jealous, bitter fool – and how many hours would they be on this godforsaken train together? Nor, with her injury, was there any credible way for him to once more, like a coward, leave her behind. He stepped into the next carriage, acutely aware of the eyes of each passenger – all seemed to have woken – sliding suspiciously over him as he passed. Still no sign of the guard. Svenson stepped through the far door onto the platform.

The wind was freezing, and, as he stood with his hands on the rail, Svenson felt every bit as helpless as he was certain he appeared. He stared down at the black sleepers, flashing past too fast to see, and exhaled deeply, doing his level best to empty his heart along with his lungs. He breathed in the unmistakable odour of indigo clay.

He yanked the pistol from his belt, but all he could see was the night sky and the coal wagon. He crouched below the rail, sniffing again – faint, but any whiff of indigo clay was enough to prickle a man's throat . . . yet where was the source? He lifted his boots – something spilt onto the platform? No . . . it was from *below*. There were cross-braces under each carriage, and indigent fellows bold – or desperate – enough to travel that way . . . but how could he be smelling something under his own carriage with this wind, which ought to whisk any smell immediately behind them? Svenson screwed in his monocle, peering *ahead* beneath the coal wagon. He could not see a damned thing.

Svenson returned to the carriage for a lantern, but the hook was empty. One of the businessmen looked out of his compartment, blanching to see Svenson advancing at such speed.

'Where is the guard?' the Doctor called, his voice low but sharply urgent.

'I – I have not seen him this hour,' stammered the man.

But Svenson was already past, convinced the guard had been thrown off the train or beneath its wheels after inadvertently discovering Xonck's hiding place. And if Xonck *was* hiding under the coal wagon, what did that mean as far as the Contessa's fate – or Miss Temple's? Had they been despatched like so many others? Or could *they* be on the train? That would put Xonck in the same situation as Svenson with regard to the goods vans and the brake van . . . unless – and Svenson cursed himself once more – Xonck had not been asleep when they'd stopped. Of course not – Xonck would have been waiting, leaping at once from hiding and loping like a wolf down the length of the train. Perhaps even now he was warming himself at the stove in the brake van, having slaughtered every other occupant! And if Miss Temple or the Contessa had sought refuge there – was there a thing they could have done to stop him?

Svenson stalked through to the second carriage without finding a lantern. Upon reaching Elöise's compartment, he found its door open and one of the young men travelling to the southern mills standing inside. Beyond the man, Svenson saw Elöise, the bandage in place, her hands held tightly together. The young man spun round to Svenson, eyes caught by the pistol in his hand.

'I – we heard the lady cry out,' he managed. 'For help.'

'Elöise?' Svenson called past the man to her, fixing the interfering fool with an openly vicious gaze.

'I was asleep . . . I do not know . . . dreaming – perhaps I did.'

'Excellent – most kind of you to help.' Svenson stepped aside to allow the man to exit with all the crispness of a Macklenburg soldier on parade. 'If you will excuse us.'

The young man did not move, his gaze still fixed on the weapon. 'Is there something wrong on the train?' he asked.

'I cannot locate the guard,' replied Svenson, in as mild a voice as he could manage. 'Perhaps he walked up to the engine when last we stopped.'

The young man nodded, waiting for Svenson to say more, and then nodded again when it became clear that Svenson had no plans to do so. He

edged into the corridor and walked quickly away, looking back once to find
Doctor Svenson glaring. The man bobbed his head a third time as he left
the carriage.

'I am sure he was only trying to help,' whispered Elöise.

'A man of his age alone with an injured woman', observed Svenson, 'is
no more worthy of trust than an asp let into a child's nursery.'

She did not reply, giving him the clear impression that his entire manner
only made things worse.

'How do you feel?' he asked.

'I have been thinking,' she replied, not to his question at all. 'You asked
me of Francis Xonck. Whatever glass he used to stab me, I know it was
from a book that had been imprinted. Because I felt myself – my flesh but
also my *mind* – being penetrated, not by a blade but by . . . *experiences.*'

'Do you recall them?'

Elöise sighed. 'Will you come in and put that thing away?'

Svenson looked down at the pistol. 'You do not understand. The guard
is missing.'

'Yet if he has only gone to the engine –'

'Xonck is on the train – *somehow*, I am not certain where. The guard
may have discovered him and paid the price.'

'You should not have lied to that boy – you ought to have enlisted his
help!'

'There is no time, Elöise, and too much to explain. He and everyone else
on this train would think me mad –'

'It *would* be mad to face Francis Xonck alone when there is no need! Or
are you set on some ridiculous notion of *revenge?*'

Svenson swallowed an angry reply. That she could so easily mock the
very notion of revenge, that he might be owed anything, or that he was
incapable of taking it – or even that despite everything she might be *correct*
– He slapped the metal door frame with an open palm. The anger was
pointless, and he let it go, his emotion stalling like a Sisyphean stone at the
crest. She was waiting for an answer. Svenson seized on the first unkempt
thought that came to mind. 'You . . . yes, before – you mentioned the glass,
dreaming – the fragment. Do you recall what you saw?'

'I do,' she sniffed, shuffling to a sitting position. 'Though I cannot see it helps us.'

'Why?'

'Because it was *broken*. The thoughts inside, the sense of the memory . . . the *content* of the glass had been deranged. Like the ink running on a waterlogged page, but in one's *mind* – I cannot describe it –'

'It was a very small piece –'

Elöise shook her head. 'The matter is not *size*. There was no logic – as if five memories, or five *minds*, were overlaid one on top of another, like patterns of paper held to a window.'

'Was there any detail to suggest who might have been the source?'

She shook her head again. 'It was too full of contradiction – all tumbled into one place, which was *not* one place . . . and all the time . . . I had forgotten, music . . .' Her voice dropped to a whisper. 'It means nothing – though I'm certain the memories themselves are true. Each portion *flickered* . . . overlapping the seams between them.'

'And none of these . . . *elements* seemed . . . *significant*?'

'I do not believe so,' she said. 'Indeed, now that I try, I can scarcely recall a thing –'

'No no, this is useful,' said Svenson, nodding without conviction. 'A wound with the blue glass – as contact with blood creates *more* glass – necessitates some exclusive contact between the glass and the victim, do you see? Blood congeals against the original glass and is itself crystallized – the flesh becomes solid. But what is the nature of this *newly made* glass? Since it is in – is *of* – your body, does it contain some memory from *you*? How is this raw glass different from that smelted by the Comte?'

Svenson's mind genuinely raced with the consequences of Elöise's broken shard, and what this implied about the structure and workings of the glass books. A torn piece of paper would show only the fragment of type printed upon it, but a similarly sized spear from a blue glass page – apparently – contained an overlay of multiple memories. It meant that the books were not read (or 'written') in any linear way, but that the memories were shot through the glass like colour in paint, or seasoning in soup, or even tiny capillaries in flesh. Whatever aspect of the glass that normally allowed a person to experience the memories in sequence had been dislodged on the broken fragment, and the different memories it contained had been jammed into one jagged, unnatural whole.

He looked over at Elöise. 'On the airship, the mere touch of a glass book on her bare skin drove the Contessa to distraction –'

'She killed the Prince and Lydia for no reason but *pique* –'

'Francis Xonck has used broken glass to cauterize a bullet wound, and now carries that glass *within* his body. He may well be insane.' Svenson winced to think of it. Given the wound, the lump of glass would be the size of a child's fist – what visions gnawed – no, *tore* – at Francis Xonck's mind? 'He also possesses a glass book, saved in particular from the wreckage. I do not know what that book holds – I can only say that a perfectly sound man who *did* look into it was turned to a gibbering wreck. That Xonck has selected this of *all* books must mean something.'

He knelt near her. 'Elöise, you may be closer to his thoughts than any other soul alive –'

'And I have *told* you –'

'He knows the glass will kill him,' said Svenson coldly. 'In the Comte's absence, he will attempt to find the man's notes, his tools – anything to reverse what has been done. I must find him.'

'Abelard, he will kill you.'

'If you know anything more, Elöise. Anything at all, his aims, his – his *cares* . . .'

But she shook her head.

At the far door he finally found a lantern on a hook. Svenson struck a match, tamped the wick to a steady glow, and stepped out to face the blank wooden wall of the goods van. He sniffed the air to no avail, then leant cautiously over the rail with the lantern. An iron ladder was bolted to the van, but he saw no sign of blood or indigo discharge. He returned to the corridor, striding wilfully past Elöise and the other occupants, back to the front of the train. He drew out the revolver, took a breath, and then – acutely aware of being watched by the businessmen – realized he could not open the door with both hands occupied. He fumbled the lantern handle into his gun hand and groped for the knob.

The ceiling above him *thumped* with an impact. Someone had leapt onto the carriage from the coal wagon – in itself a prodigious feat – and was racing towards the goods vans. Svenson broke into a run. He clawed open the connecting door, just as a second thudding impact echoed Xonck's leap from the first passenger carriage to the second.

Svenson sped down the corridor, just a few steps behind the man on the roof, and shouted for Elöise to stay where she was. He reached the rear door and yanked it wide. The footsteps were gone. Xonck must have leapt ahead onto the goods van, but Svenson could not see him, or, above the clattering wheels, hear a thing. He spun round to find that all four of the young labourers had followed.

'Mrs Dujong!' he called to them. 'She is in danger! There is a man aboard the train – the roof – a murderer!'

Before they could reply, he stepped fully onto the platform. With the lantern at arm's length, he judged the distance between the platform and the ladder, swallowing already with fear. Svenson stuffed the pistol into his belt and, gripping tightly to the rail, swung one leg over it. He shifted his grip, too aware of the vibrating rail, how the fluttering stripe of train sleepers whipped past beneath him, the slippery soles of his boots. He jammed his toes between the bars of the railing – and swung his other leg over. The ladder was still too far away. He would have to jump.

A lurch of the train caused Svenson to lose his balance completely, and he flew into space between the carriages. His body cannoned into the iron rungs and slid towards the flashing wheels. The lantern burst onto the rocky trackside, a bloom of flame gone instantly from view. He cried out like a child as his right boot heel was kicked by a sleeper. His hands finally seized hold, tight as a rigorous corpse, of a cold, rust-chipped bar.

The sound of the train had changed . . . it was slowing down.

The train came to a halt with a final great wheeze of steam. Svenson dropped trembling to the track and looked towards the engine – a small station platform, men with lanterns, perhaps other passengers. He turned the other way, pulled the revolver from his belt, and ran for the brake van. There were at least fifteen closed goods vans, each with a wide door shut with a heavy metal hasp. He raced past, sparing only a glance to see whether they might have been prised open, but saw nothing untoward. Svenson looked back to the engine, wondering how long they would be stopped. If he did not return, Elöise would be at Xonck's mercy.

The Doctor's breath heaved as he hauled himself onto the brake van's platform and rapped on the door with the pistol butt. Without waiting for an answer, the Doctor pushed the door open, the revolver before him. A small man in a blue coat, his pink face scumbled with an uneven swathe of bristle, looked up with alarm, a metal mug in one hand and a blackened teapot in the other.

'Good-evening,' said Doctor Svenson. 'I am so sorry to intrude.'

The trainman's arms rose higher, still holding the mug and teapot. 'There is no m-money,' he stammered. 'The ore is still raw – p-please –'

'It could not be further from my mind,' said Svenson, peering in each corner: a table, a stove, chairs, maps, a rack of shelves stuffed with tools, but no place another person might hide. 'Where is the guard?'

'Who?' replied the trainman.

'I am looking for a man.'

'The guard would be up front.'

'Yes, *another* man, dangerous, even mad, and perhaps a lady, or two ladies, one younger, small, and the other taller, black hair – possibly injured, even – ah – killed.'

The trainman did not answer.

Svenson smiled brightly. 'And where are we – this station?'

'Sterridge.'

'And what is Sterridge?'

'Sheep country.'

'How far to the city?'

'Three hours?'

'And what other stops before we reach it?'

'Only one, at the canals.'

'What canals?'

'Parchfeldt junction, of course.'

'Of *course*,' echoed Svenson, with the annoyance of every traveller confronted with benign native idiocy. 'How long until the train moves on?'

'Any minute.' The man poked the teapot at the revolver. 'You're a foreign soldier.'

'Not at all,' answered Svenson. 'Still, I should advise you to lock the door and let no one inside. I apologize again for the disruption.'

The Doctor leapt off the van's platform, gazing to its rooftop, the revolver raised. He saw nothing. Svenson wheeled towards the front of the train. Far in front of him – and by its posture *sniffing* – a sinuous figure in a black cloak stood pressed at the door of a goods van like a fox against a hen-house. Svenson broke into a run.

Xonck looked up, alerted by the nearing bootsteps, the lower half of his face just visible beneath the hood of his cloak, both hands wrestling with the rusted iron clasp that held the van door fast. Svenson raised the pistol but stumbled badly on the rocks, just barely keeping his feet. He looked up, and Xonck was gone. Had the man darted beneath the carriages – or between them to lay in wait as he passed? Or was he already scrambling to the roof? If Xonck was on the roof, he might well reach the passenger carriages, and Elöise, before Svenson could cut him off. The Doctor ran past the goods van, sparing one brief glance beneath it, wondering what Xonck had smelt inside.

Xonck was not in wait – Xonck was nowhere at all. Svenson reached the landing, out of breath, just as the men at the front of the train blew their whistles. He slithered his legs over the railing with a groan. The train pulled forward, and Doctor Svenson fell into the corridor, the revolver still in his hand. Staggering towards Elöise's compartment, he again felt the dread lancing his spine – he was too late, she was dead, Xonck crouched at her open throat like a ghoul. But then he was at the door. Elöise lay where she had before, asleep. Across from her, looking up with defiant expressions, were two of the four young men.

Svenson rolled away from the doorway to lean his back against the wall, eyes closed, with a sigh. His every effort was a mindless grope in the dark.

They would reach the Parchfeldt canals in the next two hours. Elöise would know how far from the city they were, for this would be near to her uncle's cottage, but he did not want to wake her, or yet confront the young men of such galling good intent. Doctor Svenson allowed himself another cigarette. He shook out the match and stared out the opposite windows, at the carpet of fog that clung to the dark grassland. He blew smoke at the glass, as if to add it to the fog, and wondered what had happened to Cardinal Chang. Was he in the city? Was he alive? Svenson inhaled again and shook his head. He knew this feeling from his naval service, where men who had bonded as shipmates would, upon shifting to another vessel, leave every friendship or pledge of trust behind like the crusts and bones at the end of a meal. Svenson tapped his ash to the floor. How long had he known Chang or Miss Temple compared to the crew of the *Hannaniah* – men who never crossed his mind, though he'd sailed with them for three years?

He remembered his own advice to Miss Temple in the silence of the spiralling airship: that she ought to face Roger Bascombe while she could, or she might for ever regret it . . . and the girl had killed the man. Had he known that would happen – had he spurred her on to murder? Bascombe was nothing. What pricked his conscience was the burden the death had set on Miss Temple's soul. Doctor Svenson recalled every death – far too many – he himself had managed with a mortified regret. Yet he knew his advice had been correct. If Miss Temple had simply let the man drown, some vital question for her character – one that their entire adventure had, like some enormous alchemical equation, served to compound and lay before her – might not have had its answer. Did his own journey demand a similar accounting with Elöise Dujong?

He ground the butt out with the toe of his left boot and returned to the doorway of the compartment, signalling with a jerk of his chin for the two young men to return to their compartment. Svenson smiled bitterly that his adoption of the behaviour of braver, harder men – like Chang or Major

Blach – was so *successful*, for the pair did exactly as he demanded, sullen but fully deferential. He stood in the corridor until the far door had closed, listening to the muffled racket of the train and fighting the urge for yet another smoke.

Slumping onto a seat opposite the sleeping woman, Doctor Svenson reached into his tunic and pulled out his crumpled and bloodstained hand-kerchief, unfolding it carefully on his palm to reveal the broken sliver of blue glass he had removed from Elöise's flesh. The sliver had been altered – no longer merely a smooth shard snapped from the rendered page of a glass book. One side now bore a whorled ridging grown from contact with Elöise's body, her blood congealing like stiff beads of sap on a new-sliced wedge of oak. He picked up the sliver between his forefinger and thumb, and held it up to the dim light. Svenson felt a pressing behind his eyes and the urge to swallow, as if his throat were suddenly dry – but the glass did not absorb him. It could have been the size of the fragment, but he sensed at least some of what Elöise had said: that its contents were not *whole*, and as such perhaps offered no real point of entry. Svenson sighed. He pulled up the sleeve of his tunic and then the shirt beneath it, exposing his left arm – above the wrist, well clear of the artery. He took the glass piece delicately in his right hand and, with a quick glance to make sure Elöise still slept, stabbed the sliver's tip firmly into the meat.

The prick of pain was immediately swallowed by a freezing sensation that spread with astonishing speed, and with such chilling force that Doctor Svenson very nearly lost his ability to think. He fought the sudden certainty that he had done something incalculably stupid and forced his eyes to focus on the wound: the gripping cold, though he felt it extending along his veins, did not mean the flesh of his entire arm was being turned to glass. On the contrary, the altered area was actually quite small, perhaps the size of a child's fingernail. Svenson's relief came with a growing dizziness. He blinked, aware that time had become unnaturally expanded with sensation, that each breath felt trackless, and fought down another rush of panic. There . . . at the edge of his attention, roiling like rats in the hold of a ship, lurked the visions he had sought – but the worlds they contained were utterly unlike the seductive realms he had found in the blue glass before. These were sharp, even painful, unhinged, without *coherence*. Again Doctor Svenson was sure he had made a grave mistake. Then the visions were upon him.

The first was a thick black slab of stone, carved with characters Svenson did not know (and the person whose memory this was did not know either), at once overlaid, from another mind, with a harsher carving on paler, softer stone, a creature from some primitive time, with a bulbous head and too many arms – and then overlaid again with a fossilized stretch of an enormously large cephalopod, with suction cups as wide as a grown man's eye . . . and then strangest of all came a sound, a chanting he understood was a wicked, wicked *prayer*. Each element bled sharply into the next, colliding in nauseous diagonals, as if the scattered bits of memory had been sliced with a scissors and reshuffled at random, or hammered together like a ball of wire and nails. Even as he winced, Svenson knew the strange carved language was located on a different stone altogether, that the music had not been heard on a deserted rocky shore at all, but in the close confines of a thickly carpeted drawing room, that –

Just as the entire head-splitting and meaningless sequence was about to be repeated in his mind, Svenson sensed another strain in the mixture – a different *palpable* quality altogether . . . *female* . . . Although the woman's presence was the merest impression, a whisper in his ear, his senses cleaved to those of *her* body – her own inhabitation. And finally, like ghosts taking shape from the fog on a fearful heath, Doctor Svenson isolated three successive instants, clear as whipcracks, three tableaux so sharp in a maelstrom of lesser visions they might have been etched by lightning . . .

A uniformed man in a side chair waiting, head in hands, as a woman's voice rose in anger on the opposite side of a door – the man looked up, his eyes red – Arthur Trapping . . .

Francis Xonck within a grove of trees, kneeling to whisper to three children gathered round him . . .

Holding the hand of a nervous, determined Charlotte Trapping, a servant opening a door to reveal another woman waiting at the far end of a table, her dark hair tied simply with a black ribbon – Caroline Stearne – and in her hand –

Doctor Svenson opened his eyes. The frost in his arm had reached his shoulder, the arm gone numb. He flung the sliver of glass away and with a grimace worked the thumb of his right hand beneath the button of congealed flesh that surrounded the puncture. With a wrench that hurt far more than he was prepared to withstand, the lump of crystallized flesh came free. The Doctor stabbed his handkerchief into the wound and then held it tightly, biting the inside of his cheek at the pain. He shut his eyes and rocked back and forth in his seat. Already the cold was ebbing away in his arm, and he could flex his fingers. He let out a long and rueful sigh. He had taken a terrible risk.

He looked up and found Elöise staring at him. 'What have you done?' she whispered.

'I had a small idea,' Svenson replied with a tight smile. 'It has come to nothing.'

'Abelard –'

'Hush, now. I promise you, there is no harm.'

She watched him closely, hesitating on the edge of difficult questions. It was evident to them both he had not told the truth.

Yet, as he watched Elöise settle back to sleep, Doctor Svenson knew he should have confronted her. The final three tableaux were memories from Elöise herself, transmitted through the congealed residue of her own blood. Were these memories she herself recalled and had hidden from him – or had they been hidden from her as well, buried like a hidden seam of silver in the fibres of her body? It was another fundamental question about how the blue glass worked. Elöise was missing pieces of her mind, given over to a glass book . . . but what if memories taken into a book disappeared only from the forebrain, from a person's ready memory, but not necessarily altogether? Did that mean the mind of a man like Robert Vandaariff or Henry Xonck might be reclaimed?

And if those experiences *could* be restored . . . what sort of person would Elöise be? Did she even know herself?

The Doctor woke to brighter light and a canal streaming past the window, a shining ribbon between the rail tracks and a dense green forest beyond. Elöise still slept, rolling partially onto her side to face him, which – as he could see no bleeding on her bandage – spoke to a lack of discomfort with her incision. He sat up, the pistol still in his hand but the hand itself half asleep, tucked into an awkward position between his torso and the seat. How long had he slept? It could not have been more than a doze, and yet, he ruefully realized, however short or long, such laxity would have given Xonck ample time to eliminate them both. But they both lived. Even if Xonck was kindly disposed towards Elöise, did it follow he would scruple to kill Svenson? It did not.

Svenson leant forward and cracked the knuckles of each hand as he thought. The goods van where Xonck had been interrupted, sniffing and pawing to get inside . . . such a man would have no interest in any set of *goods* from these northern towns – in ore, or oil, in dried fish, or furs. If he traced Francis Xonck from murder to murder, each act had been in the express interest of returning to the city, or in recovering the glass book. Could it really be as simple as that?

The Doctor knelt next to Elöise and gently shook her arm. She opened her eyes, saw him, and then – with a speed that pierced his heart – composed her features into a cautious mask.

'I need to know how you feel,' he said. 'If you can stand, or travel.'

'Where are we?' she asked.

'Nearing Parchfeldt Park,' answered Svenson. 'I have reason to believe it may be in our interests to leave the train when we stop there.'

'To reach my uncle's cottage?'

'In time, perhaps,' said the Doctor. 'But I must open one of the goods vans, and I would not leave you alone, in case the train continues on before I am finished. If all goes well and quickly, we may reboard. But it may be that the hidden shelter of your cottage is exactly what you need. Certainly it will aid your recovery.' He looked down at her, his eyes touching on the bandage. 'And yet, if you cannot stand, all is moot –'

'What is in this van?' asked Elöise.

Svenson met her eyes and replied as casually as he was able. 'Ah, well, it may be the Contessa di Lacquer-Sforza.'

'I see.'

'My thought is to reach her before Francis Xonck.'

'Then I had best be getting ready,' said Elöise.

Her incision had closed cleanly and well before Svenson would have expected, given how close she had been to death. The lasting trouble was the dizzying effect of the glass, and Doctor Svenson was dismayed to find his own head swimming as he helped her walk – just a trace, almost as if he had consumed too many cigarettes at a sitting, yet he knew that he hadn't, just as he knew the sharp taste in his throat was not tobacco but the acrid tang of indigo clay. But it moved him to still more patience and more care. When he took a moment to tighten the handkerchief he'd tied across his wrist, Elöise noticed the gesture but did not comment. He caught her glance, but, as if they both knew it would be a complicated conversation – for she did not know why he had done such a thing or, having done it, what he had discovered – neither pressed the matter. Instead they found themselves at the rear platform. His hands were on the rail, his eyes focused on the passing track below. He sensed Elöise turning towards him but did not look up.

'It is beautiful here,' she said, just loud enough to be heard above the wheels. 'I knew the park as a girl. The entire place felt like it was mine, of course, the way the whole of anything feels like yours as a child, simply because you desire it so fully. I am sure I intended to desire my husband quite as much, and for a time perhaps I did. I did love him, but then he died, and so far away, and so uselessly –' She laughed ruefully and plucked at the epaulette of Svenson's uniform. 'And here I am standing with another soldier.'

Svenson turned to her. 'I am not –'

'Of course not, no.' She smiled. 'A doctor is very different, and a captain-surgeon even more. But that is not what I meant to say. And now I no longer know what it was . . . I have misplaced the thread. ' She sighed. 'Something *profound*, no doubt, about how dreams retreat, about how knowing more of a thing – about one's self – invariably means more pain. And the pain of smaller dreams is, I find, especially acute.'

Doctor Svenson knew that he ought to reply – that his reply was the exact opportunity to bare, without rancour and for the first time in his life, the merest glimpse of his own struggles about Corinna and his squandered years, about Elöise herself – but his thoughts were swimming. What was the whole of a life anyway? What was the measure of his own against a life like Elöise's? What, after everything, through everything – what seemed like years of bitter remembrance – did one look back *on*, apart from love? He was taking too long, the silence stretching out between them, and felt a new urgency to speak, to let her know that he had been happy for her words.

But he could not find the way to begin, and then the train began to slow.

'It seems we are stopping,' he said, and reached for the ladder.

The moment of conversation was gone. Elöise smiled somewhat sadly, nodding to let him know she was ready. Svenson swung a leg over the rail, waiting. The train came to a halt, and he heard the relieved exhale of steam from the engine.

Svenson dropped to the train track and stumbled onto the sloped gravel track bed, looking down to the goods van. Towards the engine a cluster of people waited to board – there would be some time at least to search. He returned to Elöise. Above them a dark figure sailed over the gap between their carriage and the next, landing with a heavy thud. Svenson spun, knowing he was too late even as he did so, and snapped off a shot that flew harmlessly behind Xonck's disappearing figure, the flat crack echoing loudly down the tracks. Elöise cried out in surprise and fell into the ladder, grunting with pain. Svenson caught her waist and eased her down.

'This way,' he said, and pulled her as gently as he could, wanting to run full out but knowing Elöise could not. At the far end of the train the trainman from the brake van appeared, staring at them – had he heard the shot?

'Where are we going?' called Elöise, as Svenson crouched down, peering past the wheels to the far side of the train.

'She is in a goods van,' he said, 'directly in the middle of the line –'

'The Contessa?' asked Elöise.

'Yes.'

'That one?'

Doctor Svenson looked up to where she pointed. The door of the van had been pushed open wide enough for the woman to exit – or for Xonck to enter. Svenson swore in German beneath his breath, still pulling Elöise along. The rushes between the canal and the sloping gravel of the track were high enough to hide the water. He swept his gaze beyond the canal to the trees – though how the Contessa might have crossed the water he did not know – but saw nothing. What he could see of the van's interior lay dark and empty. The trainman came towards him, waving. Back near the engine, the various figures seemed stopped. Had they heard the pistol too?

He turned at an audible *plunk* of canal water. The Contessa.

Elöise gasped aloud and pulled at his hand, and Svenson spun back to see Francis Xonck – through the underside of the carriage – on the far side of the train, having just dropped from some hidden perch. He was on hands and knees. With a rasping, hacking rale Xonck vomited a bilious stream of dark liquid onto the stones. Svenson extended the pistol, unsure of his aim through the intervening cables and wheels, and Xonck reeled to his knees, the hood falling back onto his shoulders. Elöise gasped again, and her fingers dug into Svenson's hand. Xonck's face had been savaged by his ordeal – eyes rimmed red as two open wounds, lips blue, face streaked like a sweat-smeared actor's greasepaint. Doctor Svenson hesitated, and then Xonck's torso convulsed and he fell forward again, spewing another vile splashing bolt. The Doctor looked away with a wince – it was almost as if the sight conjured the smell – then saw the flash of a woman – black hair, dark dress, white hand – vanish into the trees on the canal's opposite side.

He pulled Elöise's hand and leapt into the rushes, the high green stalks slapping against them.

'But – Francis – the goods van –' cried Elöise.

'It is empty!' shouted Svenson. 'Xonck is dying – the Contessa is more important!'

Her reply was curtailed by a stab of pain as they stumbled abruptly into the low brick barrier that lined the canal. The bricked border of the canal was slick with dead reeds, flattened and brown, dangling into the dark green water.

'How did she cross?' asked Elöise.

'Perhaps she swam.'

'Never so quickly,' replied Elöise. 'And not in any dress.'

The canal was not excessively wide, perhaps ten yards, but far enough for a woman's swimming to have made some noise – simply her climbing out would have dripped and splashed enough to draw their attention – and yet they had not heard a thing. He scanned both banks in either direction, looking for any rope or ferry box that might be pulled across. Once more Elöise pulled at his arm. She pointed further down the canal, where the current flowed. Svenson screwed in his monocle and saw it for himself – a small flat-bottomed launch. The Contessa had taken it across and then pushed it away downstream.

'Can we catch it?' asked Elöise.

'We have little choice, save swimming,' replied Svenson.

Behind them the train whistle sounded its shrill and forlorn cry. They both looked back, hesitating, but reaching the train before it pulled forward, even if they had wanted to, was impossible. The iron wheels ground into motion with a shriek.

'Let us find our way across,' Elöise said.

As it happened, they did not need the little boat. Thirty yards away they found a narrow bridge of ingenious construction: it could be folded when the water traffic needed to pass, and then laid out again as necessary to reach the other side. As the Contessa's boat drifted further from their view, Doctor Svenson wrestled with the knots securing the planking. Once loosed, the network of pulleys and weights and cords stretched itself like some sort of·wood-and-hemp mantis across the green canal, falling on the far bank with a slap.

He took Elöise's hand, helping her climb the short rise through the rushes. They had entered the vast and isolated woods of Parchfeldt Park.

'Do you know where we are?' he asked.

She squeezed his hand and pulled hers free. Doctor Svenson fussed in his pocket for a handkerchief to wipe his monocle.

'I am not sure,' said Elöise, taking a deep breath of the country air and exhaling with a smile, as if to displace the tension between them. 'You see how dense the forest is. The canals are to the south – as is my uncle's cottage, but I have always come by the road. We could be within two hundred yards of the place or twenty miles . . . I've truly no idea.'

'The Contessa has not run so far only to escape Xonck. If she was intent on reaching the city, that woman would have clawed his eyes out rather than leave the train. She has entered the park for a reason. Can you think what it might be?'

'I cannot.'

'But did she ever – when speaking to you –'

'She *never* spoke to me.'

'But did she see you – did she know you were on the train?'

'I'm sure I've no idea!'

Doctor Svenson was torn between shaking her hard by the shoulders and caressing her face with sympathy. He diverted both urges by rewiping his monocle.

'I'm afraid that will not do, my dear. Though I am an ignorant foreigner, I can at least make speculations. If it is a royal preserve, is there some royal presence – the hunting lodge of the Duke of Stäelmaere, for example? Some other estate where the Contessa might hope to find rescue?'

'I do not know the whole park, only one small portion –'

'But if we are near that portion –'

'I do not know –'

'But if we *are* – what other tenants, what other possibilities?'

'There are none. The Rookery is all that remains of an estate house that burnt some years ago. There are villages and wardens but wholly unremarkable. Certainly a woman such as the Contessa might convince them to give her food –'

'She did not leave the train to find food in a village,' said Svenson.

'If you say so,' snapped Elöise.

'It will not help to get angry.'

'If I am angry, it is because – because all of this – my mind and my body –'

She was breathing quickly, her face flushed, one hand in the air and the other protectively touching the bandage below her breasts.

'Listen to me.' The Doctor's sharp tone brought her eyes to his. 'I am here – in this wood – because I am trying to recover my sense of duty. This woman we chase – the man in the train – the dead Ministry man at Karthe –'

'*Who?*'

He waved her question away. 'If the Contessa escapes, other people will die – *we* will die. I am not thinking of myself – or of *us* – it is the last of my concerns – whatever I once thought, or hoped – I have put it away.'

'Abelard –'

'There is a hole in your mind you cannot help. That is a fact. And yet there are other facts you have not shared. Perhaps you have your reasons – but thus, you must see, comes my own dilemma. With some distress I must admit that we do not truly know each other at all. For example, I know that you met Caroline Stearne in a private room of the St Royale Hotel, in the company of Charlotte Trapping.'

He waited for her to respond. She did not.

'You did not mention it,' he said.

Elöise looked away to the trees. After another hopeless silence Svenson indicated the way before them.

It took ten minutes of thrashing through a dew-soaked thicket of young beech trees before their way broke into a band of taller oaks, beneath whose broad canopies the ground was more bare and easy to cross. More than once Svenson caught Elöise's arm as she stumbled. After each stumble she thanked him quietly and he released her, stepping ahead and doing his best to clear the branches from her path. Aside from this they did not speak, though once the Doctor risked an observation on the majesty of the mighty oak in general and, with a nod to a darting red squirrel, how each tree functioned within the forest as a sort of miniature city, supporting inhabitants of all stations, from grubs to squirrels, from songbirds to even hawks in its heights. It would have been possible for him to continue – the relation of oak to oak being certainly comparable to the various tiny duchies that together formed a sort of German nation – yet at her silence he did not, allowing the last sentence to dissipate flatly in the empty woods.

Beyond the oaks they met a path, wide enough for a horse and wagon, but so covered with leaves that it was clear traffic was rare.

'You recognize nothing?' he asked.

She shook her head and then gestured to their left. 'There is perhaps a better chance if we continue west.'

'As you wish,' said Svenson, and they began to walk.

They walked in an unbearable silence. Doctor Svenson tried to distract himself with the birdsong and the rustles of invisible wind. When he could stand it no more, yet upon opening his mouth found nothing to say, he indicated their leaf-strewn path. 'Our way is as thickly padded as a Turkish carpet – I find it impossible to tell if the Contessa has preceded us.'

Elöise turned to face him quickly. 'Do you think she has?'

'She has gone *some* place.'

'But why here?'

'We are walking west. Is not west more towards the city?'

'If she sought the city, she would have remained on the train – you said so yourself.'

'I did.' Such stupidity was exactly what came of making conversation to no purpose. 'Still, the park is large. We can only hope.'

'Hope?'

'To catch her, of course. To stop her.'

'Of course,' nodded Elöise, with a sigh.

'You would prefer her free?' asked Svenson, somewhat tartly.

'I would prefer her vanished from my life.'

Doctor Svenson could not stop himself. 'And what life is that? Your master is dead – your mistress in turmoil – your enemies everywhere. And yet what life *was* it before, Elöise? Can you even remember what you embrace with such determination – or why?'

'One might say the same', she answered, her voice swift and low, 'to a man whose Prince is dead, whose Prince was a fool, whose wasted efforts on an idiot's behalf have left only bitterness and shame.'

Svenson barked with disgust, looking to the trees for any retort, but nothing came. Her words were exact as a scalpel.

'You are of course correct –' he began, but stopped at her exasperated sigh.

'I am an idiot whose life has been saved countless times by your precise foolishness. I have no right to say one word.'

Before he could disagree Elöise stopped walking. He stopped with her. She turned to look behind them.

'What is it?' he asked.

Elöise pointed off the path. Through the new green trees Svenson saw a grey stone wall, perhaps the height of his shoulder.

'We have passed something,' said Elöise. 'Perhaps it is a house.'

On the far side of the wall they found the ruins of what might have been an abbey, the stones draped with vines, the windows empty holes through which he could see trees that had grown up inside, nurtured on the decayed beams of the ceiling. Svenson recognized several fruit trees, gnarled and unkempt, the remnants of some abbot's orchard or lady's garden, and then, as they neared, pointed out an even thinner line of wide stepping-stones that led beyond the ruins.

'Do you know what this place is?' Svenson asked.

Elöise shook her head. She had stopped, staring ahead into the trees.

Svenson nodded to the new flagstone path. 'Shall we not see where it goes?'

'It is a ruin,' she said.

'I find ruins stirring,' he replied; 'each holds its own secret tale. And besides, these stones seem quite well kept.'

He stepped forward, and she followed without answer. Ruins of any kind, but most particularly those overcome by nature, spoke to Svenson's heart deeply – and he glanced at Elöise with an encouraging smile. She did her best to smile in return, and he reached back to take her hand, which she allowed with a defeated look that left him wishing he could, without even sharper embarrassment, let it go again.

The path of stones wound to a wooden gate, set with an iron latch.

The square flagstone below the gate showed a fading, wet mark . . . a small footprint . . . a woman's boot . . . or a man's that had evaporated to a smaller size. Svenson slipped the pistol into his hand. He motioned that Elöise should keep behind him and reached for the iron latch.

Beyond the gate, the flagstone walk threaded a pair of well-tended flower beds (pruned rose bushes to the left and new budding tulips – red and yellow – to the right) and ended at a low stone house with a thatched roof whose edges hung out far enough to cast the walls of the house, its two rounded windows, and its wooden door into shadow. The green turf that lined the walkway was wet with dew, the stones ahead marked with more footprints. The air was silent save for the birds.

'Do you know this place?' he whispered again.

Again Elöise shook her head. Svenson crept to the nearest print, crouching down to study it. This was unquestionably left by a woman's boot, for even a young man's would not show such a pointed toe. He motioned towards the rose bushes, where a small spade had been set against a stake. Elöise pulled it from the ground and somewhat uncertainly shifted it in her hands to find the proper grip for swinging.

They had been standing in the garden too long, and, with a nod to Elöise, the Doctor advanced quickly to the doorway, darting to one side and indicating that she should stand opposite – which at least hid them from the windows. She hefted the shovel gamely, but he saw she was entirely without confidence. For all he knew her wound had reopened and was bleeding. He must capture the Contessa by himself. The less any situation asked of Elöise the better.

He reached for the iron latch. The door swung wide without a squeak onto a room exuding both intimate care (the hearth dotted with porcelain keepsakes, the furniture waxed and gleaming, and the plaster walls covered with framed engravings) and abandonment, for the flowers on the table had died and the flagstones beneath Svenson's feet showed streaks of dust the wind had blown beneath the door. The Doctor entered carefully and crossed to the hearth. The grate was empty and cold.

He turned to Elöise, standing stiffly in the door with her shovel, and motioned her inside. The Doctor led the way into a humble kitchen. No one was there, nor were there signs of recent occupation, but his eye caught, stuffed behind a butcher's block, a shapeless pile covered with cloth. He pulled back the cloth. Heaped beneath, without the sensitive regard their maker might have demanded, lay the *Annunciation* canvases of Oskar Veilandt, Comte d'Orkancz, last seen, face to the wall, in the laboratory at Harschmort House.

He looked up to see Elöise's gaze fixed on the topmost painting – one Svenson had not seen before, showing the haloed face of the angel. The awful man's brushwork really was exquisite – the flesh of the ecstatic woman seemed as real as that of Elöise across the room, and the blue surface of the menacing angel shone like glass itself. The angel's mouth was open, almost in mid-bite, or perhaps this was only the hissing exhortation of its message. The teeth were sharp and, to the Doctor's dismay, bright orange. Like a Roman statue, the eyes bore no iris or pupil, and were as entirely blue as the skin around them, only more liquid, giving the unpleasant impression that, were he to touch a finger to its surface, it might penetrate full length into the eye. He lifted the painting, flipping it over to study the bright inscriptions on the back. Despite there being the odd legible word – 'incept' . . . 'marrowes' . . . 'contigular' – Svenson could perceive no larger meaning, bristling as it was with symbols, some no doubt unique to the Comte alone. He shivered to recall the slick blue discharge as it coated Lydia Vandaariff's quivering chin, and set the painting back onto the pile.

Elöise was no longer there.

Svenson was through the doorway in two strides. She stood across the main room, having clearly just taken a peek through its far curtained door. He spoke in the barest whisper. 'I did not see you leave.' He nodded to the curtain. 'Did you see anything?'

'Perhaps we should go,' Elöise whispered back.

She was trembling. Had she seen something? Or had he lost track of her frailty in his pursuit of the Contessa?

'We cannot. She must have come here. The footprint.'

He pushed aside the curtain for himself, revealing a dark unlit corridor lined with high, ebony cupboards. At the far end was a second curtain, sketched out by the light beneath. He crept down the passage, resisting the urge to open the cupboards – there was plenty of time for that later – and a creak from the floorboards told him Elöise had followed. He held up his pistol hand for silence as his other reached for the curtain and twitched it aside: iron-frame bed, seaman's trunk at its foot, another tall cupboard, writing desk with a bevel-edged mirror above.

Svenson crossed to a small door, left open to a rear garden. Beyond its threshold lay another smeared footprint, and another trail of step-stones leading deeper into the woods.

'She has escaped,' he called to Elöise. 'She cannot have stayed long. Why did she not simply go around?'

'Perhaps she wanted food,' said Elöise, still in a whisper.

'More likely a weapon.' The Doctor stepped back into the bedroom. 'If only the occupants might provide some sense of where we are, and where she might be *going* – hopefully they have not come to harm –'

He paused at a muted scuffle from within the bedroom's tall wardrobe. Svenson yanked it open and shoved his pistol into the face of the man who crouched there, gazing up without concern – indeed without any expression whatsoever. His clothes gave off the distinct reek of a fire. It was Robert Vandaariff.

The blow caught Doctor Svenson square across the side of his head and sent him straight into the wardrobe, where, aside from a mixture of camphor and smoke, his last sensation was of a doubled shadow in the room behind him . . . a second woman standing next to Elöise.

Whatever camphor had been laid in the wardrobe only evidenced a struggle lost, for, as the Doctor woke, stifling the simultaneous urges to groan aloud and to be sick, he looked down to see his tunic covered with the detritus of moths – spent cocoons, corpses, dusty webbing. He batted at it, realizing as he did so that his arms were free, and that he was no longer in the wardrobe. He had been laid onto the bed and a thick towel set beneath his bleeding head. He explored the wound with his fingers – a mild enough cut, though extremely sensitive – and discerned that no bones had been staved in, though he was certainly suffering some degree of concussion. Vandaariff was no longer in the wardrobe. The revolver was nowhere in sight. Nor was Elöise.

He sat up and felt a dizzying rush. He patiently allowed the rush to subside, then swung his legs over the bed. On the desk lay a piece of paper. It had not been there before. He picked it up, squinted, and took a moment to insert his monocle. A woman's writing . . . 'Forgive me.' He folded the paper absently into quarters and then folded it again, smoothing each edge as his mind sought some sensible purchase on his emotions. He stuffed the folded bolt of paper into his pocket and took out his silver case. The Doctor lit a cigarette and smoked it through, leaning so his thighs were braced against the desk, tapping the ash into a dish half full of pins, and gazing into the bevelled glass. His face, as leached of pride as a thrice-whipped dog, did nothing to jog his heart into some response – anger, scorn, even despair.

He weaved through the dark passageway of cupboards into the main room and from there to the kitchen. The paintings had been taken as well. Svenson found an earthenware dish of cool water, bathed his head, mopped it with another towel – the spotting of blood gave way soon enough – and then took a long drink. His thoughts were chessmen made of lead, impossible to push into motion. He had saved her life on the train – for what? So she could refrain from taking his, an even trade.

He lit another cigarette, knowing it might cause him to vomit, and dropped the match on the table, hoping vaguely it would leave a mark. There was a clock on the mantel, but it had not been wound. The cigarette burnt to ash in his fingers.

He was not dead, though he was not sure his mortification – how *many* times must he fail at the same hurdle?'– was preferable to oblivion. Dull-minded but grimly determined, he returned to the bedroom and sorted through the papers in the writing desk, finding a ribbon-wrapped bundle in a wooden slot. Svenson recognized the same hand that had written 'Forgive me' and opened the letter, dated two years previously and addressed to Augustus Sparck . . . '*Dear Uncle* . . .' Svenson dropped the letter back onto the desk, feeling stupid. Her uncle's cottage after all. Of course it was – and she had allowed him to playact each step of protecting her, pistol in hand, knowing at every instant what the end must be.

The room was too close. He walked out the still-open door into the garden, blinking, the sounds of birds in the tree branches above him.

Doctor Svenson patted his pockets for a handkerchief and winced at the pain in his left arm. He had forgotten stabbing himself with the glass, and now felt a flicker of sensation throughout his body, a twitching ribbon infused with the revolting amalgamation of visions – the cenotaph, the glade, the fossilized creature . . . but there was something else, something apart from these, like the strain of a sweet violin within a chorus of martial brass. He had not fully appreciated it in the train carriage . . . an exquisite sensuous redolence of Elöise's own body, momentary memories of being *her*. This was from the new glass, created from her own blood. The memories were almost too much to bear, but he could not resist them. He sat down on a wooden stool, his head in his hands, eyes shut.

The first tableau had been a parlour: Colonel Arthur Trapping, miserable, powerless – and Elöise – overhearing a bitter disagreement in another room . . . a man and a woman. Svenson recognized neither voice – which meant, he realized, that the man in the quarrel was *not* Francis Xonck. Could it be his brother, Henry? And could the woman be Charlotte Trapping? Trapping wore his uniform . . . could it be about the transfer of the dragoons to the Palace? Or was it something simpler – the payment of his debts? But then why was Elöise present?

The second was a grove of trees. Francis Xonck knelt with the three

Trapping children, Elöise's charges. Xonck chatted with them, the wry playful uncle, but then looked up at Elöise . . . and his expression changed. At first Svenson assumed it to be conspiratorial, but by concentrating, steeping himself in Elöise's memory, he felt something else . . . a lick of fear, as if Elöise had been caught out. But what could Xonck have known? Or was it the other way round? Had she learnt one of *his* secrets – and now he knew it?

The third image was the most disturbing: Elöise and Charlotte Trapping with Caroline Stearne, the Contessa's particular minion, in a private room at the St Royale. Svenson knew no more than that: the two women holding hands, Charlotte Trapping's obvious fear . . . but he'd no idea if the two women knew Mrs Stearne – knew her connection to the Cabal – or were meeting her for the first time, or what the interview was about, or . . . Svenson frowned. Just as the image faded from his mind, Mrs Stearne had been turning towards them . . . something, yes . . . in her hand, just catching the lamplight . . . a blue glass card.

Svenson sat back on the stool, blinking up at the sky, these three glimpses rendering palpable how little he knew of Elöise's life. He felt intolerably alone. He lurched to his feet. How had the Contessa known of this cottage? When had Elöise told her – in Karthe? Or before? With a chill in his heart he realized Miss Temple was even more likely to be dead. Yet . . . he thought back to the cottage of Sorge and Lina, and he was sure – he was *sure* – that Elöise's affection, her *devotion*, to tending Miss Temple had been real. But he had been sure of so many things.

The wardrobe! He had forgotten all about Robert Vandaariff. What was *he* doing here, of all people? How had he travelled from Harschmort to Parchfeldt? It could not have been on his own power, but who else could have managed it – and then what had happened to *them*? And how could the Contessa have sent word so far in advance to arrange this as a destination?

He retreated into the cottage and, paying closer attention, searched fruitlessly for any clue as to where the women had gone. Did he even *want* to follow them? Did he want to risk a night freezing to death in a strange forest? With a bitter determination he rummaged through the drawers of the writing desk until he found one fitted with a secret inner niche that was locked. The Doctor popped the lock with a pen-knife and collected the small amount of money, mainly gold coins, that had been hidden away. From there he stalked to the kitchen and pulled open the various drawers and cupboards in search of some useful weapon. At last he found a heavy hammer – tenderizing meat? killing fowl? – he could swing with one hand. He stuck the handle through his belt, took another drink of water, and went out the front door, following the flagstone path back to the leaf-covered track he had walked with Elöise.

Once there, it was with a sudden urgency that the Doctor began to retrace his steps to the canal. He assumed the women had taken the opposite direction. Perhaps succumbing to cowardice, perhaps to common sense, Svenson fixed his thoughts on Chang waiting at Stropping. He would return to the city.

As always, it seemed to take less time to return than to arrive, and soon, despite the Doctor's still-thrashing thoughts, he found himself at the dark canal's edge. It was not quite the same spot where he had crossed – he could not find the little bridge – but as he looked in its direction he saw this might not matter. Sailing towards him was a low barge, wide enough so that even he could hop easily aboard, cross its deck, and just as simply step off onto the far bank. The man waved in a cautious manner – perhaps taken aback by the Doctor's sudden emergence from the wood – and glanced over his shoulder. He whistled, sharp and shrill like an angry jay, and then returned his gaze to Svenson, who was doing his best to smile pleasantly.

'May I use your craft to cross?' he called, pointing to the far bank.

Three other men emerged around a line of large awkward shapes stretched with canvas and lashed to the deck, like a battery of field cannon – for, as the bow swept past, the Doctor saw the long deck was covered with this strange, hidden cargo. One of these three, more burly and immediately daunting, stretched a hand to Svenson, who caught the man's forearm and leapt aboard. The man clapped Svenson soundly on the back, and with a general conspiratorial grinning they walked him to the other side and hovered, waiting for a clear spot where the Doctor could easily leap away.

'Belay that, there!'

An older bargeman in a black peaked cap had shouted from the stern. But instead of saying anything further he lowered his head, deferring to a slim, tall man wrapped in a brown topcoat, face pensive, holding a thin cigar some inches from his mouth.

'What is that uniform?' this second man called out.

Svenson paused, then brushed his tunic before the men around him noticed his hesitation.

'The Duchy of Macklenburg!' he shouted back, thickening his accent deliberately. 'I would not expect you to know it.'

'On the contrary,' announced the man in a flat voice, the cigar still hovering. 'Perhaps you will do me the *service* of conversation.'

Svenson looked longingly at the far bank, but the muscular bargeman had gracefully interposed his body between the Doctor and the shore.

The barge had nothing so formal as a cabin, but there was a wheel and beyond it a depression in the deck where more canvas had been stretched to shield a small stove. Svenson was directed, not unkindly, to a wooden crate where he might sit. The man in the black cap, the barge master, placed a clay mug of tea in his hands and then left the two gentlemen alone. The man in the coat sat on a crate of his own and deliberately smoothed his side whiskers with both hands.

Svenson gestured vaguely towards the train tracks, by now invisible beyond the trees. 'You may wonder, if you know Macklenburg, at how far you find me from it. The fact is, this morning I was on a train, but it stopped – some difficulty with *valves* – and I took it upon myself to explore these lovely woods.' Svenson waved his hand vaguely. 'North country – mining has always been an interest, as I hail from our own hills, where there are many minerals. And of course the lives of fishermen. You will see from my buttons that I am of the Macklenburg Navy. One cannot keep a sailor too long from the sea! But I really ought to return, as the train must continue soon – I have no timepiece, you see, and would very much hate to miss it –'

'You are Karl-Horst von Maasmärck's doctor,' said the man.

'Goodness,' Svenson laughed, 'you speak as if you had studied the roster of the Prince's whole party!'

'And where is your Prince now?'

'In Macklenburg, of course,' said Svenson. 'Where else could he be? Unless you know more than I do.'

The man narrowed his eyes.

The Doctor allowed himself to become visibly exasperated. 'If there has been other news, I beg you do not trifle with me –'

He made to rise, hoping more than anything to get a current sense of where the other bargemen stood, but the man in the topcoat pulled him back onto the crate. 'Do not *distress* yourself,' the man hissed.

'If you will excuse me! My train –'

'Forget your damnable train!' barked the man, but the force of his words was mixed with peevish displeasure, as if he resented the necessity of their entire conversation, and even his own presence on this barge to begin with.

'Will you *constrain* me?'

'What happened to your head?' the man demanded. 'There is blood!'

'There were difficulties with the train, as I *told* you – a sudden stop, falling luggage –'

'Then perhaps you can tell me instead who made up the travelling party for the Prince's return.'

The man had spoken too easily, as if the question meant nothing.

Svenson shrugged, again exaggerating his accent. 'Is that any secret? I am sure your own newspapers –'

'Newspapers are trash.'

'And yet for these simple facts –'

'*I insist that you tell me!*'

The man balled both hands together in his lap and squeezed his fists. Svenson looked away to give himself time – was the situation so unpleasant already?

'*Well* . . . since you make such a *demand* . . . let me see . . . the Prince's intended bride, of course. Who else? Diplomats – your own Deputy Minister Crabbé, his assistant Mr Bascombe . . . dignitaries – the Contessa di Lacquer-Sforza, the Comte d'Orkancz, both new friends of the Prince,

Mr Francis Xonck –' He stopped at the subtle catch of his captor's breath.

The man leant closer, speaking low. 'And, if you will indulge me . . . just exactly *how* did they travel?'

'You will understand,' replied the Doctor, 'that however strange it may seem to find a Macklenburg naval surgeon in this forest, it is just as odd for me to find not only a man who knows me, but one engaged on an equally mysterious journey of . . . commerce.'

'Nothing mysterious at all!' snapped the man. 'It is a commercial canal.'

The man took his own moment to peer over the canvas. The canal had twisted more deeply into the forest, and the overhanging branches blotted out so much of the pallid light that it seemed near dusk. With the thickening trees came less wind, and Svenson saw the entirety of the crew, save the master, had taken up poles. The man sat back down on his own crate, frowning that his captive had seen fit to rise along with him.

Svenson studied his adversary. The brown topcoat was of an excellent cloth, but cautious in its cut, just like the cravat – silk, but the inoffensive colour of orange pith. The man's thinning hair had been pasted to his scalp that morning with pomade, but with the breeze now sported an insolent fringe.

'What a strange cargo you seem to be carrying.' The Doctor waved a hand towards the front of the barge. 'All wrapped up and odd-shaped, rather like different cuts of meat from a butcher's –'

The man seized Svenson's knee. Svenson glared at the point of contact. His host removed his hand, then cleared his throat and stuck out his chin. 'You will tell me what you know of Robert Vandaariff.'

'I do not know anything.'

'Did he travel with your Prince?'

'Was there not some story of fever – that Harschmort was under quarantine?'

The man thrust his face close to Svenson's, his lips pursed and white. 'I will ask you again. If he did not travel with the Prince in secret, where is Robert Vandaariff?'

'Could he not be in the city? Or elsewhere in the country – surely he owns many –'

'He is *nowhere!*'

'Perhaps if I knew why you *need* him –'

'No, *you* will answer *me!*'

'O come,' sighed Svenson. 'You are no policeman – and nor am I. We are not fitted for *interrogation*. I am a foreigner in an unfamiliar country – an unfamiliar language –'

'You speak it perfectly well,' muttered the man.

'But I possess no *subtlety*. I can only be plain, Mr . . . come now, your name cannot be so precious . . .' Svenson raised his eyebrows hopefully.

'Mr – ah – Mr . . . Fruitricks.'

Svenson nodded, as if this were not an especially obvious fabrication. 'Well, Mr *Fruitricks* . . . it would seem, and I offer this out of pure scientific deductive reasoning, that you are in – as it is said amongst your people – a *spot*.'

'I'm sure I am in no such thing.'

'As you insist. And yet, even the crates we are sitting on –'

'Crates are common on a barge.'

'Come, sir. I am also a soldier, though I should hardly need to be to recognize so famous a seal as the one beneath your seat.'

The man looked awkwardly between his legs. The crate was stamped with a simple coat of arms in black: three running hounds, with crossed cannon barrels below.

'Are you insolent?' the man bleated.

'The only question that *matters*', continued Svenson mildly, 'is which member of the Xonck family you serve.'

'You did not say what happened to your head,' said Mr Fruitricks sullenly.

'I am sure I mentioned luggage.'

'You wander in a forest without any possessions! Without hat or coat –'

'Again, sir, all of this was left on the train.'

'I do not believe you!'

'What *else* would I be doing here?'

Svenson gestured at the trees with exasperation. The canal had curved more deeply into the park, and when Svenson looked through a small break in the trees, there was no longer any sign of the track bed. The pain in his arm was pulsing again, the disturbing overlay of images seeping up through his thoughts like bubbles of corruption in swamp water – the cenotaph, the fossil, Elöise . . . Svenson felt dizzy. He nodded to the stove. 'Would there be any more tea?'

'There would not,' replied Mr Fruitricks, whose mood had soured even more. He sniffed at Svenson like a thin, suspicious dog. 'You seem unwell.'

'The . . . ah . . .' The Doctor motioned vaguely towards the back of his head. 'Blow . . . bag . . . hitting me –'

'You will not vomit on my barge. It has new brass fittings.'

'Wouldn't dream of it,' rasped Svenson, his throat tightening. He stood. The barge master, who had approached without any warning at all, caught his shoulder and steadied him from pitching over the side. Svenson looked down at Fruitricks's crate. 'That has been opened,' he said.

'The Prince would not travel without you,' snarled Fruitricks, petulantly throwing his cigar into the water. 'You know where he is, where they all are, what has happened! Who has attacked them? Why have I heard nothing? Why have they said *nothing* to the Palace?'

The questions flew at Svenson with such speed and invective that each one caused him to blink. His tongue was thick, but he knew that the situation ought not to be beyond him. Fruitricks was exactly the sort of desperate man – officious courtiers, ambitious minions – he had spent years doggedly manipulating in the service of the Macklenburg court.

The sky spun, as if a very large bird had silently swept past. Doctor Svenson lay on his back. He squeezed his eyes tightly, embracing the dark.

Svenson woke slowly, his entire body stiff and chilled, and attempted to lift his arm. He could not. He craned his aching head – which felt the size of a moderate sweet melon – and saw the arm had been bound to a bolt on the deck with hemp rope. His other arm was tied as well, and both legs lashed together at the ankle and the knee: he lay cruciform between two of the canvas-wrapped objects. The sky was empty and white. He closed his eyes again and did his best to concentrate. The barge was no longer moving. He heard no footstep, call, or conversation. He opened his eyes and turned to the nearest piece of cargo. From within the canvas Svenson smelt indigo clay.

The hammer was gone from his belt. He brought his legs up and bent forward. The knot binding his knees came well within the reach of his teeth. The Doctor's naval service did not call for any particular knowledge of sailing, yet he had often found his interest piqued by older members of the crews he tended, and the earlier, vanished world those men had known. His awkward but honest attempts at friendship were often met with some practical demonstration – easier than conversation for all concerned – and in more than one instance this had involved knots and ropework. With some satisfaction, biting at the fraying hemp like a crow at a sinewy carcass, Svenson realized he knew both the knot in question – what seaman Ungar called a 'Norwegian horse' – and the simplest way to pluck it apart.

With his knees free and his legs beneath him, he could bend to reach his right hand. The knot was the same – he had no high opinion of his captors' creativity – and, a few moments aside for spitting out hemp fibre, his hand was quickly free, then the second hand, and at last his ankles. Doctor Svenson crouched at a gap between the swathed pieces of cargo, working the stiffness from his wrists.

The barge was tied at a dockside of freshly cut timber, and the road that led from the water was recently enough laid to show an even depth of gravel across its width. He saw no one on the landing. He quickly untied one of the canvas flaps, uncovering a gleaming steel foot pierced with empty bolt holes. Svenson reached into his pocket for a match, then stopped as his fingers found an empty pocket. His cigarette case, his filthy handkerchief, the matches . . . all missing. With a surge of rage at being plundered, the Doctor caught the canvas with both hands and pulled it away from the machinery. A brass-bound column of steel – studded, like a jewelled monarch's sceptre, with dials and gauges – liquid-filled chambers and copper coil. Svenson attacked the tall bundle to his other side: an examination table dangling black hose, like the legs of five wasps all overlaid onto a single sickening thorax, each hose end tipped with a ring of blue glass. He recalled the imprints on Angelique's body. This cargo had been removed from the great cathedral chamber at Harschmort.

*

The road narrowed between natural hedgerows of thick underbrush, and so the Doctor nearly missed it, rising above the trees: a dark curling plume against the white sky. Only then did he notice the rough path, simply made by a large man pushing his way through the foliage. He looked back towards the barge. Could it perhaps be a watch fire? But why would a watchman have set himself so far from the cargo? He took the time to dig out his monocle and screw it into place, and looked down the road.

The road curved, he realized. From the barge one could not see to its furthest end. But from the curve Svenson could see both behind to the barge and ahead to a distant white-brick building. Feeling suddenly exposed – was someone watching with a telescope? – he darted off the road. At the trees he sank to a crouch, peering through the leaves of a weeping beech at a ring of stones and a smoking knot of blackened wood. The fire had been allowed to gutter out. On a blanket next to the fire pit lay a bottle, a checked handkerchief containing what looked like bread and meat, and a flat silver square . . . his cigarette case.

Next to it lay the purple stone, a pencil stub, coins, his handkerchief . . . and something else he did not recognize, reflecting light in a different way than the case. Where was the man who had taken them?

Svenson crept carefully forward, towards the fire, and snatched up his things, hesitating at the last new object, which took him utterly aback. It was a blue glass card, exactly like the one he had found in the Prince's flower vase – the first glimpse of his charge's entanglement with the Cabal. The Doctor had later found another, on the body of Arthur Trapping, but both those other cards were long lost. What was another card now doing amongst his things?

Someone had slipped a blue glass card into his pocket without his knowing – but when? And who – for who could *have* such a thing? The cards were created by the Comte – enticing tokens to seduce potential adherents, each inscribed with the events of a few lurid moments . . . each as much a trap as a first exquisite taste of opium.

Svenson frowned. He had not had the purple stone in his pocket either. He had given it back to Elöise on the train . . .

He was an idiot – it was a *message*! She had tried to communicate with him! If only he had examined his pockets at the cottage! What if the blue card explained exactly what he ought to have done? What if the Contessa had forced Elöise – what if he had doubted her wrongly? What if it was not too late?

He grazed the cool surface of the glass with one fingertip, and at once felt an icy pressure at his mind. He licked his lips –

The Doctor spun at a noise on the other side of the fire. He stuffed the card into his tunic and snatched up a piece of unburnt wood. The sound came from behind an alder tree. He advanced cautiously. A pair of legs, half visible in the underbrush . . . the black-capped barge master, the kerchief round his neck soaked with blood and already a dark locus for flies. Svenson took a clasp knife from the man's belt, snapping it open. He shifted the piece of wood into his other hand, feeling a little foolish, as if he were apeing a true, battling man of action.

Another noise, now near the fire. While Svenson had been examining the body, the killer had quite silently circled round.

Svenson forced himself to walk, no longer caring for silence, directly towards the fire. A twig tugged insolently across his ear. Someone was there.

On the blanket, one hand picking at the food in the chequered handker-chief, the other tucked out of sight to her side, knelt the Contessa di Lacquer-Sforza. She met his arrival with a mocking smirk.

'Doctor Svenson. I confess, you are no one I expected in this particular wood – apart, one supposes, from *symmetry* – and yet having seen you approach so *earnestly* . . .'

Her dress was of poor-quality silk, dyed deep maroon. Her black boots were smeared with mud, and above the left he could see her white calf. She swept her hand across the blanket, as if to welcome him, indicating the exact spot where the blue card had been set, and spoke again, careful as any cobra. 'Will you not sit? Such old acquaintances like ourselves must have so very much to talk about – we should scarcely notice if it were the end of the world.'

SEVEN

CINDERS

As a girl Miss Temple had once, after insisting upon it for a steady hour, tagging along at his side as he surveyed the fields from the raised high road, been given a puff from the pipe of Mr Groft, the overseer of her father's plantation. She had immediately become sick – realizing the puff was not likely to be repeated, the young Miss Temple had made it a mighty one – dropping to her knees as the overseer spat oaths above her, for if her father found out he would be sacked. She had stumbled back to her rooms with a splitting pain behind her eyes and a reeking taste that would not leave her mouth, no matter how she scrubbed it with lemon slices. Mr Groft was indeed sacked, but that was the following month and had involved improprieties with housegirls, three of whom had been promptly sold (including a sweet fat thing, always kind but whose name Miss Temple had since forgotten), for her father's authority brooked no challenge whatsoever.

It was some years later, preparatory to her voyage to the Continent, when Miss Temple, goaded by that same iron cagework of rule, found herself in her father's study. Despite her imminent departure he had ridden to the far side of the island to inspect a new planting and was not expected to return before she sailed, simplifying everything for them both. She had wandered through the house and along the paths of the garden and the open balconies, smelling the sweet, musky fields. She knew she might never return. But in the study, sitting in her father's large leather chair – the horsehair stuffing clumped and flat and kept this way precisely because her father believed a lack of ease sharpened the mind – Miss Temple was suddenly restless, and looked to the closed study door, wondering if she ought to lock it even before she formed any sense of what she was going to do.

One of her hands had idly traced a path, finger by finger, up the inside of her thigh. Despite a fullness of tension in her flesh, not yet demanding but palpable, she pulled her hand away, for she did not choose – since it seemed that she had wandered now pointedly to the heart of her father's domain – to so expend her desires. Instead she opened the cedar box of cigars, wrinkling her nose. With a shocking and scandalous presumption she took one out and bit off the end, just as she had seen her father do on hundreds of occasions – and she knew, had she been male, this would have been a common occurrence, even such a thing as to bring two men together. She picked the bitter flakes from her mouth and wiped them onto the cracked leather of the chair, then leant to the candle on the desktop. She puffed four times before the thing took fire, gagged, spat out the smoke, and puffed twice more, swallowing the smoke with a cough. Her eyes watered. After another puff she erupted with a hacking that would not stop. The awful taste was back in her mouth. But she continued to inhale, determined, until there was an inch of tightly coiled grey ash at the end. Miss Temple wiped her lips on her sleeve, feeling dizzy.

It was enough, her edge of restlessness blunted by disgust – with both the tobacco and her own desire. She set the smoking cigar on the metal ash tray and collected her candle, walking unsteadily from the room – uncaring whether a servant would clear it away before her father returned or if he would find the evidence of her invasion himself . . . a last fittingly oblique communication between them.

The foulness of these old memories was but a childish shadow to what she had so foolishly just opened herself. Miss Temple lay on her back beyond the gardens of Harschmort, panting hard, staring up without registering the slightest detail of cloud or sky, insensible to any cries that might have echoed beyond the hedgerows, to gunshots, and to time. She reached up slowly, as if the air had become gelatinous with dread, and touched her dripping mouth. Her fingers were wet with saliva and a clotted string of black bile. With a concentrated effort she turned her head and saw, gleaming where it had fallen, the blue glass book. She swallowed, her throat raw from retching, and sank back again, feeling the stalks of tall grass poking at her hair, her will sapped, with all the sickness in her mind rising again like a flooding mire.

Since looking into the glass book in the Contessa's rooms, Miss Temple had been determined that its insistent, delirious memories not overwhelm her, knowing such an initial surrender could easily stretch into a span of days. But Miss Temple's disapproval of a world so defined was primarily fearful, for such surrender frightened her very much. Miss Temple did not consider herself as priggish – she did not tremble at her own natural appetites – yet she knew some pleasures were different. When she imagined them inside her mind, she imagined her mind stained.

But the second book changed all of this. It had coloured Miss Temple's thoughts to the same extreme degree as the first – or recoloured them, overlaying every vivid impulse ash grey. The Contessa's book had been compiled from countless lives, while the book on the grass contained the memories of a single man – but his memories had been harvested at the very moment of death, infecting each instant of his captured experience with a toxic, corrupting, nauseating dread. It was not unlike the pageants one saw carved on medieval churches – lines of people, from princesses to peasants to popes, trailing hand in hand after Death, the trappings of their lives exposed as vanity. Scenes of lust – and what scenes they were! – became disgusting charades of rotting meat, sumptuous banquets became fashioned whole from human filth, every strain of sweet, sweet music became restrung to the coarse calling of blood-fed crows. Miss Temple had never imagined such despair, such utter hopelessness, such bottomless bankruptcy. The first book's bright empire of sensation, its unstable riot beneath her skin, had been mirrored by bitter futility, with the acrid dust that was every person's inheritance.

But Miss Temple understood why Francis Xonck had chosen this book to keep. How quick his thoughts must have flown just to see the possibility, to seize an empty glass book. He had preserved in its unfeeling depths – the freezing glass no doubt pressed to the dying man's face – all the alchemical knowledge of the Comte d'Orkancz.

She shoved her body onto one elbow, pursing her lips with a twinge of irritation that hinted at recovery, and looked over her shoulder at the book,

whose surface had taken on a satisfied glow. Miss Temple doubted there
was any person – even Xonck, even Chang – strong enough to actually
immerse themselves in its contents without being utterly overwhelmed.
Mrs Marchmoor's hand had passed into it without harm . . . but what did
that mean? The glass woman may have learnt the book contained the Comte
– why else would she have gone to Harschmort? – but if she had been able
to absorb the actual contents of the Comte's mind, then she would have
had no need for Miss Temple and no reason to seek the Comte's tools and
machines. Miss Temple recalled the three glass women ransacking the
minds of everyone in the Harschmort ballroom – invisibly passing everything they saw to the Comte . . . it only made sense that he had forbidden
them to enter his *own* mind. Could that taboo extend to his mind when
encased in the book? Mrs Marchmoor had come to Harschmort to insert
the book into another body – one the glass woman believed she *could*
control. But that must mean she had no idea of the taint, the corruption
colouring all of its contents.

And what of Francis Xonck? He had rescued the book from the sinking
airship, his own body a sickening ruin, in the hope of reversing his
condition. Had *he* looked into it? Miss Temple did not think so. Had
not Xonck come to Harschmort – just like Mrs Marchmoor – to find the
necessary machines to open the book and thus save his life?

Again Miss Temple wondered who had set the fires, foiling them both.

She curled her legs beneath her and peeked over the wall. The actual
clearing where Xonck and Mrs Marchmoor had struggled was far beyond
view, but there were no signs of anyone searching in the garden. With a
fretful grimace – as if she were managing an especially wicked-looking cane
spider – Miss Temple carefully scooped the glass book back into the canvas
sack. Harschmort was surrounded by miles of fen country. She was alone,
hungry, and her appearance would have dismayed a fishwife. Miss Temple
wound the top of the sack around her palm and pushed her way through
the high grass. She had no idea of cross-country escapes and pursuing
soldiers, but what she knew quite well were large houses run by servants,
riddled with ways to pass unseen.

Near the stone wall's end lay a collection of low sheds. She saw no one – and this was strange, for even with the family not present, routine upkeep of Harschmort's house and grounds ought to necessitate all manner of effort, and Miss Temple was confident – unless she had discovered an epidemic of shirking – that these sheds were a hive of everyday activity. Yet now they seemed to be abandoned.

She scampered quickly between the sheds to the nearest glass double doors of the house. The lock had been broken. This must be where Francis Xonck had forced his way in. Miss Temple slipped into the ballroom. She had last seen it full of the Cabal's minions, dressed in finery and wearing masks, cheering their masters off to Macklenburg. Now the great wooden floor and the line of bright windows were coated with dust from the fire. She crossed quickly and found herself in the very same ante-room where the Contessa had licked the port stains from her eyes. Miss Temple shivered, stopping where she was. The memory of the Contessa's tongue led directly to the goods van, the woman's lips on her own . . . and to Miss Temple's spiralling shame she could not stop her mind from ploughing on. At once those kisses bloomed like a gushing artery into a hundred more, kisses of all kinds between too many different people to separate, erupting from the Contessa's book. Miss Temple stuffed one hand in her mouth, the tips of her body ablaze, aghast at how quickly she had been so overwhelmed. On desperate impulse, she opened her reeling senses to the second book, to the bilious tang of the Comte's despair. As it collided with her pleasure, Miss Temple lurched into the cover of a decorative philodendron, where she crouched and rocked helplessly, hugging her knees.

In time, both waves ebbed away. She heard shouting in another part of the house. Miss Temple staggered up. In the corridor lay the older servant, toppled by Mrs Marchmoor, his face still dark with blood. The voices were far away and the hallways too conducive to echo for her to place them. She crept past the fallen man to what looked like a painted wall panel and found the inset hook to pull it open, revealing a narrow maid's staircase. She climbed past two landings before leaving it to enter a thickly carpeted corridor with a low ceiling, almost as if she had boarded an especially luxurious ship – though she knew this to be an architectural remnant of

Harschmort Prison. With a spark of anticipation Miss Temple padded
towards Lydia Vandaariff's suite of rooms.

She passed quietly through the Lady of Harschmort's private parlour,
attiring room, bedchamber, and finally to her astonishingly spacious closet.
The walls were lined with hanging garments and tightly stuffed shelving –
enough clothing for a regiment of ladies. Satisfied no one was here – she
had feared a lingering maid – Miss Temple lifted the chair from the heiress's
writing desk and, recalling Chang's precautions at the Boniface, wedged it
fast under the door knob.

She returned to the closet, plucking at her dress – not intending any
commentary on the late Mrs Jorgens but more than sick of it, the smell of
her own sweat having permeated the fabric. Miss Temple dislodged the
final buttons with impatience, pulled it over her head and then balled the
thing up to throw across the room.

She stopped. As she wadded the fabric . . . on the side of the bodice,
along the seam . . . she stepped closer to the light and removed a scrap of
parchment paper torn to a neat square and folded over. She wondered if it
was from Mrs Jorgens – a shopping list or love note – for the writing first
struck her as an unschooled scrawl. But that was wrong . . . not so much a
scrawl as that its author was utterly careless of how it appeared. As she
thought back to the littered ruin of the suite at the St Royale, such an
intemperate script for the Contessa di Lacquer-Sforza made perfect sense.

My Dear Celeste,

Forgive my Departure. Were I to stay I must eat you to the Bones.

*Islands are Precious Domains. This is my way of saying Do Not
Follow. That is your Choice now, as it was mine before you. There
is no Shame in Retreat.*

*If you Ignore good Advice, I will see you Again. Our Business is
not Finished.*

    RLS

Miss Temple folded the note, then unfolded it and read it again, sucking her lip at each overly dramatic capital, sensing that even in this disturbing little note (and how long had it taken the woman to find that pocket, she wondered, imagining those nimble fingers searching across her body . . .) the Contessa's foremost goal had been to find some measure of delight. It was as if, in a mist of woodland air that anyone else would find refreshing, the Contessa di Lacquer-Sforza would locate some extra thread of scent (a flower or a rotting stag – or flowers growing *from* a stag's carcass) so the tips of her black hair might twist another curl.

Miss Temple did not consider herself an object of change – she had always been the same bundle of impulses and moods, however unpredictable these might appear to others – but now she found herself surprised, in the very midst of her anger, by the sudden memory of the Contessa's gashed shoulder, and an urge to draw her own tongue along its ragged, coppery length. The problem was not the impulse itself, but the necessary connection to another person.

Miss Temple had become very accustomed to the fact that, in her life, almost no one *liked* her. She was served, flattered, distrusted, disapproved of, coveted, envied, despised, but she had never, with the illusory exceptions of certain servants when she was a girl, enjoyed any particular friendship. The closest she had come was her fiancé, Roger Bascombe, but that had been a mere three months sparked by physical hunger (and had turned out horribly). She thought of Chang and Svenson, even Elöise . . . but friendship was hardly the same thing as loyalty or duty. Would the two men die for her? She had no doubt. Did they *like* her? A nut-hard part of Miss Temple's heart would not believe it – and she could have easily convinced herself the question did not matter, save for the Contessa's disorienting attentions in the goods van, no matter how mercenary those attentions undoubtedly had been.

But then, for she could not help it, Miss Temple read through the note again, this time fixing on the word 'Choice', and the very intriguing phrase that followed it, 'as it was mine before you' . . . she had never heard even one reference to the Contessa's life *before* . . . nor entertained the notion that there *was* a before for such a creature. Miss Temple's throat went dry to imagine what the Contessa could have possibly been like as a *girl*. And what *choice* could any girl have made to become that woman?

And how *dare* she suggest that Miss Temple herself faced anything resembling the same crossroads?

Suitably affronted to set the paper back down, Miss Temple turned her attentions elsewhere. Lydia Vandaariff's closet had a metal hip bath and a very large Chinese pitcher of water. To either side of a tall mirror stood elegant tables, three-tiered like cakes and entirely cluttered with pins, ribbons, bottles, powders, paints, and perfumes. She tore off the corset and ill-fitting shift she had worn since her bath in Lina's kitchen and then, quite determined to be clean once more, sat naked on the carpet to unlace her boots.

Though the water was unheated there was still a splendid array of sponges and soaps, and Miss Temple took the opportunity to scrub the whole of her body without any impediment of time. She must leave Harschmort eventually, but did it not make sense to wait until nightfall – a decision which, once made, allowed her *hours*? After having washed and towelled at some leisure, she entered into a scrupulous investigation of Lydia's wide array of scents. While Miss Temple could not but view so many choices as emblematic of Lydia's essential lack of character, she was nevertheless curious as to whether her own sensible routine might be improved. Out of deliberately minded perversity, she settled upon a concoction of frangipani flowers, the Contessa's signature scent, placing a drop behind each ear and on each wrist, and then dragging one wet fingertip from the join of her collarbones down between her breasts.

Though Lydia had been taller than she, Miss Temple found several dresses that fitted and one in particular that would allow her to run. This was a murky shade of violet that went quite well with both her boots (she was committed to her boots) and with her hair. That the fabric was dark meant it would not so eagerly show the dirt her actions must acquire; that it was sensible wool meant she would not be cold – practical insights that pleased Miss Temple very much.

Yet before the dress came an exacting selection of undergarments, and here, more than anywhere, the late Miss Vandaariff had not skimped. The possibilities presented to Miss Temple became quite literally overwhelming, as each new garment opened lurid implications – a veritable advent calendar of wickedness – in her mind. She was forced to pause, eyes open, cheeks flushed, and thighs tight together, until the fluttering tide had passed. With trembling fingers she selected silk replacements for her long-lost little pants and bodice, then petticoats, and a corset, which she put on backwards, tightened as well as she could, and then inched round until the laces were behind her. This done, Miss Temple sat at Lydia's mirror and did her steady best, availing herself freely of pins, ribbon, and a tortoiseshell comb, to strip the knots from her hair and restore the sausage curls she associated with her own accustomed *presentation*. She was not her maid Marthe – and, had she been asked, might well have admitted it – but possessed some skill with her own hair (and since it had before been *such* a fright, the merest measure of success was welcome). Another half an hour slipped past before Miss Temple was at last presentable, the canvas sack exchanged for an elegant leather travel case, the glass book inside doubly wrapped within two silk pillowcases.

She knew she was dawdling, to keep away from outright danger and to indulge herself in the luxury to which she had been for far too long denied. She had even, as she washed herself and patted powder along her limbs, enjoyed the sensual tension of the Contessa's book, hovering like a cloud of golden bees just beyond reach, testing the limits of what she might allow and when she must bite the inside of her mouth to quell the sweetening tides. But then she became aware of another strain – an impatience with the petty vanity of her toilette; and she watched with fascination, both within the emotion and sufficiently apart to see it, as the impatience grew into anger – with herself, with the luxury around her, with everything the useless life of Lydia Vandaariff had stood for. She shot home the latches on the case and picked it up. Without any thought but bitter disapproval Miss Temple's hand lashed out at an especially over-glazed Chinese ginger jar and boxed it from its stand. The jar broke on the floor like a disconsolate egg, and she smiled. She stopped and snatched up another just like it. With grim satisfaction Miss Temple hurled the thing all the way back into

the closet's mahogany door, the completeness of its destruction the exact
expression of sharp justice she had desired.

Miss Temple, now unsettled and sour, retraced her path down the corridor.
If she could suppress the glass books' active interference with her thoughts,
Miss Temple could not expunge the *fact* of their encroachment — nor
pretend that suppression was any lasting victory. As she walked, she sensed
the prison's bones behind the paint and powder of Harschmort's splendour.
Was she any different? Just as the lurid memories from the Contessa's book
mocked Miss Temple's most secret desires, the Comte's book made clear
its own web of grim connection – that death was shot through her past, her
family, her wealth, and in her every morsel of anger or condescension or
contempt.

   She glanced into a mirror on the wall, its heavy gold frame carved with
impossibly lush paeonies, the blossoms blown open in a way that made
Miss Temple uncomfortable. But what caused her to stop before the glass
and rise to her toes was the pallor of her face. There had been mirrors in
Lydia's chamber, and she had naturally glanced at her own body as she
bathed – the shape of her legs, the appearance of her bosom, the tightly
curled hair between her legs when it was wet and soaped – but this was a
way of looking and not seeing. Miss Temple poked a finger into the skin
below her eye and took it away – there was a brief impression of pink where
the fingertip had been, but it faded at once, leaving her complexion waxy
and drawn. She bared her teeth and was distressed to see the edges of her
gums were red as the flesh of a fresh-cut strawberry.

Miss Temple peeked over the railing of the main staircase, her newly set curls hanging over her face, and saw a passing line of bright red uniforms far below. There had been no soldiers accompanying their coach, which meant others had arrived. Did this mean Colonel Aspiche? She could not descend to the foyer if there was anyone there who might recognize her. She quickly darted down one flight, just to the next landing. She would cut along this hallway, stay out sight, and find a servant's staircase to the ground. But when Miss Temple hurried around the first corner she nearly collided with a captain of dragoons.

He was fair-haired with an elegantly curled moustache and side whiskers. It was the officer she'd seen in the corridor of Stäelmaere House, sick and tottering after his audience with the Duke. Behind him in a line, the oldest holding hands with the Captain, were three primly dressed children.

'Good-afternoon,' said Miss Temple, bobbing in a tardy sketch of a curtsy.

'Closer to evening, I think,' replied the Captain. His voice was soft but sharp, like a talking fox in a tale.

'And who are all of you?' asked Miss Temple (who did not appreciate foxes), smiling past the officer at the three children. She did not especially appreciate children either, but could be kind to them when they were silent. All three watched her with wide, solemn eyes.

'I am Charles,' said the middle child, a ginger-haired boy in a brushed black velvet suit. He sniffed. 'Master Charles Trapping.'

'Hello, Charles.' Miss Temple loathed the boy at once.

'I am Francesca,' said the eldest, a girl with hair near the colour of Miss Temple's own. Her chin was small and her eyes too round, but her dress was a shade of lilac Miss Temple very much approved of. The girl's voice was low, as if she was not at all confident of her surroundings but as the eldest needed to assert precedence over her brash younger brother. Francesca turned to the third, a boy of perhaps three years, also in a velvet suit, holding in one hand the remains of a chocolate biscuit. 'That is Ronald.'

'Hello, Ronald.'

Ronald looked at his feet in silence.

'Who are *you*?' demanded Charles.

Miss Temple smiled. 'I am a dear friend of Miss Lydia Vandaariff, whose house you are in. She has journeyed to Macklenburg to be married.'

'Did she forget something?' Charles pointed to her case.

'She did not,' replied Miss Temple. '*I* did.'

'Don't you have servants to fetch it for you?'

Miss Temple smiled icily, wanting to strike him. 'One does not simply send servants to Harschmort House. We had been celebrating Lydia's engagement –'

'My mother has a case just like that,' said Francesca. 'For her silver bracelets.'

'Is that full of silver bracelets?' the officer asked Miss Temple. His gaze gently ranged across her body. He negligently met her eyes and smiled, but the smile seemed unconnected to his thoughts.

'What I forgot', Miss Temple replied with a winning smile, 'was a set of combs and brushes. As a *treat*, Lydia's closest friends all prepared her for the *gala evening*. But now I need them back again.'

'Haven't you a maid?' asked Charles.

'I have as many maids as I like,' snapped Miss Temple. 'But one is accustomed to a particular degree of *bristle*. I'm sure your sister under-stands.' She smiled at Francesca, but the girl was rubbing her eye.

'When Maria brushes Ronald's hair it makes him *cry*,' announced Charles.

Ronald said nothing, but looked at Miss Temple with hopeless little eyes.

'And what brings all of *you* to Harschmort?' Miss Temple asked brightly.

'I don't believe I heard your name,' interrupted the officer.

'I am Miss Stearne.' Miss Temple raised her eyebrow to let him know she held it to be an impertinent question. 'Miss Isobel Stearne.'

'David Tackham, Captain of Dragoons.' The officer clicked his heels with another wry smile. 'A pleasure to make your acquaintance, Miss Stearne. Are you related to *Caroline* Stearne?'

'I beg your pardon?'

'Caroline Stearne. Also an intimate of Miss Vandaariff, I believe.'

'We are cousins,' said Miss Temple tartly. 'Caroline is presently travelling

with Miss Vandaariff, as they are especially close to one another. Do you
know her? She did not mention you.'

'I know *of* her only. A handsome woman, I am told.'

Tackham's blue eyes were both lovely and absent. Miss Temple looked
at them for just a touch too long, and they began to appear inhuman – blue
eyes so often *did* that, Miss Temple felt.

'Were you off to anywhere in particular, Miss Stearne?' he asked.

Miss Temple did not reply, bending forward to Francesca with a smile.
'Where is your mother, darling?'

'I do not know,' answered the girl, her lip quivering.

Miss Temple turned at a sound on the main stairs. A young man in a black
coat with a yellow waxed moustache and blue eyes approached them, a
sheaf of papers under one arm. In his Ministry topcoat, he could have been
a lesser cousin of Roger Bascombe, but as he came nearer Miss Temple saw
the pallor of his skin, and the bloodied nails on the hand that held the
white papers.

'There you are.' He noted Miss Temple's presence with an irritated
frown. 'Who is this?'

'I am Miss Stearne.'

'What is she doing here?' the man asked Tackham.

'I am a friend of Lydia Vandaariff,' Miss Temple answered him. 'What
are *you* doing so freely in *my* friend's house?'

'This is Miss Stearne.' Captain Tackham smiled.

The Ministry man ignored her. 'You are well behind schedule, Captain.
There is no time –'

'If there's so little time, where in hell have you been?' Tackham snapped.

The other man's eyes shot wide at such language in front of the children,
but he erupted in a wicked sneeze, and then two more in rapid succession,
even as he shifted the papers to his other arm and pulled a handkerchief
from his pocket. He finally wiped his nose but not before they had all seen
the first smear of blood on the yellow waxed hair on his upper lip.

'I'll not have this impertinence. Mr Phelps is waiting with the Duke.'

'Will you join us?' Captain Tackham asked Miss Temple.

'Yes, please,' said Francesca in a small voice.

'Of course she will not,' snapped the man from the Ministry.

'She has a case of hairbrushes,' announced Charles, as if this were especially significant. The Ministry man ignored him and folded his handkerchief away.

'Captain Tackham! The *Duke*!'

'What is *your* name?' Miss Temple asked the man.

'He is Mr Harcourt,' replied Tackham.

'Mr Harcourt has not answered my question about what he is doing with another man's children in my good friend's house.'

Harcourt fixed her with an unpleasant glare. 'Perhaps you'd like to come with us after all? Perhaps you'd care to explain' – he sniffed again, for the dark pearl of blood had reappeared – 'to the *Duke* just where your good friend's *father* has gone off to!'

Harcourt wheeled towards the stairs. Tackham snapped his fingers for Francesca's hand without shifting his gaze from Miss Temple, who was shocked to see, as the girl extended her arm to the officer, the sleeve of the child's dress slide up to reveal a blot of cotton wool stuck to the hollow of her elbow with blood. As the unlikely party disappeared behind the balcony rail, all three children looked back to her, like lambs on a leash to market.

It had been gratifying how easily her being disagreeable to Harcourt had resulted in his leaving her behind – but, unless the Captain was a fool, there would be immediate enquiries about one Isobel Stearne and soldiers sent to find her. That the children were being brought to the Duke – that the Duke was still in play – meant Mrs Marchmoor had survived, and that the children were being brought to *her*. Yet the shock Miss Temple had felt in her mind as she fled the garden had been real. Something *had* hurt the glass woman dearly, but not dearly enough.

She smiled at Harcourt's slip revealing that they'd *still* no idea how Robert Vandaariff had disappeared, pleased with an opportunity to puzzle something out for herself – such puzzling being an excellent distraction from the distressing urges of her body (had it been necessary to so notice the delicate curve of Captain Tackham's throat?) and the foul taste that would not leave the back of her throat. Vandaariff's absence must be related to the fires at Harschmort – but had he been taken, or murdered?

Miss Temple paused on the landing, wondering why a dragoon officer had been guarding children – and then what the Trapping children were doing here to begin with. Had they been taken hostage to ensure their mother's cooperation? Why waste time kidnapping the children of a power-less woman? Thus, Charlotte Trapping was *not* powerless, but a person Mrs Marchmoor needed to control . . . could *she* be the new adversary? With the death of her husband she surely had a motive.

On the carpet lay a crumble of chocolate biscuit, directly outside a door. Miss Temple walked to the door and opened it. On a spindle-legged side table next to a mirror-fronted cabinet sat an unfinished snifter of brandy and a half-smoked cheroot in a ceramic dish. Clearly Captain Tackham had found his own distractions. Further into the room were two uncomfortable-looking armchairs with yellow cushions, and across from these (beneath a strange painting of an old man glaring oddly at two half-dressed young women) was a fancily carved camp bed, with a long, blue-striped bolster. Beneath it lay more chocolate crumbs.

Beyond the camp bed was another doorway. Through it came the scuffling of papers, and then a dry voice croaking with impatience. 'Are you back again, Tackham? What have you cocked up *this* time?'

Miss Temple clapped a hand across her mouth to stifle a gasp. In the mirrored cabinet, she could see, reflected from the far side of the doorway – dishevelled, sickly, but still unquestionably recognizable – of all people, Andrew Rawsbarthe, Roger Bascombe's aide. On his desktop lay an open leather case lined with orange felt and containing inset depressions for small glass-stoppered vials. Three of these spaces were empty. These vials, their ruby contents glowing darkly, lay before Rawsbarthe, who was in the midst of glueing to each, with shaking fingers (each ending in a ragged and split purpled nail), small labels. To the side lay jumbled wads of cotton wool, streaked with still-bright blood. He finished the last label, slipped the vials into the case, and snapped it closed.

'Captain Tackham! I am in no state for *teasing.*'

The chair scraped as Mr Rawsbarthe stood. He would know her – they had been in each other's company a score of times. Had Roger taken him into his confidence? Or was he another of Mrs Marchmoor's minions, to be occupied and consumed? Did he know of Miss Temple's actions against the Cabal? Ought she to snatch up the brandy bottle and crack him on the head?

Rawsbarthe called, less certain. 'Mr Fochtmann?'

He appeared in the doorway, the leather case tucked under one arm. Miss Temple had not moved. They stared at one another.

'Hello, Mr Rawsbarthe. I'm sure I did not expect to find you *here*.'

'Miss Temple! Nor I – of all people – *you*!'

Andrew Rawsbarthe had always been the servile functionary hovering at Roger's right arm, and, as a young woman inured to servantry from an early age – and servantry of an especially abject status – Miss Temple had regarded him as merely a more animated, speaking species of footstool.

'Permit me to observe you do not look at all well.'

'A smithereen of fatigue,' offered Rawsbarthe, plucking at his shirt collar. 'Extra duties with this recent *unrest*. It will pass.'

'You have lost a tooth.'

'But I have found *you*,' the man replied, his tongue reflexively sliding over the gap. 'In Harschmort House.'

'I believe it is *I* have done the finding . . .'

Miss Temple noticed Mr Rawsbarthe's eyes upon her bosom . . . and was shocked that instead of sparking her bitter ire, she sensed with a mocking pleasure what power his covetous desire granted her, and what she might now be able to *do*.

His eyes flicked to the open door behind her.

Sensing that Rawsbarthe sought to prevent her exit, she reached for the door herself and swung it closed, the clasp catching with a well-greased click to shut them in together.

'That is a new coat you wear,' said Miss Temple. 'And of a finer cut. Do you know where Mr Bascombe – your superior – *is*?'

Mr Rawsbarthe cleared his throat and swallowed. 'Do *you*?'

'Do you know why you moult to pieces like a dying parrot?'

'Roger Bascombe is *dead*!' blurted Rawsbarthe, openly gauging her reaction to this news.

'Is he?'

'Do you deny it?'

'Why should I?'

'Because Bascombe was murdered! He accompanied Deputy Foreign Minister Crabbé to Macklenburg, but they never arrived – cables from Warnemünde have confirmed it!'

'Not arriving does not make him dead, much less murdered.'

Rawsbarthe stepped closer, shaking his head with a cloying tolerance.

'Do you imagine the Queen's Privy Council and her Ministries remain idle when so much hangs in the balance? I know you were this very morning found at Stropping Station and taken to the Palace. I know your disfigured criminal accomplice – O yes, we are *aware* of your *activities* – has re-emerged from the gutters where he fled. And the German spy? His own government has issued papers for his arrest – by now he's been dragged home in chains, or had his throat cut by his countrymen! You know about Roger Bascombe! You know about Arthur Trapping!'

'Ah, well then, it is impossible to dissemble.' Miss Temple found herself smiling enigmatically and batting her eyes. 'I put a bullet through Roger Bascombe's heart myself.'

Rawsbarthe was silent. Miss Temple deliberately inhaled, the small swell of her breasts momentarily confounding the man's attention, and then let out a poor little sigh. 'You will undoubtedly want to arrest me – it is natural. And yet . . . have we not made enough amiable conversation between us – at the Ministry, at Mr Bascombe's home, at so many very dull receptions – to possess between us *some* understanding?'

'You . . . *shot* him?'

'Dear Mr Rawsbarthe . . . what I *mean* to say – and I may be wrong, and if that is so, we must proceed to unfortunate outcomes –'

'The murder of Roger Bascombe –'

'Enough about Bascombe.'

'Miss Temple, as much as I might prefer –'

'Mr Rawsbarthe, I do not believe you are a fool.'

'I am gratified by the sentiment, I'm sure.'

'Indeed, so – please – if you could just step . . . *here.*'

She took his arm – causing him to nervously lick his lips – and guided him two steps to the mirrored cabinet. Rawsbarthe flinched.

'Look at my skin.' Miss Temple nodded to her mirrored image. 'Below the eyes.'

'You are a perfectly attractive young woman –'

'O Andrew – normally I should blushingly agree with you, but the two of us must be honest . . . I look ill.'

'People often do.'

'Not me.'

'No doubt the toll of your recent *immorality* –'

'Andrew . . . look at yourself.'

At once he pulled away. 'I – I am a representative of the Foreign Ministry, and I insist that you accompany me downstairs. You must see the Duke –'

'How do you think I arrived?'

Rawsbarthe put a hand to his mouth. 'You saw the Duke? You spoke with him? Impossible, he speaks to no one –'

'Of course he doesn't –'

'But how are you free? Did they not know you?'

'Of course they did!'

'How can that be?'

'Have you *seen* the Duke? Andrew – listen to me, for your own sake –'

Rawsbarthe's eyes shirked away from hers, and he squeezed the leather case.

'Andrew, answer me! Have you *seen* the Duke?'

Rawsbarthe waved at the mirror without looking at it. 'If you refer to His Grace's illness – most definitely not the blood fever that has been rumoured, rumoured to infect all Harschmort, and yet here we are! – it is but an ague that will pass! If in the meantime others of us shake under His Grace's chills, it is another sort of loyalty, of *service* –'

Rawsbarthe took another step away, staring at the carpet like a shamed dog, his voice coloured by an unpersuasive chuckle.

'Whatever you have *assumed* – well, trust you are not the first to make the error. Indeed, the inner workings of a modern government must appear a veritable *spider's web* of influence and compulsion to the humble citizen, and so the commonplace – an ague! – turns into mystery, crisis, plague! I do not know what Mr Bascombe ever explained to you – very little I should think, you being, indeed, a w-w-woman –'

'Mr Rawsbarthe –'

'Now I must take you downstairs with all despatch. Mr Bascombe spoke at all times with discretion – I have heeded no insinuations about what compromised your engagement, even now, despite those questionable men who have become your *companions* –'

Miss Temple stepped nearer, and he began to stammer. She could smell the frangipani perfume on her skin and wondered if he could as well. Rawsbarthe took a breath with a quivering determination, as if he had been abruptly pushed to some inner precipice.

'A great deal has changed, Miss Temple. I do not promise I am in a position to help you – but yet it may be that I am not wholly without influence. I *have* been summoned to Stäelmaere House . . . on several occasions . . . a sign of favour I should not have dreamt of one week ago.'

'I have just been there myself,' observed Miss Temple.

'Then you know!' he said quickly, and then caught himself. 'Or perhaps not – perhaps you did not – cannot . . . truly appreciate –'

'Appreciate *what*, exactly?' She came closer, despite the unclean odour of his mouth.

'How bold you are, I see that – even if you try to influence me – towards, ah, leniency – but – but nevertheless, because you know – *knew* – Mr Bascombe, you can at least appreciate my good fortune, even to be *invited* –'

'O I *do* appreciate it,' she whispered.

'Do you truly?'

'I should like every detail! Once you entered Stäelmaere House . . . the seat of the Privy Council itself . . . the corridor with the glass cases and those awful old paintings – were you ushered to a room? Come, Andrew . . . what do you *remember*?'

'Naturally, I was not alone –'

'Were you with Mr Soames?'

'How do you know Soames?' Rawsbarthe's voice was pinched. 'Soames is *new*! *He* didn't see the Duke? Soames is hardly worthy of –'

'Soames does not matter,' she assured him. 'The *room*. It was dark?'

'His Grace is notoriously particular.'

'So you did see the Duke?'

'Of *course*! And we *heard* him –'

'What did he say?'

'I . . . I . . . the words themselves . . .'

She waited. Rawsbarthe clutched his hands.

'Andrew . . . surely you *remember*?'

'Ah . . . well –'

'How can you not remember what the Duke of Stäelmaere said to you *personally*? The highest achievement of your career?'

Rawsbarthe was silent. Her lips almost touched his blood-scabbed ear. 'I will tell you why, Andrew. You fell asleep. Every one of you. You had dreams. A pain in your head . . . the taste of copper in your throat. You knew exactly what you must do, though you cannot recall receiving any instruction. And afterwards none of you said a word –'

'Silence b-bespeaks the high respect –'

'Listen to yourself! It is Mrs Marchmoor!'

'I beg your pardon? I am unacquainted with any M-M-Mrs –'

'*The glass woman.*'

Rawsbarthe attempted a blanched smile. 'I must assure you again there are no *women* in Stäelmaere House – the Duke's, ah, *martial* proclivities –'

She took his shoulder and thrust him again towards the mirror. Mr Rawsbarthe bleated his protest and squeezed shut his eyes.

'Andrew! Mrs Marchmoor has rummaged in your thinking like it was a *bag*!'

'Miss Temple –'

'*Look at yourself!*'

He did, but at once burst free with a stricken cry, shoving past and knocking Miss Temple across one of the chairs. By the time she pulled herself upright, there was no sign or sound of Andrew Rawsbarthe at all.

Miss Temple found her side staircase. The walls were lined with painted niches aping the shadowed passageways of a cathedral, each holding allegorical figures that Miss Temple – whose biblical education had been attended to with a gratifying indifference – nevertheless recognized as the ten plagues visited upon Egypt. Despite her hurry she could not help but stare as she went down, the toads, blood, lice, and fire presaging her own descent into the stinking mire than had already swallowed poor Rawsbarthe. But the final landing stopped her cold, for the wider section of wall allowed for a more elaborate tableau, and she stood there, Francesca Trapping's bandaged arm fresh in her mind, facing the death of the Egyptian first-born, where pitiless angels dangled lifeless children from both hands, hovering above a crowd of keening women.

At the base of the stairs was a door on a swing. She was near the kitchens. The corridor wound past rooms stuffed with barrels and crates and dishes and bottles and baskets and burlap sacks, rooms storing pots and pans both massive enough to cook a wild boar whole and comedically small, as if for a Roman banquet of larks. Yet every room she passed, in what ought to have been the busiest part of the household, was devoid of servants.

At a larger archway she wrinkled her nose and looked about her for the source of the smell – matted straw thrown onto the mess, the actual cleaning laid aside for some luckless drudge – perhaps a soup bowl's worth of mustard-yellow vomit. Miss Temple had reached the enormous central kitchen hearth, radiating heat from a bed of white flaking coals. The benches and tables that filled the room had all been pushed aside, as if making room for . . . something. She advanced slowly, and the smells of gastric excrescence gave way to the stench of indigo clay. A pebble crunched beneath her foot – a fleck of blue glass. The smell was thicker at the hearth itself, the heat against her face. On the brick border of the oven lay a dusting of tiny blue needles . . .

What *had* happened in the garden? And where was everybody *now*?

She staggered and put a hand over her mouth, turning her face and groping for the nearest table to support her. What had just happened?

She had framed the questions in her mind . . . and then suddenly received a sickening flick of an answer . . . the glass woman had been in here, and in such distress that the agony projected from her mind had sickened the minions around her. The knowledge had come from the Comte's memories – Miss Temple's own mind drawing unbidden from that pool, dangerously and without warning –

Miss Temple bent over and did her best to rid herself of the nausea, but nothing came. She felt the blood rushing to her head and stood, grim and once more consumed with an anger not altogether hers.

The corridor ended at another swinging door, and she pushed through to an elegant dining room. A crystal chandelier in the shape of a three-masted frigate hung over an enormous long dark table. The glass craft floated like a ghost ship, bearing a mere half-dozen candles, their glow abetted by a standing candelabrum on the table itself, set next to a man in his shirt-sleeves. He sat in the master's own throne-like seat and busied himself amidst a mass of papers. One ink-stained hand held an old-fashioned quill and the other a metal tool she had seen used on a ship to measure distance. Beyond him lay the doorway out.

The man was not Robert Vandaariff.

Miss Temple cleared her throat. He looked up and showed himself to be younger than she'd first assumed. His hair had receded to the rear of his skull — but upon seeing his face she doubted he was much older than Chang, and his firm jaw and strong hands bespoke a masculinity that made her twitch. He set down the quill and the metal tool, and stood, a politeness that took her by surprise.

'I did not know there were any ladies in the house . . .'

'I am Miss Stearne, a friend of Lydia Vandaariff. I fear I am interrupting all sorts of things everywhere.'

'Not at all, I'm sure.'

'There seems to have been a fire.'

The man gestured broadly with a wry smile. 'And yet the house is of a size that some fifty rooms remain for civilized occupation. Would you care for tea?'

'No, thank you.' The last thing Miss Temple wanted was to be introduced to a servant as a friend of Lydia's. 'I trust I am not disturbing your work.'

'Not at all.'

A silence hung between them, to her mind, fetid with possibility.

'You have not said your name,' said Miss Temple, a little appalled for blinking her eyes as she did so.

'My apologies. I am Mr Fochtmann.'

'What a very interesting mass of papers,' she said, pointing. 'They look very . . . goodness . . . *mechanical* and *scientific*.'

Still smiling, Mr Fochtmann turned the top page of each pile face down, hiding their contents from her eyes. 'A woman like yourself cannot be interested in anything so tiresome. Will you sit?'

'No, thank you. I'm sure I will be late for the train –'

'Caroline Stearne I am aware of,' he said. 'But you said "Isobel" –'

'We are cousins,' said Miss Temple easily. 'Caroline has travelled with Lydia to Macklenburg.'

Miss Temple wondered if Captain Tackham and his dragoons were searching for her, whether they might appear at any time.

'Apparently there has been no word sent from her party,' Fochtmann observed. 'Though they are gone now over a week.'

'Who writes postcards after getting married?' The skin above her breasts flushed with memories from the glass book (. . . a blindfolded man straining at the touch of two tongues at once . . . the careful liquid insertion, one at a time, of a string of amber beads . . .). She blinked to find he had cocked his head, watching her.

'But there *has* been word. From the court at Macklenburg. The party did not arrive.'

'Not arrive? That is impossible.'

'It is at the least strange.'

'Sir, it is difficult to credit at all! Where is the outcry? Where are the journalists – the naval search parties, troops of lancers scouring the coasts?

If the heir to Macklenburg is *missing* –' She stopped, staring at Mr Fochtmann quite seriously. 'Has anyone told Lydia's *father*?'

'Her father cannot be found.'

'But he is Robert Vandaariff!'

'Is he, though?'

'I beg your pardon?'

'Will you not take a seat, Miss Stearne?'

'I have told you I cannot.'

'And yet I think you should. I would go so far as to recommend it for
your health.'

Fochtmann's voice remained as pleasant as ever. 'You have been exposed to
the glass. I can see it in your skin. Perhaps the exposure has been minimal –
it has not caused you to lose any of your lovely hair. But you *do* know what
I am talking about, and I must insist that you answer my questions.'

'What questions?'

Fochtmann glanced to the door, then back to her, staring hard, as if
what he found in her countenance would determine his choice – that he
was making a choice, right then. Miss Temple smothered another spasm
of nausea. A cold shaft of understanding from the Comte's memories
pierced her thoughts, the tip of a blade shoving past a cupboard lock and
splintering it open.

The hearth. The man was in his shirtsleeves. *He* had cauterized Mrs
Marchmoor's shattered wrist in the kitchen hearth fire.

Fochtmann indicated the papers before them on the table. 'It is an entire
world of the "mechanical and scientific". These are times when opportunity
rides side by side with disaster.'

'And you would avoid the disaster.'

'For myself, to be sure.'

'And your . . . employers?'

'I only know what I've been told – nothing a man can *trust*. There are
fissures between them – it can be the only reason I am engaged.'

Miss Temple nodded slowly. 'And perhaps . . . I am not . . . exactly . . .
who you take me to be,' she said.

Fochtmann rapped the papers sharply, as if some inner gamble had been won. 'So which of them sent you? It is all very well to replace Lorenz, but before anything else I must know whether the blue glass has killed him. No one will hazard a guess – especially since all of *them* are sick as well –'

'Dr Lorenz dead? Well, Doctor Lorenz was nothing – the Comte's dogsbody only.'

'You know the Comte? You knew him?'

'Knew? You do not mean the Comte is dead?'

Fochtmann squinted at her as if she were a strangely behaving insect. 'I wonder at your indifference. Your own cousin, Caroline Stearne, was part of the same party. She is most likely dead as well.'

Miss Temple did her best to gasp aloud.

'Do not pretend!' he scoffed, pleased at catching her out. 'You yourself bear signs of this indigo decay – and here by luck you have blundered into the only man who can save you!' He snatched up his pen and searched for clean paper. 'Tell me whatever you have heard them say – Lorenz, the Comte, anyone – I will make sense of it myself. Obviously a young woman has not come all this way on her own initiative – whom do you serve?'

He looked up suddenly.

'No no – I'm a fool! It's Vandaariff!'

He stabbed the quill at her clasped hands. 'What is in that case?'

Miss Temple raised it with a shrug and waggled the handle between her fingers. 'It is empty. I was instructed to collect a particular item, from the Comte's laboratory. But it is already gone.'

'Do you expect me to believe that? Who else but Vandaariff could marshal the resources to steal away so many machines? But he lacks something and was forced to send *you* to retrieve it – someone harmless who would attract no suspicion –'

'Why would Vandaariff destroy his own house?'

'Why scruple at the house when he has already sacrificed his *daughter*? The stakes must be beyond imagination! What were you instructed to retrieve? Where are you to take it?'

'I do not know. It was a . . . a *thing*. I was told no more.'

'But you were given details – a description –'

'I was told it was bright metal, and perhaps the size of . . .'

She held out her hands and extended her fingers to indicate triggers and knobs. She thought of the wicked snouty implement the Comte had employed to violate Lydia Vandaariff and began to describe it. As she spoke, Fochtmann set down the quill and began to search through the piled documents.

'And it would fit in your case?' he asked.

'Apparently the item *folds*.'

'Ah . . . as I *assumed* . . .'

Fochtmann pushed one wide page of foolscap across the table to her. She turned it right side up and saw a cross-section diagram of the exact object, labelled in the Comte's hand an 'ethereal irrigator'. Miss Temple inhaled sharply through both nostrils and met Fochtmann's gaze – anything to look away from the diagram. At the sight of it her flesh crawled, imagining its usage – the prone form of Lydia Vandaariff, limbs secured, legs forced apart, the thickened blue mixture to be extruded from the metal snout at the exactly right temperature. She bit back her disgust – at Lydia's weakness, at the uselessness of women, at the arrogance of human effort, at Fochtmann's idiotic pride. Miss Temple set the page back down.

'Aren't you curious where it is?' he asked.

'Not any more.'

'Do not be downhearted. I have seen others far worse off than you –'

'Where is the Duke of Stäelmaere?'

'*Indeed*,' said Fochtmann, as if her question illustrated his point. 'Having done a minimal examination, I have to admit, the dynamic properties of this indigo clay *are* singular. To turn a little thing like death on its damned head –'

Miss Temple ignored him, suppressing the burn in her throat.

'And where is Colonel Aspiche?' she croaked.

Fochtmann frowned at the interruption. 'Where is Robert Vandaariff?' he demanded.

'Where is Mrs Marchmoor?'

'Where did he take all the machinery?'

'Where is Mrs *Marchmoor*?'

'No, you must answer me! Where is Robert Vandaariff? Why does he want this particular tool? Why did he send *you*?' He slammed both fists onto the table, his long arms like the forelegs of a powerful horse. 'You cannot brave me unless you are prepared to brave Mrs Marchmoor! However . . . if you cooperate with me *now* . . .'

Miss Temple shivered to recall the glass woman hammering her mind.

'You have no choice,' he said, gently as a farmer easing a lamb onto the block.

'It's because you can see, isn't it?' she said. 'You understand what this glass can do, perhaps now more than any man alive . . . they have employed you like a coachman, but they do not comprehend that *you* will gain an advantage over them all . . . over her, over the *world*.'

Fochtmann smiled tightly, immensely pleased with her description.

'What will you do with me?' Miss Temple asked.

'That depends. You must do what I say.'

'Must I?'

He chuckled. Miss Temple leant across the table, as if to share a final secret, daring him to hear it. Despite himself, Fochtmann leant down to meet her.

Her voice was a whisper. '*You were given a chance.*'

She swung the case with all her strength, for it was well made, with sharp metal corners – one of which caught Mr Fochtmann's shining forehead like the spike of a chisel. He reeled with a cry, one hand to the wound, blood already pouring through his fingers and across the Comte's papers.

'O! O damn you to hell! Help! Help me – *help*!'

Instead of running to the door, which had been her first impulse, Miss Temple instead went directly at the weaving, keening man. He saw her coming and croaked his defiance, waving a spattered palm to ward her off, but she swung the case again, hard with both hands, cracking it straight into his right kneecap. Fochtmann toppled with a squawk at her feet. Miss Temple felt the sickening black presence in the back of her throat. She brought the case down once more on Mr Fochtmann's head and stopped his movements altogether.

*

He was still alive, for the bellows of his chest beat like the wet wings of a newborn insect. Miss Temple seriously considered cutting his throat with the knife in her boot – inflamed without her even noticing by seven different memories of that very action, nose thick with the remembered smell, hands twitching at how *hot* the spray – but instead she sensibly crossed to the door and locked it. She returned to the prone man – curious at how out of their element a tall person seems when on the ground, like fish on a tar-baked dock. Ignoring the dark coagulated smears above his face, she stepped to his topcoat, hung on a chair: cigars, matches, a scented handkerchief, a brass case of visiting cards printed with swirling script on a pale green bond paper (*Marcus Fochtmann, Theoretical Engineer, 19 Swedter Street*).

The outer pocket contained something heavy and clinking, and Miss Temple extracted a canvas pouch, sewn shut, like a bag of grapeshot for a tiny cannon. She sensed a glimmer of nauseating memory and forced it away – any more and she would vomit. What did every detail matter – no doubt the bag held machine parts – and she shoved it angrily back into his coat.

The final pocket was custom-made, for it was long and perfectly suited for what in fact it held: a rolled piece of stiff vellum. Miss Temple hesitated, but could not prevent herself from unrolling the paper. The sheet held an elegant sketch by the Comte d'Orkancz of a slotted brass pedestal, trailing thick metal tubes and black hoses. At the sight of the sketch a black acrid surge brought Miss Temple to her knees, gagging, but the harsh strain on her throat was subsumed by a wave of perception as to the pedestal's *function*. The slot held a glass book. The tubes and hoses were attached to a person, laid out upon a table – the machine serving to connect the glass book to that person's mind. Depending on how one set the seven brass knobs, alchemic energy could flow in either direction. If the energy was directed towards the *book*, the person's mind was drained and the book inscribed with their memories. If the energy was directed towards the *person*, the book's contents were imprinted on the person's mind, obliterating their own memory – and possibly, if one chose to use the word, their soul.

Miss Temple gasped as if she had been submerged in water, and with desperate fury she ripped the vellum drawing in half and then half again, pulling the pieces to ragged bits. Her mind swam with black loathing, and when her eyes found Fochtmann laid out next to her, his eyelids fluttering, she was at once caught between the futility of any action and the sharp urge to end his life. The knife lay in her boot. Fochtmann's right hand feebly groped the carpet. He was an enemy. If one saw the world with open eyes, was it anything but cowardice to halt half-way? Chang would not have scrupled to kill him. The Contessa would have slain the man without a qualm. Miss Temple wanted to believe her rage was her own, but, as she swayed on her feet, she knew it had been contaminated every bit as much as her desire.

With a tremor of fear she tried to remember some moment of her *own* – some instant she could claim – but found only a new swirl of visions, like the flutters of a dovecote, set loose inside her head. She squeezed her thighs together and sucked hard on her lower lip, appalled at the sudden rush of sweetness in her loins, and groaned (. . . smooth cool marble against her bare buttocks, her fingers, heavy with ecclesiastical signets, forced into a grunting man's mouth . . .), willing her thoughts to something else – to some*one* else – but it seemed as if every bit of care and affection in her heart had been translated to mere hunger, the impulse of animals, a callous cycle of need and dissipation, of emptiness and death at the end of every-thing, woven into each moment, inevitable and cruel. She remembered Chang's hand on her body and gagged, steeped in the horrid futility of each morsel of longing.

Miss Temple wiped her eyes on a sleeve, wishing herself back to a time when everything had always seemed so clear. But how long ago was that? Before leaving her island? Before Roger's letter ended their engagement? Before the glass book? Miss Temple was not one to care about *causes*, or about cares in the first place – it was a simpler life without them – but she could not bear being so *subject* to forces she insisted on seeing as external, as unthinkable plagues. A larger thought hung within her reach: the differ-ences between one death and another, or between her killing of Roger and the hanging of a renegade by her father's overseer – her benefit from each, her *participation* in each. More examples flared from the Contessa's book, murders and executions and desperate struggles, those collected lives rising to mirror a secret history she could not deny . . . how violence, rather than gold, was the true currency of her world – and how in such a world, to her sharp shame, she remained a very wealthy girl indeed.

But Miss Temple appreciated shame no more than criticism, and shoved this unwelcome conclusion away as if it were a malingering servant in her path. On her way to the door she paused to wipe the edges of Lydia's case on the carpet. The last thing she needed was to stain her dress.

Miss Temple realized she had not properly understood the glass woman. Fochtmann must have been sought out some time ago, perhaps as soon as the airship had been aloft. Even if only in the interests of survival, Mrs Marchmoor was casting a wider net: hiring her own expert on the glass, hunting down Charlotte Trapping, ransacking the minds around her for diplomatic advantages. But the Duke's usefulness was only a matter of time, and the glass woman would need another mouthpiece.

At once Miss Temple saw the glass woman's plan – and the reason she had come to Harschmort: to implant the contents of the book – the Comte's memories and sensibility – *into* the vacant mind of Robert Vandaariff. With both the Comte's knowledge and Vandaariff's vast fortune at her call, what need she fear from any survivor of the Cabal – what from any quarter anywhere?

Yet this book was now Miss Temple's. And the Comte's machinery – whose now was that? And where was Robert Vandaariff? Every element of the glass woman's plan had gone wrong. Miss Temple's torment of minutes before was shoved aside by her own ably working mind – these *plagues* would prove as tractable as any other apparently devastating tragedy. Did the loss of a mother or a father's violence dog her every step as a woman? Of course not – she scarcely recalled either to mind at all.

Her intention had been to climb through a window and hike across the fens to the train. Yet, as she sought the proper ground-floor room, Miss Temple was aware of another possibility, like the echo of her boots against the marble. If Harschmort was riddled with her foes, they were now scattered and beset: Fochtmann bloodied, Rawsbarthe debased, Mrs Marchmoor perhaps quite literally broken ... she asked herself what Chang would do in the same circumstances and knew he would hunt down whoever had offended him. Miss Temple turned to the more rational Doctor Svenson, and immediately remembered the sad face of young Francesca Trapping. If he were here, the Doctor would no more leave Harschmort now than take the child's life himself.

She allowed herself a sneer at the Doctor's tractability, just on the off chance such sneering might convince her that she could in fact walk on, but it did not, and so Miss Temple stopped, besieged all the more by her own meanness of spirit. There really was nothing wrong with simply saving herself. Indeed, she was certain both the Doctor and Chang would advise this exact course of action for *her*, while never once considering it for themselves. This realization settled the matter at once.

She reached an odd hallway lined with marble heads (Romans – a doomed cruelty marked the faces, like animals still ferocious in a cage), and she stopped. On the floor lay a jumble of clothing and broken glass – shattered champagne flutes, by what remained of the stems. The wine was dried but still tacky against her boots. Miss Temple stepped over the mess, but as she went she found more debris – spilt food that had been stepped on, broken masks from the final night's ball, female undergarments – the corridor looking as if it had not been visited once by a servant in the whole intervening week. Finally she reached a set of double doors left ajar, and heard running water, the murmurs of voices, and, strangest of all, the plink of an out-of-tune piano.

She entered an entirely lovely atrium, with a glass ceiling and a stone fountain set into the floor, the whole surrounded by tall potted trees. The piano sat beneath the wide, splitting leaves of a banana plant and the man slumped against it – thick-waisted, in his shirtsleeves and stockinged feet, a gold-leather mask pulled down around his neck – did not *play*, but picked at the keyboard with one index finger, like a sated chicken amongst scattered seed. The atrium held at least twenty more people, lolling on chairs and benches or on the tiles – men and women kissing each other quite openly, others fast asleep, half dressed, the floor more littered than the hallway with bottles and plates and rotting food. Every third person still wore a mask. All had once been arrayed in the finest evening attire, now rumpled or discarded – or even exchanged, for more than one woman wore a topcoat or evening jacket, and at least one man – the opened bodice strange against the hair on his chest – a lady's gown. This was the last band of the Cabal's adherents, confounded by appetite and the excess that Harschmort could supply. Miss Temple studied the still bodies she first assumed were asleep and wondered how many might be dead.

Her foot kicked a toppled wineglass. The man at the piano stopped, turning to her. Others looked up from their absorptions, and soon they were all staring.

'Who is it?' one fellow whispered to a bearded, shirtless man crouched at his feet.

'Have they come back?' called an older woman, her petticoats pulled up above vein-mottled thighs. 'Is it time?'

'You don't have a mask,' a young woman chided Miss Temple. Another next to her poured brandy into teacups. Both their chins were matted with dried slime. 'Everyone has been instructed to wear *masks*.'

'I have just arrived,' replied Miss Temple. 'I am looking for three children.'

The young woman with the brandy bottle begin to snigger. Miss Temple kept on, stepping round groping couples – in one case groping *men* – and felt the rising flush in her limbs. She reached the fountain – happy to find nothing worse than a sunken pair of shoes in the water. They all continued to stare at her.

'There has been a fire,' she told them. 'Lord Vandaariff is gone.'

The woman with the bottle sniggered again.

'The soldiers are coming,' Miss Temple said. 'You should be ready – all of you –'

But, with the exception of the man at the piano, the tattered adherents had gone back to their dissipation. Miss Temple met the man's gaze, and then he too resumed his distended, internal melody.

*

If Tackham had been taking the children to the main floor – and Mrs Marchmoor's hand had been mended in the kitchens – then that meant her enemies were gathered in the centre part of the house. Miss Temple had just decided to cross the next hallway and try what doors she could, for the people behind her – like animals in a human zoo – made her shiver, when something caught her eye. At first she was frightened to turn, fearing it was another assignation that would bring her to her knees, but it was only a dark mark on the wall, a broken vertical line that indicated a hidden door. She could not stop herself, even if she assumed it to be full of more revellers. Miss Temple went to the door and opened it wide.

The room was very small, sized for a servant, with a daybed, standing cabinet, writing desk, and several lamps with brightly coloured shades. The door from the atrium lacked a knob, opening instead by the pressing of a button; from the outside, it posed as merely another wall panel. Miss Temple laughed aloud, for the purpose of such a hidden bed chamber directly off such a romantic space as the garden conservatory was suddenly obvious. The bed covers had been remade but not cleanly, and the writing desk lay cluttered with items more redolent of assignation than correspondence – ointments, a hairbrush, wineglasses, one of which was smeared with lipstick. Indulging her naughtiness this much, Miss Temple crossed to the bed and sat on it, bouncing to test the firmness. Flushing at the memories this action kicked up, she quickly stood again, grinning despite an uncomfortably growing itch.

Before her on the green blotter was a letter in the unmistakable hand of Roger Bascombe. It was addressed to Mrs Caroline Stearne.

The letter itself, read with a studied revulsion, as if she were peeling up a bandage to peek at her own half-healed wound, contained no particular point of interest, simply informing Mrs Stearne – at no point did the familiar, Ministry-schooled tone of Roger's prose presume to 'Caroline' – of the arrangements for Lydia's gala engagement party: that she would be collected by coach at the St Royale Hotel, taken to Stropping – Roger himself would see her on the train – and from there to Harschmort, where she would be met by the Contessa di Lacquer-Sforza. He instructed her as to dress and closed with a simple congratulation on her imminent embrace of the Process. Miss Temple read it again and set the paper onto the blotter so as not to notice her own shaking hands. Her eyes fell onto the rumpled bed, mocked by the book within her, knowing that upon it Roger and Caroline must have surely acted those visions out in flesh.

That the letter contained no evidence of affection meant nothing. Roger would not have crossed the street to bid good-day to his mother if it meant appearing less than properly poised. And yet . . . She read the note a third time, and noted with a sour curdle in her stomach the appearance of certain words. Roger loved words very much, and took care to polish a handful of favourites, the pleasure they gave him attaching to the object of his affection, and here they were. She could imagine his tender smile at the writing of each one . . . 'piquant' . . . 'exactitude' . . . 'tulle' . . .

She pushed the letter aside and roughly pawed through the other papers, sweeping what did not interest her to the floor, only preventing herself by deliberate will from toppling the entire little desk altogether. She stopped. She had crumpled and thrown another letter without looking at it closely, but not before a name had leapt out to her eye. She kicked awkwardly through the scattered pile until she found the one she sought. She would have liked to sit but could not now bring herself to further touch *any* piece of furniture, given what gymnastic purposes they might have served. Miss Temple smoothed out the paper against her thigh.

The looping script matched the note in her dress. Miss Temple scanned the text for the name she was sure she'd seen . . . and there it was . . . Elöise Dujong.

Sweet Caroline,

As we discussed, Husband and Family are your Skeleton Keys.

She will come at your Request, I am Sure, if the Invitation appears by way of her Companion, Mrs Elöise Dujong. A Room has been laid ready at the St Royale tomorrow night. Our Allies understand you do my Business, so you must justify your Travels. Thus go first

*to the Ministry to give the enclosed List of Invitees to Mr Roger
Bascombe.*

*They will do the work Themselves. Be genuinely their Friend.
There is always Time for Everything.*

  RLS

The note bore no date. Some elements were obvious enough – if Elöise was
'Companion' to 'she', then 'she' must be Charlotte Trapping. The husband
and family were the late Colonel and the three children now in the care of
Captain Tackham. The Contessa's reference to 'Our Allies' made clear that,
to the rest of the Cabal, Caroline was the Contessa's creature and thus
needed to seemingly embark on normal business with Roger (the 'Invitees'
being those figures from the highest levels of society they planned to
assimilate into books) to conceal the Contessa's *private* business. And this
private business had to do with Charlotte Trapping and Elöise. Had Elöise
truly met with Charlotte Trapping and Caroline Stearne at the St Royale?
Surely Elöise would have said something about it to her, or to the Doctor
– surely she must have recognized Caroline Stearne on the airship, or at
Harschmort when she was taken prisoner!

  But was that the case? When Elöise had been captured in the Comte's
laboratory . . . Caroline had been elsewhere. They had all been on the
rooftop and in the airship, but with the chaos of the battle was it possible
that Elöise and Caroline had not recognized one another? Miss Temple
huffed. Anything was possible, but was it *likely*? Was it not *more* likely
that Elöise remembered the meeting perfectly well, that she had merely
kept the knowledge to herself? As they walked from the Jorgens' cabin
Miss Temple had spoken of Caroline Stearne, about her murder . . . and
Elöise had not said a word.

She looked around her at the tiny room with a colder sense of pride.
Caroline Stearne, like Elöise, had been a creature in service, and indeed,
the room appeared now every bit as provisional and undistinguished as a
military barracks or a cramped cabin on a trading ship. And this had been

the woman's final home – these were her things, still strewn about because there existed no one in the world to claim them, no one who cared to know her fate – whether she might be dancing in a Macklenburg ballroom or a frozen, crab-chewn corpse at the bottom of the sea. Miss Temple walked out, stepping over the rubbish in the atrium and past the debauchery, accepting the taste of death in her throat and unfettered desire coursing through her veins. These people were *nothing*.

Miss Temple marched through Harschmort at a rapid pace, determined to find the Trapping children and extricate them from the glass woman's clutches. She swept into a suite of offices – thick with filing cabinets and bookcases and workdesks – and looked down to see her feet kicking through loose papers as if they were autumn leaves. The cabinets and desks had been pulled open and ransacked without care. Then through a large doorway she heard a crash and raised voices. Miss Temple threw back her shoulders and deliberately walked towards the noise, the knife in one hand and the case in the other.

Robert Vandaariff's private office was full of soldiers. Red-coated dragoons – with their brass helmets and clanking sabres half like machines themselves – were tearing through every expensively appointed inch as uncaringly as a thresher pounding grain. Hovering ineffectually around them were Lord Vandaariff's own people, doing their vain best to preserve his files from destruction.

Miss Temple darted back from view.

'I do not care, sir!' bellowed a harsh voice. 'We will find it! We will find *him*!'

'But we have told you – we have told you all – we do not –'

'Pig swill! Barrows – have a look through these, from his own desk!'

There followed a *whump*, as another column of paper was dropped without ceremony onto a table.

The second voice yelped in protest. 'Colonel! I cannot allow you –'

'Foster!'

'Sir!'

Aspiche, for it was none other, ignored Vandaariff's secretary, barking to Foster: 'Where is Phelps?'

'With Mr Fochtmann, sir.'

'Tackham?'

'The Captain is with the . . . ah . . . children, sir.'

'What word from Lieutenant Thorpe?'

'None yet, sir. If they searched as far as the canal –'

'I am well aware of it! Carry on.'

'Sir!'

This last was echoed by a snapping click of Foster's boot heels, and the renewed protests of Vandaariff's man. Miss Temple risked another look. She caught the Colonel's receding form, tall and fierce, stalking to the far end of the wide office . . . Robert Vandaariff's own office, being ransacked like a Byzantine jewel house for clues as to where he had vanished. Miss Temple darted across the open doorway, paused for any corresponding cry of alarm, and then crept on to the next open door.

Before she reached it, a man stepped through, stopping abruptly at the sight of her.

'Mr Harcourt,' she said, and bobbed her knees, for it was the same young Ministry official from the upstairs hallway. 'Miss Stearne. We met with Captain Tackham.'

'I am aware of it. Why are you still at Harschmort? I am sure you have no one's permission.'

'My good friend Lydia Vandaariff –'

'Lydia Vandaariff is not here!'

Mr Harcourt looked past her to Lord Vandaariff's office. He would call for soldiers. She would be seen by Aspiche.

'What of *Lord* Vandaariff?' she asked quickly.

'Lord Vandaariff is *gone*.'

'You do not know where he is?'

Harcourt gestured angrily towards the sound of the ransacking soldiers. 'Of course not!'

'Goodness,' she said, smiling brightly. 'Would such information be worth while?'

As she hoped, Harcourt hustled her back whence he had emerged, the better to make her capture his own. It was another office, its furniture covered with dust cloths. His grip remained hard on the arm that held the case, and he shook her when he spoke. 'Where is he? *Tell* me! Lord Vandaariff has five estates within two days' travel. Soldiers have searched each one.'

Miss Temple chuckled and shook her head. 'Mr Harcourt, I am not a girl to take the efforts of the Queen's own army lightly! Believe me when I say, with sober respect –'

Harcourt shook her arm again. She looked down at his hand and her voice became cold. 'It is merely a matter of logic –'

'*Logic?* Are you just *guessing*? If you think to mock me –'

'Mr Harcourt, contain yourself! If Lord Robert Vandaariff is not here at Harschmort, then two things have unquestionably taken place.'

'What *things*?'

'First, *someone* has lost him. And second, someone *else* . . . has *taken* him.'

Harcourt sputtered with exasperation. Her knife-hand was still tucked behind her back.

'You said you knew where he was!'

'I said I was looking for Captain Tackham.'

'I am right here,' called Tackham from the inner door.

Miss Temple and Mr Harcourt both spun towards the officer. He smirked at their expressions, then pushed himself towards a tall piece of furniture from which the white cloth had been pulled, a sideboard stocked with bottles. The Captain sorted amongst the brandy as Harcourt sputtered.

'Are they finished? Why did no one call?'

'Where are the children?' asked Miss Temple.

Tackham pulled the cork from a squat square bottle and poured an inch of amber liquid into a glass. 'What is *she* doing here?' he asked.

Harcourt's reply was stopped by a cry from the inner room, the high-pitched voice of a child. Miss Temple took a step towards the door. Tackham quite casually reached back and pulled it tight with a click.

'What is being done to them?' she cried.

Harcourt called past her to Tackham. 'She claims to know how to find Lord Vandaariff.'

'*What is being done?*'

'Does she *really*?' asked Tackham with amusement.

'But now she will not say!'

'I say she knows as much as my boot.'

'Any *idiot* knows,' sneered Miss Temple.

Tackham cocked his head with some amusement, but she saw the shift of weight between his legs and the snifter slip easily into his left hand, leaving his empty right hand ready to catch her arm.

'Call me idiot, then,' he said. 'I've no damned idea.'

'You are a swearing rogue,' she spat.

Captain Tackham extravagantly drained his glass. Recognizing the gesture for a distraction, Miss Temple wheeled to find Harcourt had crept up behind her.

'She has something in her hand,' called Tackham sharply, but Miss Temple had already slashed the little blade at Harcourt, ripping a two-inch line across his coat sleeve. Harcourt stumbled clear and stared at her in shock, pulling at the sleeve and its dangling button to make sure he was unhurt.

Captain Tackham chuckled. Miss Temple turned back to him with contempt. 'You are a beast. I will be happy to see your skin melt off with each rise in rank.'

Tackham's face hardened, and she knew he was about to come for her. Miss Temple gripped the knife tightly, but the conversation was interrupted yet again.

'What is this?' croaked a peevish voice from the corridor.

'It is Miss Stearne!' called Harcourt. 'She knows the location of Lord Vandaariff but will not say.' He raised his sleeve. 'And she has cut my coat!'

Andrew Rawsbarthe entered unsteadily, drawing a noticeably more gelid gaze across Harcourt, Miss Temple, and the blade in her hand, before settling it on Captain Tackham.

'Captain?'

'The lady insists upon seeing the children.'

'What children? It surprises me to hear you speak of children in Harschmort House.'

Tackham shifted uncomfortably. 'She encountered them in the upstairs hallway.'

'I *see*,' said Rawsbarthe gravely. 'You first failed in your assignment, compromising your orders – and then you said nothing about this breach, to protect yourself!'

'She's only a feather-headed nothing of Lydia Vandaariff –'

'I did not know you made these decisions, Captain. I was not aware you were in command.'

Tackham pursed his lips, angry but silent. Harcourt cleared his throat and gestured to the door. 'If you would like me to inform the Colonel –'

'I would like nothing of the kind!' Rawsbarthe's fatigue showed through his anger like bones protruding in an old man's hand. 'I will be obliged, sir, if you would shut the door to the corridor and then sit on that chair.'

Harcourt looked once at Tackham and then – as he was clearly junior to Rawsbarthe, no matter the man's condition – closed the door and then perched himself on an armless side chair, looking altogether childish. Rawsbarthe himself fell onto a divan. His palm left a rusty streak on the white cover.

'Miss *Stearne* . . . is it?' he asked.

'It is,' said Miss Temple.

'A companion of Lydia Vandaariff,' offered Harcourt.

'She should be brought to Mr Phelps,' insisted Tackham.

'I disagree, Captain,' Rawsbarthe answered sharply. 'Miss Stearne . . . perhaps you will lower your weapon. There are no highwaymen here, and no lady is in peril.'

Miss Temple looked to Tackham, who smoothly adopted a posture of casual disinterest and poured himself more brandy. She lowered the knife but did not put it away.

'I am indeed acquainted with Lydia Vandaariff.' She indicated the case in her left hand. 'I am here to collect certain hairbrushes to be sent on to Macklenburg. I came upon the Captain and his charges, and have expressed my concern. You have three children – under arms – mistreated –'

'What of Lord Vandaariff?' Rawsbarthe wheezed. 'Do you indeed know where he might be?'

Miss Temple did not answer him, glaring again at Tackham. Rawsbarthe leant forward with difficulty. His chin quivered and suddenly Miss Temple wondered where he had been in the house all this intervening time. Even from the upstairs room, his condition had precipitously declined.

'Will you *tell* us?' he croaked.

'Why should I, given these peremptory gentlemen?'

'It would be indelicate to *say*,' smirked Tackham, 'but I should be more than happy to *show* you.'

'Captain Tackham!' cried Rawsbarthe. 'I believe you have tasks other than drunken insolence! You will enquire as to the readiness of your charges, at once!'

'I was told to wait –'

'And I am telling you to go!'

The officer met Rawsbarthe's gaze – and his trembling jaw – and then mockingly clicked his heels. He cast a last glance on Miss Temple. Then he was gone.

'Mr Harcourt, as soon as Miss Stearne reveals Lord Vandaariff's location, you will take the news to Mr Phelps *alone*.'

'Yes, sir.'

'If I tell you,' Miss Temple asked, 'will you let me see the children?'

'It is not your place to *bargain*,' wheezed Rawsbarthe.

Miss Temple was certain that as they stood talking, no matter what Rawsbarthe intended to do, Captain Tackham would carry the children further and further from her grasp.

'*Well*, then.' She tugged on a dangling chestnut curl, and then exhaled with a tinge of boredom. 'It is the *simplest* thing to learn where a person is – one merely has to know where he *isn't*. Lord Vandaariff is not at any dwelling or place of business, or you would have found him long ago. He is not anywhere related to his business or his family. His daughter is gone. His recent companions of close council are gone as well, all off to Macklenburg. Of course such a man has *secrets* – yet with the destruction of his home, he must suppose those secrets *compromised*. He must turn to others, and so one returns to these absent companions. Which of *them* possesses resources he might rely upon . . . or take outright?'

'If he was in the shelter of Crabbé,' whispered Rawsbarthe, 'the Ministry would know it.'

'So he is not,' said Miss Temple. 'And neither the Contessa nor the Comte have an organization of *people*. It leaves only Francis Xonck, and the power of Xonck Armaments.'

'But . . . but Francis Xonck . . .' Harcourt looked nervously to Raws-barthe.

'Was here this very day,' said Miss Temple. 'I know it.'

'Yet if Francis Xonck could not find him . . .' began Rawsbarthe.

'Then it is not *Francis* Xonck Lord Vandaariff is with.'

Neither man spoke. Rawsbarthe stared at Miss Temple, his fingers gripping the divan at some internal pang.

'Go to Phelps,' he hissed. 'It is the sister after all.'

Harcourt rushed from the room. Miss Temple followed him to the door and locked it. From the corridor she heard Colonel Aspiche roaring to his men. She turned to the wheezing man on the divan.

'You are not well, Andrew. And now you have quite compromised yourself. When it is known who I am, *she* will be angry.'

'Then she must not know.'

'She knows already. Have you not sent Tackham to her? She will snatch my image from his mind.'

'I resent this very much indeed,' Rawsbarthe muttered. He coughed weakly. Tears glazed his eyes.

'Come, come,' she said, with a brightness that would not convince a trusting dog. 'You forget that I am well acquainted with the woman. Indeed, I am acquainted with her *as* a woman. Up you go!'

She took his arm carefully with her case hand, guiding him from the divan and towards the inner door.

'We cannot –'

'If I leave you here, you will simply die like Mr Soames.'

'And the Duke,' he sighed, as if this were a terrible admission.

'And the horrid Duke,' she agreed. 'But the truth is, Andrew, the Duke of Stäelmaere was killed some days ago. He was shot through the heart in the quarry at Tarr Manor, and by the lover of a Macklenburg spy at that.'

Rawsbarthe wobbled as Miss Temple reached for the door knob.

'I had no idea.'

'It is a *world* of secrets.'

*

They passed through another shuttered parlour and another after that, Miss Temple closing each door behind with a flick of her boot.

'I have always found you beautiful,' wheezed Rawsbarthe.

'Well, that is most kind of you, I'm sure.'

'What you said to me, earlier – about my being ushered into a room, and not remembering –'

'The truth is better for us all, Mr Rawsbarthe.'

'That is a terrible lie! The truth is a plague!'

'Mr Rawsbarthe –'

'*Andrew!*'

She felt the claw-like grip of his fingers on her arm as she opened the next door. Beyond lay a table spread with a white cloth, dotted with small reddish stains.

'Can you smell her?' she asked.

'I cannot smell myself,' he whimpered. 'Though any mirror says I ought to.'

'She has left with Captain Tackham and the children.'

'What does she look like exactly?'

'You have seen her yourself, Mr Rawsbarthe.'

'*Andrew*,' he whined.

'*Andrew* – you have seen her. She has seen you. Have you no memory at all?'

He shook his head dumbly. 'I saw your man,' he said.

'What *man*?' Miss Temple had grown impatient and pulled him round the table to the door. '*Roger?*'

'Roger is dead. And I have been thinking, since we spoke – you will wonder that I have come back to find you – but all of what you said has been gnawing at my mind, and – I will say it – at my body. I can imagine where you have been, what you have done, what experiences you have cast yourself open to, what wanton impulses –'

'Mr Rawsbarthe –'

'Do not deny it! I am speaking of your *criminal!*'

Miss Temple's hand was on the knob but stopped mid-turn.

'You saw Cardinal Chang? At the station?'

'Of course not. At the Trappings'.'

'When was that? What were you doing? What was *Chang* doing?'

'Looking for her.'

'Mrs Trapping?'

'Why should you care for him?' Rawsbarthe whined. 'He is a brute! Your curls are so beautiful –'

Rawsbarthe erupted in a coughing fit. His face was bright with fever. Clumps of hair fringed his lapels. His eyes had acquired a slick cerulean oil, and she doubted he could see a thing. Miss Temple pulled free. He sank against the table. She retreated to the far door.

'Where are you going?' he rasped, his voice shrill with concern.

'I must find Captain Tackham. I will return, I promise!'

'You will not!' Rawsbarthe moaned, then toppled. He scrabbled to steady himself but found only the table cloth, balling up in his hands. He collapsed to the floor with a shriek, pulling the white sheet on top of him. Miss Temple plunged into the darkness of another room.

Rawsbarthe's plaintive cries (*'Celeste! Celeste!'*) penetrated the door at Miss Temple's back, but she did not pause. She followed Mrs Marchmoor's path, the smell growing more bitter and the stains more bright, until she finally emerged in a far part of the garden, lined with hedges. Crushed on the threshold was a broken chocolate biscuit.

The glass woman's journey to Harschmort had yielded nothing. In the absence of the book, and the Comte's machines, and Vandaariff, was Mrs Marchmoor in flight? Or was she following some desperate strategy? One thing was sure: since the children had been taken out this way, not back through the house, Mrs Marchmoor did not intend a return via carriage or train . . .

So much pointed to Charlotte Trapping. Yet if the children were only hostages to their mother's cooperation, what could one make of the vials and blood-stained cotton wool? With a grimace Miss Temple opened her mind to the memories of the Comte d'Orkancz – the three children, their mother, the vials . . . but was rewarded only with bitter retching and tears in her eyes. She wiped her mouth on the back of her hand. She must rely on her own wits. The children had been brought *here* . . . and now they were being taken away. *Why?*

When she ran out of lawn – the house now a darkening shadow behind her – Miss Temple tumbled into the beach grass without a break in stride. Another two minutes of running, her pace now spurred by fear, and she dropped into a sudden crouch. Ahead stood a silhouetted man smoking a cigar, its tip winking red. It was Captain Tackham. Miss Temple flung herself down.

Tackham stood scanning the high grass, turning his head stiffly like a marionette, his face emptied of all expression and intelligence. She held her breath. Another ten seconds and Tackham erupted into a fit of coughing. He raised both hands to his head, gagging like a man given poison.

From behind him came a call: 'Captain Tackham!'

Tackham wiped his mouth with dismay. 'In a moment!'

He threw his shoulders back and staggered from Miss Temple's view. Quietly, she slipped after him. She could hear bootsteps on planking and creaking ropes . . . another few yards and she could see the canal itself. To either side of a long barge scurried shadowed figures – soldiers on deck and others, actual bargemen, readying sails and coiling the ropes that bound the craft to the canal side. Miss Temple saw nothing of the Trapping children, or of Mrs Marchmoor, but the glass woman had just inhabited Tackham in order to search the dunes. She must be in a cabin below deck. Tackham strode up the gangway to a knot of men. She recognized Mr Phelps, Colonel Aspiche, and – his forehead wrapped with gauze – the ambitious engineer, Mr Fochtmann.

Captain Tackham saluted the Colonel, gave some minimal report, and then stood back from the others, who talked on. Tackham's gaze was restless, studying the sailors, sweeping the dock, then returning to the grassy dunes. He raised a hand, and the other men at once followed his gaze. Miss Temple plunged her head down to the sand, too terrified to move.

'Where have you been?' Mr Phelps called directly towards her. 'We have been waiting!'

Miss Temple pressed her body closer to the ground, hoping it was all a mistake, fighting the urge to leap up and run.

'Did you find Rawsbarthe?' called Phelps again.

'I did,' gasped a voice right behind her. Miss Temple nearly yelped with surprise. Not inches away, his feet kicking grass into her face, appeared the young Ministry man, Mr Harcourt.

'My apologies to you all!' Harcourt was out of breath as he stumbled down to them. Phelps turned to the others.

'I suppose we can rendezvous with Rawsbarthe tomorrow –'

'I cannot think he will see morning,' gasped Harcourt, as he reached the gangway. 'Mr Rawsbarthe is overcome. He is quite unable to travel.'

'Lord preserve us,' muttered Phelps, and rubbed his eyes.

'What happened to this girl – this Miss Stearne?' asked Colonel Aspiche, his voice low.

'I questioned Mr Rawsbarthe – but, to be frank, he was no longer lucid.' Harcourt's voice was heavy with concern.

'Miss *Stearne*, indeed!' snapped Phelps. 'We have all been fools –'

Phelps stopped speaking, for Harcourt had suddenly begun to weave on the gangway, dangerously near to pitching head first into the water. Tackham took a step away, but Phelps caught Harcourt's arm. Harcourt tottered, then slowly spun, surveying the canal side and the darkened dunes. He seemed to stare directly at her. Miss Temple did not breathe.

'Gentlemen . . .' announced Harcourt, still facing into the night, his voice unpleasantly hollow. 'Is it not time to set off?'

'We were only waiting for Mr Harcourt,' replied Phelps.

'Has he seen Miss Stearne?' asked Fochtmann, his voice stiffly conversational.

'Mr Harcourt has not,' said Harcourt, a phrasing that made the men visibly uncomfortable.

'She is dangerous,' said Fochtmann firmly. 'She must be found.'

'Perhaps some soldiers could continue the search here,' offered Phelps.

'She is nothing,' announced Harcourt, his voice hollow. 'An insignificant liar. Mr Phelps is required in the forward cabin with Mr Fochtmann and the Colonel. Captain Tackham will see to his men.'

'May I suggest that Mr Harcourt remain on deck?' offered Phelps delicately. 'I expect he will feel . . . unwell.'

'As you like,' intoned Harcourt. 'It makes no difference.'

The younger man staggered again, and Phelps rushed to catch his arm, guiding him off the gangway. Tackham hovered, but Phelps turned to him sharply. 'You have your orders – get below! I will follow in a moment.' Tackham went with a curt nod. Phelps looked down at Harcourt – dazed and distractedly sniffing – and then shouted at the bargemen, startling them back to duty. 'Cast off at once! Barge master! Make sail!'

Miss Temple knew very well that she could stay where she was, allow the barge to go, and walk back to the house and then to the train station – that her journey could end in a suite at the Anburne, with a proper bath and a proper pot of tea. Yet, when she pushed herself up and drove her body on, it was towards the canal. The bargemen pulled the gangplank onto the deck, but Miss Temple kept running. With a stitch in her throat came an awareness of how delicate the blue glass was. She cradled the case in both arms, holding it tight against her chest, and leapt the distance onto a pile of netting, the rough hemp biting into the soft skin of her knees and forearms. She rolled quickly off the ropes and into the shadow of a sail, out of sight but dangerously near to where Mr Harcourt sat slumped.

The bargemen ran back and forth around her, their hard bare feet slapping the deck, gathering lines. She could see the pale hair above Harcourt's stiff collar. The knife was at hand and the ease of his murder fluttered atop her thoughts, a rippling pennant of cruelty. She imagined the man's shirtless back . . . she wondered if there would be scars – Chang would have all sorts of scars . . . even the Doctor might have them, as a soldier . . . ugly things . . . disfigurements – she felt a desire to trace her fingers down Mr Harcourt's spine . . . or someone else's, anyone else's . . . and slide her hand beneath his belt like a knife into an envelope.

Miss Temple slipped from her shadow to a hatchway at the rear of the barge. She stuffed the knife into her boot and pushed the hatchway wide, wrinkling her nose at the stink of bilge water below her in the dark. She slid the hatchway closed above her, perched in pitch black, listening. Footsteps thumped past above . . . but no cries of alarm, nor was the hatch flung wide. She groped around her – boxes, bales of moist cloth, coiled rope – and then wormed her way behind the ladder so that anyone looking down would not see her, no matter that they had a light. Shifting with her buttocks and shoulders made room between the bales where she could sit, and Miss Temple did so, leaning back, Lydia's case on her lap.

No doubt the barge was rife with rats. She snorted. If the rats knew what was good for them, they would steer clear.

Miss Temple snorted again. For the very first time she understood the Contessa di Lacquer-Sforza's slovenly room at the St Royale. With death and desire such constant companions, what attention would a woman like *that* possibly waste on *décor*?

Or indeed, thought Miss Temple – curling onto her side to sleep, an animal in its lair – a woman like herself?

EIGHT

RETICENCE

The shouting from the open French doors must have been very loud, for it penetrated – like the first perceived drop of rain out of a thousand others – just enough to disrupt Chang's velvet enthralment. He was on his knees in Harschmort's garden. Someone was pulling his hand. He turned – his glasses askew on his nose, half his head still surrounded by morning light and perfume, the voices of young women – as the pistol was wrenched from his fingers.

Before him lay the Duke. Francis Xonck slithered from view behind an ornamental boxed juniper. The black-coated Ministry man fired the pistol, the bullet splintering the box near Xonck's foot. Bodies rushed past Chang to cluster around the glass woman, her shattered wrist waving above their heads and steaming blue. The Ministry man's pistol clicked on an empty chamber.

'Reload, Mr Phelps! Where can he hide?'

Too slowly Chang spun on his knees. The sharp toe of Colonel Aspiche's boot caught him square on the shoulder. The blow knocked Chang onto his back, the whole of his left arm gone numb. Aspiche swept out his sabre. Chang scuttled further away, feet hopelessly tangled, still unable to stand, raising his stick as Aspiche came on with his blade. Chang knew from experience that stabbing or slashing at a man on his back was more difficult than one might assume – cold comfort when he still felt half asleep. Aspiche cut at Chang's left knee, to maim him. Chang deflected the blow on his stick, cracking the wood.

'Ought I to shoot him?' asked Phelps. He stood quite prudently beyond Chang's reach, the cylinder of the revolver opened out, digging in his waistcoat for brass cartridges. Both men gasped at another sharp silent spasm from Mrs Marchmoor – some tall fellow grappled to wrap her hand. Chang rose to one knee. Again the impact of her distress had passed him by.

'Cardinal Chang is entirely my business,' barked the Colonel. 'Find Mr Xonck. Predators are most dangerous when they are hurt . . .'

Aspiche did not bother to feint, but hacked directly at Chang's head. Chang dodged to the side, another chip of wood flying out from his stick. Around them dashed more servants and soldiers, as if he were nothing but an animal being put down in a corner.

He called to Aspiche: 'How can *you* kill Xonck? You underwent the Process! Where is your loyalty?'

'Ask me rather why he – like *you* – has lived so long!'

Aspiche's curved blade lanced viciously at Chang's stomach. Chang slashed the stick desperately across his body, splintering the tip, and the sabre's deflected point disappeared into the earth. Behind them came two more pistol shots – Phelps putting Xonck from his misery – but their sudden sound launched another shattering vibration from Mrs Marchmoor's mind, and Aspiche flinched.

But the vibration did not stop Chang. He flung himself forward. The Colonel stumbled back, flailing wickedly with the blade, but Chang rolled free. Around him a nest of dragoons and servants and Ministry men all took sudden notice of his presence – blades swept from scabbards in every direction. Chang plunged after Xonck around the same boxed juniper – but in three long steps came to an abrupt halt, arms circling to keep his balance, at the sudden edge of the collapsed cathedral chamber, a dizzying slope of jagged, smoking wreckage beneath his feet, dropping at least a hundred feet. Not five yards away stood Phelps. The man raised the pistol straight at Chang's head. Without a second's thought, Cardinal Chang launched himself out into the void.

He landed ten feet down on a blackened iron beam and without pause sprung recklessly onto the shattered remains of a jail cell, a fall of perhaps fifteen more feet, the breath driven from his body. His stick flew from his hand, and before he could see where it landed a shot crashed out from

above, the bullet pinging like a hammer near his head. Chang writhed over
the twisted prison bars, hanging so the metal floor of the cell shielded him
– at least until Phelps moved to a better angle. He looked past his dangling
legs – a straight drop some sixty feet into a wicked pile of sharp steel that
would finish him as neatly as the press of an iron maiden.

Phelps fired again – the bastard *had* moved round – the bullet sparking
near Chang's left hand. Chang swore and began to vigorously swing his
body back and forth. The earth wall had fallen in some yards away, creating
at least the pretence of a slope. If he could reach that, there was a chance.
He looked up. Phelps stood directly above him, Aspiche at the Ministry
man's side. Phelps extended the pistol. Chang kicked out his feet and
let go.

When his body came to rest – after perhaps as brief a time as ten seconds,
but seconds as eventful and bone-shaking as any Chang had ever known –
he lay on his back with his legs, fortunately unbroken, stretched out above
him. His knees were bleeding and his gloves torn, and he could feel
abrasions on his face that would unpleasantly scab. His dark spectacles had
remarkably remained in place (Chang had long ago learnt the virtues of a
well-tightened earpiece), but his stick was lost in the heights above. Roused
to his danger, Chang scrambled into the cover of a buckled sheet of steel –
part of the cathedral tower's skin, half embedded in the ground like the
blade of a gigantic shovel. The wreckage around him was so complete and
his passage down so chaotic that he'd no idea where he was, or whether his
enemies could see him. He peeked around the metal sheet. A shot rang
out, and he darted back, the bullet ringing harmlessly off the debris. That
was one question answered.

In the silence, and quite near, Cardinal Chang heard a distinctive and
odious chuckle.

The chuckle was followed by an even more disgusting gagging swallow.
Francis Xonck crouched in a nook of mangled ducts and prison bars, just
across the clearing where Chang had come to rest. The wound in his chest
had congealed to a sticky cobalt.

By now, Phelps might have been joined by twenty dragoons with carbines.

'I thought you'd been shot,' he called casually to Xonck, keeping his voice low.

'My apologies,' sneered Xonck. 'It is a younger son's natural talent to disappoint.'

Chang studied the man, taking his time, since neither of them seemed likely to be going anywhere soon. Xonck's face was more altered than he'd realized. The eyes were wild with fever, nostrils crusted, and his blue lips blistered raw. Where his skin was not discoloured it was pale as chalk.

The glass woman's fingers had been inside Xonck's *body* . . . when her wrist had broken, had they come *out*? Or were they still *inside*? What delirium must be swimming through Xonck's head, bearing so much glass in direct proximity to his heart, his lungs, his rushing blood? Yet, during their own recent battle in the train carriage, he'd shown no weakness . . .

'But you were shot before . . . I see you've dressed the wound in an extremely sensible fashion.'

Xonck spat a ribbon of clotted indigo onto the broken stones.

'I can only imagine what it's doing to your *mind*,' continued Chang. 'One recalls those African weevils that chew from ear to ear, right through a man's brain. Their victim stays alive the entire time, losing control of his limbs, unable to speak, to reason, no longer noticing when he's fouled himself –'

Xonck laughed, eyes shut tight against his mirth, and playfully stabbed his plaster-cast arm at Chang. 'The sensations *are* singular, Cardinal – you have no idea! The *pleasure* in action, the *impact* of feeling, even *pain* . . . like having opium smoke for blood – except there is no sleep in it. No – one is most viciously awake!' His laughter stopped short in a cough and he spat again.

'Your mood seems strangely merry,' said Chang.

'Why shouldn't it be? Because I am dying? It was always possible. Because I'm a stinking leper? Was that not always possible too? Look at yourself, Cardinal. Did your mother breed you for such work? Would her eyes shine with pride at your fine habit? Your high-placed companions? Your *virtue*?'

'It does not seem you are anyone to speak of *family*. What are you but an inheritance, and the debauchery that came with it?'

'*I could not agree more*,' growled Xonck, with all the spite of a viper that has bitten itself in its rage.

Chang risked another glance at the high crater's edge. No bullet followed, but he tucked his head back into cover. Xonck's eyes were closed but twitched like a dreaming dog's. Chang called to him: 'Your former associates have not welcomed you with affection.'

'Why should they?' Xonck muttered hoarsely.

'Does not your Process ensure loyalty? Slavish devotion?'

'Don't be a fool, the Process harnesses *ambition*. That is the risk of ruling by fear. As long as they know disobedience will be crushed, our *adherents* remain fiercely loyal. If however' – and here Xonck chuckled too giddily – 'the *masters* lose their hold – or become so ill mannered as to *die* – these restraints vanish. We are sunk to their level – or they raised to ours . . . all the more since knowledge itself is the most levelled field of all.'

'Because the Comte is dead?'

'Very bad form, in my own opinion.'

Xonck thrashed his head – as if struggling with an unseen hand around his neck – and then gasped aloud. 'But Cardinal, you forget my family business – I am not such a *dilettante* as I may appear. Perhaps for all your reputation for learning, *you* are . . .'

Xonck nudged his plastered arm at the destruction around them. To his chagrin, Chang registered for the first time the striations of force amidst the fire . . . clear signs of an initial and massive point of ignition.

'An explosive shell.'

'Perhaps even two,' replied Xonck. 'Detonated after the Comte's machinery had been removed. Not one of his infernal machines is here. Just as in his laboratory –'

'You're wrong.'

'I am not! Smell the cordite within the ash!'

'I do not mean *here*.' Chang could not smell anything and was annoyed to have missed so obvious a clue. 'In the laboratory there was no detonation. That *was* a fire, started with the Comte's chemicals. Though again, his things – or at least the paintings – had been removed.'

'Perhaps they did not care to set off ordnance indoors.'

'This destruction is not the act of someone who *cares*.'

Xonck smiled. 'So . . . we have two sources of fire. Then there must also be two *perpetrators*, for anyone with access to our munitions has access to *quantities*. Neither deed can be laid to our surviving glass creature, for she very convincingly asked me these very same questions in the garden.'

'Then who has done it?'

'Lord knows. Where are your own earnest compatriots?'

'I have no idea. Dead?'

'How *cold* you are, Cardinal.'

'I thought you were an ardent admirer of the Contessa.'

'Well, you know, who *isn't*?'

'You tried to kill her before my eyes.'

'Again, who doesn't – eventually? Did you not yourself, on several occasions?'

'Actually, I never did,' replied Chang, surprised that this was actually true. 'I should be happy to do so now.'

'How lovely to have things in common.'

Xonck looked up at the lip of the crater. There were no gunshots.

'The Contessa took your little trunk, didn't she?' Chang called.

Xonck winced at some internal pain – the blue glass ripping at the flesh it was frozen against – and merely grunted his assent.

'What was inside it?' asked Chang. 'The Comte's device?'

Xonck grunted again at a still sharper pain and then, when the pain did not give way, kicked his boot at the ground, muffling a louder cry through force of will, breathing through his nose like a bull. When the attack at last subsided, the man's face was even more spent, the red around his eyes deepened to scarlet and his teeth the colour – whether this was the enamel itself or the slick discharge, Chang could not tell – of lapis lazuli stones. Strands of blue stretched between his lips with each huffing breath.

'It is true,' Xonck whispered at last. 'I must recover it . . . as I must recover my book . . . as I must locate the requisite power . . . and the requisite *vessel* . . . all true . . . and all unlikely. I am not a fool, Chang. If I hate the proud virtue of a *real* fool, like – I lose the name – your Captain of Dragoons – men the likes of whom I would happily shoot every day before breakfast . . . if I hate such virtue it is because . . . for all my rank and privilege, I have been defined by exclusion. I have studied the limits of what human beings can endure – a study undertaken without scruple, indeed, well aware that such pursuits might consume my own soul away . . . like Brazilian fish strip the carcass of a bull . . . have you been to Brazil?'

Chang snorted.

'A pity,' sniffed Xonck. 'It is a crucible – destruction of men, of men's *souls*, on *such* a scale . . . An idiot can see what drives his enemies . . . only a rare man perceives what drives himself. But when men and women are bought and sold so openly . . . one is oneself devalued . . . yet made wise. In our *civilized* society we actually compete for the privilege of being owned by the very foulest of masters. As I am from a family of the foul, I know this to be true.'

'I thought you were describing how you were doomed,' observed Chang drily.

'Of course,' Xonck laughed thickly. 'If only one could put such a thing in a play, its audience must be *huge*! "Francis Xonck to Perish: Extra Performances Added!"'

He shook his head and coughed, but almost immediately Chang could see the man had become rueful again, resistance to self-pity never being – in Chang's observation – a priority of the rich.

'But perhaps I *should* have died with the rest and been swept beneath the sea. I could have lain still and allowed the water to rise over my face with a hideous serenity. But I do not possess that sort of *mind* . . . and so, before you and I make our compact of survival, Cardinal – as it seems we must – I will tell you . . . a little story.'

Xonck wiped his face. When he spoke again his voice was calm.

*

'Three children, the eldest by enough years to seem more an uncle, never one with whom the younger two shared interests or exchanged secrets – a figure who from his own youth had been occupied with making business out of air – that is, quite literally, from conversation, from cunning speeches both made and overheard . . . for the father of all three – a sort of king, or more exactly a sort of magician – had left behind a secret . . . a treasure hoard. It was the eldest child's skill to inflame this treasure into an empire, where the secret was sold and resold and refined and resold again, innumerable times, until he became more like a king than their father ever could have hoped, and all around him kings in truth were made to kneel.

'The second and third children were nearly twins, growing up in the shadow not of their father but of their fearsome elder sibling. They had their own portion of inheritance but not, for he would not allow it, any role in the kingdom. Their lives became nothing but appetite and ease, and no one paid either any mind, save to condemn their sloth, or blanch with disapproval at what new tastes they found. But each possessed an *innate* inheritance from their father, like the eldest's skill with commerce. The middle child glimpsed the father's secret itself, though she was not schooled, because she was a girl. The youngest saw only the father's lack of fear . . .'

Xonck paused. 'Or perhaps it was not from the father at all, but the mother . . . she who had been slain by his birth, giving him life no matter that she would die.'

Xonck spat and went on more heartily.

'And for his empire the eldest son received an idiot wife, compliant whores, and children he could barely name. For her seclusion, the second child received a husband she despised, a life of craven envy, and children she could barely see without tears. For his ferocity, the third received no wife at all, unceasing hunger, and no child to ever call his own . . .'

'Not much of a story at all, of course,' added Xonck, after a moment of silence, 'but it is a degraded plane, and one grows attached to one's fancies.'

He spun his face from Chang, cocked his head, and sniffed several times like an animal. 'It is a draught of air,' Xonck whispered, already pawing at

the wreckage. 'A tunnel blocked with debris. The stones are too large –
I cannot shift them alone!'

Against all his best instincts, Chang scrambled across the open blast
space into Xonck's shelter. Working together they cleared the aperture:
one of the large metal ducts, the sort through which Chang had descended
from the garden urn into the boiler room.

'That there is air shows the way is still open,' said Xonck.

'It can lead only to the lower levels of the house. All those going up have
been destroyed.'

Xonck smiled. 'Which means it may be crawled. If I go first, I am of
course vulnerable to a knife from behind. If I go second, I may as easily be
ambushed at the end.'

'As may I.'

'Indeed. I offer you the choice.'

'What if I let you depart on your own and attempt to make my own way
up the walls?'

'You cannot. There is no other way.'

Chang was silent, disliking that Xonck was right, disliking their very
proximity.

'Then I will follow,' he said.

Xonck wormed into the shaft, his arms ahead of his body, and disappeared. Chang dived in afterwards. The pipe was greasy with soot, just
wide enough to squirm through, and pitch black. Chang's attention was
rooted to the scuffles and grunts of Xonck's progress. Whenever Xonck
paused, he readied himself for a trick, but each time the man simply pushed
ahead into the darkness.

Then Xonck stopped, and Chang heard him whisper: 'There is a turn.
It goes down – you will have to keep hold of my feet, for if the way is
blocked, I will not be able to climb backwards.'

Without waiting for Chang's answer – not that Chang had intended to
make one – Xonck slithered ahead, positioning himself at the turn. Chang
crawled up and took hold of Xonck's ankles with both hands. He did not
know how this might prove a trap, but he nevertheless held himself ready
to release the man at a moment's notice.

Xonck dropped into the new passage, and Chang felt the man's weight hit his grip. He heard Xonck's knuckles knocking the metal.

'Let me go,' called Xonck. 'There is a hatch just ahead.'

With misgivings, Chang released his hold. Xonck slid away. Before following, Chang drew Lieutenant Sapp's razor. The pipe was suddenly pierced by a beam of light. Xonck had found a hatch after all. Chang lowered his body into the turn, holding himself in place with his legs. Xonck opened the hatch all the way and began to climb out. Chang slid down in a rush and shot out his left hand, catching Xonck's boot before it disappeared. Xonck paused, taken by surprise, and Chang flipped open the razor, ready to strike if Xonck attempted to pull free. But Xonck did not move his leg, nor did Chang creep forward. To move further would place Chang's head in the open space of the hatchway, where Xonck might bring the hammer of his plaster cast – or a knife, or a shard of glass – down onto Chang's skull.

'An interesting situation,' chuckled Xonck. 'You cannot come through without risking my attack . . . and yet if I attempt to free myself, no doubt you will cut the cords at the back of my knee?'

'It seems a sensible precaution.'

'Wholly unnecessary, I assure you. Come out, Cardinal – I shall do nothing to prevent it.'

'Permit me to doubt your word.'

'Do you think I fear you?' Xonck rasped wickedly. 'Do you think I *need* you at a disadvantage? You have survived me several times on luck alone – we both know it. Climb out and meet me – the real question is whether you have the courage.'

'On the contrary,' sneered Chang, 'I am too in awe of your prowess.'

Xonck sucked at a blister on his lip. Chang saw a flicker of blue through his cloak: Xonck's free hand held one of the blue glass spikes. If he released Xonck's leg, nothing prevented Xonck from hacking away at Chang as he tried to crawl out, utterly unable to defend himself.

'Withdraw your leg slowly,' said Chang. 'If you try anything at all I will do my best to sever your knee.'

Xonck removed his hand from his cloak, revealing the glass dagger.

'If you do that I will stab you through.'

'And you will still bleed to death in this stinking hole,' said Chang. 'The choice is now yours.'

'It is no choice at all,' huffed Xonck, and he quite deliberately raised both arms and then very slowly pulled his leg free of the pipe, allowing Chang, the razor pressed close, to extricate first his arm and then his upper torso from the hatch.

'Drop your weapon,' said Chang.

'As you will.'

Xonck released the glass dagger. Chang's eyes flicked towards its impact – he wanted to be sure it shattered and could not be snatched up again – and Xonck swept his plastered arm at Chang's wrist and knocked the razor away from his knee. Chang swore, his legs still caught in the pipe. Xonck clawed his free hand at Chang's face, and Chang wrenched his left forearm up to block it. Exchanging blows like a pair of boxers, Chang cut the razor at Xonck and dredged a thin line across the plaster.

Xonck swept up a leather fire bucket full of sand and swung it at Chang's body like a heavy mace. Chang bent to his right and the bucket only jarred his shoulder and showered them both with sand. Xonck dropped the bucket and reached into his cloak for more glass. Chang curled his legs beneath him and shot forward, barking both ankles hard on the metal hatch rim but trapping Xonck's arm against his body and bringing him down. Xonck thrashed to his feet, eyes wild, a new glass dagger finally ready. Chang rolled to his knees, his back to the cold iron furnace, waiting for the attack . . .

But Xonck's eyes had not followed his movement – the man still stared, blue saliva hanging off his chin, at the floor where Chang had been. Xonck snorted in a panic, then wrenched his face to Chang's. With a swirl of his black cloak, Xonck was gone through the door.

If Xonck's illness had the best of him, then now was the time to cut him down. Chang dashed after him into the curving stone corridor and towards the staircase door. But Xonck had shot the lock – there was blue fluid on the knob – and it took four strong kicks to break it wide. The circular stairs offered too many doors to either side for Chang to blunder past in safety, and his caution allowed Xonck, wherever he had vanished, to slip free.

It was always annoying when, having decided to kill, the work could not be done, but perhaps it did not matter. Chang knew the exact task to justify his journey to Harschmort – long overdue, and his alone.

At the main level Chang entered a long formal ante-room, whose far end held an archway hung with a heavy red curtain, like a private proscenium. Chang knew it was far more likely to hide servants than a stage, and so he sidled quietly to the curtain's edge. He heard voices on the other side and the clinking of cutlery, and saw that the thick carpet of the ante-room continued on to the far side . . . was it a private dining chamber? Who could have the leisure for a meal at a time like this?

He came through the curtain with a sudden rush. Three men in black smocks and knee-breeches looked up with surprise from their work, laying meat and cheese and pickled vegetables in piles onto vast silver platters. Chang struck the nearest with the heel of his fist hard across the ear, knocking the man into a line of wooden chairs. The second – gripping a cleaver half deep into a wheel of thick-rinded cheese – he kicked without ceremony in the stomach and then hurled by his smock onto the groaning carcass of the first. The third, younger than the other two, stood gaping with his hands full of translucent onions, like the disembodied eyes of drowned sailors. Chang took him by the throat. 'Where is she? Be quick about it!'

'Who?'

Chang hurled him into the wall – the onions slathered away on impact – and hauled him up again, this time placing the razor flat against the man's cheek. 'The Ministry officials – where are they?'

Chang spun to the second man, the cleaver wrested from the wheel, foolish – or angry – enough to attack. Chang's razor flashed forward. The man yanked back his arm, too late, his face going white as he looked down, for the slice across his fingers was so clean that the blood took a good two seconds to flow – but then the flow would not stop. The servant dropped the cleaver and held the wound tightly with his other hand, the blood seeping through those fingers as well. Chang yanked his captive peremptorily towards the kitchens.

'You are making their food – where is it to go?'

'The green drawing room – just outside –'

'What would they be doing in the kitchens if you're preparing their food here?'

'I don't know – they made us leave!'

'Where are their other prisoners?'

'What prisoners?'

'Where are the dragoons?'

'Outside – something happened in the garden.'

Chang shoved him back where they had come.

'Tell no one, or I *will* return to cut your throat.'

The next red curtain led to a formal saloon, with a mirrored wall and a massive sideboard lined with bottles. Its tables lay littered with papers, glasses, cigar butts, and at least one cardboard box of carbine cartridges. Chang crossed the carpet in silence to another curtain – he imagined how, with all the curtains drawn, the whole suite of connecting rooms would appear as one massive reception hall – and heard two men speaking low . . . guards?

'Allow me . . . your nose . . .'

'Ah! I do beg your pardon. It is no doubt the fen grass, one *always* sets to sneezing at Harschmort. Good Lord – this is blood!'

'It is.'

'Good Lord.'

'Did you see Mr Soames?'

'Soames? Who is Soames?'

'With Phelps.'

'Who is Phelps? I am hopelessly at sea – and my head aches like a night of gin –'

'Phelps is with the *Duke*.'

'The Duke is *here*?'

'The Duke was in the *garden*.'

'Good Lord. Was not the garden where –'

'His Grace –'

The second man cut him off with a sneeze. Chang flicked the curtain aside. The two men wore black coats, and each held a handkerchief – one tight against its owner's nose and the other, the target of the sneeze, using his cloth to wipe blood from his cravat. They looked at Chang with surprise.

'Where is the Duke?' he snarled.

'Who are you?' asked the man no longer wiping his front.

Chang snapped his fist into his face. The man staggered and dropped to his knees, clutching his nose. His companion took a prudent step away from both Chang and his toppled fellow.

'I will raise the alarm!' he cried.

'Where is the glass woman?'

'Who?'

'Where is the Colonel? What has happened in this house to make you bleed like lepers?'

The men looked at one another, and Chang flicked out the razor.

'Get away while you can.' He nodded behind him to the dining room. '*That* way.'

The men dashed out. Chang did not give them another thought – time was short and his tactics doomed to fail. At some point *someone* would stand up to him, others would gather, the dragoons would appear, and that would be that. Around a corner the carpet ended and a gleaming waxed wood floor began, which told Chang he had entered the domain of servants. He must be close to the kitchens. Another turn brought a set of swinging double doors, and he stepped through, aware he could not lock them behind him.

It was a more formal preparation room, and Chang supposed it might be used for flower arrangements as well as to dress meat. There were several long tables topped with grey marble. On the nearest were laid two men as if for a mortician's care. The Duke of Stäelmaere was stretched next to the other Ministry functionary Chang had seen on the grass in the garden, a dark stain obscuring one side of the man's face where the temporal bone had been crushed. The functionary showed the same peeling veneer of disease he had seen on Aspiche. The Duke, on the other hand, looked as if he had been dead for a fortnight, bloated and discoloured, eyes disgustingly gummed.

The doors on the far side of the room pushed open. Mr Phelps, now holding a sheaf of papers, entered side by side with Colonel Aspiche. Behind them floated Mrs Marchmoor. She was wrapped in a cloak, its hood slipped back on her shoulders. Chang could see the transformation with more clarity: the solid blue eyes, plump indigo lips, and her once lustrous hair, still brown but stiffened, a mocking vestige of a different life, like a eunuch's beard. From the side of the cloak emerged her right arm, the hand gone, the stump bound tightly with blue-stained cloth.

The instant was over. The Colonel leapt forward, sweeping out his blade. Phelps dug in his topcoat for the pistol. This was going very badly, very fast.

'*Stop!*'

The two men paused, glancing at one another. Chang realized that the word had not been spoken aloud.

'It is Cardinal Chang!' cried Aspiche. 'He must be killed!'

At once Aspiche's sword arm fell to his side, like the limb of a mechanical man on a clock. The Ministry man had his revolver free, but apparently could not bring it to bear.

The voice buzzed in Chang's head. 'We are in no *danger*, Colonel. Be *patient* . . .'

Mrs Marchmoor floated forward, her gait tender. The two men stepped aside with unease. It did not seem they found Mrs Marchmoor's company any more welcome than a tiger's – and yet, what choice did they have? Chang braced himself . . . her felt her pushing at his mind . . . he felt her pushing at him . . . but without success, like a strong wind shaking a window. Mrs Marchmoor paused, tried again, and failed. Her swimming eyes narrowed.

'*What is this?*'

Chang remembered Angelique's words in his head, pricking his brain like needle points. Something was wrong – the glass woman's voice was blunted, less astringent. Was it her injury?

Chang took a step towards her. At once she retreated and dragged Colonel Aspiche directly between them, the sabre in his hand sawing the air like a puppet's. It was not the injury at all, Chang realized – her power over the *other* men had not dimmed.

'Let me take him myself!' cried Aspiche. Chang feinted with the razor. Aspiche's arm leapt at his movement, abruptly and without aim.

Chang chuckled. 'This sort of . . . street fight is a tricky thing, Margaret. Without *any* experience, one is simply ordering trouble on a plate.'

'What have you done?' she hissed. 'How do you resist me?'

'Why don't you release Mr Phelps and his pistol so he can shoot me? Why not release the Colonel and his sabre? Surely you don't doubt *their* loyalty – just because they've seen it's possible to defy you?'

'I do not release them because they will kill you too soon.'

Chang feinted, and she brought up the Colonel's arm, again too awkwardly and too late.

'An afternoon of setbacks, Margaret. My defiance . . . Harschmort burnt . . . your poor hand . . . and you seem to have fallen out with Francis Xonck.'

'Francis Xonck will be dead in two days. Like all of the others. I will not be anyone's slave.'

'No, now you require slaves of your own – an ever-replenished supply, the way you corrode them like acid.'

'That can be undone!'

Chang turned to the Duke's body on the table top. 'Your puppet doesn't look so *spry*, Margaret . . .'

In a sudden movement Chang seized the Duke's long hair and dragged the dead peer's head and shoulders off the edge of the table. He dropped his right forearm onto the extended neck like a hammer, snapping the half-rotten vertebrae with a crack. He stepped away, leaving the head in a morbid dangle. Mrs Marchmoor cried out, and lost her possession of the two men. Aspiche leapt to the side, the sabre raised high, his eyes flashing first at Chang and then at the glass woman. Behind him Phelps had his pistol raised, knowing no more than the officer where it ought to be aimed.

'A moment!'

This was Aspiche, his left arm extended to the glass woman, the sabre in his right aimed at Chang.

'The man's a villain – do not listen to his lies. Simply allow me to kill him –'

'No, we need his information!' said Phelps, and he called sternly to Chang, 'Where is Francis Xonck?'

'Such *loyalty*,' said Chang. He felt the cold pressure batting ineffectually at his thought and laughed. 'Neither of you is even curious as to how I confound her? Perhaps if you consulted a mirror you'd change your mind . . .'

Mrs Marchmoor jutted her brittle chin at Chang. 'His essence . . . *tastes* of Xonck's . . . *proximity*.'

'Where did he go?' Phelps asked again.

'Where do you *think*?'

'He recovered the book!'

'By finding that young woman!' cried Aspiche. 'She escaped back to the train! Xonck knew we did not have her, or the book –'

Their blurted words were exactly what Chang had hoped for but too much to make sense of in the moment. Young woman? Book?

'How would Francis Xonck know *any* of that?'

This was Mrs Marchmoor. She took a halting step forward, gesturing with the stump of her right arm.

'I saw into his mind. Francis did not notice *her* at all, no more than he takes note of *anyone*. To him I am a whore – the Colonel a pompous dupe – Cardinal Chang a rabid dog in need of poison –'

'Did he know about the *children*?' asked Chang.

She cocked her head and studied Chang carefully. 'He did not . . .'

Her eyes slid closed and her body went abruptly still. It took Phelps and

Aspiche a moment to realize her attention had been directed elsewhere, but neither man knew whether their opportunity lay in killing Chang or freeing themselves from their mistress. Chang discounted Phelps – the man was too schooled by reason to act on his own – but he watched Aspiche warily. Yet the Colonel hesitated as well – had sickness broken the soldier's nerve? The glass woman's eyes slid open again, one layer of a glass onion peeling away to reveal another, and her moist blue lips curled with disdain.

'The children are perfectly well. Captain Tackham – with whom I see you are *acquainted* – has them in hand. Francis Xonck has abandoned Harschmort House like a whipped cur.'

'Francis Xonck is many things,' said Aspiche, 'and most far worse than any scorpion. But we believe him beaten at our peril –'

Chang barely listened. It was as one tasted intuition in a fight – on impulse lunging on when a sane man would retreat, throwing all to the attack when others would flee – as a swordsman balances all in an instant, the position of each limb, the weight of the blade, and the nearness of each adversary . . .

'We have men watching Hadrian Square, and his brother's houses in town and in the country, his club, his bank, his tailor, the Old Palace, his own rooms at the Caracalla –'

'The *Caracalla*?' asked Mr Phelps. 'He has rooms *there*?'

'He does,' replied Aspiche.

'But it is horrible.'

'It is perhaps *notorious*.'

'It is *louche*,' insisted Phelps, 'and *foul*.'

'So', observed Aspiche, 'is the man in question –'

The wooden chair caught the Colonel across the legs, but Chang took care – whipping it with one arm from behind a table – to aim so it would not bounce in the direction of Mrs Marchmoor. Aspiche went down with a shocked cry of pain, and as the man groped for his sabre Chang stepped on the blade. Again, his reaction far too slow, Phelps raised his revolver, but Chang had already hauled Aspiche up by the collar, holding him as a shield.

Mrs Marchmoor had not moved.

'Take control of your man,' Chang snarled, 'before he hatches an *idea*.'

Phelps lurched and then settled like a stack of jostled crockery, his face blank. Aspiche's body stiffened beneath Chang's grip, ensuring the same degree of silence and cooperation.

'I have others at my call,' she whispered, 'in every direction throughout this house. You will not escape, no matter what you believe.'

'Whoever you call will only find a pile of broken shards.'

'I can have Mr Phelps shoot you.'

'You can have him try.'

He scooped up Aspiche's sabre and felt the desperate thrust of her mind. Two steps gave Chang the range to take her head.

'If I had decided to harm *you*, Margaret, I would not have thrown the chair at the Colonel.'

The glass flesh conveyed no more *feeling* than marble – or less, as marble at least presented a coherent surface. Chang's gaze penetrated beyond his ability to measure, into a swirling well whose depths he could not resolve.

'Of course, Cardinal . . . perhaps, we can aid each other . . . there must be so much you want to know . . .'

Chang sneered at the need in her grating, acid-etched voice.

'Why have you taken Charlotte Trapping's children?'

'To force the cooperation of their mother, of course.'

'Why should you *need* the cooperation of Charlotte Trapping?'

He could feel her presence again, more gently, like the flickers of an annoying breeze.

'Stop that, Margaret. *Answer* me.'

The coldness fell away but her eyes still watched him closely.

'I should think it obvious. I need her because the *Grand Design* depended on shipments of munitions – how else were we to make sure of Macklenburg, much less our own city? With Henry Xonck lacking a mind and Francis Xonck ruined, Charlotte Trapping takes their place.'

'You're a liar.'

'How dare you!'

'When your masters left for Macklenburg, Henry Xonck was exactly as empty-minded as he is now, and Francis Xonck as unavailable – *nothing* has changed to require Mrs Trapping's participation. All munitions were to be managed by Francis Xonck's hand-picked man, Alfred Leveret – whom *you* have driven away. But that is not what I asked! I asked why you have taken that woman's *children*!'

Chang's voice had become too loud, and in the silence that followed he feared some earnest minion or other would take it upon themselves to intrude – or perhaps those intrusions were just what Mrs Marchmoor was preventing as she paused.

'Think of all I can tell *you*, Margaret,' he whispered. 'Just answer this first. You sent Rawsbarthe into her home –'

'Charlotte Trapping is not important,' she barked, like a nail scraping porcelain. 'But there is too much for me to manage – the Duke, the Council, all the *adherent* minions awaiting instructions – so many tasks – and I am alone, without help –'

'Without help? You have the servants of a pharaoh.'

'But they must not see me! They would rebel! They would break my body!'

'Why is that?'

'Because they are all as ambitious as I once was!'

'*Once?*'

'You cannot begin to understand what has been done to me!'

'What has been *done*? What you *desired*!'

'But so much has changed . . . I was not to be alone . . .'

'Everyone's alone, Margaret.'

'No, not everyone.' Her voice had gone disturbingly still. 'Some are fortunate enough to carry their loved ones with them always . . .'

Chang sensed the pressure of her thought entering his palm like a key into a lockhole, and before he could react the same vision of Angelique that had overborne him in the garden swallowed his awareness again. Chang shook his head, but it was too late. When he saw the room once more, Colonel Aspiche had been pulled away, his body positioned to shield her. Chang stood utterly open to a bullet from Phelps, who extended the revolver with an arm of stone. How had she done it?

'All you can tell *me*?' Mrs Marchmoor mocked him. 'Will you begin – or will Mr Phelps shoot your leg?'

'I should prefer he didn't.'

'How do *you* know of Leveret? Where is he now? I need the machines! I need the power!'

'You need a book too, I believe. *Xonck's* book.'

'*She* has it. And she is already mine! I have been inside her mind, your proud little island *rat* – and left my stain upon it. Will it disgust you when *her* hair falls out – or her teeth? Will the stench of her decay revolt you more than *I* do?'

The glass woman's laughter came in brittle snaps. Chang felt the heat on his face, wanting to break her graceful neck. Mrs Marchmoor leant even closer and hissed again. 'How is it you were able to resist me?'

'I find you *vulgar*, Margaret,' he replied. 'Why should a little glass change that?'

In answer, Mrs Marchmoor poured all her energy into his palm – could there still be glass in the wound? Once more Chang was drowned in Angelique's incomparably sweet memory . . . once more, with a near nauseating pang of loss, he dredged his mind free . . .

He looked up, breathing hard. Why was he not dead? Aspiche had returned his sabre to its scabbard. Chang wiped his mouth on the back of his glove.

'Madam,' began Phelps, 'we should not allow him to –'

'He wants nothing more than all our deaths,' Aspiche croaked. 'He is our *enemy*.'

She did not reply. Chang looked into Mrs Marchmoor's expressionless eyes. He took a step backwards.

'Where would you go now, Cardinal Chang?' she hissed.

'There's nowhere he can go,' said Phelps.

'Do not believe it. Cardinal Chang is *resourceful*.' He felt her loathing, her open hatred, her clear memory of his every insult. 'He may even escape from Harschmort House alive. Who can say when we will encounter him again . . . each party having accomplished so much in the meantime?'

As he cut through Harschmort's maze, he met not a single servant or soldier. Had the glass woman cleared his path of any possible obstacles?

Mrs Marchmoor would find Miss Temple. For Celeste to survive, Chang needed to deliver someone of equal value. He had been released to find Charlotte Trapping. Was their understanding so naked?

As he walked, Chang brought his injured palm up to his mouth and tore off the bandage with his teeth. He stepped into a small mirrored alcove and took out the razor. He opened his hand wide, stretching the skin, and dipped the square corner of the razor into wound, pressing delicately until blood was flowing over his fingers. The metal touched something hard . . . Chang shifted the blade and braced himself against the insistent, pulsing memory of Angelique. He gouged the last splinter of glass free, winking and wet on the flat blade . . . the final shred of Angelique. Chang flicked the blade at the mirror, spattering it red, the blue fragment sent who knew where. He'd have no further shackling.

He kept walking until he finally reached what seemed like an acre of black and white tiles, the entryway to Harschmort, a crossroads usually thronged with servants and guests, now empty. He made his exit without incident, trotting down the wide stone steps, certain he was being observed. In the courtyard were at least five coaches laid in a line, but their drivers stood clustered together, watching him descend.

No one had cleared the hallways for Francis Xonck, yet Chang was sure the man had escaped. In the Library, Chang relied on the archivists to limit his own effort and spare his eyes – could he not use Xonck the same way? Xonck's first priority would be to locate his book and thus Miss Temple. This *ought* to have meant following her path through the garden, slavering after his prize like a pig after truffles . . . but Aspiche's dragoons were combing the land between the gardens and the shoreline, from the farm-lands to the canal – and the Colonel, odious but not incompetent, would have sent patrols to the train stations at both Orange Canal and Orange

Locks. Yet they had *not* found her. Nor had they found Xonck – what did he know that his pursuers did not? Chang returned the impassive gazes of the gathered coachmen and strode towards them.

The coachmen were wary of someone – by his clothes at least – so obviously of a lower rung. But once he stood with them, their caution was punctured by both discomfort at Chang's scars and a curious compulsion, for his questions were so specific and assured that only afterwards did the more careful amongst them realize they had answered the strange figure as if he were a policeman. Having learnt where each coach had come from, and with whom, Chang asked if any had returned to the station. He was told they had not, nor had anyone approached them to do so. The men waited for another question. Chang cleared his throat.

'It will be obvious that I am being observed from the house – do not look at the windows, you will see no one – and were any one of you to go so far as drive me to the train station, another would be immediately drafted to follow in pursuit. I thus apologize for not being able to employ you. I *would* be much obliged if you might point me in the direction of the canals . . .'

In saying this to men he knew would be interrogated, Chang was simply attempting to save time. He knew the way perfectly well – and while the canals were a reasonable, even clever, destination for a man seeking escape from Harschmort, Xonck would avoid them, for the canals would be thick with dragoons. Since Xonck had also avoided the coachmen, that left Cardinal Chang with a single place to pick up his trail: the Harschmort stables.

He jogged towards the outbuildings, but then deliberately overshot them, so anyone watching would assume he had passed the stables by. At the next row of sheds he darted to the right and broke into a dead run to get around the far wall, where he paused, waiting. Soon enough a rumble of bootsteps on the gravel reached his ears and then faded in the distance. Chang hurried back, slipping the razor from his coat.

He need not have bothered. The stable door swung ajar, and a black-coated groom lay face down in a heap of straw not two yards away. Beyond

the groom gaped an open stall, no horse within. The boards at Chang's feet
were sticky. Chang scuffed new straw into the goo and saw its vivid blue
colour. He sighed. Horses were not, to Chang, any source of comfort or
pleasure. A rustle caused him to turn – a second groom in the doorway,
obviously on the verge of shouting for help.

'Be quiet!' Chang snarled. 'Who has done this to your fellow?'

The confused groom looked at the fallen man and then back to Chang.
'But – I – *you* –'

'If it had been me, I would not be here. There was a horse there, yes?
He has taken it!'

The groom nodded dumbly.

'A saddle! Another mount! Your friend will revive,' Chang said firmly.
'I must catch his assailant – it is the only hope we have! As fast as you can
or we are *finished*!'

As the groom leapt to his task, Chang risked a glance outside. No one
had come back to search. He picked up the fallen man from the straw and
turned him over. White flecks from Xonck's plaster fist dotted the raw skin
along the jaw. Chang slapped the young man lightly and stepped away,
letting him grope to awareness on his own.

Minutes later a saddled mare was brought forward for his approval.
Chang nodded gravely – what did he know of horses? – and did his best to
mount the thing on the proper side on the first attempt. This done and
Chang's feet having found the stirrups, the groom guided the horse through
the door and pointed to the only path Xonck could have taken – then
slapped the mare's flank. Fast as a rifle shot the animal leapt forward.
Chang squeezed with his knees to keep his seat, expecting at every moment
to break his head like a melon.

Within minutes, the cobbles of Harschmort gave way to a grassy path.
At the end of the immediate estate grounds the grassy path forked, the left
side clearly turning towards the railway station at Orange Canal. He pulled
the horse to a halt and awkwardly – for he did not trust himself to dismount
and remount with any success – paced the mare along each path of the
fork. If Xonck had gone to the station, he had gone back to the city. But
without the machines Xonck needed to survive, the city was just a place to

die. It took Chang another three minutes, glancing over his own shoulder
for pursuing dragoons, to find a smear of blue on the bright grass, like the
excrement of some especially exotic African bird, on the fork going north.
Chang wheeled the horse and dug in his heels.

He bounced past meadows dotted with the gnarled survivors of abandoned apple orchards, testament to the unpredictable flooding of the fen-
land. He thought back to the confrontation with the glass woman and her
mocking description, 'resourceful' . . . he was smart enough to realize that
whatever hopes she had that he might deliver Charlotte Trapping would
keep Miss Temple alive. Was it possible that Miss Temple had escaped?
She had been in the garden – no doubt he'd been blinded to her presence
by his fit. With the damage to Mrs Marchmoor and the rush to shoot Xonck
and himself, the search might have been delayed some five or even ten
minutes. How much ground could she have made with such a start – against
the determination of organized soldiers? Chang gripped the reins more
tightly. She would stick out against the dunes and fen grass like a fox on
a croquet lawn.

He kept riding. Mrs Marchmoor – two weeks before a whore named Margaret Hooke – had somehow become his keenest enemy. She was vulnerable,
to be sure, and hot-tempered – but she was learning. *She* had taken personal
control of the Ministries. *She* had launched Tackham on his search. And
she was willing to sacrifice *anyone*. It would be insane to underestimate
her – insane to come within a hundred yards of the woman without a coatful
of orange rings. Woman? Margaret Hooke had been a woman. *This* was a
creature, the abhorrent residue of one man's diseased imagination. Who
knew when she might become unstoppable altogether?

This thought pricked his memory . . . something else the glass woman
had said, that she 'needed the machines . . . needed the power . . .' He had
taken it to mean power in the broadest sense – domination over an invisible
octopus of minions. But what if Mrs Marchmoor had been speaking literally?
The Comte's laboratory held paintings, chemicals, papers, the man's *knowledge*. But the cathedral chamber had contained not only the machines,
but also the *power* to run them, through Harschmort's fantastic network of

ducts and furnaces and boilers. Whoever had taken those massive machines would find them useless without an equal source of power.

At once Cardinal Chang knew where Xonck was riding, and where he was bound to follow. The clue had been before him from the moment he'd seen the striations of shell-blast. The explosives had been courtesy of Alfred Leveret – the same man who had overseen the refitted factory near Parchfeldt Park, a factory specifically remade to house all the Comte's machines . . . machines no doubt already arrived on the newly made canal and set into position.

The meadows lasted another three miles, and Chang began to worry about the horse, knowing nothing of their care, and so eased the animal's pace. He passed a stand of birch trees, planted as an estate boundary, but all of the surrounding lands had been gobbled up by Vandaariff's agents to ensure his privacy. Beyond the birches was a proper road, and on that road an inn. Chang pulled up and walked the horse to a trough of water. He was debating whether to slide from the saddle himself when a boy ran out from the inn with a mug of beer and a wadded cloth. He handed the mug to Chang and began at once to rub the horse with the cloth. Feeling he had been given a role to play – and since it only required drinking beer – Chang drank deeply, suddenly aware of how thirsty he was. He returned the empty mug, feeling one could enjoy country life after all, and dug in his coat for a coin, asking the boy in an idle tone where the road might take him. One direction looped back towards the Orange Canal Station, and the other led all the way to the lonely coastal fortifications at Maxim-Leduc. He wondered aloud that the inn must not see many travellers, and the boy shook his head, accepting the tarnished old florin – he'd seen no other rider stop all day. Chang flicked his heels and nearly lost his perch as the mare shot forward, appalled at the figure he made, but far too occupied with staying aboard the animal to care.

He clattered across a small wooden bridge, children fishing down in the reeds to either side, thinking to enquire about Xonck but not wanting again to wrestle with a horse that had no inclination to stop. The road topped a gentle hill. At its crest Chang stood in the stirrups and saw, miles ahead, what must be Parchfeldt's thick green canopy. Then the road dropped down into an even denser wood, and Chang felt the air grow colder.

With a determined tug, Chang reined the mare until she walked, slow enough to study each side of the path as they went. If Xonck knew he was being followed, this was the best location so far for an ambush. Chang tried to remember what else he knew of Parchfeldt, from the maps and the newspapers, and from whatever Elöise had told them about the cottage of her uncle . . . *Elöise* . . . the woman had slipped from Chang's thoughts.

Where was she now? He had not, frankly, expected to see her again – any more than a hundred others that had crossed his path on one unsavoury matter or another: the widow Cogsall . . . the old ship's clerk . . . the basement-dwelling apothecary . . . or that Russian cook . . . or was she Hungarian? He remained haunted by her arm – the inch-long scar, from a stove. The ragged diffusion of his memory was echoed in the colours of the forest, trees in such number and variety as to make him think he had never truly seen one in life before. But the vivid density of the wood only drove Chang's thoughts deeper. He pulled his collar up against the chill. Moisture leached into the earth here, giving off a cold that touched his very bones. In nature's eyes, human desire seemed a brief-lived thing, no more notable than the blind hopes of a fox for its cubs or a lark for the contents of each fragile egg.

The road was barred by a low wrought-iron gate, beyond which lay a wooden landing and the brick-lined canal. Chang listened in vain for any voices or recognizable sounds, then gripped tight to the saddle and swung himself to the ground. He patted the mare's neck as he had seen other horsemen do, and walked her to the gate.

The gate's clasp was sticky – he could imagine Xonck wiping his mouth on a sleeve, the slick fluid brushed onto the metal – but there was no lock. Chang looped the mare's reins around the gate post to examine the situation unencumbered: there was no bridge, or any towpath to a bridge further down. Chang peered into the black swirling water, seeing his own reflection with distaste. There was no further sign of Xonck, nor of Xonck's horse, which meant the beast had not been abandoned. Had they *swum* across? The drop from the facement to the water was perhaps two feet – easy enough to leap into, but to climb out again? Chang glanced back at the mare, contentedly watching him with her placid brown eyes, and shuddered. He pushed up his glasses and squinted at the far bank. Was it possible? Xonck *was* a gentleman, and could ride even a crazed horse to its limit . . .

Directly opposite the wooden landing was another just like it, and a continuing path. Chang dropped to a crouch. Beneath the other landing was some sort of ironwork, hanging down . . . after a moment of feeling especially dim he craned his head below his own landing and found a cast-iron lever. Chang pulled it and jerked back as the bridge speared forward across the black canal, slamming into the far couplings with enough force to skewer a wild boar. He stood and studied it with dislike: the bridge was but a yard in width and did not look to hold a man, much less a horse. Yet on the centre plank, smeared by retraction and extension, gleamed another patch of blue.

The mare crossed as blithely as she had borne his ignorance. It took Chang three attempts to regain the saddle, but she stood patiently through them all.

The narrow path wound uphill through trees to meet a more proper country road covered with leaves. Chang did his best to place the direction of the road by the fading light, and orient that direction with reference to the factory – or where he, without having paid special attention to the map, conjectured it as being. He clapped his heels, spurring the mare to a trot. He would only discover if he'd made a mistake in the brief time before the light was gone. He needed to hurry.

The path veered deeper into the woods, and he began to pass ruins – broken boundary fences, road markers, the remnants of walls – all echoing the gnawing discomfort of his body. The path skirted a tumbled gatehouse, but Chang could detect no sign of the manor it once had guarded. He detected no sign of Xonck and so rode on, still hoping to reach De Groot's factory. And who would he find there? And what did Chang expect to do? Destroy the machines? See to it that Xonck's illness consumed him? That the Comte's legacy disappeared? Chang felt a fresh spark of irritation that he was so very out of his element, while the Doctor and Elöise might be – who knew, perhaps not two stones' throws away – settling in with cups of tea before a warm fire, the woman blinking shyly as Svenson did his level, failing best not to stare at the single button undone at the top of her black dress. Chang clutched tightly at the mare's mane and snarled, nearly slipping again.

When he looked up, something caught the corner of his eye. He pushed his dark glasses down his nose, for the curling plume of white smoke blended so cleanly into the colour of the dying sky that he could not at first be sure it was fire or cloud. Chang clumsily slid from the saddle and walked the mare off the road. He looped the reins over a low branch, saw with satisfaction that there was thick grass around the tree for the horse to eat, and then rolled his eyes at his own solicitousness.

The ground fell steeply towards a trickling watercourse, edged on either bank by a trough of rich black mud. Chang slid down through a moist layer of last year's leaves, doing his best to avoid snapping twigs or low hanging branches, along the tight muddy valley to where the smoke seemed to rise. He had assumed it was a campfire – woodsmen or hunters – but was surprised to meet the crumbled remnants of an outlying wall, netted with vines that seemed intent on pulling the stones back to the torpid earth. Over the wall lay an abandoned garden, thick with high grown weeds. Beyond the garden stood the roofless frame of a red brick house, the windows empty . . . yet out of its still-standing chimney rose the white plume.

Crossing the tangled garden in silence was impossible, so Chang crept around the wall, sinking to his ankles in the black mire. The watercourse fed an unkempt pool lined with stonework and once fitted with a mill wheel, now toppled half rotted to one side. The pool's surface was thick with green scum, like the spittle of toads, and the air above it beset by hovering insects. On the bank near the ruined house lay a small flagged yard. The stones would allow a silent approach.

Chang studied the back of the house: two windows with a doorway leading out between them. One window had been covered with planking, and the other draped with oilcloth. He looked up at the smoking chimney – most likely it was a refuge for gypsies, or a rough lodge for hunters. Had it not been for the lack of any sign of another horse, he would have thought it a perfect temporary refuge for Xonck. Chang advanced to the oilcloth-covered window and listened.

The last thing he expected was the sound of a woman in tears.

'There, there . . .' It was the voice of a man, hesitant and low. 'There, there . . .'

'I am fine, thank you,' the woman whispered. 'Do sit down.'

A scrape of a chair and then silence. Chang reached up to the oilcloth, pausing as he heard new footsteps.

'A cup of tea,' announced a clipped new voice. Another woman. Chang could hear the fatigue and impatience beneath her simple words. 'One for each of you.'

'Thank you,' said the man, and at once he whimpered.

'It is *hot*,' the second woman snapped. 'Take it by the *handle*! It is lemon verbena.' The woman sighed bitterly after a sip of her own. 'Too weak.'

'It will do perfectly well,' said the first woman. Chang felt a spark on the back of his neck. He knew her. Why was she crying? And who was the man?

'I'm sure it will have to,' responded the other tartly. 'I am not used to making tea at all, of course – still less in such a pot, on such a fire. Any more than I am used to any of what has happened to my former existence! Though what has truly changed after all? Am I not still a shuttlecock batted back and forth by the more powerful?'

To this opinion the other two had no answer.

'I do not mean to compare my losses to yours,' the woman went on. 'Whatever your losses might be, I'm sure I do not fully comprehend them – who comprehends *anyone*? – but from what you *have* told me and what I have in the meantime guessed – I am not *wholly* without deductive powers – I do not know *why* you find yourself still so *distraught*. Indeed, Elöise, it is most difficult to bear.'

'I am sorry.'

'It has been *some time*. No matter what you say about *memory* and *forgetting*, all of which you take *so* seriously – of course a *measure* of seriousness does credit to a person, but not an excess – yet here we are, flown from what seemed a perfectly fine cottage, *because of you*. It is nearly dark – I suppose we shall *sleep* here! I myself am enduring all manner of outright tiresome privations.'

'Of course you are.'

'I *am*. And yet *you* are the one in tears! They are *pernicious!*'

Elöise did not answer. It was obvious to Chang that the other woman was as terrified as she was arrogant.

'And who *was* he again? That *fellow?*'

'Doctor Svenson,' replied Elöise softly.

'O yes, the Prince's man. Lord *above* –'

'He has saved my life repeatedly.'

'So you intimated. Or,' the woman added drily, 'so you *remember . . .*'

'He saved my life from *Francis.*'

'Why would Francis hurt *you?*'

'Charlotte –'

'Why would Francis hurt any one of us? What *nonsense!*'

'Charlotte,' Elöise sighed with some forbearance, 'Charlotte, that is not *true.*'

To Chang's astonishment, Charlotte Trapping *laughed.*

'Ah, well, there you have me,' she chuckled quite merrily. 'Perhaps I fathom one or two elements after all!'

'Charlotte –'

'Stop blubbering! Your *dear* friend – of, goodness, ten days? – is still alive. And left behind he will remain so, and there's an end to him. What did you want instead, Elöise? A romance to sweep you away? After all you've done?'

'What I've done for you –'

'You say that – so often that I nearly believe you. Do *you* believe her?'

This last was to the man.

'She is very pretty,' he answered gently.

Charlotte Trapping huffed. '*Pretty!* What girl *isn't* pretty? *I* was perfectly pretty and look what happened! Come now, Elöise, did you really expect – and from a *German* –'

'He is very decent –'

'Decent!' Mrs Trapping crowed. 'A word to describe a churchman! Elöise – a woman cannot put her hope in a man she *pities!*'

'I do not pity him. Doctor Svenson –'

'He struck me as – O I don't know – rather *weedy* –'

'He was injured!'

'Not like Arthur. Arthur was a strapping man, with very broad shoulders. Even if you grant your Doctor his uniform – though it was extremely shabby – you cannot allow his shoulders are anywhere near as broad. What's more, your fellow's hair was unpleasantly fair – not like Arthur with his very thick whiskers. I do not believe this Doctor possessed any whiskers at all. You approved of Arthur's shoulders and his whiskers yourself, didn't you, Elöise? I am sure you said something very much like that – perhaps you did not know that I could hear you. I made a point to hear *everything*, you know –'

'Yes, Charlotte –'

'*Arthur*. My husband promised to save me, but he was always promising things he didn't understand.'

'I am *sorry*, Charlotte –'

'Everyone is always sorry for everything.'

'Not Francis,' said Elöise.

To this, Charlotte Trapping was silent.

'The tea is hot,' said the man quietly, as if he had been waiting for some time to speak. Both women ignored him.

Chang eased two fingers to the oilcloth and edged it aside with glacial patience. Elöise sat on a broken-backed wood chair. She still wore her black dress, but had added a dark shawl. Her hair had become curled with the moisture of the woods and rough travel. There was a lost look in her eyes Chang had not, even in their determined struggles aboard the airship, seen before. The veil of kindness and care that had been so customary had gone, and a frank, bitter clarity had taken its place.

To her right, on a rotting upholstered bench, the still steaming mug of tea held tightly between his palms, sat Robert Vandaariff, hatless, in a black topcoat with silk lapels and the muddy shoes and trouser cuffs of a sheep farmer. Like a child for whom an absent parent bears responsibility, the mindless magnate's hair was uncombed, and his cravat had gone askew.

Charlotte Trapping sat with her back to Chang, in what was obviously the only whole chair in the ruined house. The widow's hair was pale with a touch of red (he would have taken it to be a henna wash had he not known her brother), silhouetted against the light of the glowing fire. She wore a well-cut jacket of blue wool over a warm straight dress. Next to her chair was a leather travel case, a hat, and long gloves, all spelling out that Mrs Trapping had attired herself for travel and difficulty. A patterned velvet clutch bag had been looped around her wrist and hung heavily. When Mrs Trapping raised her mug of tea, the bag clacked as if it were stuffed with Chinese ivory tiles. Near to Vandaariff lay another awkward bundle, wrapped in a blanket and bound with twine.

'So you have *seen* Francis,' remarked Charlotte Trapping.

'I have,' replied Elöise. 'Have you seen your brother Henry?'

Mrs Trapping waved her hand towards Vandaariff with a sniff. 'The world will lose no sleep over *Henry*,' she said, and then too lightly, 'I did not know if Francis was alive.'

Elöise did not respond, and once more Chang noted the dull hardness of her gaze. Mrs Trapping must have noticed it too, for she muttered with disapproval: 'I thought you *liked* Francis . . .'

'Charlotte . . . your brother Francis . . . has *changed* –'

'But that is where you are ignorant, Elöise. Francis has *always* changed – it is why he is the opposite of Henry! You would not have known him before he went to school, or again before each of his celebrated travels. Every time he returned he appeared entirely new – and each time he made new friends with no inkling of how strange or dissipated he had become. It was as if portions of his character kept vanishing one after another – given over in exchange for . . . well . . . *something*. And what did he have to show for it – for all his boasting? Land? A title? I will tell you, Elöise, and it is Francis all over: nothing but more wicked stories . . . more cruel *tricks* –'

'But this is different, Charlotte. It is physical. It is *monstrous* –'

'Really, Elöise –'

'Francis is beyond whims and cruelties – it is the blue glass!'

Mrs Trapping pursed her lips and took an unsatisfying sip of tea. 'I

am heartily sick of this blue glass. Is it true that especially nasty man
is dead?'

'The Comte? Yes.'

'And who killed him?'

'Cardinal Chang.'

Mrs Trapping snorted. 'Are you sure you remember correctly? Are you
sure it was not my brother?'

'Your brother and the Comte were fast allies!'

'I very much doubt it.' Mrs Trapping smirked. 'Francis is not one to
keep promises. He was never the *Comte's* true friend! And who can blame
him? I never liked the way that man smelt. Just like a *Russian* – or how
one *imagines* a Russian –'

'*Charlotte* –'

'If you take that tone with me, Mrs Dujong, I will forbid you shelter in
even this crude ruin! We find ourselves at liberty – and you find yourself
rescued – precisely because I have learnt all there is to know about this
blue glass, about this supposedly alchemical *woman* – and these apparently
all-powerful books. Not that I have *seen* any of them, you understand, but
I have done my share of work. You will not perhaps credit that, as children,
I always got the better of Francis playing chess, and always got the better
of Henry too – whenever he would play me, which was very rarely, because
he hated to lose! Do you think I spent my time at those dreadful Harschmort
galas worrying about my evening gown? I watched Henry, and I studied
Robert Vandaariff. Look at him now, Elöise! Smarter than Henry, smarter
even than Francis, though of course without Francis's *appetites* –'

'I saw Francis shot in the chest. Yet he lives.'

Mrs Trapping stopped talking.

'I thought him dead,' Elöise said. 'We all did – and drowned beneath
the sea. But then there were signs, Charlotte, murders – innocent people,
terrible attacks made to look like those of an animal. Then I saw him
myself. He has poisoned himself to stay alive, and the only man who could
cure him is dead. It is all hopeless. You must abandon this business. You
must go home. You have other responsibilities. Francesca needs you, and
Charles, and Ronald. They have no one else.'

Mrs Trapping remained silent.

'I am sorry,' continued Elöise. 'I know how – how – how –'

'Who shot him?'

Elöise's face fell. The woman had not heard a word.

'Charlotte –'

'*Who shot my brother Francis?*'

'It was Doctor Svenson,' said Elöise heavily.

Mrs Trapping stood up and emptied the whole of her tea mug into Elöise's face.

Taking this as the best opportunity he might find, Cardinal Chang took the sill with both hands and vaulted through the window, shooting past the oilcloth to land in a crouch. Charlotte Trapping wheeled to face him, quite obviously wishing she had not just emptied her cup on such a lesser target. Vandaariff stood as well, but this was in mere imitation of the woman, for the man did nothing other than stare as Chang rose, the razor slipped from his pocket.

'It is Cardinal Chang,' said Elöise quickly, her face wet, taking a warning step towards Mrs Trapping.

'Is he your lover as well?'

'Charlotte, come *away* from the window –'

Elöise gently reached both hands for Mrs Trapping's arm, but at her touch the woman sharply shrugged herself free.

'So you are the one who killed that odious Comte,' she cried to Chang, her eyes bright and glittering. 'I daresay it has saved me the effort, and yet the *timing* has proved most unfortunate. Ought I to be frightened by your fearsome appearance? I am *not*. What do you intend with that implement?'

She nodded at the razor. Chang looked at his hand as if he had not known what it held.

'This? I suppose I hold it out of instinct – like an animal. Or because I do not choose to share the fate of Doctor Svenson.' Chang kicked Mrs Trapping's chair across the room with enough force to make both women flinch. 'You will sit down until I tell you otherwise.'

The women did so, Elöise moving hastily to right the chair and brush off the seat. Chang watched with disgust, wondering what could possibly drive her to abandon the Doctor, who had saved her life, in favour of an *employer*. He turned to Vandaariff, still standing with an expression of blank concern.

'Sit down, Lord Robert.'

Vandaariff did. Chang plucked the tea mug from the man's grasp and drank it down, then handed it back with a nod of thanks.

'I think you *are* an animal –' began Charlotte Trapping.

'Be quiet,' growled Chang, and turned to Elöise. 'Where is Miss Temple?'

'How on earth are you here?'

'Dry your face and answer my question.'

'Elöise, do not tell this man one thing.'

Chang shot out his hand and slashed Mrs Trapping's jacket – trusting the razor would not cut through the whalebone in her corset – clean across her torso, causing the blue fabric to hang, the gash made before the woman could even squeak.

'Do not speak again until I am asking questions of *you*. I promise, we *will* talk, for I have spoken to your brother. Elöise?'

Elöise looked into Chang's black lenses for the first time since his entry, her gaze grim and beaten. 'I left Miss Temple at the town of Karthe. We became separated. We had quarrelled. The Contessa was there, and Francis Xonck. If you have truly seen him –'

'I have seen him.'

'I believe he took me for the Contessa. He attacked me, with a sliver of glass . . .'

'Elöise,' muttered Charlotte Trapping, '*really* . . .'

But Elöise had already prised free the third button down between her breasts and pulled the fabric open with her hands. Chang saw the bandage, and its coin-sized stain of blood.

'The Doctor found me –'

'What was Svenson doing in Karthe?'

'I have no idea. He left the fishing village not long after you yourself – we had quarrelled –'

'Elöise quarrels with *everyone*,' whispered Mrs Trapping.

'When I woke I was on the train. The Doctor removed the glass. He saved my life –'

'Again,' said Chang.

'*Again*,' echoed Elöise miserably.

'I found him rather *weedy*,' whispered Mrs Trapping.

'Charlotte, *please!*' cried Elöise, her voice a whisper.

'Francis Xonck was also on that train,' said Chang.

Mrs Trapping looked up.

'And the Contessa,' sighed Elöise, 'hiding in a goods van. When the train stopped at Parchfeldt, she fled, and the Doctor and I went to find her. The last we saw, Francis was bent double on the trackside, sick as a sailor. The Contessa escaped into the park. Abelard insisted that we follow.'

'And what of you? Did you want to follow?'

'I believe I more wanted to die,' sighed Elöise, and she covered her face with both hands.

Chang looked down at the unhappy Elöise, whose dismay only inflamed his desire to cuff her face. Instead, he stepped to the bound bundle. He flicked the razor at the blanket and then ripped enough of an opening to see the vivid colours of the painted canvas beneath it. Charlotte Trapping had gone to Harschmort, burnt the laboratory, taken the paintings, and captured Robert Vandaariff all by herself. He had taken her for a society ninny. He glanced up, met her fierce, determined gaze – the green eyes unpleasantly like her brother's – and recalled Xonck's story, in which the second child inherited the intelligence of their powerful father. From the conversation he had just overheard he knew she was whimsical, cruel, and insufferably proud . . . that she was here at all proved her bravery and determination . . . and that she was a Xonck meant she was also probably insane.

But he was not finished with Elöise Dujong.

'Where is the Doctor now?' he demanded harshly.

'We left him at my uncle's cottage.'

'Struck on the head,' added Mrs Trapping.

'He will be safe,' said Elöise quickly. 'The cottage is warm, and there is food and firewood and a bed – Lord knows he deserves an excuse to let all of this go – to let me go –'

'I'm certain he feels the same way,' said Chang.

'He is *alive*,' said Charlotte Trapping haughtily. 'He need not be.'

'And how long will he stay there, do you think?' Chang ignored her, directing his words to Elöise. 'And where will he go? The Prince is dead. The Doctor has been declared an outlaw by his own government – and *our* Ministries, presently in the hands of his enemies, are more than happy to capture or execute him. I do not imagine he has any money. A destitute foreigner hunted by the law? Your *Abelard* will be lucky not to be hanged on the spot by the first country sheriff to run him down!'

Elöise began to sob before he finished.

'You're an ugly fellow, aren't you?' observed Mrs Trapping.

Chang took hold of Elöise's jaw, tugging her face up so their eyes met. 'I've been to your room – I *know*. Were you Xonck's spy from the beginning? Or was it the Contessa's?'

'Cardinal –'

'Of course none of this was worth mentioning! When people were dying! When people were saving your life!'

He released his grip with a push.

'Caroline Stearne summoned you both to a private room in the St Royale,' Chang went on. 'Doing the Contessa's bidding – was it only blackmail, or something else? What did she demand in exchange? Who else did you *betray*?'

Tears streamed down Elöise's cheeks. He turned away from her to Mrs Trapping. 'Why don't *you* tell me – there are no holes in *your* memory, are there?'

'I am completely capable of telling you about Caroline Stearne,' said Charlotte Trapping. 'But I want you to tell me why I *should*.'

Ironically Chang realized her blithe dismissal of his anger actually meant that, for the first time, she truly understood how dangerous he was. Was this her Xonck tenacity rising to – and there was the pity, perhaps only to – a mortal challenge?

'These are family matters,' she said coolly. 'Why should *you* be part of it?'

'Clearly I am *already*.'

'But what is your stake, sir? Is it this *Doctor*? Is it *revenge*? Or' – she allowed her eyes to traverse his ruined habit – 'merely a matter of *money*?'

With an effort Chang stopped himself from backhanding the woman across the face.

'I am here because people have tried to kill me. People like your brother.'

'But he has *not* killed you. I don't know what you're so afraid of – you must be very formidable to survive *Francis*. You must tell me where he has gone. What are his plans?'

'So you can assist him?'

She smiled almost girlishly. 'O I do not say *that* . . .'

The woman was insufferable.

'When did you last see your children?' asked Chang.

Mrs Trapping did not answer, realizing at once what the question meant.

'It is that terrible man!' she whispered. 'Noland Aspiche. Always watching, disapproving – he *never* accepted Arthur as his rightful commanding officer –'

'He hired me to *kill* your husband, actually,' said Chang drily.

'*What?*'

'Chang did *not* kill Arthur,' said Elöise quickly.

'But – but that *man* – he *hired* you –'

Chang smiled. 'Your husband was *loathed*.'

'I beg your pardon –'

'Your husband was an *undeserving ass*.'

'But – the arrogance – the *presumption* –'

'*Charlotte!*' Elöise cried. 'Your children! Could they have been taken by Francis?'

'Of course not! Why would he endanger –'

'*Charlotte!*'

'*I do not know!*'

Both women turned to Chang. To tell them what he knew was to step away from interrogation and towards alliance. Did he want that? Did he

care? What *was* his stake? Had he not been wrestling with Charlotte
Trapping's question since the first night in the fisherman's hut? Why *was*
he still involved in this business? He thought of the Doctor, with a broken
head and a ruined heart, and of Miss Temple, running for her life, a captive,
or already dead. He looked at the two women, their bundle of paintings,
their idiot tycoon, squatting in a shambles like the meanest gypsies.

'At the command of the Privy Council, your children were put on a
train to Harschmort House, under the immediate authority of a Captain
Tackham.'

Charlotte Trapping's eyes narrowed. 'David Tackham made advances to
me at a regimental function. He was not even drunk. He is an *adder*.'

'Are they still at Harschmort?' Elöise asked Chang.

'Am I?'

'Did Francis see them?'

'I do not know.'

'Did he speak of them?' pressed Elöise. 'You said the two of you talked
– did he speak of them?'

'Not at all.'

'What *did* he say?' This was Mrs Trapping, but her voice had gone cold.

'Very little that bears repeating,' replied Chang. 'The blue glass has
deranged his mind.'

'Cardinal, please!' cried Elöise. 'Francesca! The boys! Where are the
children *now*?'

'No,' he said. 'Tell me about Caroline Stearne.'

From outside the window came the sound of splashing water. Chang turned
to it, trying to pick out anything unusual within the normal noises of the
woods at night – for night had indeed fallen while they spoke – but it all
sounded strange to him. Who knew what shuffling steps would be covered
by the pond water rushing past the broken mill wheel?

He spun again and pulled his head back as sharply as any bantam rooster.
The brick in Charlotte Trapping's hand swung inches past his face. He
caught her wrist and, had the razor been open, could not have prevented
an instinctive counterstroke from opening her jugular. As the razor was

folded into his right fist, he merely snapped a blow into the woman's jaw, dropping her to the floor with a protesting grunt of pain. He looked up at Elöise, who stood with both hands over her mouth.

'I did not see her!' she whispered. 'O Cardinal Chang – O Charlotte, you fool!'

She went to her mistress, sprawled and kicking, then looked to Chang, her eyes wide. '*Cardinal!*'

The door behind was kicked open. Three dragoons filled the window, carbines aimed at his chest, while in the doorway stood an officer with his sabre drawn. Behind the officer were the shadowed forms of at least another ten soldiers.

'Whatever is in your hand, drop it,' ordered the officer – a lieutenant, by the bar on his collar and the single thin epaulette. 'You are all prisoners of the Crown.'

Chang opened his palm and let the razor fall to his feet. The Lieutenant stepped into the room, the tip of his sabre pricking Chang's breastbone. Chang retreated so he stood in a line with the two women and Vandaariff, who had leapt up at the crash of the door. The officer kicked the razor to the side with one muddied boot. Behind him four more dragoons entered, their sabre blades glinting in the firelight.

'You are Chang,' announced the Lieutenant, as if to cross the name off a list of tasks. 'Do not move.' He nodded once at Vandaariff. 'Berkins, Crimpe – take him.'

Two troopers seized Vandaariff's arms and marched him away into the darkness. The officer's blade did not waver from Chang's chest.

'Ladies. I am Lieutenant Thorpe –'

'I know you very well, sir,' said Mrs Trapping.

The Lieutenant nodded stiffly, not meeting her eyes. Instead his gaze went to Charlotte Trapping's leather travel case. Without a word he stepped to it, pulled it open, and sorted carefully through the clothing inside. He stood and then saw the clutch bag around her wrist. The Lieutenant held out his hand for it – the woman handed the thing across with a huff of indignation – and then pulled open the top. Chang heard clinking from inside, and then saw a glint of blue light reflecting off Thorpe's face. The bag was stuffed with blue glass cards . . . no doubt all looted from secret corners in Arthur Trapping's study.

Lieutenant Thorpe closed the bag and hardened his voice. 'I have been pursuing this criminal from Harschmort House. That I have located your party as well is a kind coincidence. Sergeant!'

From the doorway came a massive man. He placed an iron hand around an elbow of each woman.

As she was pulled past Chang, Elöise whispered, 'I am so sorry, so very sorry –'

Chang had no answer, and then she was gone. Thorpe sheathed his sabre with a sweeping ring and followed the women outside, where he whispered in his sergeant's ear. Chang stood alone, facing the firing squad of carbines in the window. Then Thorpe returned, studying him with a professional detachment.

'It was the horse, you know. We saw it from the road.'

'I know little of horses,' Chang replied.

'And that has cost you. Take off those glasses.'

Chang did so, having no other option, and took some satisfaction in the discomfort on the faces of the soldiers at the revelation of his scars. He folded the glasses into his pocket.

'I am obliged,' said Thorpe, and called behind him, 'Corporal!'

A young soldier stepped forward, yellow chevrons on his sleeves. Chang smiled bitterly. The man's left leg was wet above his boot – here was the oaf who'd tripped into the pool.

'Secure him.'

The Corporal quite savagely drove a fist into Chang's abdomen, doubling him over, then stepped behind and laced his arms with Chang's, pinning them tight. With a brutal shove he drove Chang onto his knees. Chang looked up, fighting for breath. The three troopers had left the window. Thorpe was tugging on a thick pair of leather gauntlets, and the dragoon next to him held an open leather satchel. Another dragoon stood with a drawn sabre to Thorpe's other side, but Chang could no longer see any troopers through the door.

Had they all left with the sergeant and the prisoners? So they wouldn't see him die?

'My orders are simple,' said Thorpe. 'You are too dangerous to keep alive, and yet what you know is extremely valuable. Therefore I have been instructed to *take* it.'

He reached carefully into the satchel and removed a square parcel wrapped in cloth. He looked at Chang, measuring him, and then spoke generally to his men.

'If one word of this is breathed to any other soul, I will see *all* your backs whipped raw.' Thorpe nodded to the dragoon with the satchel. 'Help hold him fast.'

Thorpe picked the cloth away with thick leather fingertips. The blue glass book flickered in the firelight. He knelt in front of Chang, so their faces were at a level, and delicately opened the book. Chang glanced once into the swirling blue depths and wrenched his eyes away.

'I am *told*,' the Lieutenant said, 'that after this, when you are killed, you will not feel a thing. I have no relish for executions, so I hope it is true. Corporal?'

Chang felt a hand grip the hair on the back of his head and push him down. He twisted his face and shut his eyes, resisting with all his strength. This was an empty book. Gazing into it, or touching it with his flesh, would cause the whole of his memory to be drained like a wine cask.

And why was he fighting it – merely pride? Was this not what he had wanted – oblivion after Angelique's destruction? Was this not what he sought in opium, in poetry, in the brothels? It was not a decision he cared to be made *for* him . . . yet . . . his eyes drifted closer to the swirling blue plate, daring to be seized . . .

The Corporal pushed down even harder. Chang's face was inches away. Would the orange rings in his pocket protect him? Or merely prolong his agony? He could feel the cold emanating from the slick surface –

The dragoon standing guard with a sabre shrieked like a woman and thrashed forward onto his face. Thorpe leapt free of the man's weapon, cradling the fragile book beneath his body. Chang just glimpsed a glittering spike of blue sticking out of the dying trooper's spine before a black-cloaked figure hurdled the body and tackled the Lieutenant into the rotting bench where Vandaariff had perched. The two men landed with a hideous crash, but then the shadowed figure rose and swept the cloak aside to reach for another blue stiletto. The officer's mouth gaped with harsh astonishment, the bulk of his torso frozen stiff, for the book had been crushed on impact and the broken sheets driven deep into his chest.

The men holding Chang went for their blades. Chang dived for the razor and slashed wildly behind him. The Corporal howled, blood spitting from his wrist, and Chang drove a heel into his groin. The Corporal doubled over, and Chang kicked the man brutally across the jaw. Francis Xonck stood over the second soldier – whose open eyes gazed unnaturally backwards from his twisted head – a dragoon's sabre in his non-plastered hand. Chang rolled to his feet, dropping the razor to seize the Corporal's blade.

But Xonck's face was a death mask, chin and neck dark with blue discharge, and his eyes fluttered, as if the room before him made up but a portion of what he saw, as if the effort of the attack – of controlling his mind enough to make it – had been too much. He stabbed the sabre into the dirt and held out an empty hand.

'There will be too many for myself alone . . . too many for you . . . perhaps you will accept . . . a temporary . . . *expedience.*' The words emerged from Xonck's mouth as if through a sack full of slick stones.

'These soldiers,' said Chang. 'Mrs Marchmoor . . . Margaret . . . she is coming.'

'I should think so.' Drool covered Xonck's lips. 'That means she's found your little Miss.'

An hour later, twisting through the woods until even with the moon above them Chang had no idea of where they'd gone, and stopping twice for Xonck to be ill, they reached a ridge, and upon it a sudden gap of meadow. Far below curled a gleaming snake of canal water. From the canal a pale road had been cut through the trees, at the end of which loomed a bright building. Its high windows bled enough light into the black air for a royal christening.

In the silence Chang could hear the thrum of machines.

'Frightfully bad form,' Xonck rasped next to him. 'The swine have begun without us.'

NINE

INCISION

Doctor Svenson refused to consider himself the sort of man who might kill a woman, under even the most heinous of circumstances, 'heinous' being a perfectly apt word to describe the woman before him. The Contessa had requested a cigarette from the Doctor's case and was deftly inserting it into her black lacquered holder. She caught the Doctor's gaze and shyly smiled. 'Would you have any matches?'

Svenson slipped the dead barge master's clasp knife into his trouser pocket and pulled out a box of matches. He lit one and offered it to her, nodding to his own case, still in her hand.

'May I?'

'It is very lovely,' she remarked. 'I suppose the laws of salvage compel me to return it.'

She held it out and his fingers just barely grazed hers – cool, soft – as he took it.

'As if you were one for laws.'

The Contessa blew a plume of smoke towards the guttering fire.

'These are quite raw,' she said. 'Where do you get them?'

'Purchased from a fisherman,' replied the Doctor. 'Danish.'

'In the city, you were smoking something else. They were black.'

'Russian,' said Svenson. 'I buy them from an agent in Riga. I used to call on him when my ship stopped in port. Being no longer with a ship, I order them over land.'

'I'm sure you could acquire them nearer.'

'But not from him. Herr Karoschka – one so rarely finds a decent man of business –'

'Rubbish.' The Contessa tapped her ash towards the fire. 'The world is ankle-deep with decent men of business – it is exactly why so many are so poor. Their delusion is merely the *ordure* in which more hardy crops thrive.'

Svenson nodded in the direction of the barge master's body. 'Are you always so merry after killing a man?'

'I am this merry when I have *survived*. Will we speak like reasonable people or not? The food is wholesome, the bottle contains – it is the country, one condescends – a clean-tasting cider, and if you put more wood on the fire like a kindly person it might well revive.'

'Madam –'

'Doctor Svenson, *please*. Your querulous niceties only make it more awkward to speak freely, as we *must*. Unless you have decided to dash out my brains after all . . .'

Her tone was arch and impatient, but Svenson could see the fatigue in her face – and it surprised him. The Contessa's normal temperament was so fully *armoured* – he naturally thought of her as a seductress or a killer, but never anything so fragile as a *woman*. Yet here the Contessa di Lacquer-Sforza had been reduced to cutting a man's throat for his dinner and a meagre fire.

'Where is Elöise Dujong?' he asked, his voice even.

The Contessa burst out laughing. '*Who?*'

'You were with her, madam. In her uncle's cottage – you arranged –'

'Arranged *what*? And *when*?'

'Do not hope to lie to me! You saw her –'

The Contessa choked gleefully on her cigarette.

'Madam! She directed you to Parchfeldt Park –'

'We did not meet at all. I saw *her* in Karthe, I admit it – a slag-heap I have scrubbed from my memory – but she did not see *me*. She was skulking after some man.'

'She was attacked by Francis Xonck.'

'I don't suppose it was fatal?'

'He mistook her for *you*.'

The Contessa shrugged as if to say this meant nothing, but then met the Doctor's cold gaze. Her smile faded away. 'And so Francis followed on the train – not reaching the goods van before I was gone. It was you that prevented him from doing so, wasn't it? That gunshot.'

Doctor Svenson was silent. The Contessa exhaled again, wearily.

'Being obliged in any way is hateful. Very well. I have not seen Elöise Dujong since the train yard at Karthe. Miss Temple travelled with me. I left her quite alive, free to re-enter her cocoon of respectable hotels and tractable fiancés. Now will you please *sit down*?'

He knew the Contessa to be the worst of women, and yet whenever she spoke, even if he knew it to be a honey spun of nightshade, it was as if her candour was meant for him alone. He stuffed the kindling into what remained of the embers. Could she truly not have been at the cottage? The Contessa uncorked the cider, took an unhurried pull, and held out the bottle. He felt the dizzy throb at the back of his skull and drank, reflexively wiping the bottle with his sleeve – at which the Contessa chuckled. She pushed across the barge master's dinner: a half-loaf of coarse brown bread, a block of cheese, its edges scumbled with mould, and perhaps six inches of blood sausage. The Contessa raised her eyebrows with a knowing expectation. He looked at the sausage, then met her eyes again and felt his face grow warm.

'You have the fellow's knife, I believe,' she said.

'*Ah.*'

Doctor Svenson cut sausage and cheese for them both and then returned the clasp knife to his pocket. The Contessa piled a slice of each onto a torn hank of bread and took a small, estimatory bite.

'A bit of mustard would do well,' she said with a shrug. 'Or caviar on ice with vodka – but what can one do?'

They ate in silence – like Svenson, the Contessa was evidently starving. But it was enough to simply watch her *chew*, or her nimble fingers pluck together each mouthful, or the action of her swallowing throat – the display of the Contessa di Lacquer-Sforza as a human machine. While this brought her status in his mind as an especially splendid creature somewhat down to earth, it also – combined with the lines lack of sleep and comfort had sketched around her eyes, the dull bloody colour of her unpainted lips, and the untucked strands of black hair that fell about her face – made her seem so much more a palpable *woman*. He sawed apart the rest of the meat and cheese, and smiled as she snatched the slices away as they appeared, marvelling at how effortlessly *companionable* she had become. Doctor Svenson caught himself staring at her hands. The pain in his head had eased, he realized, only to by replaced by a growing, embarrassing ardour. He reached for the bottle and shifted what had grown to an uncomfortable position, drank, and groped to change the subject in his own internal conversation.

'What did you think of the glass card?' he asked. 'It was taken from my pockets. Don't tell me you didn't look into it.'

'Why should I tell you that?' She reached for the bottle, drank, and set it down. 'I think she does her best to warn you.'

'Why?'

'Because she is an idiot.'

'You mean she wants to save my life.'

The Contessa shrugged. 'If she cared for you truly, if she had a scruple of genuine sympathy for your soul, she would have instead provided you with the experience of Arthur Trapping having his beastly way with her on the floor of his children's schoolroom. You would have felt their pleasure – it would have aroused you, but sickened you even more. No doubt your skin crawls to think of it, of *them*, those little chairs, the room smelling first of notebooks and chalk, but then, more pungent, the air thick with *her* – the barnyard grunting, the secretions – my goodness, you must know each by its Latin name!'

She stopped at once, her eyes innocently round.

'If Mrs Dujong cared for you, she would have done her level best to drive you away by whatever means might be at hand. She has instead attempted to *explain* . . . and thus sent along your own death warrant.'

'Do you think so?'

'Listen to yourself defend her! The only question is whether she did so knowingly or is stupid. In either case, again – really, Doctor – *pah*!'

*

Svenson had no answer. The blue card had been placed in his pocket by
Elöise . . . but what justification could it possibly offer? How other to read
the attack in her uncle's cottage save as the tipping point where she had
been forced to reveal her *true* allegiance? But why should he trust the
Contessa? He glanced once more towards the shadows where the barge
master's cooling body lay hidden.

'Is it likely we will receive visitors from the large building down the
road?'

'That depends on whether the fellow whose dinner we eat was merely a
guard to mind the barge or someone with a task, the non-doing of which
will draw notice.' She reached for a last slice of cheese. 'One reason to
maintain the fire of course is to preserve the illusion of his continued
presence.'

'And if I had not arrived?'

'But you *did* arrive, Doctor.'

'You credit the notion of destiny, then?'

The Contessa smiled. 'I credit the need to face facts. I am not one to
entertain phantasms when I can entertain the real.'

'The objects on the blanket told you they had encountered me.'

'Why should I care?'

'Why indeed?'

Doctor Svenson reached for the cider. The bottle was two thirds gone.
'And what *is* this building? Surely it is your *object* in Parchfeldt Park?'

'To so arrantly reveal your ignorance, Doctor Svenson – it shows bad
form.'

'Rubbish yourself, madam.' Could mere cider be going to his head so
quickly? 'Do you think I cannot see the stiffness in your right shoulder?'

'I assure you, I am quite well.'

'You have taken the bottle each time with your right hand, even when I
have placed it much nearer the left. If you have been injured, I should see
what I can do – it will only make it easier for you take my life when you
finally decide.'

'Or for you to take mine directly.'

'If that were a worry, you would not be here.'

In a sudden afterthought to his logic, Svenson realized that he had taken a blow square to the right side of his head, from a woman directly behind him – which meant she must have used the full force of her arm, which strongly suggested his assailant had used her right arm. It could not have been the Contessa at the cottage – just as the Contessa could not have extricated Robert Vandaariff from Harschmort. But if the woman he had glimpsed next to Elöise *had* taken Robert Vandaariff from Harschmort, along with the Comte's paintings . . . at once the Doctor suddenly knew he had been knocked into the wardrobe by Trapping's wife, Charlotte.

The Contessa glanced to the road, then back to Doctor Svenson, her violet eyes inhabited by a curious gleam. As if she had come to a wicked decision, she reached into a canvas bag behind her and came out with a bottle and a rag.

'Such professional concern. You must give me a moment to undo my dress . . .'

He could see the wound would scar. At another time he would have certainly stitched the gash together, but here he soaked it with the alcohol.

'This was not from the glass,' he said, as the Contessa flinched – not from pain but from the cold drips that ran beneath her dress to the small of her back.

'Not from Francis, you mean?' Her hair hung over her face to provide a clearer view of the wound. 'No. I had the misfortune of passing through a window.'

'A few inches higher and it would have cut your throat.'

She had removed her right arm from the dress, and the purple silk bunched in a rustling diagonal, revealing the Contessa's corset and a good deal of her body – even paler for the blackness of her hair.

'What is your *opinion* of my bandage?' she asked.

'I think you did very well to tie it yourself,' he answered, reaching carefully beneath her arm to redo the knot.

'It was not me at all,' said the Contessa, 'but someone with much smaller fingers. It was a very long journey, you see, and just the two of us together.'

For an unguarded second Svenson imagined himself trapped in a goods van with the Contessa. Sharing an open fire was difficult enough. But the woman alone with Celeste Temple . . . what had they spoken of – and what . . . what else . . . it did not matter – nothing mattered as long as Miss Temple had emerged alive and unscathed. If only he could believe it.

'There you are,' said Doctor Svenson, sitting back on his knees.

She turned to face him, testing the ease of her arm and the tightness of the bandage, but not moving to do up her dress. Doctor Svenson swallowed, his medical objectivity steadily more confounded, like distant moonlight disappearing under cloud, as he stared. He forced his gaze up to hers, expecting a twinkling mockery, but the Contessa's eyes were warm and clear.

'If any girl could ever be dear to me, I can imagine Celeste Temple such a one, though my first impulse on seeing such a determined little beast was to snap her neck between my teeth. So to speak, you understand . . . and yet . . . perhaps it was this wound . . . perhaps the need to huddle together for warmth . . .'

'She – she *is* ferocious,' the Doctor stammered. 'But still innocent.'

'I think *you* retain some innocence as well,' whispered the Contessa.

The moment was as dangerous as any Doctor Svenson had ever known. Despite all perspective and sense, her violet eyes remained pools into which he could, even now, be utterly lost, and in that losing give over all loyalty, all faith, all decency to her uncaring purpose. If he leant forward to her lips, would she kiss him? Would she laugh? He licked his lips and dipped his gaze across her body. He could no longer recall the colour of Elöise's eyes.

Doctor Svenson sprang to his feet, wiping his hands on his trousers, and at once stumbled on a stone and toppled backwards into the undergrowth, landing with a grunt as the air was knocked from his lungs. He lay gasping, the green leaves of forest ivy brushing at his face, and shoved himself onto his elbows. The Contessa had returned her arm to her dress, and was doing up the shining black buttons with her left hand.

'Are you quite alive?' she asked.

'My apologies.'

'Come back to the fire,' she said. 'We have little time after all, and urgent matters to discuss.'

Doctor Svenson took a cigarette from his case and lit it before he sat down, as if his habit might shield his weakness, but her expression made plain he was the least of her concerns. Grateful, if also childishly stung at his peripherality, he returned to his place across the fire.

'Where is Cardinal Chang?'

It was not at all what Svenson expected her to say, and he was strangely crestfallen.

'I have no idea.'

The Contessa was silent. Svenson exhaled and tapped his ash onto the stones.

'If you hope Chang will aid you any more than I –'

'*Aid?*' she snapped. 'You are a presumptuous Teuton . . .'

Her mood had sharpened, or she had stopped bothering to hide it.

'Upon surviving the airship, madam, you must have assumed you were the only one of your Cabal –'

'*Cabal?*'

'What else does one call you and your . . . associates?'

'*Anything* else. The word smacks of businessmen playing with corn harvests.'

'My *point*', continued the Doctor, 'is that your allies must have been few – thus your enlistment of the poor boy in Karthe. He was quite badly killed, you know –'

The Contessa's eyes were harder. 'The subject is not diverting.'

'You ask for Chang because you are alone and seek greater numbers – and since you do ask, since you do expect my help –'

'How very *dramatic*,' she sneered. '*Ganz tragisch.*'

Svenson's cigarette had nearly burnt to his fingers. He took one last puff and dropped it into the fire. He looked the Contessa in the eye. 'You left the train deliberately to come here, to this spot in Parchfeldt Park. While this building is of a size to be a manor house, the construction is made for industry. The location of the canal allows the swift passage of goods – and yet the road and the canal are new-made. That you are here suggests *you* are one of the people who has new-made it – just as it is *you* who have made Xonck your enemy. You met him – in the village or on the way to Karthe. You most likely stole his horse, you certainly stole his book – and yet even after recovering it he was still doing his level best to find you.'

'Once wronged, Francis is most persistent in his rage. As you put a bullet in his chest, you might bear it in mind.'

The Doctor ignored her mocking smile. 'He has had several opportunities to take my life, yet I am here. Which means this place too is entirely related to Xonck.'

This last did not come from any deduction about the Contessa, but from the crates of Xonck munitions on the barge with Mr Fruitricks. Svenson was sure now that Fruitricks was an agent of Francis Xonck, who had intended all along to seize control of the Comte's machinery. And now Charlotte Trapping had the Comte's paintings along with Vandaariff. Whatever she knew of the Cabal – through her brother or her husband or even, he had to admit it, Elöise – had been enough to send her on her own extreme journey. Did the woman hope to challenge Fruitricks? Or was she hoping only to survive?

Svenson swallowed. Would he see Elöise again after all?

'In any event,' he muttered, 'you must expect Xonck here, if he still lives.'

'I do. And you and I have been here far too long.'

The Contessa stood, reached behind for her bag, and smiled as Svenson struggled to his feet.

'You have caused me so much trouble, Abelard Svenson, yet, as you say, you *are* here.' She flicked a bit of grime from his hair. 'It shows something more than your *decency* – passion, lust, despair, one scarcely cares – but something in you uncontrolled. I find it spurs my trust.'

'But I do not trust *you* at all.'

'If you did, I should think you quite a worm,' she replied. 'The fire will die on its own, and by now we will be unseen on the road. Come, it is time.'

*

They walked without speaking to the gravel road, a rough carpet threading the wood to either side. With night fallen full, the building glowed even more brightly. The Contessa reached for his arm, and then her touch became a tug on his uniform sleeve. He quickly followed her off the path, crouching low and keeping silent. A thin glimmer of yellow drifted towards them from the white building: the gleam from a mostly closed lantern. Svenson had not even glimpsed it – without the Contessa he would have blundered on and been taken. Behind the lantern came a double line of figures dragging two low, flat carts. These were the bargemen going back for the final load from the canal. Once they had passed, the Contessa's lips touched his ear. 'They will find him. We must hurry.'

In a rustle of leaves she was back on the road and walking as quickly as the dark and her injury would allow, and Svenson broke into a rapid jog to catch up.

'What is this place? I know they have brought the Comte's machines –'

She ignored him. Svenson caught the Contessa's uninjured shoulder and pulled the woman to a stop, her furious glare causing him to take back his hand at once.

'If you expect my help you must say.' He gestured at the bright building. 'You and Xonck were *both* to have been cavorting in Macklenburg for how long? Another month? Two? All *this* was set in motion without regard to your present state *or* his. It is either Xonck's secret plan against you all, or it is mutiny in his absence.'

'Francis *is* coming – that is all that matters.'

'Whatever of his you have – whatever his book contains – can you really want it for yourself?'

'Really, Doctor, I want him not to *kill* me – whether Francis dies or we make peace I care little. But at this moment I care least of all to be *caught* on the road!'

Behind them Svenson heard a cry – distant but telling. The barge master had been found. The Contessa picked up her dress and quickened her pace to a run. Svenson dashed after her.

'We must hide!' he hissed.

'Not yet!'

'They will see us –'

She did not reply, bearing straight towards the house. Over his shoulder Svenson saw a lantern wink on and off in sequence. Figures silhouetted in an upper window of the white building replied with their own signal. With a sinking realization he knew the bargemen would assume *him* to be the murderer.

Abruptly the Contessa dodged from the road. The Doctor followed, the undergrowth whipping around his knees. The Contessa vanished into the trees. An instant afterwards the branches were slapping Svenson's face in the dark. The double doors of the building had opened wide – pools of light bobbed forward and over the trees. Then the Contessa stopped and he was right upon her, nearly knocking her down.

'There is a party, coming down the road,' he whispered, 'from the – the –'

'Factory,' she said, finishing his sentence. 'Follow me. Walk on the leaves!'

She darted ahead again, not quite so fast, moving with hushed footfalls under a line of high, old elms. He followed, making up the ground with his longer strides, and saw she held her dress with only one hand, to favour her injury. The minutes passed in silence, the moonlight flickering through the treetops onto her shoulders. With a puncturing loneliness, Svenson marvelled at how delicate a woman the Contessa truly was, in contrast to the enormity of her character. He tried to imagine possessing the same determination, for he too had driven himself to extremes, but it had always been in the service of someone else.

The Contessa reached with her good left arm and took hold of Svenson's tunic, slowing them both to a stop. Through the trees before them he could see torchlight. He reached carefully into his pocket for his monocle and fitted it over his eye. The torches were moving – figures on the march down a different forest road . . . but marching *towards* the factory. Was this a second search party? Had they been cut off? He looked behind him, but saw no one following under the trees.

He turned back to the roadway, screwed in his monocle more tightly, and frowned. The party walked with the serious intent of soldiers on a forced march — except, by their dress, these were evidently figures of *quality*. At least thirty people had passed . . . and the stream showed no sign of failing.

'This is no search,' he breathed into the Contessa's ear, his concentration even then pricked by the smell of her hair. She nodded, but did not shift her gaze.

The line of figures finally came to an end. As if the decision had been made together, both the Doctor and the Contessa·inched forward. The road indeed led straight to the large brick building — fronted here by a high wooden wall and an iron-bound gate. They turned to look in the other direction, to where the strange crowd had appeared. Perhaps fifty yards away *another* set of torches was bobbing towards them.

'Now!' the Contessa whispered. 'Keep low!'

They broke from their shelter and dashed across the road — horribly exposed for an instant — and stumbled into another grove of trees, this one more tangled with broken limbs. They threw themselves down in the shadows.

'You know those people,' whispered Svenson.

The Contessa did not answer.

'I believe the preferred term is *adherents*,' he hissed, 'those fools who have pledged their loyalty to you and your associates — and had it seared into their souls by the Process. One wonders what in the world such a collection of people is doing so far out in the countryside — almost as much as one wonders why you did not reveal yourself to them. It would seem the answer to all your present difficulties. That you did not tells me their presence here is a mystery — and that you fear they retain no loyalty to *you* at all.'

The Contessa only pushed past him into the trees.

When they emerged on the other side, another road crossed before them, overgrown with grass and knee-high saplings. Svenson realized it must have pre-dated the canal, for it curved away around the forest, and recalled all the ruins he had passed in the woods while walking with Elöise. Parchfeldt Park was a sort of graveyard — like any forest perhaps, where every new tree fed on the pulped-up corpses beneath it. But as graveyards always brought to the Doctor's mind his own mortality, so standing on the derelict road placed all the new life and effort he had seen – the barge, the refitted factory, its master's blazing ambition – within the heavy shadows of time.

The Contessa had not spoken since they'd seen the torch-led crowds. Doctor Svenson cleared his throat and she turned to him.

'If I had not appeared, did you intend to simply approach the front door and charm the inhabitants to your will?'

He was aware that sharp questions and a mocking tone must be strange to her, and did not doubt he was angering the woman – and yet his questions were also plainly meant. What *had* she expected? What seeds of defeat or despair might find purchase in her heart?

'You're a strange man,' she at last replied. 'I remember first meeting you at the St Royale, where it was immediately obvious you were an intelligent, dutiful, tractable fool. I do not think I was wrong –'

'I admit Cardinal Chang cuts a more *spectacular* figure.'

'Cardinal Chang is merely another stripe of heart-sop idiot – you could each learn a thing from your little provincial ice floe. Yet I am not speaking of *them*, Doctor, but of *you*.'

'What you think cannot be my concern.'

The Contessa gazed at him, so wan and simple it made him blanch.

'I will find the proper word for you some day, Doctor. And when I do, I shall whisper that word into your ear.'

The Contessa turned and began to walk towards the factory.

'Where are you going?' he cried. 'We do not know who is there! We do not know why – if you have not called them – these people – your *minions* – have assembled!'

The Contessa looked over her shoulder – an action he was certain caused her pain.

'Content yourself with your card,' she called back to him. 'The ideals you place upon the world are broken. There is nothing *necessary* here at all.'

The shimmer of her silk dress caught the moon even after he could no longer distinguish her shadow from the surrounding dark, and then she was around the curve and gone. He did not follow, wondering why, and looked back at the trees where they had come, and then down the overgrown road as it led away from the factory . . . a path he might follow to another world. He reached into his pocket for his cigarette case and felt his fingertips touch the cold glass card. Was there enough moonlight to see? Was it not an intensely stupid thing to do in such open ground?

Doctor Svenson sighed, regretting the act already (what had Elöise said, that knowing more of a thing invariably meant more pain?), and turned his gaze into the glass.

When he finally looked up again the world around him seemed unreal, as if he had been staring into the sun. He felt the sweat on the back of his neck and a stiffness in his fingers from gripping the glass rectangle so tightly. He slipped it back into his tunic pocket and rubbed his eyes, which seemed to be moist . . . tears? Or merely his body's response to not blinking? He began walking towards the factory.

The card had been infused with Trapping's memory, but that made sense, since the man would have taken part in many gatherings where the Cabal recruited its intimates, where the cards were a prominent lure. Svenson had looked into two cards before this, each different from the other in the manner of captured experience. The first contained one specific event – the Prince's intimacy with Mrs Marchmoor, when the woman's sensations had been bled into the glass on the spot. The second card, holding the experiences of Roger Bascombe, had been an assemblage of impressions and memories, from his groping of Miss Temple on a sofa to the quarry at Tarr Manor. To fabricate it, the memories must have been distilled into the card well after the fact, from Bascombe's mind.

Trapping's card – as the Doctor now thought of it – was different from each of these. Its experience was not rooted in images, or even in tactile sensations. Instead, it conveyed – and to a hideous degree – an emotional state alone. There *was* context – and here the card was similar to Bascombe's card, with an apparently random flow of trivial incidents: the foyer table of the Trappings' house at Hadrian Square . . . the Colonel's red uniform reflected in polished silver as he ate a solitary breakfast . . . the house's rear garden, where he watched his children from a cushioned chair. Yet suffusing each of these moments was a feeling of bitterness, of selfish need and brutish reaction, of exile and isolation, of a man whose bluff, unthinking complacency had been punctured by sorrow sharp as an iron nail.

Mrs Trapping appeared nowhere, yet her absence was not its source. What reason did Arthur Trapping have to be so bitter? His ambition had been handsomely rewarded . . . and suddenly Svenson placed Colonel Trapping's bottomless resentment: he *owed* the Xonck brothers for *everything* he had achieved. Each gleaming point of disgust spelt it out: a calling card in the foyer from Francis, Trapping's red uniform a disgraceful sign of Henry's patronage, the very house itself a wedding present, the children . . . even *these*, Svenson shuddered, came under Trapping's eyes with guilty sparks of hatred, before the lightness of their voices spun the anger into a binding net of grief. And this struck Svenson most of all: that the lasting impression from Colonel Trapping was not rage but unanswerable sadness.

If Mrs Trapping was absent from the card, Elöise Dujong was even more so – was she not the man's mistress? This was convenient if Elöise hoped to assuage Svenson's anger, but Doctor Svenson was not truly angry – perhaps, he thought drily, it was a life-long failing. The choices Elöise had made, however much apart from his own desires, were too easily seen to be contingent and human. She had done what she had done – though he did not especially want to *think* about it – just as he had buried his own grief for Corinna in useless service. And yet, to present him with the experience of *this* man – was that not simply *cruel*? Being the object of such cruelty deadened his heart. What else would she expect? What could trump the visceral distaste of being placed *within* his rival's body? That Trapping was sad? That Trapping loathed his in-laws? What did either of these matter when Svenson would have happily seen Trapping horsewhipped by both brothers and thrown into a salt bath?

The light still blazed through the factory's windows, and Svenson could see the shadows of a gathered crowd against the wooden wall. As he came nearer, he heard a buzz of discontentment, affronted mutters, and calls of disbelief. The gate had not opened, a turn of events the crowd found altogether unexplainable. The men with torches held them high, the better to shout to the unanswering windows. Their dress was not as formal as when he'd seen these same people at the final Harschmort gala, but there was no question they represented the highest levels of the professions and the military. There was also a rank of younger faces within the whole – those for whom profession was but a path to pass the time, high-born siblings or cousins, living near enough to taste the titles they would never hold, for ever nursing jealousies and resentments. Svenson compared this gathering with the servants and clerks he'd met on the train to Tarr Manor, seduced into selling the dark secrets of their masters in exchange for what to the Cabal must have seemed like red feathers given to South Sea islanders for land – a decent place to live and enough money for a new coat in winter. What could any of the well-placed people before him lack – by what lures had they been led along? The Doctor shook his head – the terms did not matter at all. The Cabal had suborned each group by dangling before their eyes a credible prospect of *hope*.

He dropped onto his knees in the grass. The way into the factory was twice blocked – by the spreading crowd and by the wall. The crowd bunched in front of the gate, but their numbers were such that the mass had spread along the wall – perhaps as many as two hundred people altogether. Svenson could hear people knocking on the gate and calling for entrance . . . but their calls were so arrogantly presumptuous in their tone that the Doctor began to doubt that any of the crowd really knew where they were . . . or what might be inside. Did they not even register the contrast between the isolation of the factory and its fantastic new blazing inhabitation – between the derelict road and the recently raised outer wall?

Svenson did not see the Contessa.

He had seen a bust of Cleopatra once, in Berlin – his thoughts were wandering, it was getting cold – life sized, but he had been struck by how small it seemed, that she was only one woman, who, no matter how much of the world she had set aflame, remained only so many pounds of flesh

and bone, so much breath, so much warmth within one bed. He thought
of the Contessa's lacerated shoulder, her quiver of pain beneath his touch,
and laid against it like a wager her determined and rapacious – and cruel,
he could not forget it – *hunger*. What life could have constructed such a
creature? What events had shaped a man like Chang? Svenson had seen the
scars, of course, but those were only outward signs, the oil-slicked surface
of a pool. He could not be less like them, despite his own bursts of invention
or courage. Those moments were not who he *was*. And what of Miss
Temple? He compared her with the men of privilege milling about before
his eyes, discontented and hungry . . . was she not as restless and peremptory? The Doctor's mind went to Elöise, but he rubbed his eyes and shook
the entire train of thought away.

He stood and straightened his tunic. Some of these people had no doubt
witnessed him being knocked on the head at Harschmort and dragged away
to die – but that only meant they assumed he *was* dead. If the Contessa
had avoided the restive mob, as he was quite sure she had, then there
seemed all the more reason for him to do the exact opposite.

Svenson reached the crowd and shouldered his way past the rearmost
ranks before speaking aloud, in a disdainful voice borrowed from the
late Crown Prince. 'Why do they not open the gate? Do they intend we
should wait like tradesmen in the lane? Have we not travelled all these
miles?'

A man next to him, in a crisp wool overcoat, snorted in commiseration.

'No one answers at all! As if we were not even expected!'

'There can be no mistake,' whispered a thin, older fellow with gold
spectacles. 'When so many of us have received the message.'

This was met with a general murmur of agreement, but still the gate did
not open. Further down the wall – Svenson was some distance from the
gate itself – he could hear the rapping of steel-toed boots kicking hard
against the wood.

'Have you seen no one?' Svenson asked.

'When we first approached, the gate was open. They barred it shut at
the sight of us!'

'They must know we are summoned!'

'They do not act as if they do!' complained the older man. 'And now it has grown cold – and the country is so *damp* –'

'Gentlemen,' offered the Doctor, hesitating enough to make sure of their attention. 'Is it possible . . . there is trouble?'

The man in the overcoat nodded vigorously. 'I have the exact notion!'

'What if it is all a . . . a . . . a *test*?' whispered the older man.

Svenson was aware that their small conversation had attracted many listeners.

'Then it were best not to fail,' he replied, pitching his voice more loudly. 'Would you not agree?'

He was answered by nods and mutters by others around them.

'I beg your pardon,' one said, 'but your voice . . . your accent –'

'We are not to know one another any more than necessary!' the older man broke in.

'Our league is intended to be invisible in the world,' the Doctor agreed, 'like a fishing net in the ocean, yes? Yet I will say, since you hear it clear enough – that I am from the Duchy of Macklenburg, serving my Prince, who serves the same . . . *principles* . . . as you yourselves.'

'You are a soldier.' The older man indicated the Doctor's uniform.

'Perhaps we are all soldiers now,' replied Svenson gravely, feeling an absolute ass. The men around him nodded with a cloying self-satisfaction.

'Something *has* gone wrong,' announced the man in the overcoat. 'I am sure of it.'

'You were not told why you were summoned?' asked Svenson.

'Were *you*?'

Svenson felt the entire gang of men around him waiting for his answer.

'Not *told* . . .' he began carefully. 'Perhaps I overreach myself . . .'

'Tell us what you know!' urged the older man, and he was echoed by many others. Svenson surveyed their faces and then shook his head seriously, as if he too had come to a decision – to trust them all.

He lowered his voice. 'On the other side of this wall is a factory . . . the property of Xonck Armaments.' At this revelation came a gasp from the older man. 'Exactly who controls the factory at this moment is a mystery. Francis Xonck has journeyed to Macklenburg. Henry Xonck has been taken

with an attack of blood fever . . . and yet there has been a summoning.'
Svenson swatted at his less-than-scrupulous uniform. 'I say summoned, but
you will notice I am here later than you all, and after travelling for a
longer time. I have come from Harschmort House, where the miraculous
machinery of the Comte d'Orkancz has all been removed . . . removed and
relocated into this very factory, behind this very wall.'

'But is not the Comte gone to Macklenburg as well? Upon whose orders
has this been done?'

'Is that our business?' asked the older man. 'Have we not sworn to serve?'

'Serve *whom*?' called out a voice from the knot of men around them.

'If we were summoned, why are we shut *outside*?' called another.

'Clearly we were not summoned by whoever is master in this place,' said
the man in the overcoat.

'So we must ask ourselves', said Svenson, 'just who can issue such a
summons . . . and who cannot.'

The men around him erupted into mutterings that spread along the
wall like a wild fire leaping from treetop to treetop in the wind. The man
in the overcoat bent closer, but his words were lost in the growing noise –
outright shouts that the gates must be opened at once, and an explosion of
kicks and fists upon the wooden wall. He caught Svenson's arm in a
powerful grip. The Doctor stood ready to rip it free, but the man only
squeezed harder, hissing into Svenson's ear: 'What *exact* message did you
receive?'

In his other hand the man held a small volume bound in red leather –
the book given to every loyal servant of the Cabal, for deciphering coded
messages. The crowd surged closer to the wall, jostling them both.

Svenson pointed to the book. 'I am afraid I have lost mine.'

'And yet you are here.'

Svenson groped for an explanation that would not expose him further.
Before he could speak the man tugged him away from the wall, where they
might hear one another clearly. If he struck the man hard enough, might
he reach the woods before the others brought him down?

'You were at Harschmort,' the man said. 'As was I . . . but these others
. . . I do not know them, or where they have been enlisted –'

'Or by whom,' Svenson added.

'As I say, Harschmort. You were there . . .'

'*That* night?' said Svenson. 'The Duke sent off in his carriage – the Comte's *ladies* –'

'You remember them, their sifting your thoughts.'

'Not, I confess, with any pleasure,' said Svenson.

'Nor I, and yet . . .' The man looked down at the red leather book. The others were now shouting quite loudly to be let in. 'I felt it again not six hours ago.'

'I had not wanted to say. It is *she* who summoned me also.'

'She? You know which of the three has done it?'

'Only one survived the night,' said the Doctor. 'There was chaos and violence – I know this from the Prince.'

'But . . . but . . . that just makes it worse!' the man cried, now barely audible against the escalating roar. 'Who has given *her* the order to summon *us*? And who else, though you say this is a Xonck factory, bars our way?'

'What did she tell *you*, in your summons?'

'Nothing – it was not even words! Just the certain impression that I must travel at once to this place.'

'Your dedication distinguishes you,' said Svenson.

'My dedication leaves me flat,' the man replied. 'We do not know our situation – how can we serve in ignorance?'

Before Svenson could answer, the man pulled him back into the agitated crowd, raising his voice above their shouting. 'Listen! Listen all of you! Here is one who has been this day to Harschmort House. More is afoot than we know! We have been called here for a *rescue*!'

Any answer Svenson might have made stopped in his throat when he saw the crowd of angry men had all turned to him, waiting for his words.

'Ah . . . well . . . the trick of it is –'

'He is a soldier serving the Prince of *Macklenburg*!'

They gazed at Svenson with a new veneer of respect. Once more, he was appalled.

'Gentlemen – gentlemen – while that is true –'

'Send him over the wall!' It was the old man with gold spectacles, his

mouth a rictus of spite. 'These blackguards won't let us in? Let's give them
one who can sort them out!'

Before Svenson could dispute this especially stupid idea, he felt something cold and heavy pressed into his hand, and looked down to see he was
now holding a silver-plated revolver.

'Wait – a moment – all of you! We do not know –'

'You will shoot them!' cried the old man. 'You will open the gate!'

'That is *unlikely*,' snapped Doctor Svenson, but no one heard. They had
already taken hold of his arms and legs, lifting him abruptly to the level of
their shoulders and marching straight to the wall – indeed slamming him
into the planks. The men holding his legs hefted him higher with exuberant
force – the Doctor clutched the wall convulsively with both hands, ignoring
the drop to either side, and threw a leg over the top to grip tightly with all
four of his limbs.

The men behind him shouted with triumph, but the Doctor expected at
any moment to be shot at or perforated by a pike. He looked down into a
grassy compound, lit from the factory's high windows – the light streaming
so brightly he was forced to squint. They called to him: what did he see,
who was there, what had he found? Someone bounced the fence, and he
promptly lost his grip on the pistol, dropping it onto the grass inside.
Svenson swore. His outer leg was suddenly shoved upwards and toppled
over. With a grunt he caught himself before he fell completely, hanging by
one arm, but there was no way he could pull himself back up. He spat with
frustration – suspended between the louts outside and the rogues within,
all convinced he had murdered the barge master. He dropped with a squawk
into an ungainly roll. A triumphant cry soared at his disappearance – and
he groped urgently for the pistol. A door in the factory opened wide.
Someone had seen him.

Svenson looked into the glare. Perhaps ten men filed out towards him,
the gleam of polished metal in their hands. He flung himself face down,
flinching as they snapped carbines to their shoulders and fired a crashing
volley.

Svenson realized he was not dead – nor had the bullets gone into the fence above him. They had fired into the air. He heard a synchronous clacking as each rifleman advanced his next round, and then too soon a second volley – and then a third, and then a *fourth*, then a *fifth*, in what seemed like as many seconds, the shots harmless but the demonstration as cold a display of unanswerable force as a frigate's broadside.

The mob fell silent, as if they too were on their knees and trembling. What else had he expected – it was an *armaments* factory. Who knew what weapons they might possess – what explosives, what newfangled quick-firing carbines, what vicious hand-cannons stuffed with grapeshot? The glass woman's army stood helpless as lambs outside a slaughterhouse.

His groping hand found the pistol and closed about it. One soldier detached himself from the line and strode directly at Svenson, his carbine fixed on the Doctor's chest. Svenson raised his empty hand in supplication, the hand with the pistol still hidden in the grass.

'These fellows have raised me over this wall,' he stammered. 'I am not one of them –'

The soldier wore an extravagant green uniform, like that of a hotel doorman, with polished black shoes and a black belt loaded with ammunition pouches. An elaborate silver plume of flame had been embroidered on each tab of his stiff green collar – an officer, but of what force? The man's expression was stone-hard. He advanced a new shell into the carbine. The Doctor recalled the one bit of advice he had received with regard to duelling (Svenson having been challenged as a student by a drunken Prussian) from a disinterested young baron with unpleasant pink scars across each cheek. The nobleman had advised Svenson to note when his opponent *breathed* – for men typically inhaled before launching an attack – and use that very instant to attack himself. It had not worked in the duel – Svenson had been extremely fortunate to take a sabre-tip along his wrist for an honourable ending. But he found himself now transfixed by the man before him, the swelling of his chest . . . waiting for the exhale that must put a bullet into his heart.

'*Stop!*'

The cry came from the doorway, but Svenson could see only the speaker's shadow.

'There is another dead,' called Mr Fruitricks, quite perturbed. 'And *this* man cannot have done it. Bring him inside.'

The pistol's silver plating betrayed his attempt to tuck it behind his back, and it was taken away. The officer marched him into the house, the rest of the detachment following in a drill precise enough to satisfy a Tartar. The door was slammed and bolted, and the men leapt up ladders to loopholes in the wall through which they could fire upon the whole of the open yard and the wooden wall. These were not young men, not raw fellows recruited from the thousands driven from work by failed mills or ruined farms, but men with hard faces, scarred and grim. Svenson had seen them on his own ships, sailors whose service had required terrible acts – criminal in any civilian circumstance – and who after years when such work grew familiar came to inhabit another world entirely, men whose shore leave inevitably resulted in bloody mayhem and consequent whippings. Such men filled the ranks of the Xonck Armaments private militia. No doubt the company paid better than the Queen. He thought of the crowd outside the wall, its peevish assumption of privilege, and how little they understood the resolute figures arrayed to keep them out – men whose deep-set resentment for everything the privileged *adherents* stood for would find grateful outlet in the Xonck family's defence.

The officer detailed two men to escort Svenson to a perfunctory office complete with filing cabinets, a desk, and two wooden chairs. Fruitricks was already behind the desk, shoving at the ledger books on top of it. Svenson fell into a chair and reached in his tunic for his cigarettes.

'Who is killed?' he asked mildly.

'You are astonishingly insolent,' Fruitricks muttered, sorting papers without looking at his hands.

'On the contrary, I am merely a foreigner who knows not your ways.' The Doctor blew smoke towards the lantern on the desk, wishing very much that his fingers would stop trembling. 'You know I did not kill your man at his watch fire – I found him dead.'

'Then why did you run away?'

'Because your men would have shot me,' replied the Doctor. 'Who has been *killed*?'

Fruitricks sighed, his expression aggrieved and pinched. 'One of *them*.'

Svenson swivelled his head, following Fruitricks's gaze to the guards. 'The Xonck private army?'

'They are most formidable, I assure you.'

'As formidable as your new weapons can make them, at least.'

'That is *very* formidable!' Fruitricks was nearly shouting.

The Doctor sat back in his chair and looked for a spot to tap his ash. 'A very good thing they answer to your command.'

'Of course they do.'

'And not to anyone named Xonck.'

Mr Fruitricks glared at him. 'No one named Xonck is my present concern.'

'What about anyone named Trapping?'

Mr Fruitricks shot to his feet, prompting the soldiers at the door to look in. He ignored them, leaning over the desk at Svenson. 'I am a businessman, sir – and this is a place of work! Whatever your *intrigues* – we have no part of them!'

'Of course not,' replied the Doctor. 'This is an island of calm.'

Fruitricks snorted and waved with anger towards the courtyard and the gate. 'Who is that *crowd*?' he cried. 'Do they not realize we can easily kill them all? Nor how very tempting it has been to do so!'

'I think they appreciate it more than they did, before your display.'

'But who *are* they?'

'You do not know?' Svenson tapped his ash into a dish of pins. 'My goodness. All manner of people from the city – some of them very highly placed –'

'But they cannot *do* anything!' Fruitricks protested. 'We are impregnable!'

'Then why are you upset?'

'Because two men are dead! I watched you out there – speaking and plotting! They put you over my wall!'

'They assume I am of their number.'

'That is no answer! If you think I will scruple to get the information I require –'

The man was near to screaming, and Svenson's head throbbed with each shrill, miserable word. He inhaled deeply and replied as calmly as he could. 'I am no sort of interested party – while you *are*. You really do need to think while you can. This mob around your door, sir – it means that you are finished.'

'We are nothing of the kind! Our store of munitions alone –'

'Cannot hold off the Queen's entire army!' cried Svenson. 'This mob is but a vanguard – a simple delaying tactic until the greater force can arrive.'

'What greater force?'

'Whatever the Duke of Stäelmaere can command. Whole regiments. Do you think they will scruple to get *their* answers?'

Fruitricks returned to his seat, tapping his fingers on the desktop. 'But who is killing my men?' he asked.

'How should I know?' asked Svenson, fatigued by the man's inability to keep to the obvious point. 'Someone *else*.'

'But who is left? They are all dead. Or in Macklenburg.'

Svenson rubbed his eyes and sighed. 'No one ever reached Macklenburg. My Prince is dead. Lydia Vandaariff's head was cut from her body. The airship sank into the sea.'

Fruitricks's face went pale. He shrieked to the door: 'Take him to the tempering room – at once!'

Svenson was taken through a narrow corridor into an enormous chamber so crammed with machinery that he could not see the far side. He held a hand before his eyes – gas lamps had been placed along the walls, but the truly blazing light shone from the machinery itself, piercing as winter sunshine slicing off Baltic ice. He looked back to see if Fruitricks had followed – he had not – and noticed fresh sawcuts and nails. The warren of little rooms had been recently made.

The green-coated soldier behind him touched his arm – a decent enough gesture when the man perfectly well might have given him a shove – and Svenson moved on. The bulky machines he had seen on the barge, all now roaring with life, had been arranged in a jagged, radiating spiral around a hidden centre, shielded by tall rectangles of beaten steel that hung in frames. The metal sheets reflected the light off one another, and he could see that each was somehow scored with writing. At once he thought of the Comte's alchemical formulae, scrawled on the *Annunciation* paintings . . . perhaps Fruitricks had taken the plates as well from Harschmort. But the barge had only just arrived. All of this had to have been in preparation for some time, the large machines themselves dropped into place as the final pieces in a jigsaw puzzle.

On the far side of the industrial floor another hasty wall had been flung up, and Svenson was shown into a room whose every surface had been sheathed with bright metal sheets. In the centre of the room, suspended in a complicated harness strung between iron poles, was the same – or, if not the same, its double – round, helmet-like contraption the Cabal had used in Tarr Village to refine raw lumps of indigo clay into pliable bolts of glass. The burning, acrid smell told Svenson it had been successfully used. The room would for ever stink of it.

Yet the smell and the machine were nothing, the Doctor's attention captured instead by the corpse on the floor. The kerchief around the barge master's neck had been removed, and Svenson saw the wound clearly for the first time – a deep slash across the jugular and into his larynx. Svenson turned to the soldiers posted to either side of the open door. Each resolutely ignored his gaze. He fished out a cigarette and sensed by a tightening in each man's posture that they disapproved of his access – as a prisoner – to any such luxury.

'Any physician can judge from skin pallor and stiffening of the limbs how much time has passed since this man's murder,' he observed aloud. 'Enough that the event must have taken place while I was still under confinement at the canal. Your master knows this. It proves I am no killer.'

The soldiers said nothing, not that he expected they would. He lit his cigarette, wondering how long he would be confined in this especially unnatural cell. He shook out the match and tossed it to the floor. In the brilliant light he could see the yellow stains on his fingers.

He looked up at a commotion in the corridor. Two more soldiers bustled in with a second body on a stretcher. Fruitricks stood to the side, hands balled into bony fists, waiting for them to leave. As soon as the stretcher-bearers had gone, he darted at Svenson with a nervous, sour expression. 'You must tell me who has done this!'

Doctor Svenson knelt by the body – *another* body – and inhaled, feeling the copper filigrees of nicotine score into his blood. It was one of the green-coated soldiers, sporting an almost identical incision – but not yet congealed to such purples and blacks.

'This has been done while you were out *there*!' Fruitricks waved impatiently towards the front of the building. 'With *them*!'

'The wounds look . . . similar.'

'Of course they are *similar*! They are one and the same! Who is the killer?'

'You must study the clues.'

'I do not care to – I am no butcher or surgeon! It is horrid!' Fruitricks stabbed a finger at the barge master. 'That is Mr Brandt! He is *dead*!'

'If you do not look, you will not learn. This is the world you have entered. *Here*.' Svenson indicated with his right hand – the cigarette between his fingers, a translucent ribbon of smoke fluttering above it – Mr Brandt's opened throat. Fruitricks winced in protest, but knelt beside him.

'From the angle of the cut it is clear that his assailant stood before him – from where the blade enters to where the cut leaves off . . . it is unlikely for anyone to have done it from behind.'

'He saw his killer? But there was no cry, no signal!'

'Look closer, at the actual angle of the blade – excuse me, I mean no disrespect . . . but to illustrate my point . . .'

Svenson took out the dead man's own clasp knife and snapped it open. If Fruitricks recognized the weapon, he kept silent. Svenson delicately pressed the flat blade into the sticky wound. 'To make this incision the blade must be pointing *up*.'

'What does *that* signify? If I were to attack you with a knife, my hands would be below your throat – my hands hang below my waist – they would rise in the same way!'

'No,' said Svenson. 'Stand.'

They rose. Svenson put the blade into the other man's hand and then took hold of that hand's wrist, moving the blade slowly towards his own throat to sketch an attack.

'In making your stroke, your arm is actually much more likely to swing the blade from your shoulder, like a fist, and so the angle of entry is more a flat gash than what we see.'

Fruitricks looked down at the knife in his hand with distaste. 'What does that mean?'

'Only that whoever killed the man was a good deal *shorter*.'

Svenson took back the clasp knife and knelt by the newly dead soldier, pressing aside the wound in much the same way – the fresher gash seeping unpleasantly over the blade.

'It is the same – from the front, and from below. I assume there was no cry or signal from this man either?'

'Not at all.'

'One must assume their silence comes for a reason. They might have been held at pistol-point. Or saw no reason to be afraid.'

'But they were murdered.'

'Obviously such reasoning was *wrong*. Was this man found *inside* the factory?'

'Can you say who has murdered them or not?'

Svenson imagined the ease with which the Contessa had approached each dead man, stilling their suspicions with a smile. He recalled the speed and violence – and the *glee* – with which she had murdered Harald Crabbé. Did his own reticence to name her prove she had charmed *him* as well?

The green-coated officer burst into the doorway. 'Mr Leveret! Another man! You must come directly!'

He led them all, the Doctor following 'Leveret' (since neither name meant anything to Svenson, it was as easy to call him this instead of the frankly ridiculous 'Fruitricks') out the opposite side of the building, another squad at loopholes guarding this door. On this side of the factory there was no wooden wall, but the still-standing stone border of a much older structure whose crumbled outline lay strewn beyond it, just visible through the trees, like a faded inscription on a moss-covered grave. At the base of the wall several soldiers clustered round a figure on the ground.

Leveret was already snapping for an explanation. The officer pointed to a wooden ladder fixed to the wall. Had the man simply lost his balance? Leveret wheeled on the Doctor, his mouth a tight line. 'This is monstrous!'

The Doctor glanced once at the corpse. He drew a last, long puff from the diminished stub of his cigarette before grinding it out against the stone wall. 'You must send your men away.'

'I will not!' insisted Leveret. 'You will take no more advantage of my tolerant manner!'

'As you insist . . . then they will hear the truth.'

Svenson had seen this countless times in the navy: over-promoted fools whose prideful insistence on 'having their way' resulted in a ship needlessly lost in a storm, or drifting within range of enemy batteries. Svenson glared at him, flatly contemptuous. Mr Leveret swallowed. With an impatient flipping of both hands he waved the soldiers back to their posts.

The dead soldier's eyes were open in uncomprehending terror, the corners of his mouth crusted with a blue-tinted saliva. The Doctor recalled Karthe, the blood on the rock where the boy had been mauled, the cold stench of death in the mining camp. With effort – and then with Leveret's help – he tipped the man on one side to expose his back: a shining lattice of spattered slashes and stabs, the blood, hardened to gleaming blue, suffusing the green wool coat. Svenson counted at least seven deep punctures, all made with a savage rapidity. He nodded to Leveret, and they set the body gently down. Doctor Svenson stood and dug in his pocket for his silver case.

'If you hoped for time to secure your rebellion, you will not get it. I have seen this before. In Karthe.'

'Karthe is in the *mountains*!' Leveret's face went even whiter with rage. 'You will tell me what you know, sir, and straight away! *Rebellion* indeed! You are my prisoner! I insist you tell me what has killed this man!'

'I should think it obvious.'

Leveret glanced again at the soldiers, all watching closely. Their master licked his lips.

'But – but it makes no sense . . . the others were killed by someone they trusted – or who did not scare them. However, *this* man . . .'

'*Yes?*' snapped the Doctor.

'Is it not the same killer?' Leveret asked hopelessly.

'Does it *look* like it?'

Leveret swallowed and crossed his arms. 'I suppose you doubt a man who kills like *that* would meet Mr Brandt face to face without alarming him.'

'I also doubt a man who kills like that is necessarily *sane*.'

'You said you saw this before – in the north –'

'So I did.'

'Then what must we do? How was this person stopped?'

'He wasn't stopped at all, obviously. He's come to your door.'

Leveret studied the body, flinching with distaste at the shining wounds. 'It is not possible –'

'What else did you expect?' Svenson asked. 'Who else did you think you served? When you next see Francis Xonck, will he reward you? I should think a man who makes munitions would understand how care must be taken when one's work becomes deadly. But you will learn it soon enough – since this man was killed inside the wall, your defences must be considered breached.' Svenson called to the soldiers directly and pointed to the ladder. 'Look where this man was posted! Whoever killed him is inside! You must search in force!'

'Do not instruct us,' shouted Leveret. The soldiers had Svenson's arms and were hauling him away. 'You are just like the rest of them – these social-climbing, whore-aping *adherents* – so confident, so ambitious – hoping to achieve by playing leapfrog, by climbing on the backs of others until they are lifted to the very top of their childish dreams. And lifted by *whom*? Where are these *masters*? *I am master here!*'

'I thought you served Francis Xonck!' Svenson called. He hoped for a reaction from the green-coated soldiers, but their faces did not shift.

'What you think means *nothing*!' cried Leveret. 'Take him!'

The Doctor gazed hopelessly at the silver walls of the tempering room, and at the round refining chamber hanging in its harness. He wanted to kick it. A moment after he had been escorted in, the same two soldiers resuming their stance by the door, another pair had dropped the third, glass-stabbed body at his feet, as if the murder was his doing. Perhaps these new weapons were protection enough – perhaps Francis Xonck's own soldiers would shoot him like a rabid dog. Perhaps . . . but he could still remember the earnest faces of the slaughtered townsmen of Karthe. Svenson stared at the dead man's blue-crusted lips, then turned to the men at the door, just as doomed. This little room of corpses would not do.

He dropped to one knee, gasped, then leapt up and shouted urgently to the door: 'You there – at once, run for Mr Leveret! I have discovered something on the body. He must be warned!'

The men looked at each other.

'There is no *time*!' Svenson cried. 'He may be making a terrible mistake!'

One man ran off, towards the front of the factory. The other stepped into the room, his carbine held ready. 'What mistake?' the soldier asked warily.

'Look for yourself,' said Svenson, and he knelt next to the third corpse, indicating a spot just to the back of the dead man's neck. 'The brighter light in this room that allowed me to see –'

'I do not see anything,' said the soldier, leaning.

'I'm a blind fool! *There!* Under the collar – the first point of impact – the wound!'

The soldier knelt. Tentatively, he extended one hand towards the body, his other resting the carbine on the floor for balance. 'What is it?'

Svenson stepped on the hand holding the carbine – pinning the fingers between his boot and the weapon – and brought his other knee up into the man's jaw. The sickening *clop* toppled the soldier over the bodies. Svenson dashed from the room.

He could not hope to best the soldiers around either doorway, so he dived instead towards the main chamber, straight amongst the machines. He pressed himself between bright pipes and sweating hoses, stumbling on, but once inside he was near blinded by the bright light and distracted by a very loud hissing and clanking from every direction. He would not hear the soldiers – with this light he could not even see them – while they could pot him as easily as boys shooting squirrels in a tree. A tall shadow crossed his path – one of the high metal plates. The inner face had been scored with the same dense scribbled nonsense he had seen on the paintings of Oskar Veilandt: equations, different languages, even scrawled figures like a Polynesian pictogram. The plate's reflected light fell in a pattern onto the floor. Svenson cursed his own slowness of mind – the *content* of the writing meant nothing at all! It could have been smeared with house paint – the only requirement was for the metal to reflect the glare to a specific degree. But to what purpose? The tall plates had been hung in a rough circle, but the centre of the circle . . . was only empty space, tangled with hose. He stepped inside the circle and could suddenly see. At the far edge of the room, staring directly at him, stood Leveret with at least four soldiers.

Svenson fell to his knees and cast his gaze wildly around for some way out. To his great surprise the ceiling directly above him was open, a wide round hole dangling hoses and chain. Stifling all fear and decent feeling, he leapt on top of the nearest machine, whose thrumming vibrated through his boots, and jumped at a hanging metal sheet, his heart in his mouth, catching the chains above it. His knees whacked the metal, and the weight of his body caused it to swing, his feet kicking to either side. He heard a cracking sound. The metal plate rang with the impact of a carbine bullet. Svenson stabbed out a hand for a higher chain, from the hole in the ceiling, caught it, and with a rush of vertigo let go of the sheet altogether. Another crack from the carbine, the bullet whipping who knew where, and Svenson seized the edge of the hole. He threw up an elbow with a gasp, then another, and then with a terrible heave rolled his body over the lip and lay sprawled, breathing hard. Leveret had four men with him with rapid-fire carbines, yet he'd only fired at Svenson twice and missed both times. They had held back to preserve the machines.

He had in his life seen waterfalls where one might climb between the falling water and the cliff face, and gaze out through a shimmering curtain.

It seemed he had entered a similar, though utterly unearthly, cavern. Surrounding the Doctor were dangling sheets of cable, ducts, hose, and chain – arrayed without any order he could see. The hanging mass of tubes and chain rose twenty feet – the next floor of the factory had been taken out to make room – before finally being gathered together and forced into larger metal ducts. The ceiling above held a matching circular hole, far too high for Svenson to reach by climbing.

He shoved his way through them on his hands and knees. There must be a staircase. The calling voice of Mr Leveret rose up through the open hole in the floor. 'Do not be an ass, Doctor! You cannot survive! You have no idea of your danger!'

Svenson snorted – he had *every* idea – feeling his way through a curtain of silver ducts and hoses. What was the point of so many pipes and tubes, filling the floor? It must be the height of the building! He remembered the high walls of the chamber at the Royal Institute, covered with pipes and ducts – with so much less space, Leveret had run the pipes up and down, stuffing the two storeys tight to gain the same required length. Svenson stopped. He heard footsteps on the wooden planks. He unfolded the clasp knife.

A shuffling, closer than before. Svenson squeezed through a thicket of black hoses, their condensation moist on his face. All of this to re-create the Comte's 'factory' at Harschmort – yet to what end – or, more precisely, for what *product*? What business – the steps came nearer and he slithered round a bundle of silver tubes – did Leveret have stealing the machines from Harschmort and setting up a factory of his own? He recalled Leveret's querulous reaction to the glass-slain soldier. What could a man like Leveret perceive of the workings – the *import* – of a glass book?

Svenson could hear his pursuer shoving closer and dived blindly away, disquieted by the sudden image of a steaming cavity during surgery – the cords of muscle fibre, the globular strands of lung tissue, the tender tubing of vessels and veins – shuddering at the notion of his entire body somehow swimming through *that*. Doctor Svenson spun desperately at a *second* set of steps – another soldier! Without thinking he thrust himself in a third direction, the clasp knife in his hand, ready to defend himself.

The hanging curtain gave way, and Doctor Svenson stepped out into thin air. He dropped the knife with a cry, boot heels balanced on the edge of a precipice, and snatched at a canvas hose. He tottered in one of the tall windows he had seen from the road – windows no longer glazed, wide open to the elements. What sort of insane idea was that? He looked down, swallowing nervously. It was not so very high and the fall onto grass – but for Svenson, whose outright loathing of heights only had been amplified by the airship, it was enough to fix him stiff.

The rustling sounds were directly in front of him. He had dropped the knife. An iron ladder had been bolted to the building's outer wall, running from the roof to the ground, a mere three feet away. The tubes shifted in front of him and one green arm pushed through, waving a long double-edged bayonet.

Svenson jumped, catching the cold rungs with both hands, and clambered like an untrained ape, waiting for the blade in his back.

It did not come. The hand with the bayonet slashed wildly at the air where Svenson had just been standing, but the soldier did not appear. The tubes and hoses rippled ... the man was struggling with someone the Doctor could not see. The curtain parted and the Contessa di Lacquer-Sforza shot out, surprised by the drop just as Svenson had been. She adroitly caught hold of a dangling chain and swung to the side like a circus gypsy as the soldier finally emerged. But then the man saw her – saw he was fighting not the foreign prisoner, but a breathless, beautiful woman – and hesitated. The Contessa slashed her brilliant spike into the hoses near the soldier's face and sent a spray of burning steam into his eyes. He reeled back into the shifting curtain. The Contessa dived after him and was gone.

The encounter had been totally silent, and it was strange when Mr Leveret's voice, dimmer now, called again for the Doctor's surrender. Svenson ignored it, climbing, terrified and horribly exposed, like a centipede stranded on a white-washed tropical wall. Where had the Contessa come from? He must have inadvertently drawn the soldier to her own hiding place. Svenson's head spun, and he squeezed shut his eyes, then opened them again, staring into the white bricks only inches from his face.

He clung to the rear wall, on the opposite side from the canal: to his

right was the crowd of adherents, to his left the yard where they had found
the soldier riddled with glass. From this higher vantage he could now see
over the stone wall and into the woods. Suddenly their depths were pierced
by a brace of torches . . . a snaking line with green-coated soldiers marching
at either end . . . but in between – he squinted at the flickering torchlight
– a gang of . . . *prisoners*. Two soldiers – in red, dragoons! – with their
hands bound, and then another man, hatless, in a black topcoat, and behind
the man . . . two women. Doctor Svenson's breath stopped in his throat.
The second woman was Elöise Dujong.

   Doctor Svenson's heart leapt in his chest, but he forced himself upwards,
eyes resolutely fixed to the brick. To attempt a rescue, unarmed and alone,
would merely see him delivered up to Leveret's rage. Judging by the
soldiers, Elöise's party – the other woman must be Charlotte Trapping, the
man Robert Vandaariff – had been first captured by Mrs Marchmoor's
dragoons, and then taken again by Mr Leveret's private army. As curious
as Svenson was to see Leveret's reunion with the Xonck sister – she must be
his keenest rival – it was the two dragoons that confirmed the mobilization of
the Ministries, that, as he had speculated to Leveret, the whole of the
military lay at their call . . .

   The next floor was different in that the nearest windows, also unglazed,
were blocked by iron bars. He peered closely at the bolts and saw no fresh
scrapes on the bricks – the bars had been set in place for some time, even
years. The machines here were larger, dark and oiled with heavy usage.
The Doctor had no experience with industry but had been escorted by
many a ship's engineer past turbines and boilers, enough to recognize that
here were the guts of the factory proper, the powerhouse heart that pumped
life through the rest. Leveret had adapted these mill works to animate the
Comte's metallic *fantasia*. If one sought to bring the whole place to a halt,
this was the spot to start swinging the pickaxe. Not that Svenson *had* a
pickaxe, or could penetrate iron bars. He resumed his climb.

With a shock that nearly caused him to fall, he felt the ladder shudder with
the weight of a new occupant. Svenson looked down to see the shimmering
black top of the Contessa di Lacquer-Sforza's head, and the purple silk of

her climbing arms. Svenson hurried upwards, aware that in haste his grip was not as sure and his boot heels more likely to slide off the iron. He reached the highest line of tall windows, also barred. Each opening had been stretched with sailcloth. He could smell the reek of indigo clay, as strong as it had been amongst the forest of ducts and hoses, and detected a new sound, high pitched and sustained, like the buzzing of porcelain wasps. He glanced down. His lead of two storeys had been cut in half. The woman looked up, black hair in her eyes, and as she stabbed for the next rung she bared her teeth. The back of her dress shone with blood. She caught his eye and did not smile, the iron frame of the ladder throbbing with each determined step. Svenson groped blindly for the next rung, hauling himself recklessly towards the roof.

The irony of finding a haven in a rooftop – a place where at the best of times his vertigo would drop him to his hands and knees – was not lost on him. He would have to pull himself over the lip – an awful moment of releasing the ladder entirely and taking hold of a bare – and dusty, slippery, even crumbling – crenellation of brick with his hands. What if he mistimed his reach? What if his boots slipped? And if he took too long, would the Contessa slash the back of his knee? Useless anxiety hammered his nerves. He was at the top of the ladder. He could not see beyond the lip of brick some two feet above him. With a feral snarl he thrust his arms up and took scrabbling hold, the edge of the brickwork digging awkwardly into his bicep, flailing with his legs, scuffing his knees. The Doctor clawed his way onto a gritty, soot-smeared expanse of planking, slathered with old tar.

The rooftop, an open rectangle some thirty yards across and sixty yards long, was divided lengthwise by a double line of squat brick chimneys, each perhaps the width of a barrel and twice the height of a tall man. But near to where he had emerged, on his side of the line of smokestacks, rose a squat brick hutch, with a door to the factory below. Svenson gave one quick glance at where the Contessa must momentarily emerge and dashed to the door – reasoning one fearsome woman to be less dangerous than an army of soldiers. He snatched up a length of broken wood – at one point it had been the leg of a chair (who knew how it had migrated to a rooftop, like a sheep's bone in an eyrie) – and wedged it fast between the door and the frame. He heard no steps at the door, and, peering through the line of chimneys, he saw no guards appearing from the other side of the rooftop. How could that be?

He looked back to the ladder. The Contessa's hand shot over the brick lip, fingers splayed like the claws of a clambering cat.

Doctor Svenson stepped forward. One kick and she would be done for. The Contessa tottered on the rooftop's edge, legs thrusting against their confines of silk. He reached his hand to the woman's good arm. She met his gaze, snorted, and took it. With a not entirely gentlemanly pull Doctor Svenson hauled her onto the rooftop and to her feet. She snorted again and tossed her head.

'If we had stayed together, it would have been far more sensible.'

'I am not your ally.'

'Don't be an ass! Acknowledge the world as it is – as it has become.'

'I disagree,' he replied, feeling inadequate that he had no further words.

'You have given me your hand,' the Contessa panted. 'It was that or smash your boot on my fingers and send me to hell. You did not *do* that, Doctor Svenson – you have *made* your choice, pray do not tax me with peevish distaste! Do not, or I will turn your heart's blood to a fountain!'

Doctor Svenson did not doubt the woman's rage, or her capacity – she had this night slain how many men? But he knew she had done so by virtue of surprise, by the fact that she was a beautiful woman, whom they had no reason to think a mortal threat. Svenson had no such illusions.

'Your wound has opened.' He nodded to the smear of gore that had reached the end of her right sleeve.

'Your teeth are unpleasantly stained,' sneered the Contessa. 'Neither *fact* is of the slightest use for being pointed out.'

'They will be coming for us, and very soon.'

'Again – you cleave to the obvious –'

'I must ask you something, and I will insist on an answer.'

'And I will insist on flinging your corpse from this rooftop –'

'I am not afraid of you, madam.'

With a shocking vulgarity the Contessa spat onto the stiff tar at her feet and met Svenson with a glittering expression that made it clear that, given the chance, she would carve her answer on his neck.

'By all means, then. *Ask*.'

'You arranged for Caroline Stearne to meet with Charlotte Trapping and Elöise Dujong in a private room of the St Royale Hotel. I want to know why, and I want to know what resulted.'

The Contessa rolled her eyes with disbelief. '*You want to know this now?*'

'I do.'

'My Lord, Doctor! Because of *her*? Am *I* to determine whether you throw away your life in a futile rescue? The woman does not deserve the affection one would give a chicken whose neck one was about to wring.'

'I am not interested in your opinions, madam.'

'At least let us listen at the door – it would be stupid to be surprised –'

As she spoke, the Contessa gestured with her injured hand to the rooftop door but at the same time took a sly step towards Svenson, her left hand carefully out of view behind her hip. The Doctor stepped rapidly back, beyond her reach, and spoke quite sharply. 'If you do that again, I will shout at the top of my lungs for Mr Leveret! And then, madam, I will do my very best to end your life, even if it means carrying you off the rooftop with me.'

'You would not.'

'I would consider it a service to all mankind and a sure passage to sainthood.'

The Contessa wiped her mouth with the fingertips of her left hand, a contemptuous gesture that deliberately showed him her weapon: a band of steel that fitted across all four fingers, sporting in the middle a sharp, almost triangular spike of perhaps an inch in height: enough of a blade to slash, yet the squat base also made it a vicious adjunct to the wearer's fist. One swift blow had punctured the skull of Harald Crabbé on the airship, ending his life before he could collapse to the floor. But – and the sensation caused him to marvel, for he was in his life stricken by so many things –

Doctor Svenson was *not* afraid, neither of her nor especially of dying itself
– not when survival meant so little.

'If you would,' he said to her. 'The St Royale . . .'

As if admitting she had been for the moment foxed, the Contessa smiled.
Doctor Svenson braced himself. Whatever she was about to say would form
the first step in her revenge.

'There is practically nothing to describe. You must know of her assignation with Trapping – merciful sin, Doctor, you met the man yourself. Is
there anything more dispiriting than to be the mistress of a fool?'

Svenson wanted very much to strike her, but did not move. 'I find *you*
dispiriting, madam. With all your unquestioned talents, you remain an
epitome of waste.'

'From a man who has thrown away his life for Karl-Horst von Maasmärck
. . . well, I shall bear it in mind.'

'The meeting. The hotel.'

'What is there to say? I did not want Francis or Oskar or Crabbé to know
of my suspicions, so I could not risk being seen. As I knew Charlotte
Trapping socially, it needed to be arranged by Caroline.'

'Mrs Trapping was not to know of your involvement?'

'She least of *all*,' replied the Contessa, as if this point were especially
obvious.

'But why should Elöise be present? Why, if she was' – he stammered to
say it, feeling his face grow hot with anger and shame – 'the Colonel's
mistress – and Mrs Trapping was aware of – her – their – assignations –'

'*Aware?*' laughed the Contessa.

Svenson was dumbfounded. 'But – if – why –'

The Contessa laughed again. Svenson saw her assumptions change – and
knew that what she would tell him had changed as well. Before she could
speak, he held up his hand. 'You were not getting information *from* Charlotte Trapping – *that* you would have insisted on hearing alone. Instead
Mrs Stearne was informing *her* that some deep secret was known, and
exacting a promise or payment to forestall its publication. The obvious
secret is the infidelity, the Colonel's mistress . . .'

But suddenly Svenson knew this was wrong.

'. . . and indeed such would explain the presence of Mrs Dujong. But you forget that I *have* seen the women arrive together to this building, as I have seen them together earlier this day: if the infidelity were indeed a breach between them, this would not be. You included Mrs Dujong in the invitation for two reasons: first, as a sensible, observant person who must have known the secret herself, she would make sure Charlotte Trapping showed up, and second, upon being apprised of the threat to her mistress, she would exert a prudent influence – in protecting Mrs Trapping, she would inadvertently deliver her into your control.'

It was also ironic, he thought: Elöise being made aware of the threat to Mrs Trapping – swiftly followed by the Colonel's disappearance – explained why she had been so readily persuaded by Francis Xonck to go to Tarr Manor, where the memories of that meeting, along with the very fact of her infidelities, had been removed from her mind.

'Why should I require *prudence*?' asked the Contessa. 'I find prudence *dull*.'

'Because Mrs Trapping is a Xonck,' replied Svenson. 'Proud, angry, bitter, and unpredictable as a drunken lord.'

The Contessa smiled again. 'My goodness, Doctor, your cleverness has so nearly assuaged the urge to strike you dead.'

'You have not told yet me what the secret *was*.'

'And I will not.'

'You will.'

'Unfortunately, Doctor, we are no longer *alone*.'

Svenson spun towards the rooftop door. At once, instinct firing his limbs just in time, he threw himself back to avoid the slash of the Contessa's spike across the front of his throat. The woman staggered at the force of her erring blow. Svenson's own arm was cocked in a fist when he met her eyes and saw she was once again laughing.

'You cannot blame me, Doctor – only a fool gives up easily. Strike me if you must – or if you can – but I was telling you the truth.'

She pointed with her steel-wrapped hand at the far side of the rooftop, beyond the line of chimneys. Two men stood there, one straight, one bent as if in illness, yet, however many steps apart they stood, they unquestionably stood *together*. Svenson turned back to the Contessa, wishing he still held the silver revolver. On the other side of the line of smokestacks stood Francis Xonck with – *with!* – Cardinal Chang.

The two men advanced to the line of chimneys and crossed through to Svenson's side of the tar-covered rooftop. The Contessa darted to the ladder, but once there merely leant down, sniffed, and then called to them.

'No one climbs up. As it would be evident to an infant that we are here, I must assume Mr Leveret considers us *managed*.'

How easily the woman had gone, in the matter of a minute, from dashing conversation to attempted murder, to a reunion with sworn enemies – and *then* shown the presence of mind to assert that any specific argument between them had been rendered trivial by their shared predicament.

'What weapons are they using?' growled Xonck, his voice thick and hoarse.

'Your special carbines, of course,' replied the Contessa. 'But I do not believe they have men in the trees to shoot us here.'

'They could rush us if they cared to.' Xonck nodded to the rooftop door.

'So they do *not* care to,' she snapped. 'It is *your* Mr Leveret – perhaps you know his intentions.'

Xonck hacked out a wretched blue gobbet onto the tar. For an instant his eyes lost focus and his body swayed. 'Leveret . . . merely following . . . orders –'

'I do not think so, Francis,' the Contessa said. 'Leveret remains no more your creature than Margaret Hooke is the Comte's, or Caroline Stearne my own.'

'He does not know that *I* have arrived.'

'Perhaps not – merely that a savage, stinking, monstrosity –'

'*Rosamonde –*'

'And how *bold* you were to remove Oskar's machinery from Harschmort – before anyone was even dead! Or was *everyone* to die in Macklenburg by way of a poisoned pudding?'

Standing apart from them all, Cardinal Chang chuckled. Svenson searched on his one-time ally's face for some explanation for his alliance with Xonck but found only the two implacable, flat circles of black glass.

'Francis.' The Contessa's tone was almost kindly. 'There is no time at all. You must talk to us while you are still able, and while we have time. The machines are gaining speed.'

The clatter from below, and the corresponding vibrations, had accelerated so gradually the Doctor had scarcely noticed the change. But the incremental change was actually quite extreme, like a ship's boiler driven slowly to ramming speed to break through ice.

'What of that army – those *adherents*?' Xonck growled. 'Why summon them if you are marooned with us?'

'Because she did not summon them at all,' said Chang.

'You might have said what you knew before,' hissed Xonck, swaying.

'Neither of you could have called them. You have both just arrived.'

'Nor Leveret,' said Svenson. 'He does not even know who they are.'

'It is Margaret,' said the Contessa bitterly.

'She will skin you alive yet, Rosamonde,' Xonck snorted, a garbled rueful laugh. 'Do you still have it?'

'Have what?'

'The marrow sparge,' said Chang, again causing both to turn to him.

'*Margaret* has the book,' Xonck snarled. 'She will bring it here.'

'With a damned *army* –' began Svenson, but Xonck ignored him, weaving close to the Contessa. 'If you have the marrow sparge, none of this matters!'

'Unless Margaret did *not* recover the book,' said Chang.

'Recover it from *whom*?' the Contessa asked with impatience.

'The little teapot.'

'Celeste Temple,' said Chang.

'She is alive?' cried Svenson, taking a step closer to Chang, wanting to shake the man.

'She went to Harschmort,' said Chang. 'And took the book for herself.'

'Margaret has invaded her mind!' insisted Xonck. 'The girl is marked, *finished* –'

'So all will be well!' the Contessa shot back at him. 'If your book does arrive – and if we are not killed – and if our minds are not raped – and if Margaret and Mr Leveret are both utter fools! And if *that's* the case, Francis, I suppose we must come to an agreement!'

'I am *dying*, Rosamonde.'

The Contessa's only reply was a haughty snort.

'None of this makes sense,' said Svenson. 'Leveret knows we are here. And yet he does nothing –'

'Because he fears to cross me,' rasped Xonck.

'Because he fears *us*,' cried the Contessa. 'We have defied his men, his weapons, his every defence –'

'He does nothing because he does not need to,' said Chang. 'We are birds in a cage.'

'No.' Svenson shook his head. 'He did not expect us to be here – we mean nothing to his plan. He waits for his true rivals – one he has taken captive, and the other who is on her way. The one he has is insignificant. But the one he waits for . . . the glass woman . . . when she arrives, he must be ready for her. It can be the only reason for this factory to exist.'

No one spoke, and then a moment after that they could have shouted at the top of their lungs and no one would have heard. The double line of chimneys burst into life, belching thick columns of black smoke and steam. The roar of their spewing left Doctor Svenson staggering as if a gunshot had gone off next to each ear.

It was perhaps two seconds after this that the rooftop door exploded in an almost silent flower of wood chips and flame. The Contessa fell to her knees, and Xonck, nearest to it of all, was knocked flat. Svenson flinched at the splinters blown against his face and looked up blinking. Chang carefully raised his empty hands. Svenson followed his gaze and then lifted his own arms with the exact placating caution. The ragged hole where the doorway had been was now crowded with green-coated soldiers, their bright weapons aimed in an unwavering line. Another squad of soldiers had swarmed up the ladder where he had climbed with the Contessa, and a third – following Chang and Xonck on the opposite side – had crossed the roof to take positions between the chimneys.

Xonck vomited onto the tar. The Contessa struggled to her feet, her hair in disarray. The soldiers at the ruined doorway fanned onto the rooftop, and as they did so Svenson saw a figure rise through the fingers of still-flaming wood, the black chimney smoke behind her like an infernal curtain blotting out the sky.

Charlotte Trapping stepped onto the rooftop, looking with disdain at the dishevelled Contessa and her ruined brother, then wrinkled her nose at Svenson and Chang, their arms still in the air.

'Collect them,' she cried out over the roar, a note of pleasure running through her poised demeanour like a seam of silver through cold stone. 'If any *one* so much as raises a finger . . . kill them all.'

TEN

FACTORY

When Miss Temple opened her eyes, the tiny hold was still dark. She lifted her head from a burlap sack of beans she had pulled onto the bale of wool (the moist wool being raw and still smelling of sheep) and rubbed absently at the imprint its rough surface had pressed into her cheek. The barge was not moving. They had arrived.

She sat up fully and restored Lydia's case to her lap from the crevice it had found between the bales. She bundled up her dress and wiped her face with her petticoat, then smoothed it down again. A very small amount of light crept in through an imperfection in the hatch cover, but it did not tell her whether it was safe to *emerge*.

Miss Temple felt better for sleep, though her dreams had been unpleasant. She had been once more on the roof of the sinking airship, but the sea was made of shifting plates of blue glass, and as it licked her feet she had felt them freeze and stiffen. Elöise had been there, but then Elöise had become Caroline Stearne, her neck still cruelly gashed, the ruby wound and her black hair making her skin appear achingly pale. As if to amplify this impression, Caroline had reached behind her bloody shoulders and undone the buttons on her black dress. Miss Temple had squirmed at this impropriety, but then Caroline's torso was bare, the dress draped around her hips like a funereal willow. Miss Temple swallowed, rooted by Caroline's sorrowful beauty, the gentle curve of her belly, soft, hanging breasts, nipples the colour of raw meat, and the white flesh above them flecked with dried blood. Miss Temple felt her frozen toes beginning to snap. She tottered, knowing that to fall would mean death. Caroline had changed back to Elöise, but with the same body, and the identical wound. It was suddenly vital that Elöise reveal some secret, but her ruined throat would hold no air. Each attempt to open her mouth was mocked by the puppet-like gape of the open gash below it. In a sudden spasm of dread Miss Temple reached up for her own throat and felt the tips of her fingers enter the cold incision carved across it . . .

She frowned, plucking at her hair with both hands, remembering rather more of the dream than she cared to. While she did feel restored – more physically capable, at least – this improvement was accompanied by a palpable increase in her own hunger. Not any hunger for food – though it had been some time since she had eaten, and Miss Temple would not have refused anything wholesome (save mutton) – but an erotic hunger calibrated precisely to the urges of her blue glass memories. At the same time, her sleep *had* placed some small distance between the black influence of the Comte d'Orkancz's book of death. She could taste ash in the back of her throat when she swallowed, but the impulse to *despoil* things lay not so heavily on her will.

Miss Temple swallowed again (having done so once to gauge the acrid taste, she could not prevent herself from repeating the gesture) and quietly shuffled off the bales to the ladder, climbing until she touched the hatch cover. She heard nothing, and so pushed gently with the top of her head. The cover was quite heavy and did not budge until she pushed with her hand as well, when it lurched a sharp half-inch, the sudden scrape horridly loud. She peeked through the tiny crack, but could see nothing. Miss Temple raised the hatchway another two inches, waited, then raised it more, waited again, then finally raised it enough to make any further pretence of secrecy absurd. The deck was empty. She shifted the hatch cover to the side and carefully clambered through, keeping her dress and petticoats free of her feet in case she needed to run.

The lantern whose dim light had penetrated the hold hung some yards away, and in its glow she saw they were docked at the edge of the canal. Beyond the canal's bricked border lay a cleared grassy sward and a thick, dark wall of trees whose high branches stretched over the barge, the moon and stars only visible through their whispering canopy.

Miss Temple crept to a short mast half-way up the deck, the furled sailcloth at its side making a thick column to hide behind. She heard the *clomp* of a heavy bundle dropped onto a wooden surface, and then laughter. In the glow of another lantern loomed a knot of men hauling boxes from another hatch. But they were too far away – and then Miss Temple realized her own barge had been tied directly behind another of identical width, and that it was her very good luck to have emerged just when the crew of her own vessel had chosen to plunder their unguarded neighbour. Miss Temple seized the opportunity and scuttled to her barge's gangway. She looked once more at the men, heard the thud of another box dropped on the far deck, and picked her way down the planking, each footfall silent as a fox. She padded across the grass to a gravel road, crouching low until she reached a turn that hid her from the bargemen. Miss Temple stood straight and exhaled. The dark colour of her dress and hair would hide her in the night.

The gravel road terminated at a high square building. The tall windows blazed in the darkness like a star come down to earth.

The closer she came to the bright building, the more she heard what sounded like the low roar of a fire, and the metallic clatter of pots and pans. The sky above the building was covered with cloud, yet it took Miss Temple some minutes to realize that the cloud came *from* the building, for it rose not from a single chimney stack, but in a long curtain the width of the entire structure. Once the massive scale of the industry at work became plain to her, the low roar became legible as the hum of turbines and engines, and the kitchen racket as the remorseless clanking of mill machines.

It was no great leap for Miss Temple to connect the destruction of the Comte's laboratory at Harschmort with another factory so vividly alive. Yet when she shut her eyes and opened her mind to the sickly pool of his book – which she did there on the road, despite her abhorrence, for she knew the knowledge might save her life – she detected no inkling of such a place whatsoever. But how could these works exist without the Comte's knowledge? Miss Temple walked on, dizzied again. She had seen her father's sugar works and the great coppers cooking rum – the stink of burning cane stayed with her to that day – but this would be her first *modern* mill. She did not expect to enjoy it in the least.

*

Did she expect to enjoy *anything*, any more? It was a puling thought, more suited to a helpless lady in a play than to Miss Temple's sturdy character, and yet at the core of the complaint lay something very real. She might appreciate incidental niceties – scones, for example – but these seemed merely appetite, an animal's need. Did not *pleasure* depend on an architecture of perspective – on contrast and delay, withholding and loss? Did not true enjoyment rely on facing the future? Did a cat possess such understanding? Did Miss Temple – in truth, in her soul?

It was a difficult prospect to swallow, walking alone in the dark. What of substance had she ever wanted – *genuinely*, not taken by rote from the expectations of others? A husband? Roger was gone, and even if there *had* been someone to replace Roger (not that she was the sort to stick her affections so quickly from one place to another), what then? What sort of lover – the very word was an unchewed bite she could not swallow – could she possibly be when at the first intimation of desire she vanished beneath a sea of depravity? What man would possibly have her once they glimpsed the dark lusts staining every cranny of her mind? She saw herself laying exposed on what ought to have been her marriage bed, eyes nakedly aflame with knowing desire – they would cast her away in disgust! How could she convince anyone else of her innocence when she could not convince herself?

Instead, as if in wicked confirmation of her failure, Miss Temple's brooding opened her senses to the very lurid memories that she feared: the knotted collisions of a wedding night refracting into a score of disturbingly remade memories, rooms she had been in throughout her life now repurposed to lust, every bed, every sofa, carpets, tables, her father's own garden. She staggered from the road and sank to her knees, the glow of need spreading from her hips through what felt like every stinging nerve. The sweet quickening swept on, deliciously recolouring her past – Doctor Svenson's elegant, gentle fingers and the muscles in his neck like a gazelle's ... Chang's curling lips and unshaven face ... Francis Xonck groping her body in the crowded corridor of Harschmort House ... Captain Tackham's long legs and broad shoulders ... the Comte d'Orkancz reaching underneath her dress –

She shuddered, exquisitely suspended, then exhaled with a gasp. She opened her eyes deliberately wide, forcing her mind to think, to remember where she was . . . and where she had been. This last memory had come from her coach ride with the Comte and the Contessa, from the St Royale. But it was *wrong* – the Comte's hand had been around her *throat*. The groping fingers had been the Contessa's, seeking in Miss Temple's arousal nothing more than the young woman's debasement and shame. Miss Temple had refused to be ashamed then, and with a snort she refused again now – refused the bond any of these magnetic bodies might place upon her mind or heart.

She wiped her eyes and wondered sadly at how she had placed Svenson and Chang so easily with so many obvious villains – but what did that signify, after all? Miss Temple was very sure about the hearts of men. Her blue glass memories were full of them.

A sharper noise caused her to turn towards the bright building, and then instantly throw herself down flat. A knot of jostling shadows . . . dragoons marching to the canal, at least forty soldiers in all. Before they reached her, at a crisp word from their officer the soldiers stamped to a halt, close enough for Miss Temple to place the easy, even soft, voice giving out their instructions.

'A score to each side,' began Captain Tackham. 'I will command the eastern squadron, Sergeant Bell the west. Each will advance through the wood – *quietly* – until to the west you meet the crowd at the gate, and to the east we reach the first ruined wall. These are hold points. At the signal you will then move forward in force, firing as necessary. In the west your objective is to open the gate so the men gathered there may enter. In the east, it is merely to clear the yard and prevent any retreat. Are there any questions?'

'These men at the gate, sir,' whispered the Sergeant. 'They will expect us?'

Tackham paused, and a slight weaving of his posture filled Miss Temple with dread, as if his mind had been *occupied*.

'Sir?' asked Sergeant Bell.

'They will,' said Tackham, clearing his throat. 'But if any man gives you trouble, do not hesitate to club him down. It is time. Good luck to you all.'

The soldiers poured into the woods. Miss Temple remained still. She knew that dragoons could both ride and shoot, trusted men for reconnaissance and courier missions, and yet as they vanished with the skill of practised woodsmen she was newly aware of how serious – how *real* – her enemies were. These men – *hundreds* of them, hidden all round her – were trained killers. And their officers, men like Tackham and Aspiche, were cold-eyed experts who had long ago made their accommodation with dealing out death.

Miss Temple stood, brushing at her damp-stained knees. The land surrounding the factory had been infiltrated by the glass woman's forces . . . but when a single bullet from a window – or for that matter one flung brick – could end her life, Mrs Marchmoor would be in the rear, Miss Temple was sure, with her closest minions before her like a shield. Yet their attention would be directed ahead of them, to the factory.

Miss Temple took the knife from her boot with a grim determination. She had followed them across miles and through the dark, just like a wolf. They did not *know* she was there.

She had been walking for two careful minutes, when suddenly new figures appeared, silhouetted against the white building's glare. It was not the dangerous mass she had expected, or even the glass woman by herself. Instead, a single man guarded what appeared to be a collection of baggage. Miss Temple crept closer . . . and then one of the bags yawned. She looked around to confirm there was truly only the one soldier and then strode forth, the knife held tight behind her back.

'*There* you are,' she called, causing the soldier to swivel abruptly, a carbine in his hands. Miss Temple ignored the weapon and approached the drowsy Trapping children, who struggled to stand. With a pang she saw it was only the two boys, Charles and Ronald, the latter especially cold and snivelling. Their sister was not with them.

'Who is there?' cried the guard. 'Halt!'

'O I will not,' replied Miss Temple. 'I have been following Mrs

Marchmoor these hours – *hours* I tell you – and must know where she is.
I am Miss Stearne. I have something she needs.'

She raised the leather case for the soldier to see and shifted her grip on
the knife. Was she near enough to strike him? Did she *want* to strike
him? In front of the children? She bent forward to the boys. 'We met at
Harschmort. You were with Captain Tackham.'

'You had someone's hairbrush,' replied Charles.

'My *own* hairbrush,' said Miss Temple. 'It had been borrowed. Who is
your soldier?'

'Corporal Dunn,' said Charles.

'Excellent.' Miss Temple turned to the Corporal. 'I assume you are
charged with the safety of these two young men. I met your Captain coming
the other way – he directed me to you. If you might in turn direct me . . .'

'To the Colonel?'

'The Colonel will do perfectly well.'

'How did you follow?'

'I beg your pardon?'

'Is there another barge?'

'Do I have wings? Of course there is.'

She glanced at the boys and saw that Ronald held the small leather case
she had last seen in the hands of Andrew Rawsbarthe, lined with orange
felt and holding vials of what she assumed to be the children's blood.

'Ronald,' she snapped. 'What do you have?'

'They left it behind,' the little boy sniffed, gripping the case tightly.

'Give it to me.'

'No.'

'I will return the thing, Ronald, but you must let me look at it.'

'No.'

'You must give it to me or the Corporal here will force you.'

She gave the soldier a narrow glance that warned him to cooperate. He
obligingly cleared his throat. 'Come now, master . . . the lady says she'll
give it back . . .'

Ronald wavered, looking at his elder brother, and Miss Temple took the
instant of distraction to snatch the case away. Ronald's mouth opened wide

in shock. Miss Temple leant forward with a hiss. 'If you cry out, Ronald, I will throw this into the trees – and *then* where will you be? You will go looking for it and be *eaten*!'

The boy's lower lip quivered. She nodded sharply – aware that the soldier too was curious to see inside – and snapped it open.

The three vials were exactly where they had been, but the orange felt around them was smeared and stained, the fabric stiffened . . . and blue. The vials had all been opened and replaced uncorked, but the contents had not spilt, for the blood within had been solidified into glass. Miss Temple closed the case and returned it to Ronald, who took it in sullen silence.

'What do you say to the lady?' prompted Corporal Dunn.

'Nothing,' sniffed Ronald.

'It is perfectly well,' said Miss Temple. She turned to the elder boy. 'Put an arm round your brother, Charles – he is cold. Corporal Dunn, you have been entirely helpful. Your Colonel would be where?'

Miss Temple strode confidently towards the house, measuring how far she needed to walk until the Corporal could no longer see her and fearful that by then she would have already reached Aspiche. She went as far as she could bear with her spine straight, the factory and its racket looming nearer, then looked back and saw with relief the soldier and the boys sunk in the darkness. Miss Temple dropped to a crouch and squinted towards the factory. Where was the main force of dragoons? Had they all advanced when Tackham and his men had gone into the trees? If all the glass woman's soldiers became involved in the attack, perhaps she could ambush her enemy directly.

A loud shouting erupted to the west side of the house, like the noise of a mob in a city square – Sergeant Bell and his dragoons. Miss Temple was suddenly afraid she had dawdled and missed her time. She broke into a hurried trot, the curls to either side of her head bobbing against her shoulders.

The shouts at the gate were answered by a crashing volley of gunshots. The shouting did not flag, not even after another volley. Instead the cries soared into a triumphant spike – had the mob forced the gate? A third volley was answered by screams, cutting through the shouts like a scythe. The dragoons began returning fire, and the volleys from the factory grew ragged, though most of the screaming still came from the attackers.

But then Tackham's men in the ruins opened fire in the east. The bullets spattered at the factory's defenders like hot rain on a metal roof. Yet it was as if the men in the white building had an entirely different sort of weapon, firing faster and to terrible effect, even though they were clearly out-numbered. Miss Temple could not *see* anything of either combat, but she noticed when the defenders' gunfire came from *within* the building, as if they had fallen back. Would the dragoons storm the factory so soon – would it be that simple? From the gate came a rising cry, as the crowd charged forward.

A window above the crowd spat out a tongue of flame, and directly before it – from the thick of where she imagined the crowd of men to be – a column of black smoke bloomed up like a wicked night-flower. The screams were horrific, and the charging cry faltered at once. An identical blast crashed into the ruins, with its own echoing curtain of screams and the cracking of toppled trees. With an instant of forethought Miss Temple looked up at the windows facing the gravel road – facing *her* – and flung herself down. Another crash and the earth around her kicked like a horse. She cried out but could not hear her own voice. Her body was spattered with pebbles and earth. The ground shook again and again. She could not move. The defenders had cannons facing every direction.

Smoke drifted up from the battered landscape, a scatter of riven pits. From beyond the trees rose moans and screams. The firing had ceased. Miss Temple shook the loose earth from her hair. A raw hole lay steaming in the centre of the road not ten yards away.

A sound cut through the ringing in her skull. Someone was speaking.

The voice was amplified, as the Comte's had been inside the cathedral tower at Harschmort. With a slicking of bile in her throat Miss Temple recalled the black speaking tube connected to the Comte's wicked-looking brass helmet, and how the great man's voice had then filled the massive chamber like a god's. But this voice was different – thin, and brittle, even cruel. It was a woman.

'As you have seen and felt,' cried the voice, 'our artillery can be directed anywhere we choose, from our doorstep to the canal. You cannot hide, and you cannot advance. Your men will be slaughtered. Your business here has failed. Your soldiers and your rabble will withdraw. You yourself will come forward from your shadows, madam, alone. You have five minutes, or we will begin shelling the ground in every direction. Make no mistake. If you do not come forward, you will *all* be destroyed.'

These words were followed by a rasping pop, which told Miss Temple the speaking tube had been detached and the woman's fearful pronouncement was done. Miss Temple waited for any response – orders bawled out to the dragoons, cries of retreat from the crowd around the gate – but heard nothing. Miss Temple crept forward through a line of shell holes and their rising smoke. Still she heard no response, neither to attack nor to flee. Surely staying where they were, vulnerable and in the open, was the poorest strategy of all – it could only provoke another barrage.

The smoke cleared enough for her to see that the gravel road ended at a low wooden wall, beyond which rose the factory. Its white surface seemed all windows and light, and the thin bricks the merest framework, like a flaming cage made from innumerable small bones. Shadows darted across its openings and along the edge of the rooftop, and above it the black smoke still rose in a billowing curtain.

The smoke cleared, and Miss Temple finally saw the glass woman's army, for the low wooden wall was lined with crouching figures . . . more than a hundred dragoons, with here and there an awkward fellow in Ministry black. Not one of them moved. Miss Temple went near – as if she were dreaming, for not a man acknowledged her approach – finally close enough to touch the soldiers on the face. Had Mrs Marchmoor immobilized her own minions, as she had stilled Miss Temple in the coach? Had she grown so powerful – to touch so many minds in a stroke, and with such force? But why were the men not sent away? Did this not leave them even *more* vulnerable to cannon fire? Not to retreat was direct defiance of the amplified voice's demands, and when the minutes ticked away these men must die.

She had very little time herself. Miss Temple looked up to the windows, aware there must be all sorts of eyes upon her. But no one shouted, no one shot her down. She returned the knife to her boot and stepped to the nearest of the black-coated men. It was the odious drone from Harschmort, Mr Harcourt, his blue eyes staring blankly like a fish looking up from the poaching kettle. Cradled in his hand was a small six-shot revolver. She tugged it from his grip and measured the cold iron's weight in her little palm. It would absolutely do.

She did not see Mr Phelps, Mr Fochtmann, or Colonel Aspiche, and assumed they had advanced with Mrs Marchmoor, despite Mrs Trapping's order — either willingly or dragged as automaton slaves — along with Francesca Trapping. But again, why Francesca alone? Miss Temple thought of the vials stopped up and smeared with blue. Had a sliver of glass been inserted into each little dram of blood? Or had Mrs Marchmoor transformed the vials herself with the tip of her finger, like an indigo Medusa?

To enter the factory, Miss Temple stepped over two men in green uniforms, blood smeared from their upper lips down to their chins. Beyond these bodies, the entire ground floor of the factory was occupied by rattling, blazing machinery. Miss Temple winced. Oppressed by the din and nauseated by the reek of indigo clay, she stopped where she stood, one hand to her brow. Through the Comte's memories, every machine seemed to glow before her eyes as she sensed its purpose, its hideous *capacity*. Each polished carapace vibrated like an ungainly tropical beetle bellowing for its mate. Miss Temple knew there were only rods and shafts and oiled bolts beneath their metal covers, but to the man who had made them these devices represented *life*, and somehow the shuddering things seemed ready to extend their awful legs and wings at any moment.

Where *was* everyone? She picked her way round the machines, to a nest of little rooms, past another two crumpled men in green. Why would the defenders leave their crucial machines so unprotected — were they so desperate, or so confident? Or did they know Mrs Marchmoor required them in full operation as much as they?

Miss Temple was gratified to find a staircase – wider than normal, which she supposed actually *was* normal when one had to shift, well, who knew what exactly, *material* – up and down to be worked or lathed or milled or baked – again, details escaped her. But the staircase was as dark as the rest of the factory was bright – lacking windows, lamps, lanterns, even a candle left on a plate. Miss Temple gazed up into the blackness with distaste, the mechanical roar chopping at her concentration and her nerves. Then she perceived something new in the rhythmic din, writhing through the air like a snake . . . an agonized scream.

The first landing door was locked tight. The next, up a double length of stairs, was locked as well. She pressed her ear against the door. If the massive beetles below created the rumbling buzz, here was the gnashing, hammering clatter, what she took to be the turbines – the *works* – of a proper mill. This floor must also hold the cannons – stuffed with soldiers and locked to keep their threat sure. Miss Temple did not care for cannons. It was sixteen steps to the next landing, each one carrying her closer to the keening scream.

But this landing bore a meagre light, a tiny tallow stub that allowed Miss Temple to ascend without feeling her way. She let her eyes fix first upon the little hands cupped round it, their skin glowing yellow, and then upon the ghostly small face floating above the flame. Francesca Trapping.

The girl did not speak, and so Miss Temple climbed until their heads were at the same height and did her best to smile, as if the horrid sounds around them were not there, and the simplest thing in the world would be for Miss Temple to lead the child away to safety.

'You are the lady from the house,' said Francesca. Her voice was very small, and her shoulders trembled.

'I am,' Miss Temple said, 'and I have come a very long way to find you.'

'I do not like it here,' said the girl.

'Of course not, it is entirely unwholesome. Why are you on the stairs?'

'They have put me out.'

'Are they not afraid you will run? *I* would run.'

Miss Temple peered more closely at the girl's face, but with just the one candle it was impossible to see if she had been damaged by the glass. Francesca shook her head, her lips pressed so tightly together they nearly disappeared.

'I have been told not to,' she said.

'No sort of reason at all.' The wailing cry worked to undo Miss Temple's composure like a key. 'Who *is* that?'

'I suppose it is *him*.'

'And I am certain he deserves every second of it too,' said Miss Temple. Beyond the door, the scream bubbled away . . . and there was nothing but the sound of machines. There was no time. She took Francesca's arm. The girl stood up but did not move to descend.

'O I cannot *go*!' she said.

'Of course you can.'

'But the *lady* said I must stay.'

'I will take you back to your brothers.'

'The lady doesn't want them. She wants *me*.'

'What about your mother?'

'But Mama said to stay too.'

'I'm sure she did not mean it. Parents often lie, you know.'

The little girl spoke in a rush, catches in her breath forced through the cracks in her failing courage. 'Mama was gone for so long – everyone said we would find her – and when we did find her – we heard her – she did not say anything – anything to *me* – she only talked to *them* – and I could not talk – *she* would not let me – and no one will tell me of Papa – and Mama is so different! Why won't she take me home?'

Miss Temple saw the dried tears across each cheek, and smelled the indigo reek in the girl's hair. 'I do not know. But that will not stop us. Come.'

Francesca pointed with the candle towards the door. 'We *cannot*!'

'Nonsense.'

'But the lady will *know*! I am only outside to keep watch.'

'Keep watch for what?' asked Miss Temple.

'For you!' said Francesca. 'They are all waiting!'

*

Miss Temple saw a flicker of terror in Francesca's eyes but then just as fast it was gone, and the girl's entire face went blank as stone. The muscles of the tiny arm fell slack, and the tallow light was dropped, plunging the landing into blackness. Miss Temple still held Francesca's arm, but she knew she could not carry the girl alone, not down the stairs in the dark. Such helplessness was infuriating.

The first wisp of cold flitted against her mind, like a moth past a window.

'Celeste . . .' the girl whispered.

Miss Temple heard it with revulsion, for in the twisted little voice lay the death of Soames, of Rawsbarthe, the decay of her own body. She squeezed the unresponsive little hand and awkwardly stumbled them both up the last steps to the door. She shifted the pistol and the leather case, and found the knob with her fingertips. At its touch the girl gasped and immediately began to whimper.

'Do not be afraid.' Miss Temple's voice was unpleasantly grim. 'These people are weak, and weaklings only ever want for whipping.'

She pushed on the door, and their landing was flooded with white light.

The tableau struck Miss Temple as one of those unsettling dreams in which figures from quite separate portions of one's life are thrown together, as if cut from paper and pasted together in a frame – the schoolmaster and the housemaid and the garrison soldier and wretched Cynthia Hobart from the plantation on the opposite side of the river, all eating toads on a boat that she herself was expected to steer. In dreams, such unpleasant groupings always appeared to demonstrate some unwanted *lesson* – that she was too proud, or had been cruel, or covetous of something (always the case regarding Cynthia) in truth beneath her. But what met Miss Temple in the white factory was different, not only because she knew it to be real, but because Miss Temple had finally accepted, despite every determined effort, how impossible it was to avoid consequence. She stepped through the doorway, the girl's hand in hers, with the same awareness of import as when she had first boarded the ship that would take her across the sea, when each hollow knock beneath her heels had echoed the certainty that she would never return. Her entrance brought an end to the business of all these people as surely as a little flaming match sets off a siege gun.

The open room was enormous, its far end fully taken up with bright metal ducts bundled together to feed a line of silver machines. These in turn sprouted black hoses, vibrating with gases and fluid, covering the floor like creepers from an industrial jungle. The shining casings of these machines had been peeled back and white light streamed out, each cracked carapace cradling a nugget of brilliance: super-refined bolts of indigo clay, powering the machines as they had powered the airship. Behind the machines and along each side wall were lines of green-coated soldiers with carbines. The factory's defenders had been withdrawn to this centre point, as if to maintain power in this room was to maintain it over all.

On a raised dais, like a carved figure above an altar, perched Robert Vandaariff. Three huge metal plates hung behind the financier from a lattice of chains, like panels in an indecipherable triptych. To each side were placed the buzzing brass box-stands, and at his feet lay long wooden boxes lined with orange felt – the whole arrangement like a bizarre icon for a religion, the deranged alchemy of the Comte d'Orkancz. The Comte's black memories surged within her like hounds against a leash. The scrawls on the metal plates jabbed at her thoughts, and she gagged to recognize the ruddy, purpled burn that looped around the industrialist's eyes and across his nose. The screams were now explained. Robert Vandaariff had just undergone the Process.

Next to Vandaariff, like an angel hovering near a punished soul in Purgatory, stood a slender woman with reddish hair, wearing a dark dress whose hem was crusted with dried mud. At her side lurked a man in a respectable brown topcoat, with meagre hair pasted optimistically upwards; his eyes kept flicking between the soldiers along the walls and those guarding the machines directly at his back.

Forming a triangle with Vandaariff and his keepers were two other groups, divided from each other like rival suppliants before an idiot king. On the left stood Mrs Marchmoor's party: the glass woman in her black cloak, Aspiche, and Phelps. Opposite them, in a strange little non-knot of their own – and Miss Temple did not comprehend this group at *all* – stood the Contessa, Francis Xonck, Cardinal Chang, and Doctor Svenson. They looked so depleted by their journey that even their hatreds had lost fire. She met their eyes – Xonck's insanely glazed, the Contessa's hard as a hunting bird's, the Doctor's pale with despair, and finally Chang's, mere smoked glass.

Had they been captured? By whom? What were they doing *together*?

What Miss Temple did not understand made her angry at the best of times, but now these least expected betrayals made her furious – and this fury, so like his own bitter rage, broke her last restraint on the Comte's memories. Miss Temple choked and lost her balance. She let go of Francesca Trapping and dropped to one knee, face flaming red, trying to retain her mind against the tide of despair and spite, against the crowd of facts – *sickening* facts – that split her attention into slivers. All around her the insanity of the room began to make *sense* . . . she knew that the copper filaments had burnt through, that the rattle of one machine was off by a quarter-turn, that the exact temperature of the indigo clay perceived by smell was –

'Celeste! Celeste – are you all right?'

A hand had gently taken her shoulder. Miss Temple looked up with an unladylike grunt into the face of Elöise Dujong, crouching next to her. Where had *she* come from?

Elöise shouted to the man in the brown coat: 'Mr Leveret! *Please!*'

The man did not react, but then Mrs Trapping spoke in his ear, and he waved to the soldiers behind him. They pulled brass levers on each machine and, like kettles taken off their flame, their high-pitched wailing fell away. The machines far below them still rumbled, but now the upper floor stood in silence.

Everyone was staring. How long had she been on her knees? The leather case had been taken away, and was held by Mr Phelps. The pistol was nowhere to be seen. Francesca Trapping stood with the glass woman. The child's streaked face was turned to Miss Temple without expression.

Elöise spoke urgently: 'Celeste – please listen – they know everything –'

The anger caught at the back of Miss Temple's throat like a rusted spike she could not swallow.

'What have you done, Elöise? Why does everyone stand with *them*?'

'Celeste, it is your parcel.' Elöise pointed to Lydia's case. 'You have been their pawn. She has *monitored* your passage all the way from Harschmort, the better to get both you and it here safely, away from the gunfire –'

Miss Temple felt *ill*. She was a fool, a vulgar lapdog. She began to gag again. She swatted blindly at Elöise's hand and gasped: 'Get *away* from me . . .'

'Leave her *be*, Elöise,' called the red-haired woman. 'It seems you've done something to offend her.'

'Charlotte –'

Mrs Trapping dismissed Miss Temple with a toss of her head. 'We do not care about *her*. We care that she hasn't done anything to harm that *book*.'

'Allow me to make sure of it.'

Mr Fochtmann appeared from behind Vandaariff, white shirtsleeves rolled to his elbows and his forehead bound with a plaster. The engineer strode self-importantly across to Phelps, taking the case from him. He set it on the floor. His long fingers unsnapped the clasps and opened the lid;

then Fochtmann carefully plucked at the pillowcases, one after the other, until the gleaming blue book was revealed to them all.

'You will notice I do not touch the glass,' Fochtmann announced. 'We do not know what consequences might have arisen from the circumstance of its . . . harvest, or from the circumstances of its . . . conveyance . . .'

Fochtmann studied the book carefully through slitted eyes, then picked it up – using the silk as a barrier to his skin – tipping it this way and that, as if he might penetrate its contents without risk.

Mrs Trapping's shrill voice rang out again: 'Is it what we have waited for or not? For all the time she's cost me, I should just as soon have this young *lady* flung head first out the nearest window.'

Fochtmann frowned at the book, and then stood. 'I am sorry, ma'am. I have managed the convection chambers, the aerating pathways, the distillation pipes, yet here I am blocked out. Only one of our company can divine if the book is what we hope, and whether it may be used.' He turned haughtily to Mrs Marchmoor. 'Enter her mind, madam! Enter the book! Is there any impediment to our going forward? Has she harmed it? Is there any damage?'

'Did the harvesting work at all?' added the Contessa. 'Given that Oskar was *dying* at the time –'

'Of course it worked!' Xonck's voice was thick and laboured.

'Be quiet, Francis!' shouted Mrs Trapping. She called to the glass woman, imperious and resentful. '*Tell* us!'

Against her will, Miss Temple looked at Mrs Marchmoor, flinching with dread at the invasion to come. An icy prickling resonated inside her skull . . . but then retreated at once, leaving only the chilly echo of a distant winter chime. Miss Temple braced herself for another, more savage penetration . . . but then the pressure receded altogether and along with everyone else in the room she felt only the cold slither of the glass woman's voice.

'The book . . . contains . . . the Comte d'Orkancz.'

The room was completely still, the air abruptly pregnant with discomfort. The glass woman had spoken. Miss Temple saw the reactive loathing on the faces of Leveret and Mrs Trapping, and on every soldier ringing the room. She waited for Mrs Marchmoor to say more, but she did not. Had she not sensed the corruption? Or was she laying yet another trap?

'Excellent.' Charlotte Trapping smiled icily. 'Let us move on.'

Miss Temple was forgotten. Every eye in the room was fixed on Fochtmann's meticulous efforts. Lifting it carefully from the case, the silk pillowcases between his fingers and the glass, he eased the glass book into the slotted brass box and then screwed a metal plate tight over the slot to seal it in. The glass began to glow. Miss Temple shut her eyes and swallowed against the rising burn in her throat, against the knowledge that the different plates of memory were being activated one after another, the electrical current weaving a lattice of force through a precise fusion of tempered metal and alchemical salts –

Hands slipped under her arms and heaved Miss Temple to her feet. She turned to see Chang behind her, and then Svenson took gentle hold of her jaw, gazing seriously into her eyes.

'Do nothing rash,' whispered Chang. 'Let them have at each other. Just stay alive.'

'Why should I care about that?' she replied.

'You are not well,' muttered the Doctor under his breath. 'That book is deadly. You must prevent any further contact with it, or *her* –'

'How did you simply *leave*?' The question had flown from Miss Temple's lips before she knew it.

Svenson's gaze darted up to Chang's, then back to her grey eyes. 'Ah – O – no no – it was not – truly –'

Chang tightened his grip on her arms. His whisper was curt and condescending. 'They will *hear* you –'

She turned to him. 'How did you leave? Are you such a coward?'

'Celeste,' the Doctor said, 'I am most sorry – so many things happened –'

This annoyed Miss Temple even more. She saw Elöise Dujong over the Doctor's shoulder, watching them, and spoke bitterly. 'Trust makes everyone its fool.'

Svenson followed her gaze, only to see Elöise turn away. He turned back to Miss Temple, his voice even and hard. 'What they intend to do is abominable –'

'I know it very well!'

'And I know you have been most brave –'

'You are both insane,' hissed Chang, and he pushed his knee into the back of Miss Temple's, causing her to sag suddenly into Svenson, who raised both arms to catch her. Miss Temple just saw Chang's hand slip out of the Doctor's pocket, then Chang pulled her backwards, spinning her so she lurched face first into his chest. She gasped as the Cardinal's fingers plunged directly into the bosom of her dress and felt, as his fingers just as quickly pulled away, an unfamiliar weight where they had been. Chang had deftly tucked something beneath her corset, in front of everyone.

He stepped back, straightening Miss Temple on her feet. Miss Temple looked guiltily at Mrs Marchmoor, but the glass woman was blocked by Elöise. Miss Temple looked the other way. Xonck had his head down, and was rocking back and forth on his heels, his breath whistling thickly. But the Contessa's violet eyes met Miss Temple's coldly. 'Are you back with us, Celeste?'

'She is not well,' announced Svenson. 'It is the glass.'

The Doctor's gaze flicked again to Elöise, near Francesca Trapping. The little girl did not respond to her tutor in any way. Her vacant eyes stared ahead. But Miss Temple could detect a thin halo of blue around each eye. The girl's thin lips had darkened to the colour of bruised plum-skin. At once Elöise raised one hand to her head and, stumbling backwards, extended the other towards Mrs Marchmoor as if warding off a blow. 'I'm sorry,' she cried. 'I'm sorry –'

'Get away from her, Elöise!' called Mrs Trapping. 'You must stop interfering! Francesca will be perfectly safe. Come stand by me.'

'She is *not* safe, Charlotte – look at her!'

With a reflexive defensiveness Mrs Marchmoor's remaining hand slipped from her cloak and took tight hold of the girl's shoulder. Francesca did not react, her face slack and dull, but Mrs Trapping's face went as suddenly sharp as an unsheathed blade.

'Alfred!'

'Company!' Mr Leveret shouted. '*Arms!*'

The soldiers shifted their carbines with a uniform precision, their aim fixed on the glass woman and her party.

Mr Phelps stumbled forward as if he had been pushed very hard.

'Ladies, Mr Leveret – please! There is no call for histrionics – we are nearly to the finish, I beg you – one more moment of patience! Look around you!'

Phelps sniffed loudly and dabbed at his nose with a handkerchief, careful to fold it over before anyone could detect any trace of blood, and then, back to business, gestured to Lord Vandaariff, whose scarred, livid face was wet with tears.

'In administering the *Process*, we have made proof of both Mr Fochtmann's learning and Mr Leveret's machines. What is more, this *proof* has rendered our subject's empty mind utterly compliant!'

Miss Temple remembered Roger Bascombe rhapsodizing about the Process – its gift of clarity, passage to essential truths – *claptrap* – but what *essence* did a man like Vandaariff still possess? Even without the Comte's book, she knew the main advantage of the Process for the Cabal was the insertion of a control phrase, allowing them to issue commands the subject would be forced to obey. At once she understood – a control phrase had just been implanted in Vandaariff and given to both parties.

'Charlotte, your daughter is at stake.' Elöise pointed towards Mr Leveret. 'And that man will not tell you what you need to hear.'

'And who are you?' Leveret snorted. 'That child's *tutor*!'

'Mrs Trapping knows very well what I am,' answered Elöise. 'And she *ought* to know what it has cost me. Charlotte, think! Once they get what they want, you will not matter!'

'But they have *not* got anything, Mrs Dujong,' cried Leveret hotly, 'nor will they!' He smugly snapped his fingers at a pair of crouching soldiers. 'We stand quite completely *protected* – by a Xonck Armoury 296 explosive shell!'

Leveret surveyed the silent room with satisfaction. 'A 296 explosive shell, Mrs Dujong, will shatter every piece of glass in this building. As our windows lack glazing, the only glass I refer to stands *there*.' He stabbed a long, thick-knuckled finger at Mrs Marchmoor. 'And at the first sign of – of – alchemical, mind-bludgeoning, dream-sniffing, thought-eating *nonsense*, those men will push their plunger and that creature's newest ally shall be a brush and dust pan!'

'What side are you *on*, Elöise?' called Mrs Trapping. The woman was *smiling*. Leveret broke into a confident grin looking back at her.

'Charlotte,' Elöise pleaded, gesturing to Francesca, 'it is not about mere *sides*.'

'But it *is*, Mrs Dujong,' called another voice. 'And you must get out of the centre . . . before you are killed there.'

Doctor Svenson stepped towards Elöise, his arm outstretched. His uniform was shabby and his face smeared with soot, but his blue eyes were clear. Stranded in the centre of the room, Elöise looked down at his extended hand. As if his gesture was especially unbearable, she veered away with a cry, standing alone with her arms crossed and one hand covering her mouth.

'We'll not waste more time,' announced Mrs Trapping. She turned to Fochtmann and clapped her hands together, as if she were calling a dog. 'I trust you are finished?'

The tall man bowed gravely and motioned Mrs Trapping and Mr Leveret further away. He had secured black hoses across Vandaariff's body, strapped the black rubber mask across his face, and swaddled the black webbed gloves around his hands and bare feet. Lord Vandaariff sat wrapped like a stuporous insect, stuffed away for future consumption in some spider's larder. Miss Temple wondered at how easily people – who two weeks before would have licked this man's boot heel for the merest scrap of attention – now treated him like a slave. Vandaariff's fate – pathetic, degraded – seemed only what any of them would receive, or even merit.

Fochtmann turned dramatically to face them all, pulling the brass helmet onto his head. At the wash of ash in her mouth, Miss Temple gagged. 'It will not work!' she croaked.

'Of course not!' Fochtmann barked through the helmet's voice box. 'We have not restored the power.'

Fochtmann signalled to the men, and the line of silver machines roared back into deafening life. Then he pulled down on the brass handle with the flourish of a circus showman.

Nothing happened. Fochtmann raised it up, prodded a bit of wiring, and pulled it down even harder. Nothing happened. Fochtmann waved angrily at the men, and the machines powered down. Fochtmann pulled off the helmet, his face hot and the bandage on his brow flapping loose. He strode towards Miss Temple.

'Why did you say it would fail? What do you know?'

'You lack a device . . . to manage the *flow*.' Miss Temple's words slurred.

'What *device*?' demanded Fochtmann, taking hold of her jaw.

'She does not have it,' said Chang.

'And you do?'

'No . . .'

Chang turned, and every eye in the room shifted with him, towards the Contessa.

'Once again you block our way, madam!' cried Mrs Trapping.

She snapped her fingers, but before the soldiers reached the Contessa, the woman raised her hand and delved into her clutch bag. 'My goodness, Charlotte,' the Contessa replied with an icy brightness. 'Allow me to help you all.'

She extracted a shining metal implement from the bag. With two tugs she doubled its size, stretching the device like a telescope until it took the shape of an old-fashioned pistol, with a ball-shaped handle on one end and a barrelled tube on the other.

'The marrow sparge,' said Chang.

The Contessa spared him one glacial smile and then tossed the thing in a lazy arc to Fochtmann, who caught it with both hands.

'Now, in exchange –' the Contessa began calmly, as if her words were not an explicit plea for her life.

'O do *not*!' sneered Mrs Trapping. 'Because I have been powerless you think I have seen nothing! I see *you* now – in *tatters*, like a *gypsy*! This *business* no longer requires you, madam – nor my brother, who has been a ghost these many years. You have lost your wager!'

Mrs Trapping's face was red, and her hands were clutching at her sides. Mr Leveret reached for her arm, but she shook him away. The Contessa had not moved.

'As you desire, Charlotte,' she said. 'Of course there remains much that none of you know, despite your presumption – all of Macklenburg, for example, as ripe for plunder as Peru, and richer to our interests than a continent full of silver. And even more *beyond* Macklenburg – initiatives begun in Vienna and Cadiz, in Venice –'

'What initiatives in Venice?' asked Mr Phelps, rather quickly.

'*Precisamente*,' laughed the Contessa. Then the laughter caught in her throat and the light stalled in her eyes. She clawed at the air and gasped through her open mouth, an animal panting. The glass woman withdrew. The Contessa met their gazes, eyes fierce, her voice more raw, then called to the glass woman: 'You may harvest *facts* from my brain, Margaret. But beyond fact lies an understanding you *cannot* capture – and that is my instinct. *I* outwitted Robert Vandaariff and Henry Xonck – and it *ought* to be clear to a hare-lipped infant that if you proceed without me now, it is at your peril.' She turned to Fochtmann, snorting at the metal device he held. 'I watched Oskar create the marrow sparge himself. Do you even know what it *is*?'

'It connects below the skull,' hissed Mrs Marchmoor. 'There are hidden needles.'

Fochtmann snorted upon finding the needles – at, now he had the tool, how obvious was its purpose – and set at once to its installation. Mrs Trapping watched him for a moment but then looked away, impatient and cross.

'What is a "sparge"?' she asked generally.

'A medieval term,' said Doctor Svenson, after no one else had replied. 'For the Comte, the meaning would be alchemical – to aerate, to infuse –'

'That tells me *nothing*,' Mrs Trapping muttered.

'Why ask a *German*?' Leveret replied with a sneer.

The Doctor cleared his throat. 'With this device in place, the energy from the book will be sent directly along Lord Vandaariff's spine, *infusing* the natural fluid there. This same fluid bathes the primary mass of nerves – the spinal column as well as the brain. It is the alchemical marrow.'

'Will that work?' Mrs Trapping asked doubtfully.

'If it does not also boil his brain like a trout.'

'We have seen it,' grunted Xonck from the depths of his distress. 'At the Institute – the Comte wiped the mind of a caretaker, then infused it with the memories of an African adventurer he had harvested that week at the brothel. The old man's mind became nothing but slaughtered dervishes and impregnated tribeswomen.'

'How interesting it will be to speak to Oskar once again,' said the Contessa.

'If I remember correctly,' observed Doctor Svenson, 'at the moment of his own death the Comte – beg pardon, *Oskar* – was intending to kill *you*.'

'O tush,' said the Contessa. 'The Comte d'Orkancz is, if nothing else, sophisticated.'

'You cannot think he will be your *ally*?'

'Doctor, I will be overjoyed to see my old friend.'

'But will it *be* the Comte?' asked Chang. 'That adventurer was harvested under the Comte's own care. This book was inscribed at the very worst of times –'

'Inconsequential,' rasped Xonck.

'And what of Robert Vandaariff?' asked Svenson. 'Is he truly expunged? Or will a lingering remnant dangerously shatter the Comte's *essence*?'

'And will either of these proud men submit willingly to all of *you*?' asked Chang.

'Be *quiet*!' cried Mrs Trapping. 'They do not have to submit *willingly*! The Comte must do our bidding – is that not why he underwent that horrible *Process* – so we may manage him *and* Vandaariff's money? We have acquired this power, and now we will employ it! Everyone has agreed – it is very, very *simple* – and I insist that we be finally *ready*. You, there – tall fellow –'

'I am Mr Fochtmann,' he said, aghast.

'Exactly so. *Proceed*.'

*

The handle was pulled, and the crackle of current spat across the copper wires like fat on a red-hot stove. Miss Temple clenched her fists and squinted, half turning her face away. Robert Vandaariff's voice echoed from under the black rubber mask, in unearthly yelps of terror, as high pitched and plaintive as an uncomprehending dog whose leg had been crushed by a cart. His tightly bound limbs thrashed, and his spine arched until it seemed it must break from straining. At the first touch of current, blue light glowed from the brass device that held the book, intensifying to a bright white flame; the scorching reek of indigo clay came off in clouds. Within the glare, Miss Temple saw flickers of shadow, ghost fragments, dreams flaming to life.

Then it was done. At Fochtmann's wave the machines went silent.

Vandaariff sagged against the restraints. No one else moved.

'Did it work?' whispered Charlotte Trapping.

Vandaariff lurched forward, choking. Miss Temple felt a mirroring, sympathetic spasm of nausea. Leveret cried aloud as he pulled the mask away – Vandaariff had filled it with black bile, and then vomited another ink-coloured gout across the man's trousers.

Grim and determined, Fochtmann loosened the restraints, easing Vandaariff to his knees and watching carefully as the man emptied the fouled contents of his stomach onto the planking. Leveret opened his mouth to complain, but the engineer impatiently motioned him to silence.

Vandaariff tipped his head from side to side, slowly, like a stunned bull, and flexed his fingers as if he were testing a pair of new leather gloves.

'Do not approach him,' Fochtmann warned.

Vandaariff strove to rise, grunting with effort, the livid scars accentuating the whiteness of his eyes. Fochtmann took a rag and wiped Vandaariff's face.

'Look at him!' whispered Mrs Trapping. 'What is *wrong*?'

'These are temporary effects,' said Fochtmann. 'Be patient . . .'

'Monsieur le Comte?' asked Leveret. 'Is it you?'

The Contessa took one hesitant step. 'Oskar?'

Vandaariff tried to stand but could not, slipping to his knees and elbows

like a tottering colt. He looked into the faces around him, and his eyes –
the whites tinged with a blue film his blinking pushed into beads that broke
down his cheeks – began to clear . . . and upon seeing the Contessa, a rattle
of recognition rolled from his throat.

'Oskar?' Her voice was gentle.

He swallowed, his face suddenly clouded by fear.

The Contessa sank so her face was at his level. 'You are alive again,
Oskar . . . it is not the airship. On the airship you were killed . . . but you
have been restored. You have been restored by one of your own marvellous
books, Oskar. Do not be afraid. You have come back to us . . . back from
where no man has ever returned.'

Vandaariff swung his head awkwardly, straining to make sense of her
words, of the different room and so many people – so different from the
ones he had last seen. He lurched forward. Fochtmann patiently raised him
when the spasms had stopped, once more wiping Vandaariff's chin.

'Is it truly him?' whispered Mrs Trapping.

'Of course it is,' said the Contessa easily. 'He *knows* me.'

'Did not Robert Vandaariff know you too?' asked Leveret. He peered
suspiciously into Vandaariff's face, like a farmer inspecting a pig at auction.

'Monsieur le Comte – if you *are* the Comte – my name is Leveret –'

'Tell him we need *proof*,' Mrs Trapping called over Leveret's shoulder.
'Something only *he* could know – some snip of alchemical *whatsit* –'

Mr Fochtmann insinuated himself between Leveret and Vandaariff. 'Give
him room, sir – the physical costs of the infusion are prodigious. Robert
Vandaariff has undergone this *after* the Process, nor had he a young man's
vitality to begin with –'

'The problem is not his body,' said Doctor Svenson, studying Vandaariff
with a pained disapproval, 'but his *mind*. The Comte was snatched from
the arms of death.'

'I'd expect him to be grateful,' muttered Mrs Trapping.

The Contessa sighed with irritation and shifted closer. 'Oskar . . . try to
remember . . . on the airship. The last minutes. You were very angry –
angry at me. I had behaved very badly. I had killed Lydia –'

Vandaariff's eyes flared at her words. The Contessa nodded as if to encourage his memory, as if his rage were entirely natural. 'I had ruined all of your great plans. You came at me . . . you thought to kill me . . . but then you were stabbed. Do you remember? Everything had gone wrong. We were betrayed. The airship was sinking. You were dying. Francis came to you with a book . . . an empty book, Oskar. Francis captured your soul.'

Robert Vandaariff swallowed, listening intently, watching her mouth. His lips trembled.

Once more Leveret thrust his face forward. 'This is the Xonck Armament Works in Parchfeldt Park, Monsieur. I am Mr Leveret. *You* are . . .' He grimaced with distaste and then muttered to the room at large. 'I feel a fool saying this at all – we have no certainty that anything of the sort has occurred –'

'Go *on*, Alfred,' said Mrs Trapping.

Leveret sighed, then snapped his fingers in front of Vandaariff, whose gaze had gone back to the Contessa. 'The contents of that book have been *infused* into the body of Robert Vandaariff. If you are indeed the Comte d'Orkancz, we require you to give out some sign – some *assurance* – that this is true. We require it *now*.'

Vandaariff blinked, returning Leveret's stare. Miss Temple could see the man's expression had sharpened, enough for his true thoughts to be veiled behind it – though this might bespeak no more intelligence than a cat's wary reaction to a curious child. She swallowed with a wince, like the others unable to look away from his scarred face, but unlike them dreading an echo of the corruption she had already allowed to stain too much of her own mind. But Robert Vandaariff remained mute.

'Why don't we simply *make* him answer?' Charlotte Trapping addressed Mr Fochtmann. 'What did you call it – the control phrase? Why doesn't Alfred simply speak the phrase aloud and *order* him to tell us?'

'He may not be unwilling,' began Fochtmann, 'but *unable*. If we try to imagine what this man may have *seen* –'

'Nonsense. Alfred?'

Leveret stood tall and cleared his throat. 'Indigo Pilate iris sunset Parchfeldt! Are you the Comte d'Orkancz?'

No one spoke. Instead of answering, Vandaariff attempted to stand. Fochtmann caught his arm, and so steadied Vandaariff kept his feet.

'He will not answer,' hissed Leveret. 'Look at him! He does not even acknowledge the phrase!'

'That is impossible,' said Mrs Trapping. 'At least . . . it ought to be . . .'

Leveret's face darkened with rage. 'Is this trickery? Does he presume to *trifle*?'

'For God's sake!' cried Fochtmann. 'Give him another moment! *He has only come back from the dead!*'

Miss Temple was startled by the halting clicking steps – the glass woman was advancing with great care, the little girl in tow. Vandaariff thrust Fochtmann away from him, gripping one of the brass boxes in an effort to remain upright. A line of saliva hung from his lips. He met Mrs Marchmoor's swirling blue eyes.

Then his mouth slackened, and his eyes went under a cloud. The glass woman was quite obviously probing Robert Vandaariff's new-fashioned soul.

'What do you see?' whispered Fochtmann.

'Tell us!' hissed Mrs Trapping.

The glass woman began to glow with the same cerulean sparks Miss Temple had seen that morning in the Duke of Stäelmaere's study, and her gleaming fingers tightened around the vacant girl's arm.

'Look at this marvel!' Fochtmann whispered, eagerly staring at the glass woman. 'She senses him . . . she sees what has been done – an accomplishment beyond anything I might have dreamt . . .'

Francesca's eyelids flickered like a dreaming animal's. Miss Temple looked back to Vandaariff . . . with alarm she realized that Francesca's face was now flinching and twitching exactly in time with his. Through the conduit of the glass woman's hand, the child was being completely exposed to Vandaariff's mind. Did no one else see?

Mrs Marchmoor's words curled into Miss Temple's mind like a serpent encircling a sleeping bird.

'It is done. The Comte d'Orkancz has been saved.'

*

Francesca Trapping suddenly coughed, choked, and then sprayed out a mouthful of blackened spit. Her mother screamed. As if realizing too late what had happened, Mrs Marchmoor thrust the child towards Colonel Aspiche, breaking the connection. Francesca retched again, bent over double.

'Francesca!' shrieked Mrs Trapping.

The girl looked up, eyes wide, as if she were seeing the room for the very first time. Mrs Trapping rushed towards her, but was caught about the waist by Leveret.

'What has happened?' shrieked Charlotte Trapping. 'What has she done to my child?'

'Charlotte – no, wait –'

'Do not!' cried the Colonel. He held tight to Francesca's shoulder and pointed to Mrs Marchmoor. 'Margaret – Margaret, what in heaven . . .'

Her glass hand had been sprayed with black bile. Mrs Marchmoor convulsively licked her lower lip as she stared down at the stain, as if she could taste the nauseating substance through her surface. The surprise in the glass woman's voice pierced Miss Temple's mind like a pin. 'He . . . he is . . . *unclean* . . .'

The bright slug of her blue tongue spurred another spasm in Miss Temple's stomach. The glass woman had never found the corruption, even when probing Vandaariff's mind outright, having wrongly assumed that with the change in bodies the Comte's prohibition no longer held force. Only when the taint had passed to the child could the glass woman sense it. Mrs Marchmoor retreated from Vandaariff, her blue lips drawn back.

'*Unclean?*' Leveret shook his head angrily, still holding Mrs Trapping. 'What does *that* mean?'

'It means nothing!' shouted Fochtmann. 'We all saw the sickness from the procedure – this is more of the same – it is *natural* –'

'It is *not*,' Aspiche shouted. 'Look at the child!'

Francesca trembled, held at arm's length by the Colonel. Her lips and chin were black, and her small mouth as dark as a wound.

'The child is ill,' snapped Fochtmann. 'It has no bearing on our work –'

Phelps nervously addressed the glass woman. 'You must explain, madam.

You looked into his mind – you told us the infusion worked, that this was the Comte –'

'It *is* the Comte!' insisted Fochtmann, but the glass woman's continuing distress stopped his speech.

'I could not see it in *him*,' Mrs Marchmoor hissed. 'Only in the girl . . . but it is from *his* body . . .'

'*What* is from his body?' demanded Aspiche.

'*Nothing!*' Fochtmann waved his arms. 'The girl must be diseased –'

'I was forbidden by him,' said Mrs Marchmoor. 'None of the Comte's servants could enter his mind –'

'We don't *understand* you, Margaret,' said the Contessa.

The glass woman rolled her head as if to clear it, yet her words remained too dense, as if she could not find the way to translate her present senses into language.

'I could taste that the book held him, that he had been infused with Lord Robert – but not the character of his mind . . . I was forbidden, and so the corruption . . . eluded me . . .' Mrs Marchmoor thrust her bandaged stump at Miss Temple. '*She* knew! *She* knew all along!' Her dismay rose to a keening shriek.

Fochtmann wheeled towards Miss Temple, his own frustration finally finding its object. 'Did she? It seems she has known all *sorts* of things! She was alone with the book – and alone with the girl! I suggest she tell us all *exactly* what she has done to them both!'

Miss Temple took a careful step backwards. 'The truth is before you all – the *decay*. You have not given a *man* new life . . . you have retrieved a *corpse*.'

'Truth be damned!' roared Xonck, and he careened towards Vandaariff, scattering everyone. Fochtmann turned in protest, but Xonck drove his plaster fist into the man's stomach, then took Vandaariff by the collar with his other hand.

'*Francis!*' screamed Mrs Trapping. 'Francis, we need him – step away at once! *At once or you will die!*'

'Company!' cried Leveret. '*Arms!*'

The soldiers raised their carbines. Xonck spun Vandaariff's body before him as a shield, his foul lips pressed dripping against the man's right ear. Aspiche thrust Francesca Trapping to Phelps, sweeping out his sabre as Phelps caught the girl in the crook of his cast and groped in his coat for a pistol. Leveret waved to stop the soldiers from firing, visibly furious at events being so suddenly beyond his control.

But then Xonck's whispering was answered.

From inside his raw throat came a chuckle, and the man's features settled into a heavier, petulant expression Robert Vandaariff had never worn. 'Why, Francis . . .' he rasped. 'You seem to be in . . . *a very bad way . . .*'

'Oskar?' whispered Xonck with fervent relief. 'Is it you?'

'You hold me rather tightly,' answered Vandaariff. 'I do not like it.'

'If I release you, I will be shot.'

'Why is that possibly my concern?'

'Let me enlighten you, Oskar,' Xonck snarled. 'My body is poisoned by your glass. I require you to save my life – after which I am again your willing friend. I cannot speak for Rosamonde – she too is not her best – but I can say that others, who hold the power to end both your life and mine and whose place this is, have agreed to your *restoration* only so you can be their slave.'

'That is only to be expected.' Vandaariff shrugged, surveying the room as if his gaze were a gun site, nodding with contempt as he recognized the faces around him. He reached up to wipe his face, the surprisingly delicate movements of his large hand entirely of a piece with the Comte d'Orkancz. He frowned at the black fluid wetting his fingertips. 'What is this?'

'Margaret says you're *unclean.*'

Vandaariff studied the glass woman, cocking his head at her bandaged arm. 'Does she? Well . . . poor Margaret . . . always so *emotional.*'

'They have administered the Process,' hissed Xonck impatiently.

Vandaariff reached up to the scars, his touch smearing the black fluid across the raised welts. 'A perfectly good idea, I'm sure. At any rate, worth the attempt . . .'

Mr Leveret stepped forward and shouted directly into Vandaariff's face. 'Indigo Pilate iris sunset Parchfeldt!'

Vandaariff chuckled. 'The Process *is* powerful,' he said with a wan shrug. 'But infusion from a book is even more so. One is new-laying the *essence.*'

'But – but we have remade you out of nothing!' Mrs Trapping's arrogance had taken on a plaintive whine. 'We *must* control you!'

'*Must?*' Vandaariff faced her with a sudden, low intensity. 'Control the worms in your own stomach, madam. Command the innocence of your daughter to return. Order your bankrupt heart to pump clean –'

Mr Fochtmann brought down an iron wrench on the back of Francis Xonck's head, with a sickening, crushed-pumpkin *thwock.* Xonck collapsed on the dais, utterly still.

Vandaariff looked down, abstractly curious. 'My *goodness.*'

Mrs Trapping's hand was over her mouth. 'Francis! Francis!' She strode towards Fochtmann. 'What have you done to my *brother?*'

Mr Fochtmann struck her cleanly on the jaw with his fist, knocking her into a sprawl of kicking legs.

'My God, sir!' cried Leveret, leaping to her. 'You will not hit a woman!'

'I am surely finished with them hitting *me*,' growled Fochtmann, and he called to Mrs Marchmoor: 'Enough of this nonsense.'

Colonel Aspiche extended his sabre towards Vandaariff. 'It does not sound like *nonsense* to me! If he can defy us – if he does not possess the knowledge to repair this sickness – *I* am finished with the lot of you!'

Phelp cradled the pistol in one hand and pulled the girl tighter to him with the other, addressing Mrs Marchmoor.

'Please, madam – the sickness! You call him "unclean" – does that mean we are doomed?'

'Don't be idiots,' began Fochtmann. 'There is no need for *rebellion* – we are all allies!'

Aspiche spun to Mrs Marchmoor, the naked sabre daringly near her body, his voice tight and his arm shaking. 'For pity's sake, Margaret – tell us!'

But Mrs Marchmoor said nothing. Her gaze remained locked on Robert Vandaariff. Miss Temple knew the glass woman had no answer, that she could not tell who – or what – this new person before her truly was.

Vandaariff cocked his head again and licked his lips, deliberately tasting them. He abruptly began to retch but then swallowed it down with difficulty, a display that to Miss Temple was every bit as revolting as if he had vomited outright.

Still Mrs Marchmoor said nothing, Aspiche's sabre tip dancing before her.

Charlotte Trapping cried out plaintively, 'Alfred! They have Francesca – *please*!'

Mr Leveret was startled to action. He swept his arm dramatically towards the soldiers with the concussive shell. 'No one will do anything – unless everyone here wishes to die!'

But Leveret's next shout failed on his lips. Blood burst out from the faces of the two soldiers. They dropped their wires and fuses as cleanly as if their arms had been lopped off with a scythe. Leveret stammered, and then yelled desperately for his army. He was already far too late.

Miss Temple staggered, as if she'd been cuffed hard across the ear, while all around her carbines clattered to the floor. The soldiers toppled heedless to their faces, eyes open wide, bodies entirely still. Across the entire room it was the same. Every person was incapacitated in an instant's sudden violent pulse from the glass woman's mind. Leveret and Mrs Trapping lay flattened. Phelps and Aspiche sprawled on their backs, pulling Francesca Trapping with them. Elöise groped on the floor, hair fallen about her face. Vandaariff slumped into the brass boxes. The Contessa was on all fours. Only Fochtmann had kept his feet and his senses . . . along with herself, Chang, and Svenson.

Miss Temple shook her head – her ears were ringing – taking in the swathe of destruction. A moment before it seemed as if the glass woman's impossible powers had finally reached their limit, but she had smothered the rebellion in one mighty, silent stroke. Yet whatever she had intended – to escape? to eradicate her enemies? – was for ever stalled when she saw they still stood to defy her. With a plangent whine Mrs Marchmoor retreated several rapid clicking steps. If they could withstand her mental powers, Miss Temple realized, the creature was utterly defenceless. They might be children with stones intent on crushing a tortoise. Miss Temple met the glass woman's gaze and saw in her swirling eyes incomprehension and terror.

Chang lurched towards Colonel Aspiche, groping for the insensible man's fallen sabre.

'Sir! I beg of you!'

Margaret Hooke cried out to Fochtmann, stirring him from his daze. As Chang took hold of the Colonel's weapon, Fochtmann took two strides and snatched up Mr Phelps's pistol. Doctor Svenson tackled Fochtmann, and the tall man fell, crashing to the floor in a heavy tangle. Fochtmann fought against Svenson's arms to aim the gun at Chang, who was stranded between the struggling men and Mrs Marchmoor, neither target within reach of his sabre. Miss Temple darted forward and kicked Fochtmann's hand quite cleanly. The pistol flew away from them all, skittering unimpeded across the floor . . . until it was stopped by the Contessa's foot.

The Contessa bent down unsteadily to retrieve the gun. 'Are we finished with the circus?' she asked. 'I do hope so. I am *tired*.'

She cocked the gun and held it generally, so she might as easily fire at Miss Temple or Chang as at Mrs Marchmoor.

'An interesting circumstance,' the Contessa observed. 'Like some interlocking Chinese box. Margaret can overpower *me*, but not Chang. I can shoot Chang, but then Margaret is free to overwhelm my mind. And no doubt each of us would be more than happy for the others to die.'

Before anyone could respond, another stirring on the floor caught Miss Temple's eye. Mr Leveret sputtered and struggled to rise. He looked about him, taking in the crushing vision of his soldiers all dropped to the floor, saw the glass woman and Chang, and then lastly the Contessa. He rose to his knees, his voice pinched with disapproval. 'I must protest, madam, and demand that in all *decency* –'

The Contessa's bullet caught Leveret square between the eyes, a spout of dark red blood flipping in the air as he went down. Charlotte Trapping screamed aloud, and screamed again, drawing her shaking hands up to her face. Mr Leveret did not move.

'Be quiet, Charlotte,' warned the Contessa coldly. 'Or I will kill your child.'

She extended the pistol to where Francesca lay curled, looking altogether too small. Her mother's next cry stopped in her throat with a moan.

Miss Temple turned with helpless anger to Chang. 'Will you not do *something*?'

'She is right,' he said quietly. 'If I take Margaret's head, nothing stops the Contessa from killing as many of us as she has bullets.'

The hard truth of his words fell flat upon the room, and no one spoke. Then Robert Vandaariff coughed wetly. He watched them with one open eye from where he lay slumped, the corners of his mouth touched with a distant bemusement.

The Contessa called sharply to the glass woman. 'Margaret, I would put it to you that nothing between us need prevent an understanding *now*. We have an unparalleled opportunity, you and I – to create in a stroke a new future. My former agreement lay with Harald Crabbé, Francis Xonck, and the Comte d'Orkancz. Crabbé is dead. Francis is ill. The Comte has been reborn. You and I stand opposed. You already rule the Ministries – take Crabbé's place. With the Comte reborn and Francis restored, we can begin again as equal partners.'

The depths of Mrs Marchmoor's blue eyes flickered, but she did not respond.

'Your only alternative fate is Cardinal Chang's blade. Come – together, Margaret, we will be truly unstoppable.'

'Francis Xonck tried to kill you,' said Chang.

'And I to kill him,' the Contessa replied. 'What of it? This factory is reason enough to retain Xonck Armaments within the *portfolio* – do you think I can trust Charlotte? Besides, there is also that claim of Margaret's to settle . . . that Oskar is *unclean*. In my opinion, restoring Francis to good health is a perfectly reasonable *test*, demonstrating Oskar's sound mind and intact knowledge. It is entirely *sensible*.'

Miss Temple felt the bile at the edge of her mind, curdling her concentration like tart lemon dripped in milky tea.

'But this man is *not* the Comte – not the Comte you knew!'

'Be quiet, Celeste. Come, Margaret . . . do we have an agreement?'

'If he can restore Francis . . .' The glass woman's words hung hesitant and thin, broken ice stretched across the skin of a dark pool. 'Perhaps the corruption . . . is not important . . .'

The Contessa turned towards Robert Vandaariff. 'What do you say to that, Oskar?'

'What *can* I say, Rosamonde?'

'You can agree.'

'And what of this . . . supposed "taint"?'

'Do you *feel* unclean?'

'I feel as clean as Arctic ice.'

'He is lying!' cried Miss Temple. 'For pity's sake – I touched the book – I *know*!'

'If that is so,' the Contessa rejoined, 'then we simply administer the Process once again, or find an empty book to re-vacate his mind, or wrap him in chains until the body of Robert Vandaariff is tractable once more.'

'Your sentiment is touching.' Vandaariff straightened his filthy coat with meticulous small tugs.

'Come now, Oskar, I am *overjoyed* at your return. Will you join us? Surely you would prefer not to be forced?'

'My goodness. How would you do that?'

The Contessa laughed. 'How to decide? There is no time for seduction – and no one you care for to threaten. I could put this gun against your knee – one shot and the Doctor would no doubt be forced to amputate with a pen-knife!' She laughed again. 'And think of all the money you would save, buying but one shoe!'

Vandaariff laughed with her.

'It is a very good thing we are such friends. Of course I will join you, and join Margaret. I suppose I am even in Cardinal Chang's debt for stabbing me when he did – otherwise I should surely have twisted your lovely neck clean through.'

'Is . . . is Francis *alive*?' It was the tearful voice of Charlotte Trapping.

'O certainly,' replied Robert Vandaariff mildly. 'One can see him breathe.'

He snapped his fingers at Fochtmann, who – after a wary glance back to Mrs Marchmoor – lifted Xonck into the same chair that had held Vandaariff. Under Vandaariff's instruction he reattached the nest of stinking tubes and hoses and masks to Xonck's body. As he worked, Fochtmann cut away Xonck's clothing and exposed the gleaming, dark wound in his chest. It throbbed with each heavy breath, like a parasite with intentions of its own.

'What will you do?' asked Doctor Svenson. 'The glass has fused to his heart and lungs. How can you hope to extract it?'

'The dilemma is indeed perplexing,' agreed Vandaariff, tapping the pulsing wound with his fingernail.

'If you cannot do it, let him die.' This was Cardinal Chang.

'O I can do it,' replied Vandaariff. Behind him Francis Xonck opened his eyes and groggily shook his head, pushing without comprehension against his bonds. Vandaariff tightened the mask with a tug. He turned and met Miss Temple's gaze. Her throat clenched hard, the arrangement of copper wires and hose around Xonck seeming to twist before her eyes into letters, nearly forming words . . . She was suddenly terribly afraid, but she could not quite pierce his intention – and then she burst out coughing, unable to speak. Doctor Svenson stepped to her, but Miss Temple pushed him away, waving her hand at Vandaariff.

'What is *wrong* with her?' demanded the Contessa.

'She is *ill*,' replied Vandaariff. 'An effect of the glass. Just like poor Francis. Can you hear me, Francis? Are you alive?'

'Can you truly heal him?' asked Mrs Trapping.

Vandaariff tied off the end of a black hose. 'Do you *want* me to?'

'I . . . I do,' she whispered.

An excitement leapt to Vandaariff's eyes. 'But your brother is a wicked thing. If anyone deserves an agonizing death, it is certainly Francis. No, Mrs Trapping, I'm sure I don't believe you.'

'I want him as he was,' she insisted.

'You must *convince* me . . .'

'I want him back,' she whimpered.

'*Back?*' asked Vandaariff. 'I see – so you can kill him yourself?'

'No,' sniffed Mrs Trapping, but then was overtaken by sobs. 'I do not know what I want at *all*!'

Robert Vandaariff sniggered, arch and vile.

The Contessa spoke angrily: 'When you open your mouth, Charlotte, it helps you not at all!'

'As if I had a choice! In anything!'

The Contessa snorted and pointed to the deathly pale little girl, huddled in an insensible ball at the feet of Mr Phelps. 'You might have remembered your daughter.'

'*I* might have – *I might have*?'

Mrs Trapping took three quick steps, like a high-strung dog, towards the Contessa, her hands raised, then staggered from an unseen blow. She wheeled to the glass woman in a tearful fury. 'Do not touch me!' she shrieked. 'I will not have your filthy mind in mine! I will break you to a thousand pieces! I do not care if my daughter dies! I do not care if *I* die! If you *touch* me again, this whole building can go to the devil's hottest furnace –' Mrs Trapping swayed with the same crazed ferocity her brother had shown on the roof of Harschmort. 'This is *my* factory,' she gasped, '*my* brother – you cannot –'

'Be quiet, Charlotte!' snapped the Contessa. 'Oskar, what pleasure is there in tormenting an idiotic . . .'

Her words fell silent. Vandaariff's smiling lips were slick with black fluid.

'Oskar?'

'You never did credit my alchemy, Rosamonde.'

'I beg your pardon? Who was it who took your learning to Vandaariff, to Henry Xonck – men of immense power of whom *you* had never heard –'

Vandaariff nodded dismissively, stroking his chin as if it held the Comte's beard. 'Yes, for you it was ever a means to *power*.'

'For *all* of us –'

'You lack higher goals, Rosamonde. At heart you are a *dog*. A *pretty* dog, but now look at you! You dismissed the glory of my plans for Lydia . . . for Margaret . . . even' – he giggled wickedly – 'my plans for *you*. My goodness, yes – if you'd only dreamt what truly awaited *you* in Macklenburg

. . . one limb at a time, my sweet . . . and your *womb* – O that more than anything, Rosamonde, your own sweet *legacy* . . . all given over to *me*.'

The Contessa stared at him.

'Oskar . . . you – even *you* . . . would not have *dared* –'

Vandaariff barked with contempt. 'Would not *dare*? *Would not dare?*'

He raised his arm, and Fochtmann, back at the line of machines, restored them to roaring life. The Contessa's eyes went wide. She looked with alarm at Miss Temple, still unable to speak, and shouted for him to wait, shouted for the glass woman to stop him. But Robert Vandaariff seized the handle on the brass box and pulled it down.

Miss Temple had stolen one glimpse of the Comte's cathedral chamber at
Harschmort, with all its machines at full roar and Mrs Marchmoor, Angelique, and Elspeth Poole laid out on tables awaiting transformation – and she
had seen the sickening glamour of their grand unveiling in the Vandaariffs'
ballroom later that night. But she had not witnessed the alchemical transformation itself, human flesh remade to blue glass. And so the spectacle of
Francis Xonck writhing in unspeakable agony – madly shrieking as his
body boiled away before them all – filled her with unprecedented horror.

The change began at the gleaming lump near his heart and then spread
out in twisting ropes, wriggling fingers surging up each side of his throat,
fast-growing tropical vines rippling across his sweat-slicked chest. She heard
muffled cracks, like splitting ice, as his bones were overborne, and then
came the bubbling away of muscle and sinew. The hissing glass erupted
upwards to pepper the skin in raw blue patches, a horrid dense scatter of
virulent blistering. Then these blisters fattened, pooling, colliding into one
another until the whole of Xonck's exposed flesh congealed into one gelid
gleaming sheet.

At the first jolt of current, the man screamed and thrashed his arms –
and it seemed he might tear free, so prodigious was his terror. But as his
body incrementally stiffened, his ability to struggle was curtailed. His
protests dropped at the last to a lost, vacant moan behind the rubber mask,
the sound of wind against the lip of an empty bottle, and then he was silent
altogether.

Fochtmann switched off the power.

No one spoke, and not one person moved, save for Robert Vandaariff,
who delicately leant to his new-made creature and whispered in its ear.

'What have you done?' rasped Colonel Aspiche, lifting his head from the
floor. 'What madness?'

Vandaariff did not answer. Gently peeling free the mask, he exposed
Francis Xonck's face: an inhuman swirling blue, copper hair hanging in
oily locks against his bare neck. Xonck's moustache and side whiskers were
gone. He seemed so much younger – and his corruption more stinging.
Vandaariff bared his teeth in a mirthless leer of satisfaction.

'Were you saying something, Rosamonde? I could not hear.'

'Oskar . . .' The Contessa groped for words, unable to turn from the spectacle of Xonck's body. 'O Oskar . . .'

'Oskar *indeed* – I trust any questions of *identity* can be laid to rest. As requested, I have ended Francis's struggle with the blue glass – to everyone's profit . . . or at least my own.'

'Jesus . . .' Mr Phelps seemed near tears. 'Jesus God . . .'

Vandaariff smiled. He scratched his earlobe with the nail of his right thumb. Miss Temple saw with a shudder how the sensibility that had been placed into Robert Vandaariff's body was not truly that of the Comte d'Orkancz. The Comte was an aesthete, a sensualist who rated the entire world only by its beauty. Yet, in his despairing grapple with death, that sensuality had been spoilt – like a freshly opened egg mixed with tar, like sugar frosting spun with putrid meat, like sliced fruit writhing with maggots – leaving his mind riddled with loathing and spite for everything that remained alive. Whatever ruin he could replicate in the world would merely echo the despoilment of his once-splendid dreams.

He raised an eyebrow at Mrs Marchmoor, who had not moved, and then addressed the Contessa: 'You seem reticent, Rosamonde. Did you not want to renew our compact? Or has your recent ill-fortune rendered you as tremulous as these *men*?'

The Contessa held Phelps's revolver – it was within her power to shoot Vandaariff down.

'Why do you hesitate?' hissed Miss Temple. 'After what he was saying – what he would *do* to you –'

'Be quiet, Celeste!' The Contessa licked her lips, weighing greed and arrogance and hope against the man's outright insanity. For a creature as once splendid as the Contessa even to hesitate . . . Miss Temple was appalled.

The Contessa cleared her throat and spoke in a cool, careful tone. 'I am sure the Comte was merely . . . exorcizing his old rage.'

'I was exactly,' said Vandaariff, smiling.

'Telling stories.'

'I was indeed.'

Vandaariff turned to Miss Temple and smirked at her distressed expression. 'The Contessa is my good friend – how could we not go on together? Of course, *Margaret* is a different story. *She* is imperfect, created from flawed premises, and so we see the result – beautiful enough, yet rebellious, acquisitive . . . stupid.' He called to Chang. 'Take her head, I beseech you –'

'*Enough,*' the glass woman whispered.

The chuckle stopped in Vandaariff's throat, and his body stiffened. But, despite the redness of his face and the bulging veins in his neck, he continued to smile.

'I may be yours, Margaret,' Vandaariff gasped, his face streaming with sweat. 'But Francis . . . is *mine.*'

At once Mrs Marchmoor rocked on her feet. She released Vandaariff, visibly shaking where she stood, and pivoted her attention solely on Francis Xonck. Still bound to the chair, Xonck had lifted his head to face her, his depthless eyes dark and bright. Miss Temple watched transfixed as each glass creature strained against the other – unnatural, hypnotic, battling statues – until it seemed that both must shatter. Xonck's mouth hung open, his broken teeth bared. Blue steam rose from Mrs Marchmoor's damaged arm.

'I cannot! I cannot!' wailed Mrs Marchmoor, and at once the tension snapped away, the air in the room as crisp as if it had been split by lightning. Miss Temple's eyes burnt, and she covered her mouth and nose. Mrs Marchmoor retreated to the canvas-covered window.

Vandaariff barked with hoarse laughter. 'Well done, Francis – though rather *tardy*. If you delay like that again – suffice to say that I do not tolerate *independence.*'

He took hold of Francis Xonck's right ear and with a sudden turn of his wrist snapped the upper half clean off, tossing it away to shatter behind the machines. Xonck grunted and an invisible ripple of pain shot through each unprotected mind in the room. Vandaariff mockingly addressed the steaming stub. 'Am I *understood*?'

The Contessa stepped forward, one hand to her forehead. 'Oskar –'

Vandaariff ignored her, calling gaily across the room, 'It is no use,

Margaret, you will not fit through the bars! You've been damaged – and Francis is your match!'

'What do you want?' the glass woman whispered.

'*Everything*,' Vandaariff replied. 'It would be more *efficient* to break you apart and pound the pieces into sand . . . but perhaps that arm can be mended after all. I can mend all manner of broken souls, can't I?'

He looked into Xonck's swirling depths of colour with a sour mix of delight and disdain. Miss Temple winced as Xonck's new voice entered her mind, a groping, gravelled scrape, deeper than Mrs Marchmoor's and more sad.

'Oskar . . . I . . . I . . . never –'

'Who asks for destiny?' replied Vandaariff with a strange light in his eyes. 'You have been tempered to a harder steel. And perhaps there is justice in it – we have each preserved the other by way of torment. You are quite new! The corruption is gone, the weakness burnt away – your body has undergone the true chemical marriage!'

'*You have no idea*,' whispered Xonck.

'You think not?' Vandaariff laughed coldly. 'The arrogance of this world! Your puling grief, Margaret's grasping fear – this beastly *hope* –'

Mrs Marchmoor interrupted him. 'What do you *want*?'

He did not reply. Instead, he turned at last to the Contessa, smirking at the pistol in her hand.

'What would *you* say, Rosamonde? What price to keep Margaret amongst us?'

The Contessa looked carefully at Mrs Marchmoor – her ally of just moments before – and shrugged, flinching against the pull of her shoulder. 'Her continued service,' she said. 'Even if she is no match for Francis, she remains inordinately powerful. And, in our absence, she has no doubt discovered any number of useful secrets within the Ministries.'

'Excellent *practical* reasoning, madam. I too am practical, and *I* think it is extremely important to retain control of this excellent facility – which means of all things Xonck.'

'That is nothing to do with Margaret –'

Again, Vandaariff did not seem to answer her words, but spoke from his

own urges, the same poisonous resentment. 'These machines are our future
– but my *vision*. You deprived me of Lydia, Rosamonde. Her flesh had
become my canvas.' Vandaariff's eyes sharpened. 'Now my dreams have
changed – they have deepened in astonishing ways . . . I see how I can go
so much further . . .'

His eyes settled on his target with a hungry gleam, and Miss Temple felt
her gorge rise.

'My price . . . is the *child*.'

'The child?' The Contessa shook her head. 'But she is not Lydia – she
cannot – what will you do with her?'

'Absolutely *anything*.'

Vandaariff looked to the glass woman, who met his gaze and sucked her
lower lip, measuring the foulness she had tasted against survival and a
return to servitude. She nodded, the barest dip of her chin. Vandaariff
turned to the Contessa. Her face was drawn and her mouth grimly set.

'*Done*.'

Francesca Trapping screamed. Elöise had plucked up the girl – startling
her – and run for the open door. Mrs Trapping, shocked to life as well,
shrieked after them.

'Elöise! You cannot take my daughter from me! Elöise!'

But Mrs Trapping did not stir from where she stood – wringing her
hands, tears on her cheeks – between the corpse of Mr Leveret and the
scarcely recognizable figure of her brother.

Nor was Elöise able to escape. Just at the door she stumbled – her body
stopped from afar – and toppled to the floor, face blank, pulling Francesca
down with her. The girl had not been occupied. Now she struggled against
the unmoving arms of her tutor. Her panicked eyes met those of Francis
Xonck, and she screamed even louder.

Miss Temple wheeled to the dais. It was Francis Xonck who had prevented Elöise from taking the girl.

It was not often in Miss Temple's life that she received credit for being
intelligent. She had never cared for her studies. She had participated rarely

in discussions of *substance* – business or finance or politics or religion, which was to say the discussions of men – the only sphere where *intelligence* might be seen as a factor. Instead, it was her lot to be found (and even this less often than she liked) cunning or clever, *animal* associations – as if one were to admire a badger for digging – less a compliment than a condescending description. Yet, in that instant, Miss Temple's mind made a small leap, one that she herself found startling.

It was also at that moment that she noticed a fallen soldier near Elöise move his arm.

Miss Temple took hold of the Doctor's uniform tunic with both hands and shoved him as hard as she could towards the doorway.

'The child is *Xonck's!*' Miss Temple hissed. 'Get her *away!*'

As a person who naturally thought the worst of everyone, Miss Temple never doubted the revelations about Elöise and Colonel Trapping (or Elöise and Francis Xonck), though she had not understood why Mrs Trapping still suffered Elöise's presence. She remembered the Contessa's letter to Caroline Stearne – that she possessed some secret to control Mrs Trapping. Had Mrs Marchmoor known it too? Perhaps it had been her taste of Xonck's blood in the garden. Only after *that* had Andrew Rawsbarthe been ordered to collect vials of blood from each child . . . and Mrs Marchmoor had sampled all three vials in the same fashion, turning them to glass. Yet only *Francesca* had been taken inside the factory – for only her vial had matched the glass woman's earlier taste of its *hidden* parent – brought to provide leverage against both mother *and* father. Miss Temple was dismayed by the revelation itself, but the West Indies offered innumerable examples of distressing patrimony – one was always seeing features one shouldn't on the most inconvenient faces, and she herself had studiously ignored what might be familiar noses or chins amongst her own plantation's offspring. The thought opened her heart the slightest crack to how troubled and painful the Trapping household must have been – the devastating tangle of loyalties and humiliations and betrayals, the impossibility of anything but the bitterest compromise . . .

*

'Francis!' cried Vandaariff. 'Francis – stop him!'

'Go to the devil!' barked Svenson. The Doctor stumbled as the force of Xonck's mind struck him, but then he lurched free – free of the same power that had toppled Elöise and overcome Mrs Marchmoor. Svenson leapt forward to catch the sobbing girl's hands.

'I cannot reach him!' whispered Xonck.

'Reach *her*!' commanded Vandaariff.

The girl slumped into dead weight. With an exasperated cry in German, Svenson pulled with all his strength, wrenching the slender child away from Elöise and sprawling onto his seat.

'Stop him!' Vandaariff's voice rose to a shriek. 'She is my price! She is my price to spare the lot of you! If she escapes –'

The crack of the Contessa's pistol rang in Miss Temple's ear, and a white seam of new wood was ripped from the planks near Svenson's head.

Miss Temple wheeled towards the Contessa and shrieked, desperately waving her arms.

'*The soldiers are waking up!*'

The Contessa could not help but look – and indeed the green-coated bodies were slowly writhing to life, their limbs like a welter of interlocked snakes – as did everyone else in the room.

Everyone but Chang. At Miss Temple's cry he launched himself straight for Vandaariff. Fochtmann hurled himself in front of his new master, arms outstretched. Chang struck him on the jaw with the sabre hilt, and the tall man flew back like a parasol taken apart by the wind. Vandaariff stumbled into the brass machinery and hissed with pain as his bare hand touched the hot metal. Chang raised the blade. Fochtmann, bleeding from his mouth, dived at Chang's legs, knocking him off balance and sending the stroke wide, striking sparks from a snarl of copper wire. Chang kicked Fochtmann viciously below the ribs.

Fochtmann moaned. 'You cannot! You cannot!'

Chang kicked him again, then took hold of Vandaariff's coat and threw the old man brutally to the floor. Chang raised the sabre. With horror Miss Temple saw the Contessa aiming her pistol at Chang's chest.

Too late, Miss Temple groped for the knife in her boot, but the Contessa's shot also went wide as Chang stumbled, nearly falling – kicked by Francis Xonck's glass foot. Chang wheeled as Xonck rose from the nest of machinery. Without the least hesitation he hacked the fat-bladed sabre at Xonck's head, but the edge was turned by the plaster cast still sheathing Xonck's right arm, chopping out a hank of plaster and skidding past the clear blue shoulder. Before Chang could pull the sabre back for a second blow, Xonck's plastered arm shot forward like a hammer, striking Chang's head with enough force to sever the glass arm at the elbow in a shower of sparking shards.

The mental explosion at Xonck's wilful amputation staggered Miss Temple, but she kept her senses while across the room others toppled or stood stunned. With an anguished cry she threw herself at the Contessa. Too dazed to shoot at so fast a target, the Contessa clubbed the gun wildly, clipping Miss Temple's head with the butt. Miss Temple went to her knees, but slashed out with the knife as she fell, drawing blood on the Contessa's outer thigh. The Contessa screamed and hopped away, the distance allowing her to bring the pistol to bear and fire. The bullet plucked at Miss Temple's curls and tore a jagged gash in the planking. Miss Temple launched herself at the Contessa's bleeding leg and brought the woman down in a heap, the gun bouncing across the floor. The Contessa kicked and clawed for the knife. Miss Temple stabbed her fingers blindly at the woman's eyes. The Contessa twisted her face and very nearly caught Miss Temple's thumb between her snapping teeth. With her free hand Miss Temple slammed the Contessa's bad shoulder. The Contessa screamed – as much with rage as pain – and Miss Temple rolled away towards Robert Vandaariff, who recoiled as if she were an advancing animal, an ugly resolve colouring his eyes like a greasy black film.

Miss Temple slashed at his legs and missed, falling forward. She lunged with a grunt, and missed again, her blow stopped short. The Contessa had taken hold of her foot. Miss Temple kicked fiercely and broke free, but then powerful hands caught her wrist – Fochtmann, risen again – and prised her fingers apart one at a time until her weapon fell to the floor.

*

'You really should have killed her, Rosamonde,' rasped Robert Vandaariff. 'She is a very vexing creature.'

Chang lay near her, glasses askew, blinking at the blood dripping into his dark eyes. He was alive and awake. The Doctor was gone, along with the girl. Francesca had been saved – she had done that much. Elöise had propped herself up on her arms, oblivious to the soldiers around her, all shaking their heads in the same way, all struggling to rise.

Vandaariff's forehead was bloody. He clucked his tongue absently at the blue glass scattered around him.

'Such *recklessness*, Francis . . . I do not like your being so free with *my* property . . .'

'What is *that*?' interrupted Mr Fochtmann, cocking his head towards the windows where Mrs Marchmoor had retreated.

Below, through the open windows, came a chorus of shouts . . . then a loud rhythmic smashing. The mob below had recovered their nerve and were battering the factory doors.

'The soldiers!' snapped Fochtmann. 'You must rouse them – while there's still time!' He turned to Xonck, whose impassive expression was fixed on the empty doorway. 'Order them to fire the cannons!'

'Yes, yes,' muttered Vandaariff. 'That does seem sensible . . . Francis?'

'They will not obey *Francis*,' groaned the Contessa, clutching her leg. 'They will not *know* him.'

The mob burst into another roar. The doors were down. Their cries echoed higher as the throng flooded into the factory itself.

'I suppose you are right at that,' said Vandaariff, struggling to concentrate. 'It is very vexing in *general* . . .'

'He must stop them!' cried Fochtmann. Vandaariff shut his eyes. The Contessa attempted to shift her body and grimaced. Xonck ignored them all, occupied as he was with the delicate task of stepping free of the brass boxes. Fochtmann pointed with dismay. 'What . . . what is he doing?'

Miss Temple swallowed, quite unable to avert her eyes, not only because of the man's nudity (she had not quite apprehended it for the bindings and hoses, yet was now provoked to inevitable and insistent questions about how the glass flesh actually *worked* and, as she stared, its *elasticity*), but also because she was fascinated to see another glass body *move*. For Xonck, lean and strong like Chang, was of an entirely different weight and figure to the three glass ladies. Miss Temple swallowed again, her mouth terribly dry. Watching Xonck was like watching a tiger on a chain; she marvelled at the unfamiliar muscles shifting powerfully with each step. But her gaze was drawn again to Xonck's groin as he turned, lurid memories bubbling in her mind, though this was like nothing *anyone* had ever seen . . . the dark whorls of colour, so shining and so soft, disgusting and ripe, arrogant and tender, lewd and alluring . . . she wondered if his body would be cold to the touch . . . she wondered at its *taste*. Xonck flexed the fingers of his one hand, grimacing at the steaming, shattered stump, and picked away stray flecks of glass where they clung.

The mob burst into another roar, which was followed by the high-pitched screeching of disabled machinery and a spattering of gunfire.

'If they come up here,' called Aspiche hoarsely, 'it will be finished.'

Phelps turned to Mrs Marchmoor. 'Madam – what instructions have you given to them – what summons?'

'Those men will destroy you too,' Fochtmann yelled to the glass woman. 'As soon as they see you – like any monster! You can stop them! All you represent will be needlessly lost!'

'What I *represent*?' hissed Mrs Marchmoor.

'O for God's sake!'

Fochtmann snatched up Miss Temple's knife and hurled it with all his strength across the room. The blade struck Mrs Marchmoor's cheek, snicking off a sliver of glass in a puff of blue smoke.

'She does not matter!' Aspiche shouted at Fochtmann. 'They are still coming for *you*!'

Fochtmann snorted and looked down for the Contessa's pistol, only to find Charlotte Trapping standing with the pistol in her hand. He reached out with one brusque, impatient arm.

'Mrs Trapping, I will have that weapon. If you cooperate, as a gentleman I can promise you –'

Mrs Trapping fired the pistol into Fochtmann's body, spinning the tall man headlong onto the floor. He raised his head once and she fired a second

time, the bullet spattering the top of his bald head as if it had been swatted
by a shovel.

Charlotte Trapping pointed the pistol at Vandaariff's chest . . . but then
her aim wavered to the Contessa still on the ground, and finally to the glass
monstrosity of her brother.

From the floor below came the crash of cannons and the rattle of gunfire.
Around them all the soldiers awkwardly regained their senses, collecting
their carbines, trying to make sense of the carnage before them.

Tears streamed down the face of Mrs Trapping. She opened her mouth
but then flinched as her brother's power touched her mind. She gasped as
he withdrew, and her eyes cleared with a terrible understanding of how he
could – and would, and *how fully* – now possess her. With an anguished
cry she pressed the pistol to her own head, but before her finger could
tighten on the trigger, her features went blank and the pistol clattered to
the floor.

Mrs Marchmoor had finally turned her attention to the soldiers moving
stiffly towards her. Smoke seeped from the crack on her face, and the white
bandage at her broken wrist dripped blue.

Phelps broke for the door, followed a moment later by Aspiche. Elöise
was already gone. Robert Vandaariff stared up at Xonck, dumbly enthralled
by the rebellion of his creature.

Xonck's hand slipped behind his sister's head to gather her red curls,
angling her passive face up to his. With a whimper of dread, Miss Temple
watched Xonck's blue tongue dip between Charlotte Trapping's coral lips,
just an instant of tease before the full of his ravaged mouth fell upon her.

Chang lurched up and thrust his arm across Miss Temple's chest. Before
she realized what was about to happen, he threw his body over hers, turning
his battered leather coat to where Francis Xonck, staring into the terrified
eyes of his sister Charlotte, raised one bare foot and brought it down on
the 296 shell's plunger.

Chang lifted Miss Temple to her feet, even as another volley of cannon from the floor below – felt but barely heard, her ears still ringing from the blast – made him stumble. The window bars where Mrs Marchmoor had stood were coated in fine blue dust, and the unlucky soldiers who had been nearest lay horrid and unrecognizable, blasted through and apart by innumerable razor-sharp glass grains. Charlotte Trapping's body was nothing more than red tattered shreds.

Vandaariff lay on his side in a black pool on the planking. Chang glared darkly at the man and glanced around him for a weapon.

'He must be killed –'

But then Chang spun and abruptly seized Miss Temple, bundling her desperately away just as the surging mob burst red-faced and roaring into the factory's top floor like a torrent. Mrs Marchmoor's minions swept into the crawling soldiers that remained and into the bloody spectacle of her destruction. Even as they struggled, the men, confused by the sudden loss of the glass woman's summons, shouted to each other in terror and surprise, their collection of topcoats and silk cravats utterly out place in the slaughter-house the Parchfeldt factory had become. Chang dired with Miss Temple for the doorway. She looked back over her shoulder. Through the churning crowd she saw the Contessa di Lacquer-Sforza groping like a blind beggar, feeling for the pockets of Fochtmann's topcoat.

The pitch-black stairwell echoed with shouts and gunshots. Chang tightened his grip around her and forced a path down. The doorway to the cannons had been split open – there were still screams and fighting inside – but they did not pause until the ground, the steps hellishly strewn with bodies. Many machines had been disabled – the light of the factory had dimmed, and its harsh song been reduced to the hacking clatter of a carriage with one broken wheel. Their way to the front was barred by smoking wreckage and struggling men. Chang pulled her the other way, towards the ruins, and they burst into the darkness, gasping in the cold night air, soldiers in green and red sprawled in death across the grass.

'Where are the others?' she whispered, looking around them at the empty yard.

'They have run on,' replied Chang, releasing her to pick up a fallen dragoon's bloodied sabre. He pointed with the blade to a ladder set against the rough stone wall. 'We must follow.'

'But where?' asked Miss Temple, running ahead of him, one hand on the ladder and the other gathering her dress so her feet might find the rungs. She gasped again as Chang's hands found her waist, lifting her up – which was not strictly necessary, her legs simply kicked in the air – and setting her down at a higher rung. As long as he did not meet her gaze, the man seemed perfectly able to touch her body in the most presumptuous of ways.

'What will happen to the Comte?' she cried. 'Or the Contessa?'

'They will be destroyed.' She felt Chang's weight behind her on the ladder.

'But if this mob knows them – if all this factory becomes theirs –'

'Without their mistress these minions will not stand up to the soldiers – if enough soldiers survive to face them down.'

'Is that why you would not kill her yourself?' snapped Miss Temple angrily. She reached the top of the wall and looked back over her shoulder. 'You will not be encumbered with me, but are perfectly happy to protect a pestilent *monstrosity*!'

Chang looked up as if she had spoken French and, for the first time in her memory, stammered. 'If – if I had taken her head – her power balanced the others' – without her to stop the soldiers – or the Contessa – we all would have –'

Miss Temple snorted, this being no response at all, and threw a leg over the wall, clambering down an unstable slope of tumbled stone into the darkening shadows of the wood. She reached the bottom in a rush, staggering into the undergrowth. Chang descended more carefully behind her.

'Celeste –' he began, but she did not bother to listen.

'Doctor Svenson!' she shouted into the woods. 'Doctor Svenson! Where are you?'

Chang seized her shoulder and hissed, 'Do not call out! We do not know who is here!'

'Do not be ridiculous,' she cried, 'and let me go!'

She pulled her arm free and stalked away, stumbling on a thicket of vines before locating a path.

'Celeste,' Chang whispered, following. 'There is still Aspiche – Phelps – who knows who else –'

'Then I suppose you will have to kill them. Unless you prefer I do that as well. I'm sure I have no idea of your preferences in anything.'

'Celeste –'

Miss Temple wheeled where she was and struck out with her right hand, slapping Cardinal Chang's chest. Chang caught her hand and so she struck him with the other, this time a fist across his jaw, dislodging his glasses. Chang stabbed the cavalry sabre into the ground and caught that hand as well. Miss Temple kicked his leg. He shook her.

'*Celeste!*'

Miss Temple looked up at him, her hands held tight, and saw with a piercing despair the beauty of his jaw, the broad grace of his shoulders, and his especially elegant throat, bound as it was by a filthy neck cloth. Then with a swallow she looked into Chang's eyes, visible past the skewed black lenses . . . squinting and damaged . . . confused and hideous . . . and she realized that this man was the exact image of everything that had gone so horribly wrong, of so much she had lost and could never recover.

Like a striking snake Miss Temple stabbed her face up to his, her lips finding the rough stubble of his cheek and then his mouth, which was so much softer than she ever expected.

Chang arched his back with a cry and then, his eyes finding hers once more, shoved Miss Temple away from him with all his strength. She caught her foot on another vine and tumbled to her back, watching helplessly as Chang tried to turn, groping for the sabre, only to collapse face down on the forest floor. Behind him stood the Contessa di Lacquer-Sforza. In one hand she held her recovered spike, and in the other Lydia Vandaariff's leather case . . . but had not the book been destroyed by the shell? Could it have been protected inside its brass casing? Without pausing to cut Chang's throat – a sure sign of haste and anger – the Contessa lurched straight for Miss

Temple, her face grim and cold. Miss Temple screamed aloud and kicked herself backwards through the leaves, finally rolling to her feet just as the Contessa was snatching at her dress.

Miss Temple tore away and broke into a run, careering blindly through the darkness, heart thudding in her chest, eyes streaming with tears.

She could not think at all but sobbed aloud each time she gasped for breath. Patches of moonlight pierced the treetops, but the heart of the forest remained dark. Miss Temple dodged unthinkingly between ruins and thin saplings, the branches whipping her face and limbs. She glanced behind, but saw no one – with the gash on her leg the Contessa must not be able to run.

Miss Temple knew she should go back, go die next to him – even as she kept running. What had she done? What had she lost? She sobbed again and then stumbled suddenly to a stop, blinking without comprehension.

The forest around her was flooded with light.

'Look who it is,' sneered an easy, careless voice from beyond the boxed lantern, whose gate had been flung open in a stroke to blind her. 'Little Miss Stearne. Or should I say Temple?'

Miss Temple looked over her shoulder, terrified that the Contessa would appear, and wheeled back to the clearing, crying aloud at what she had not seen. On the ground lay Colonel Aspiche, curled around a pooling wound in his chest, matched by a smaller stain on his back where a blade had run him full through.

'Didn't see him in the dark,' explained Captain Tackham. 'Terrible thing, he being my commanding officer. Still, mistakes happen in wartime – awful, *awful* mistakes.'

The men to either side of him, two dragoons, chuckled at his words.

'Are you *alone*?' asked Tackham, lifting his bloody sabre blade towards her with a frank brutality. 'We heard you call for that Doctor . . . then you screamed.'

'One . . . one of the factory soldiers,' she said breathlessly. 'I killed him . . . with a rock.'

'A rock?'

Miss Temple nodded and swallowed.

'Poor fellow. Was *he* alone?'

'I don't know. I didn't see.'

'It seems you are *pursued*.'

'I don't know – I – I am *afraid* –'

Tackham snorted and nodded to his soldiers. 'Make sure, be careful, then come back.'

The troopers pushed past Miss Temple and vanished into the darkness. Tackham pointed with his blade just past the circle of lantern light, to where Mr Phelps huddled on his knees, utterly cowed.

'I have been *told* what happened inside,' explained Tackham. 'My considered strategy is to safely wait, and then partake of what spoils remain.'

'There are no *spoils*!' cried Miss Temple.

Tackham laughed in her face. 'Darling, I am looking at one top-shelf spoil this very instant.'

Tackham spun at a rustle in the leaves behind him, sweeping his sabre to the figure who emerged . . . but when he saw who it was the Captain laughed. Doctor Svenson advanced warily with a scavenged sabre of his own, looking extremely tattered and worn. He met Tackham's gaze with contempt and then called to Miss Temple: 'Celeste . . . you've not been harmed?'

She shook her head, unable to say a thing about Chang, her throat closed tight against the words.

'Where . . .' Mr Phelps's voice was a croak. He gestured behind Svenson. 'Where is –'

'Mrs Dujong?' Doctor Svenson gestured vaguely behind him. 'I do not know. At the canal.'

'And the child?' asked Phelps.

'No longer your concern,' said Svenson.

'Put down your blade or die,' Tackham said coldly.

'Well, *one* of us will die,' said the Doctor. 'I heard your comment about spoils, you see – and if other men lack the courage to stop you, I do not.'

'How *excellent*!' Tackham hefted his blade with a wolfish smile. 'You know how to use a cavalry sabre, then?'

'As much as any surgeon of the Macklenburg Navy,' answered Svenson. Tackham laughed aloud.

'Doctor – no, no – you must not –'

'Tush, my dear. What the Captain does not understand is that, like any German university man, I have done my share of duelling . . .'

The Doctor snapped, to Miss Temple's eyes, into an extremely dubious *en garde* stance, standing at his full height with his legs together like a dancer, and his sword arm straight out above him, the blade upside down with its tip floating directly at the level of Captain Tackham's eyes. Tackham snorted and settled into a low crouch, his left hand tucked behind his back and his right hand bouncing with anticipation, as if debating just where to land his blow.

'Not the most *flexible* of stances,' Tackham observed.

'It does not need to be. The mistake *you* have made, young man, is in thinking that I give one brass farthing for my life.' Svenson's voice was both icy and forlorn. 'It is all well to fight a man whose intention is *not* to be killed. Fear makes defence his priority – it is the bedrock of every sane strategy. But since I do not care for my life at all, I tell you quite clearly that you are doomed. Strike me anywhere you can. My counterstroke *will* land. From this *inflexible* stance it takes but one turn of my wrist to open your skull like a melon.'

'You're a liar,' sneered Tackham.

'You will find out, won't you?' said the Doctor. 'Attack me anywhere . . . and die.'

'Doctor –'

'Hush now. I must concentrate.'

The two men edged slowly into the centre of the clearing, eyes locked on one another. Miss Temple trembled to see, up close, how vicious the sabre blades truly were: the wide bright steel, the indented curve of the blood gutter, the hatchet-like chop at the tip, as wide and sharp as a cleaver. It seemed the Doctor had no chance at all, yet Tackham moved with extreme care, as if the Doctor's words were at least *possibly* serious.

'Advancement by assassination?'

The Doctor nodded at the Colonel's corpse, childlike and bereft, on the ground. From the factory behind them came a spattering of gunshots. Tackham frowned and glanced over his shoulder.

'It barely matters,' said Svenson. 'You will not live to see your new rank. *They* will arrive in minutes to kill us all.'

'I beg to differ,' said Tackham.

'Celeste,' said Svenson carefully, 'please be ready to flee.'

At this Tackham feinted a cut at Svenson's head, but the Doctor either saw through the move or was simply too slow to respond and did not counter-attack as he'd promised. Tackham chuckled. Was the Doctor's threat just bluster after all? Tackham feinted again. Svenson slipped in the dirt, and Tackham swept a vicious cut at the Doctor's side that Svenson stopped – quite barely – with a parry that rang through the trees like a ship's bell.

'Counterstroke indeed,' sneered Tackham. 'You're a lying coward.'

Behind came more gunshots, closer, within the woods.

'Your men have been killed,' gasped Svenson, the tip of his blade once more floating in front of Tackham's eyes. 'You are next. Throw down your sword.'

'To hell with you,' snarled Tackham, and he lunged.

His sabre slapped Svenson's blade to the side and shot forward unopposed, slicing a bloody dark trough across the Doctor's chest. The Doctor reeled back. Tackham snapped upright, all his training to the fore, ready to launch a second blow.

But then Tackham wavered. A jet of blood spat from the side of his throat, and then, the gash primed, sprayed out like a fountain, for the Doctor had indeed taken his own desperate cut while opening himself to death.

Tackham toppled into the dirt. Svenson dropped the sabre and slipped to his knees. Miss Temple screamed and ran to him, easing his body to the ground. The Doctor's voice was already a shuddering whisper.

'No no! Run! Escape!'

Miss Temple was shoved aside by Mr Phelps, who had taken off his coat and balled it up to staunch Svenson's seething wound. More gunfire rang through the trees.

'*Go!* He has given his life for yours! Don't be a fool!'

Doctor Svenson arched in agony as Phelps tried to peel free his tunic. Miss Temple held her hand to her mouth, sobbing, and wheeled away half blind with tears.

She knew she was a coward, but she could not stop. She tripped headlong more than once, scuffing her hands, scratching her face and her arms, each time hauling herself up and running on. She cried for Chang, for the Doctor, and for herself – for every instant when she had failed – so very many of them – for how she had misplaced every part of her life that mattered.

When she fell the last time, she lay in the dirt, overtaken with sobs. She did not know how far she had run – a hundred yards or a mile – nor did she care. The sky blazed with stars. She lay in an open space ringed with ivy-covered stones . . . more ruins.

Miss Temple pushed herself to her knees, brushing the hair from her face and the tears from her eyes. Something lay on the ground, catching the light . . . a ring of orange metal. She felt the weight in her bodice and knew Chang had placed the rings there to protect her.

'Celeste,' came a hesitant whisper, 'what has happened?'

In the shadows crouched Elöise Dujong and, clasping her hand tightly, Francesca Trapping. Miss Temple spat in the dirt, weeping again, all of her bitterness and regret suddenly finding their vent.

'They are *dead*, Elöise! They are both *dead*!'

Elöise gasped, her hand over her mouth, and began to sob as well. Miss Temple rose to her feet and staggered towards the woman. As soon as she was in reach she struck her across the face with all her waning strength, knocking Elöise to the ground. The girl leapt away with a whimper of fear.

'Get up!' Miss Temple snarled at Elöise. 'They are both *dead* and you killed them as much as anyone – your foolish, prideful, reckless, selfish –'

Elöise lay on her side sobbing. Miss Temple kicked her as hard as she could and nearly fell over. She kicked Elöise again and dropped awkwardly to her knees.

'He would not come with us!' Elöise whimpered. 'He would not *come*!' Tears streamed down Miss Temple's face.

'I have tried to protect him, Celeste,' Elöise cried to her, 'to protect everyone – and not one thing has been saved! I am a fool – not one thing!' Elöise's words stopped in her throat, her shoulders rocking.

Miss Temple slumped onto her back, her ragged breath fogging in the midnight chill. Chang shoving her to safety with his last strength. The Doctor exposing his heart to a sword. Of course he had returned at her cry. Of course Chang had protected her to the end. Despair swallowed up her rage, and she felt unbearably alone.

Miss Temple heard Elöise move and knew the woman was watching her, miserable, desperate for any crumb of forgiveness or care.

'It is not your fault,' Miss Temple said finally, her voice a stricken whisper. 'It is only mine, and always has been. I am extremely sorry. I am . . . I am . . . nothing at all.'

Elöise shook her head. 'We could go back.'

'If we go back, we will die as well, and their sacrifice is made meaningless.' The words were hollow and false in Miss Temple's mouth. She felt the black coating of the Comte's book in her throat – felt the *truth* of it – and could find no other answer.

'I do not care,' shuddered Elöise.

Miss Temple turned her head and found herself staring into the face of the silent girl. Francesca Trapping's lower lip was trembling, her blue eyes frightened and remote. What nightmare had the poor girl lived? Miss Temple struggled to sit.

'You must take *her*,' she said, swallowing, kicking at Elöise's nearest leg. '*She* has to be saved, Elöise. You must take her away from this.'

'I cannot,' said Elöise, shaking her head at her own helplessness. 'I cannot go. I have been waiting –'

'You cannot wait – the Doctor is gone!'

'But – I tried to say, so many times –'

'*It has to have stood for something!*' Miss Temple cried. She surged unsteadily to her feet, shouting at the other woman. 'Get up, Elöise! Save this much! Save *her*!'

The whistle of Lydia's case as it swung in the air caused Miss Temple to turn just enough that the sharp metal corner did not punch through her skull, but the impact jarred her teeth and dropped her to the earth like a hammer. She lay without understanding, as if her head had been severed. There was blood in her mouth. She could not move.

A hissing whisper penetrated her ear like a poisonous smoke. She felt the soft lips pressed against her skin, and the warmth of each vicious word as it came.

'This is not the way, Celeste Temple – you're half dead and cannot feel a thing, cannot *think* a thing. For all your presumptions, I require that you taste your despair completely – that you *choke* on it. I want you to know to your bones when I have killed you.'

The mouth went away, and Miss Temple lay for the longest time in the cold air, stunned and drifting, though she remembered somewhere that to truly sleep was to die. She lifted an impossibly heavy head, and blinked gummed and crusted eyes.

Francesca Trapping was gone. Elöise was a shapeless huddle in the dirt, the dark wet stripe across her lolling throat reflecting the starlight.

Miss Temple retched, but nothing came. She finally stood, eyes tight closed against what she could not bear, and stumbled away. The gunshots had ceased – she must have outrun their search, it did not matter – she barely noticed. She was impossibly alone, and even the swirling visions that had for so long battered her mind could find no entrance to her shattered heart.

She would reach the canal. Beyond the canal was the train. She had money in her boot. Beyond the train was the city, her certain death, and her revenge.